Discipline
Dash Shaw
drawn
2014–2019

nyrc NEW YORK REVIEW COMICS • New York

THIS IS A NEW YORK REVIEW COMIC
PUBLISHED BY THE NEW YORK REVIEW OF BOOKS
435 Hudson Street, New York, NY 10014
www.nyrb.com/comics
Copyright © 2021 by Dash Shaw
All rights reserved.   DEC 0 6 2021

Library of Congress Cataloging-in-Publication Data

Names: Shaw, Dash, author, artist.
Title: Discipline / by Dash Shaw.
Description: New York : New York Review Books, 2021. | Series: New York
Review Comics | Identifiers: LCCN 2021005110 | ISBN 9781681375694
(paperback)
Subjects: LCSH: Quakers–Comic books, strips, etc. | Brothers and
sisters–Comic books, strips, etc. | United States–History–Civil War,
1861-1865–Comic books, strips, etc. | Graphic novels.
Classification: LCC PN6727.S4946 D57 2021 | DDC 741.5/973–dc23
LC record available at https://lccn.loc.gov/2021005110

ISBN: 978-1-68137-569-4

Printed in the United States of America

10 9 8 7 6 5 4 3 2 1

The words in **Discipline** incorporate text from actual letters and diaries of Civil War-era Quakers and soldiers.

This book would not have been possible without support from the Cullman Center at the New York Public Library and the Virginia Museum of Fine Arts.

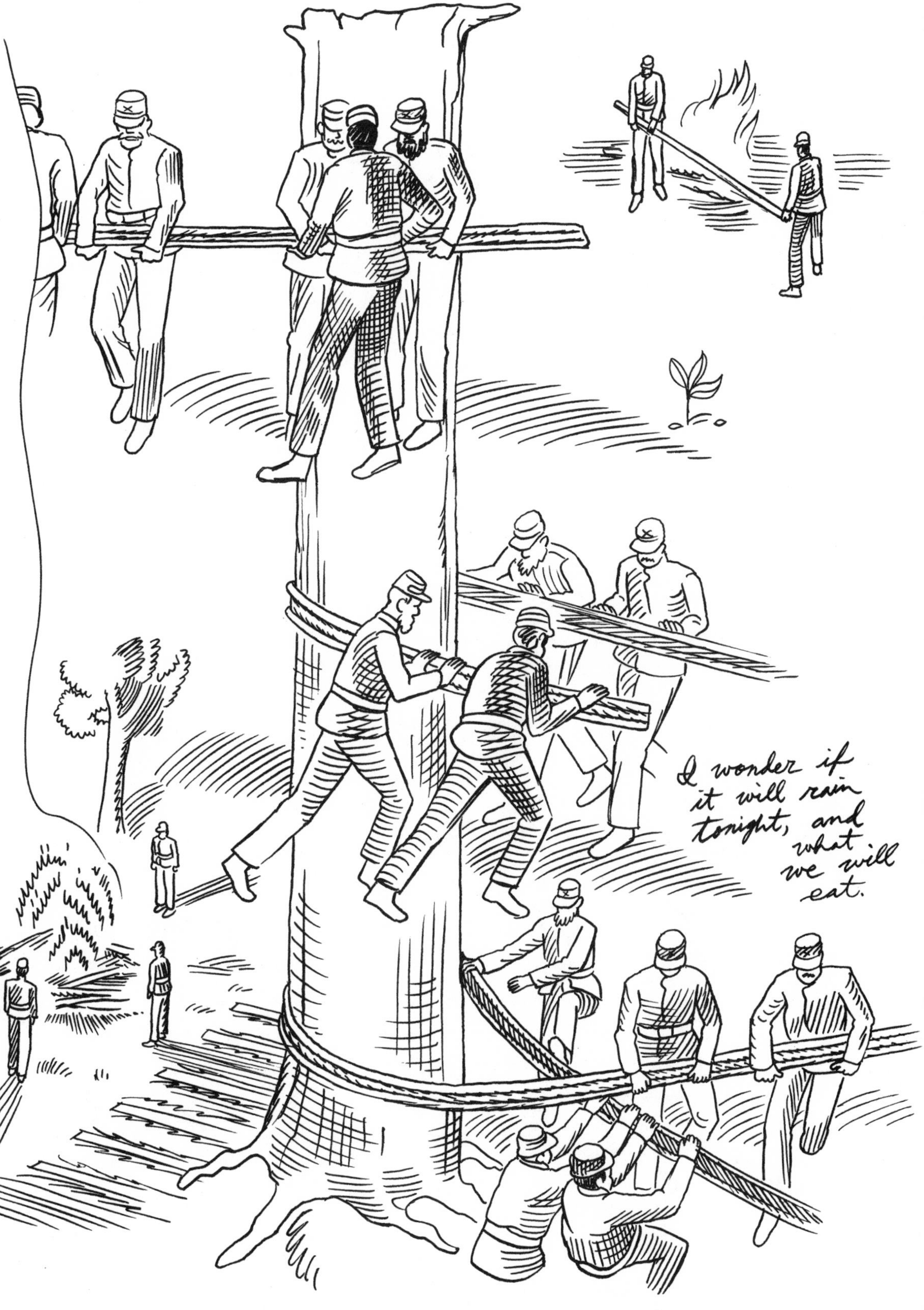
I wonder if it will rain tonight, and what we will eat.

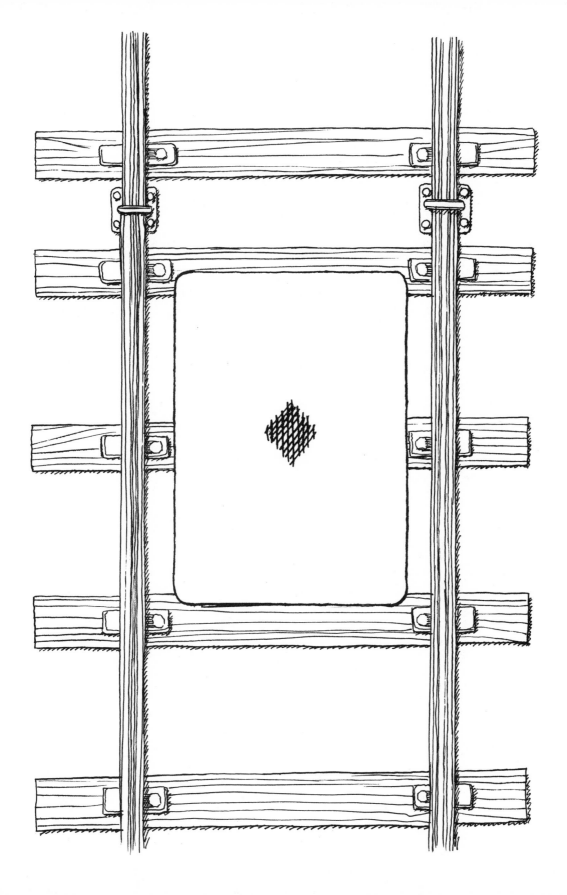

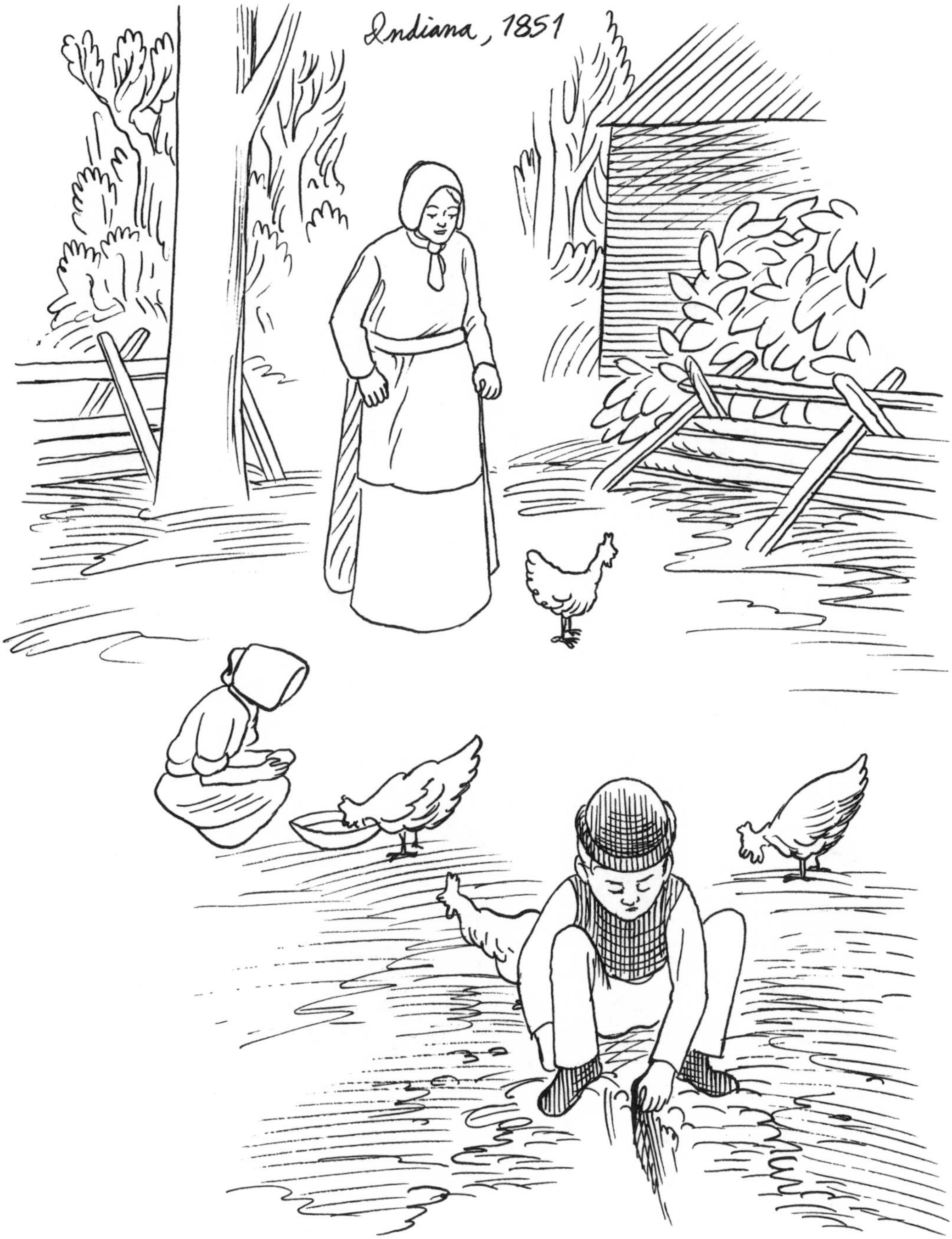
Indiana, 1851

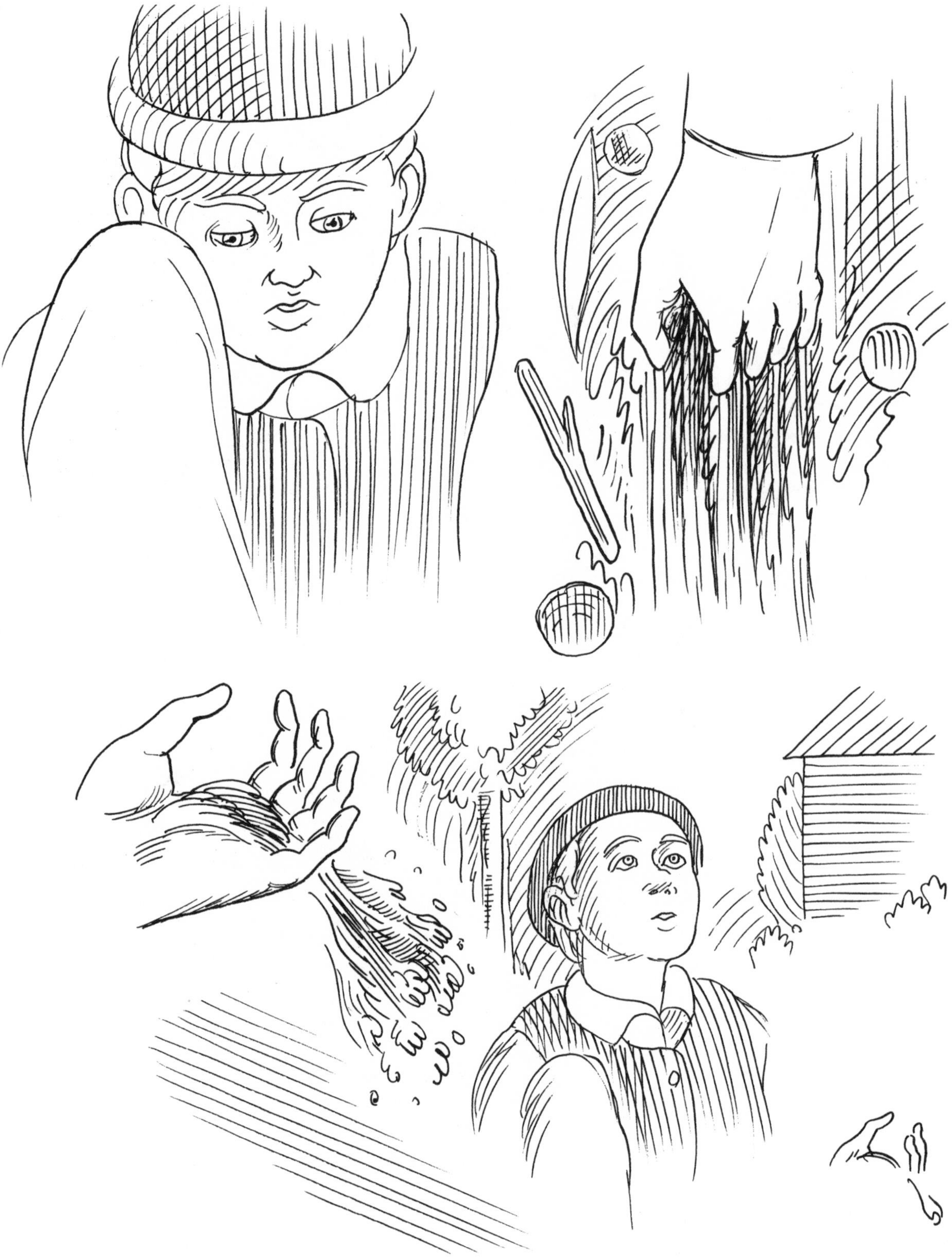

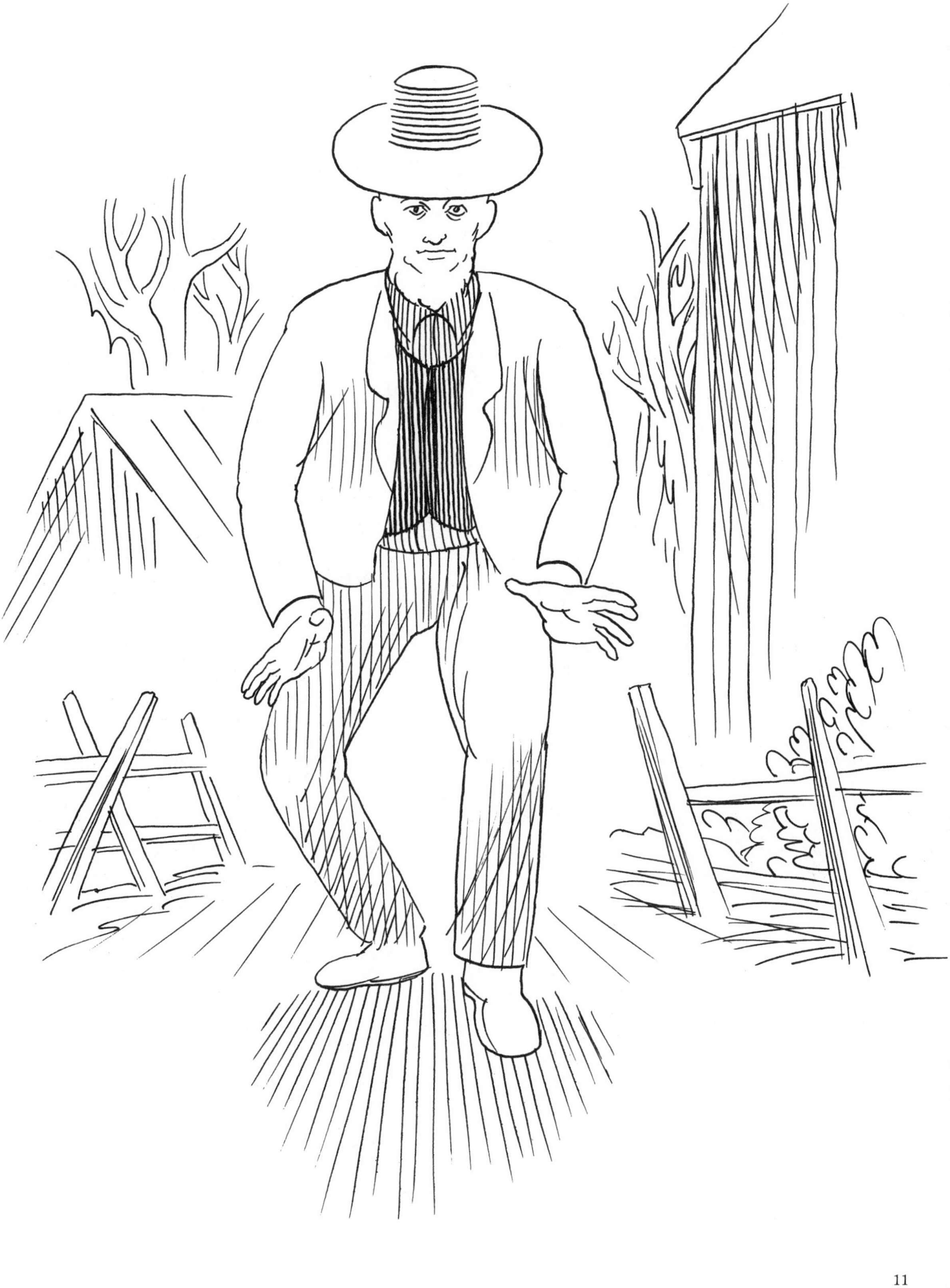

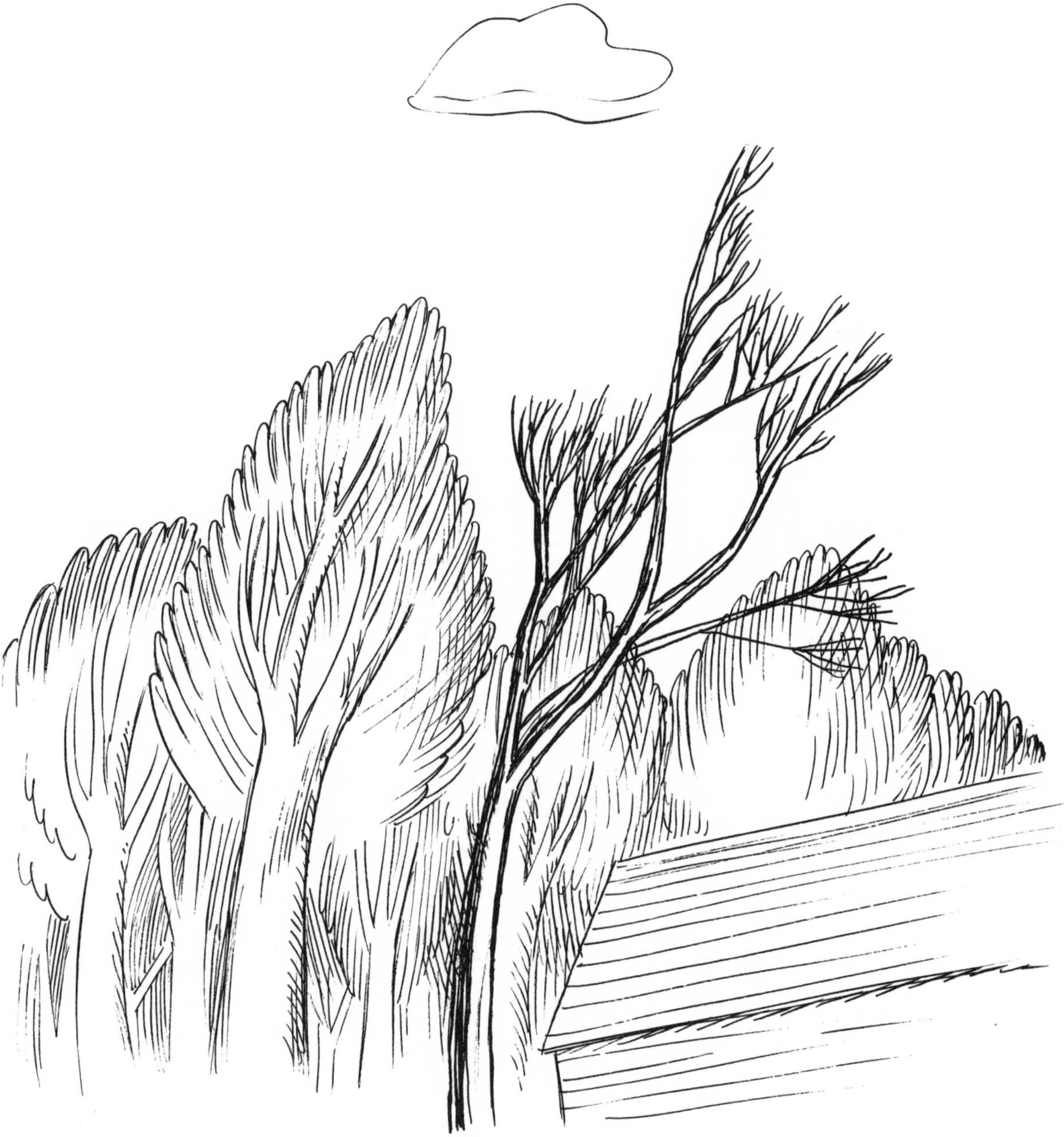

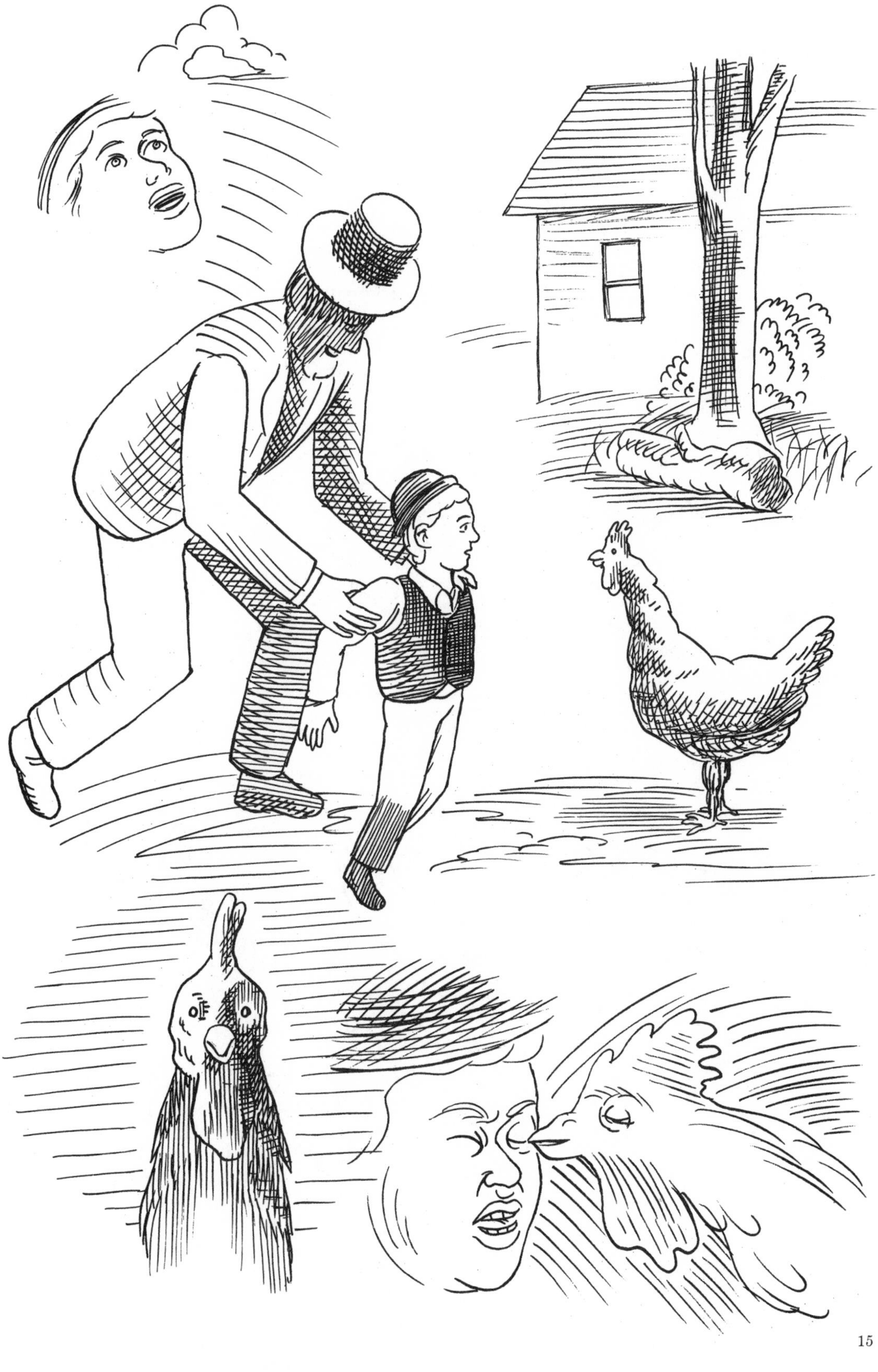

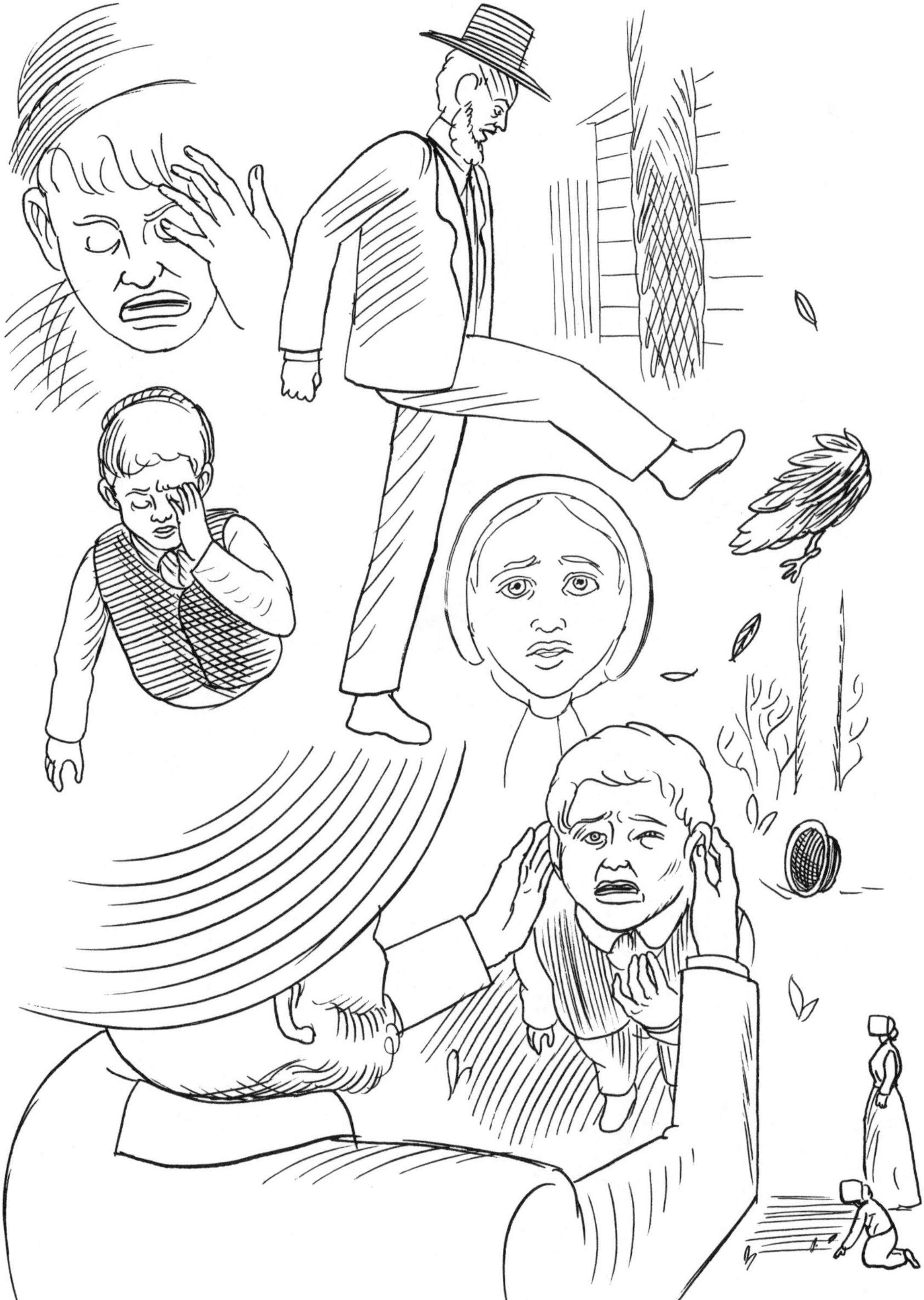

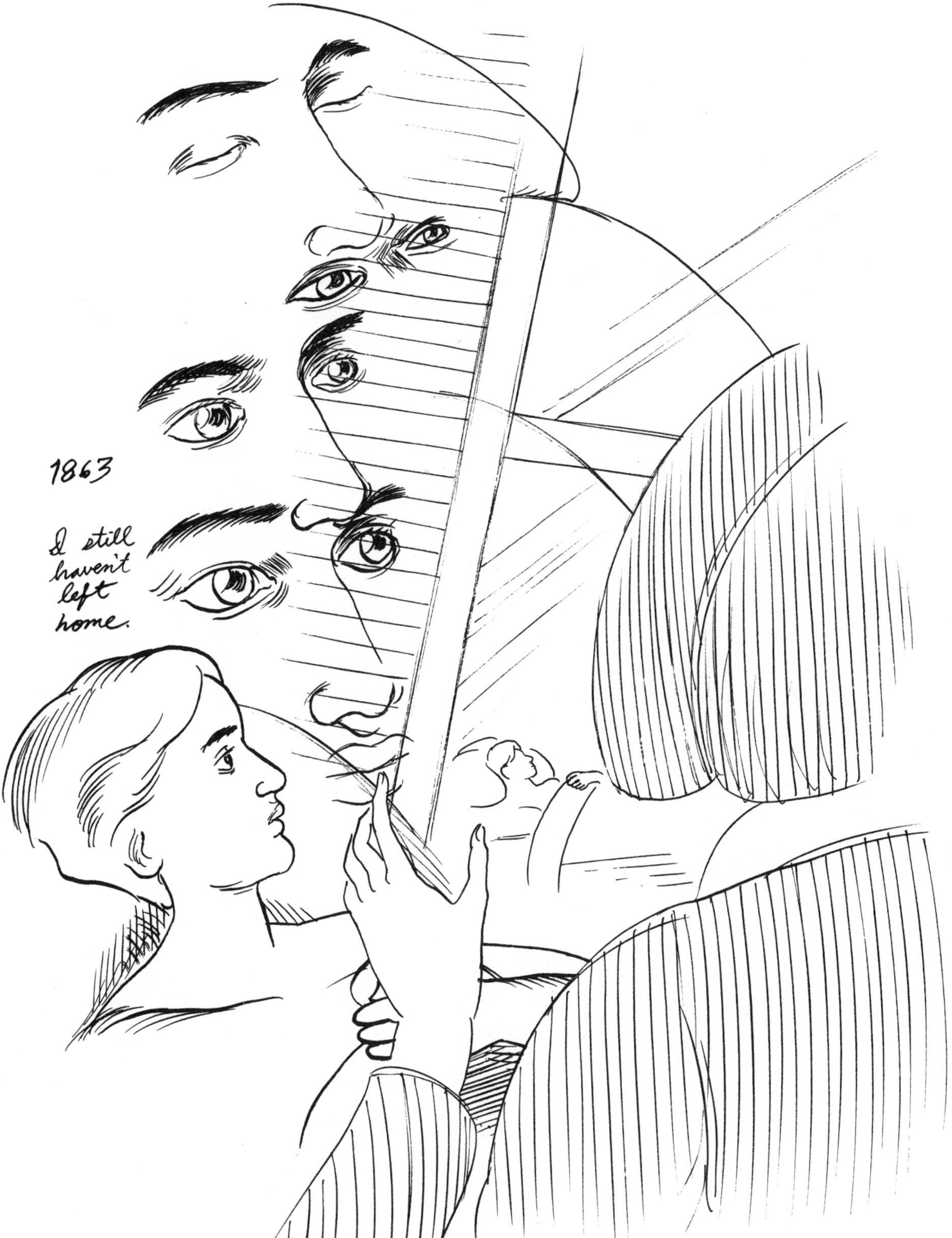
1863
I still haven't left home.

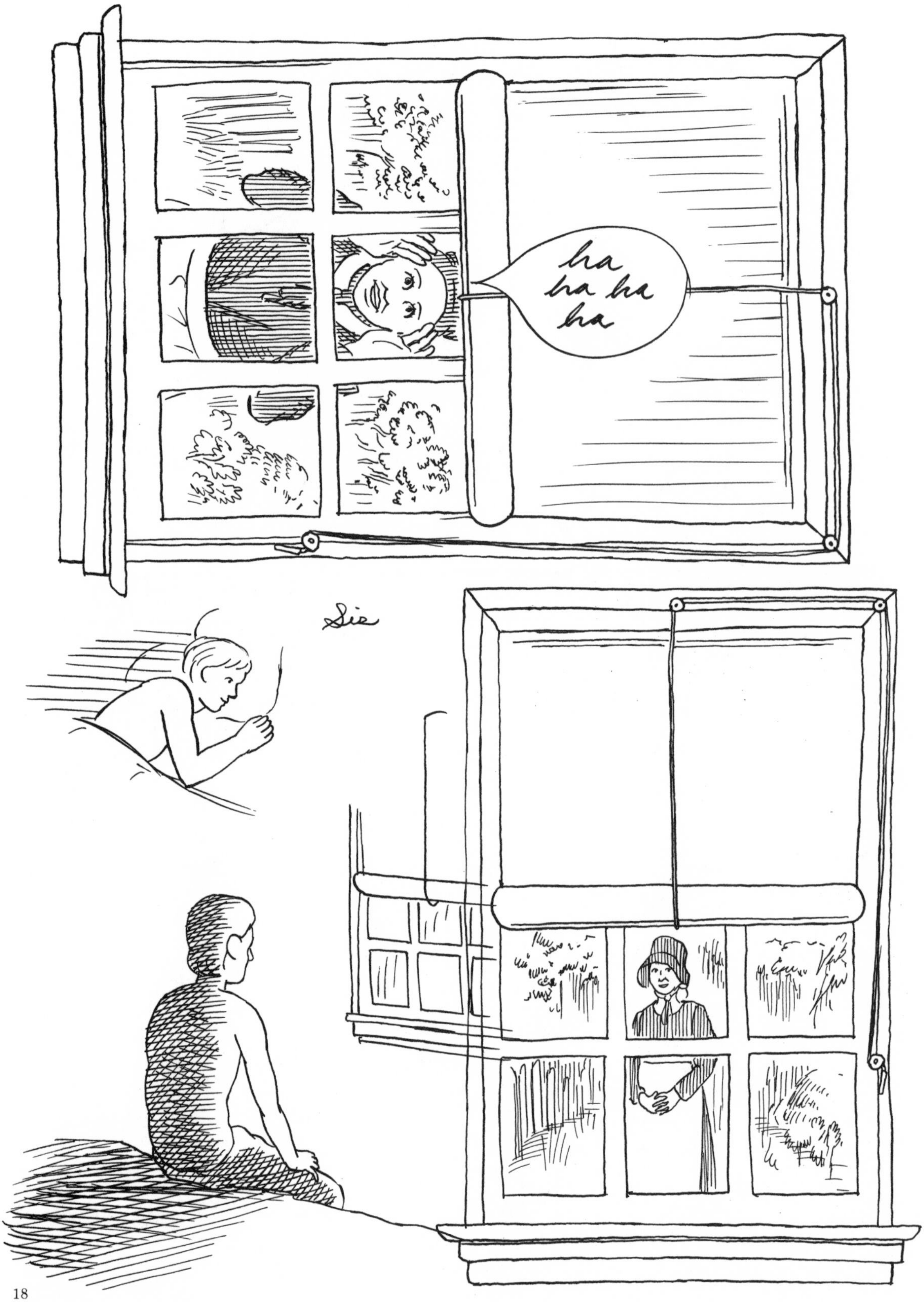
ha ha ha ha
Sis

Why do I have to go
to meeting?
My spirit does not
move me to attend.

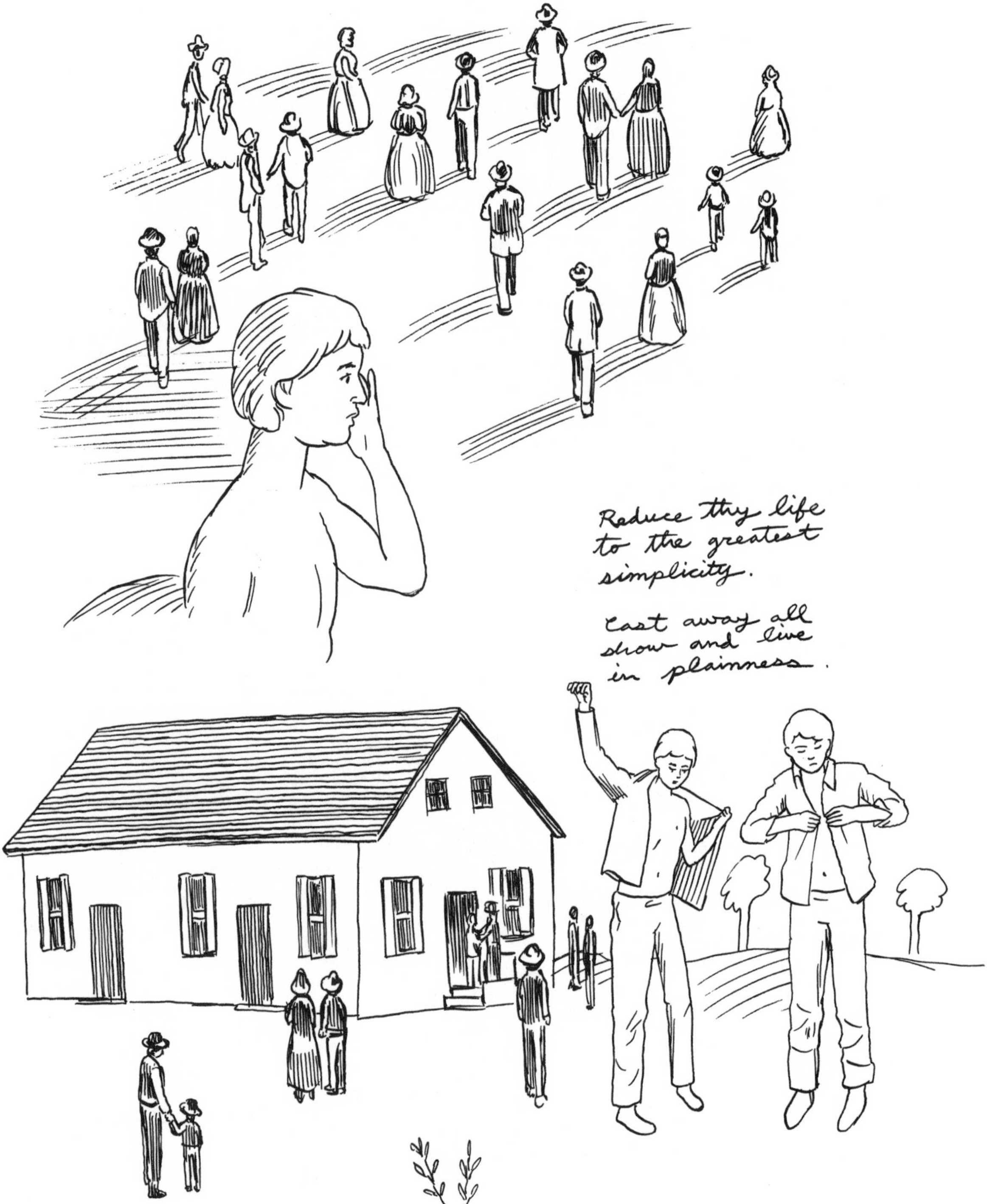
Reduce thy life to the greatest simplicity.
Cast away all show and live in plainness.

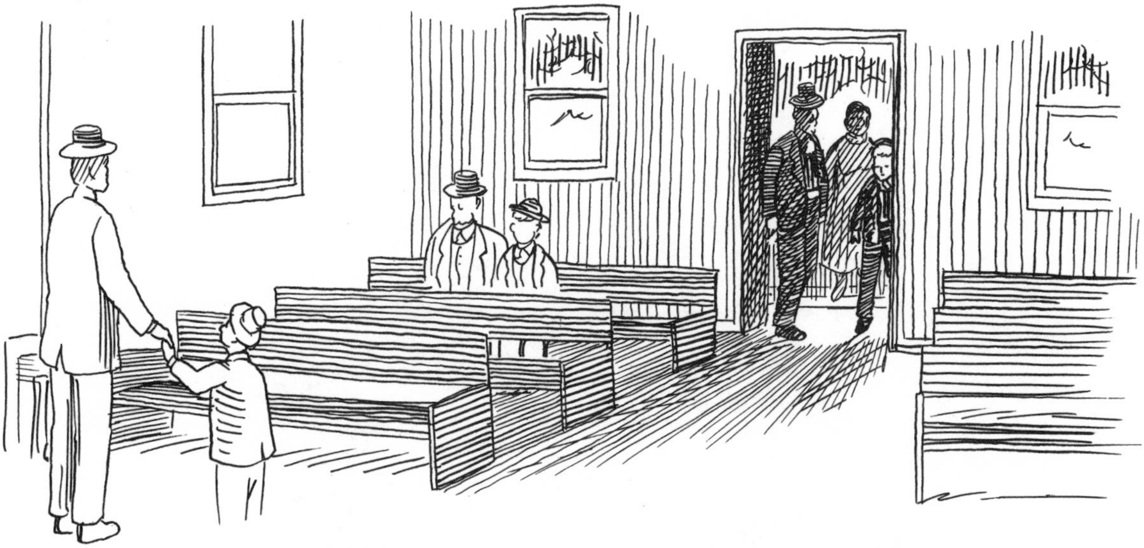

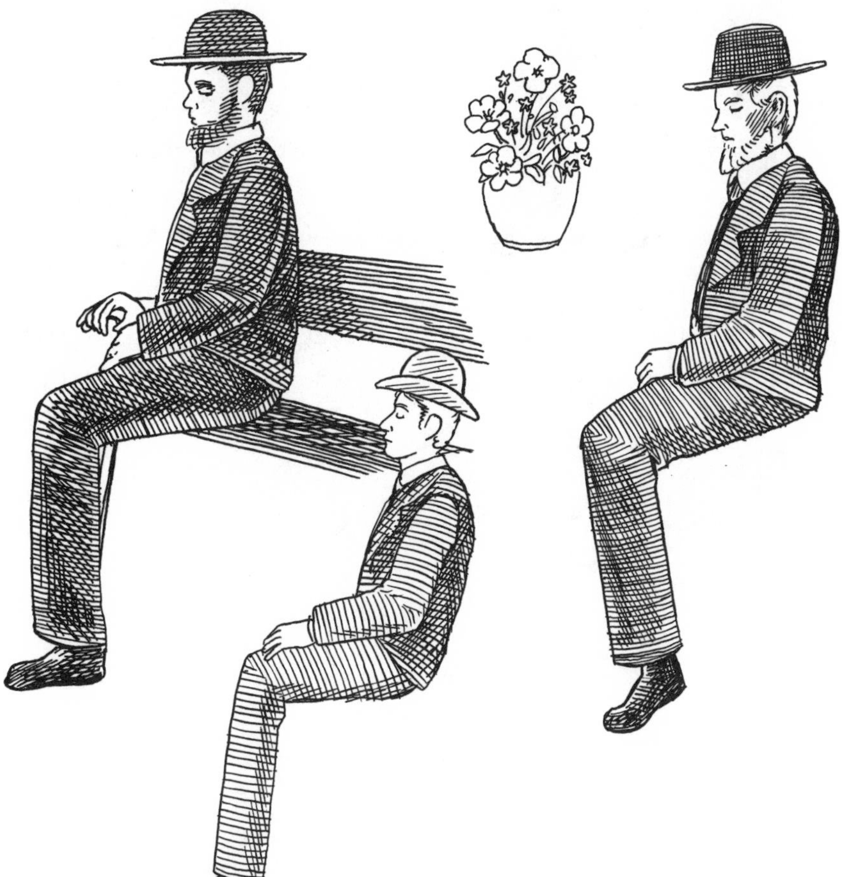

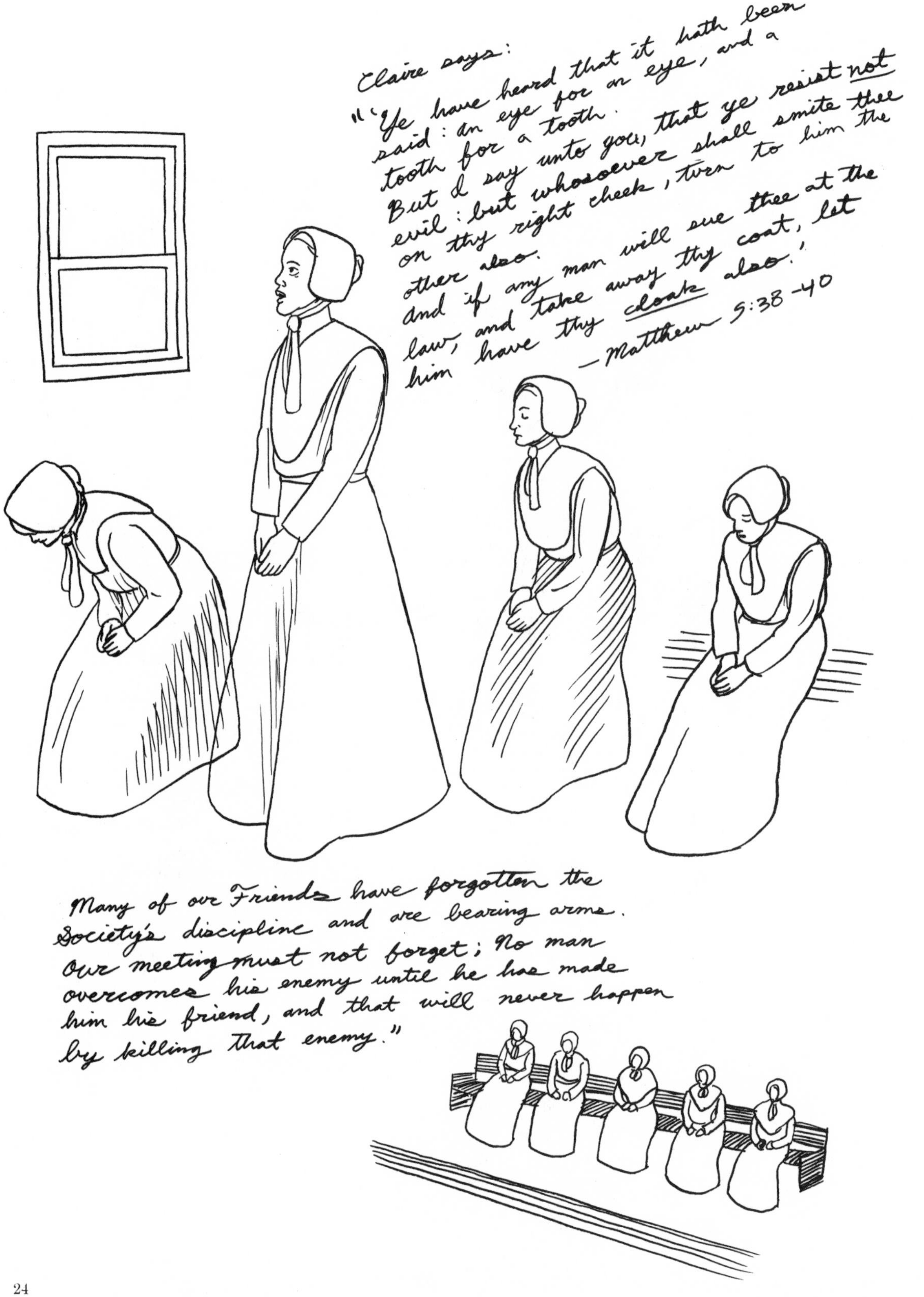
Claire says:
"'Ye have heard that it hath been said: an eye for an eye, and a tooth for a tooth.
But I say unto you, that ye resist not evil: but whosoever shall smite thee on thy right cheek, turn to him the other also.
And if any man will sue thee at the law, and take away thy coat, let him have thy cloak also.'
—Matthew 5:38-40
Many of our Friends have forgotten the Society's discipline and are bearing arms. Our meeting must not forget: No man overcomes his enemy until he has made him his friend, and that will never happen by killing that enemy."

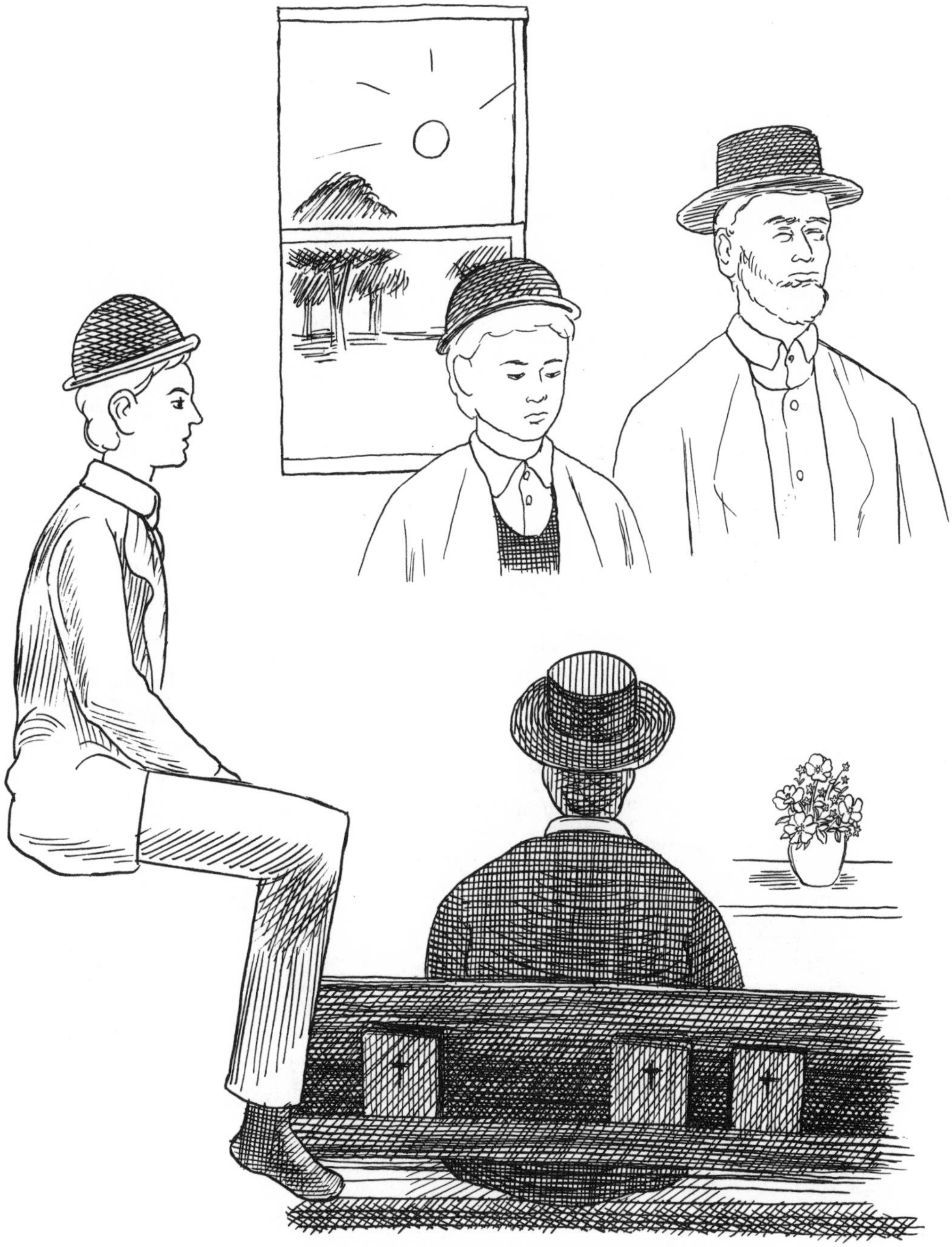

Silence.

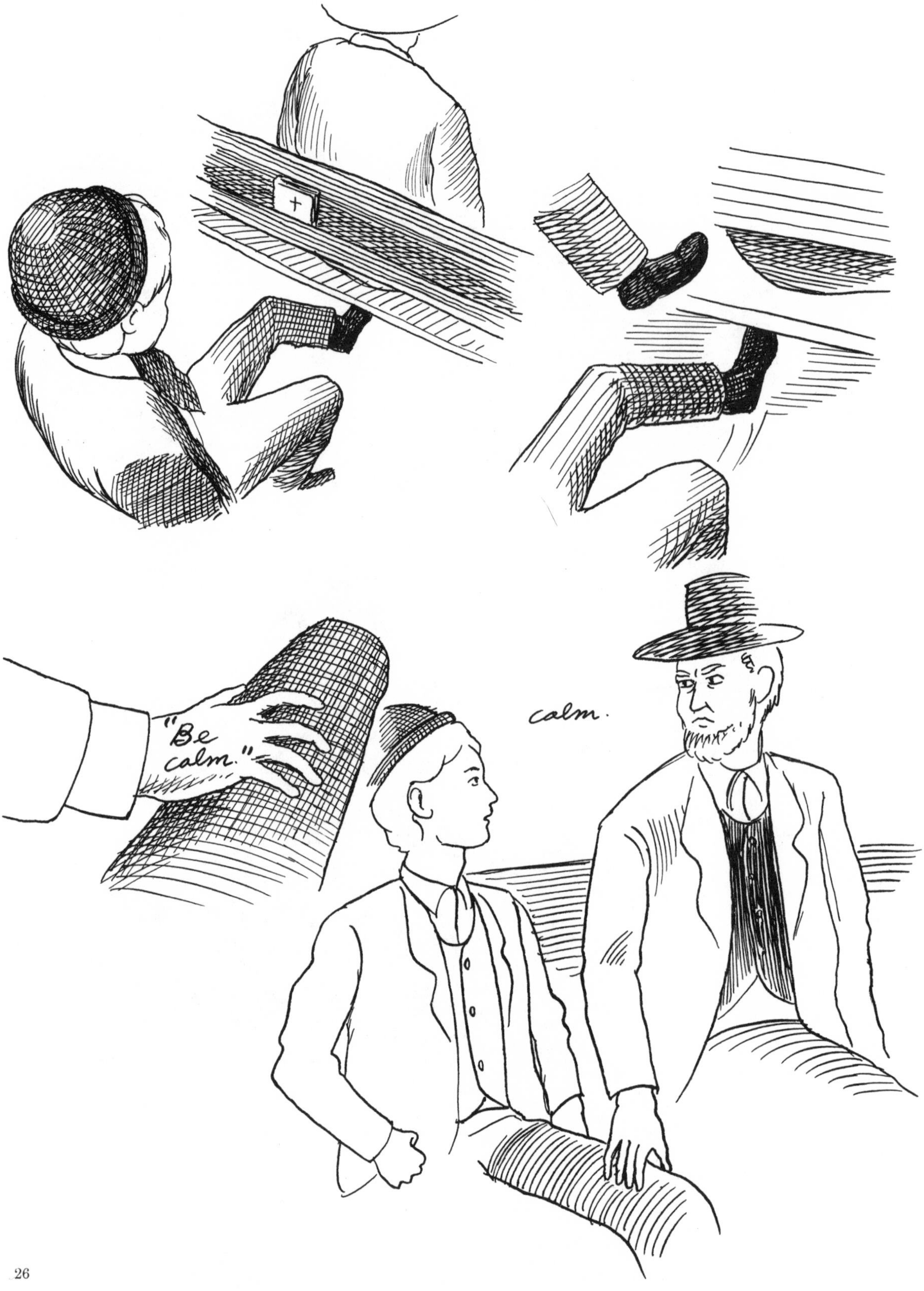
"Be calm."
calm.

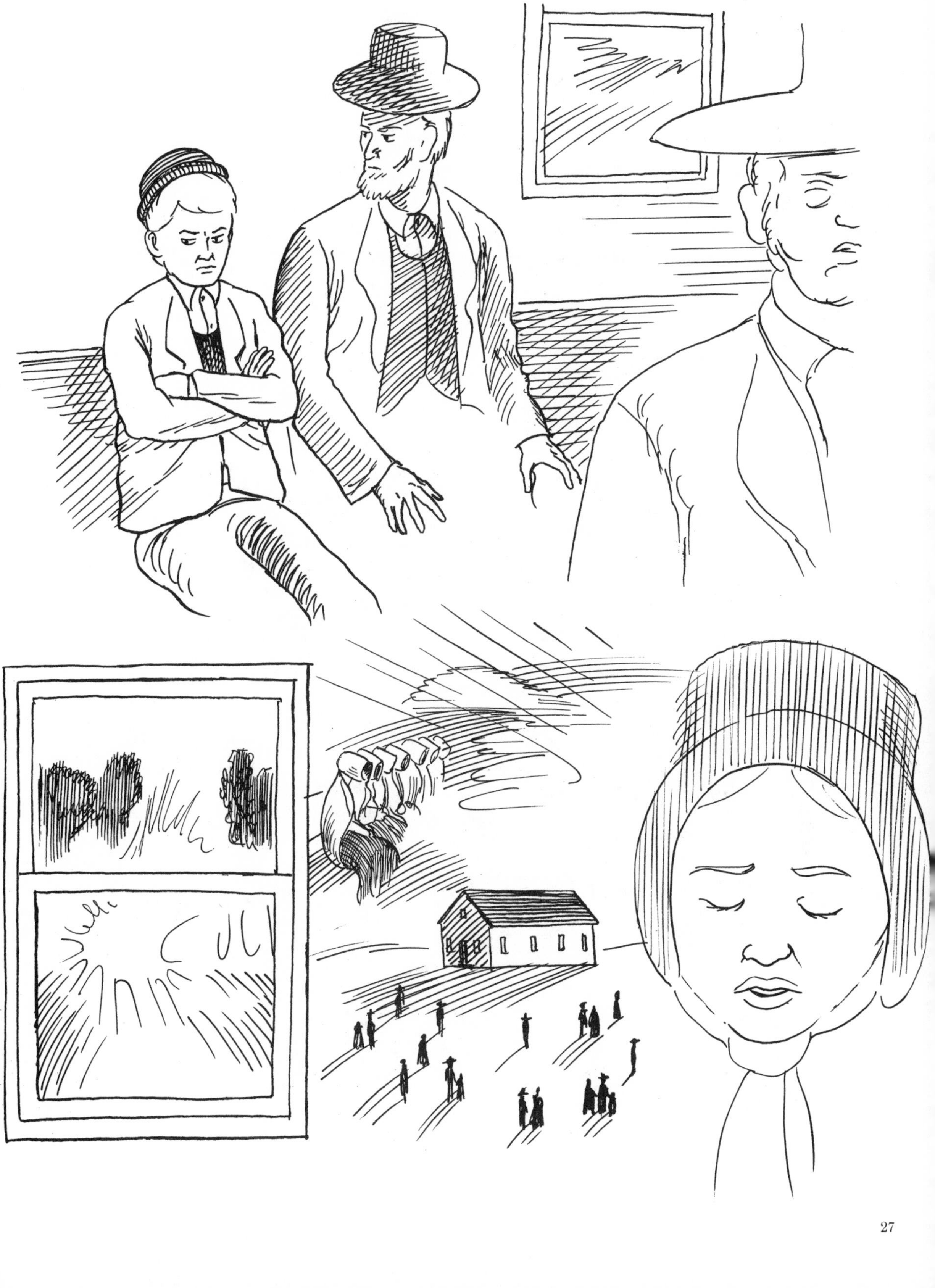

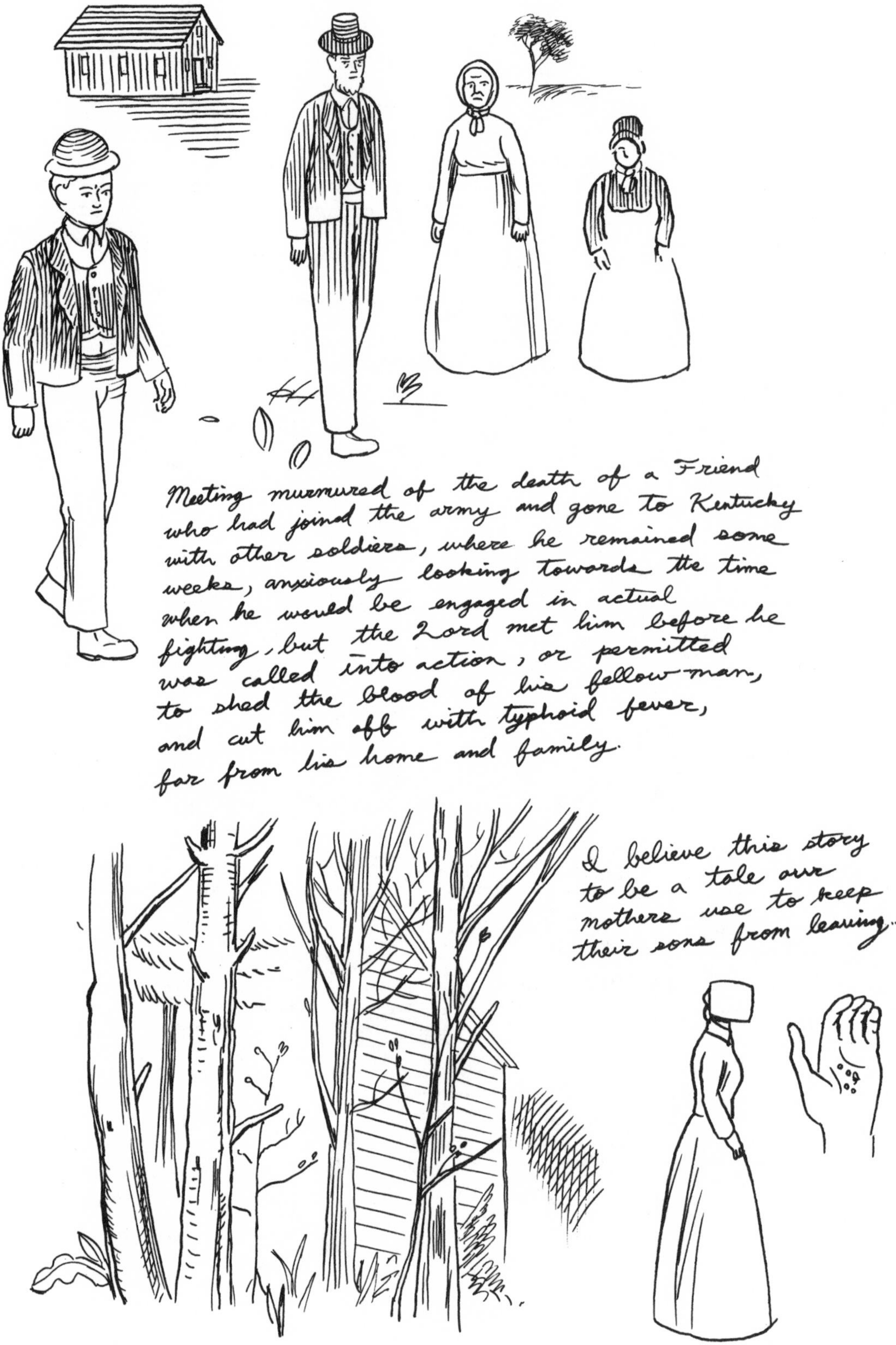
Meeting murmured of the death of a Friend who had joind the army and gone to Kentucky with other soldiers, where he remained some weeks, anxiously looking towards the time when he would be engaged in actual fighting, but the Lord met him before he was called into action, or permitted to shed the blood of his fellow man, and cut him off with typhoid fever, far from his home and family.
I believe this story to be a tale our mothers use to keep their sons from leaving...

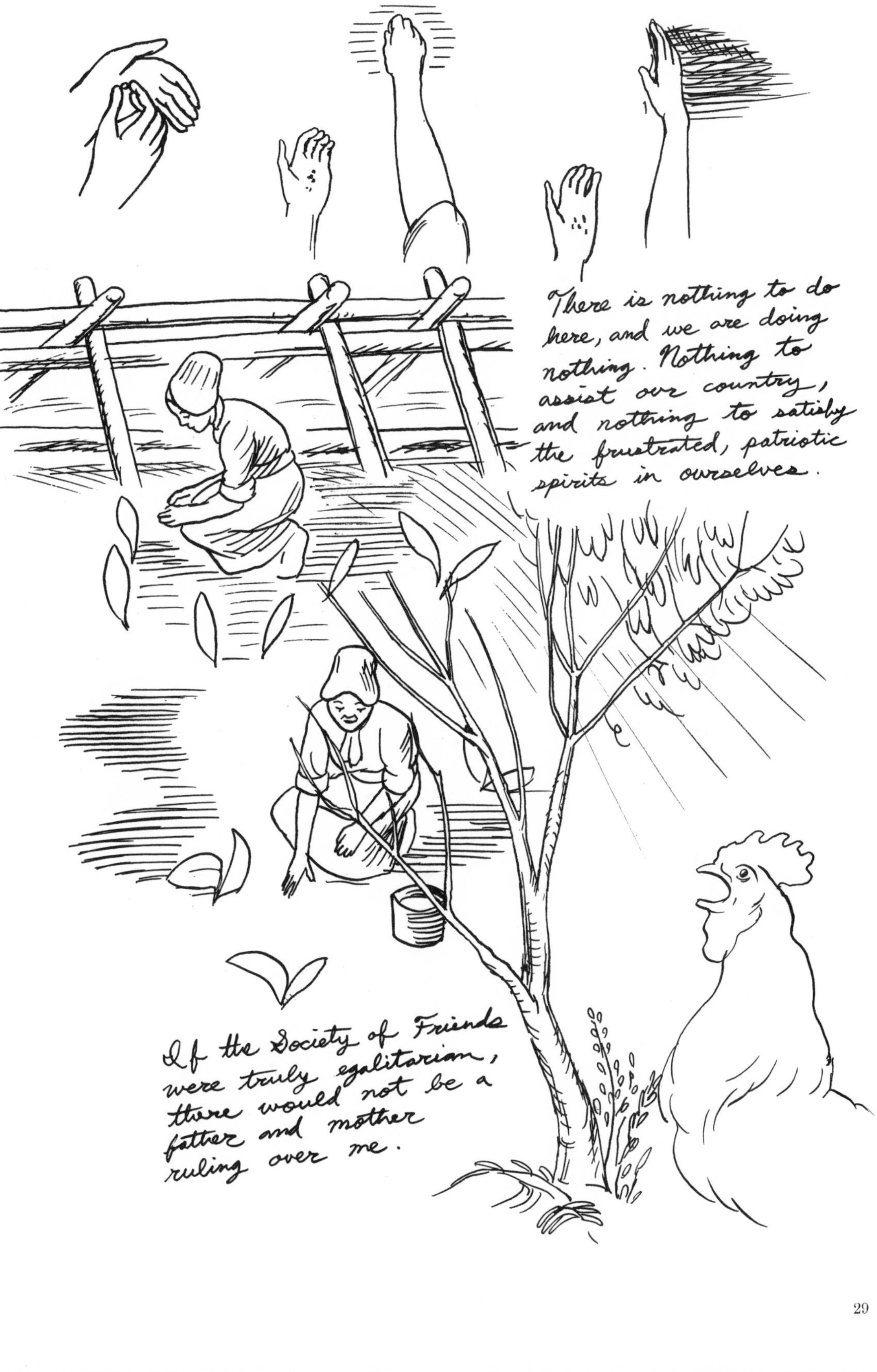
There is nothing to do here, and we are doing nothing. Nothing to nothing. Nothing to assist our country, and nothing to satisfy the frustrated, patriotic spirits in ourselves.
If the Society of Friends were truly egalitarian, there would not be a father and mother ruling over me.

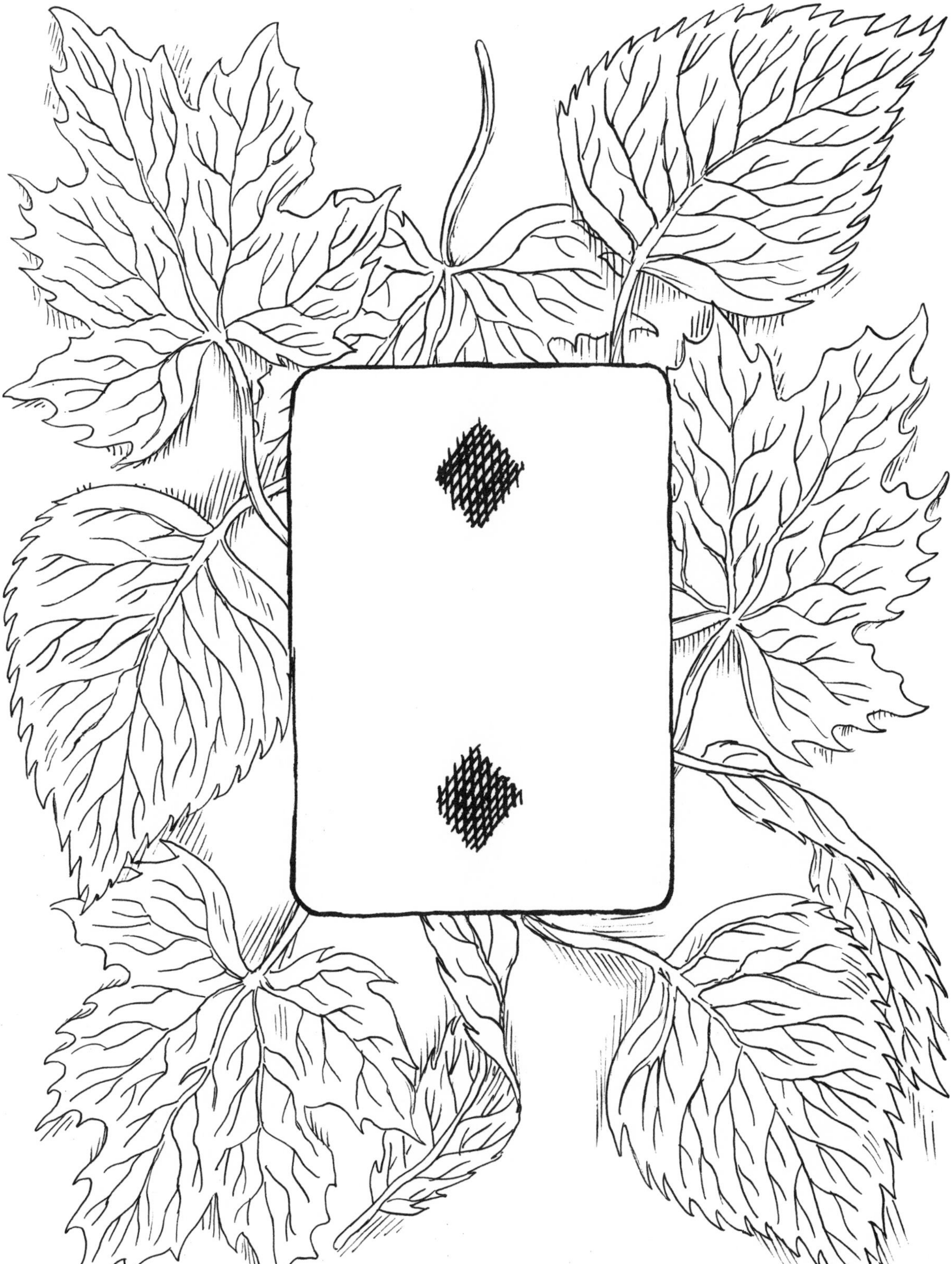

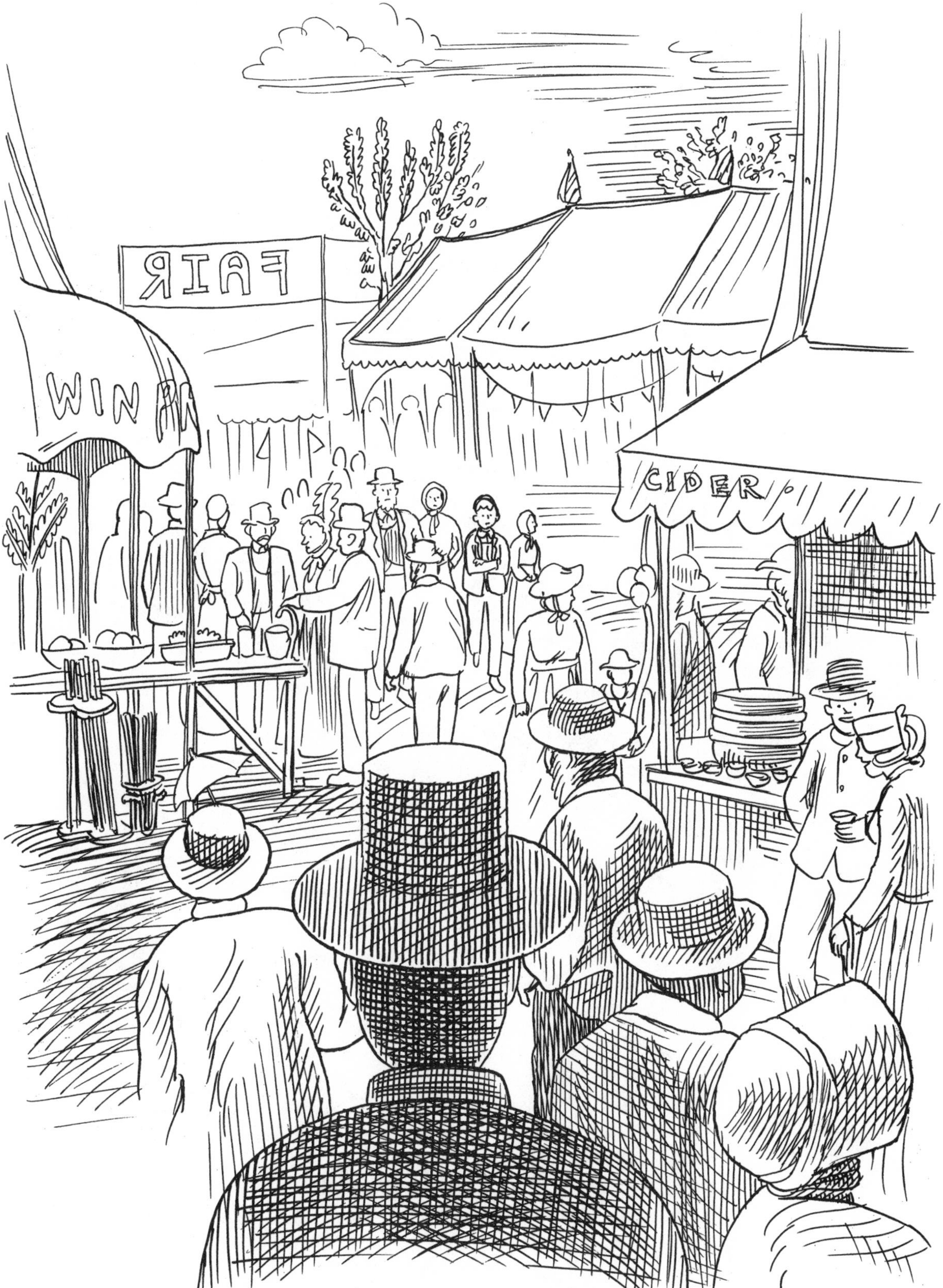
FAIR
WIN
CIDER

Yesterday at the Quarterly Meeting, mother had to deal plainly with those who were indulging in the vain fashions of the world. That the Lord's judgements were not slumbering, but would come upon them for their manifold sins and transgressions.

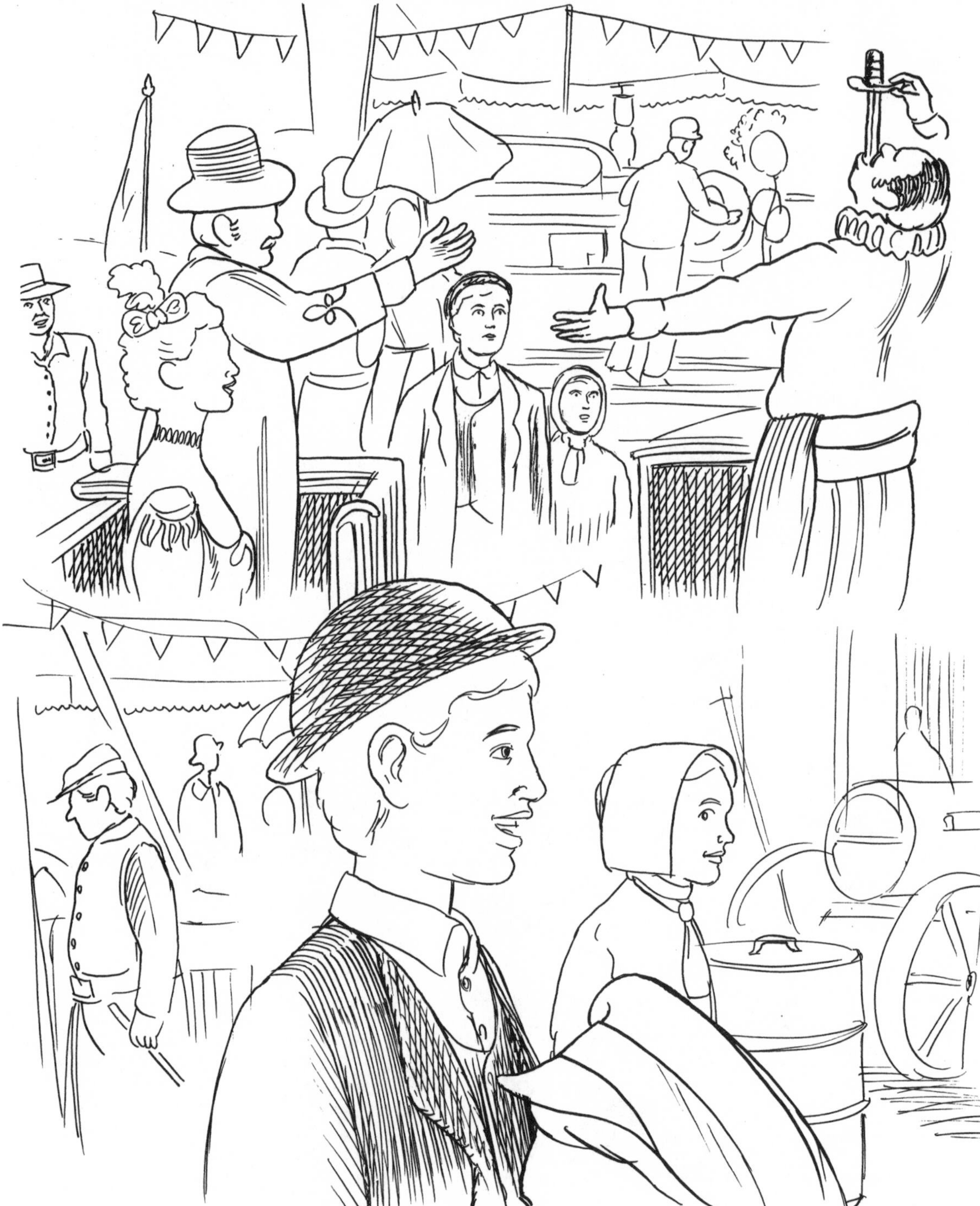

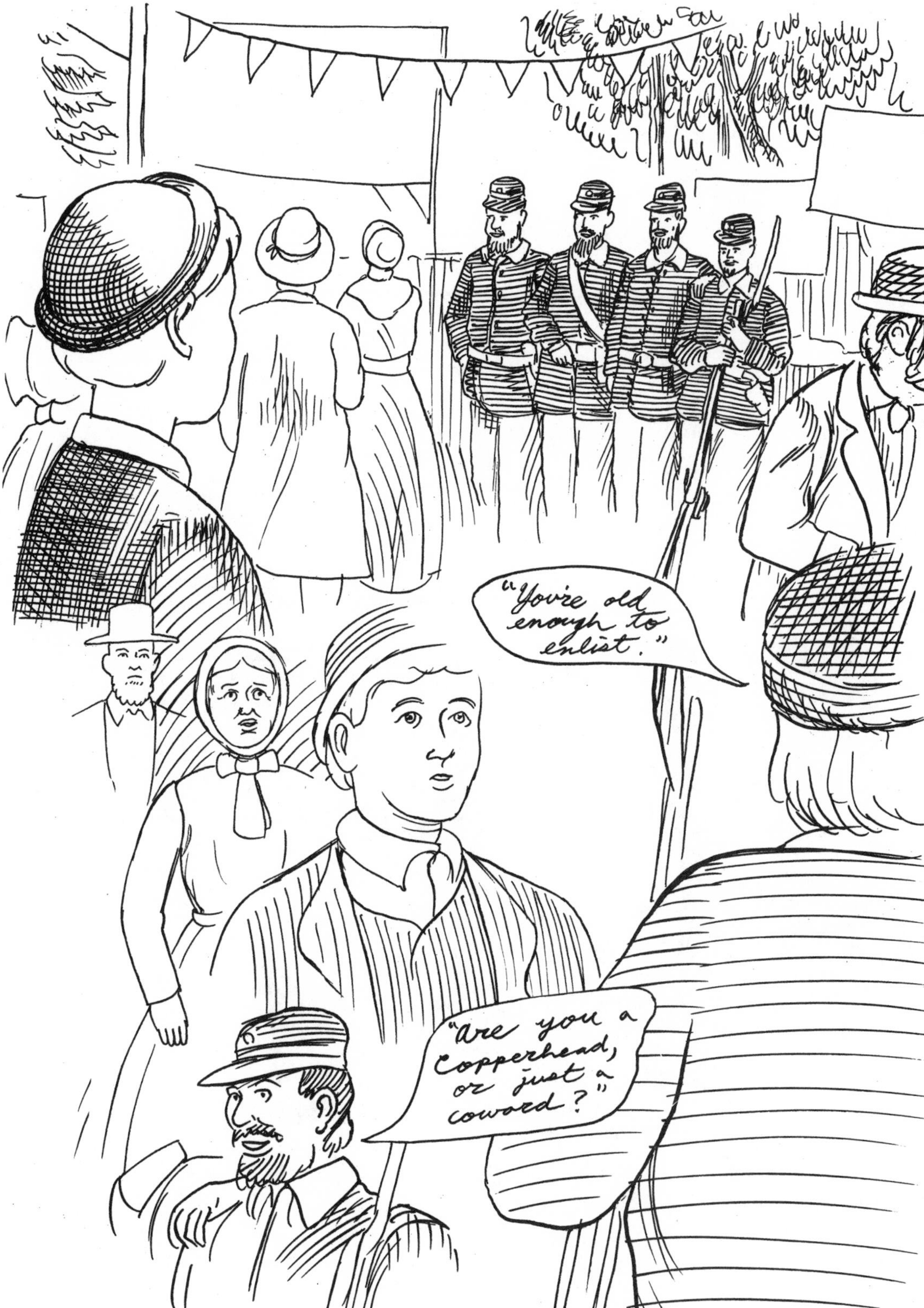
"You're old enough to enlist."
"Are you a Copperhead, or just a coward?"

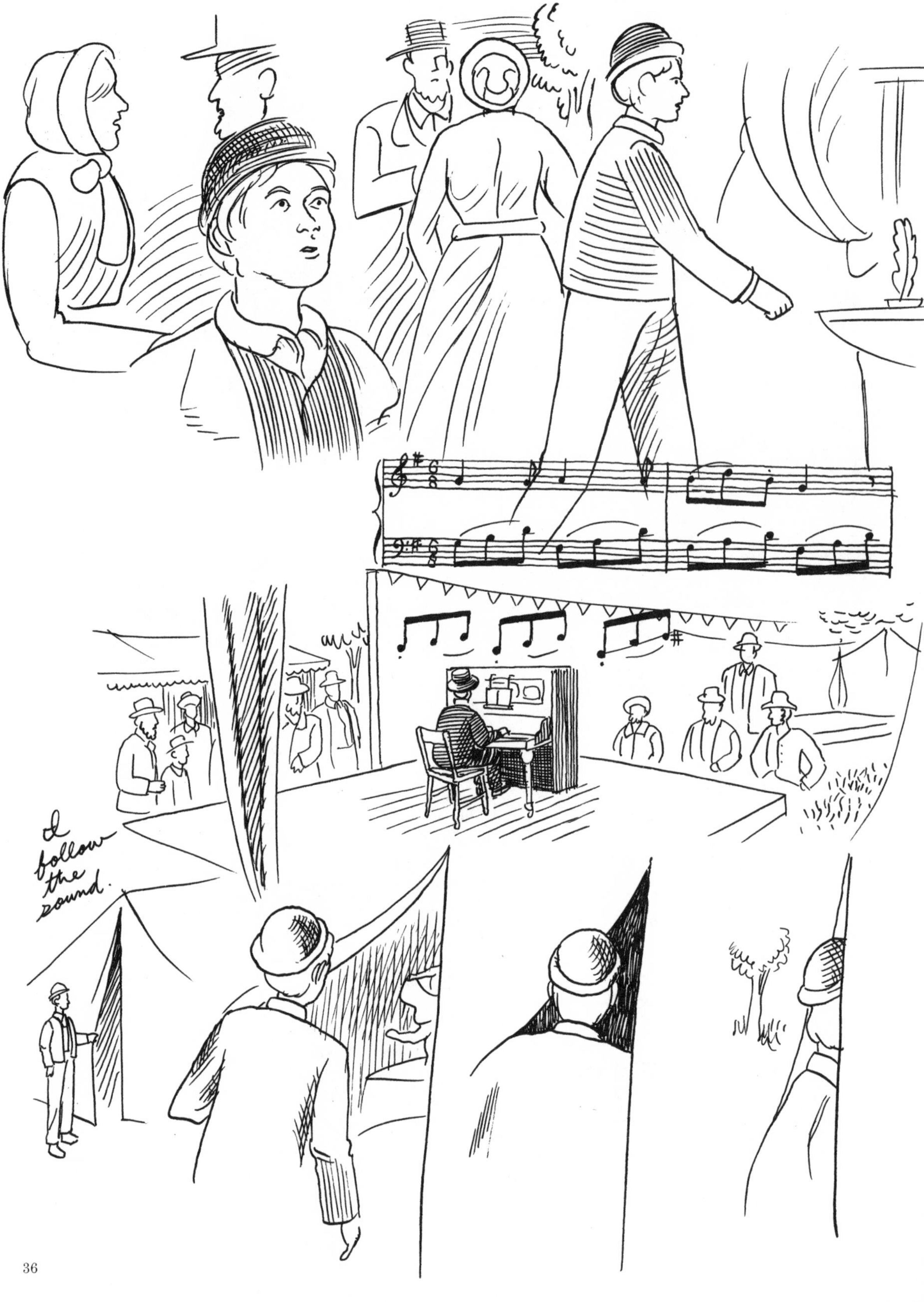
I follow the sound.

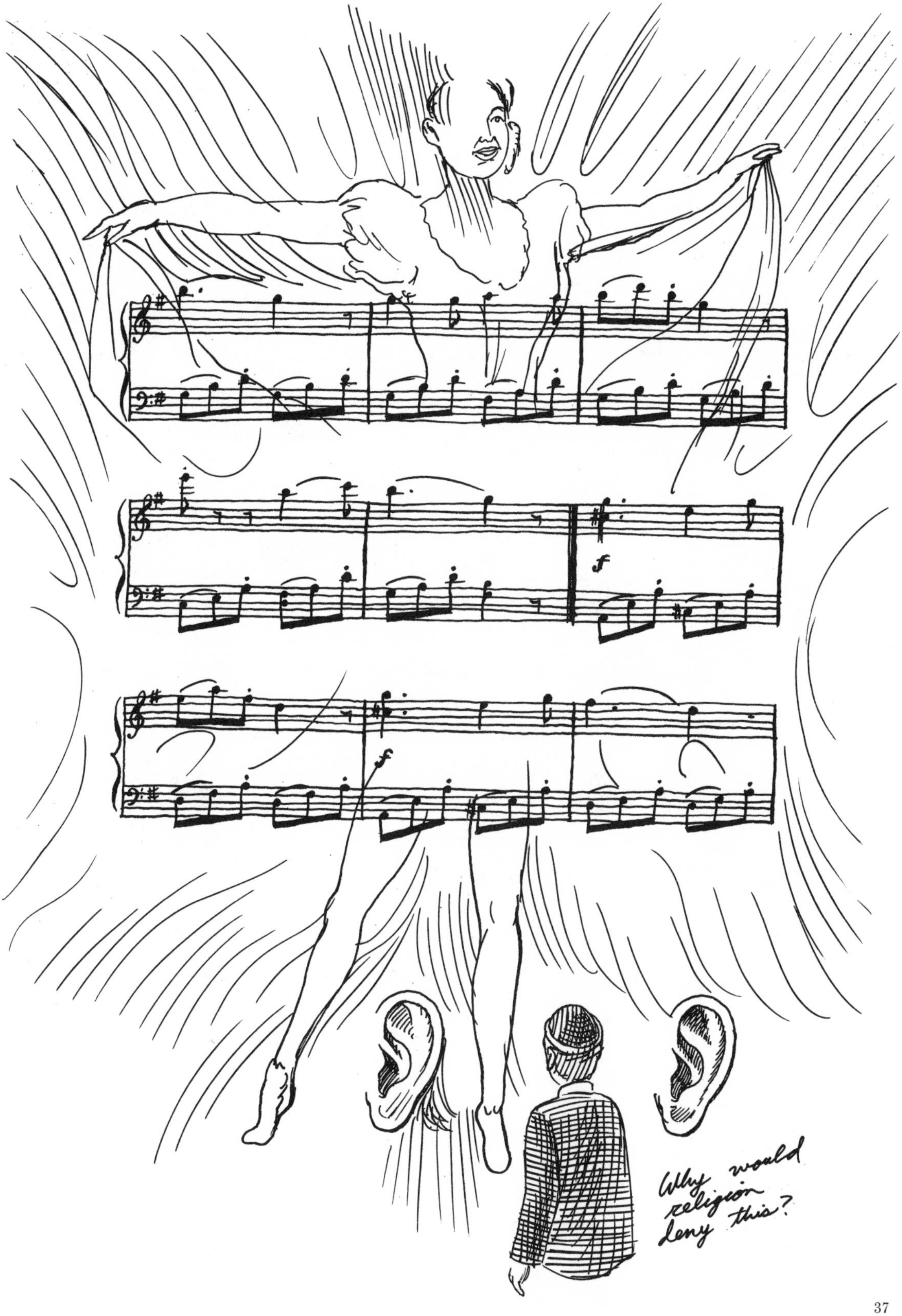
f
f
f
Why would religion deny this?

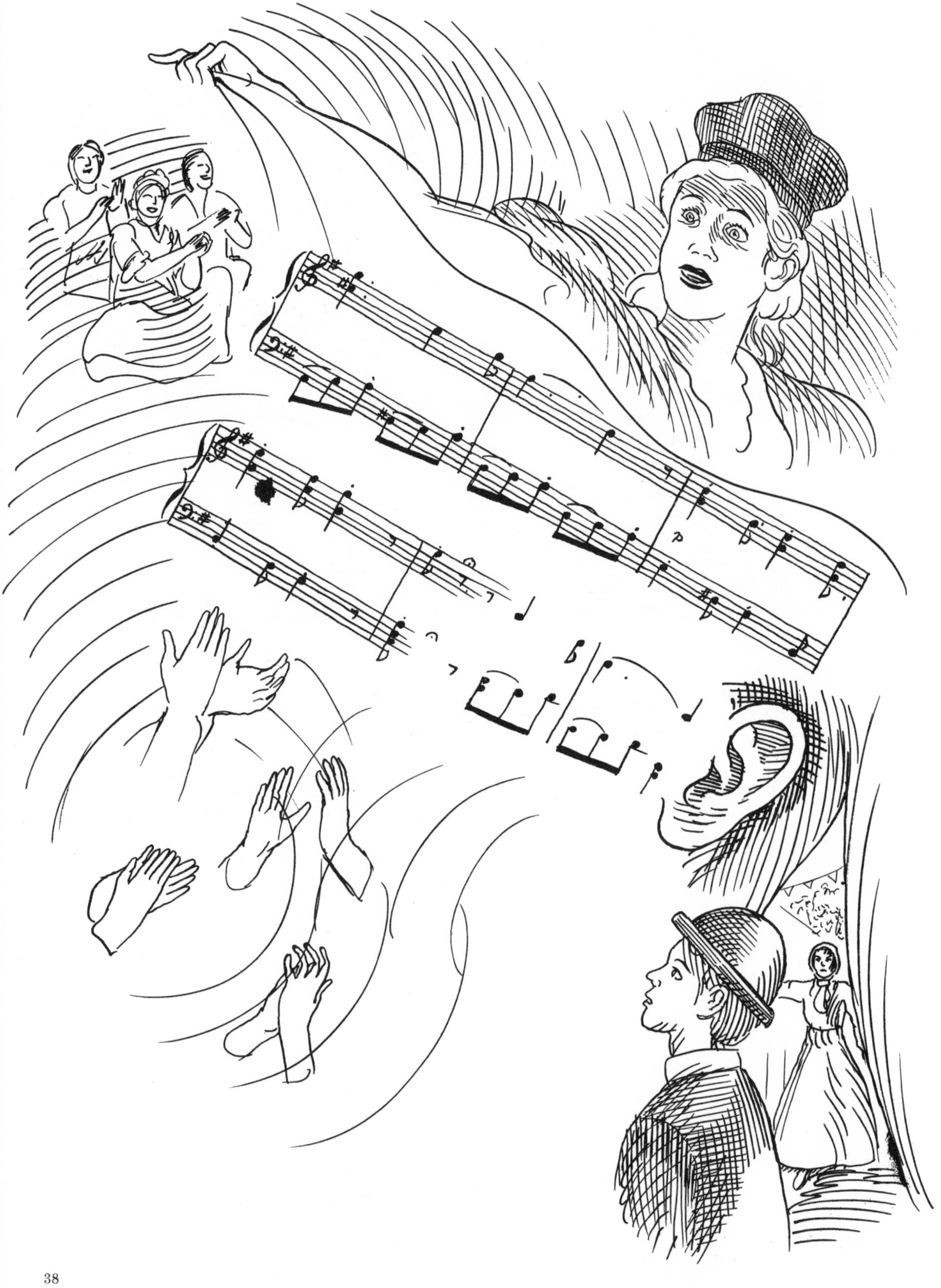

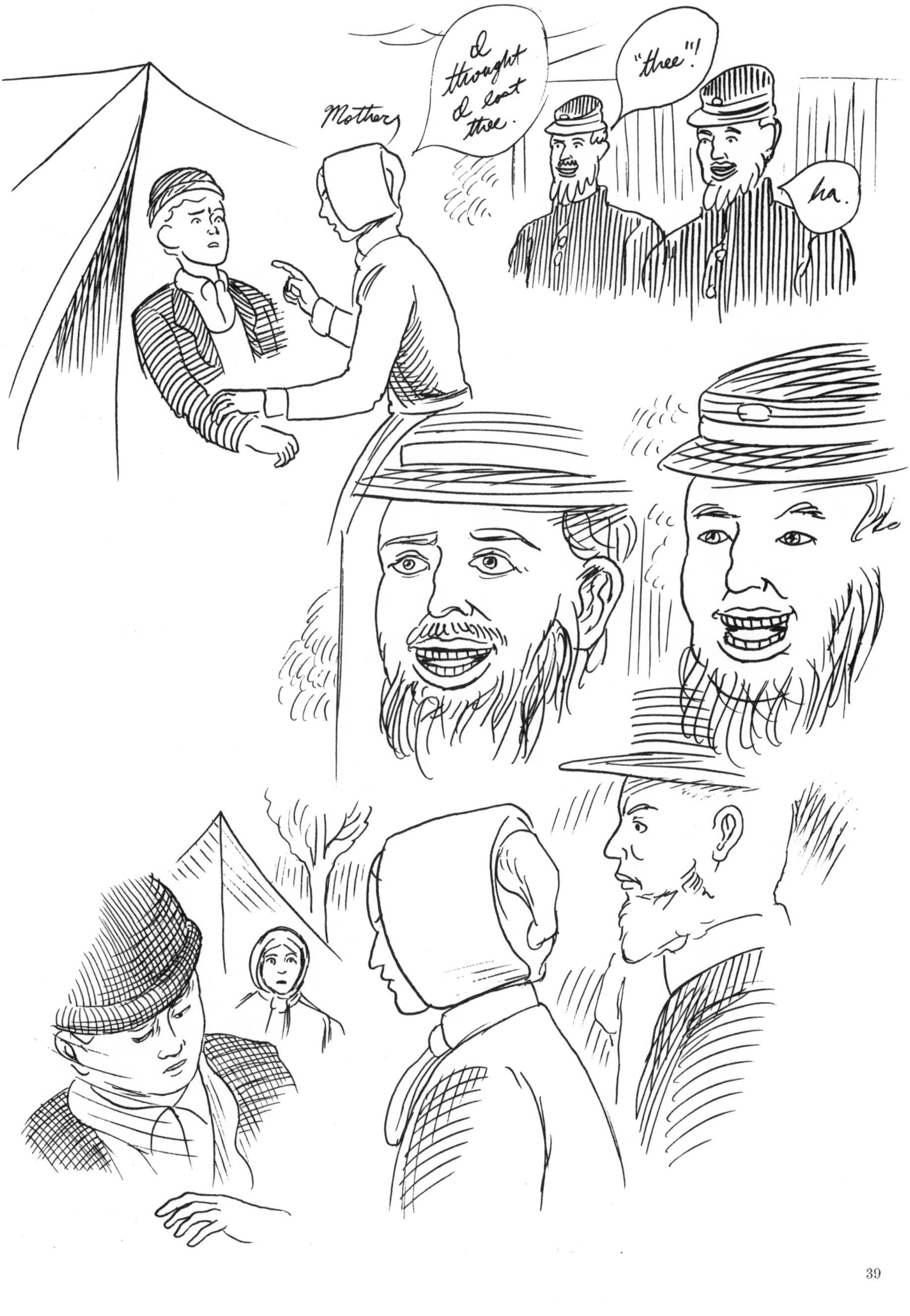
Mother,
I thought I lost thee.
"thee"!
ha.

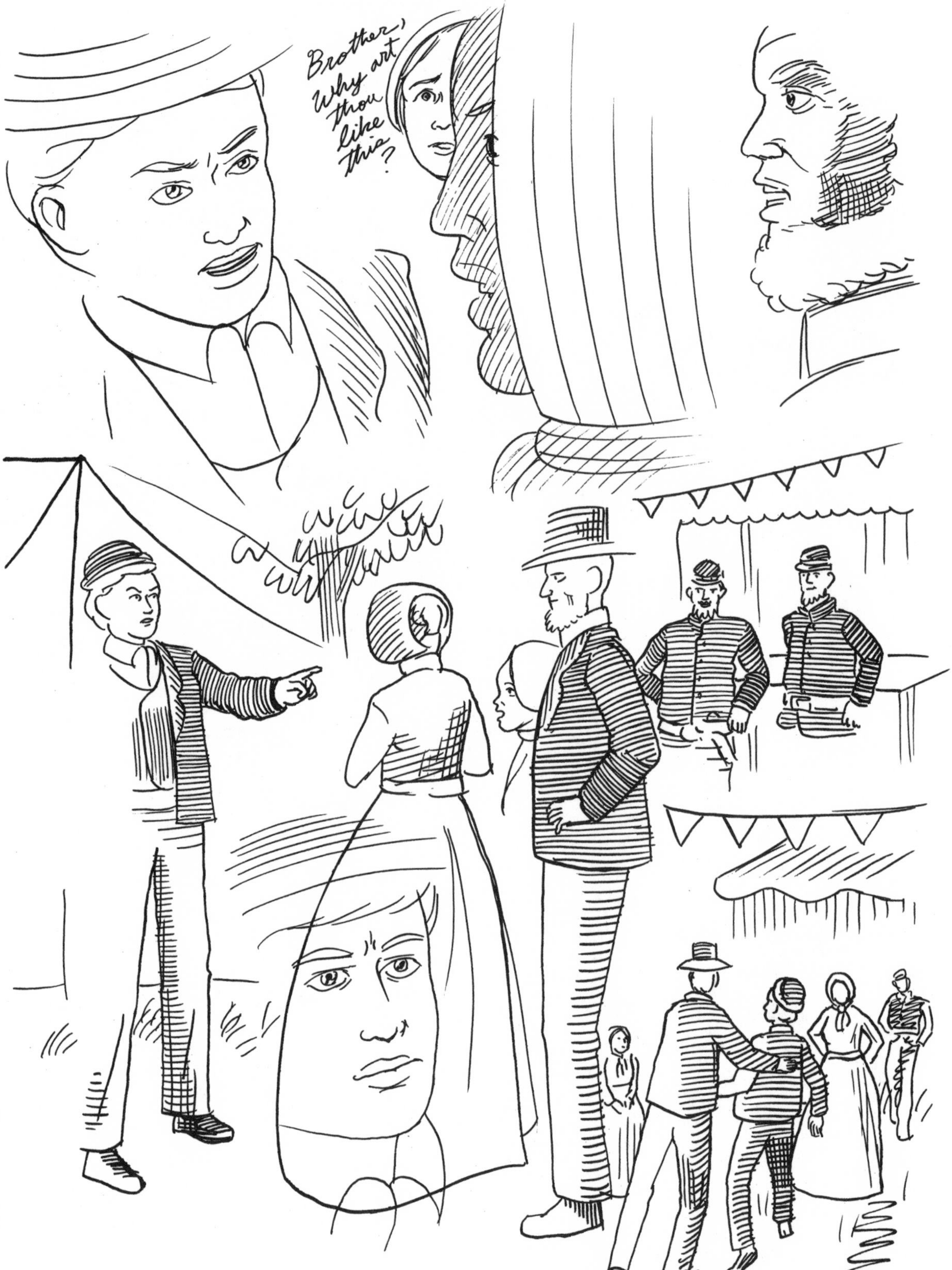
Brother, why art thou like this?

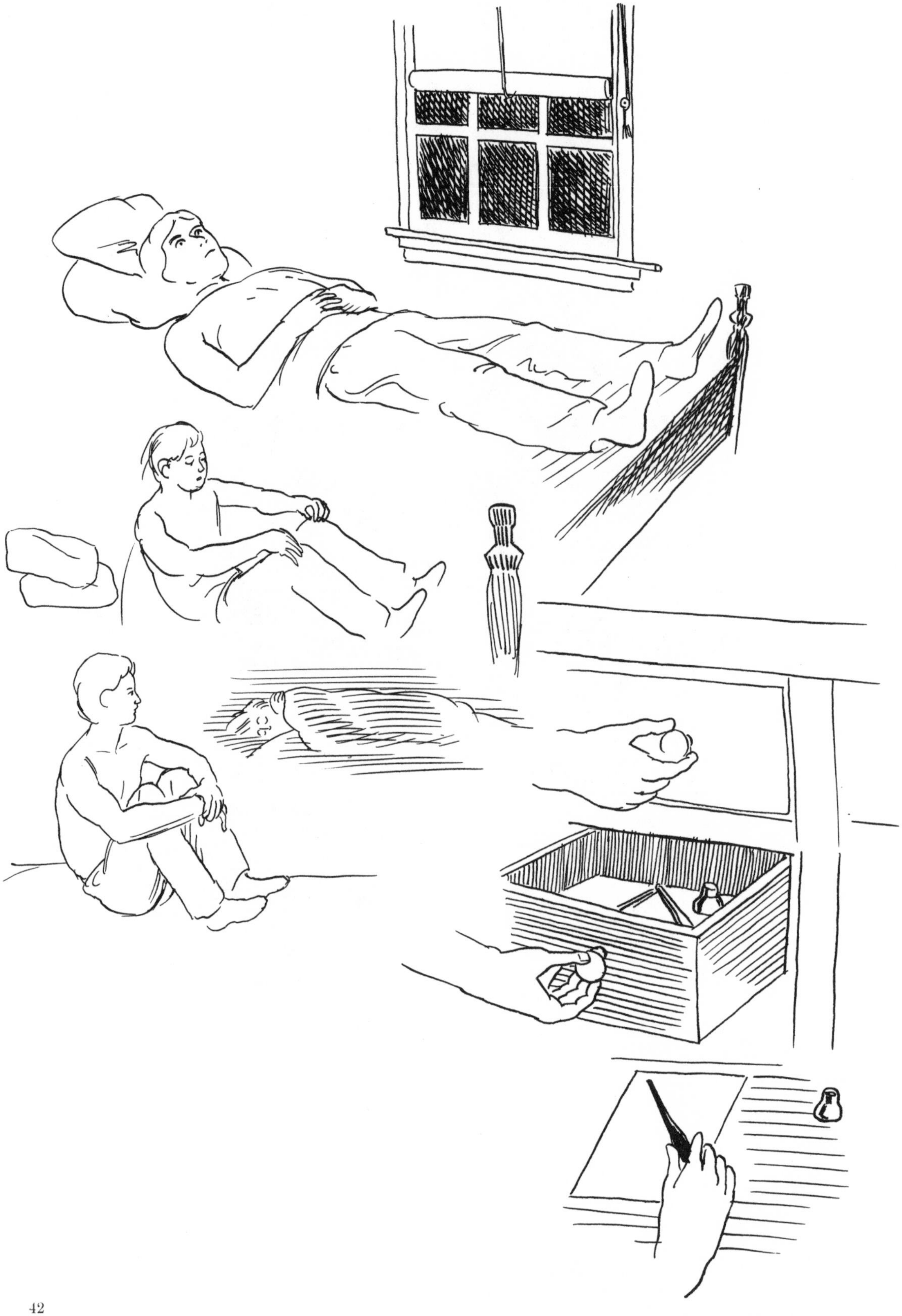

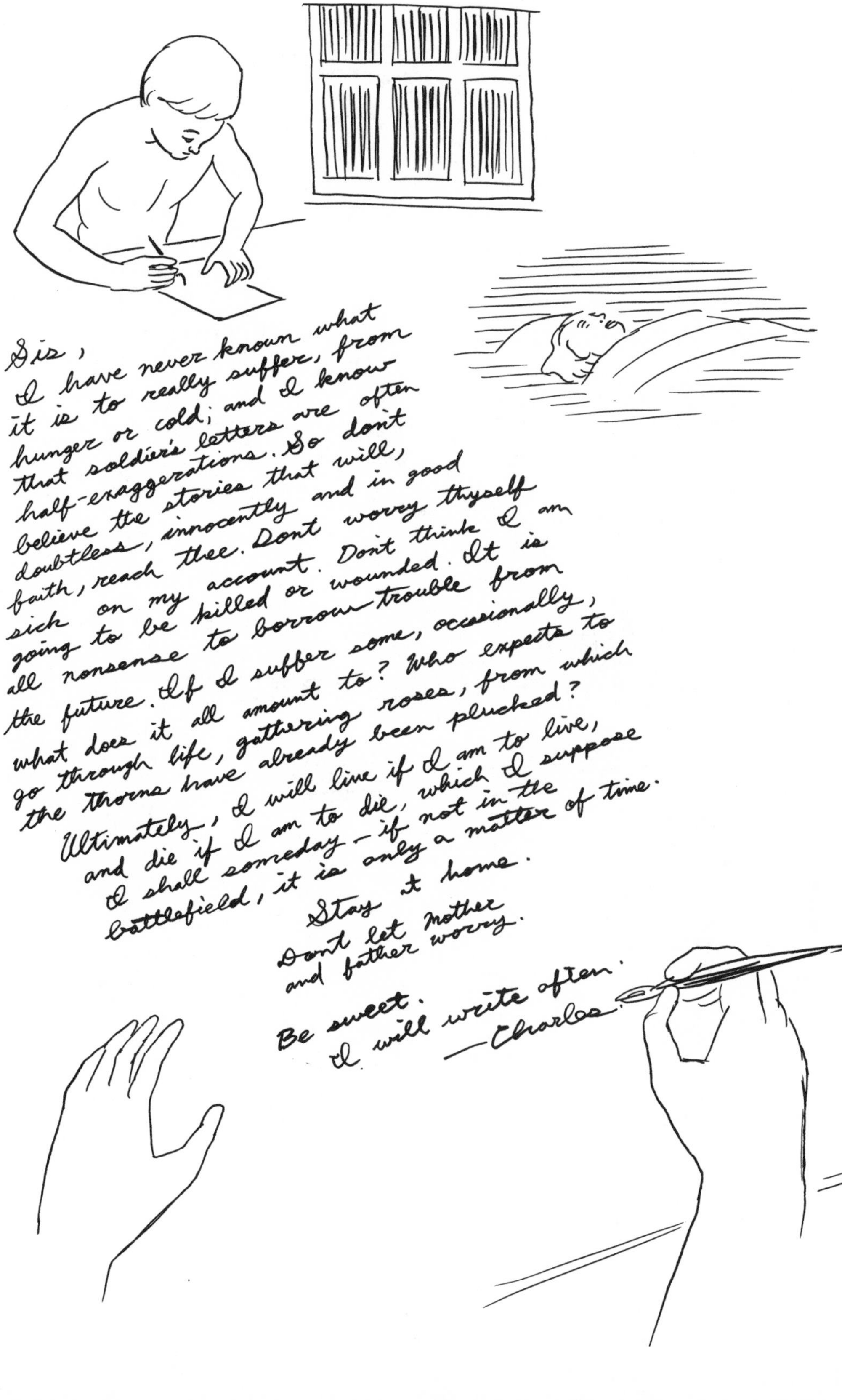
Sis,
I have never known what
it is to really suffer, from
hunger or cold; and I know
that soldier's letters are often
half-exaggerations. So don't
believe the stories that will,
doubtless, innocently and in good
faith, reach thee. Dont worry thyself
sick on my account. Don't think I am
going to be killed or wounded. It is
all nonsense to borrow trouble from
the future. If I suffer some, occasionally,
what does it all amount to? Who expects to
go through life, gathering roses, from which
the thorns have already been plucked?
Ultimately, I will live if I am to live,
and die if I am to die, which I suppose
I shall someday—if not in the
battlefield, it is only a matter of time.
Stay at home.
Don't let mother
and father worry.
Be sweet.
I will write often.
—Charles

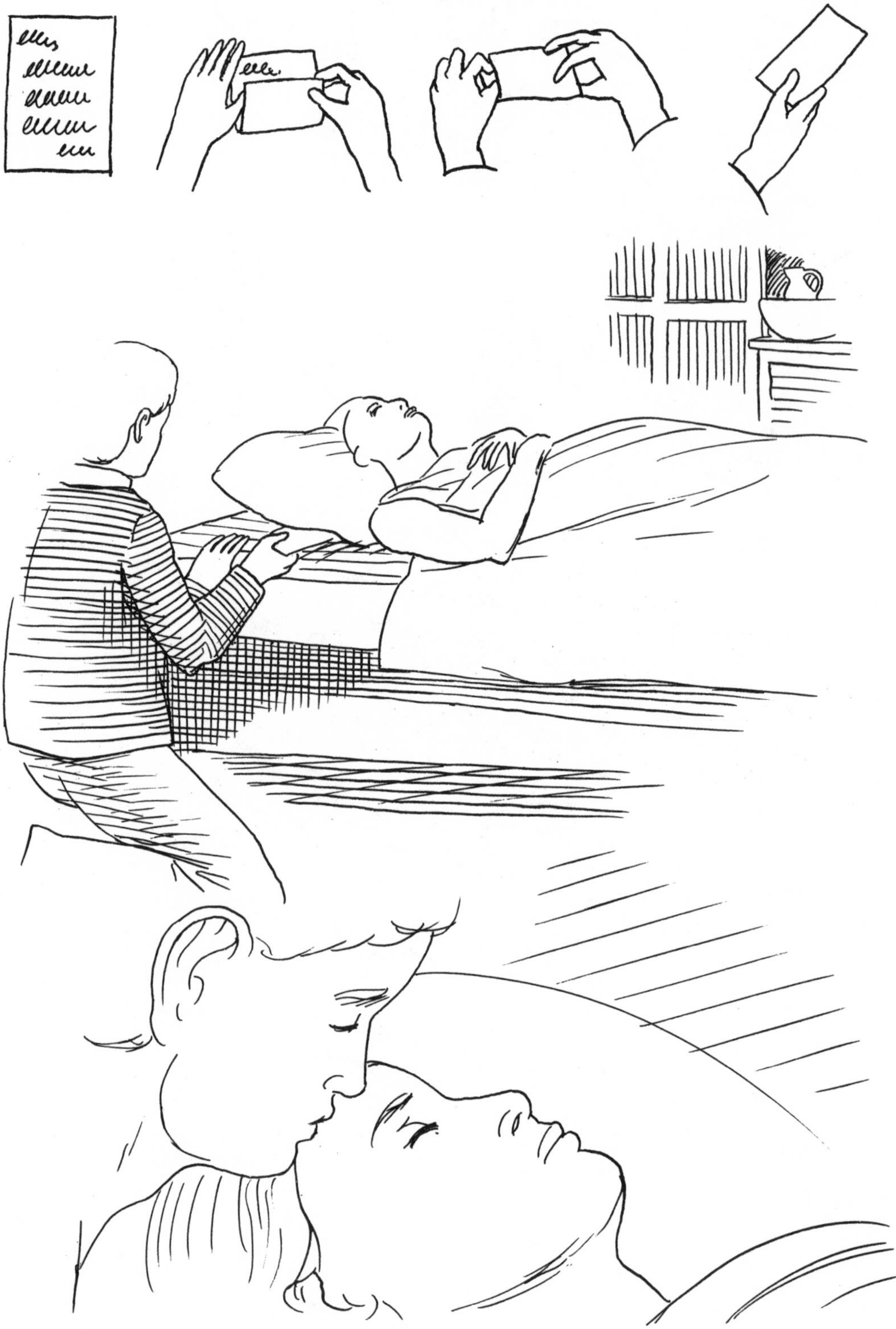

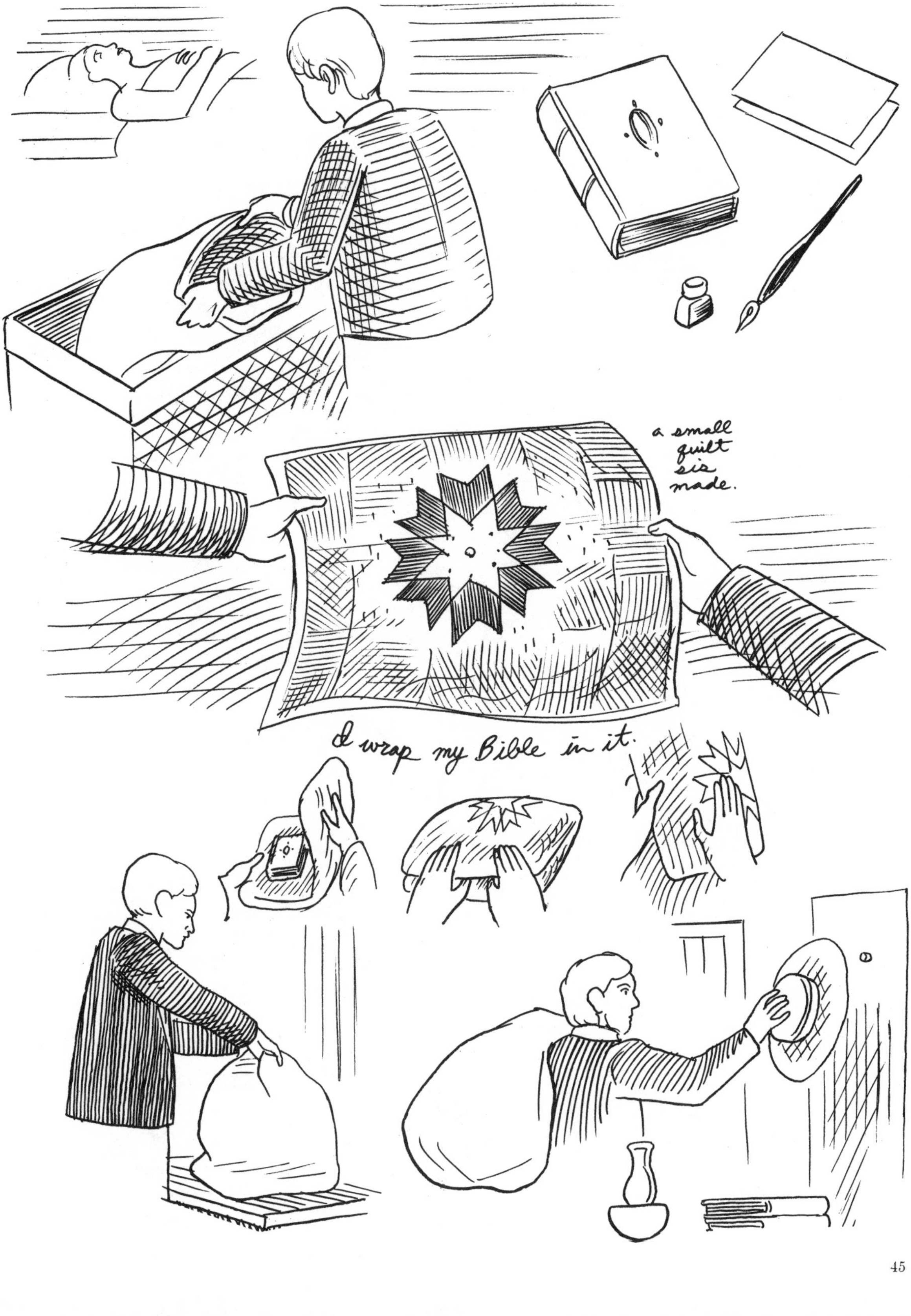
a small quilt sis made.
I wrap my Bible in it.

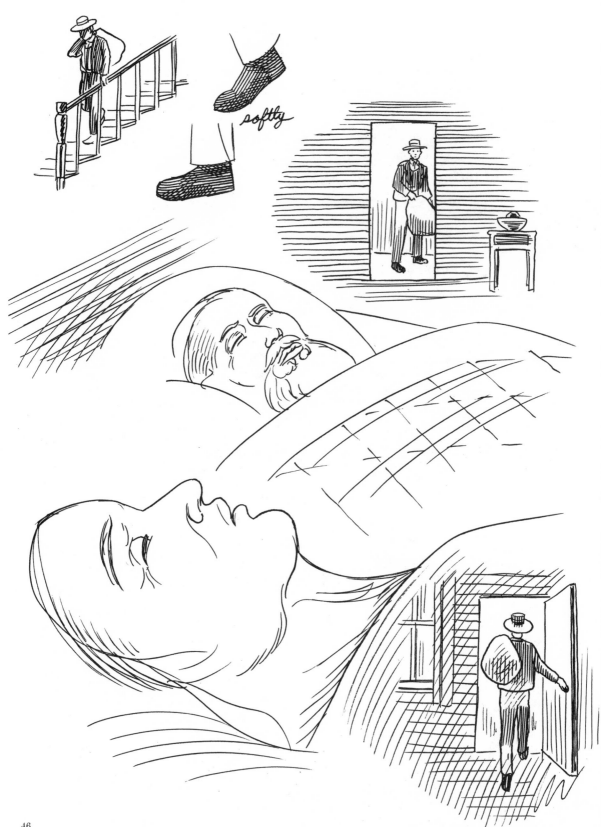

softly

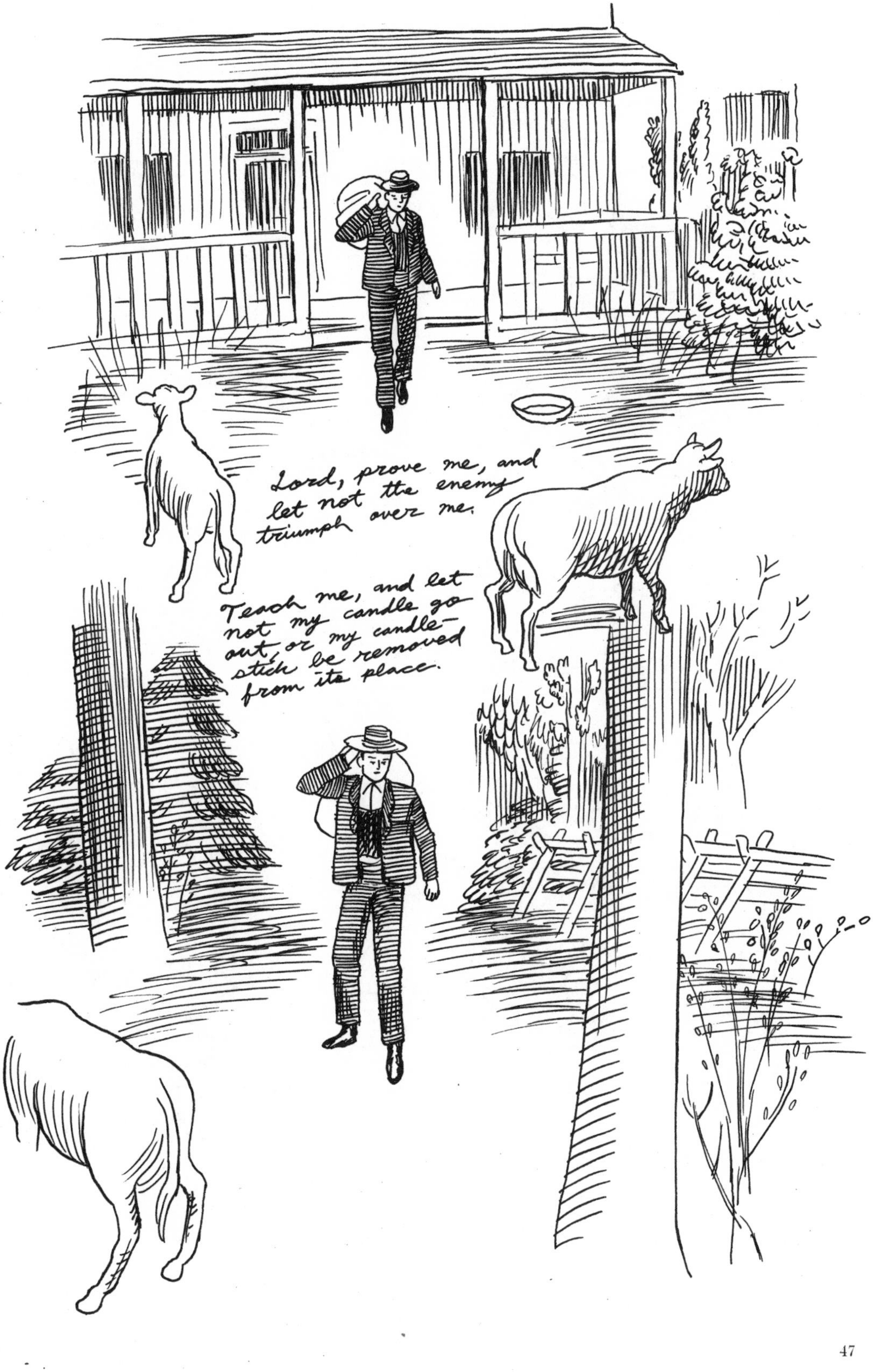
Lord, prove me, and let not the enemy triumph over me.
Teach me, and let not my candle go out, or my candlestick be removed from its place.

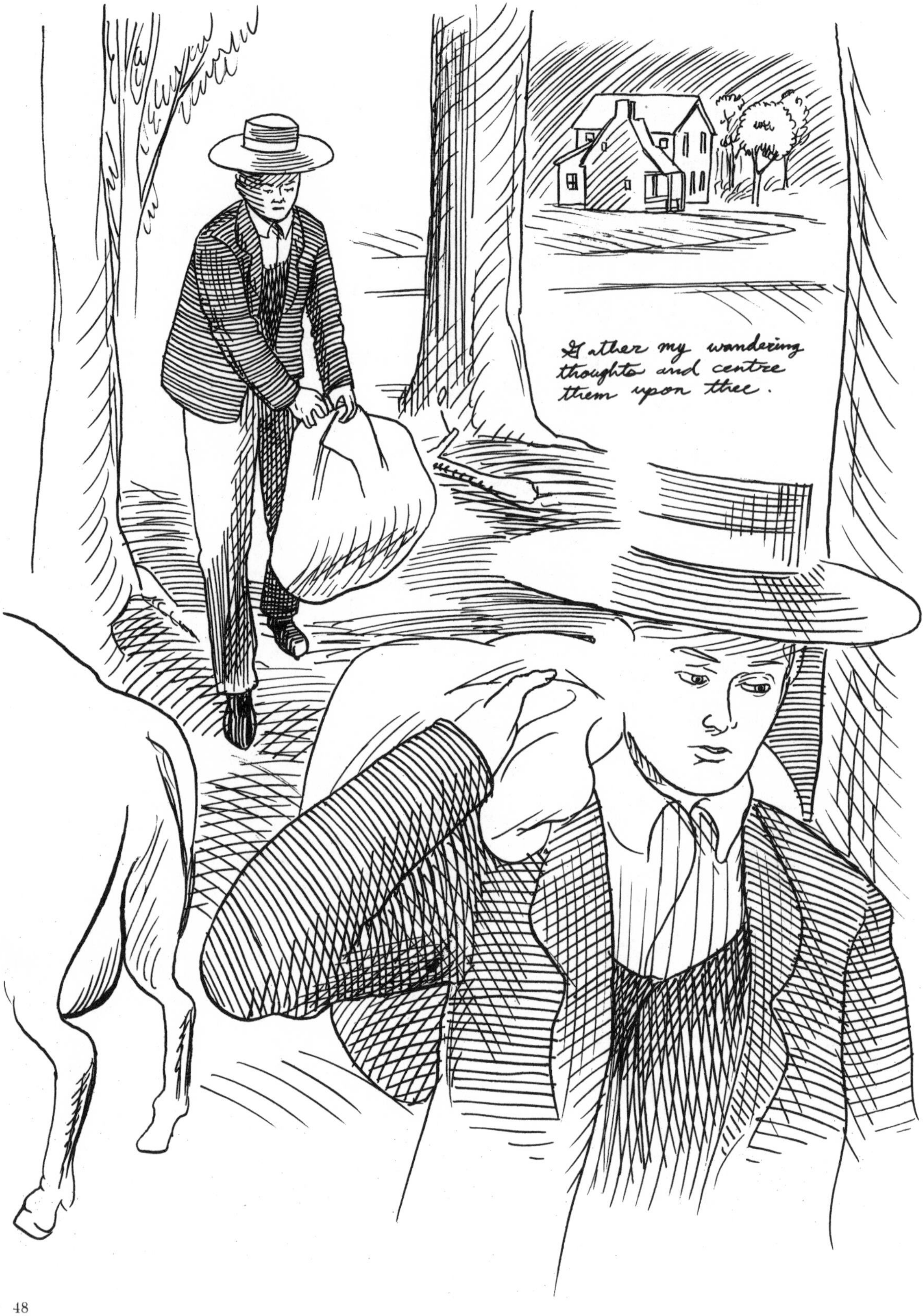
Gather my wandering
thoughts and centre
them upon thee.

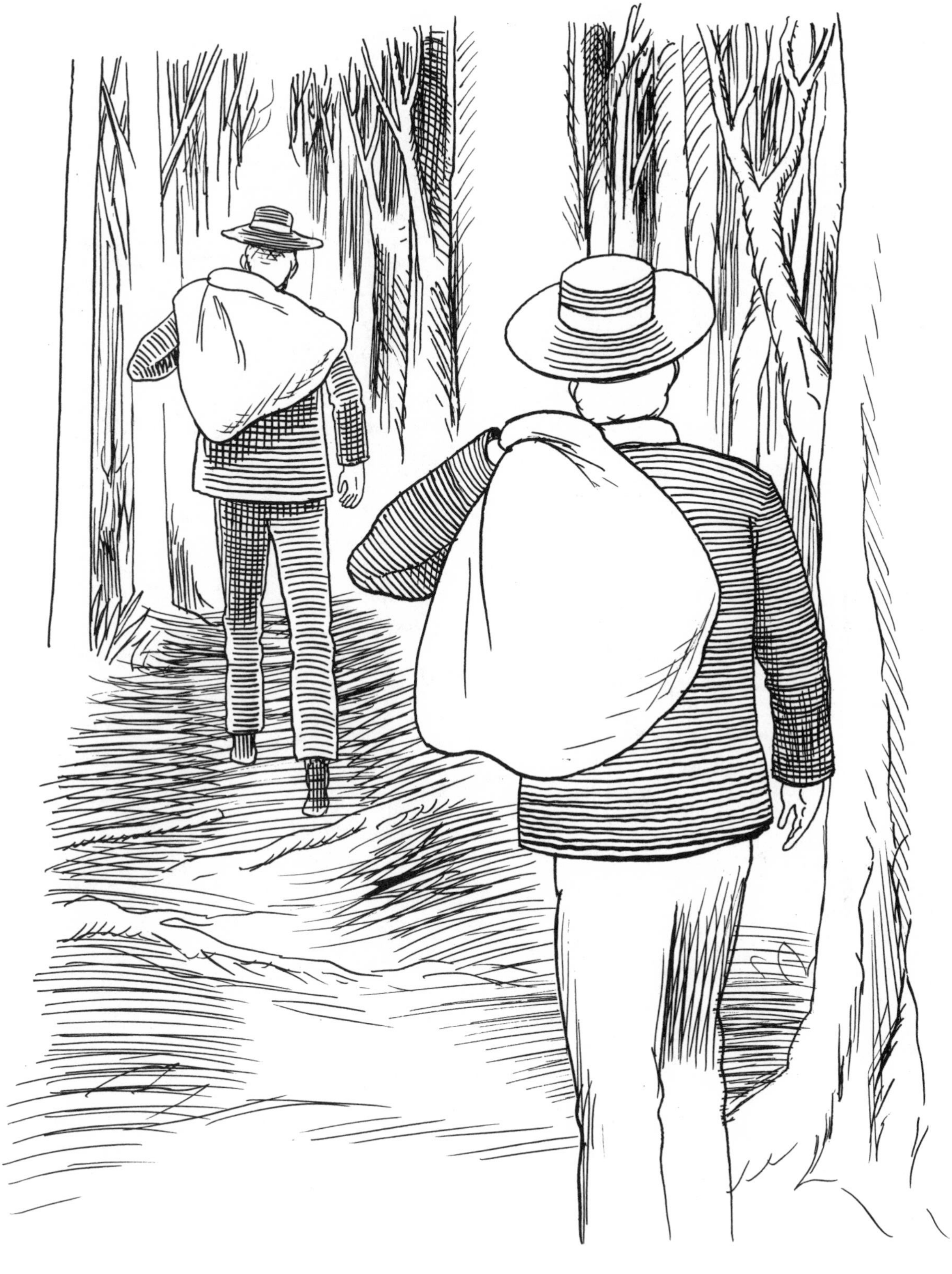

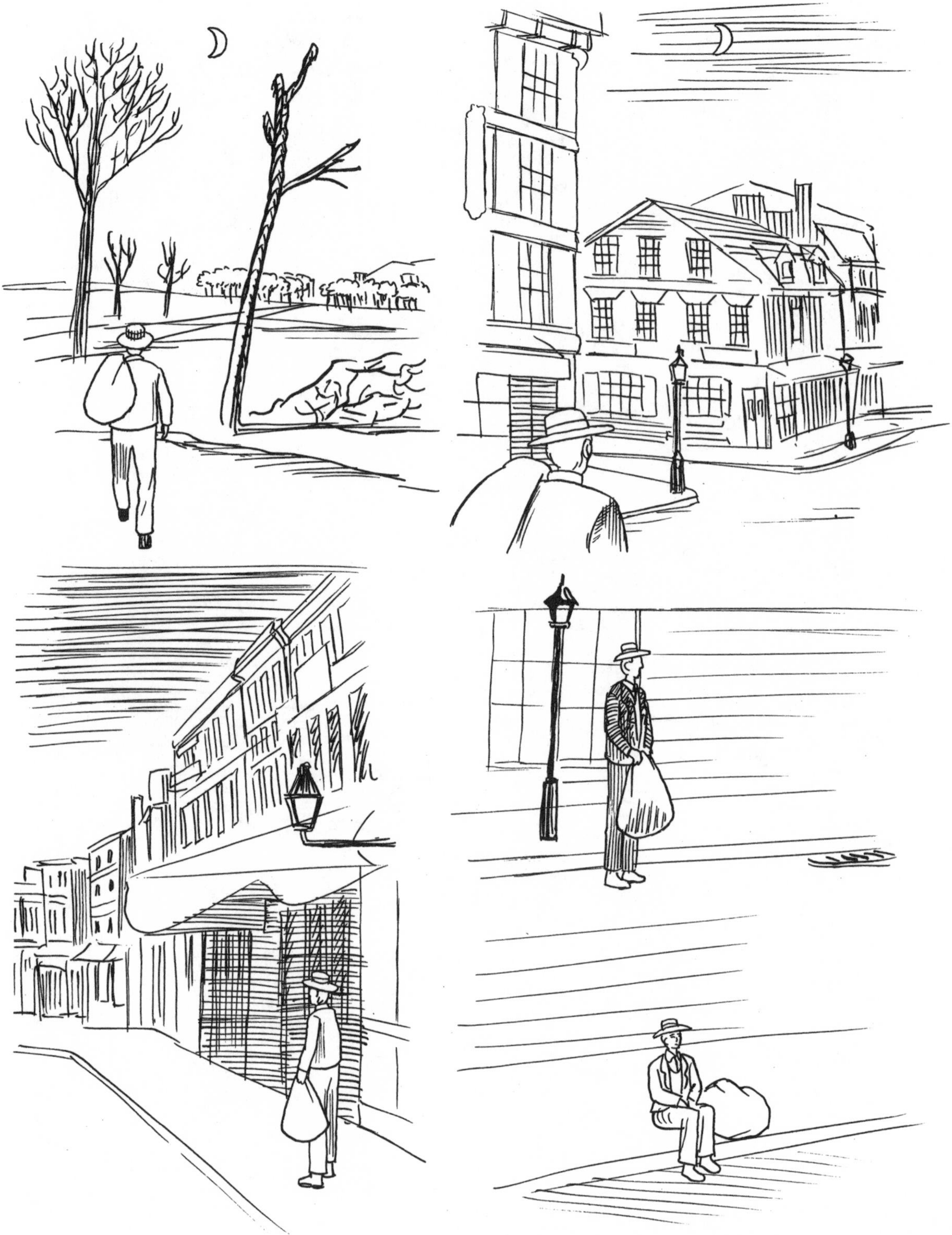

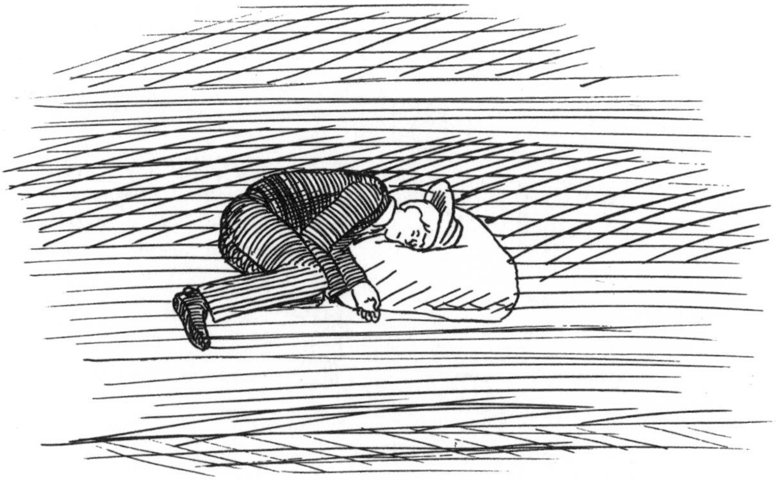

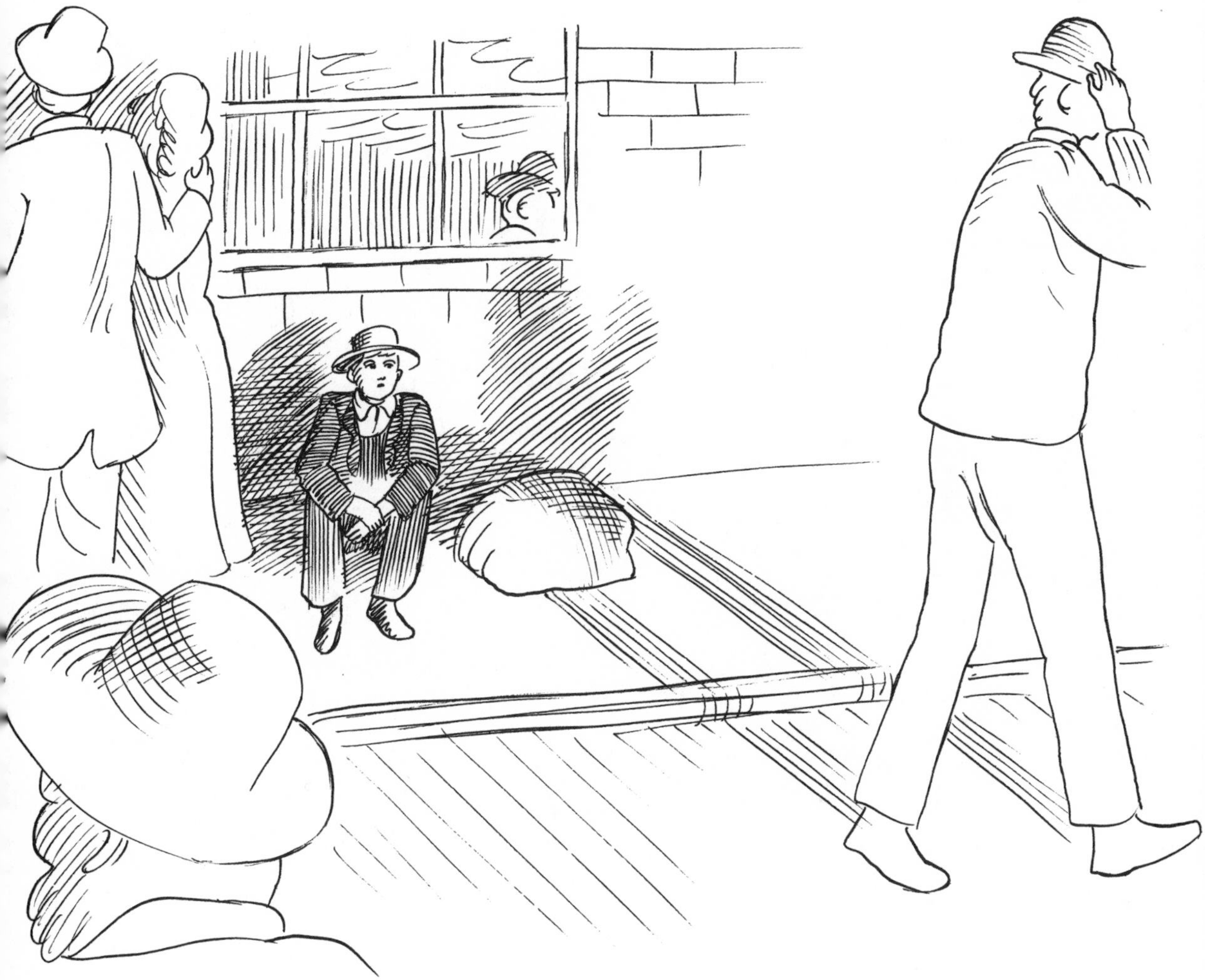

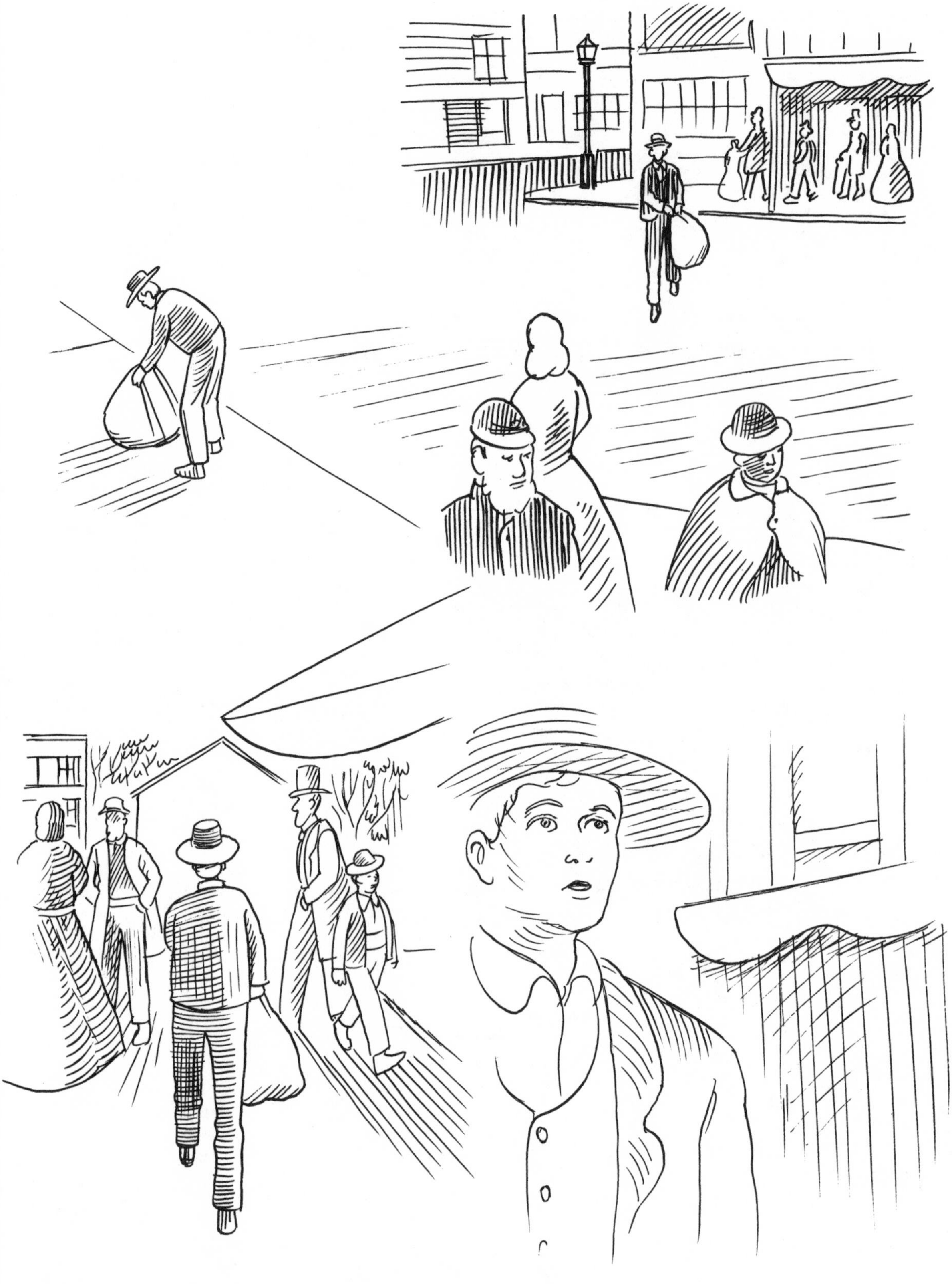

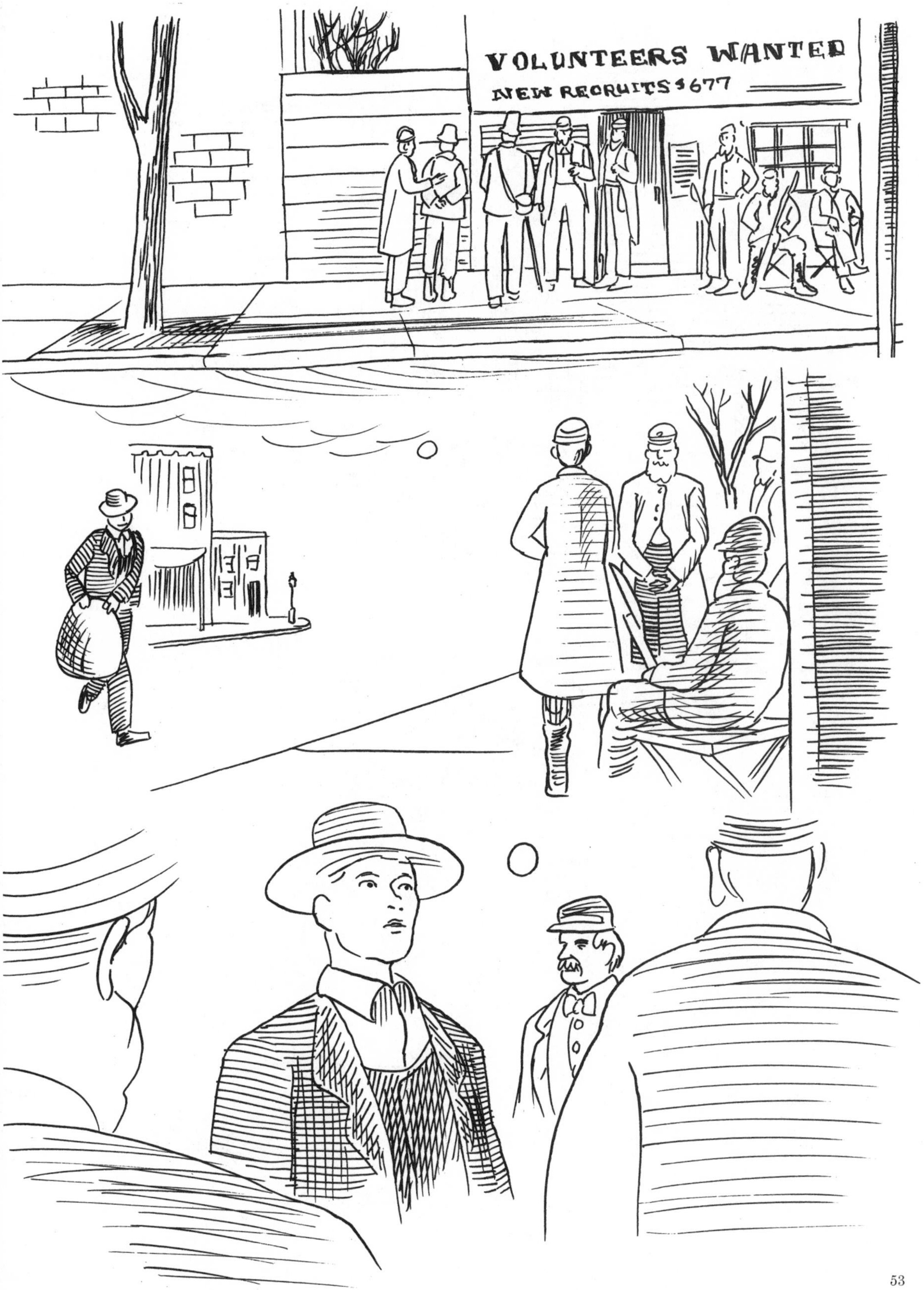
VOLUNTEERS WANTED
NEW RECRUITS $677

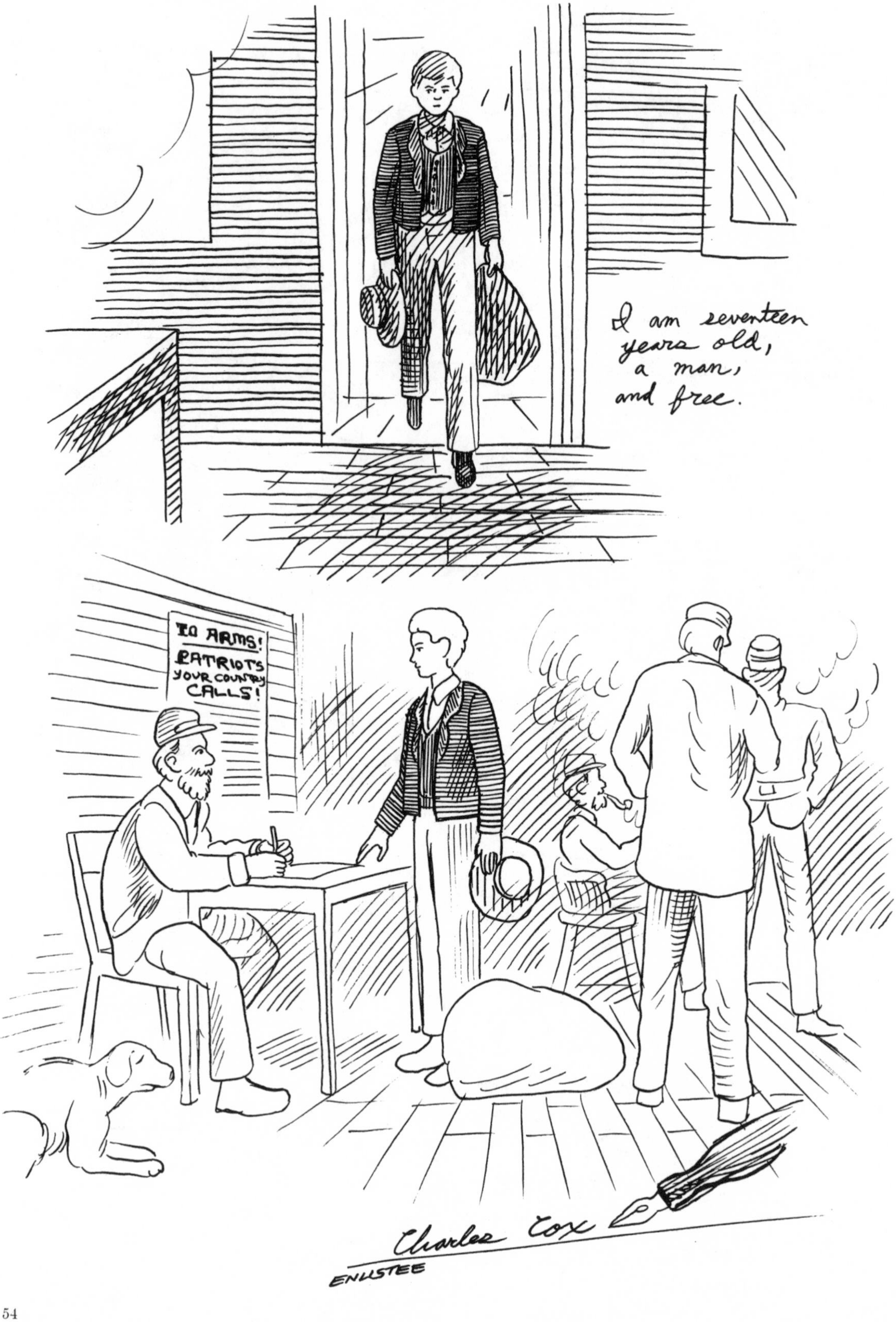
I am seventeen years old, a man, and free.
TO ARMS!
PATRIOTS YOUR COUNTRY CALLS!
Charles Cox
ENLISTEE

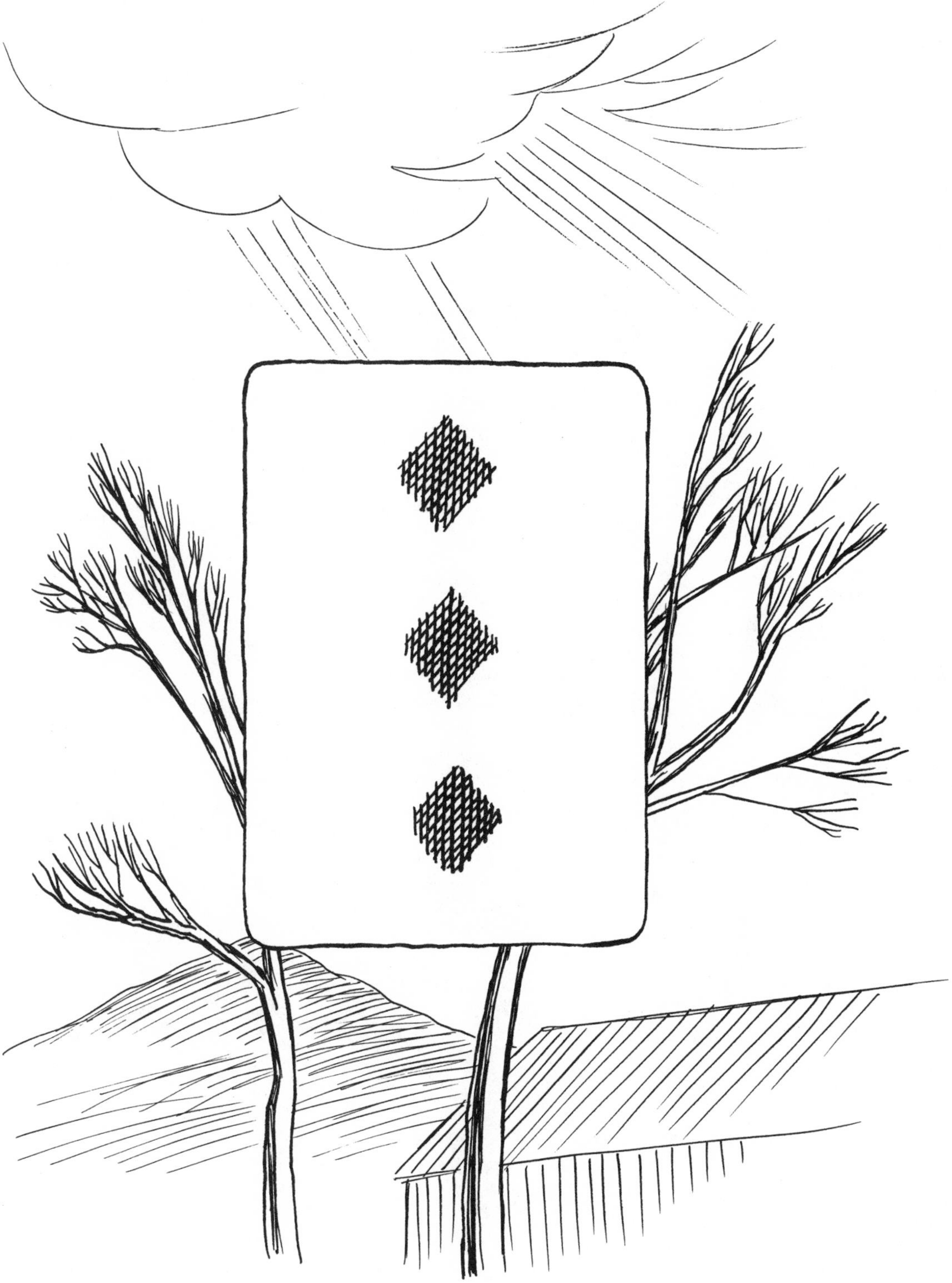

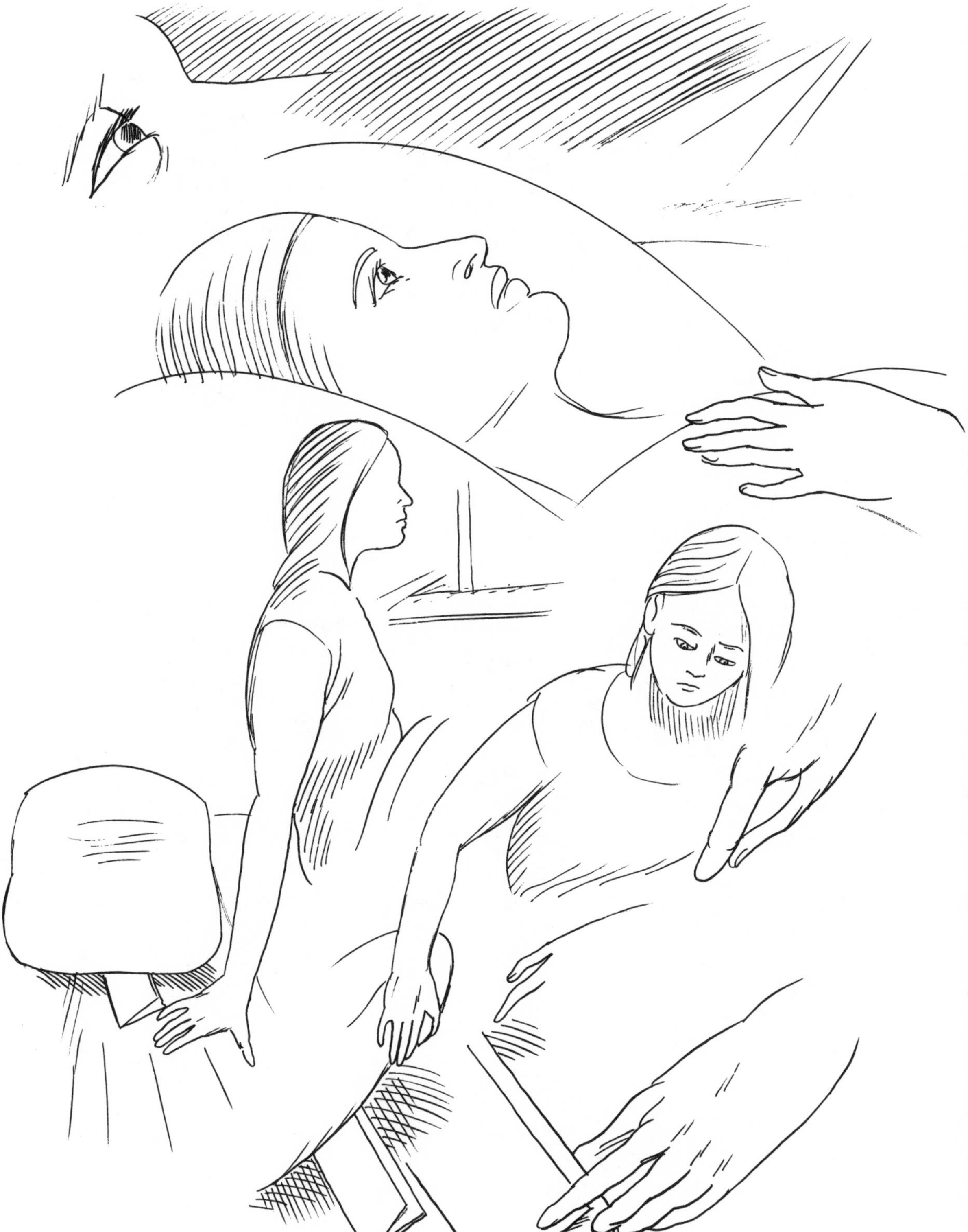

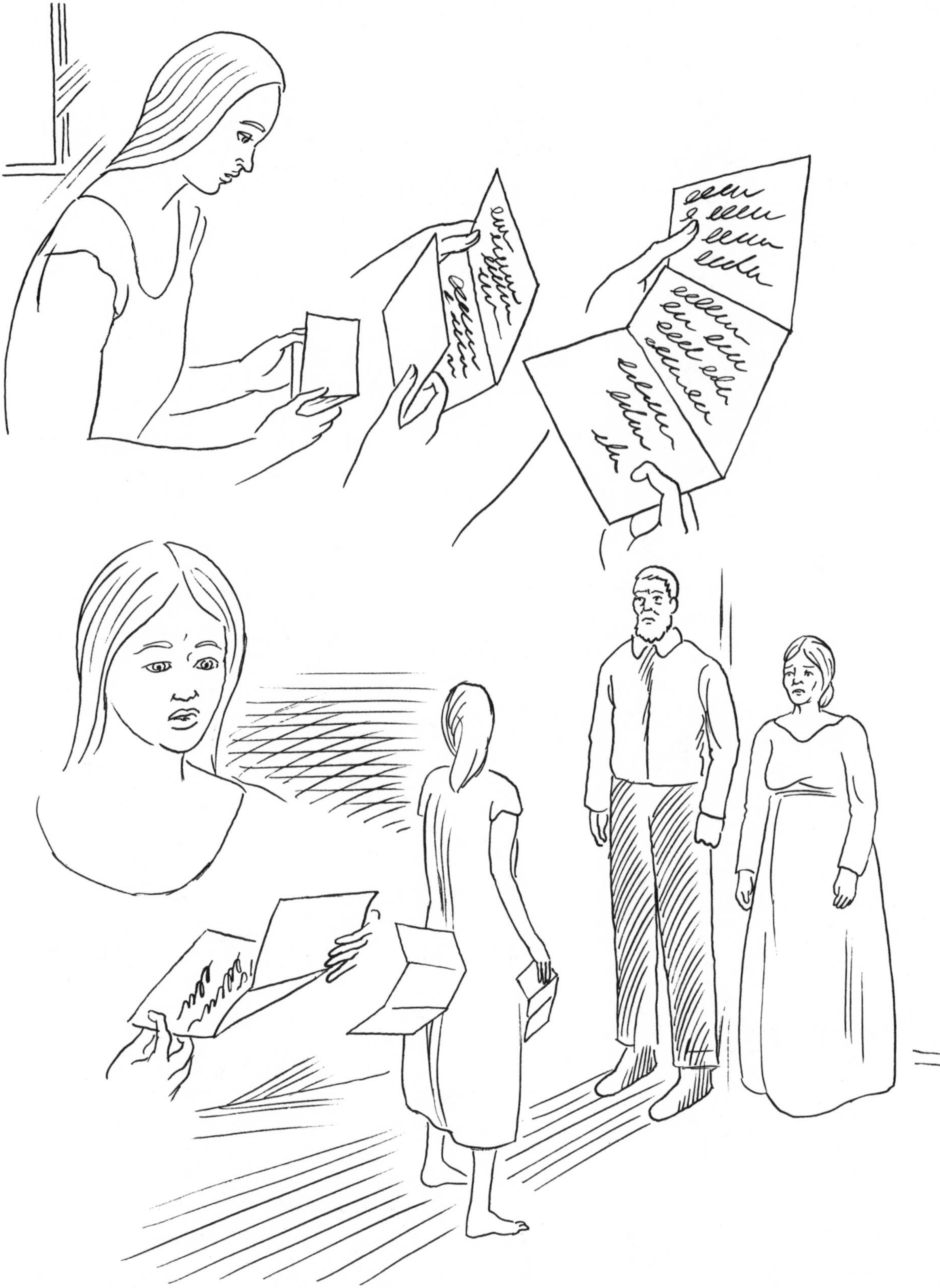

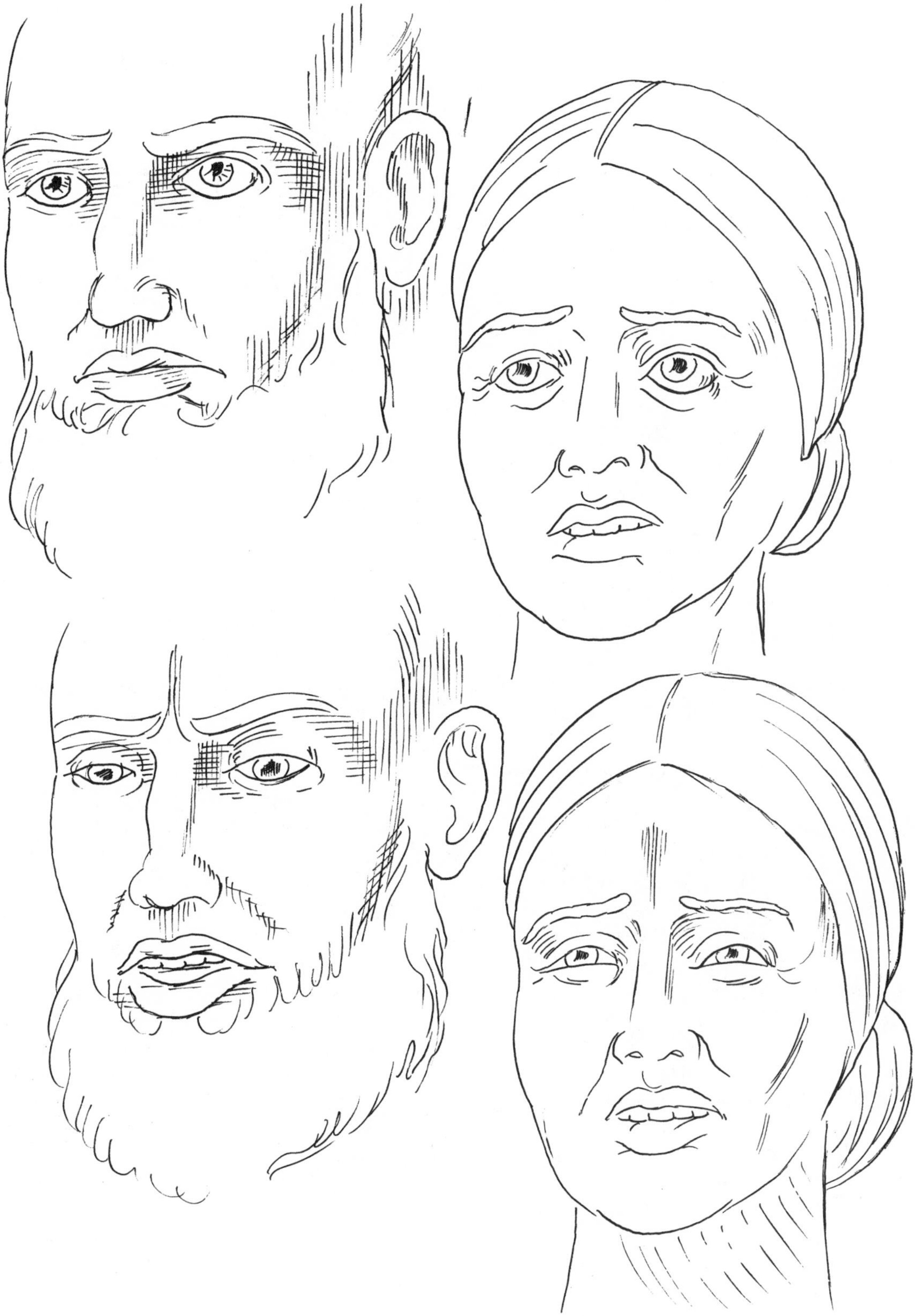

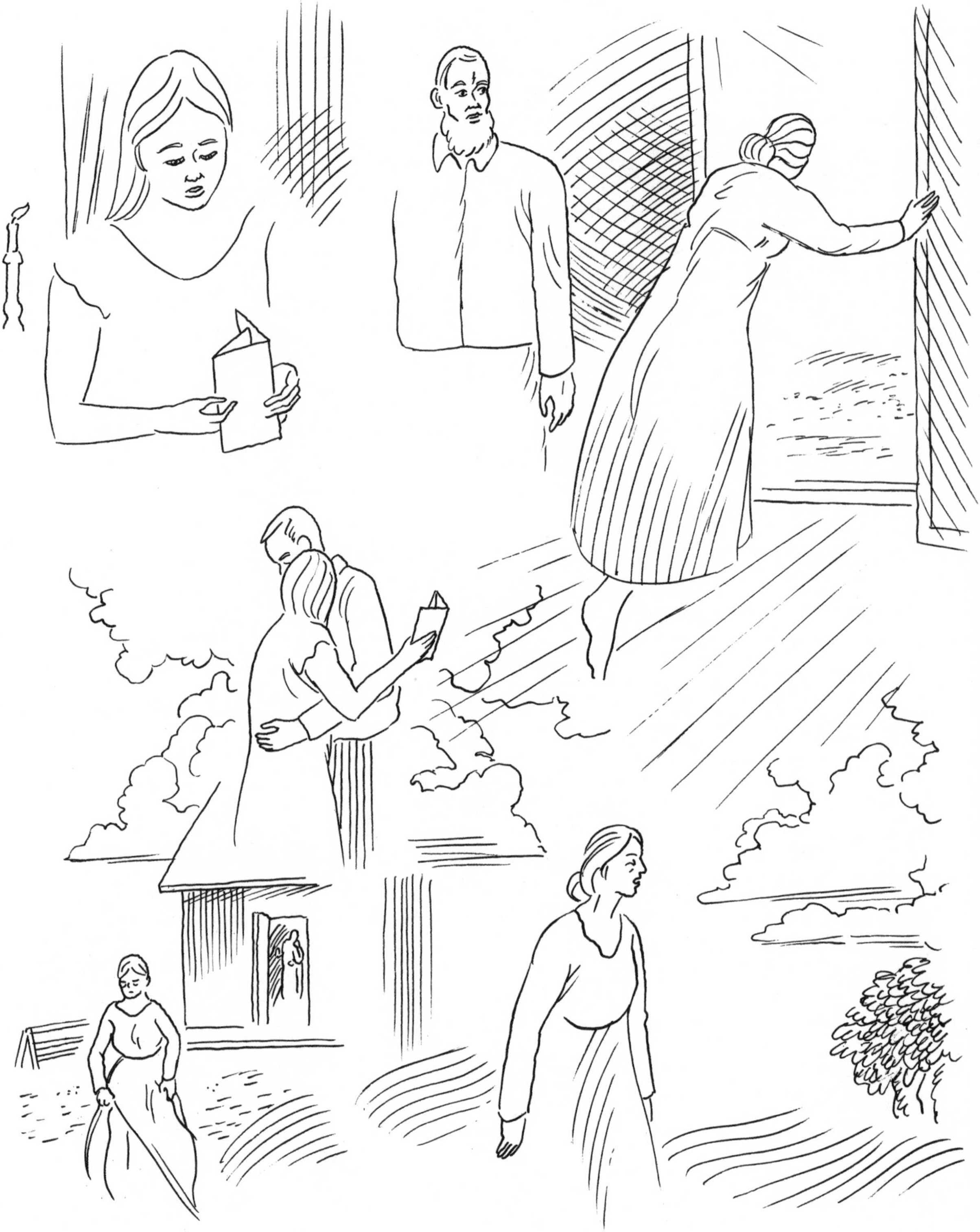

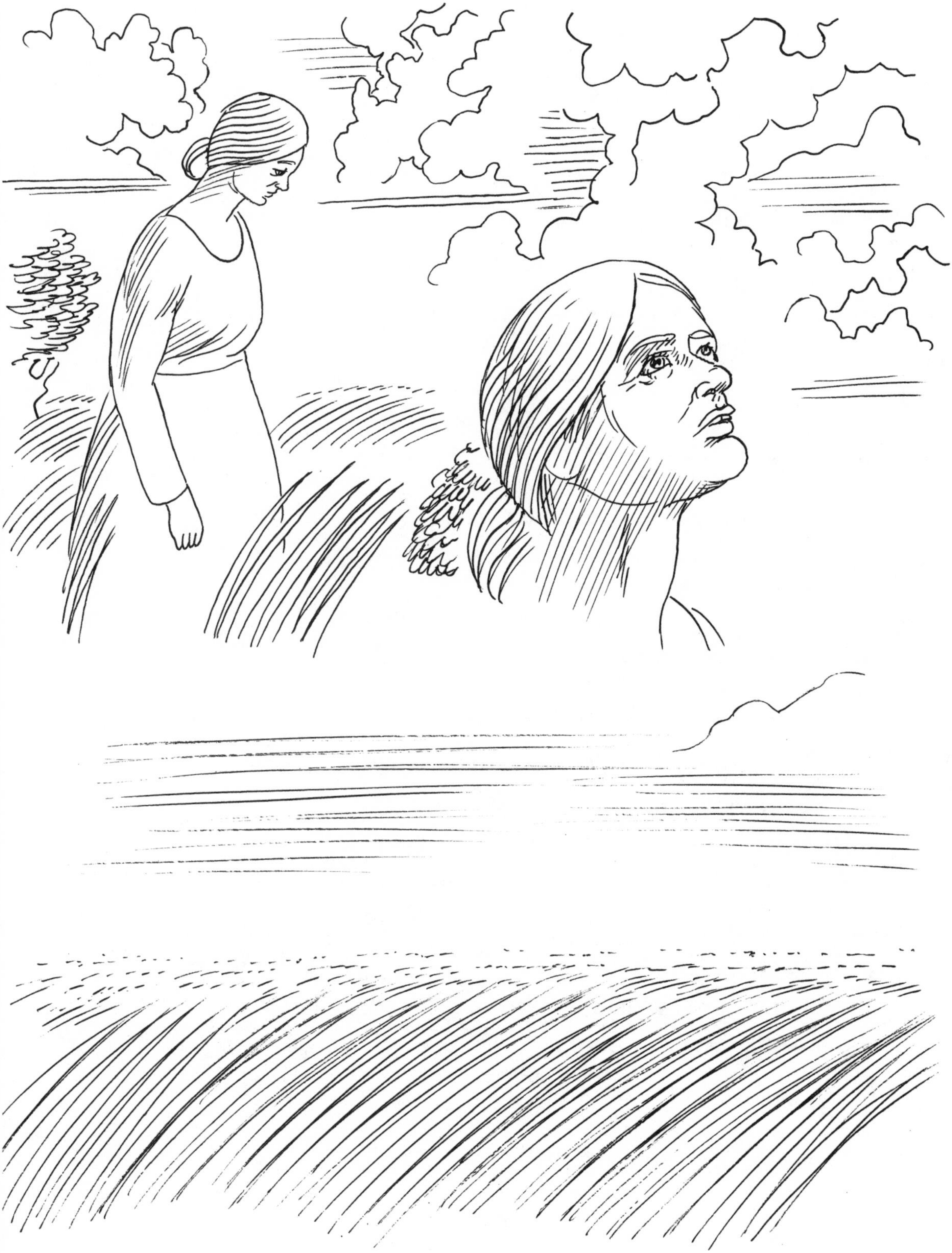

Greensville, Indiana
Military Training Camp

Outward forms represent inward life.
All of man's action is a representation of himself.
He lives out his inner life.

A body grows around man as a tree around the life it represents. If he be a fruitful tree he is known by his fruit – if not fruitful, his barrenness reveals him as much as his fruit would be fruitful.

When thou dost look at a tree, thou canst tell the kind of life that is in it, what its fruit will be, and what its use to man.

When thou dost look at a church, thou canst tell what kind of God is worshiped in it. It is the outer body of the inner idea of God.

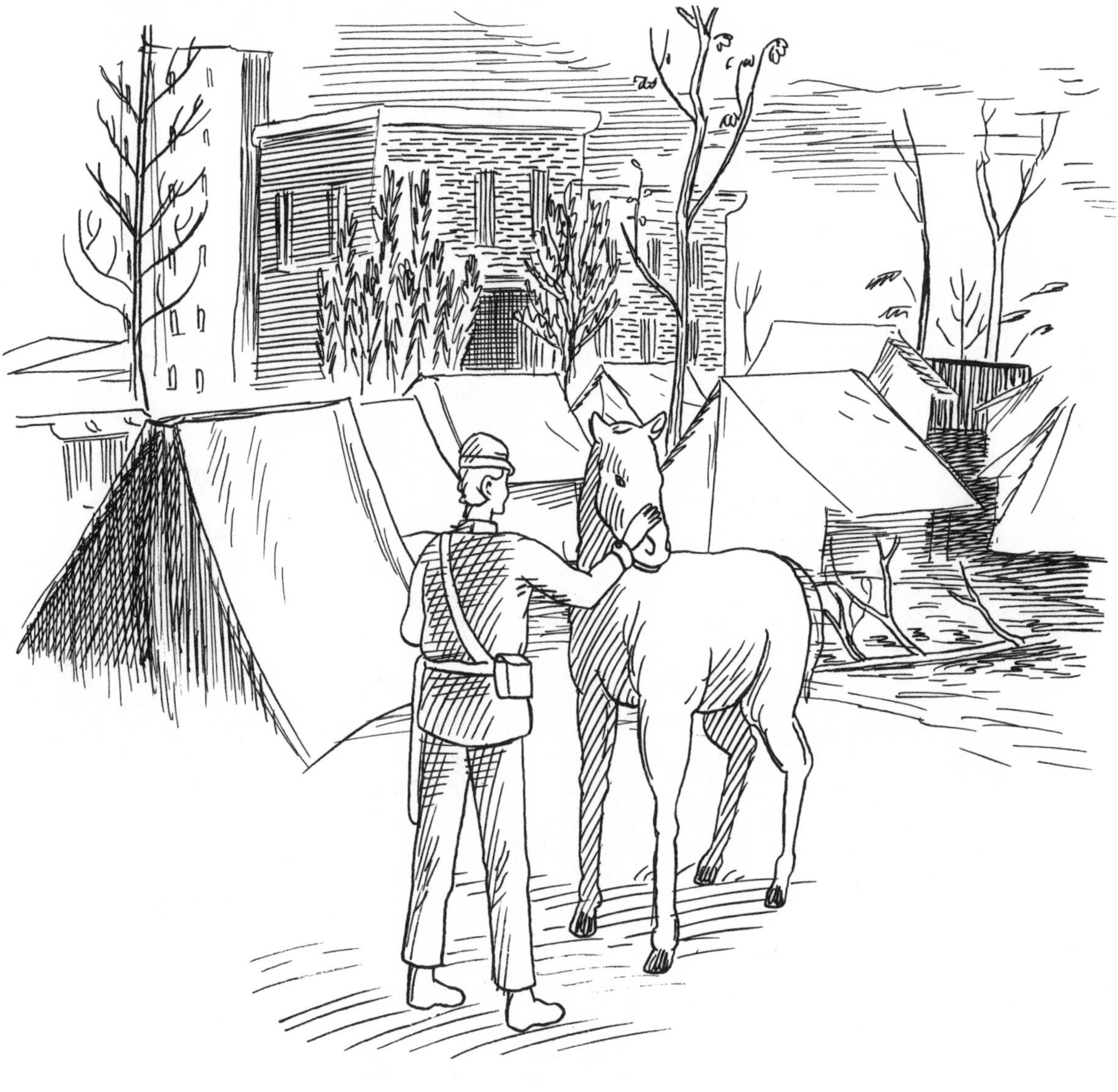

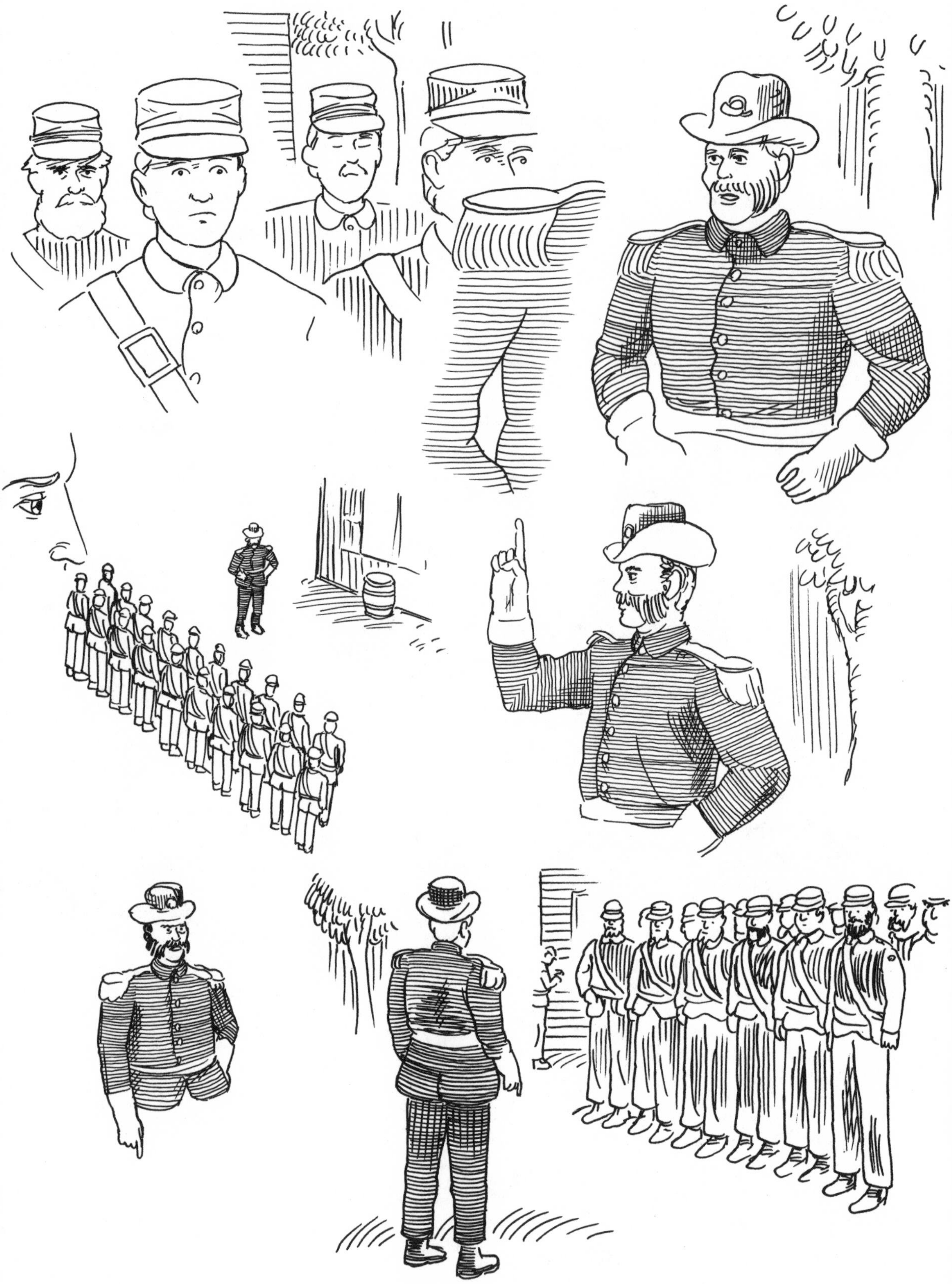

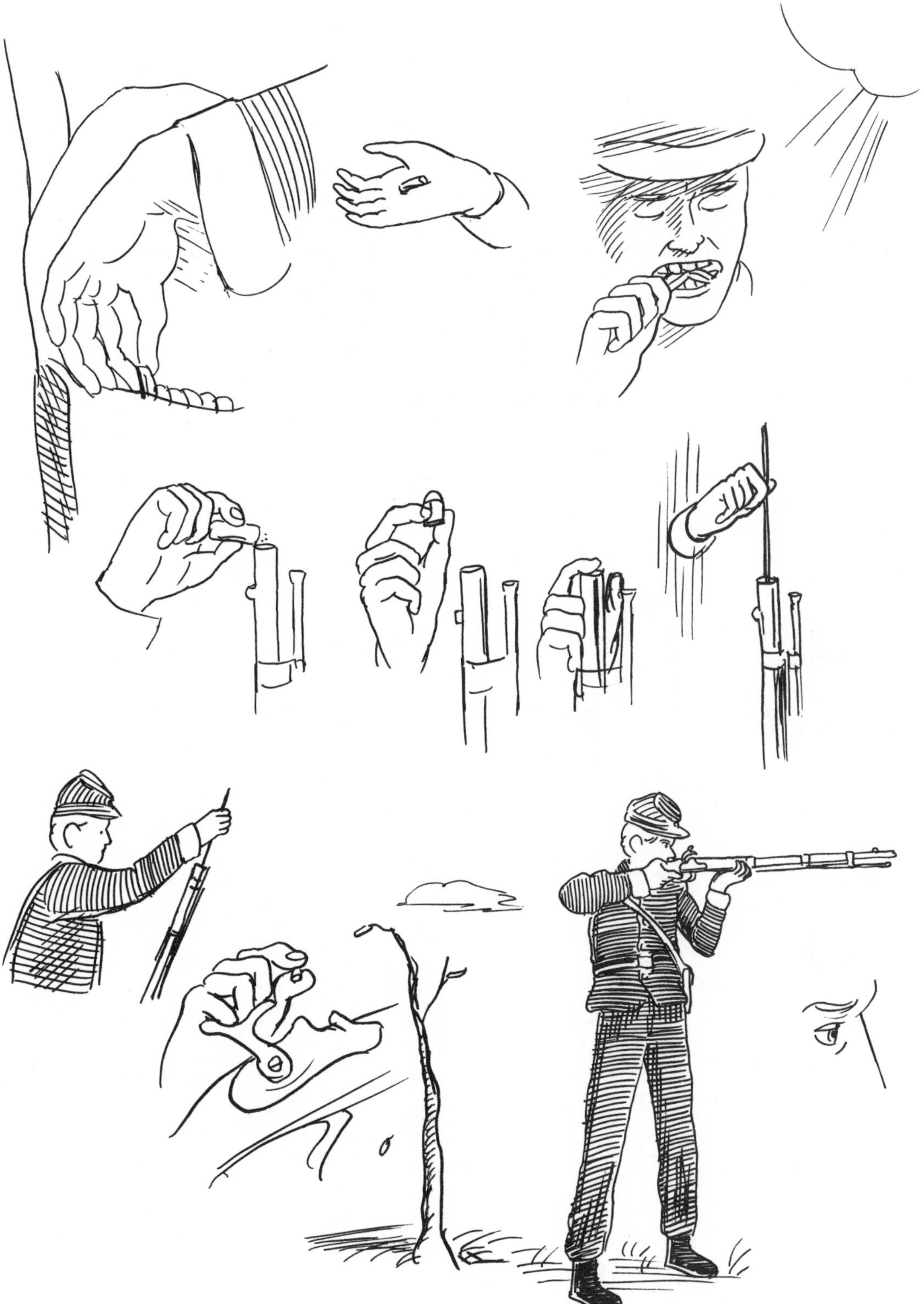

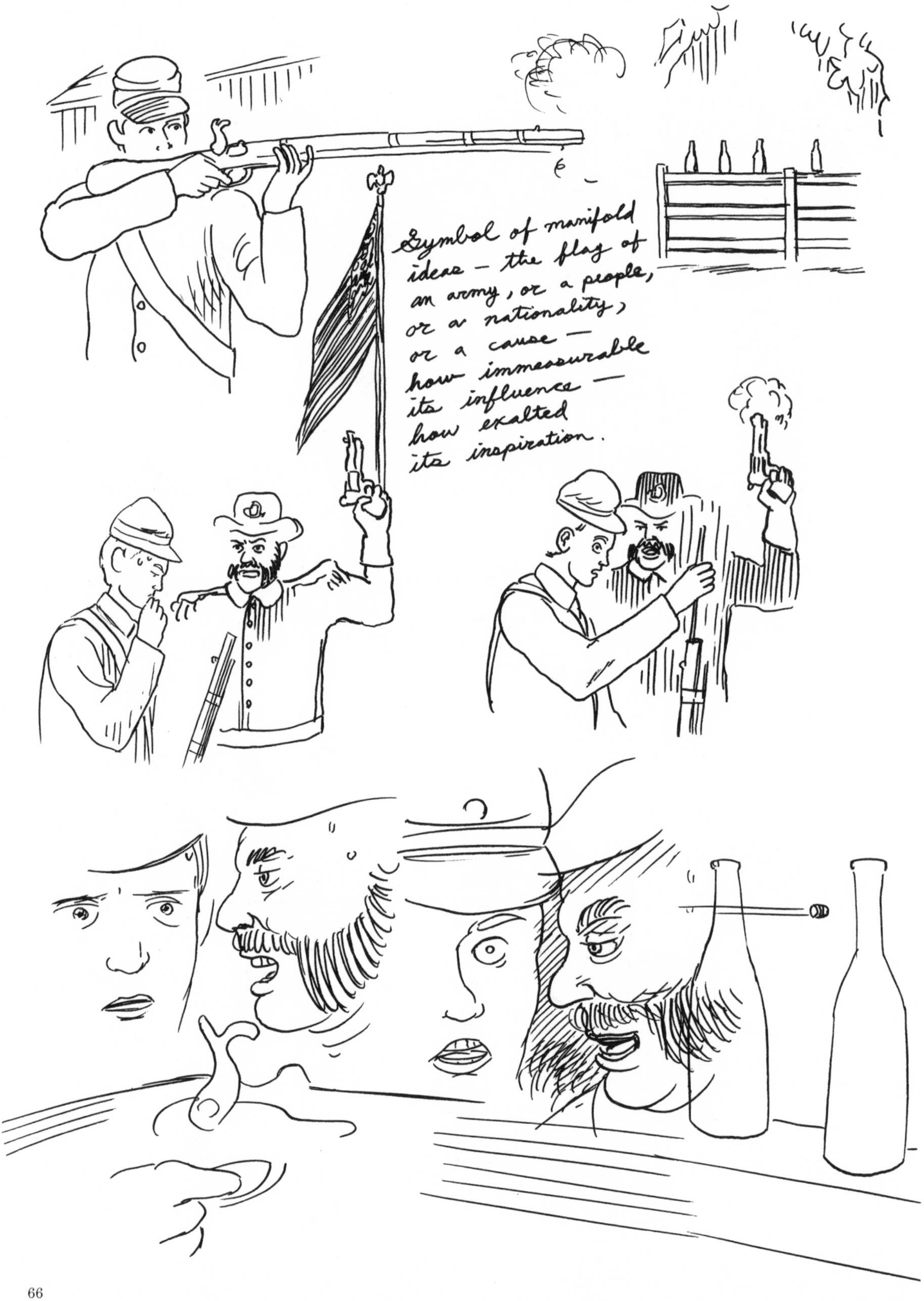
Symbol of manifold ideas — the flag of an army, or a people, or a nationality, or a cause — how immeasurable its influence — how exalted its inspiration.

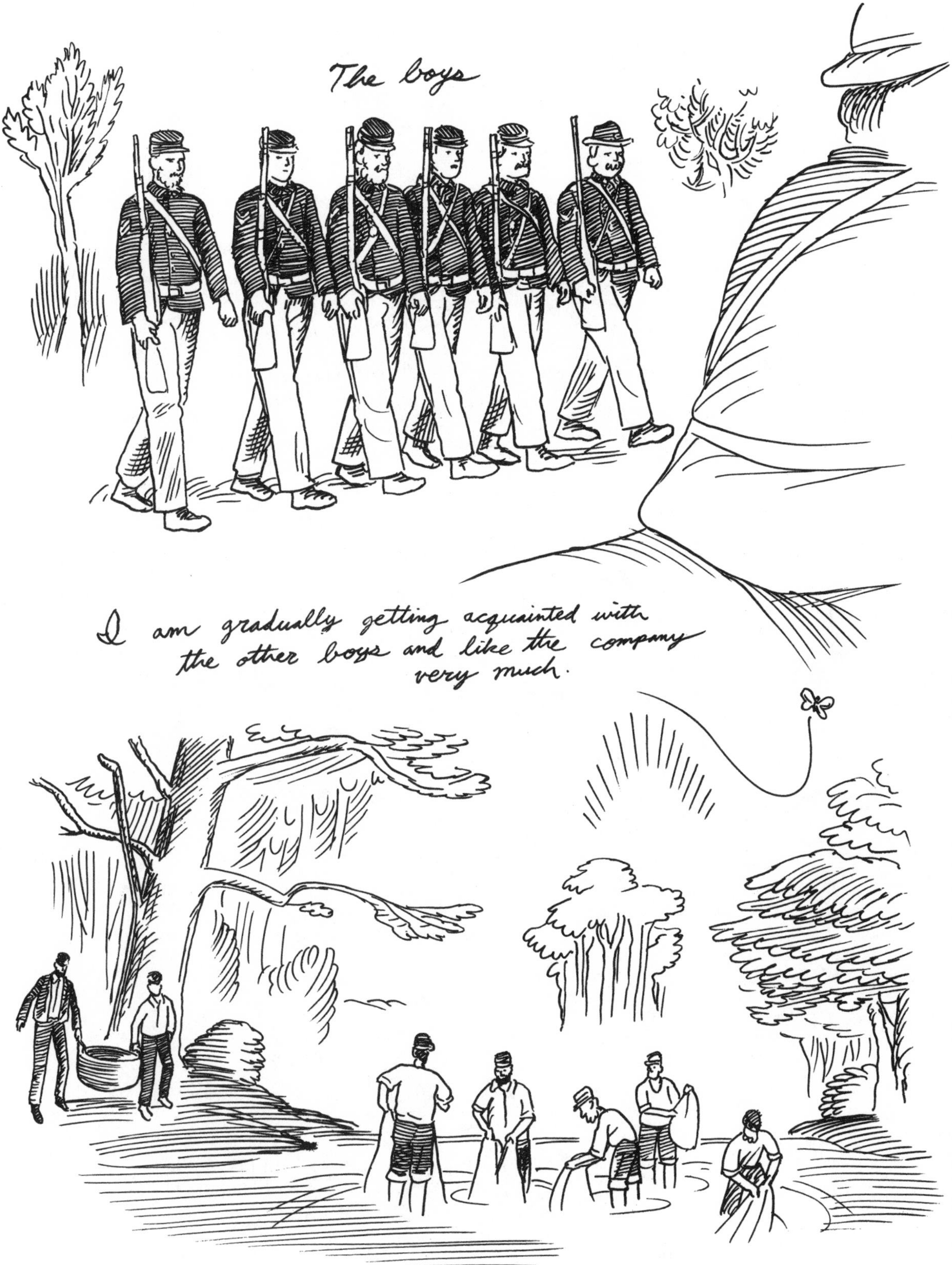
The boys
I am gradually getting acquainted with the other boys and like the company very much.

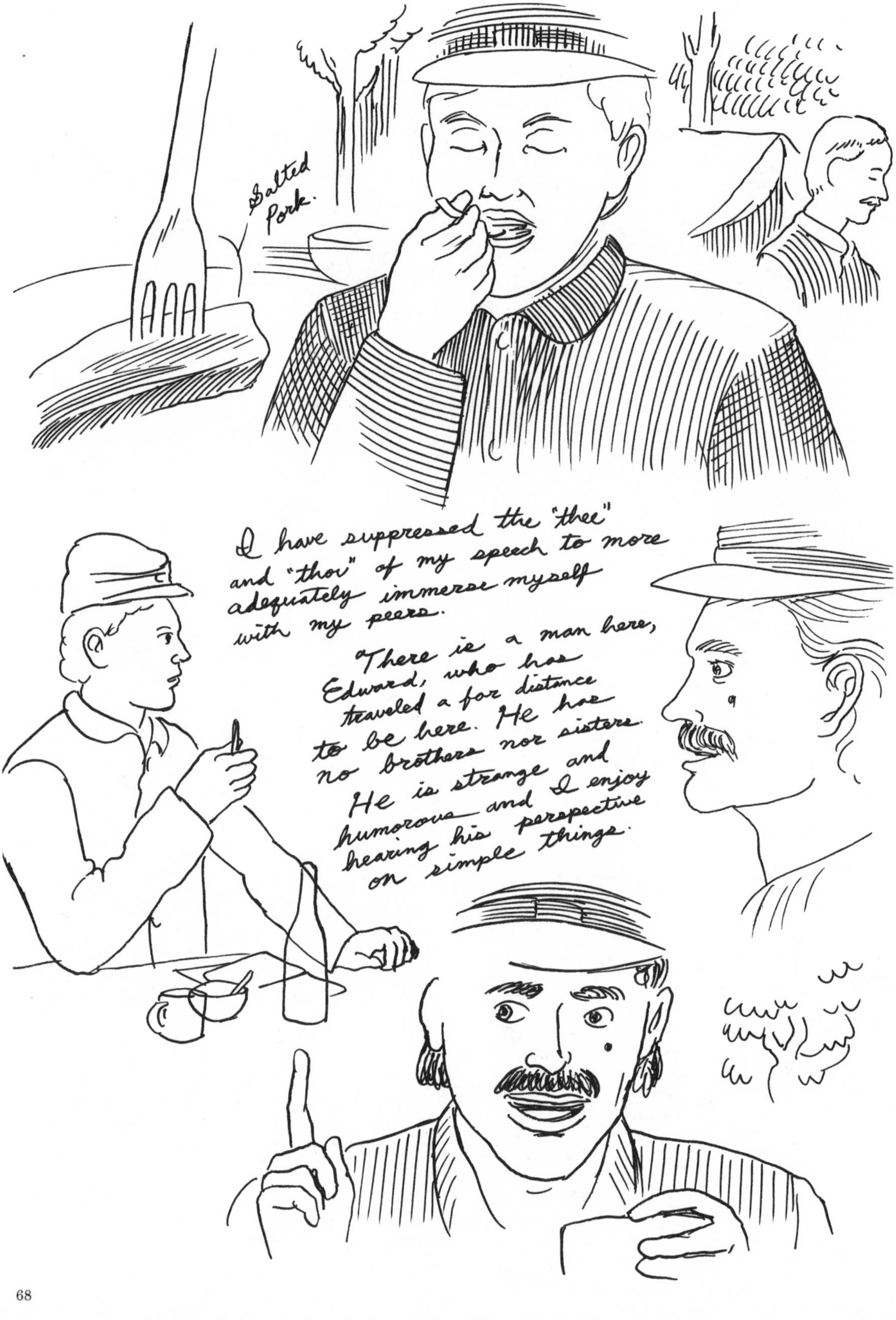
Salted Pork.
I have suppressed the "thee" and "thou" of my speech to more adequately immerse myself with my peers.
There is a man here, Edward, who has traveled a far distance to be here. He has no brothers nor sisters.
He is strange and humorous and I enjoy hearing his perspective on simple things.

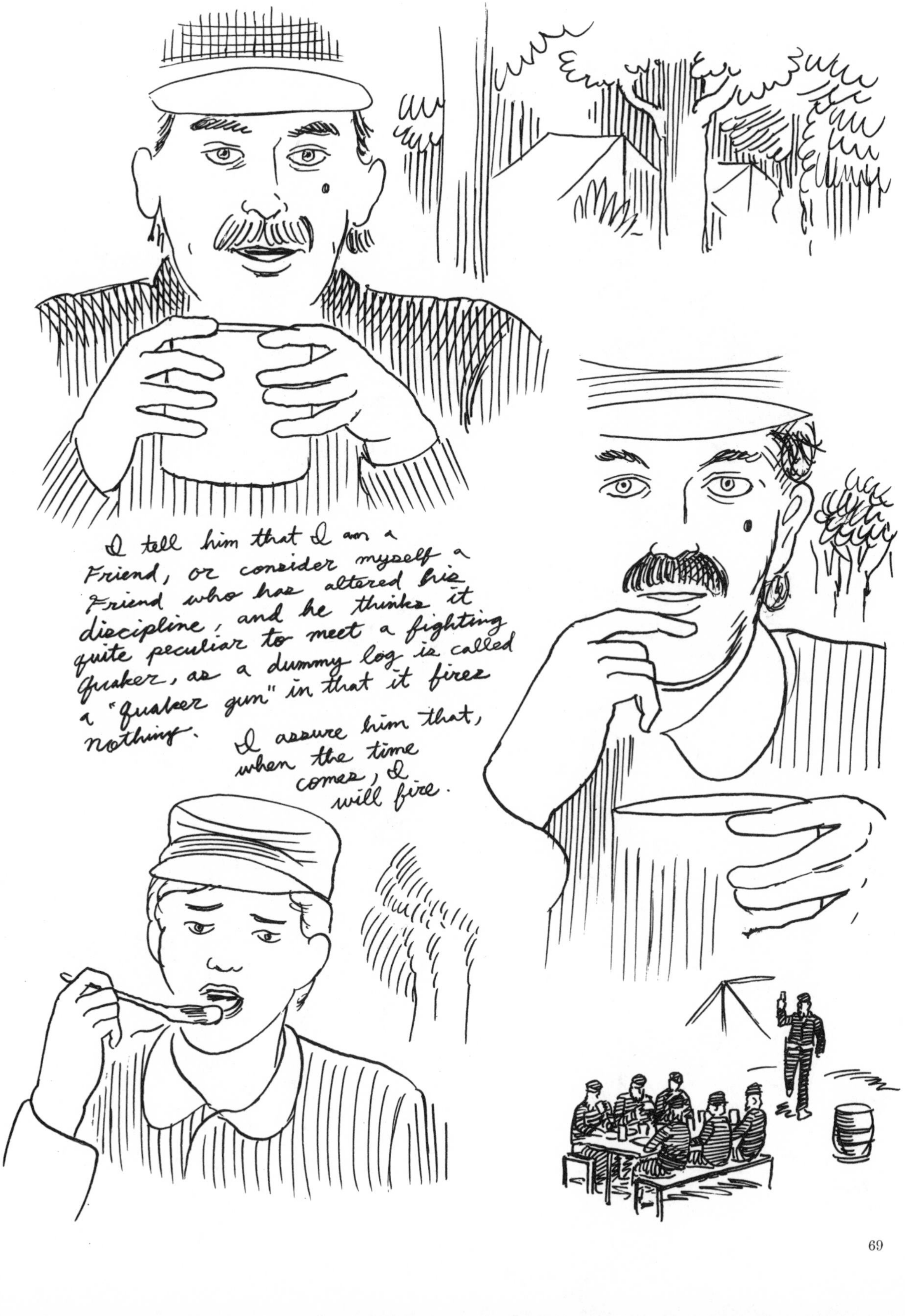
I tell him that I am a Friend, or consider myself a Friend who has altered his discipline, and he thinks it quite peculiar to meet a fighting Quaker, as a dummy log is called a "Quaker gun" in that it fires nothing.
I assure him that, when the time comes, I will fire.

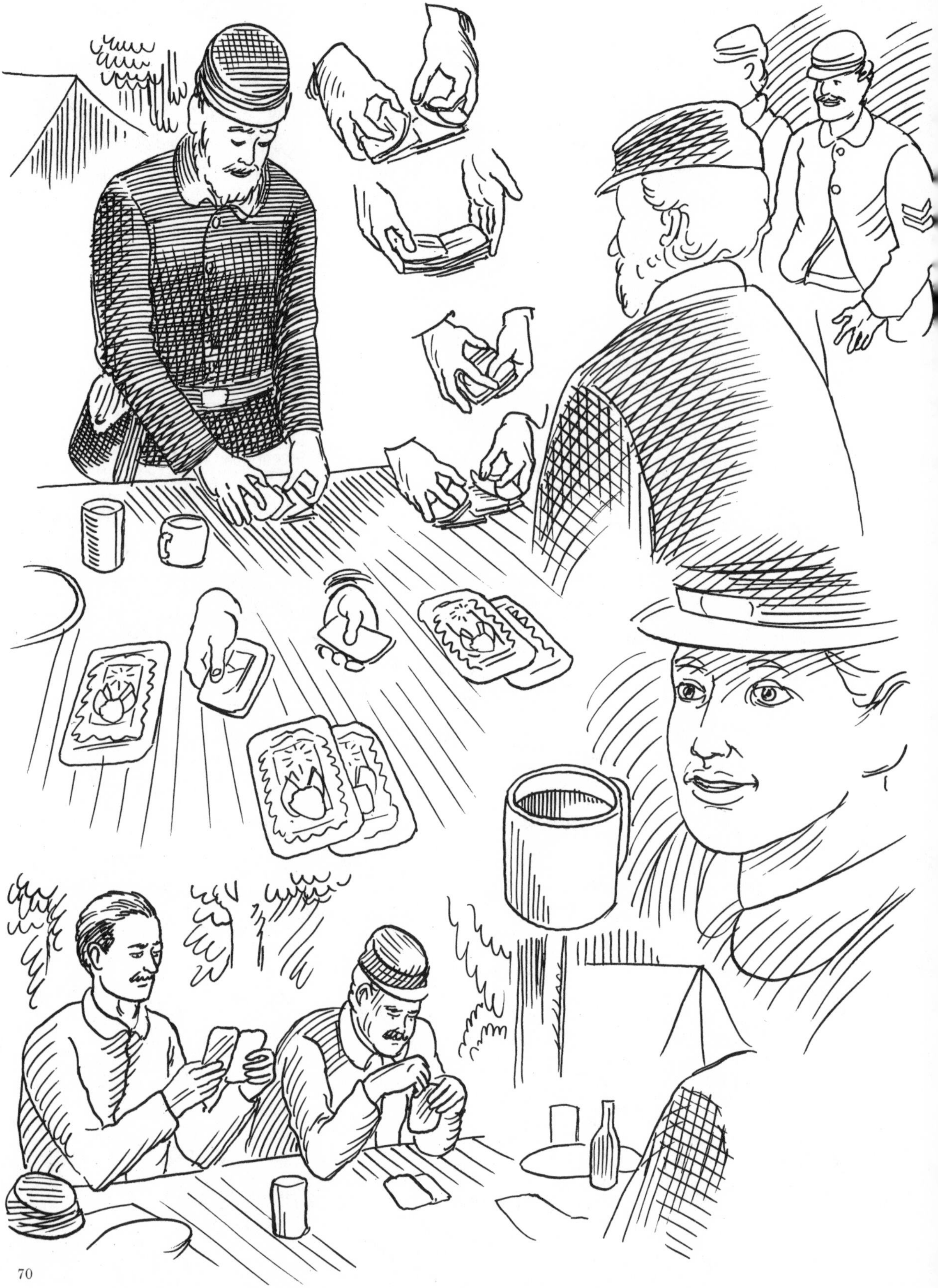

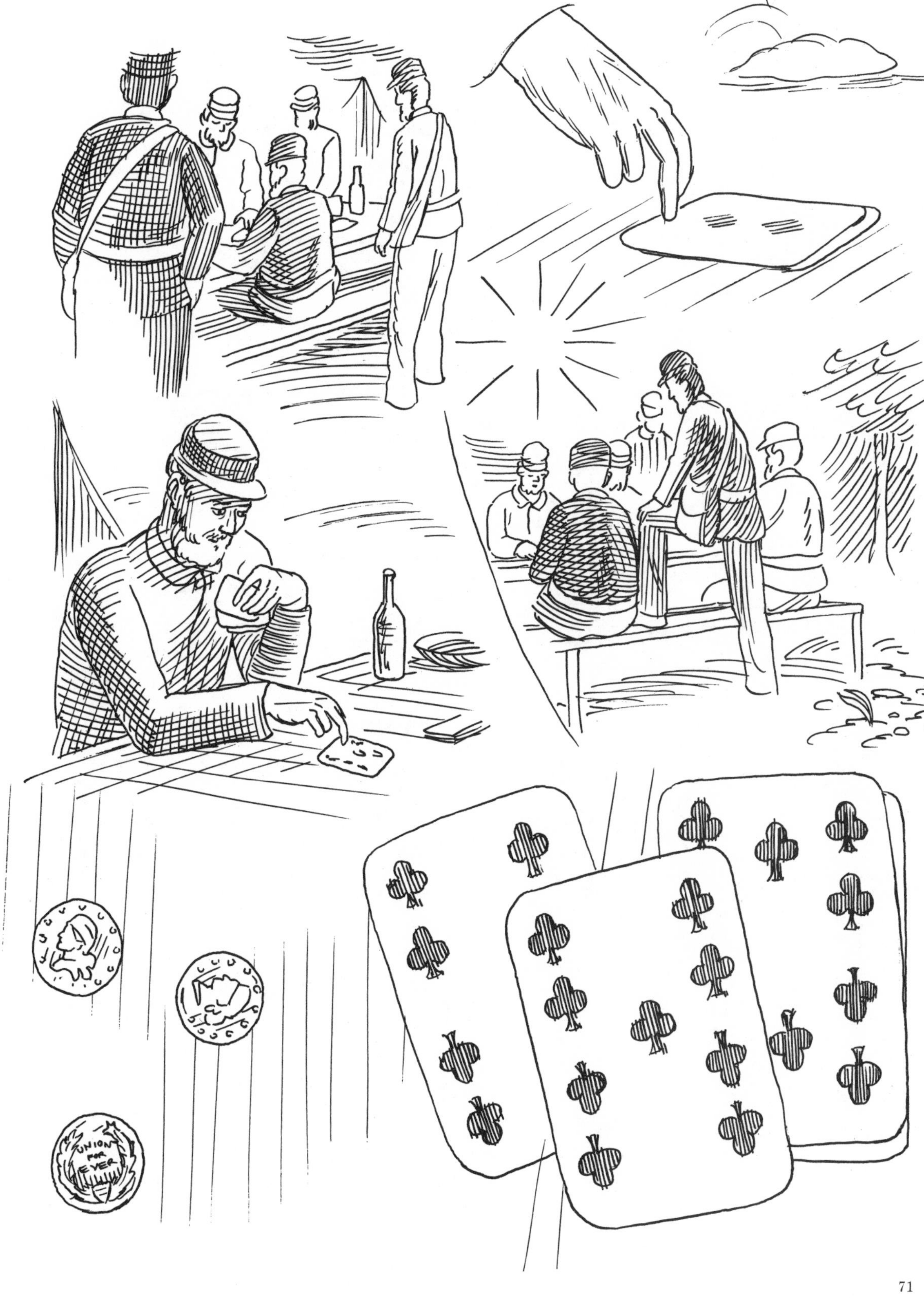
UNION
FOR
EVER

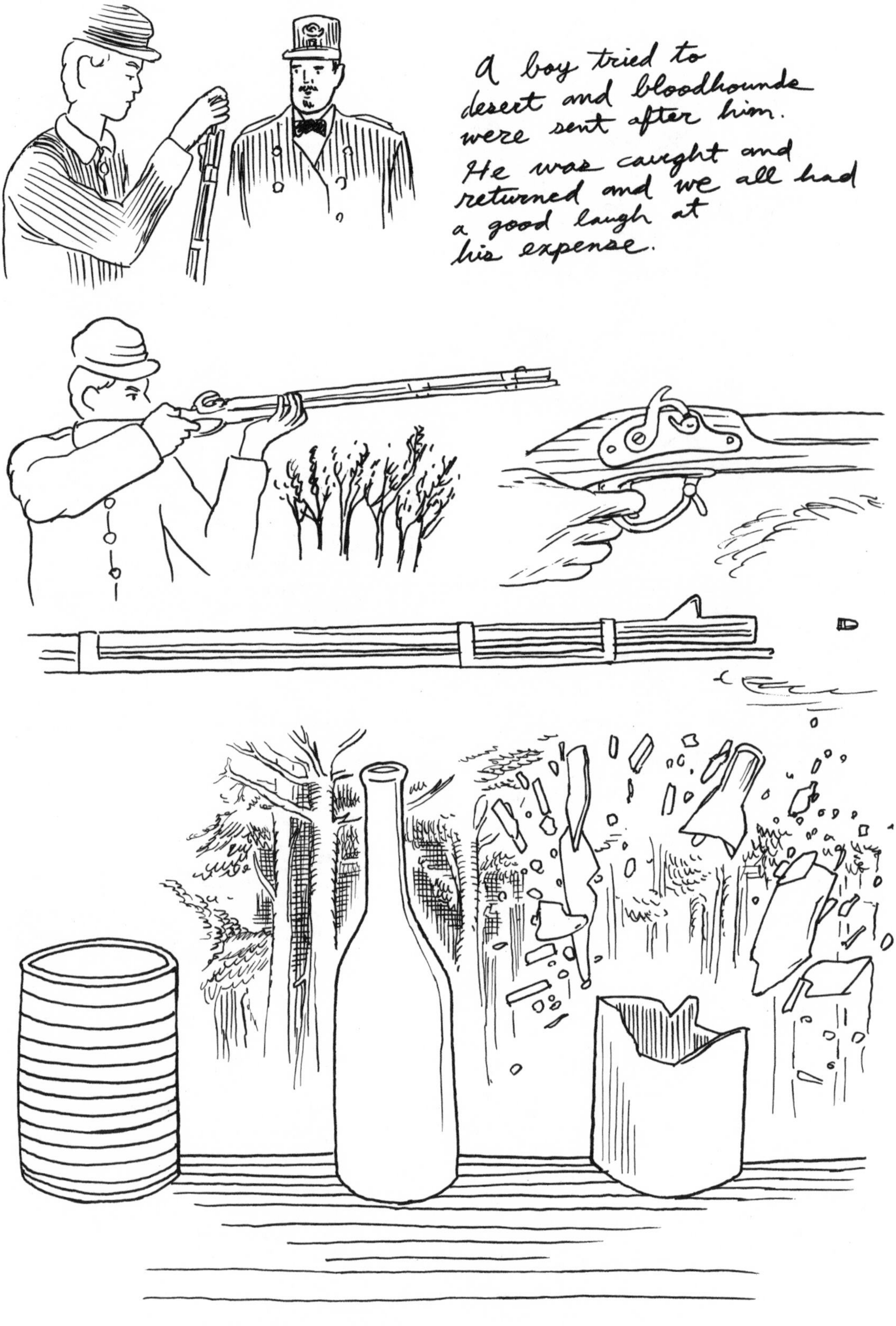
A boy tried to desert and bloodhounds were sent after him.
He was caught and returned and we all had a good laugh at his expense.

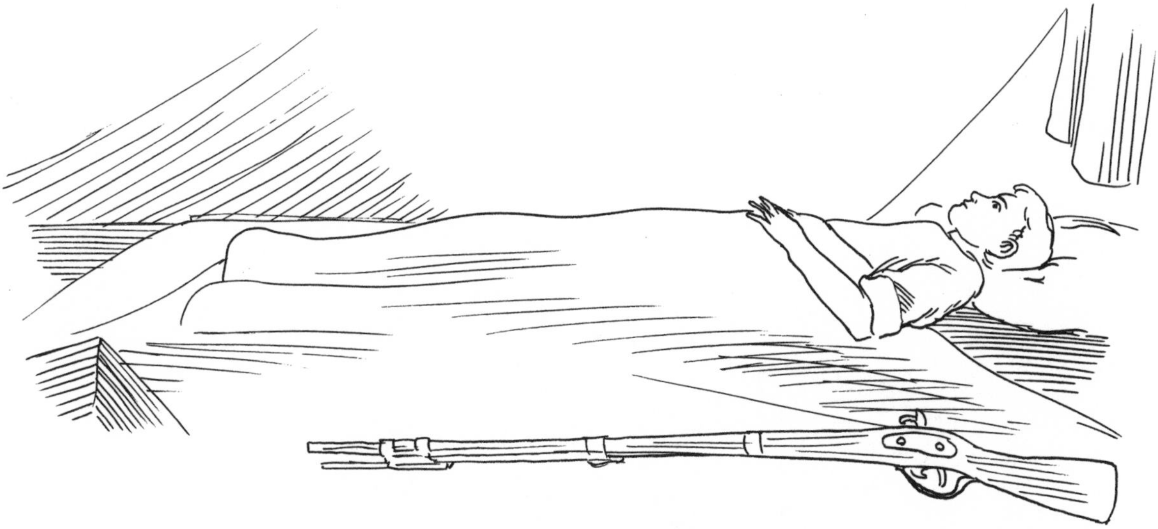

I am told that to many in the South the idea of
Liberty itself is strangely associated with that of
African Servitude. We are pitted against a demonic spirit
which has been known in all ages as Oppression: that
spirit which is so brutalizing in its influence that it
can change a woman into a fiend, and a child into
an imp of cruelty. Peace is not the answer now.
We must do wrong rather than suffer wrong.
There is no folly in expecting Satan to cast out Satan.

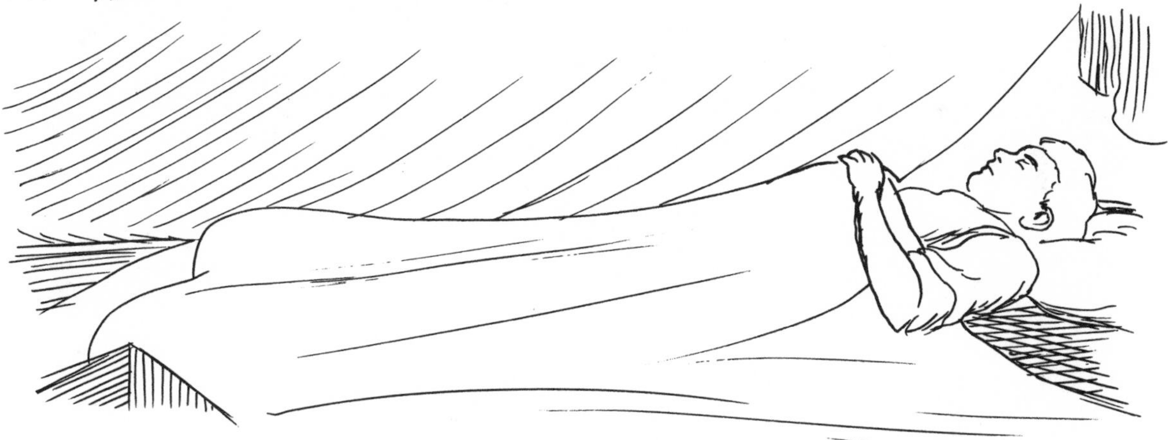

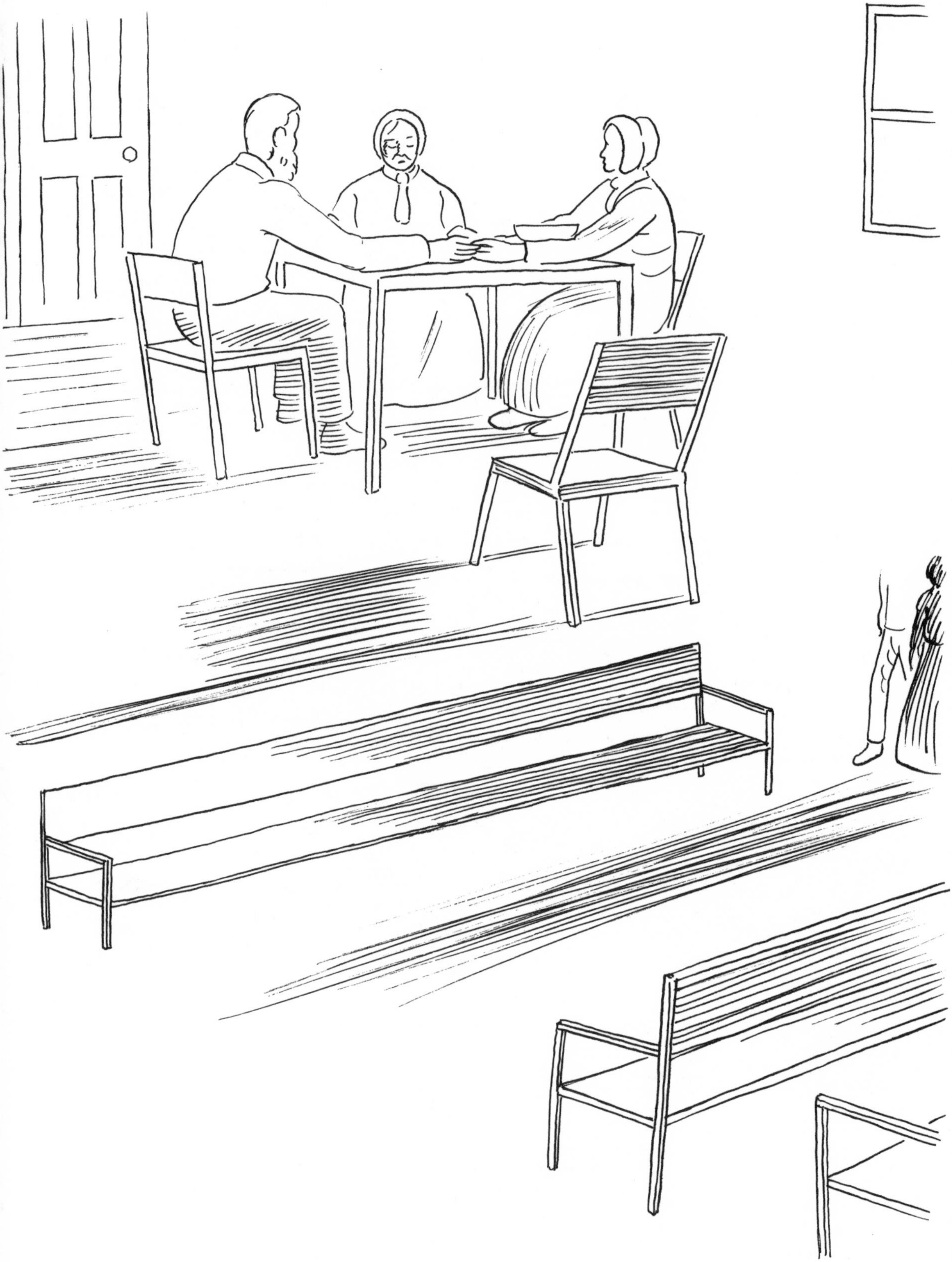

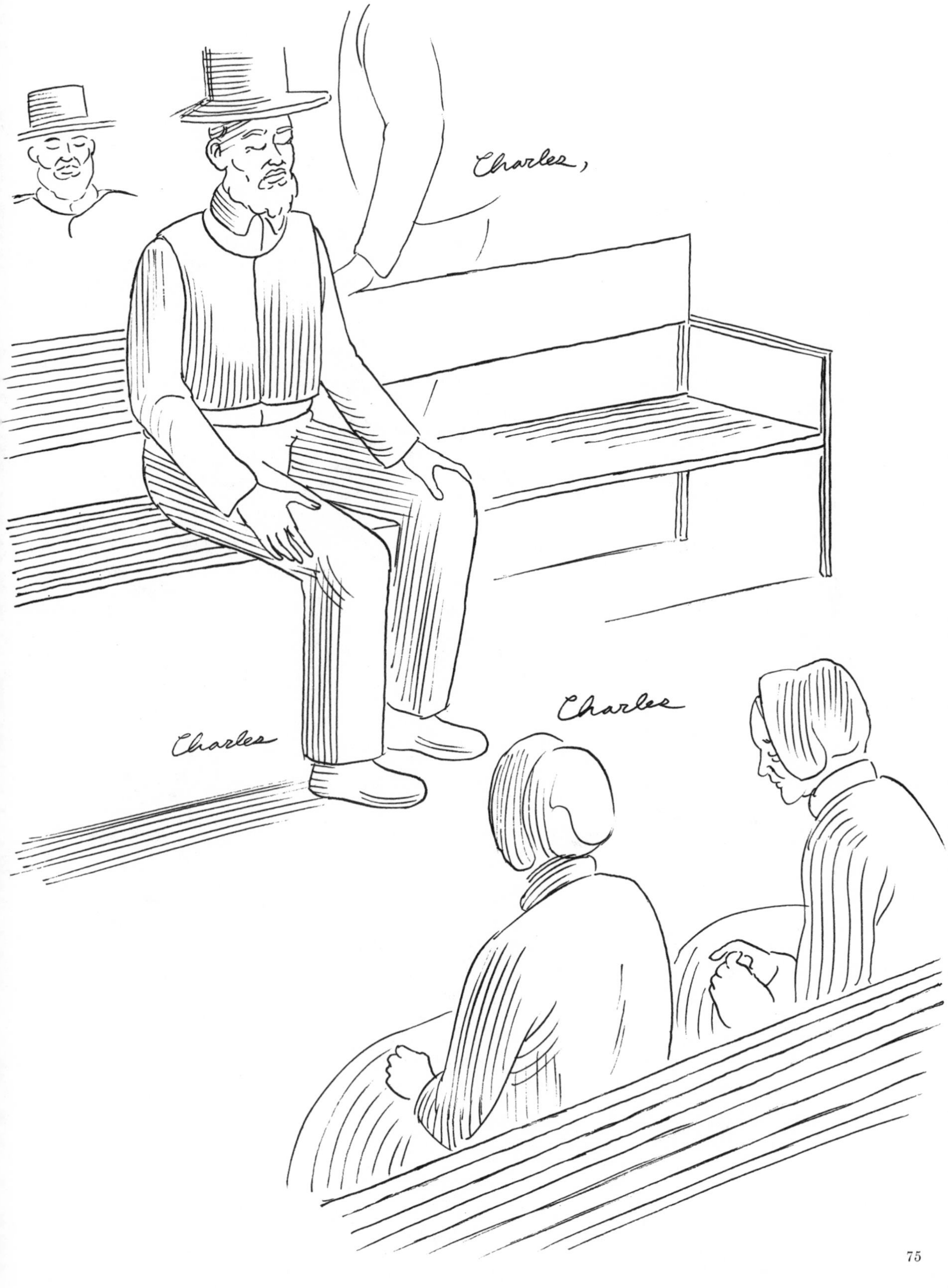
Charles,
Charles
Charles

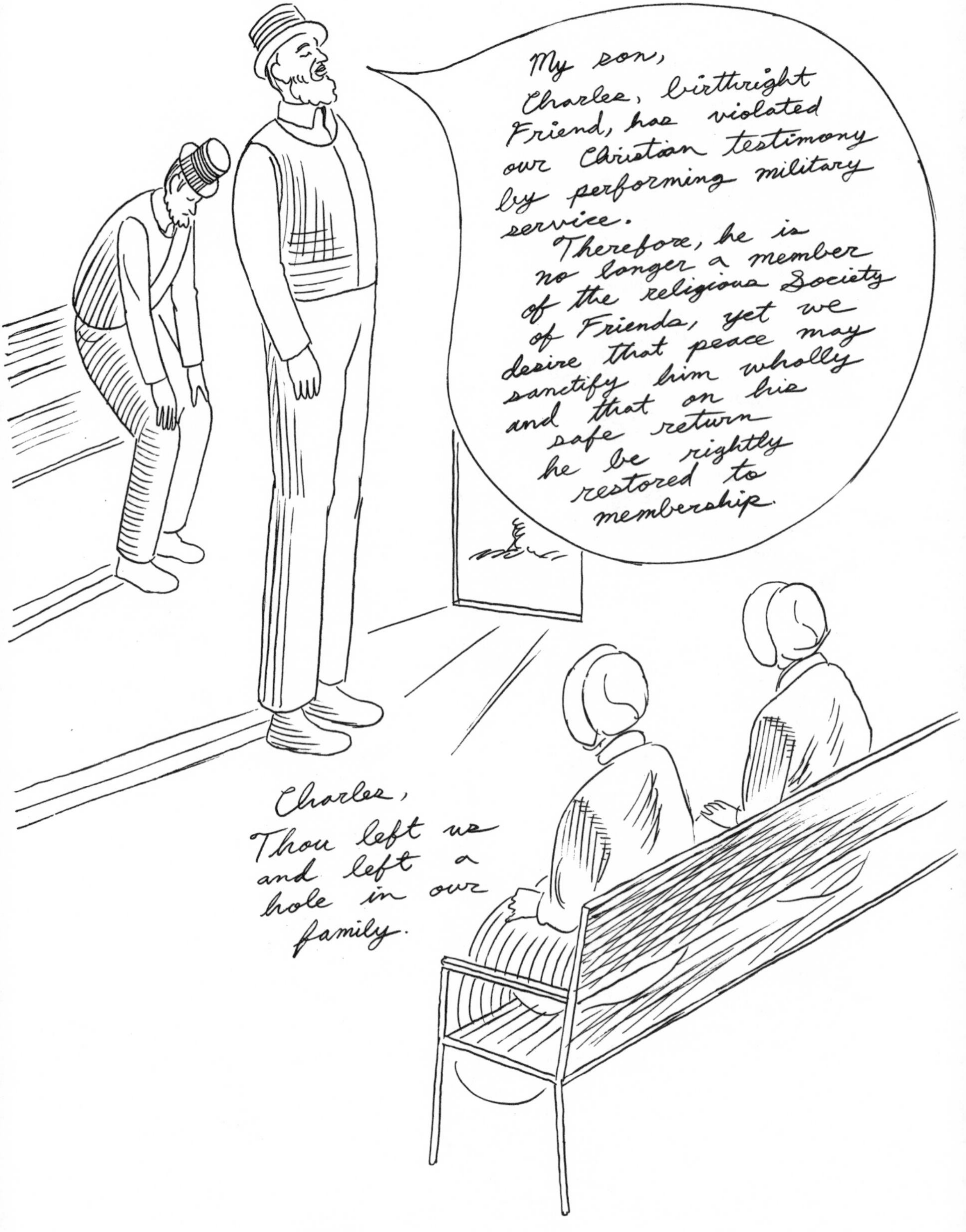
My son,
Charles, birthright Friend, has violated our Christian testimony by performing military service.
Therefore, he is no longer a member of the religious Society of Friends, yet we desire that peace may sanctify him wholly and that on his safe return he be rightly restored to membership.
Charles,
Thou left us and left a hole in our family.

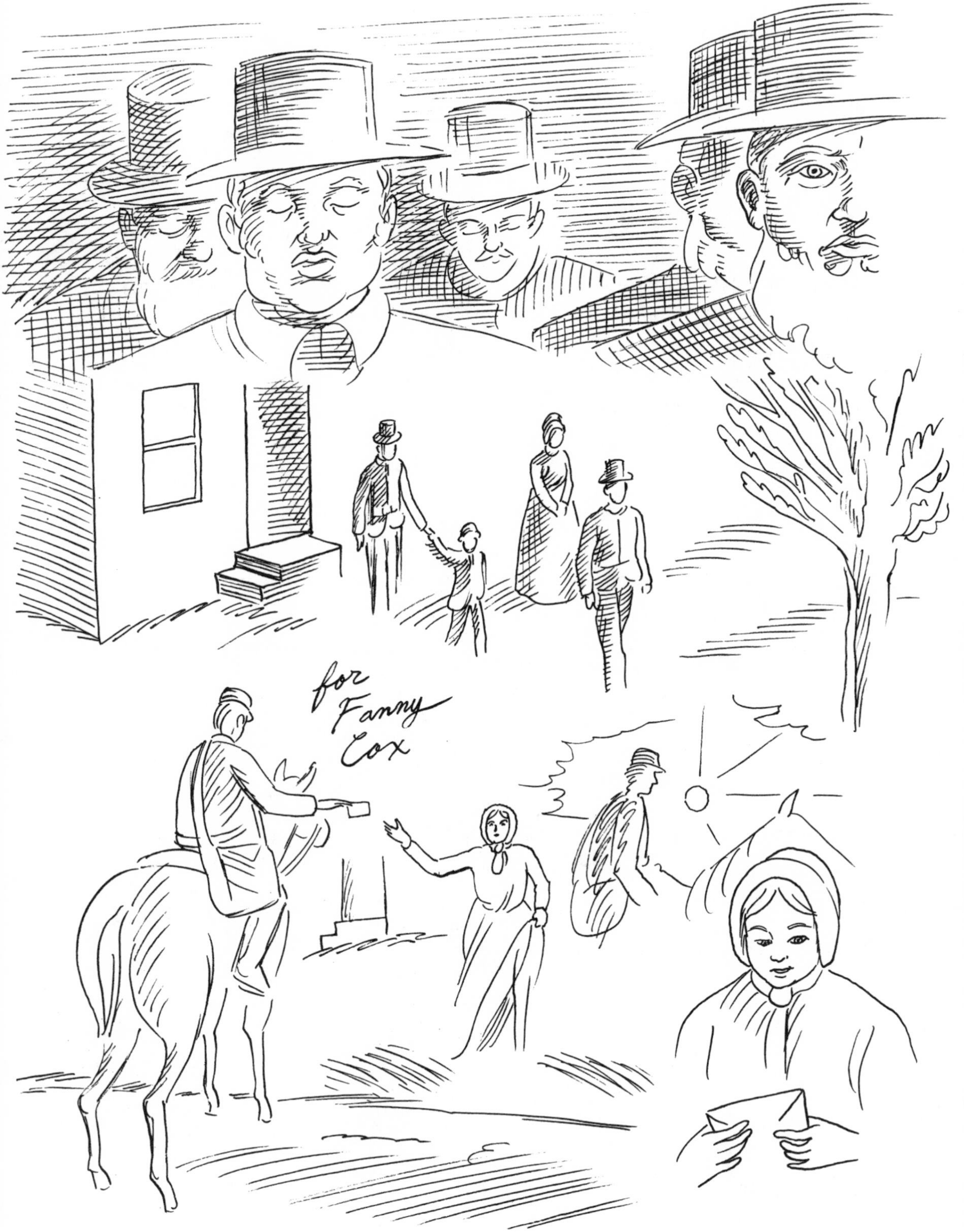
for Fanny Cox

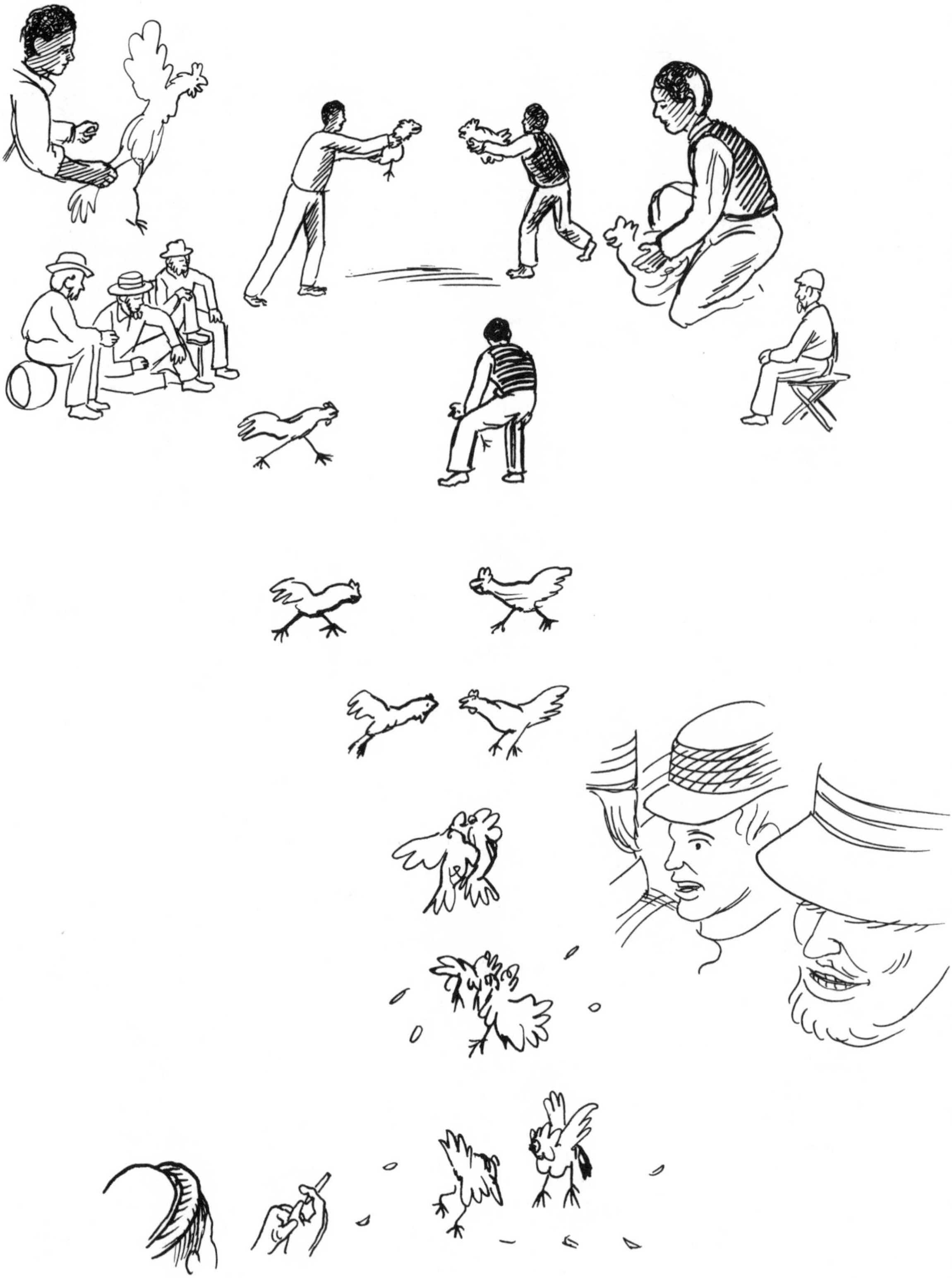

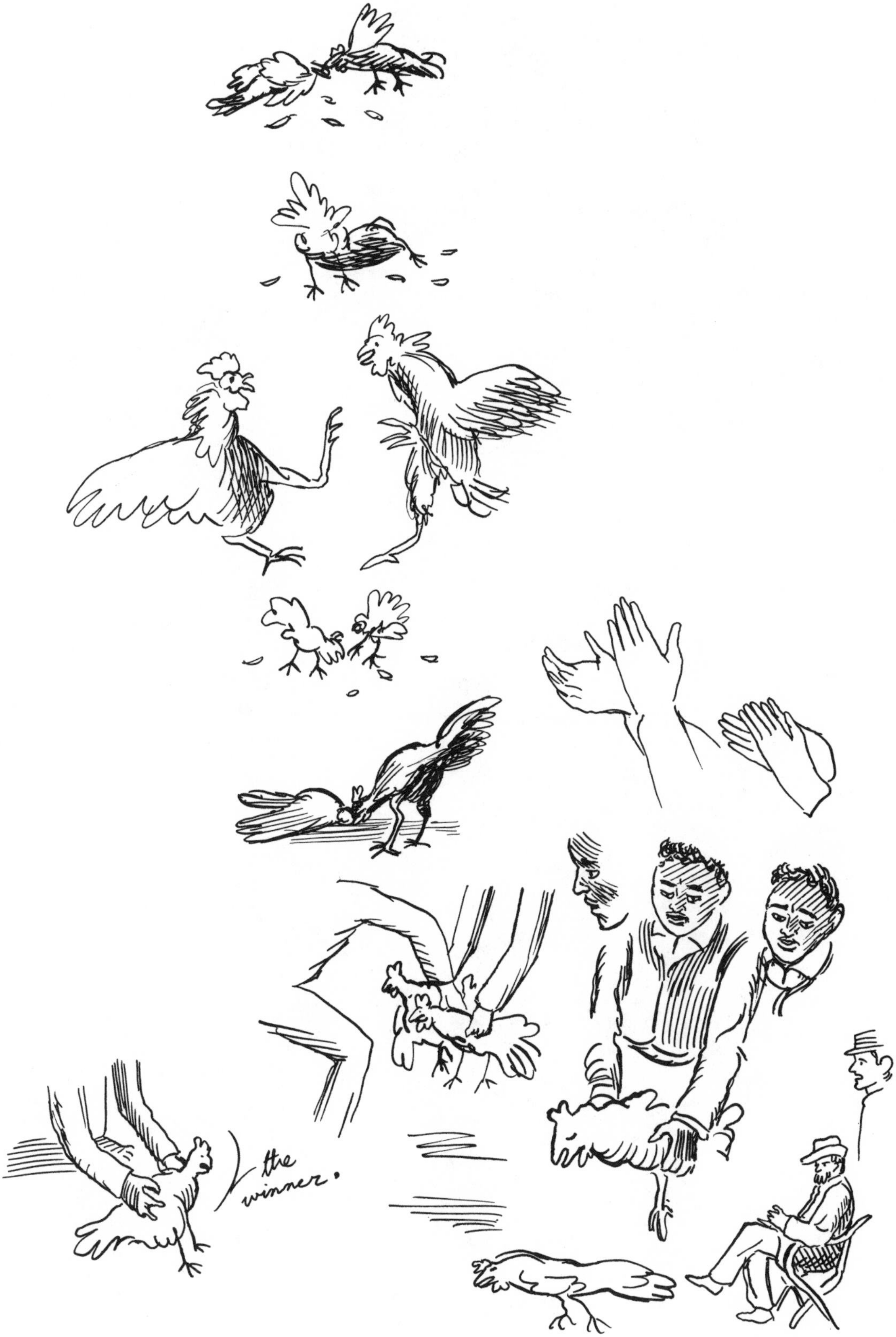
the winner.

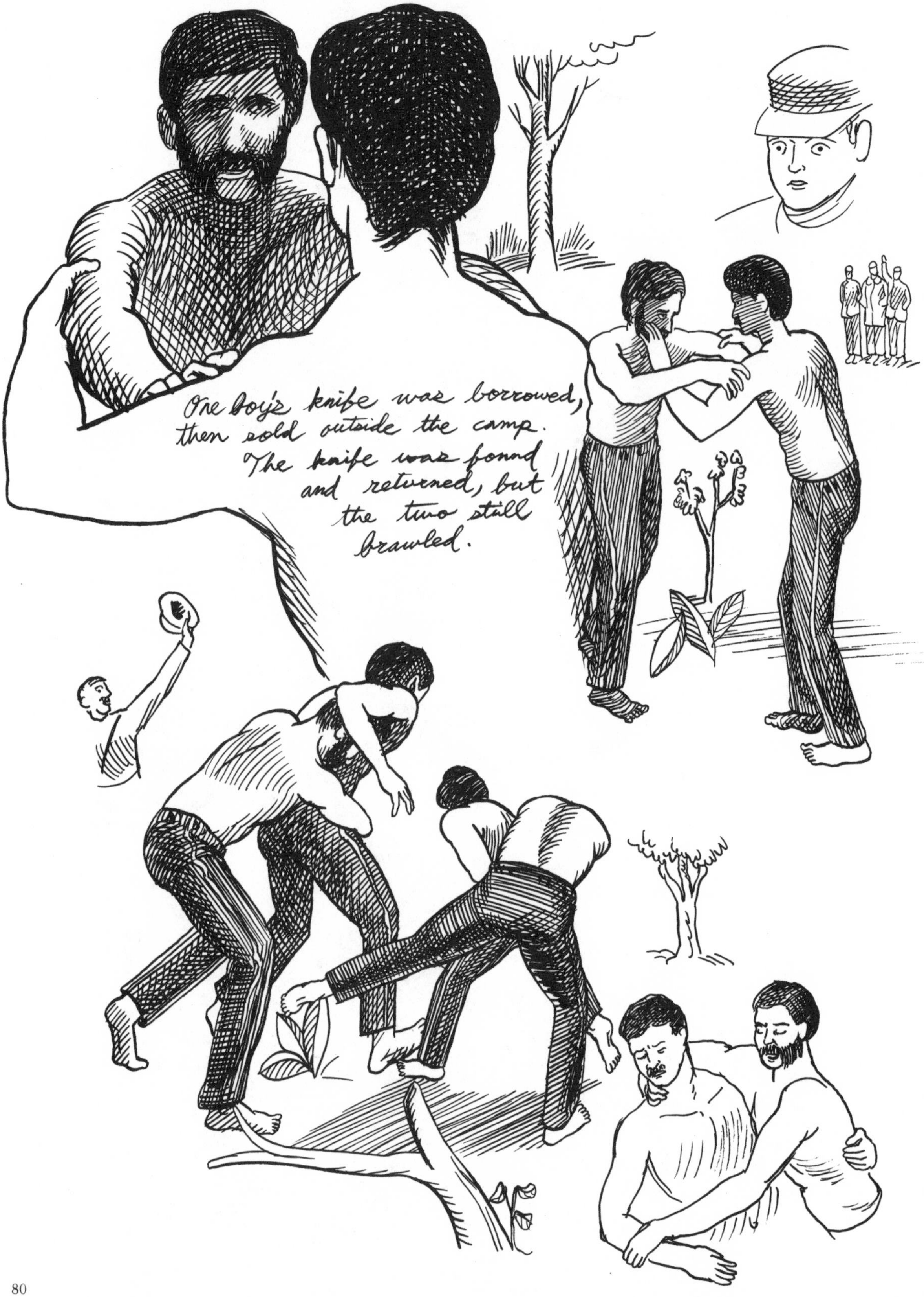
One boy's knife was borrowed, then sold outside the camp. The knife was found and returned, but the two still brawled.

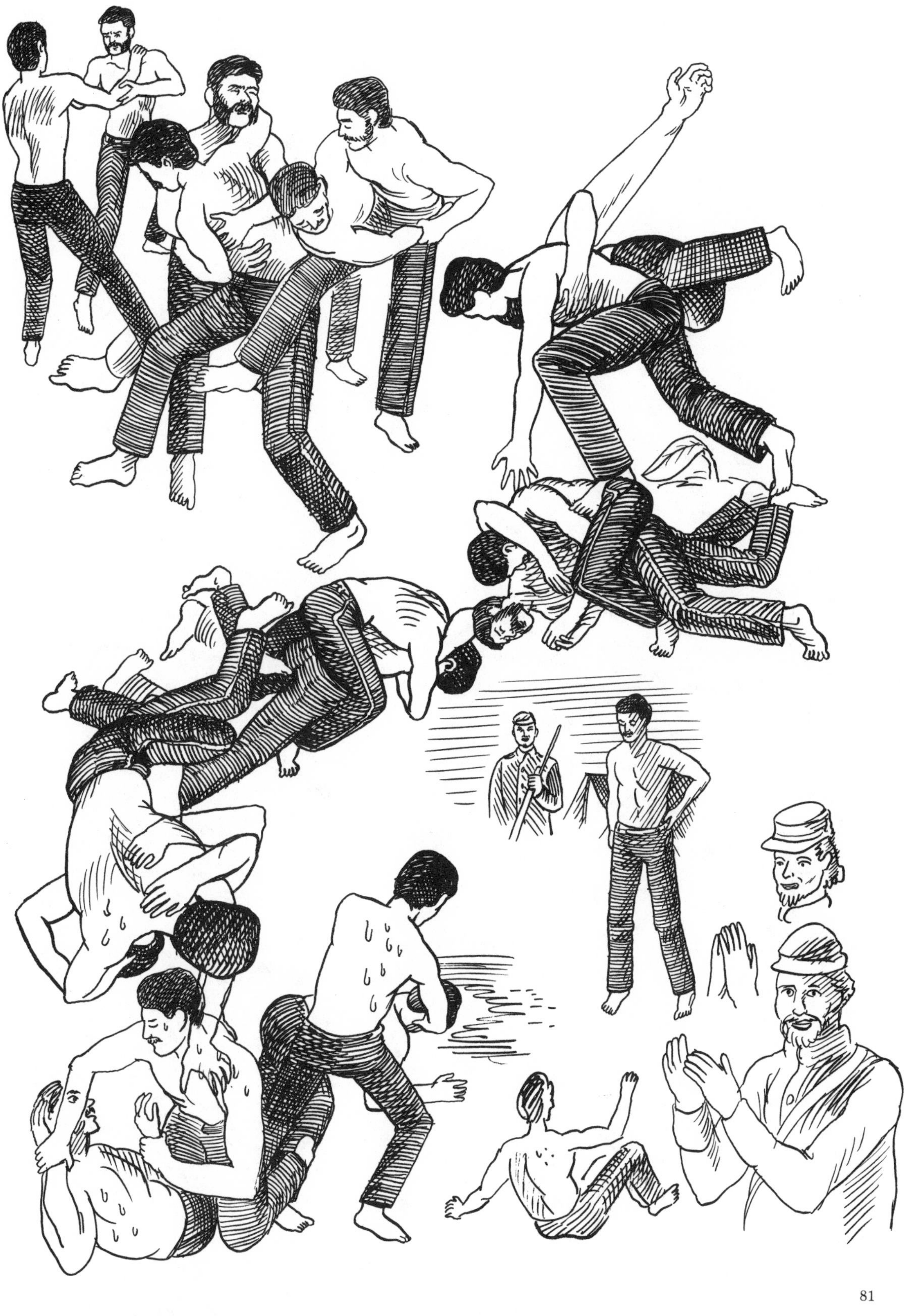

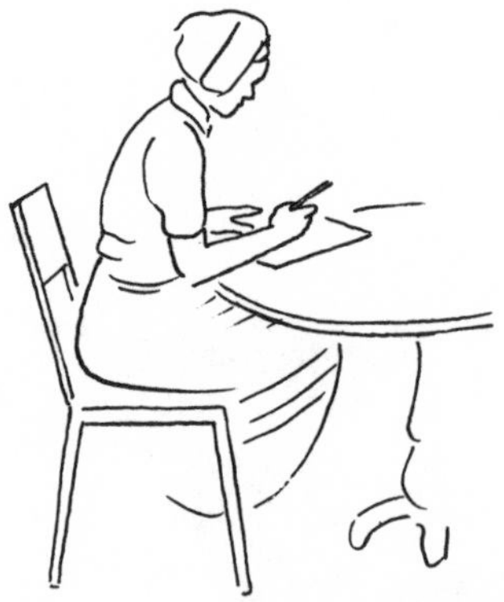

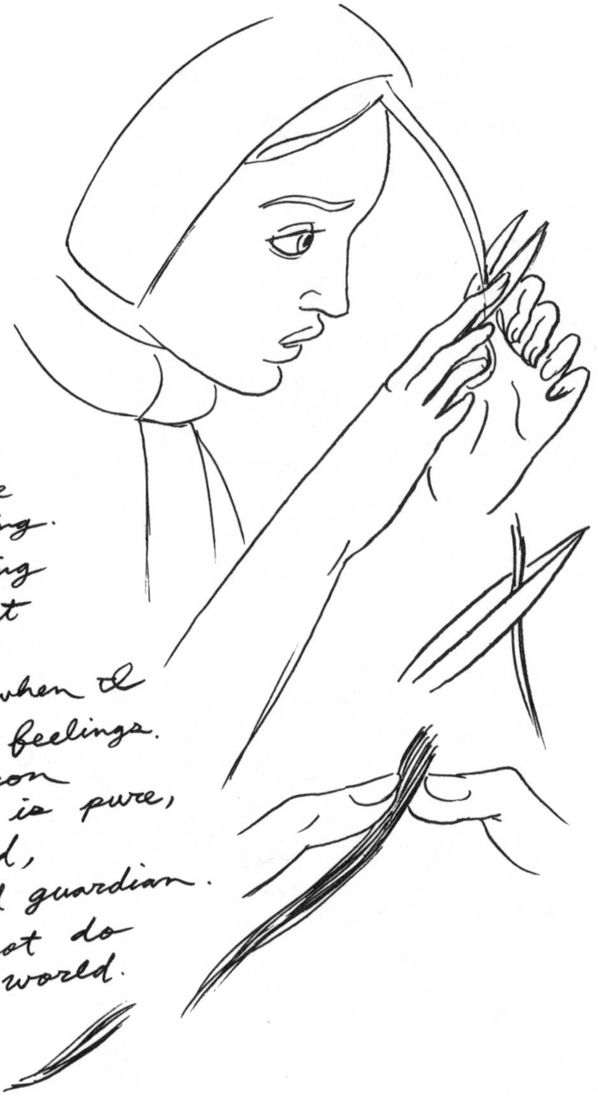

Charles,
We think of thee often,
and plenty of words are
spoken of thee in meeting.
I hope thee are finding
silence somehow, if at
least within thyself.
I often doubt myself, when I
consider my changeable feelings.
Religion is no common
enthusiasm, because it is pure,
it is a constant friend,
protector, supporter and guardian.
It is what we cannot do
well without in this world.

Thy loving
sister,
Fanny

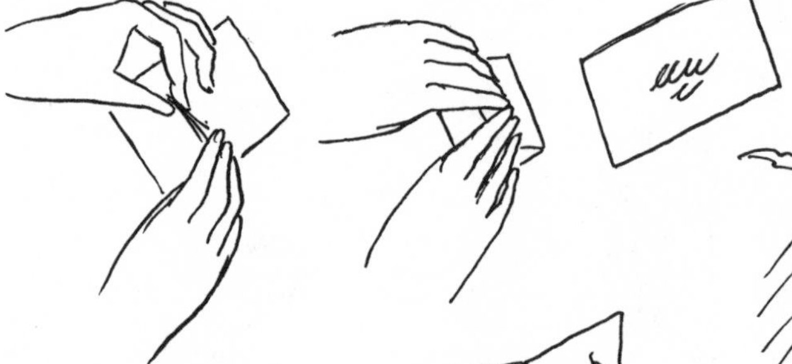

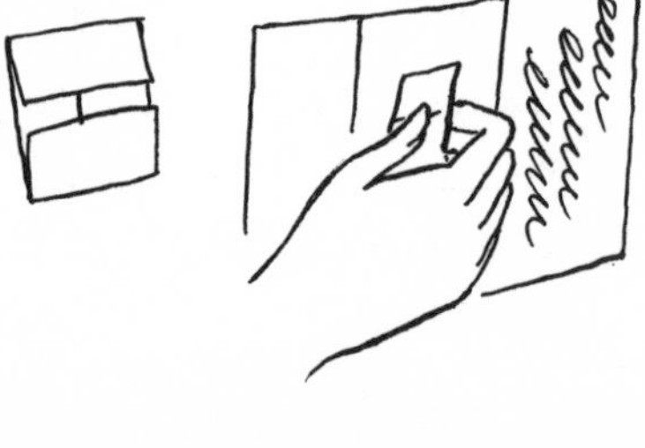

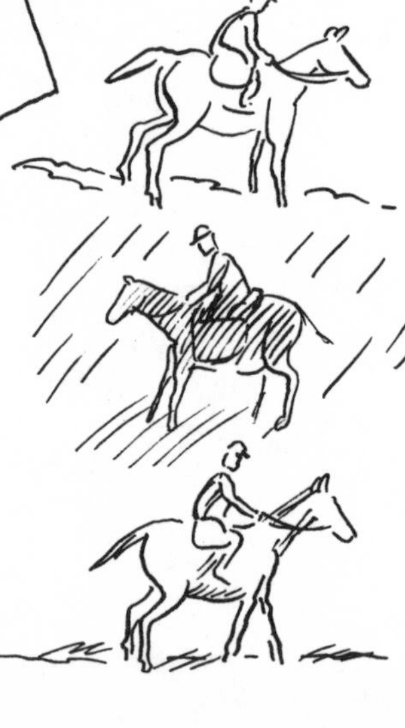

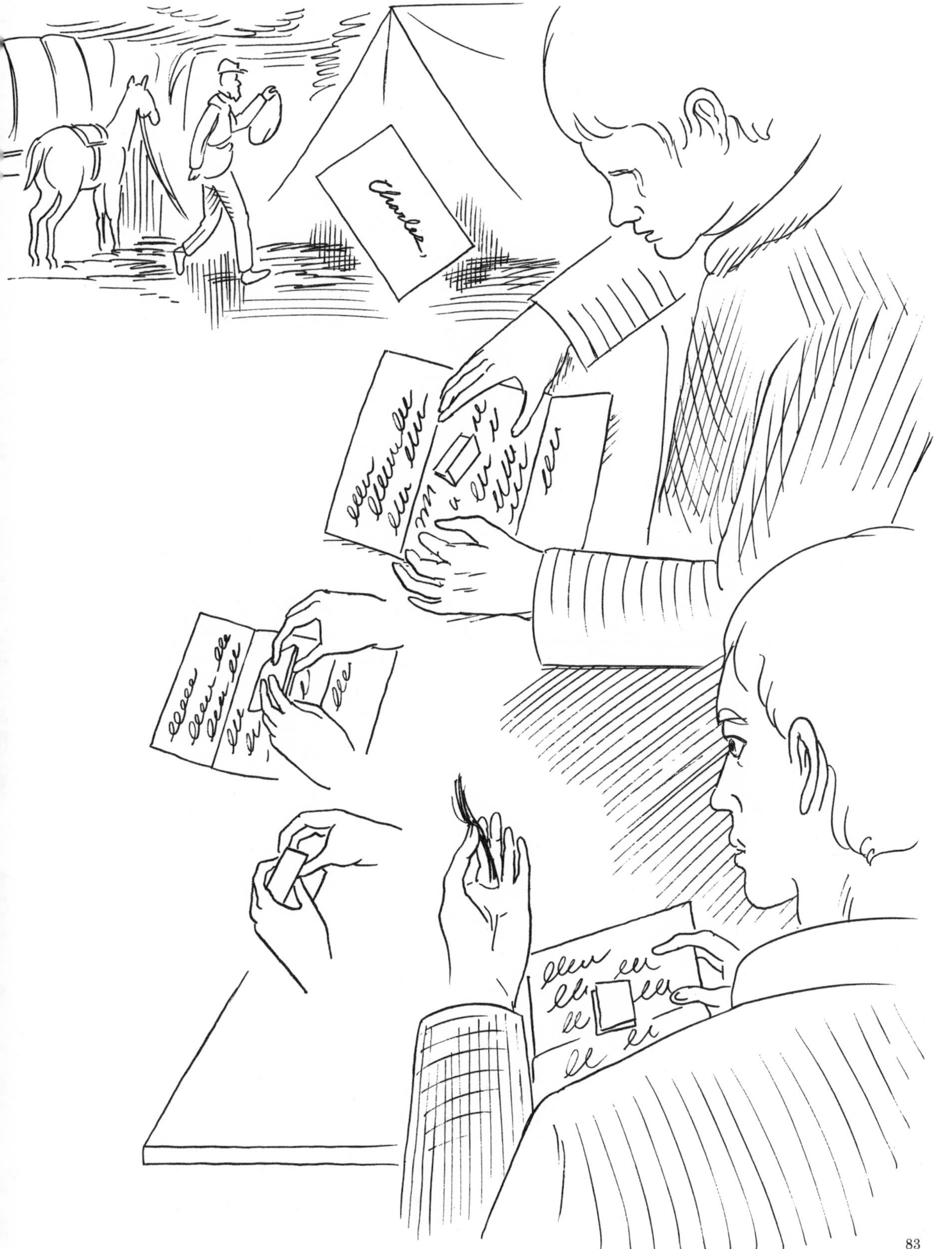
Charles

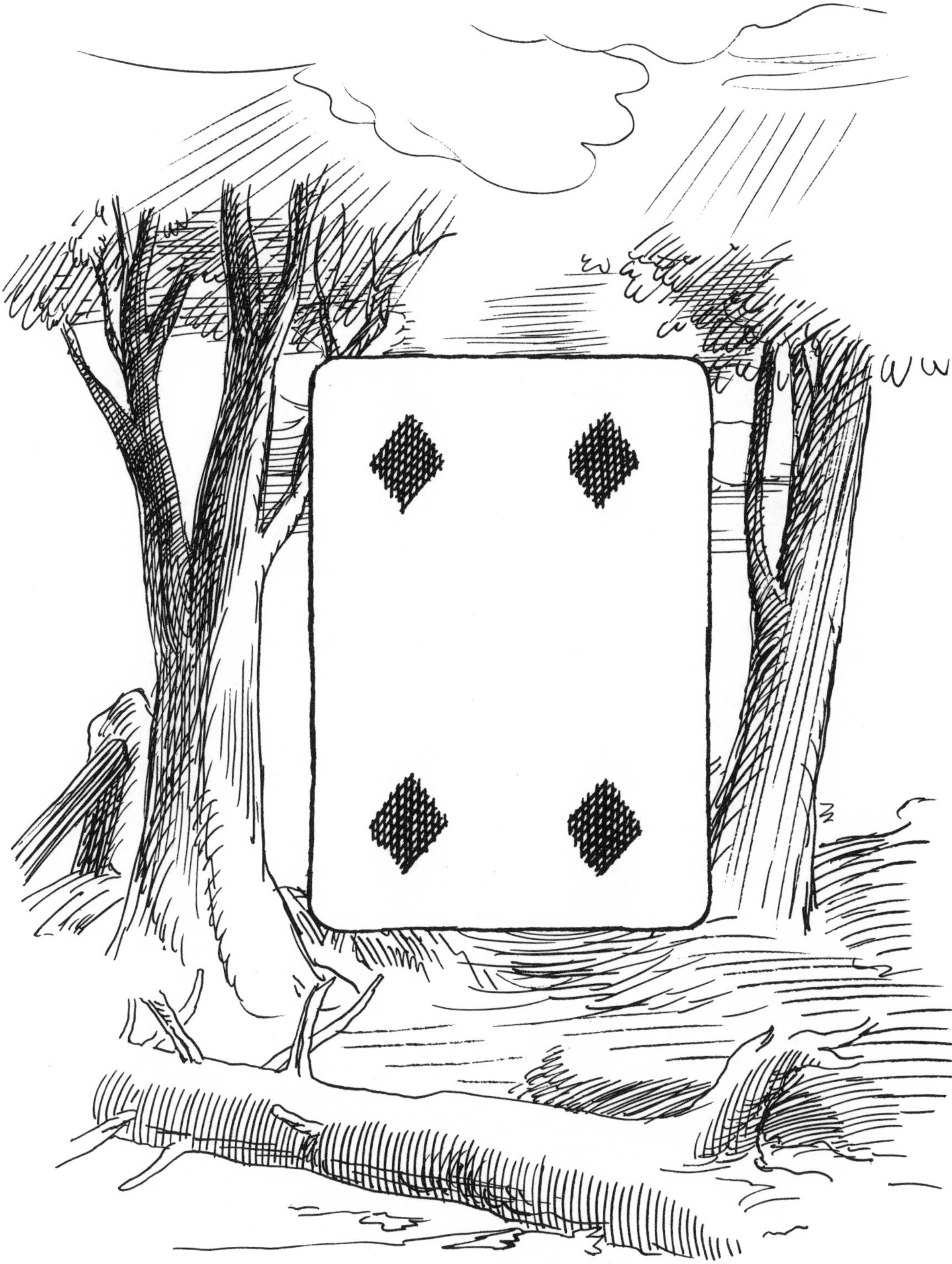

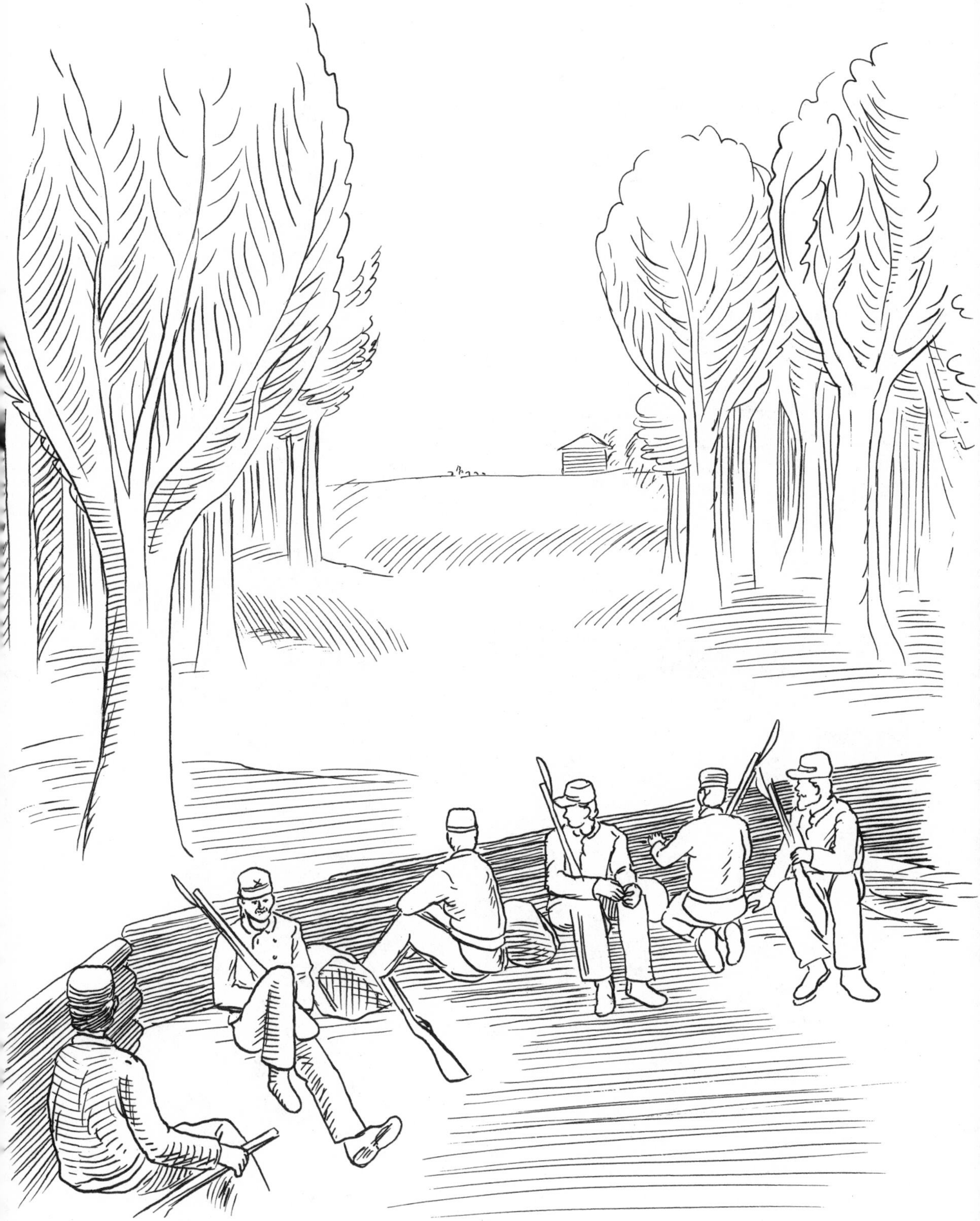

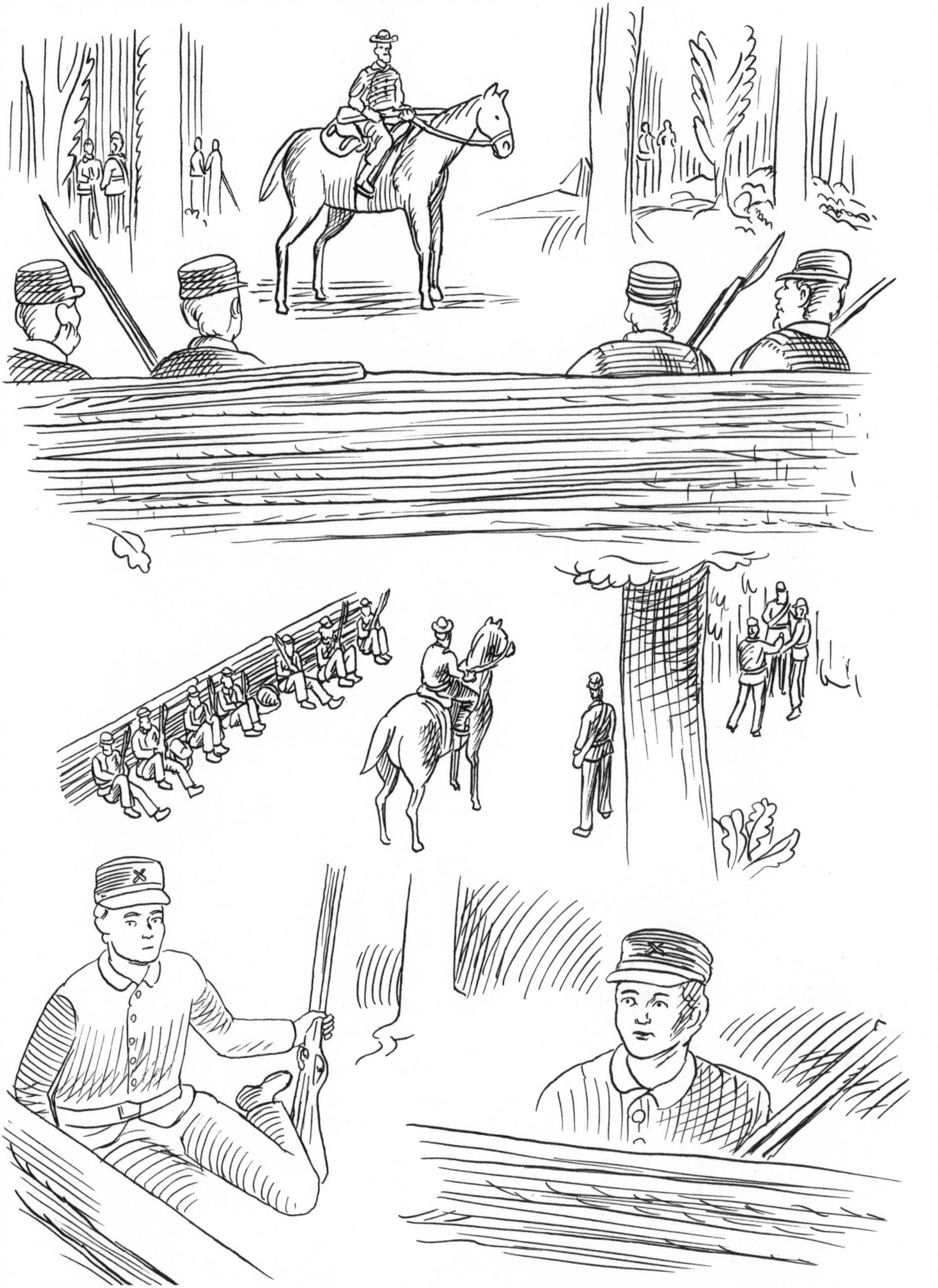

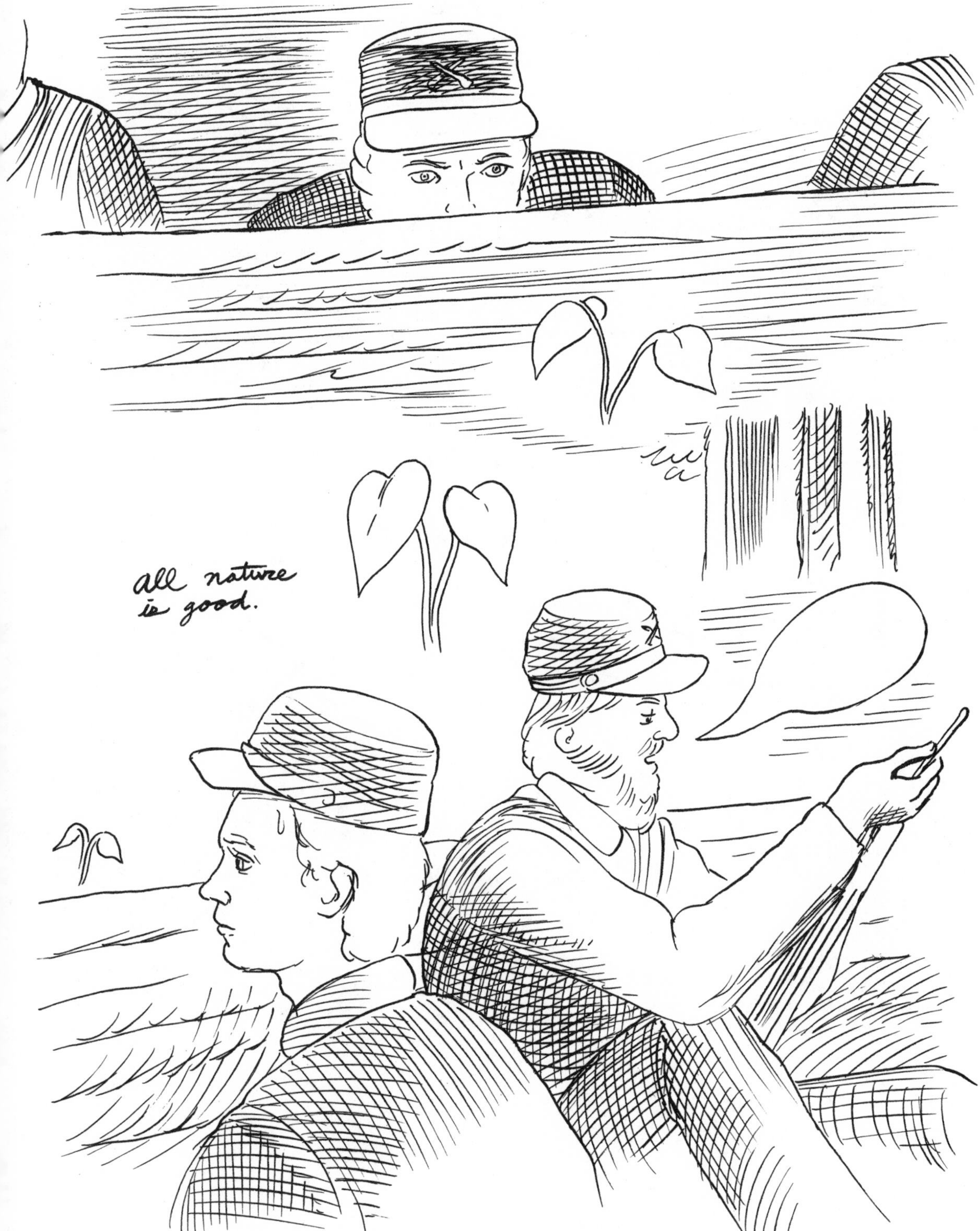
all nature
is good.

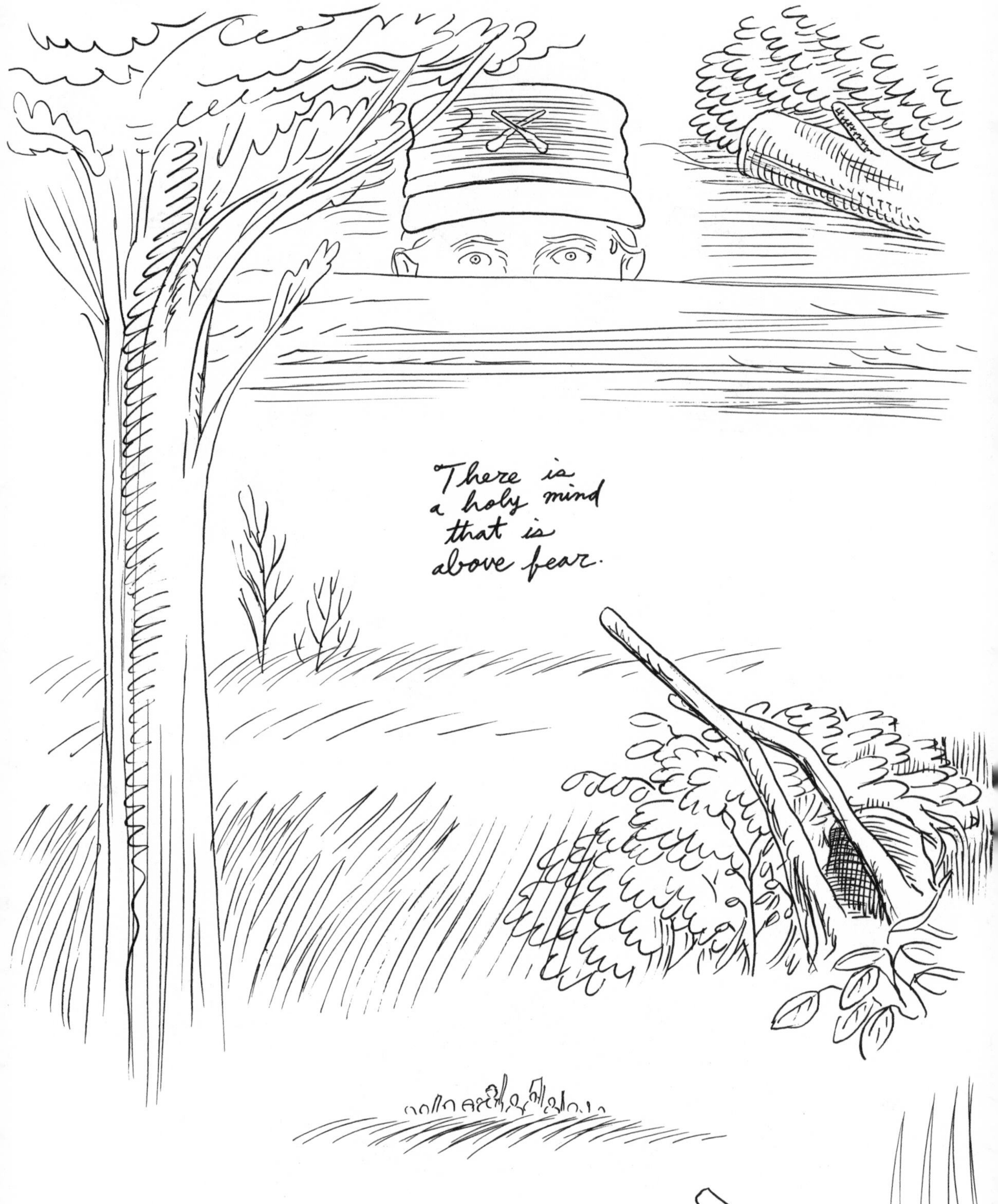
There is a holy mind that is above fear.

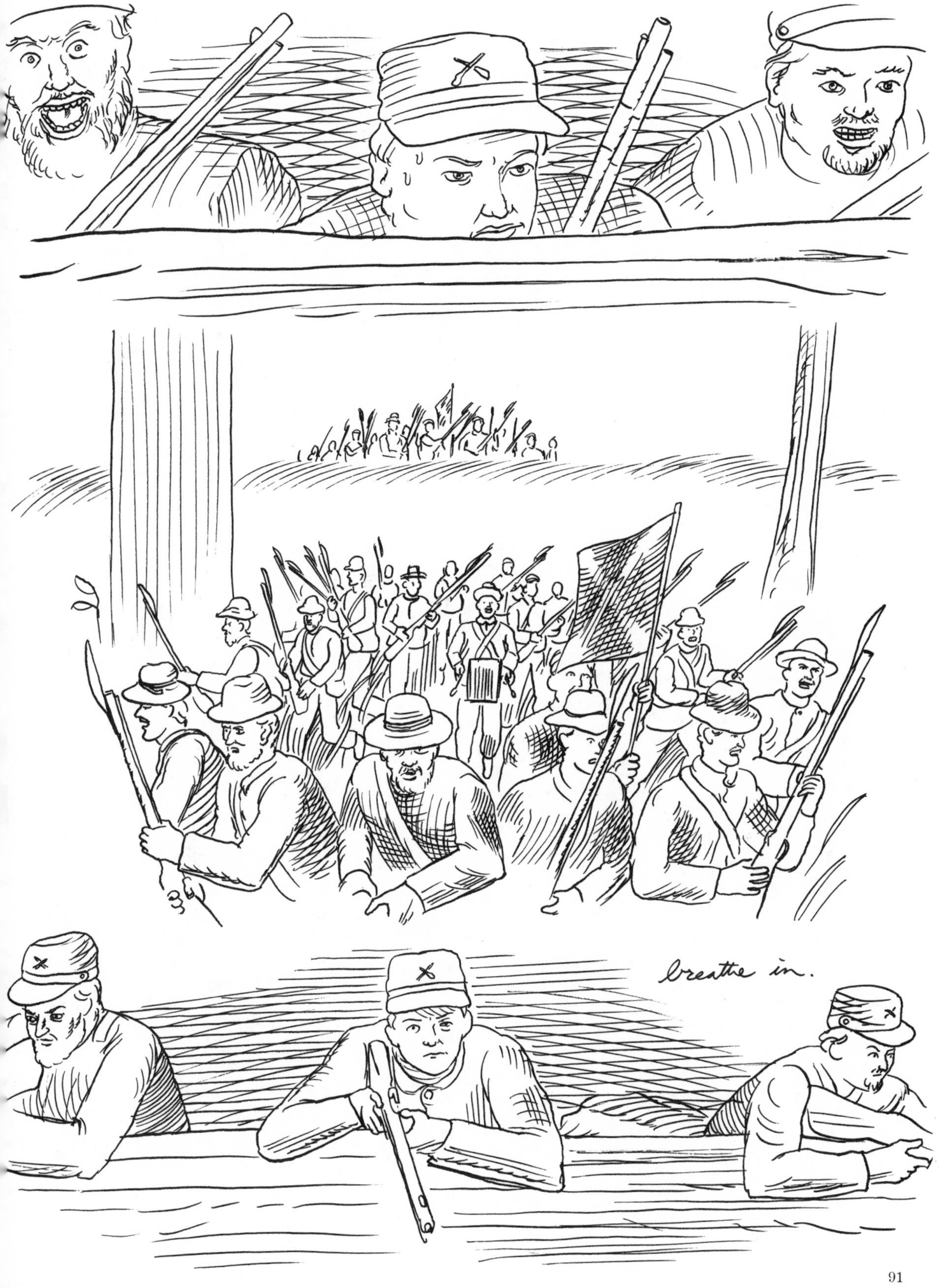
breathe in.

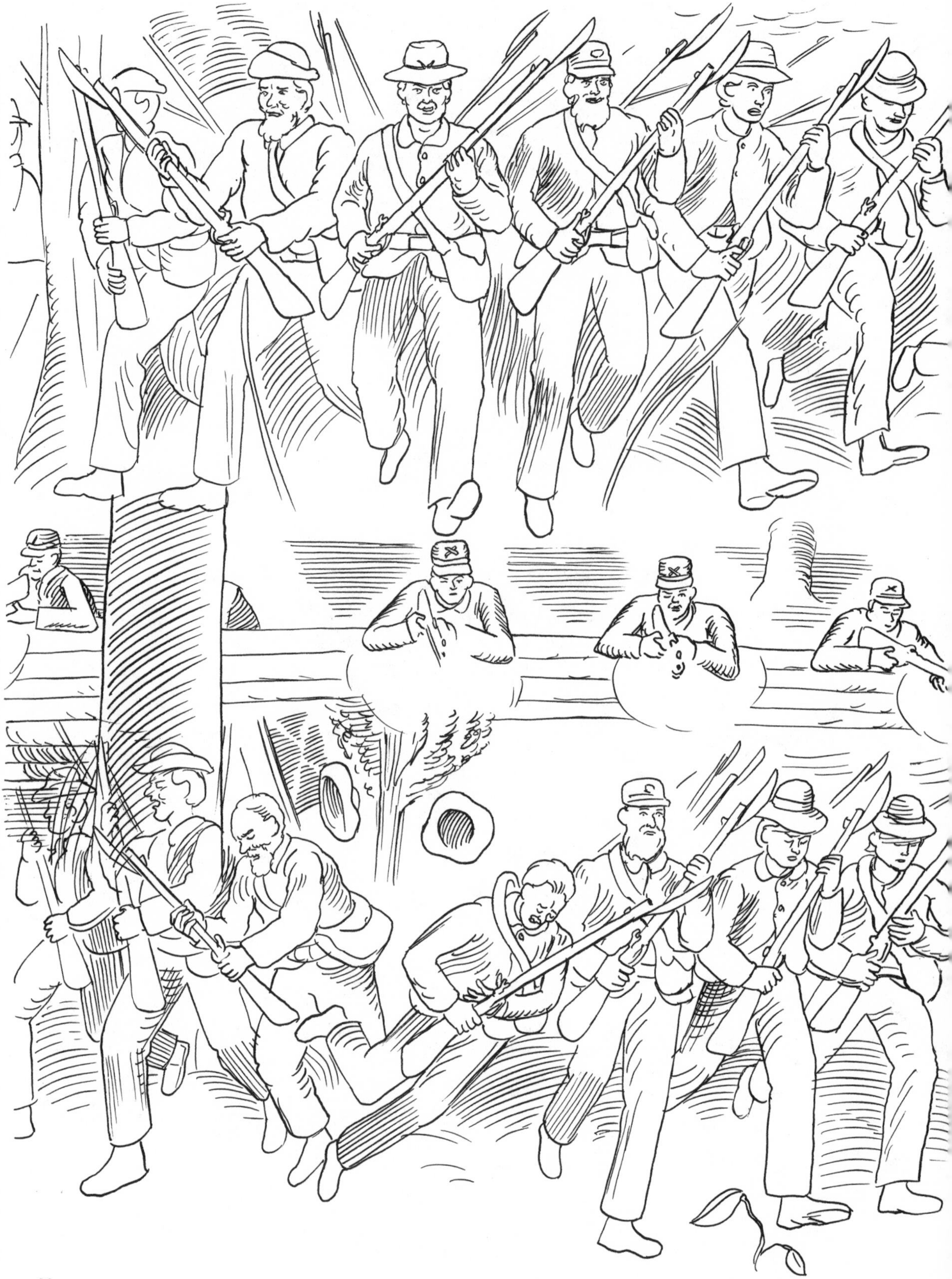

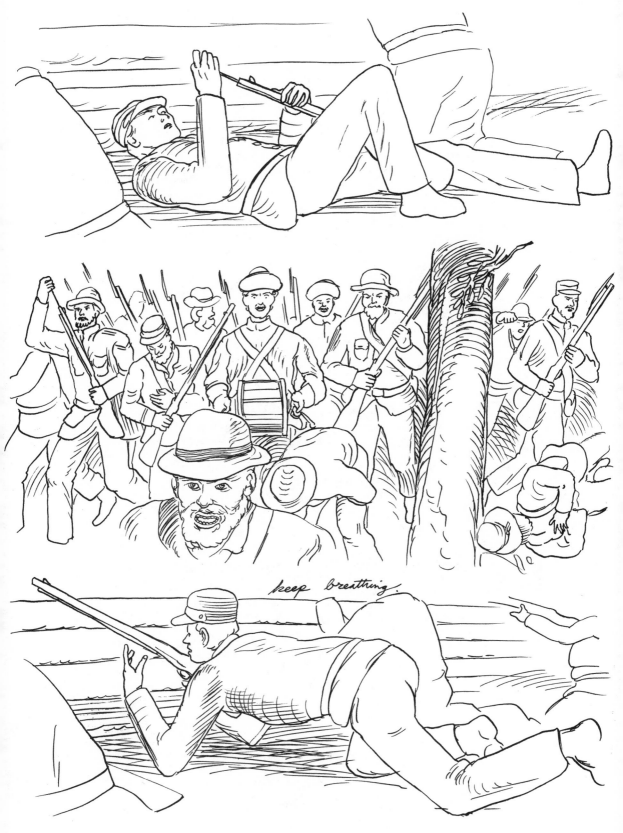

keep breathing.

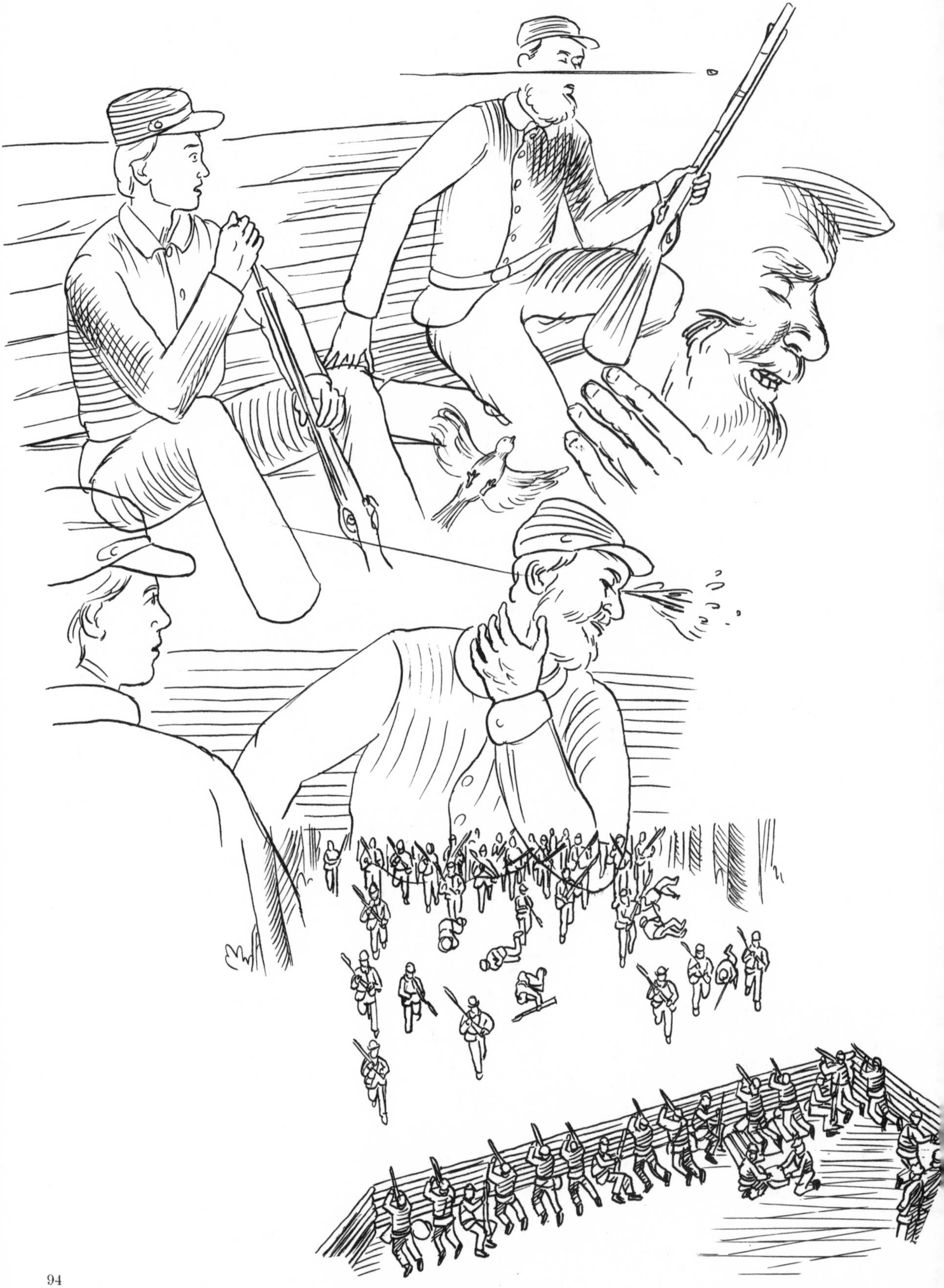

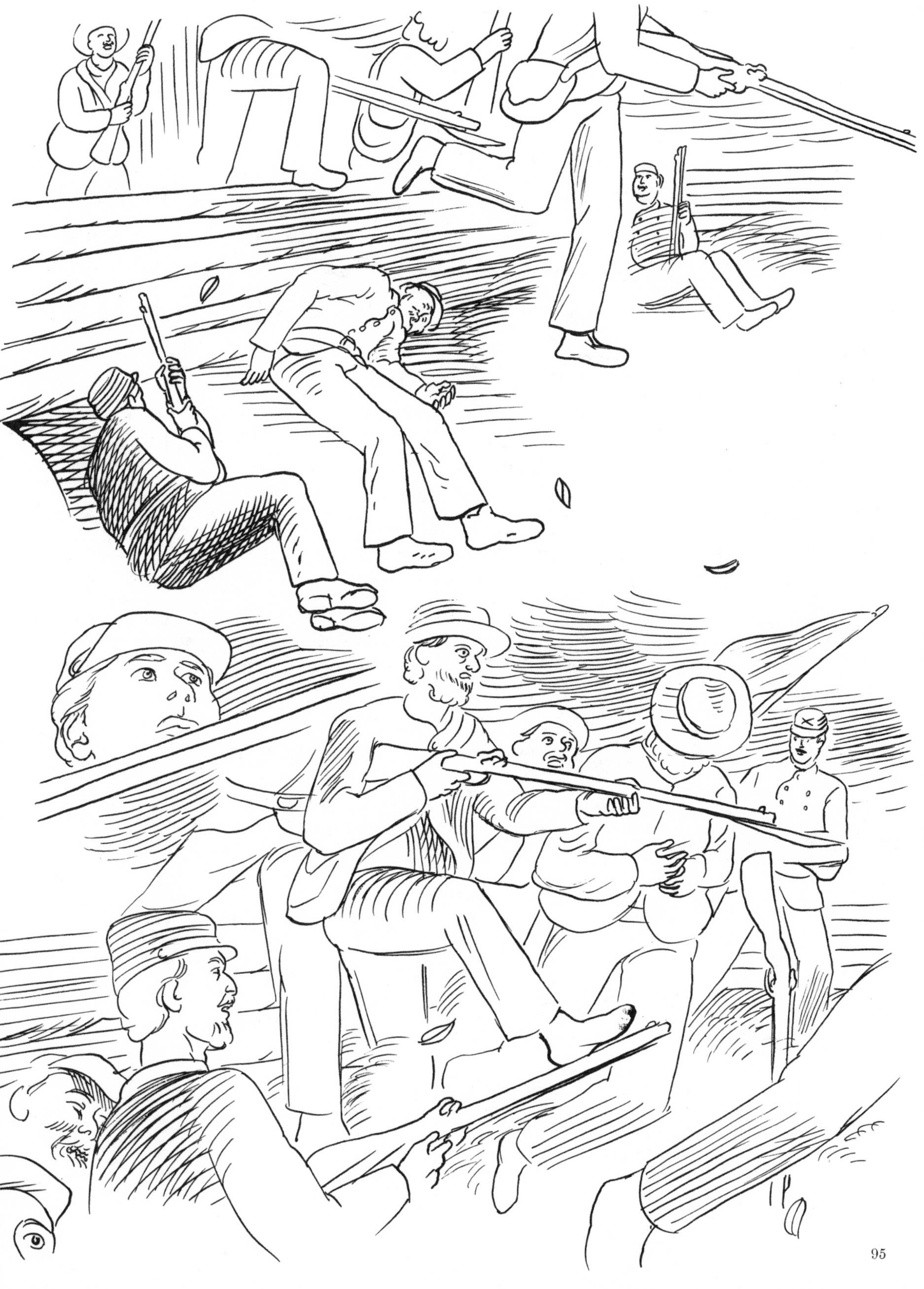

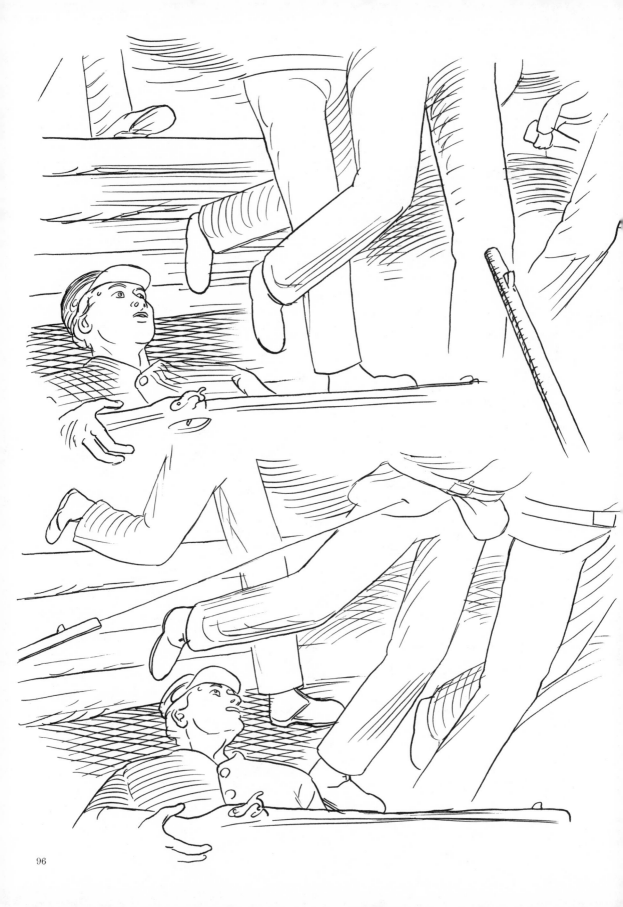

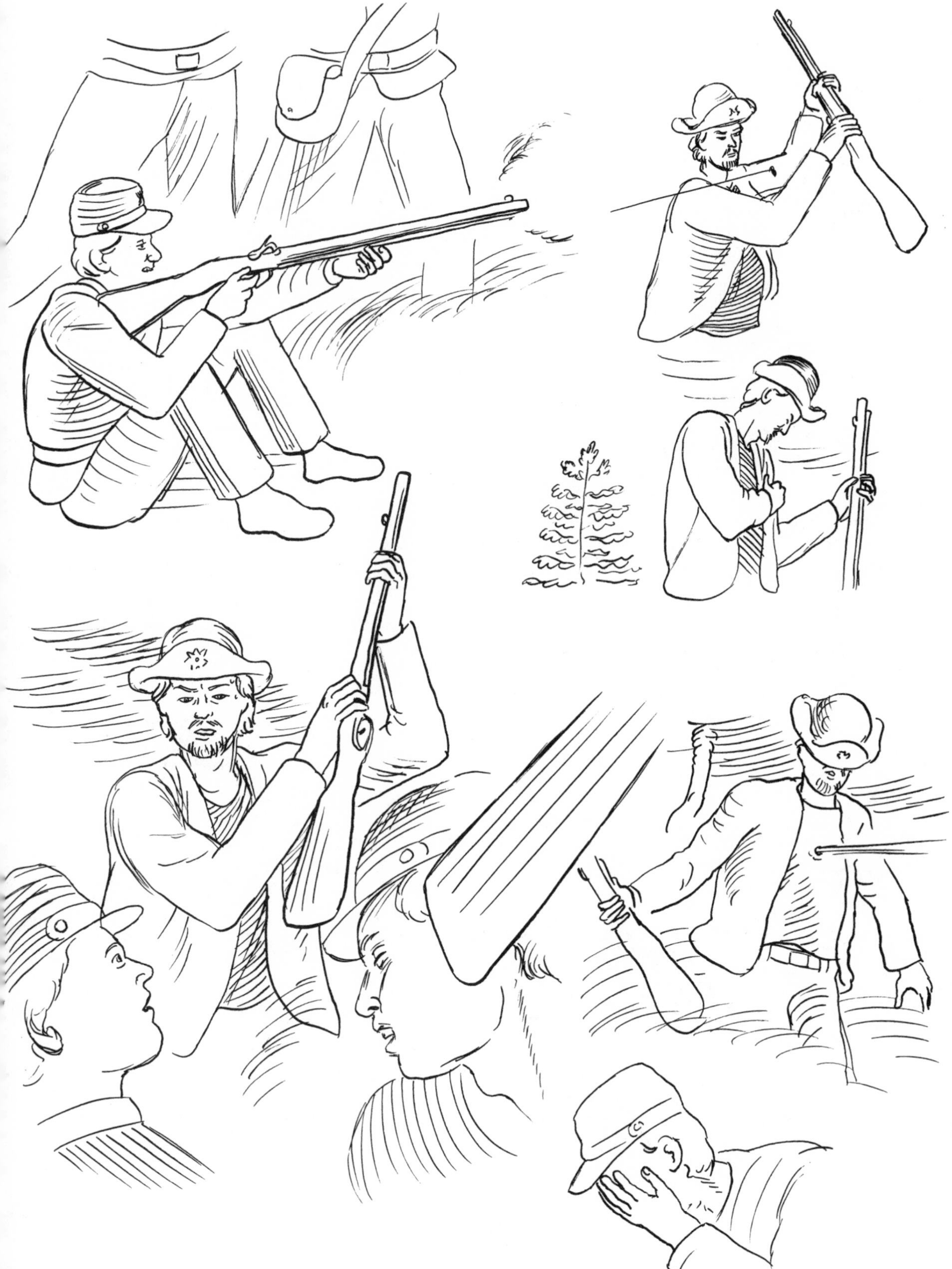

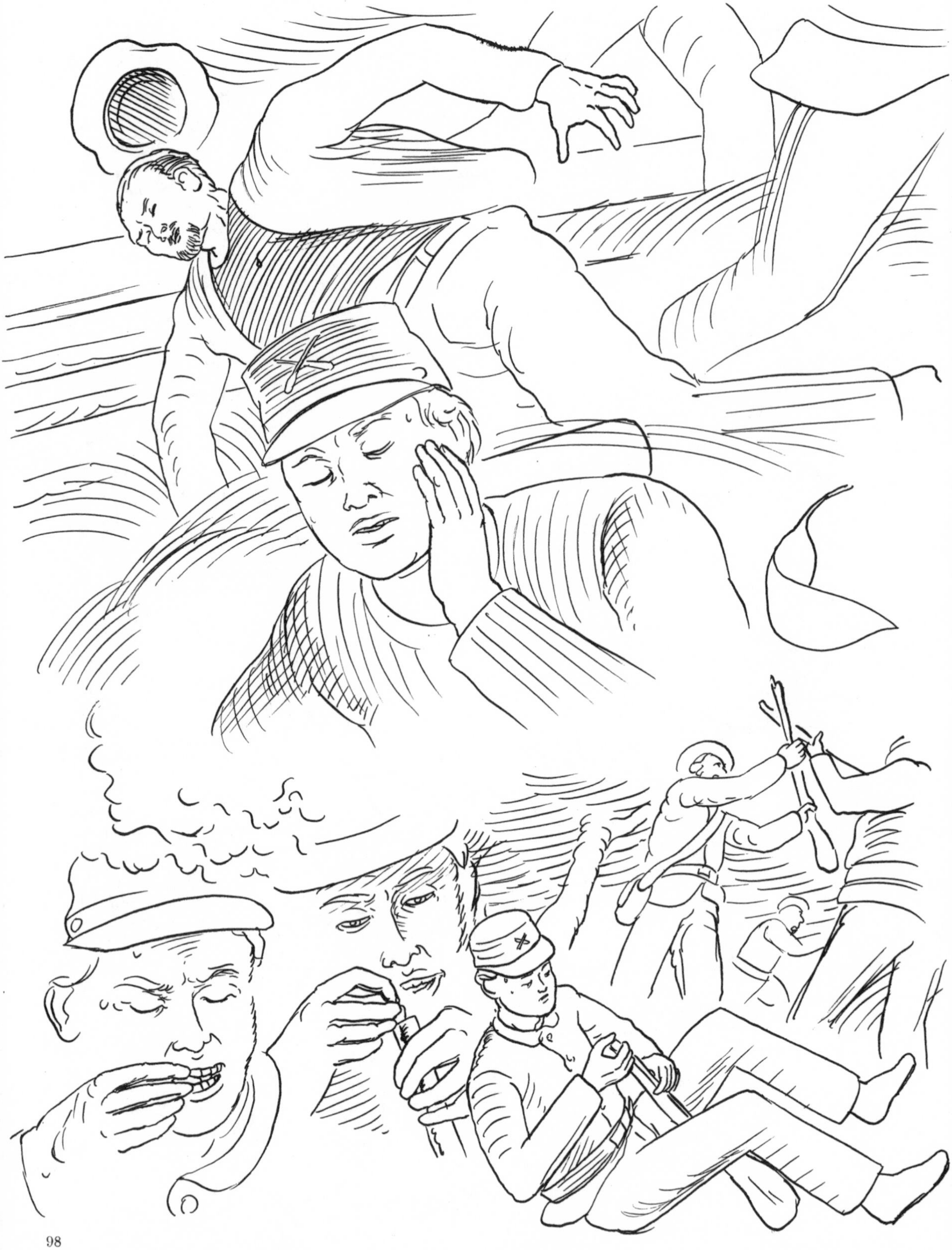

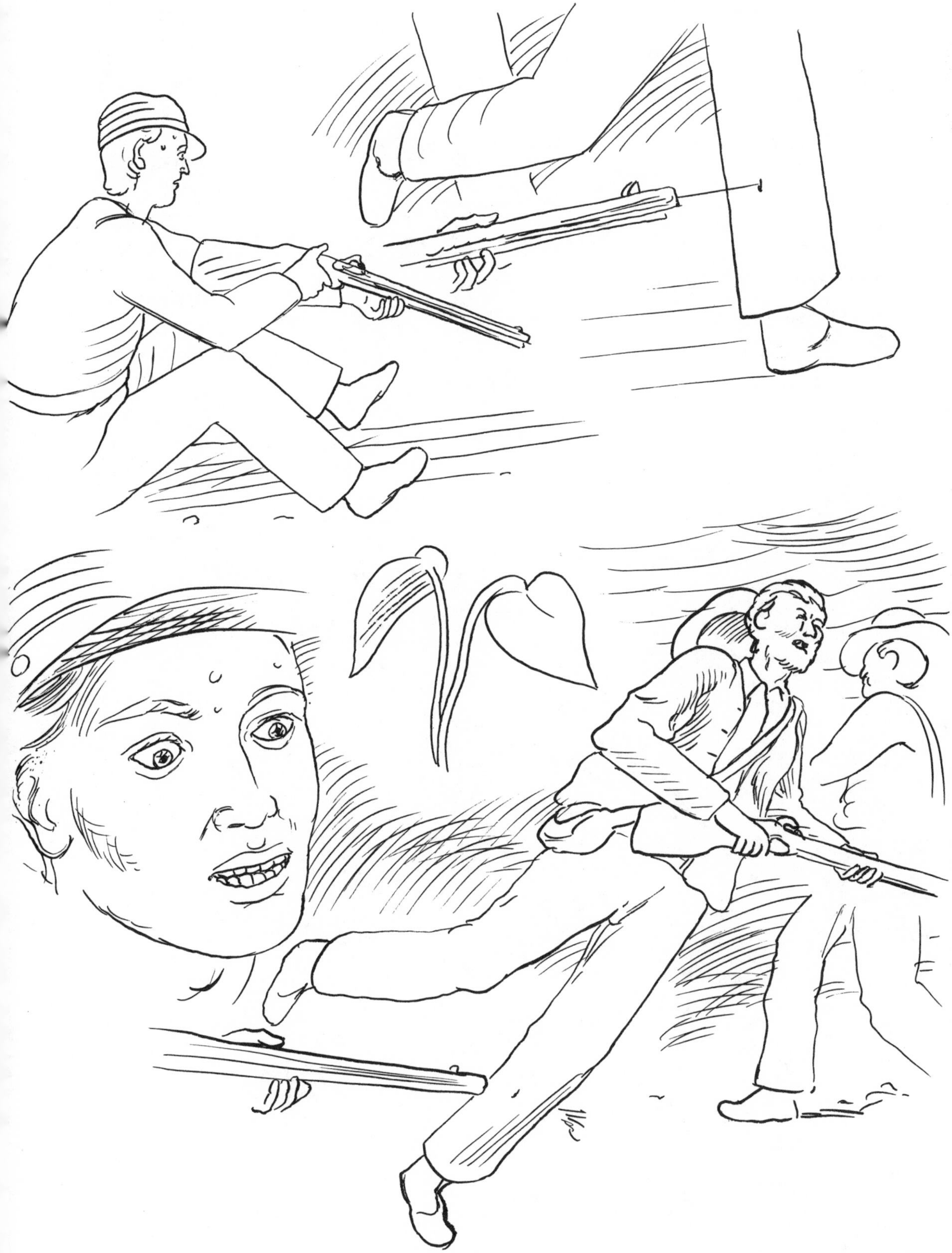

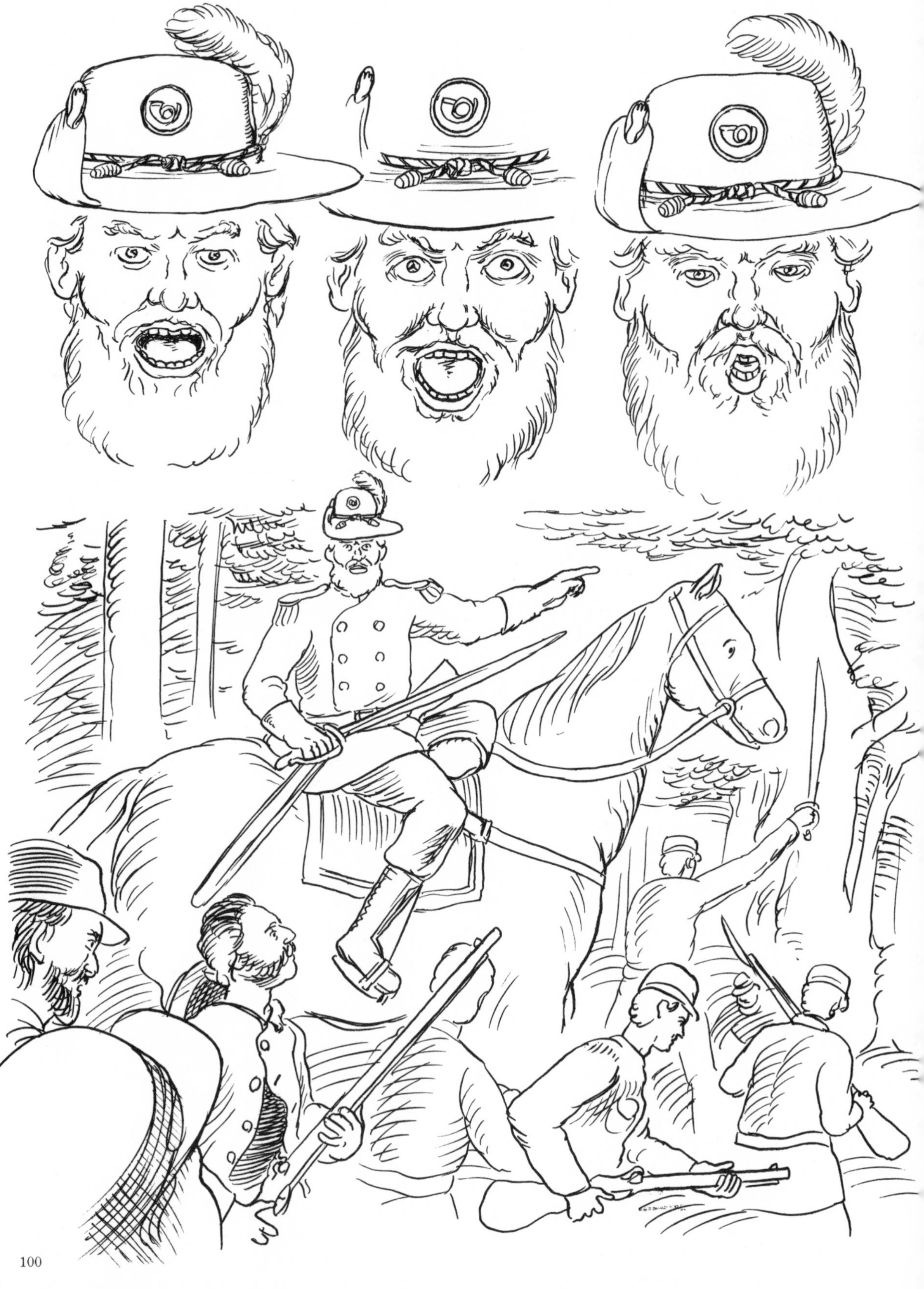

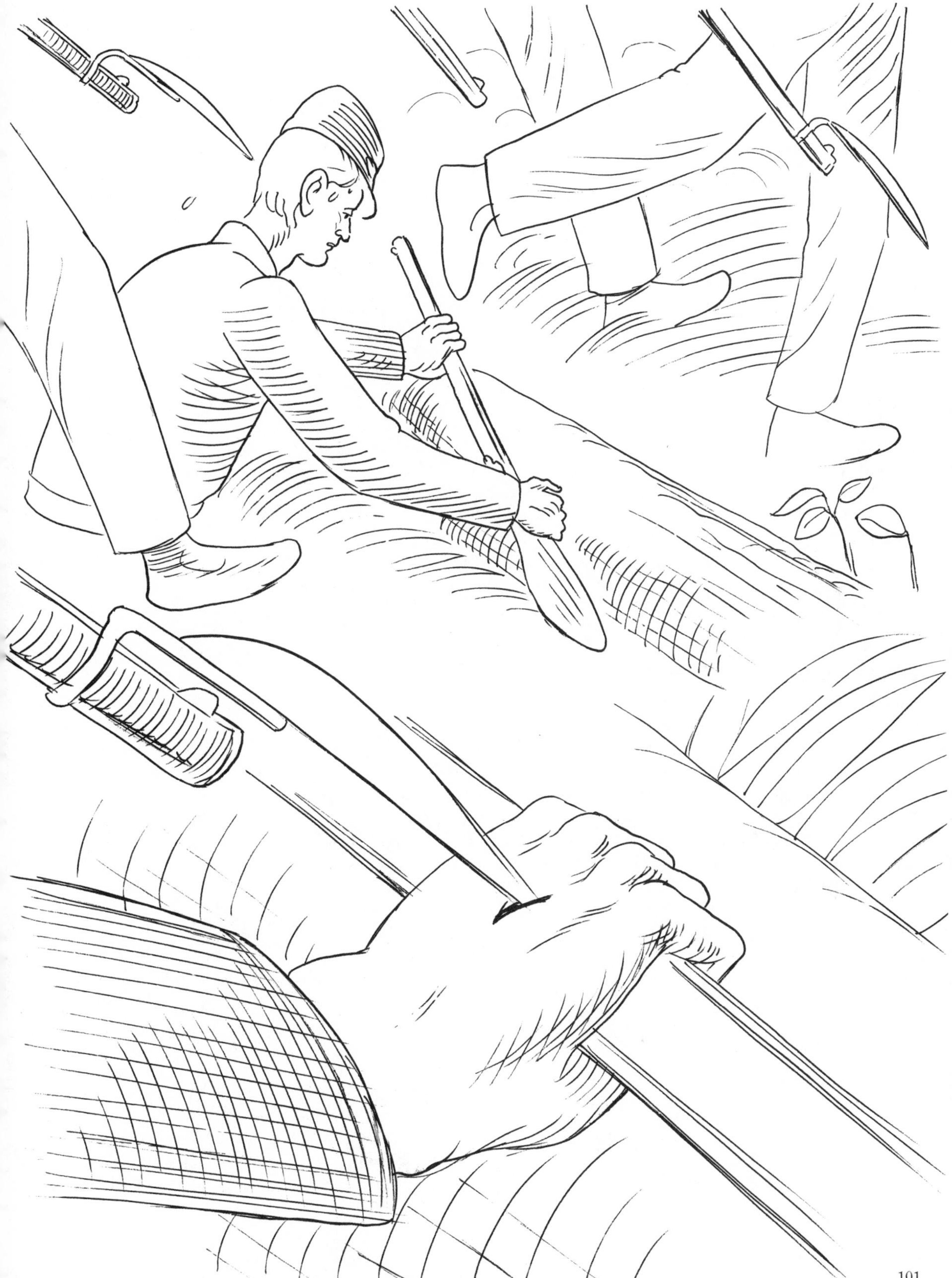

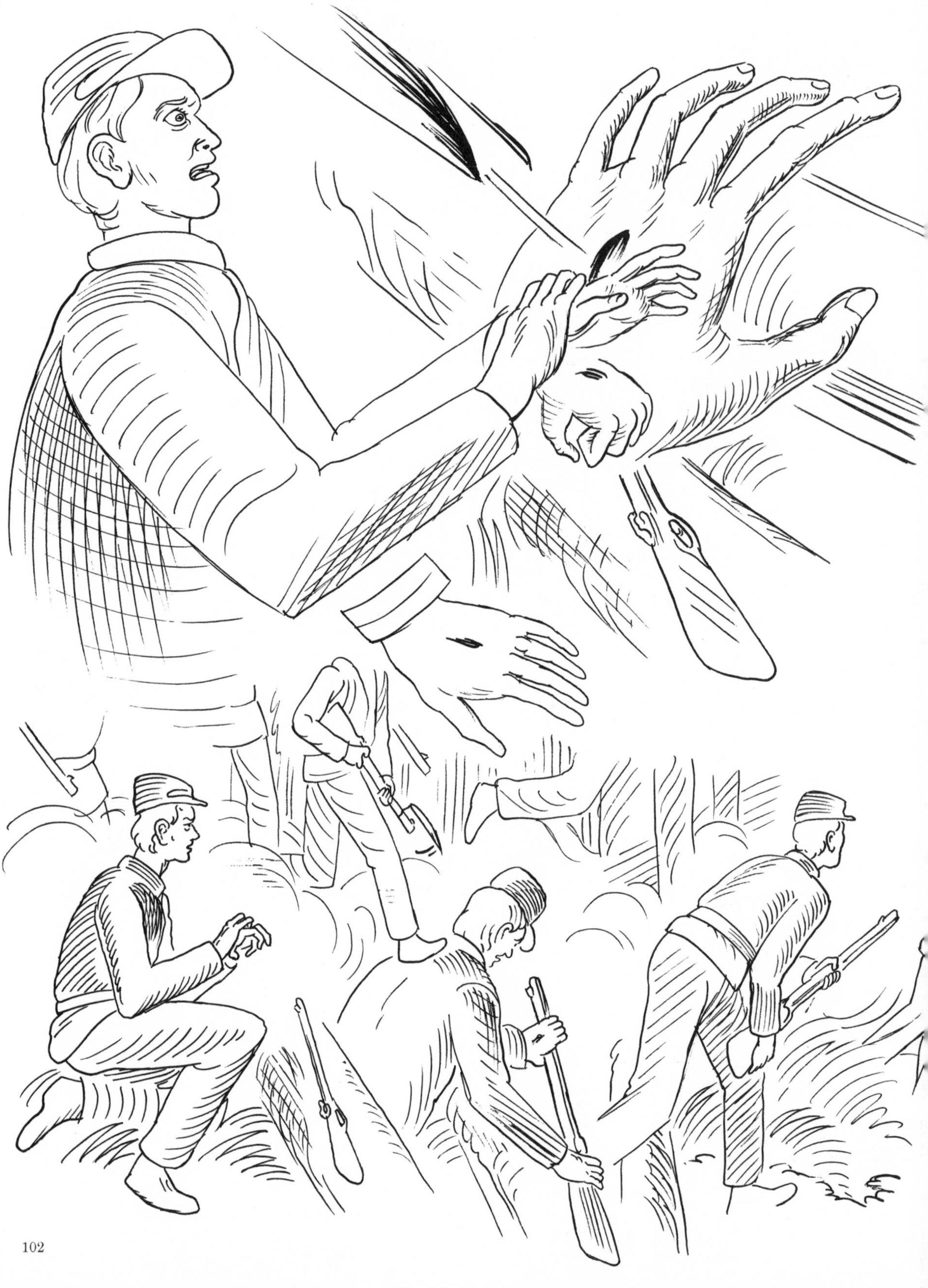

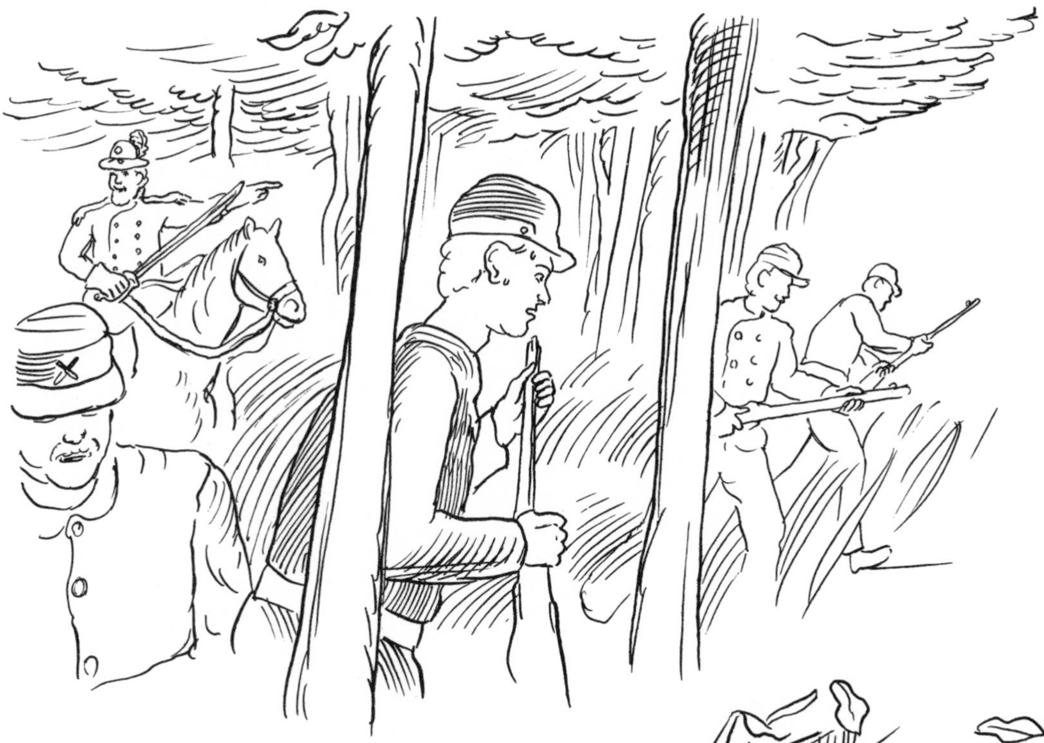

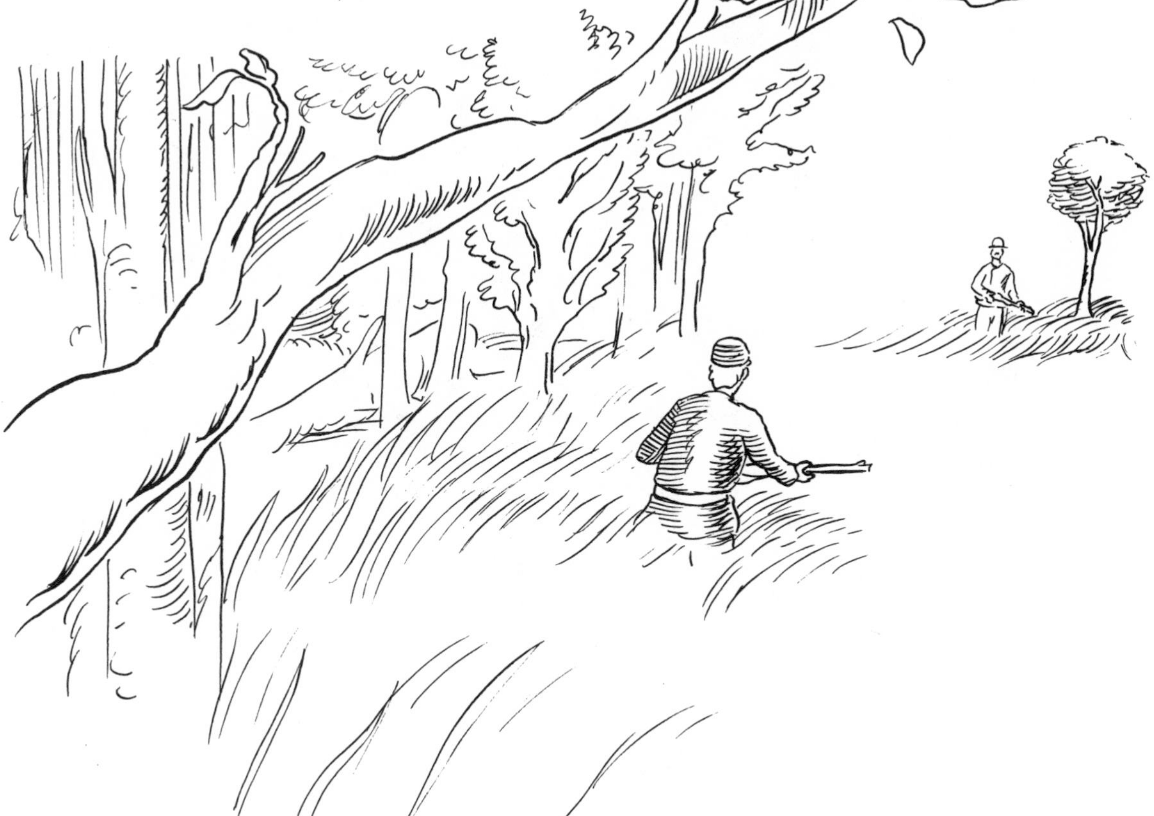

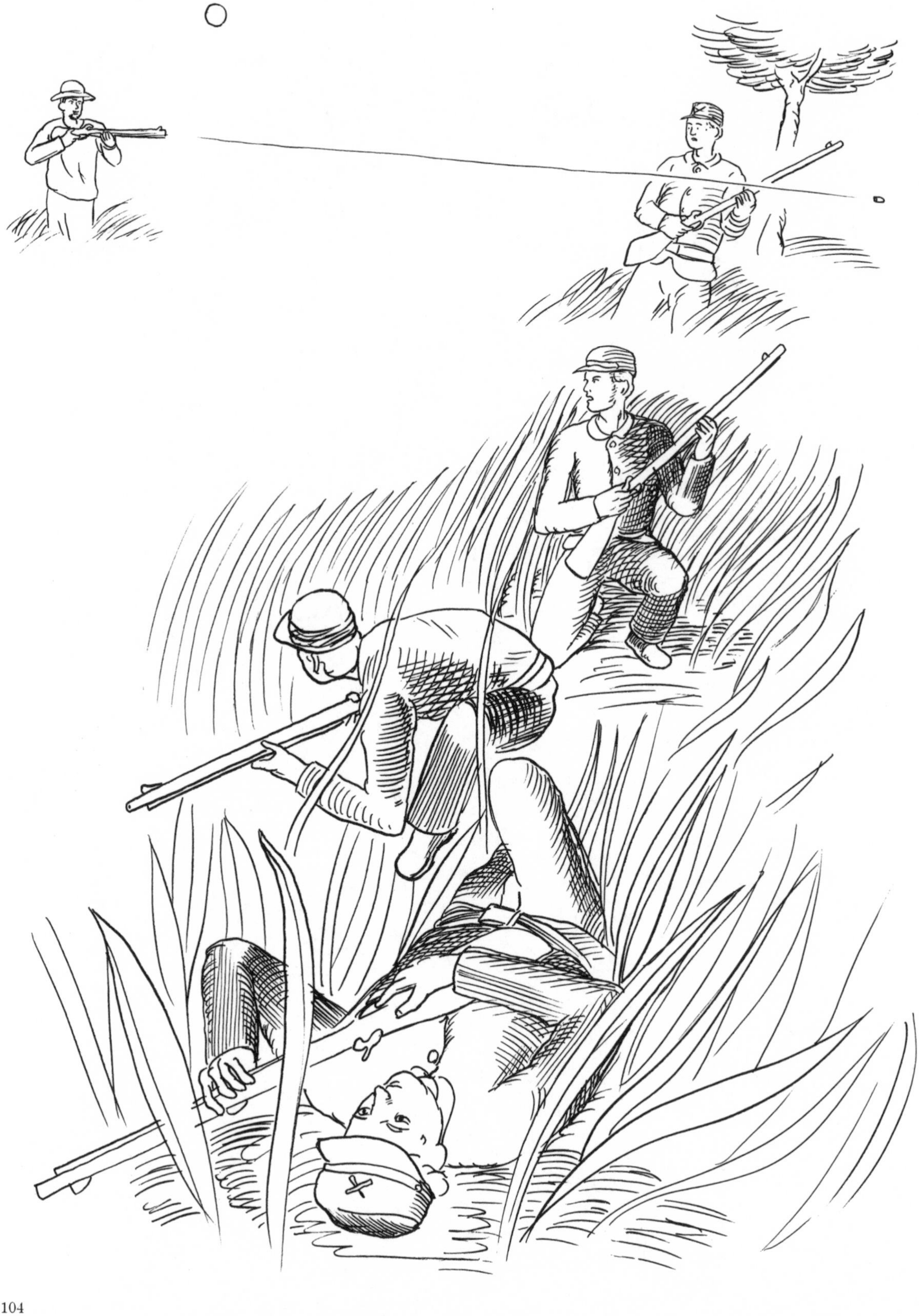

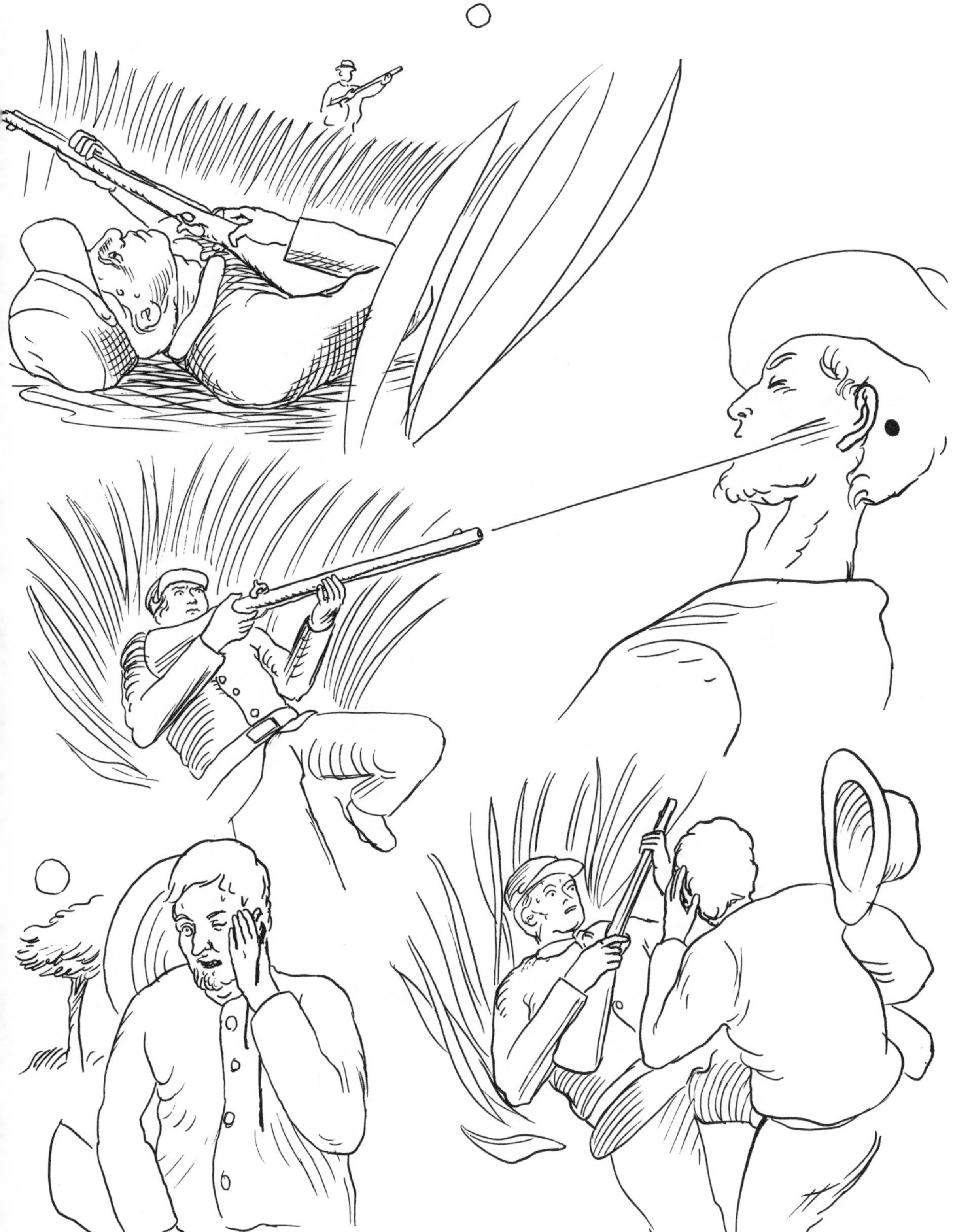

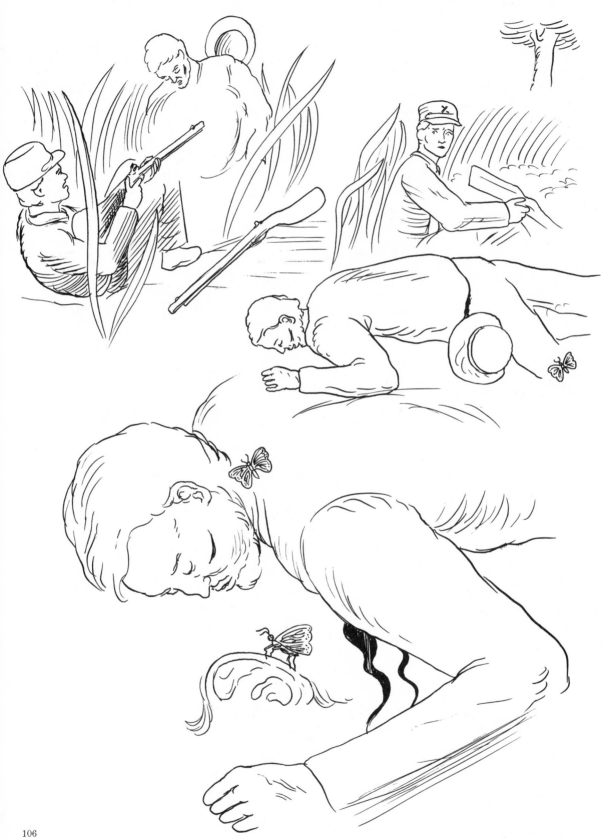

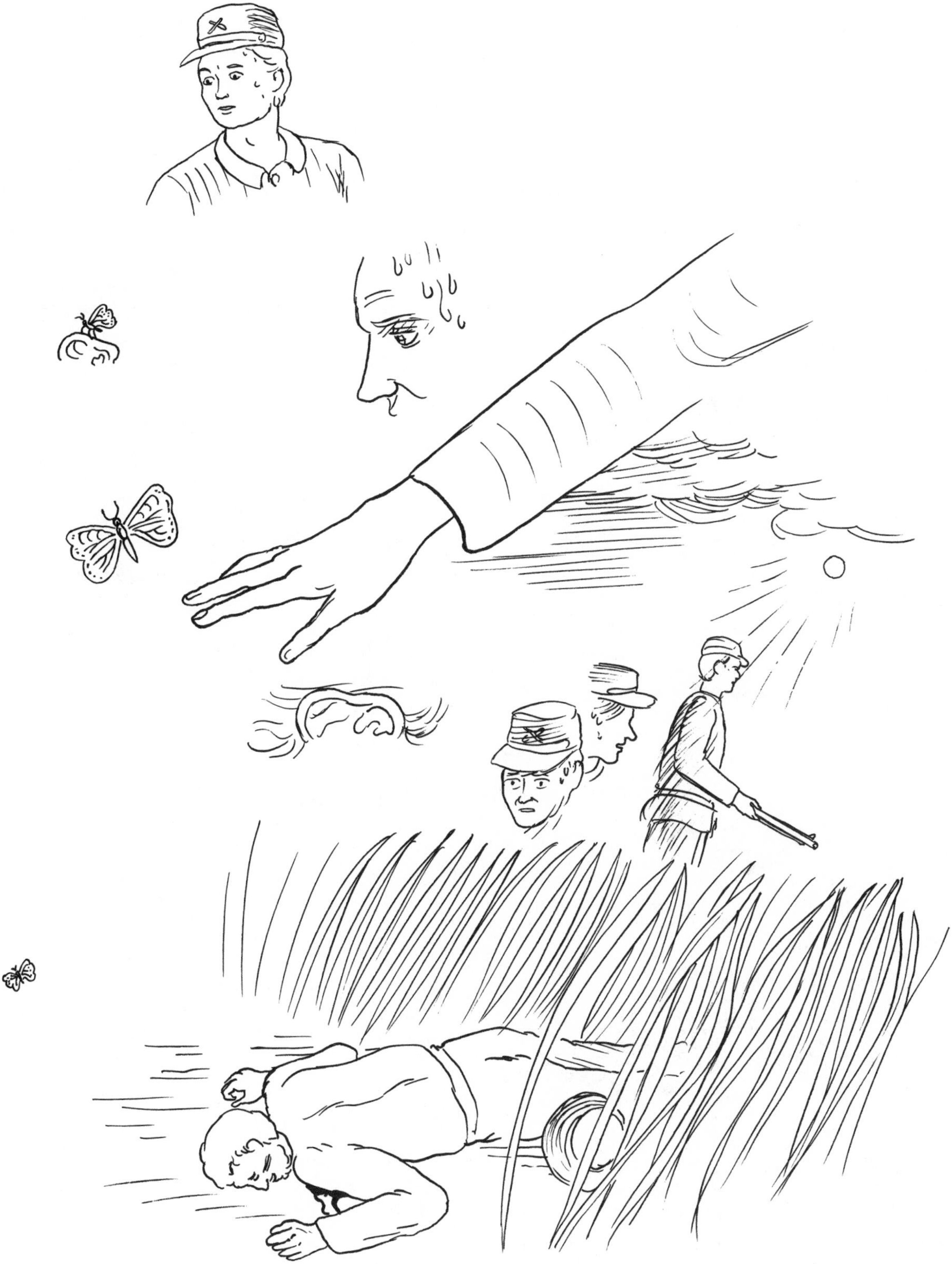

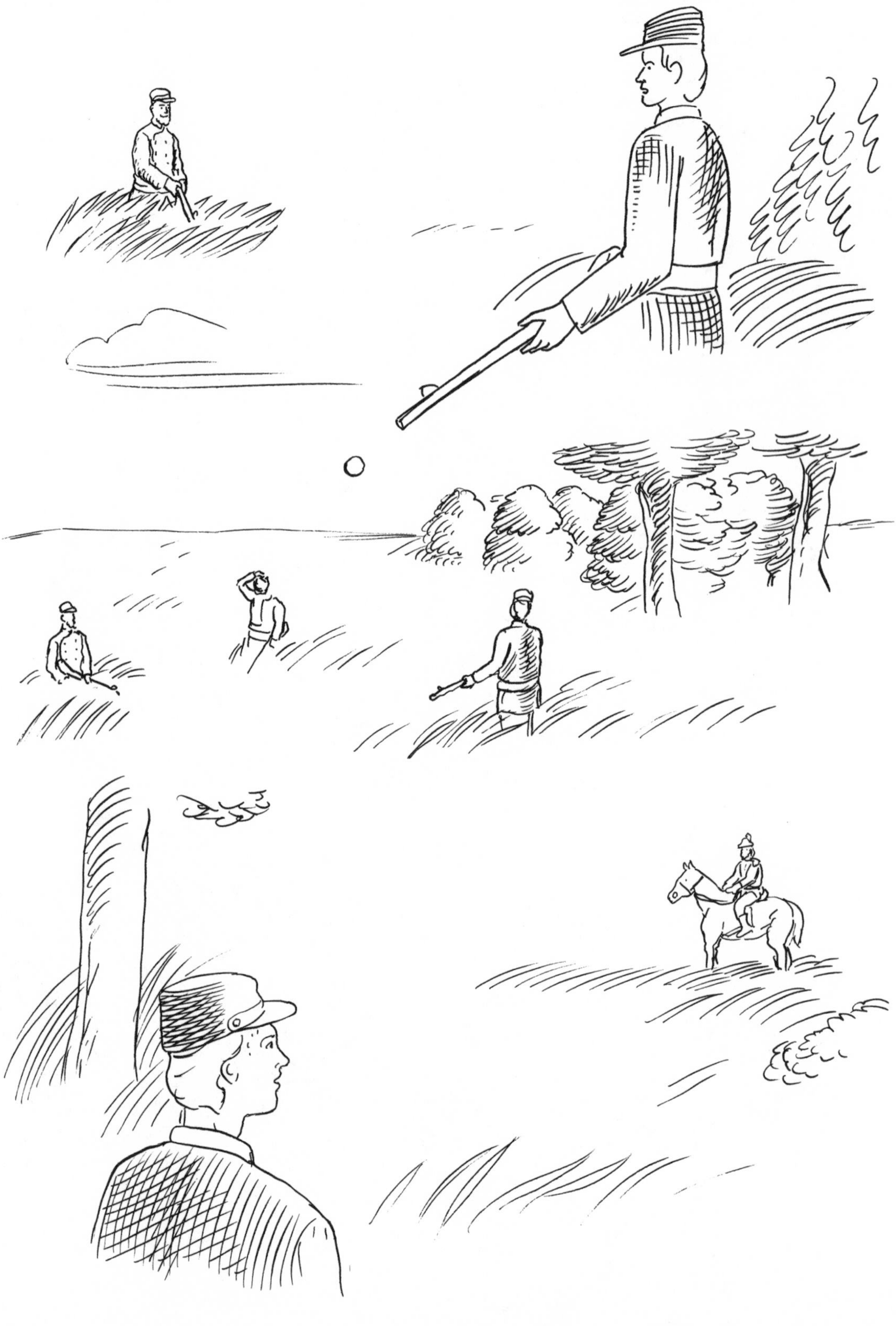

Victory
ha
Yay

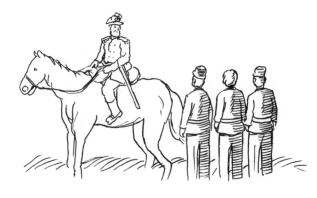

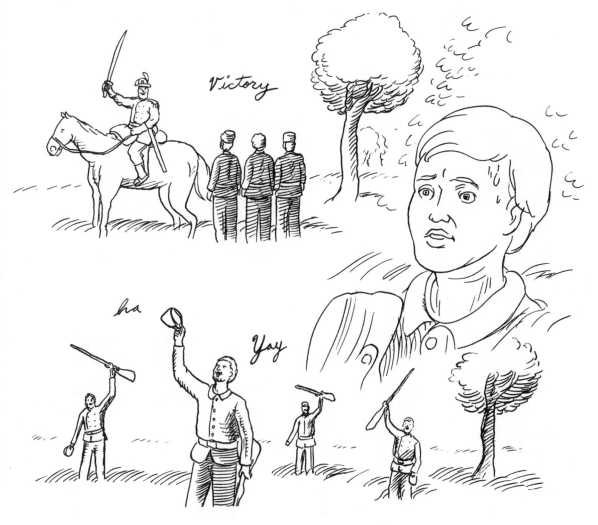

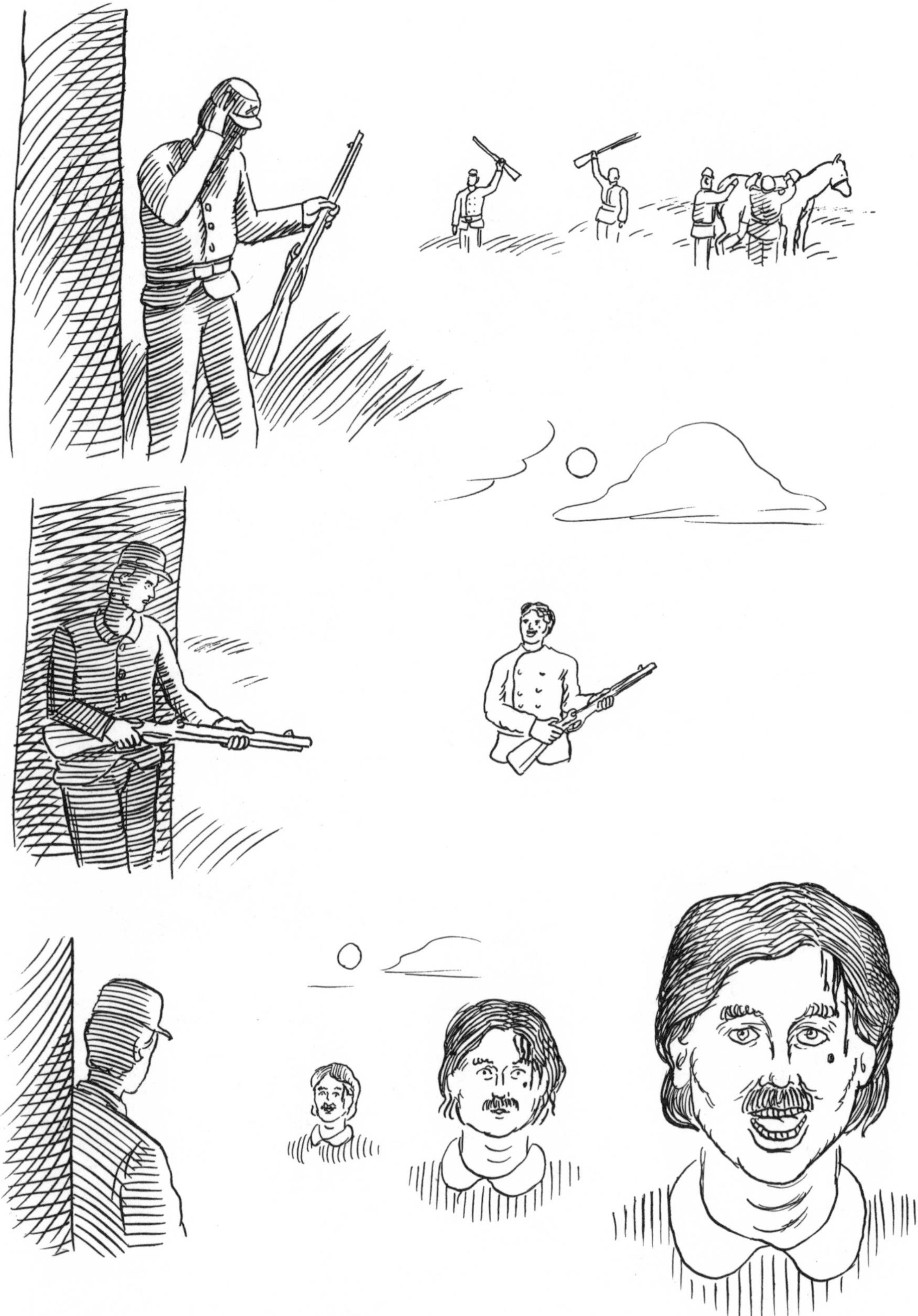

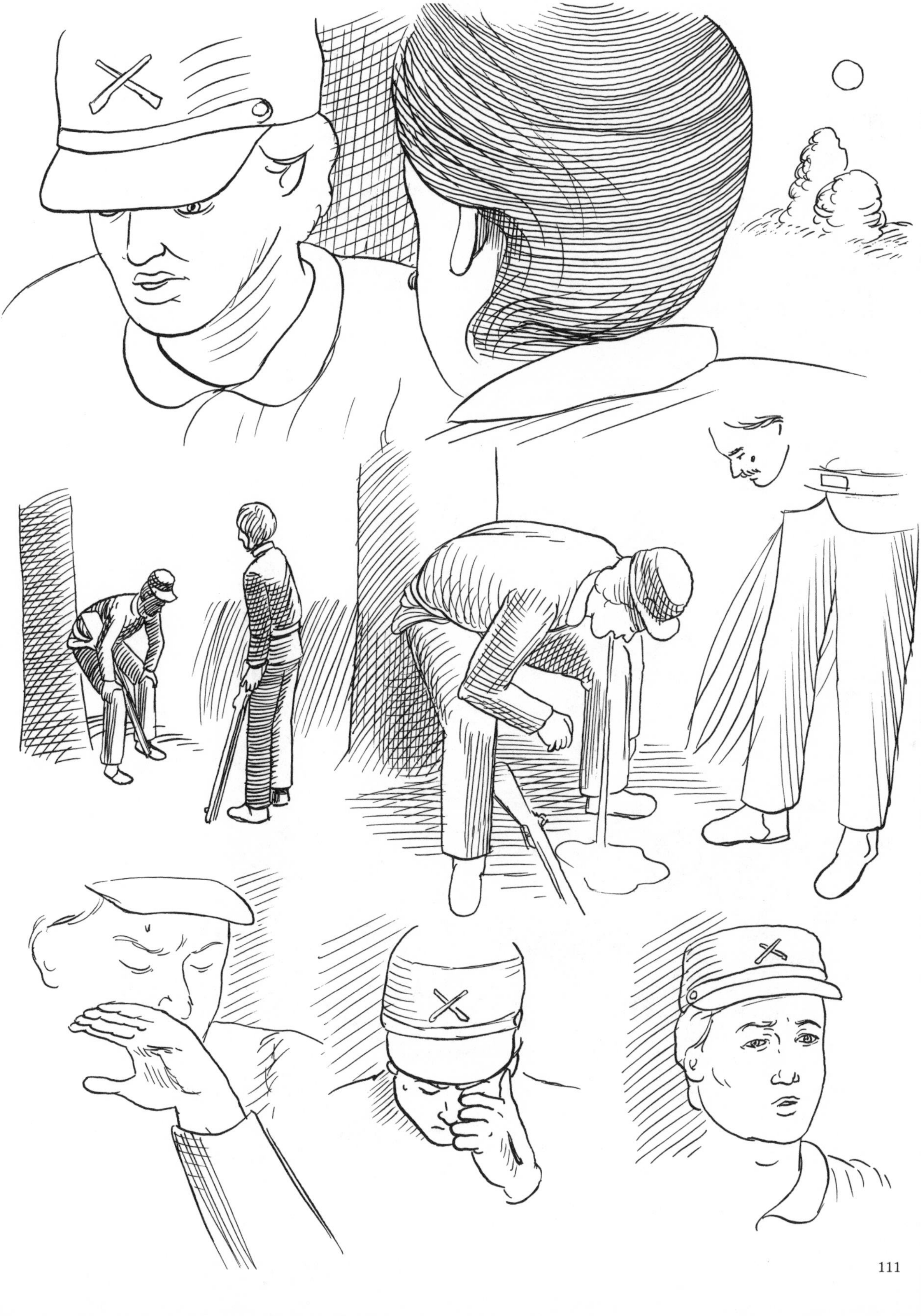

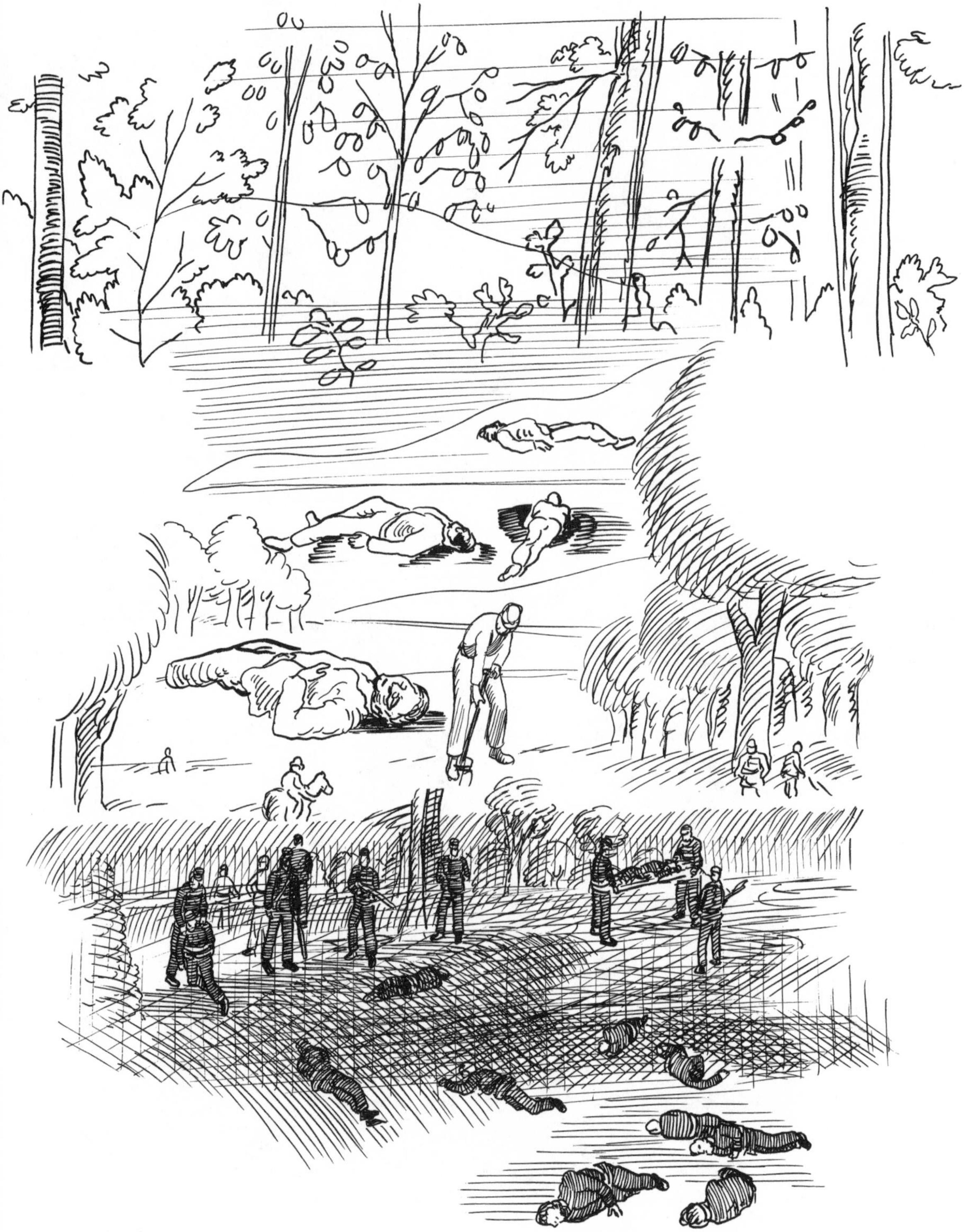

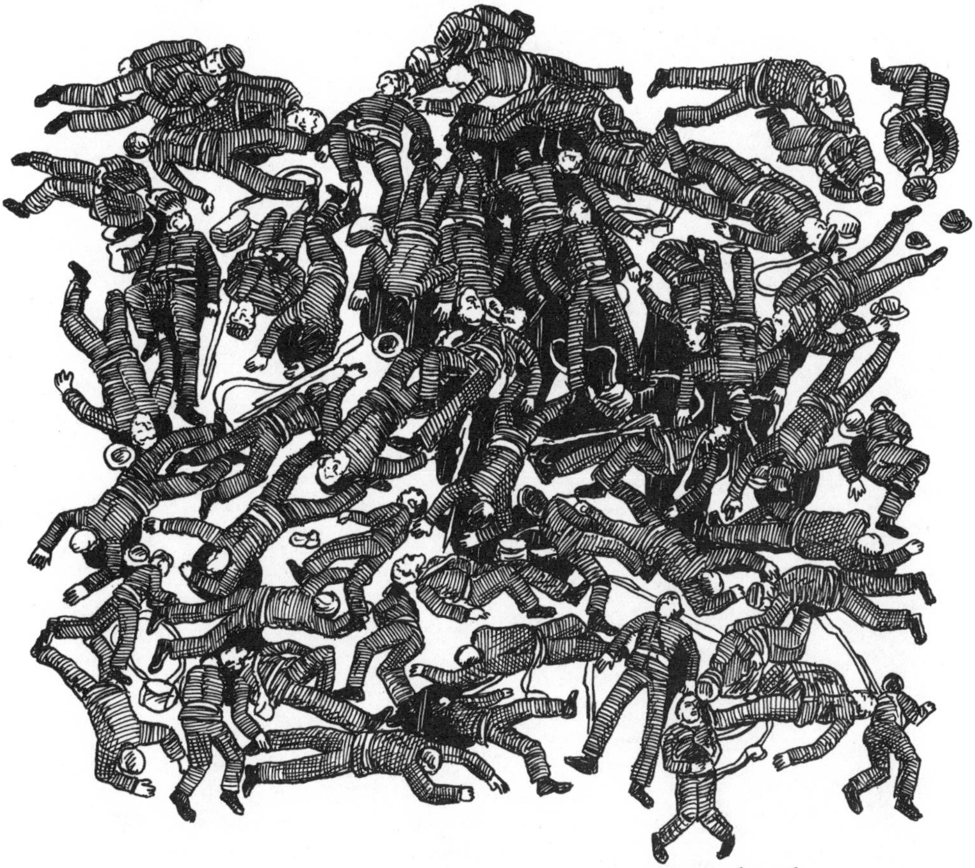

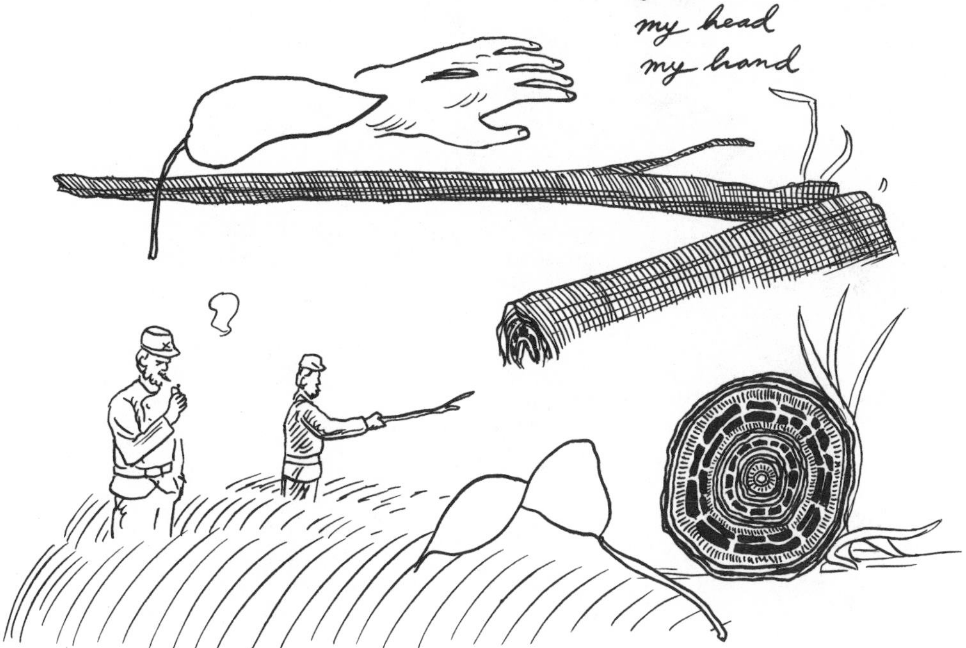
my head
my hand

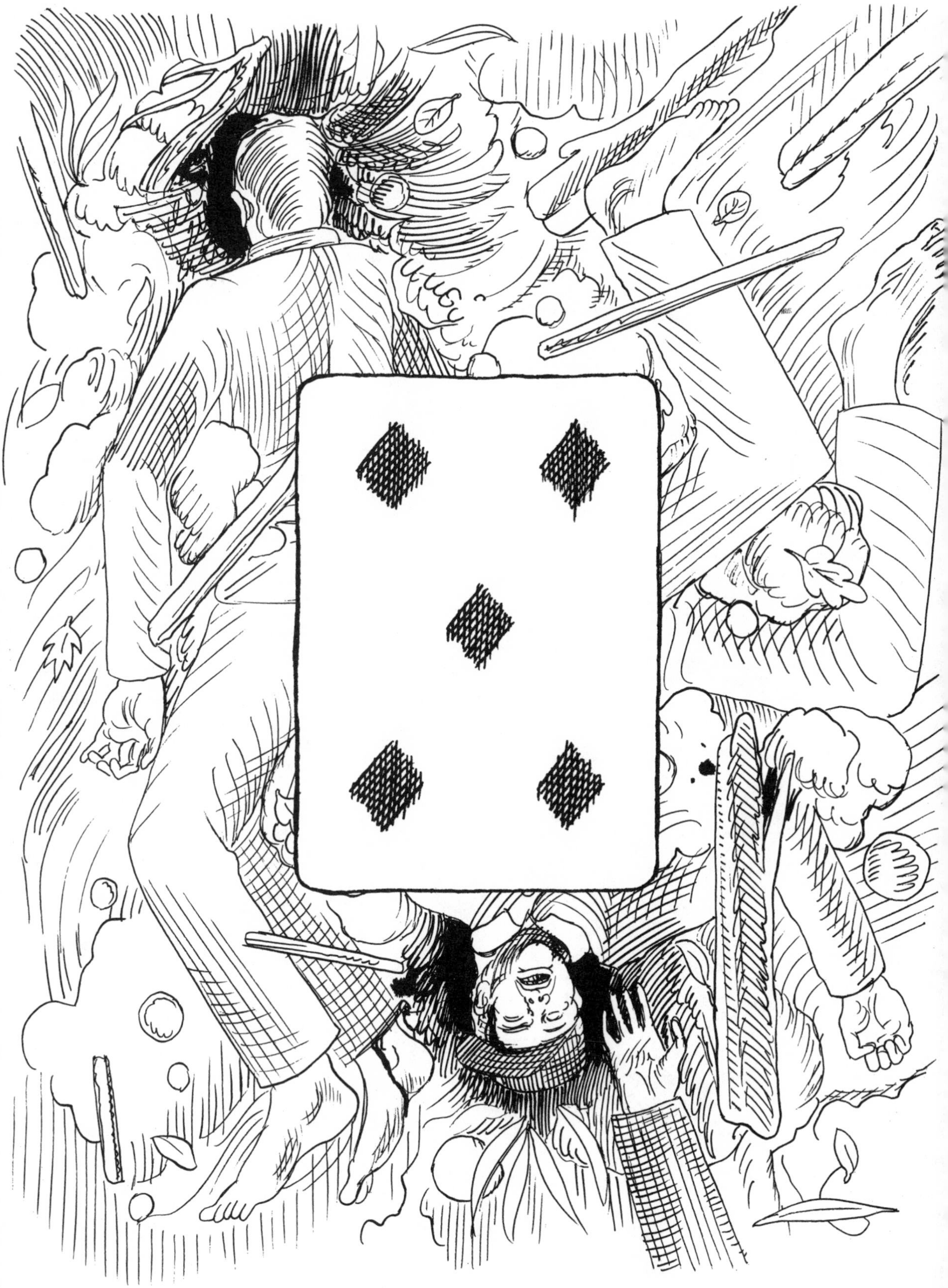

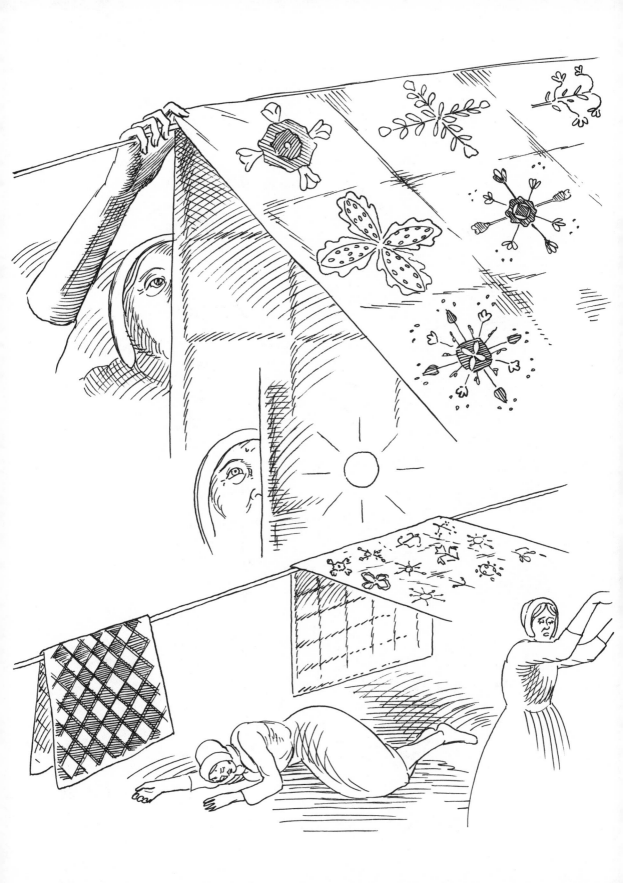

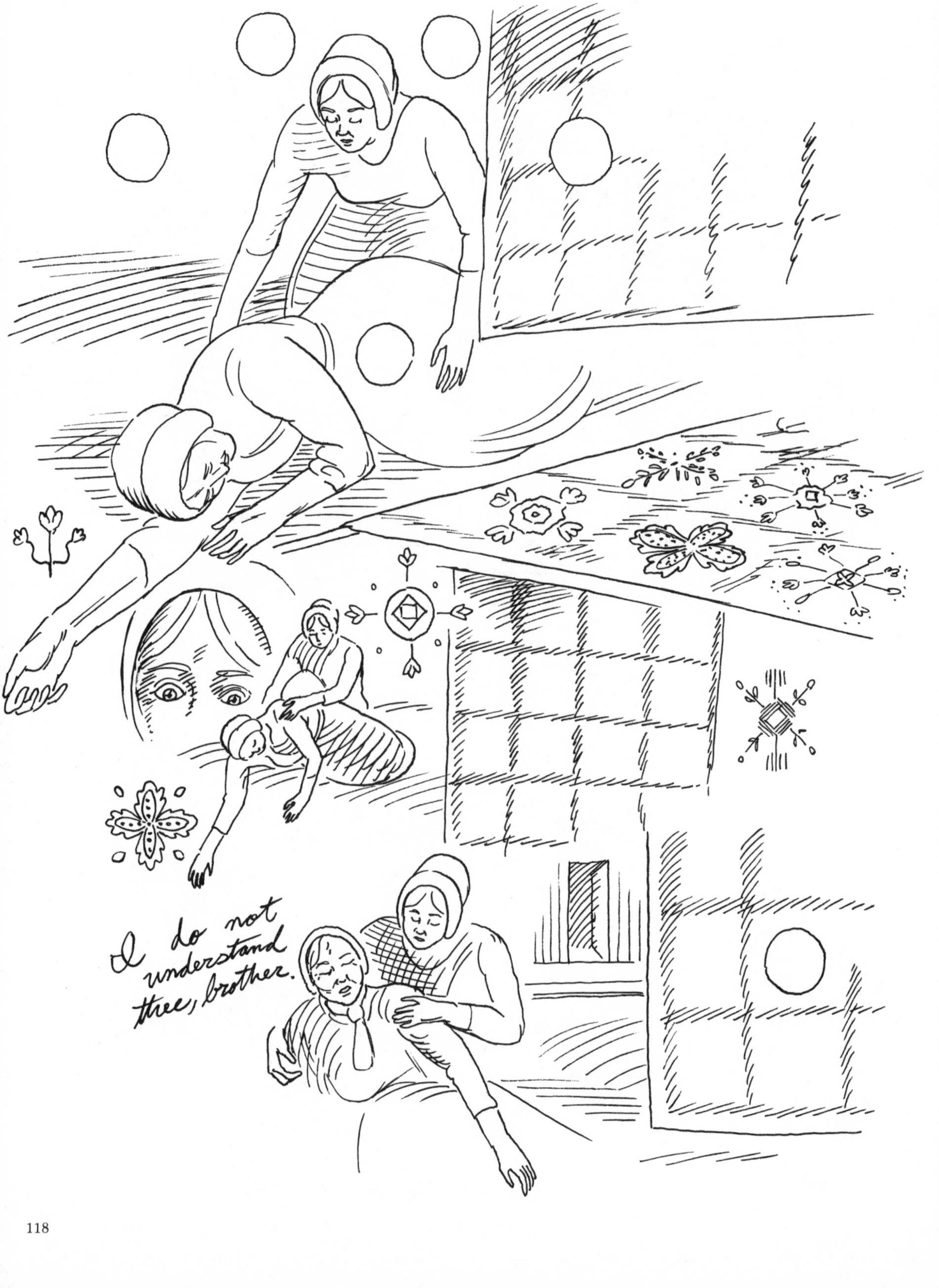
I do not understand thee, brother.

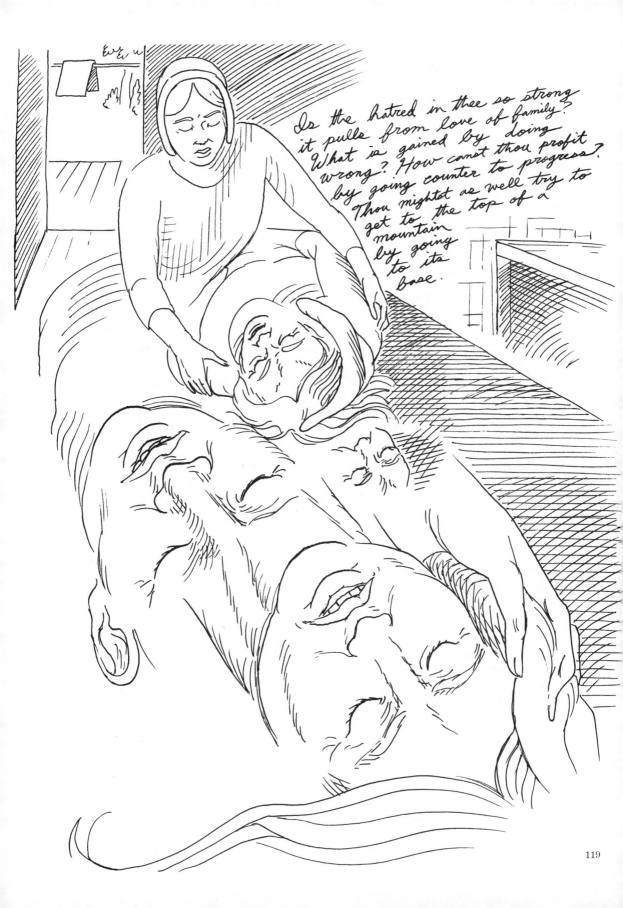

Is the hatred in thee so strong it pulls from love of family? What is gained by doing wrong? How canst thou profit by going counter to progress? Thou mightst as well try to get to the top of a mountain by going to its base.

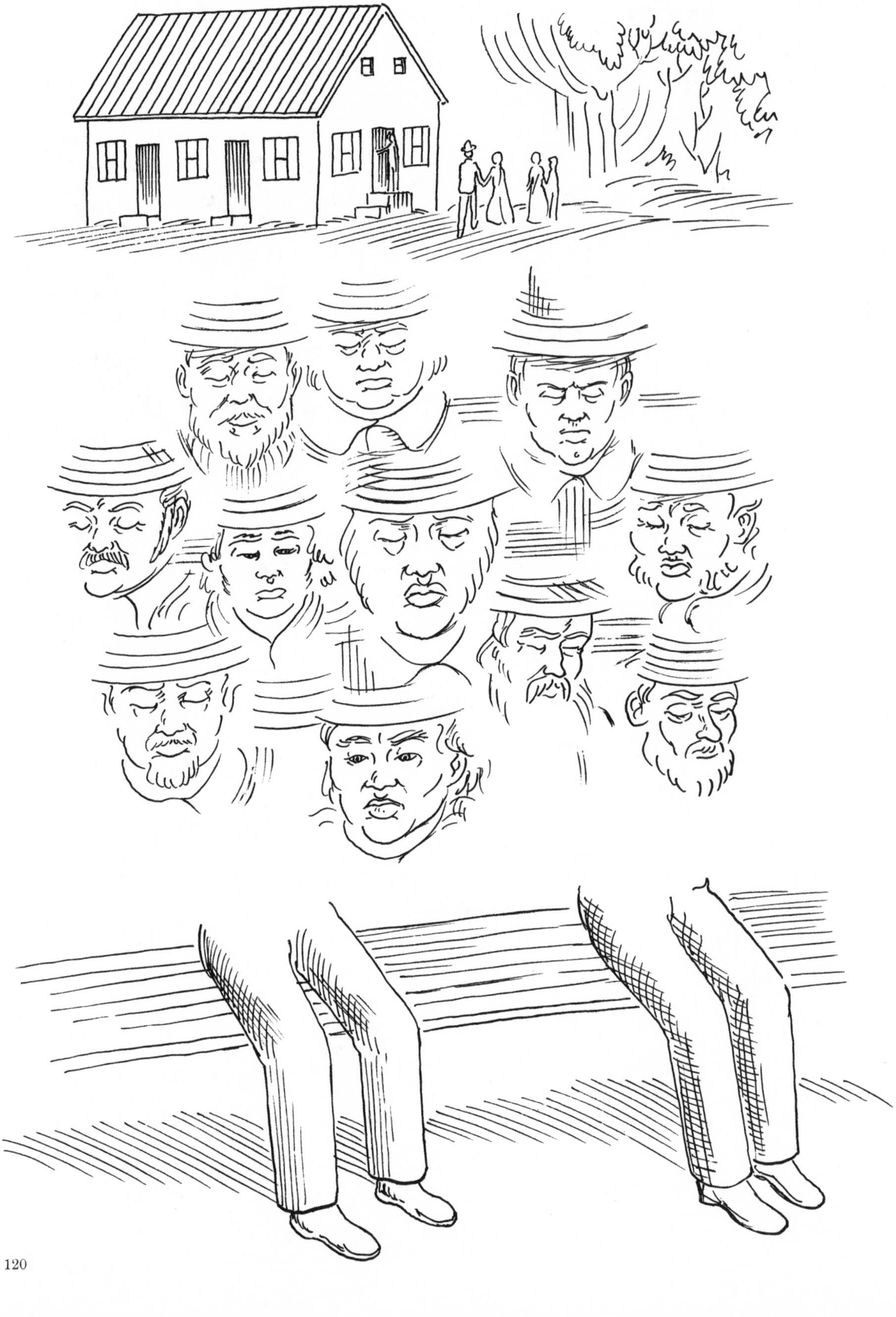

Mother is ill, but wished to speak to the increased military tax and believes we cannot conscientiously pay the specified tax. Whatever peculiar circumstances attach to the war which is now waging in our land, the testimony of the Religious Society has unambiguously been against all wars and fightings without distinction. It is our tradition to not pay portions of taxes devoted to military use, and if we slide in this regard, we may forever forfeit our well-known testimony against war.

Our mission is, at this time, to mitigate the sufferings of our countrymen, to visit and aid the sick and wounded, to relieve the necessities of the widow and the orphan and to practise economy for the sake of charity. Our Society is rich, and of those whom much is given, much will be required in this hour of proving and trial.

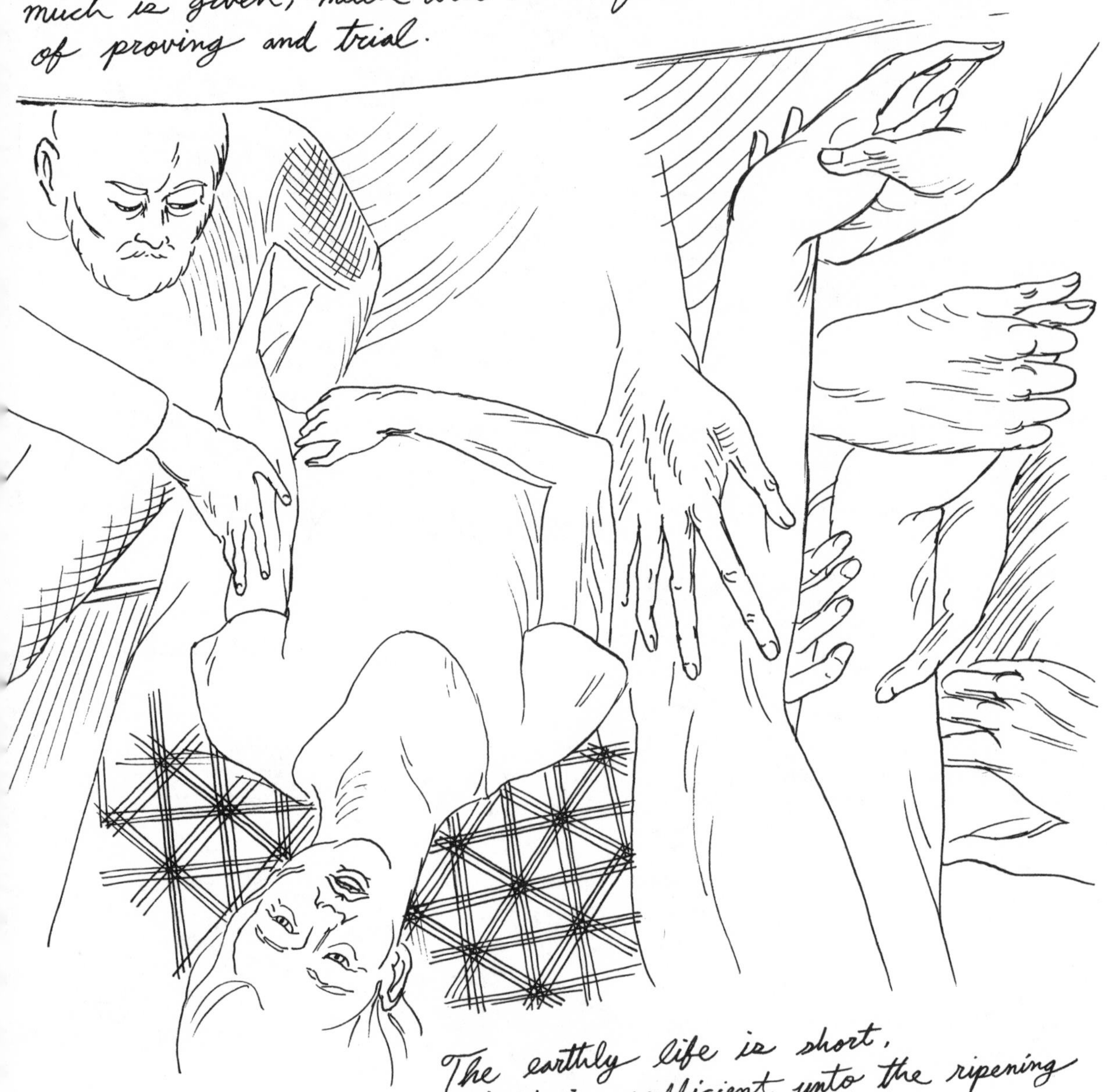

The earthly life is short, but it is sufficient unto the ripening of man or God would have made it longer.

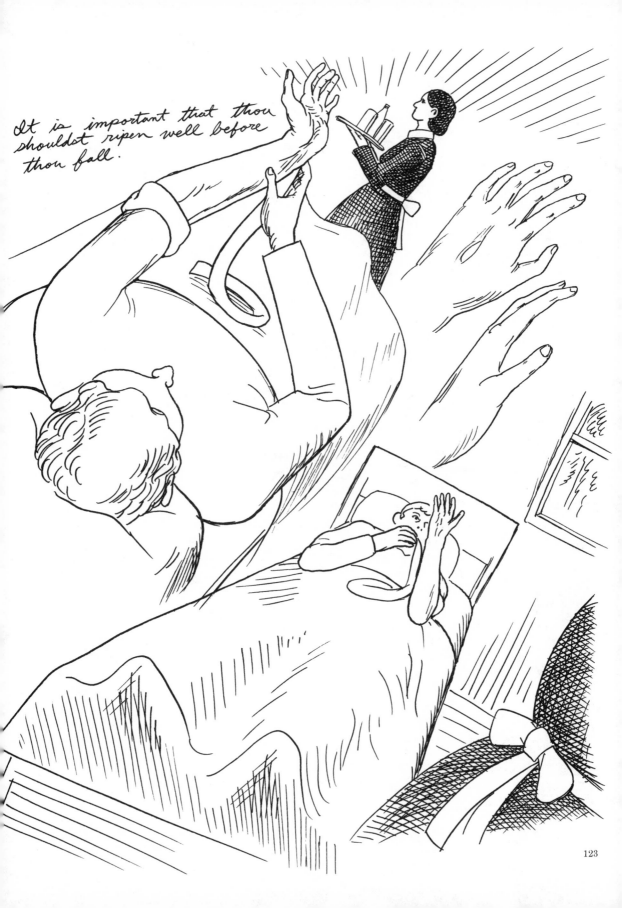

It is important that thou shouldst ripen well before thou fall.

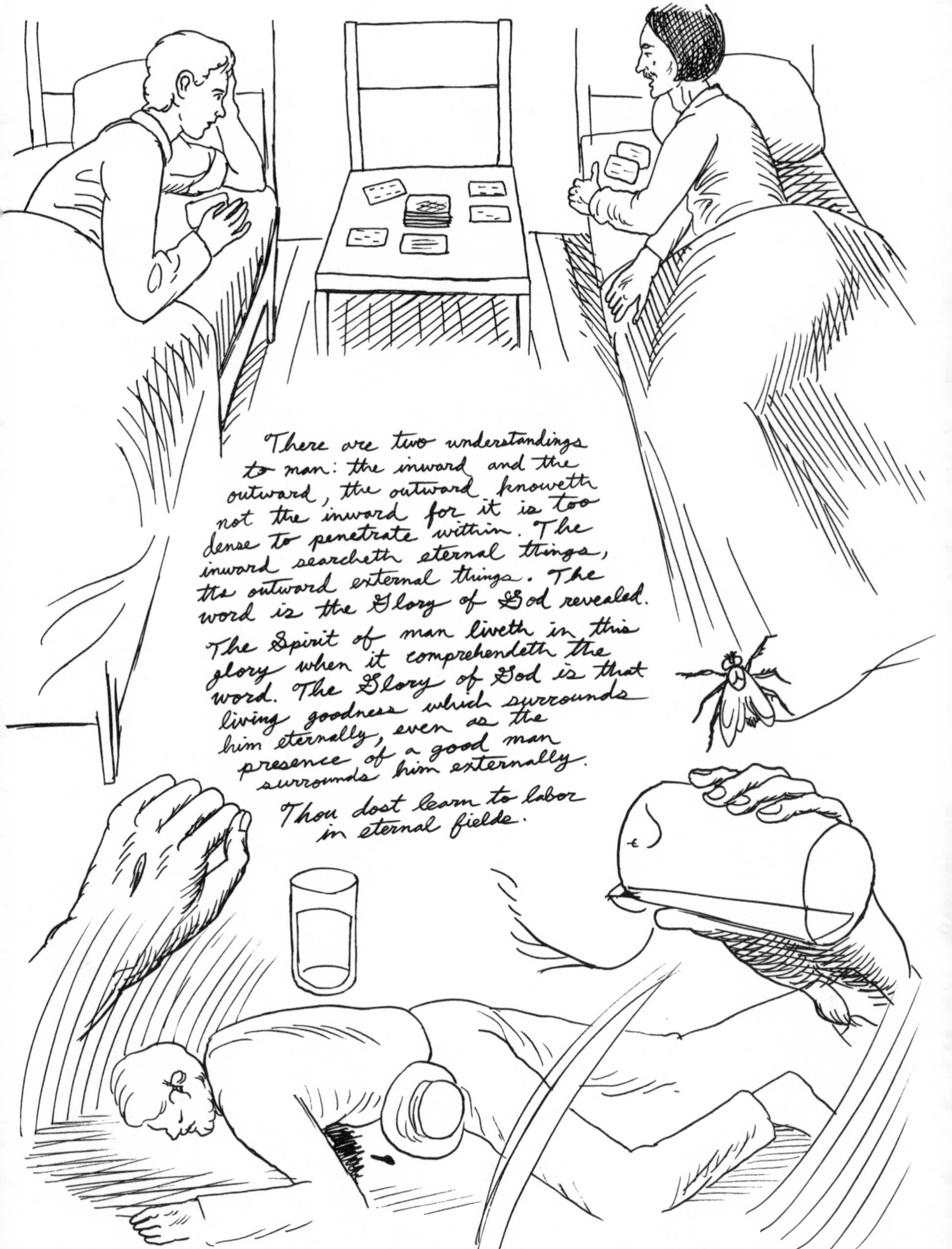
There are two understandings to man: the inward and the outward, the outward knoweth not the inward for it is too dense to penetrate within. The inward searcheth eternal things, the outward external things. The word is the Glory of God revealed.
The Spirit of man liveth in this glory when it comprehendeth the word. The Glory of God is that living goodness which surrounds him eternally, even as the presence of a good man surrounds him externally.
Thou dost learn to labor in eternal fields.

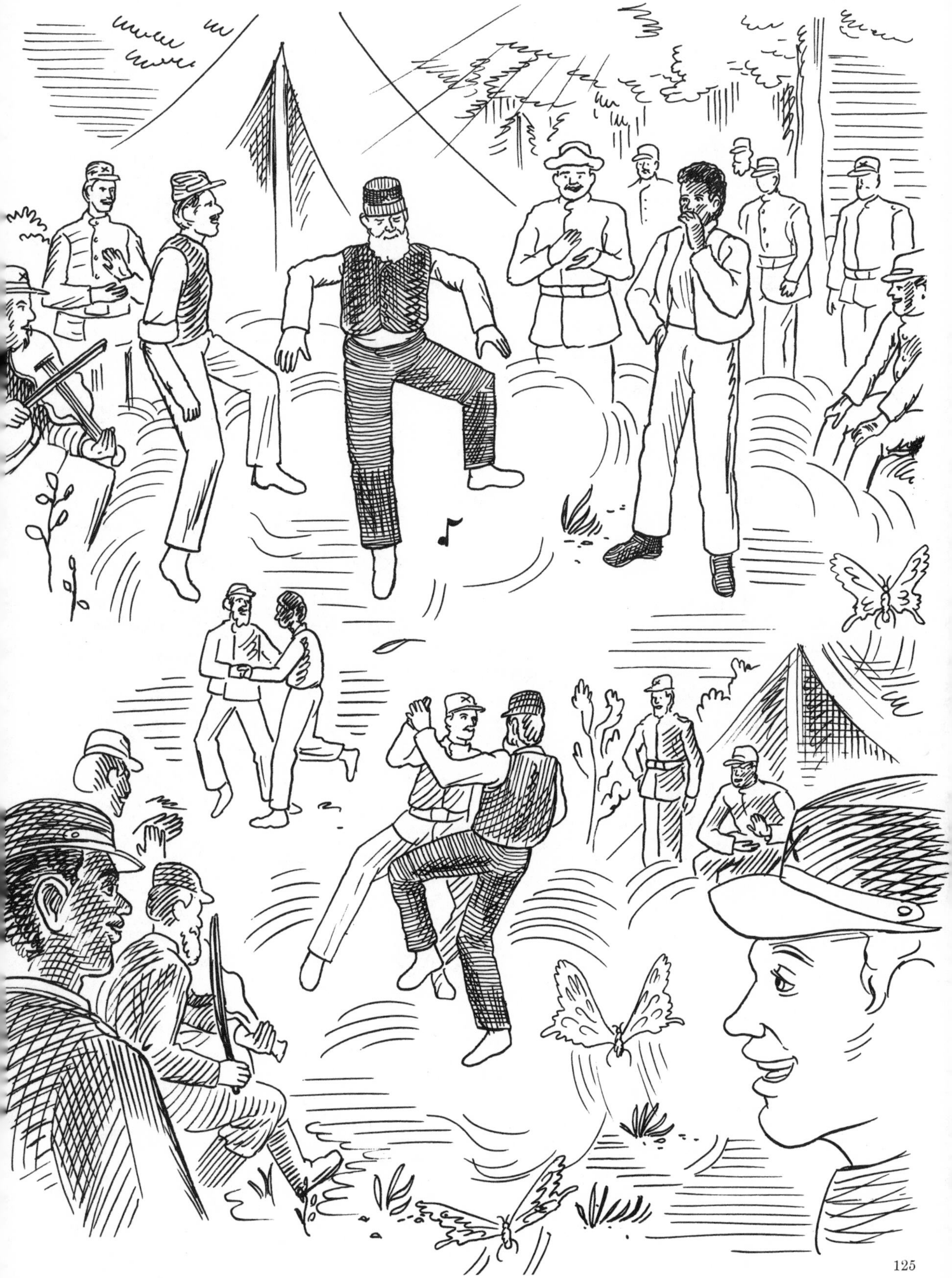

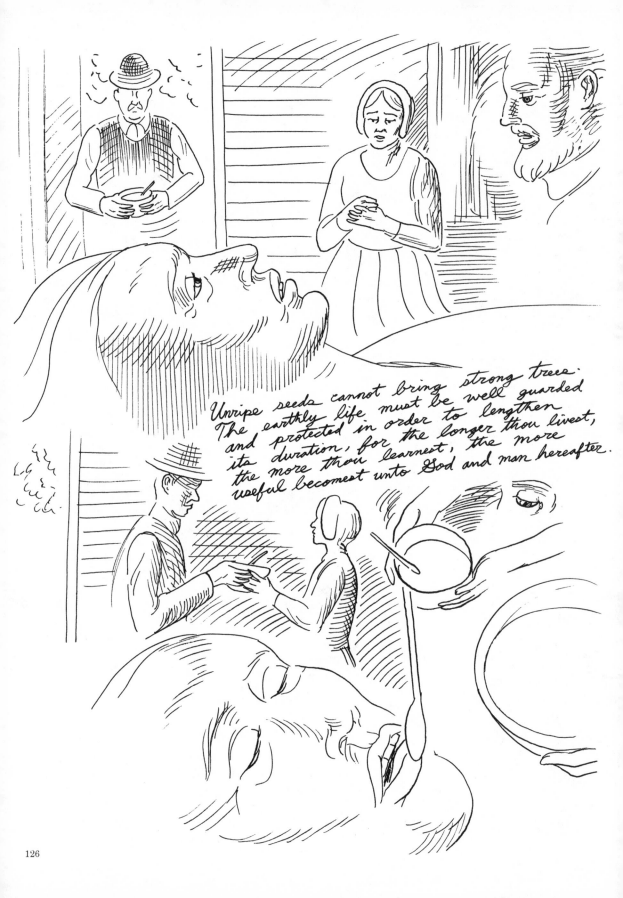

Unripe seeds cannot bring strong trees.
The earthly life must be well guarded
and protected in order to lengthen
its duration, for the longer thou livest,
the more thou learnest, the more
useful becomest unto God and man hereafter.

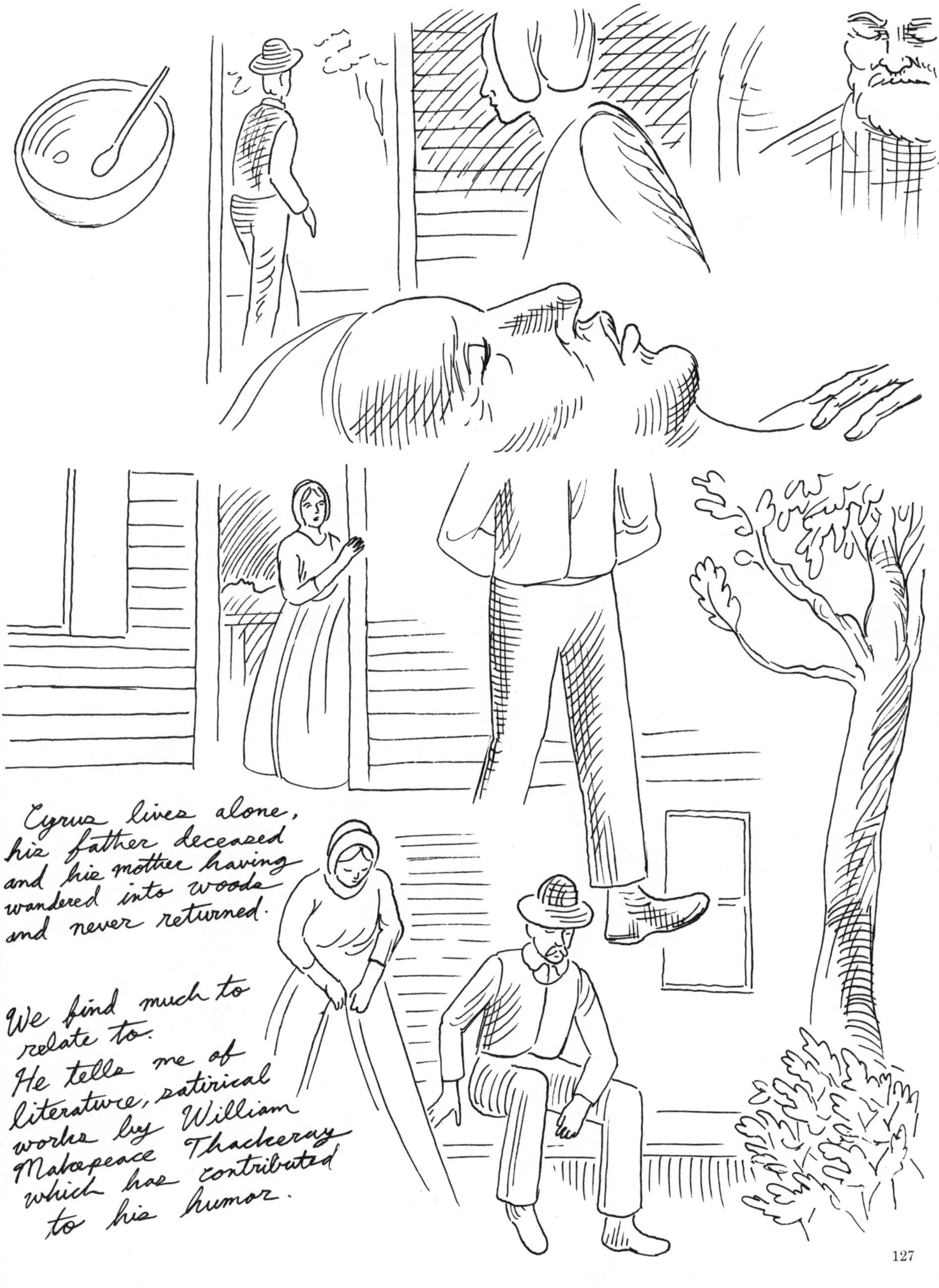
Cyrus lives alone, his father deceased and his mother having wandered into woods and never returned.
We find much to relate to.
He tells me of literature, satirical works by William Makepeace Thackeray which has contributed to his humor.

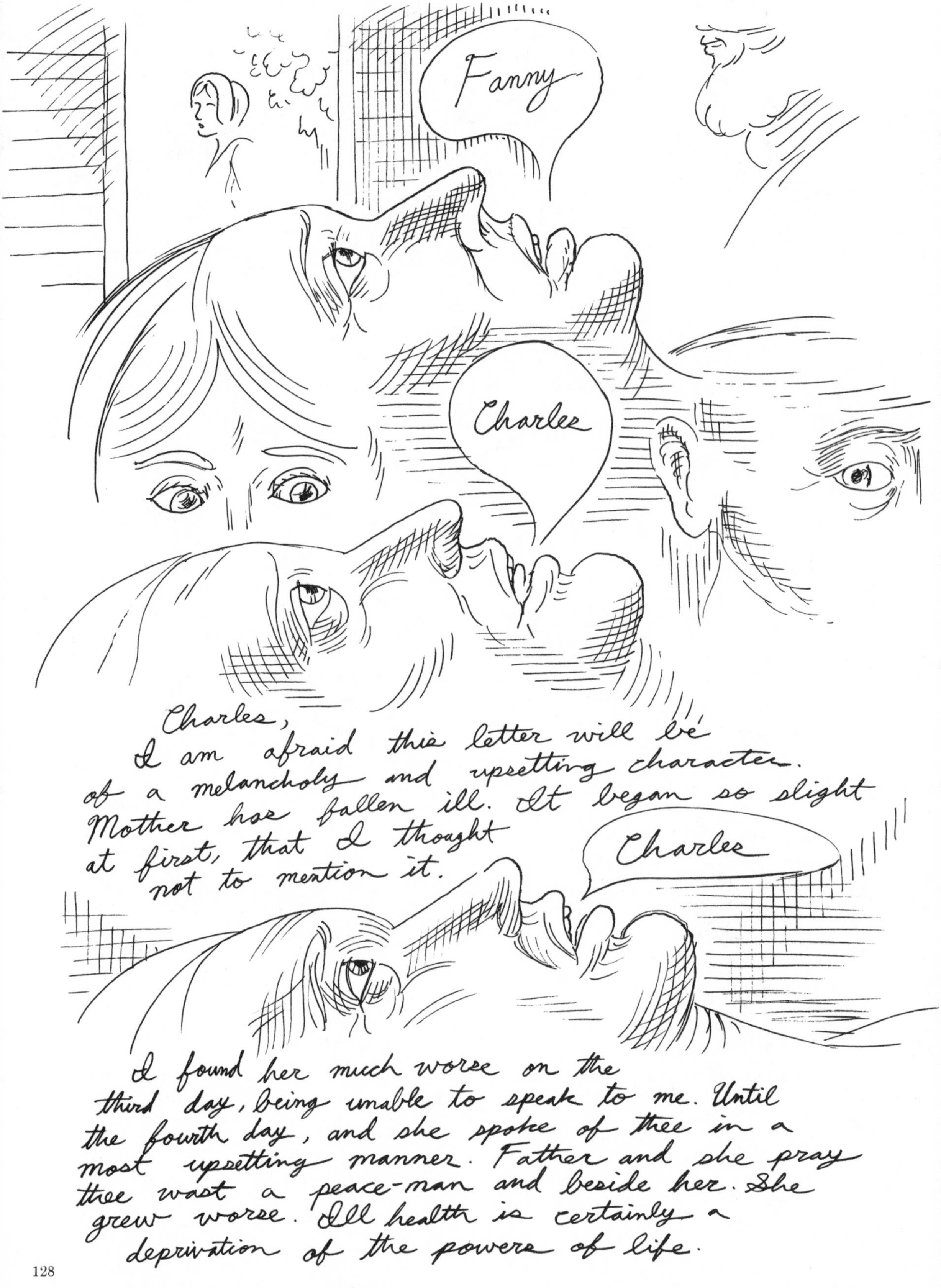
Fanny
Charles
Charles, I am afraid this letter will be of a melancholy and upsetting character. Mother has fallen ill. It began so slight at first, that I thought not to mention it.
Charles
I found her much worse on the third day, being unable to speak to me. Until the fourth day, and she spoke of thee in a most upsetting manner. Father and she pray thee wast a peace-man and beside her. She grew worse. Ill health is certainly a deprivation of the powers of life.

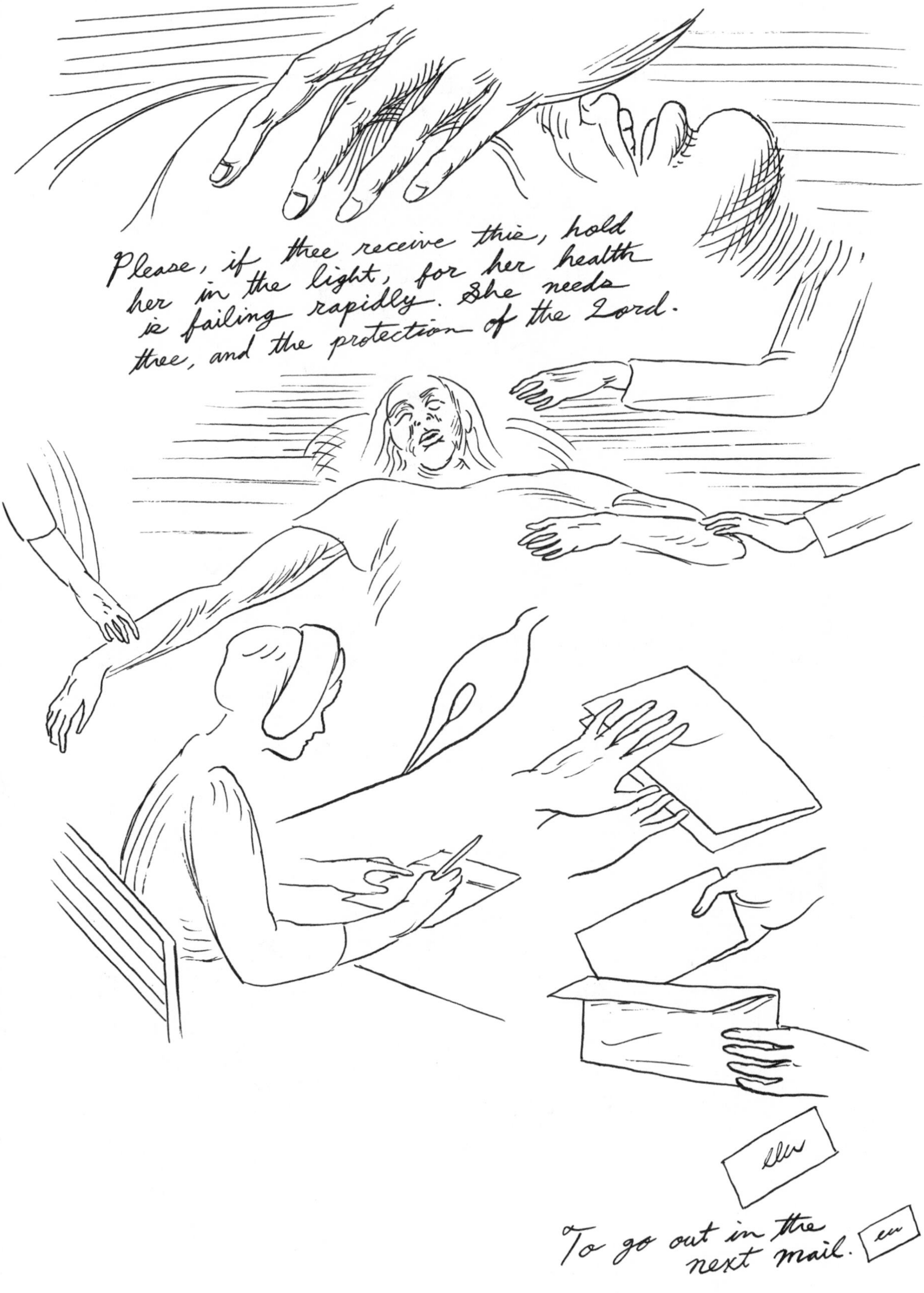
Please, if thee receive this, hold her in the light, for her health is failing rapidly. She needs thee, and the protection of the Lord.
To go out in the next mail.

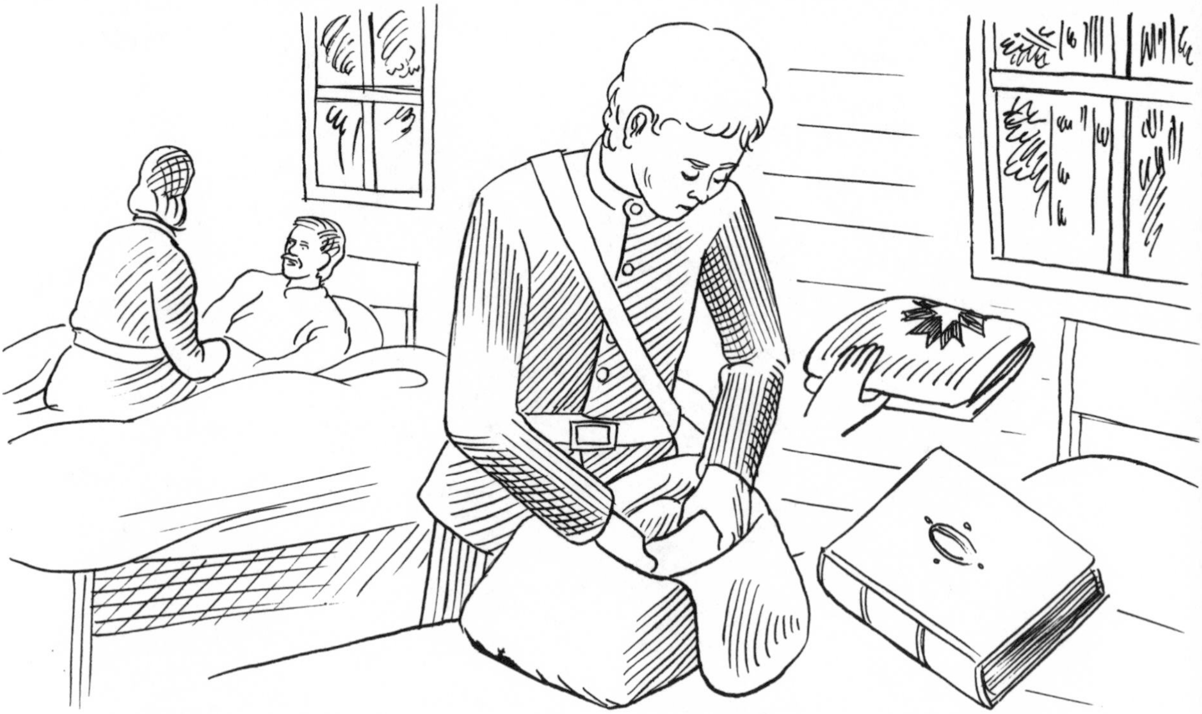

Sister,
Edward and I are leaving to join Tecumseh
Sherman in the Secession states, where he is in the
midst of a great campaign. Writing will become
less frequent, as we will be in the hell of the South,
but my thoughts will be with you always.

—Charles.

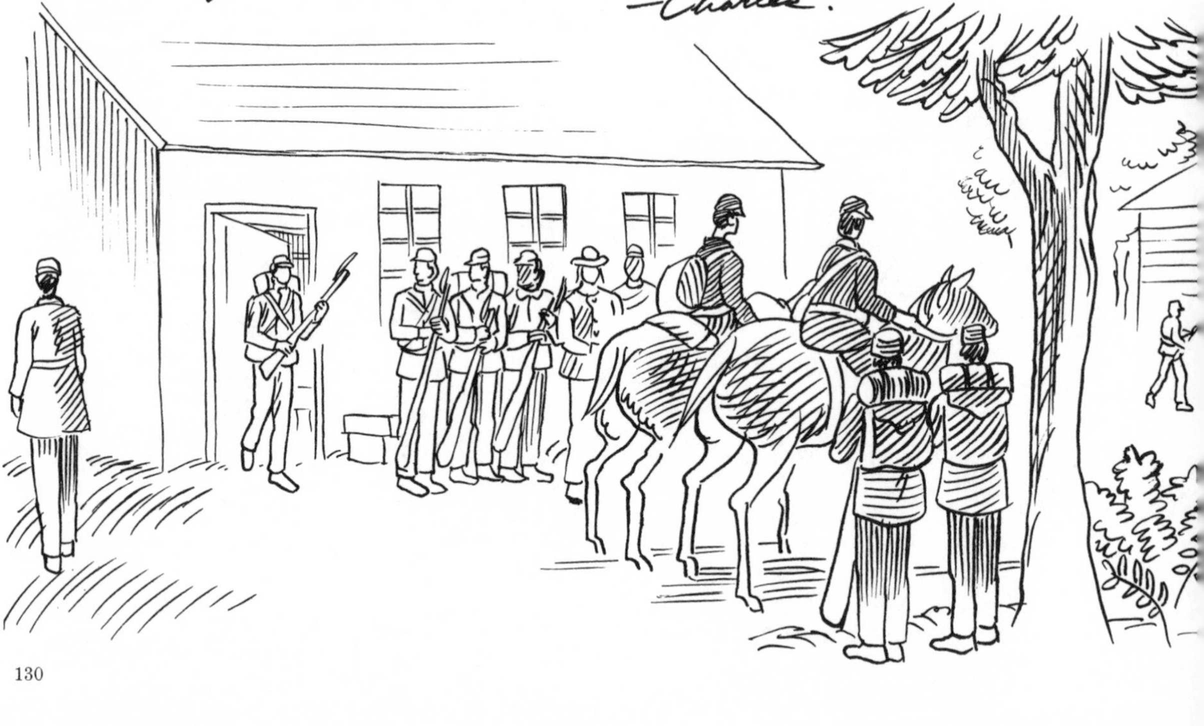

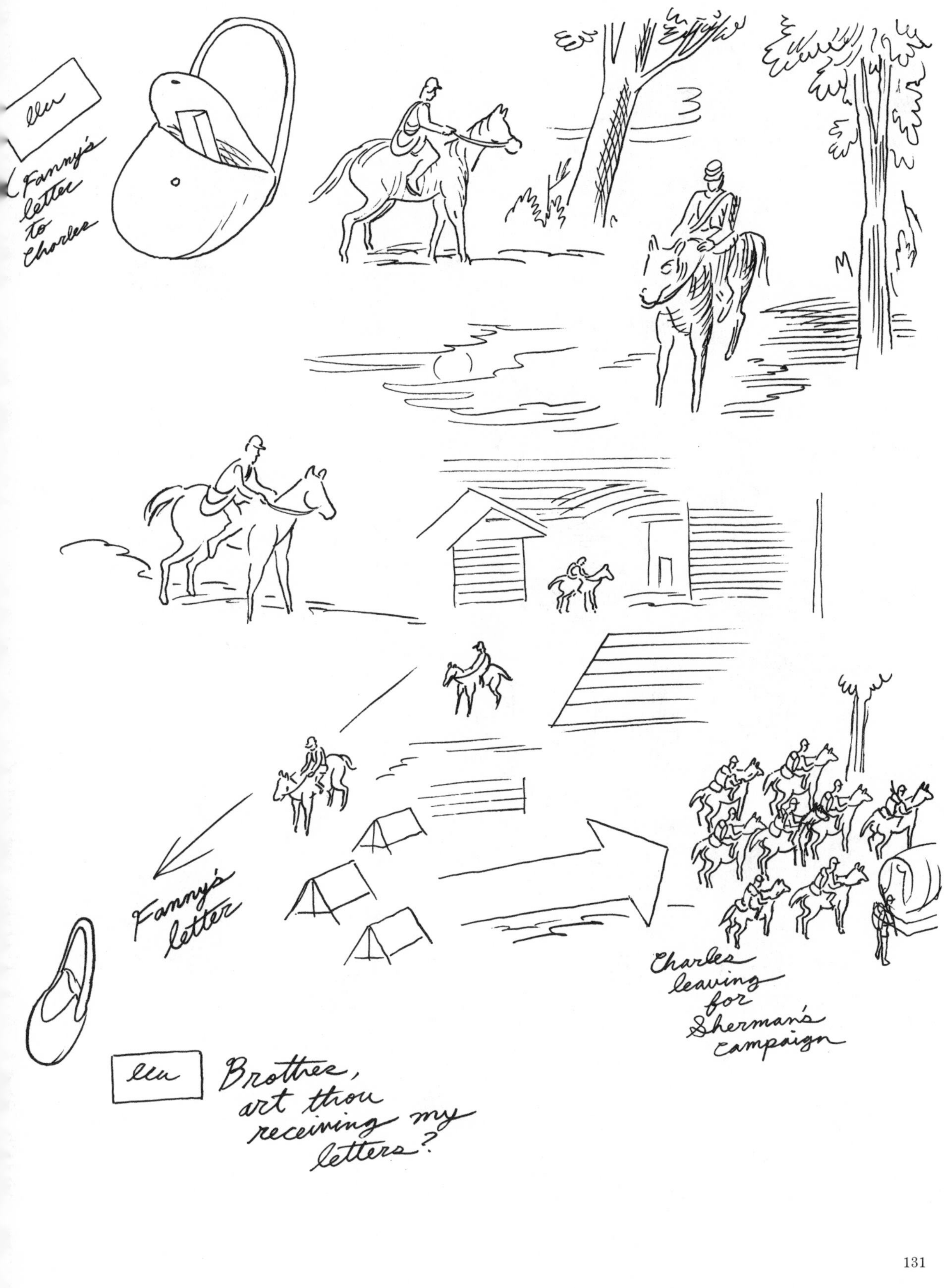
Fanny's letter to Charles
Fanny's letter
Charles leaving for Sherman's campaign
Brother, art thou receiving my letters?

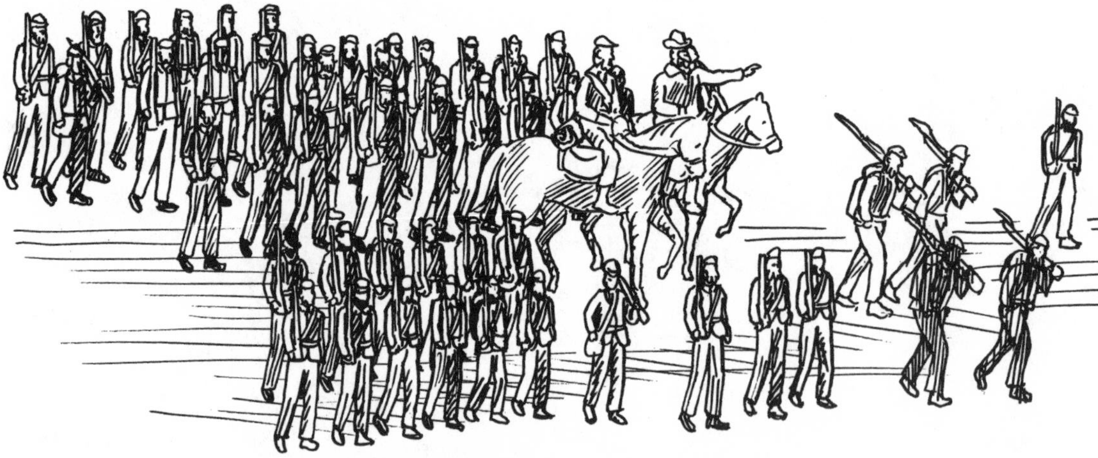

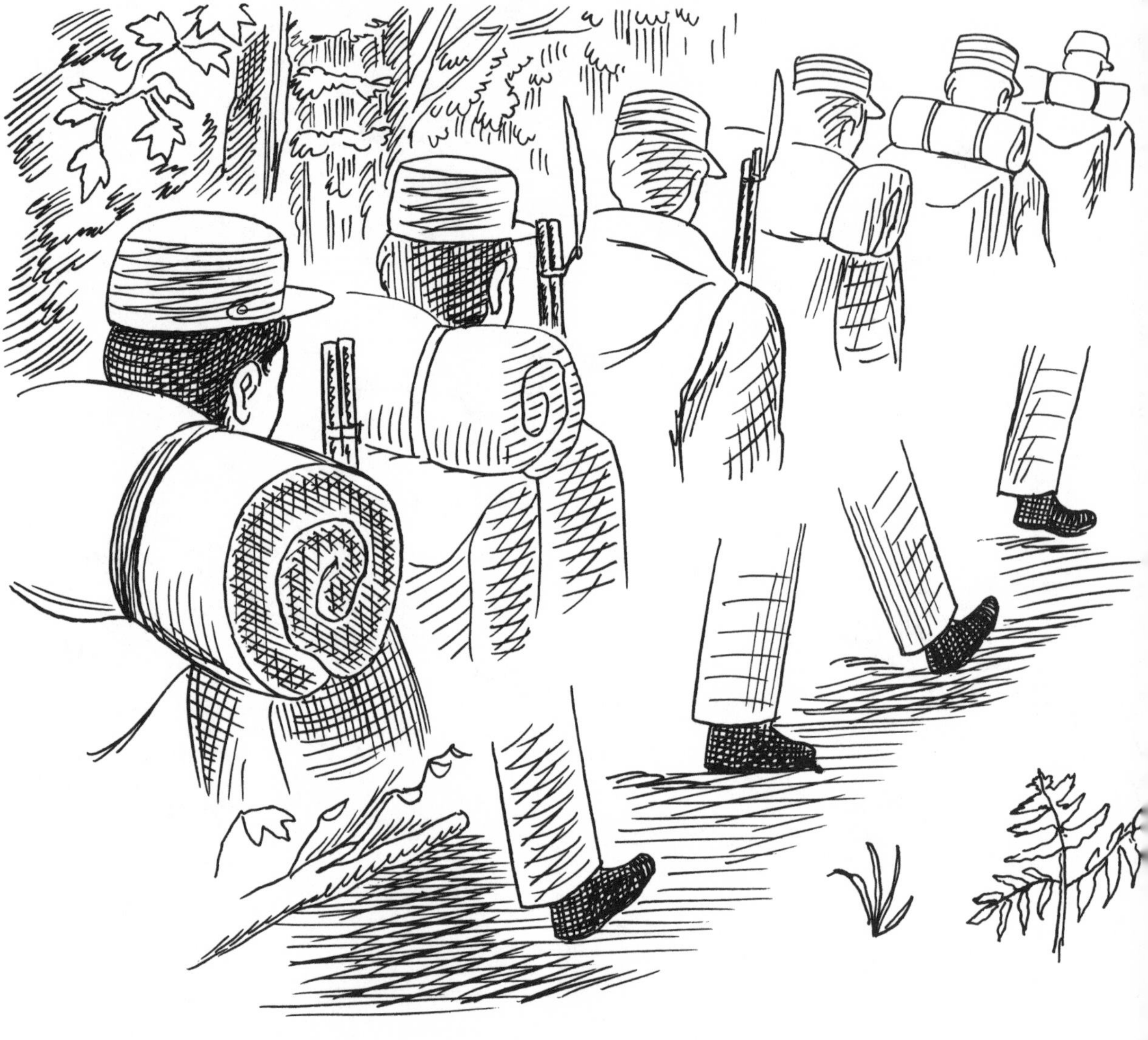

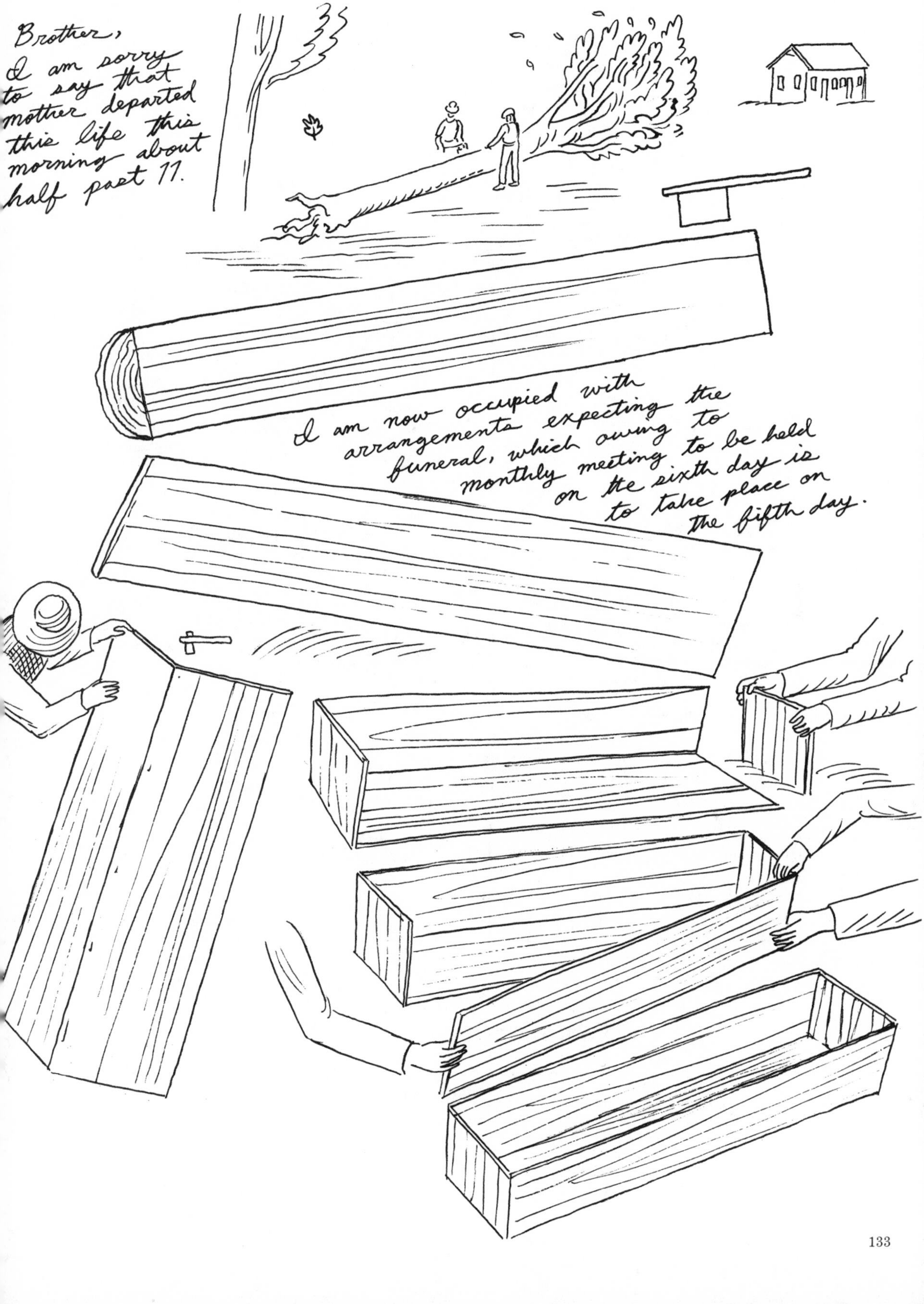
Brother,
I am sorry to say that mother departed this life this morning about half past 11.
I am now occupied with arrangements expecting the funeral, which owing to monthly meeting to be held on the sixth day is to take place on the fifth day.

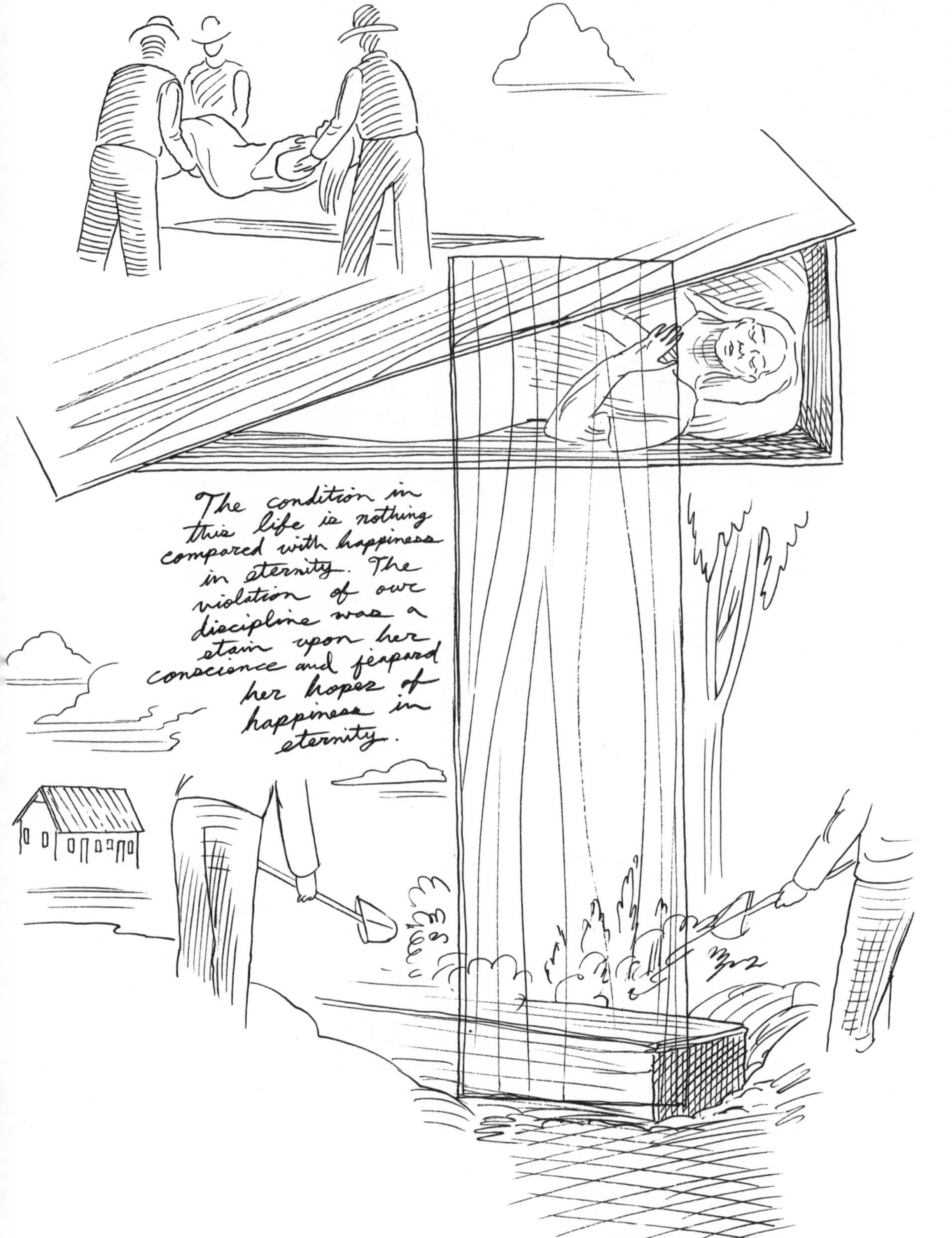
The condition in this life is nothing compared with happiness in eternity. The violation of our discipline was a stain upon her conscience and jeopard her hopes of happiness in eternity.

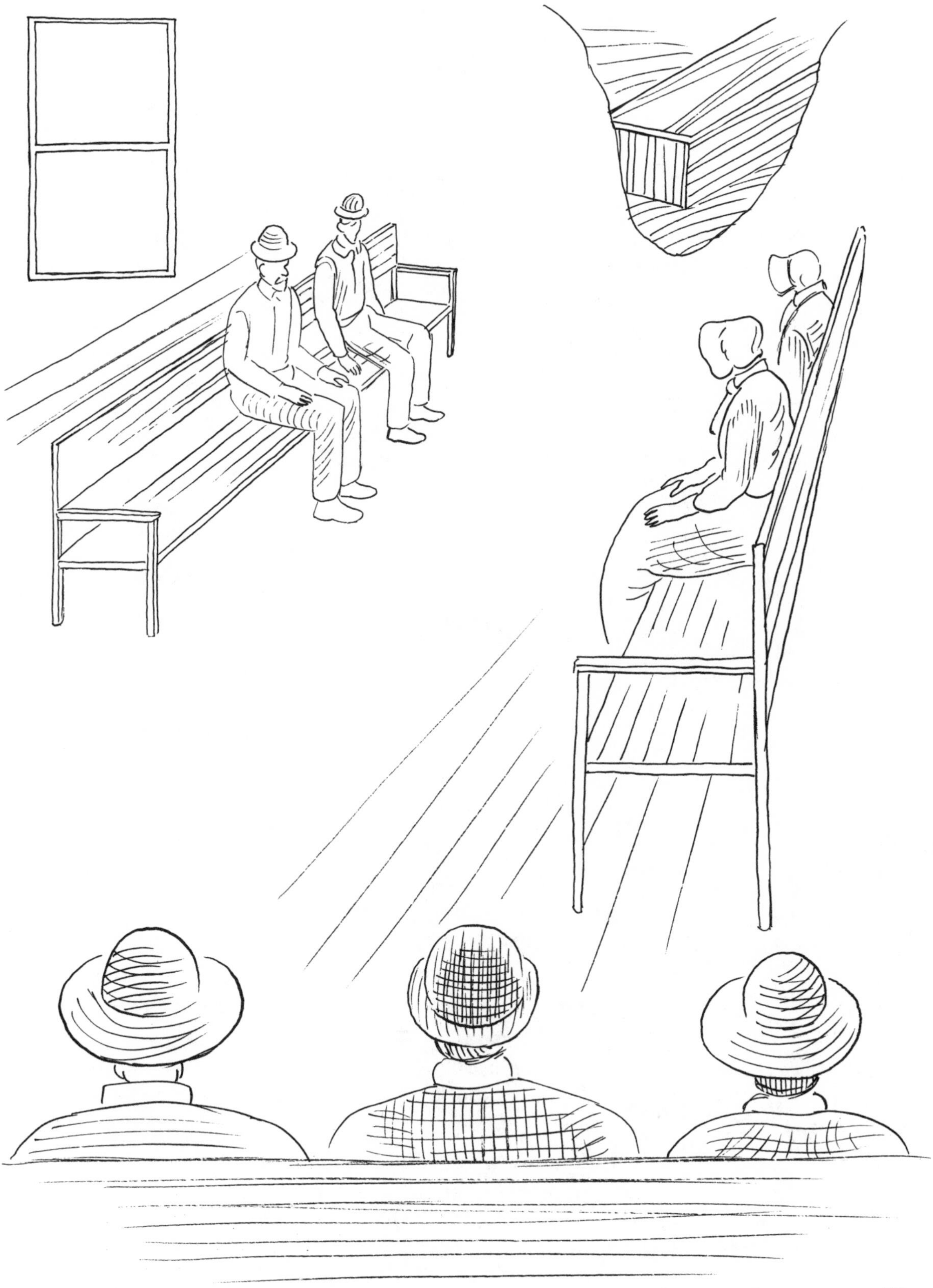

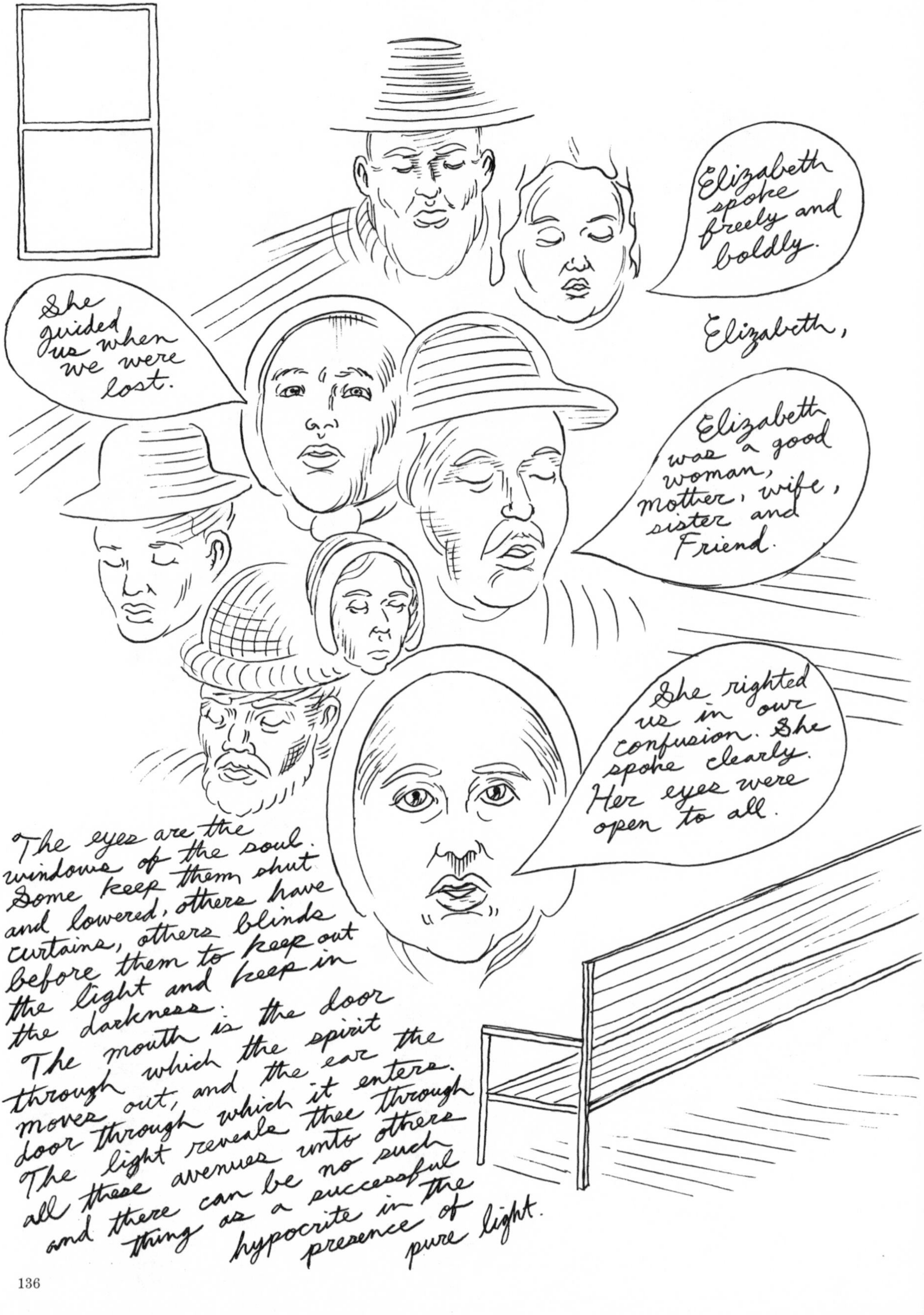

Elizabeth spoke freely and boldly.
She guided us when we were lost.
Elizabeth,
Elizabeth was a good woman, mother, wife, sister and Friend.
She righted us in our confusion. She spoke clearly. Her eyes were open to all.
The eyes are the windows of the soul. Some keep them shut and lowered, others have curtains, others blinds before them to keep out the light and keep in the darkness. The mouth is the door through which the spirit moves out, and the ear the door through which it enters. The light reveals thee through all these avenues unto others and there can be no such thing as a successful hypocrite in the presence of pure light.

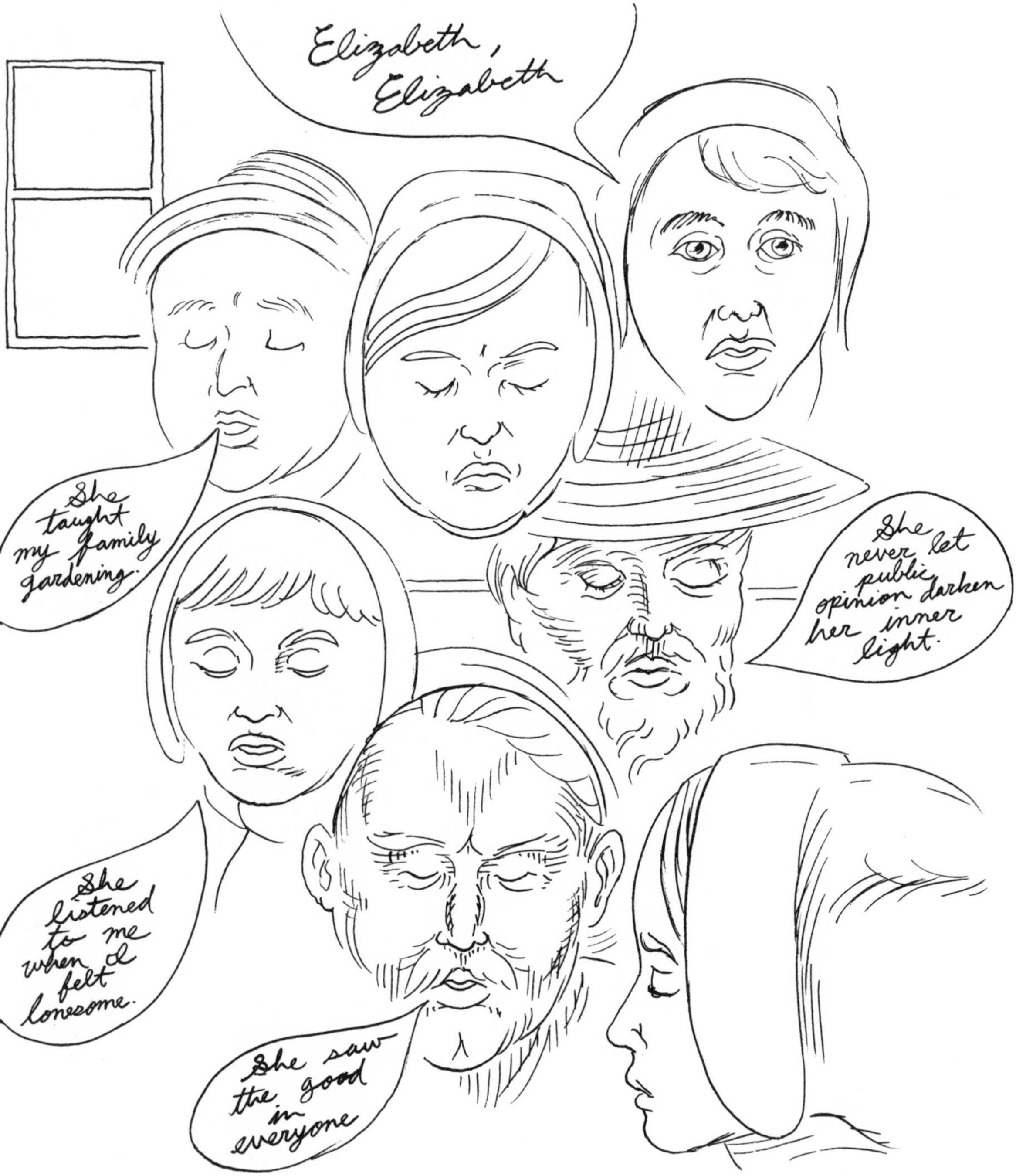
Elizabeth, Elizabeth
She taught my family gardening.
She never let public opinion darken her inner light.
She listened to me when I felt lonesome.
She saw the good in everyone

God is always extending toward us a helping hand. If we reach out for it, it helps us, and this reaching out is prayer.

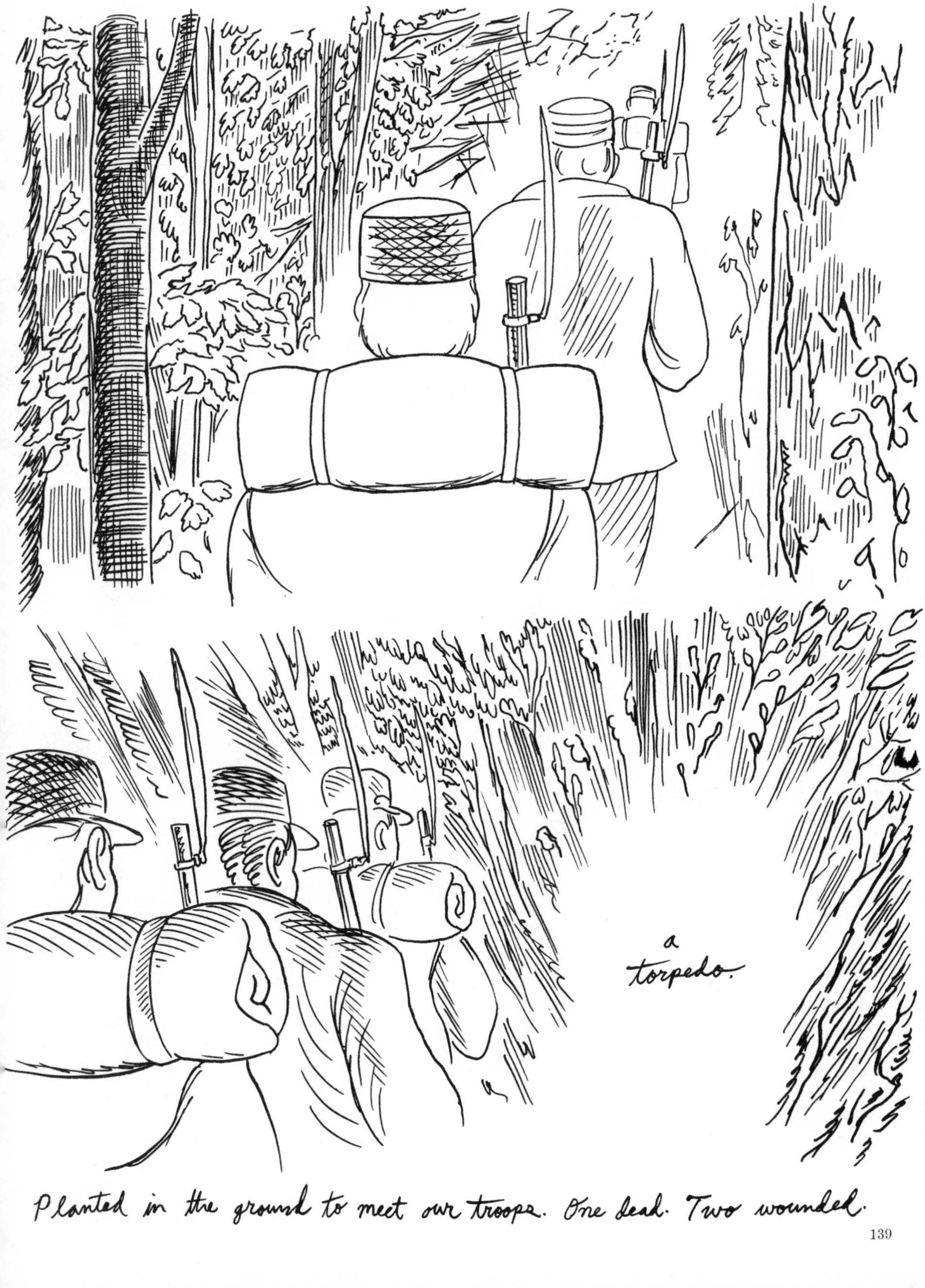
a torpedo.
Planted in the ground to meet our troops. One dead. Two wounded.

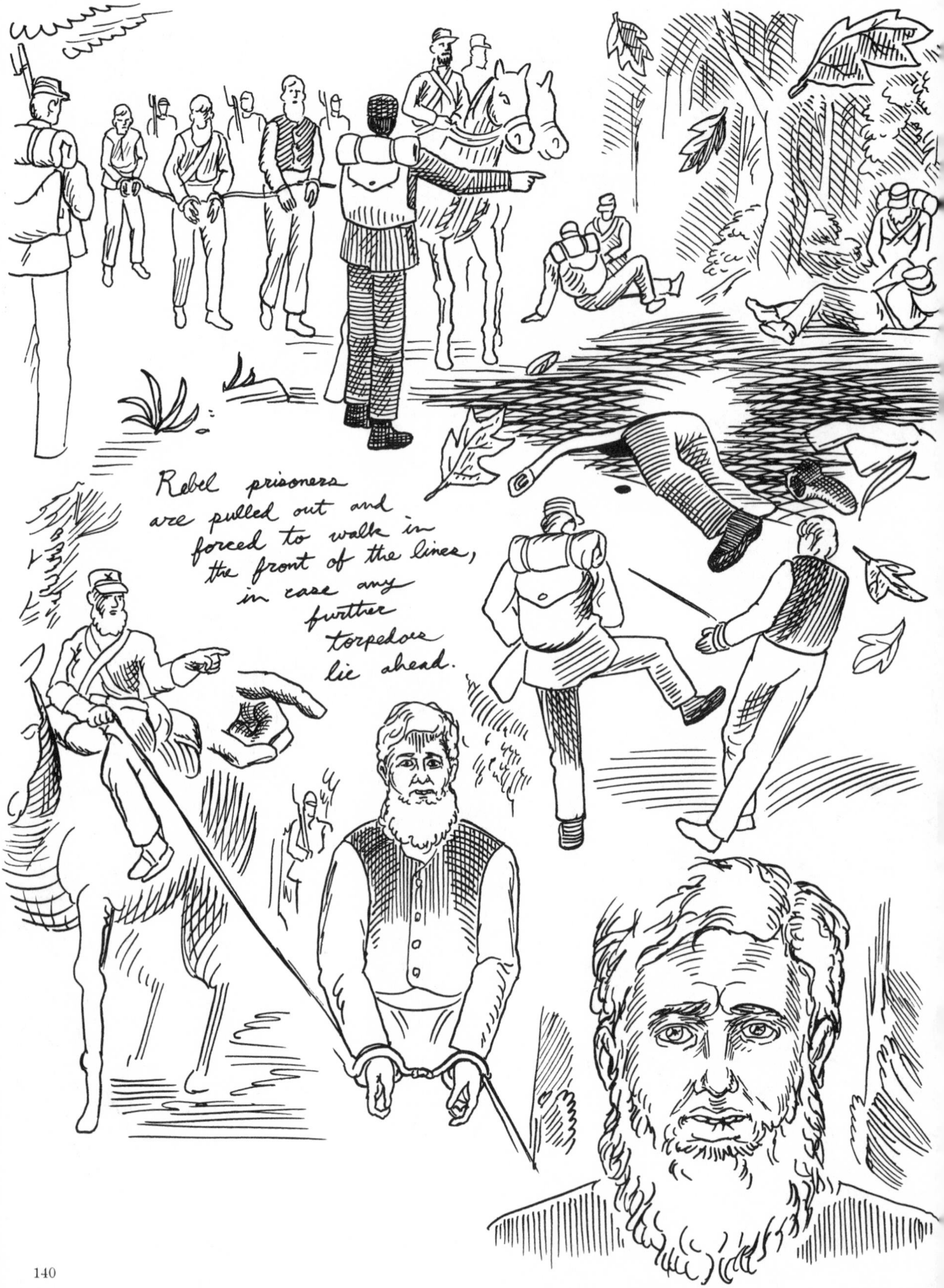
Rebel prisoners are pulled out and forced to walk in the front of the lines, in case any further torpedoes lie ahead.

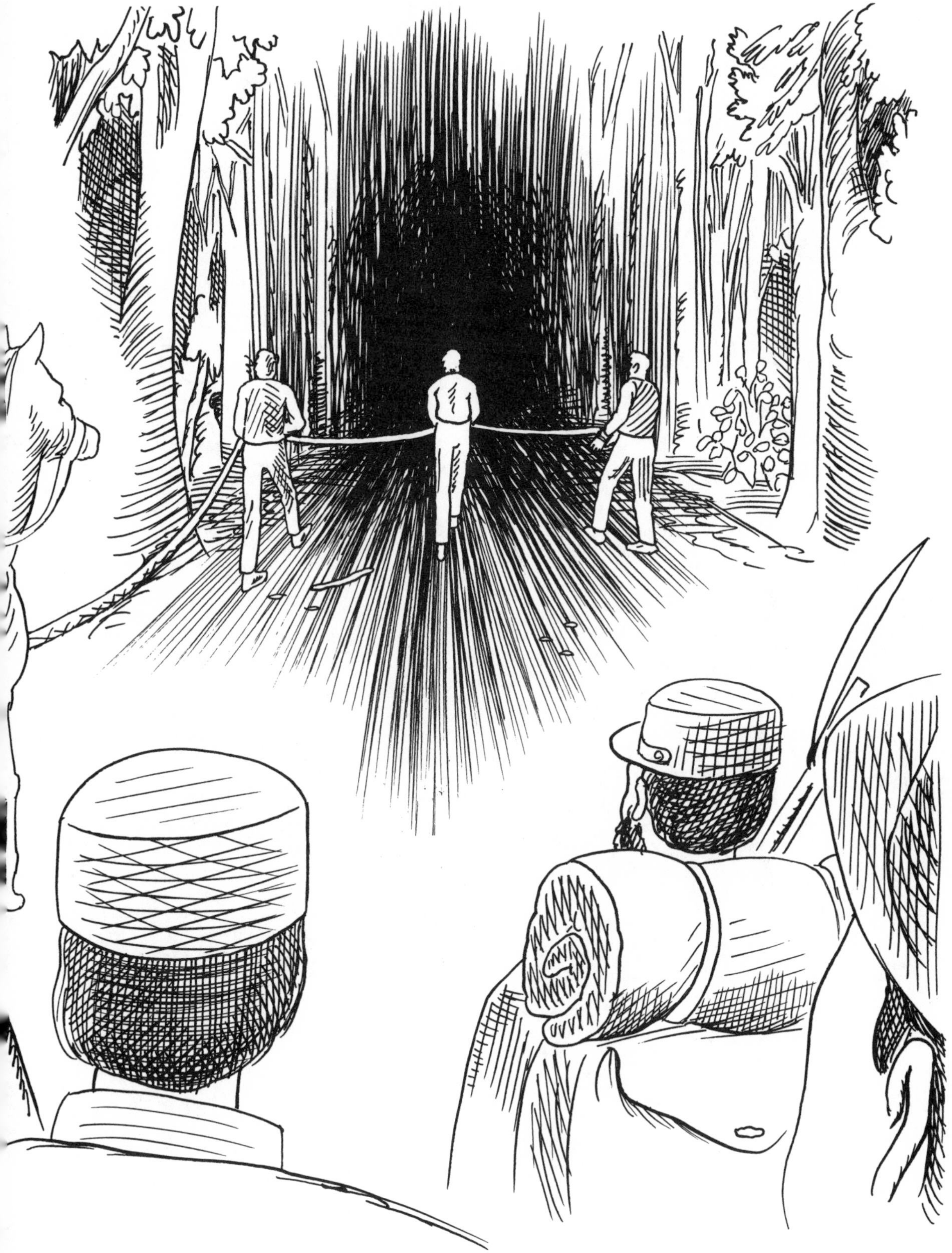

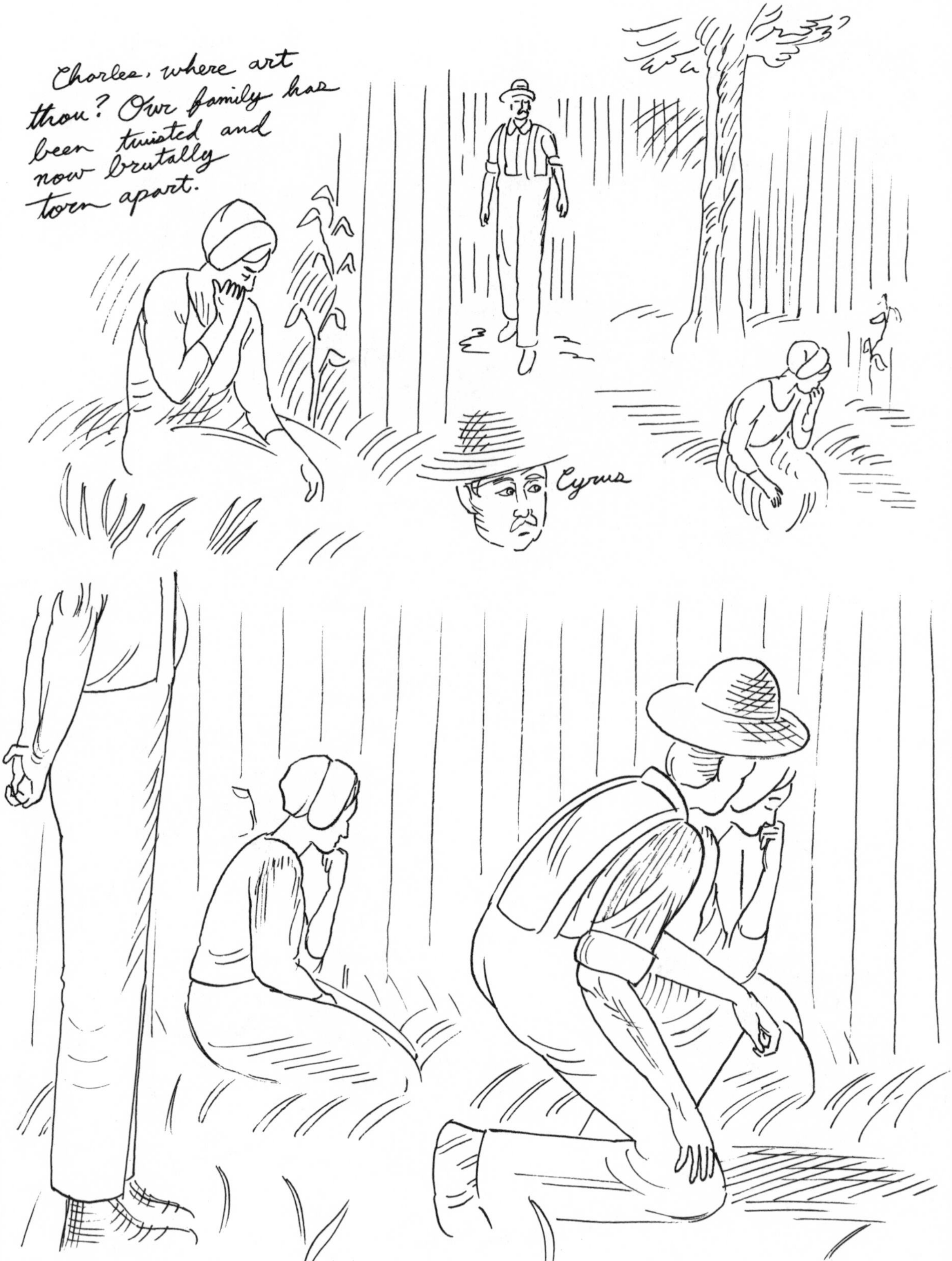
Charles, where art thou? Our family has been twisted and now brutally torn apart.
Cyrus

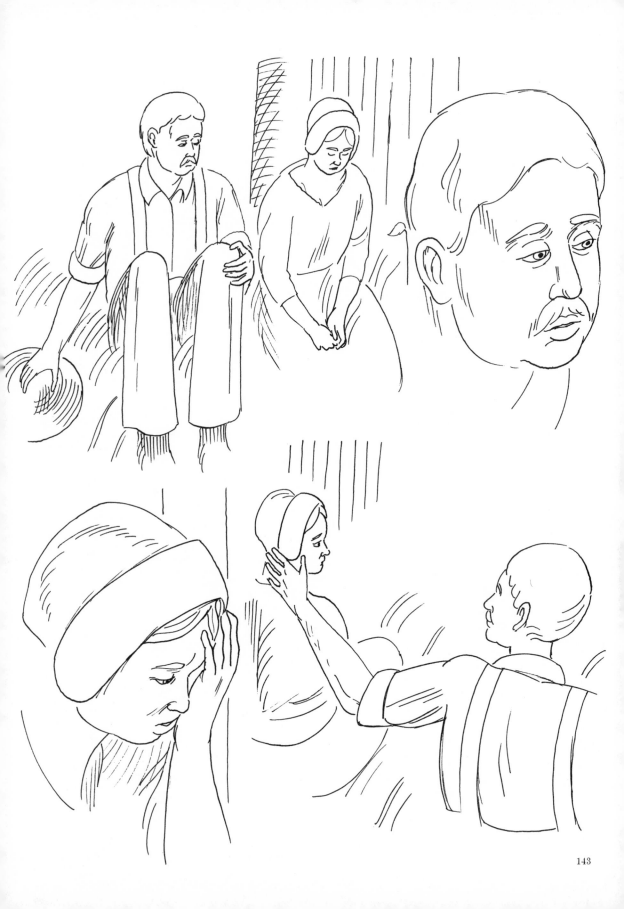

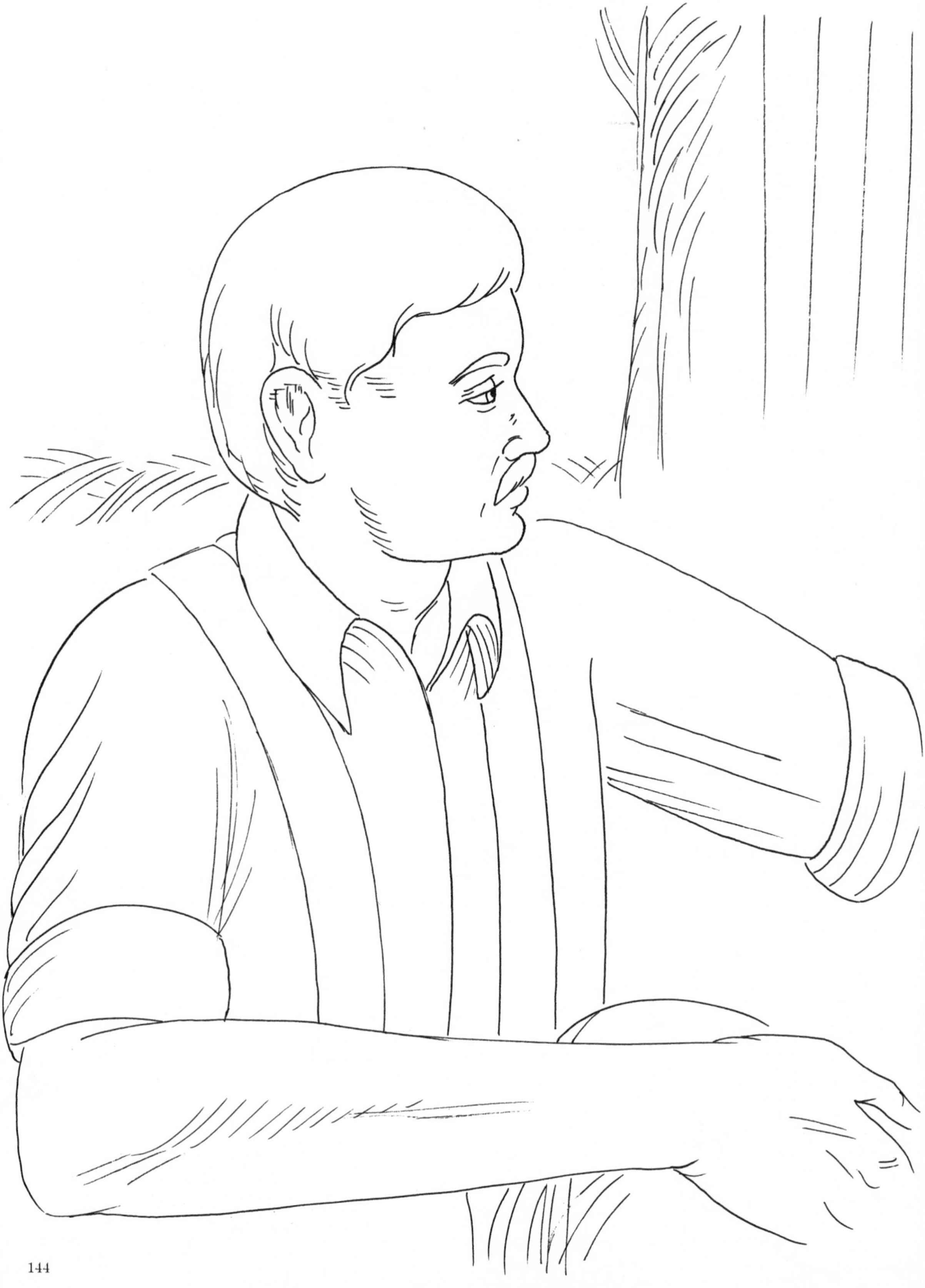

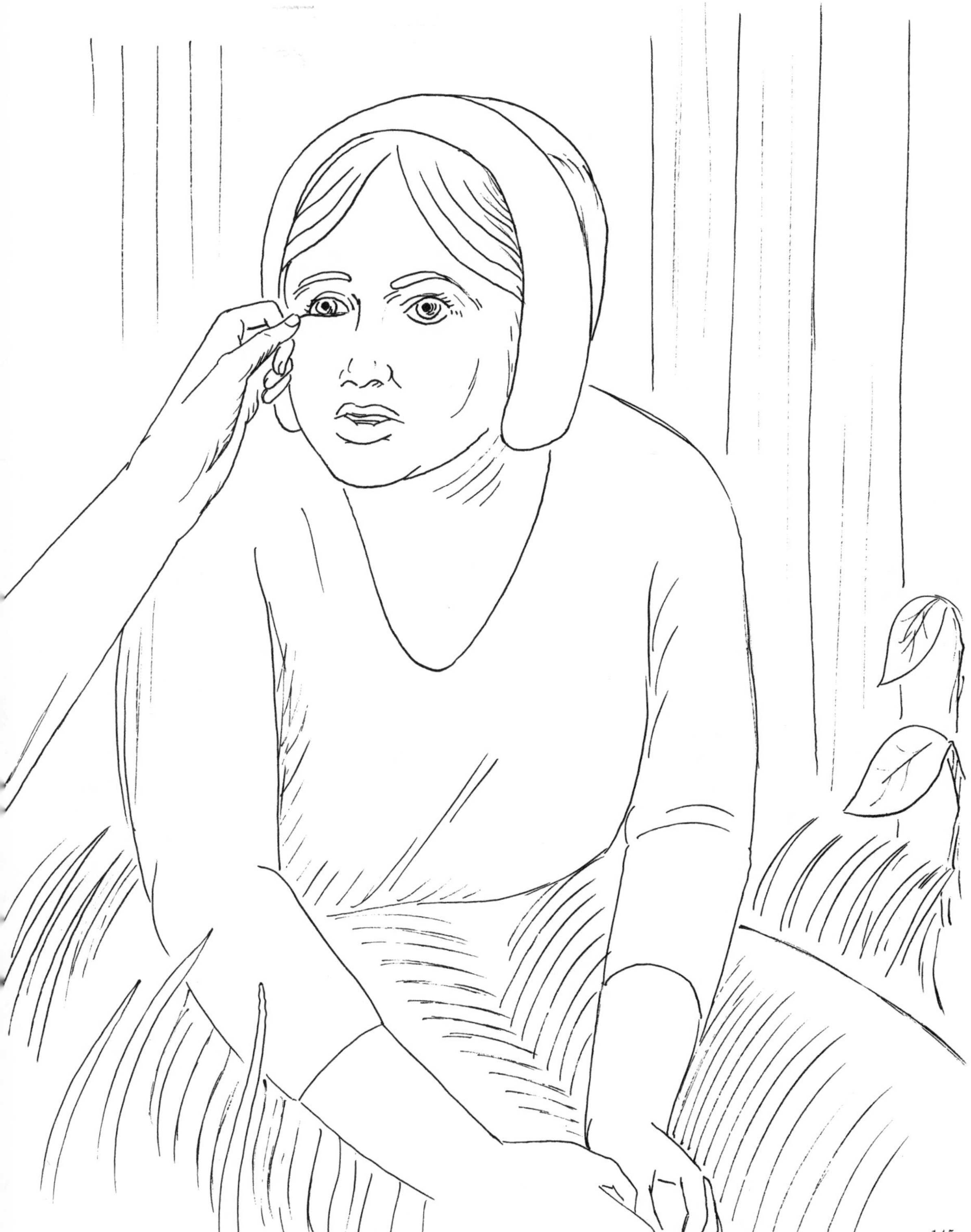

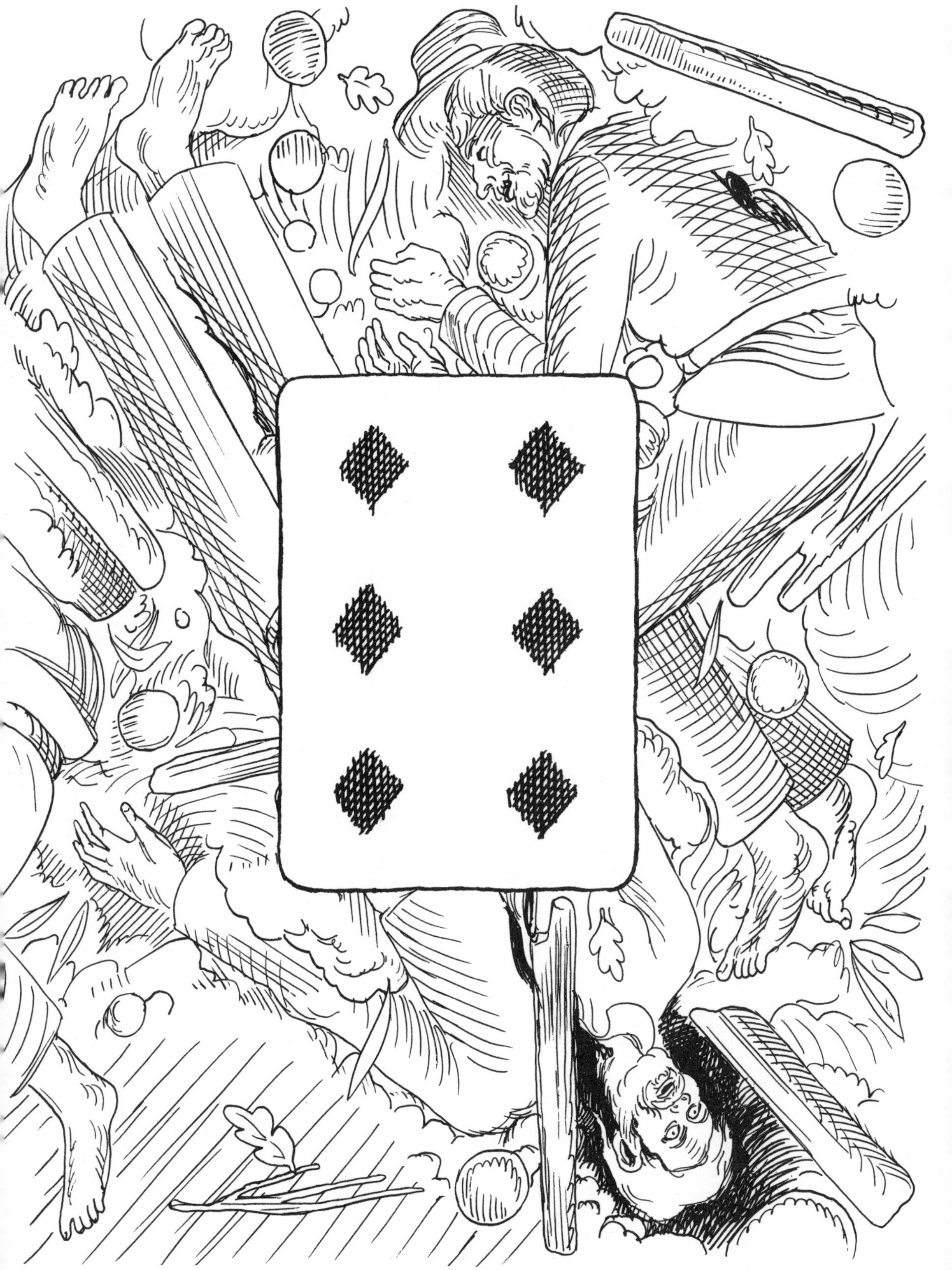

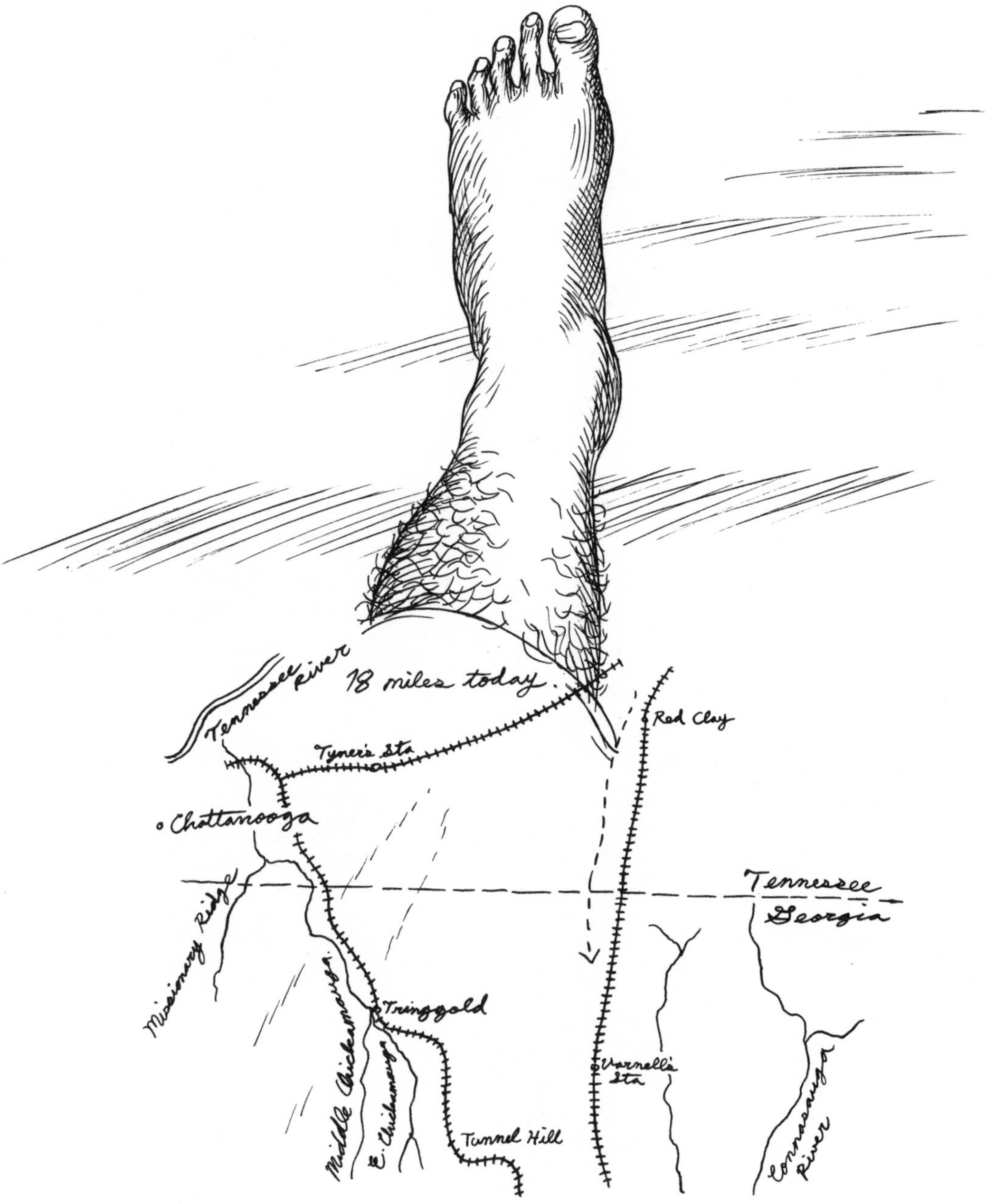
18 miles today
Tennessee River
Tyner's Sta
Red Clay
Chattanooga
Tennessee
Georgia
Missionary Ridge
Middle Chickamauga
Tringgold
E. Chickamauga
Tunnel Hill
Varnell's Sta
Connasauga River

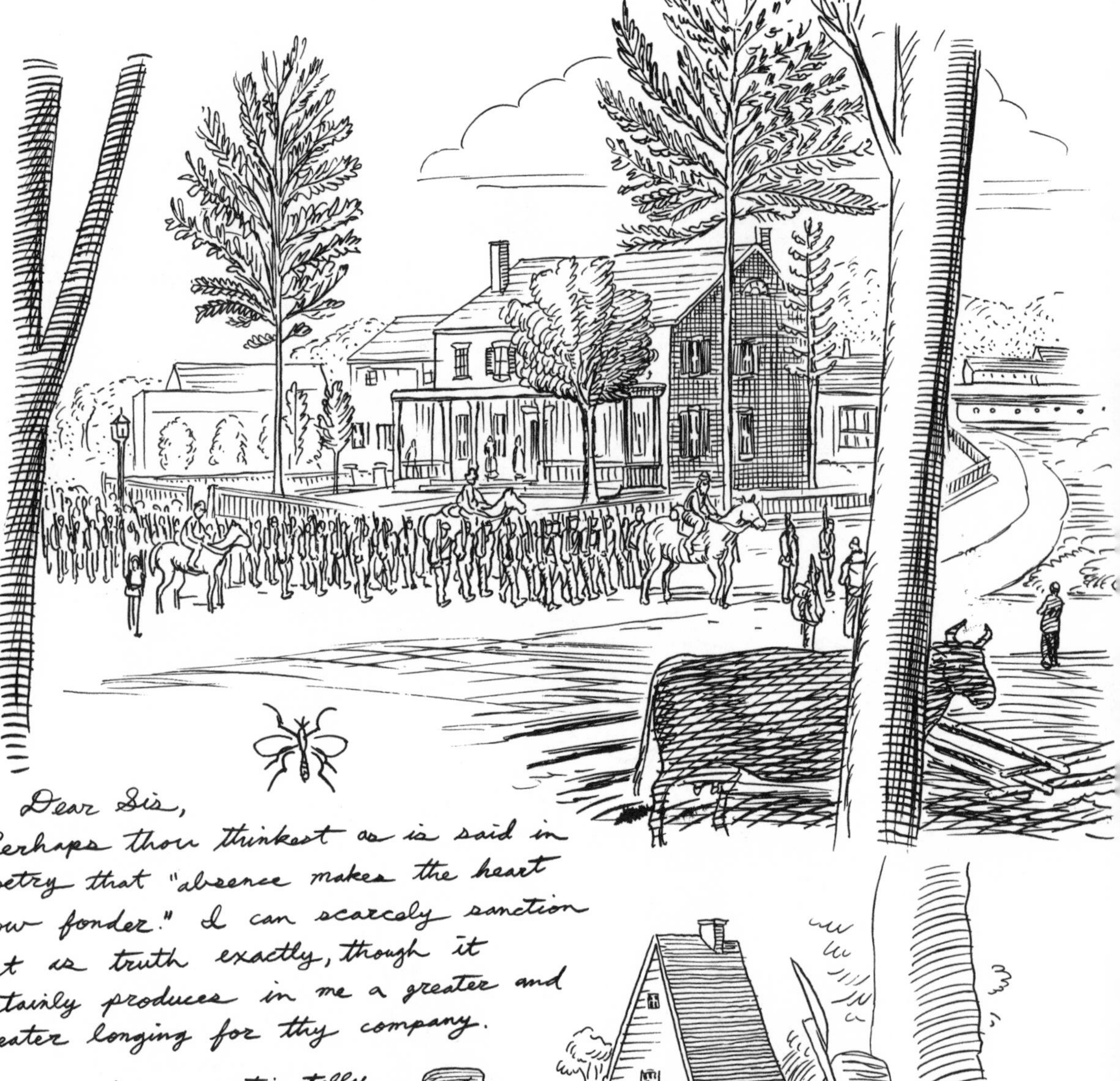

Dear Sis,
Perhaps thou thinkest as is said in poetry that "absence makes the heart grow fonder." I can scarcely sanction that as truth exactly, though it certainly produces in me a greater and greater longing for thy company.

My heart so sentimentally yearns for thou that are so near and dear to me.

Charles.

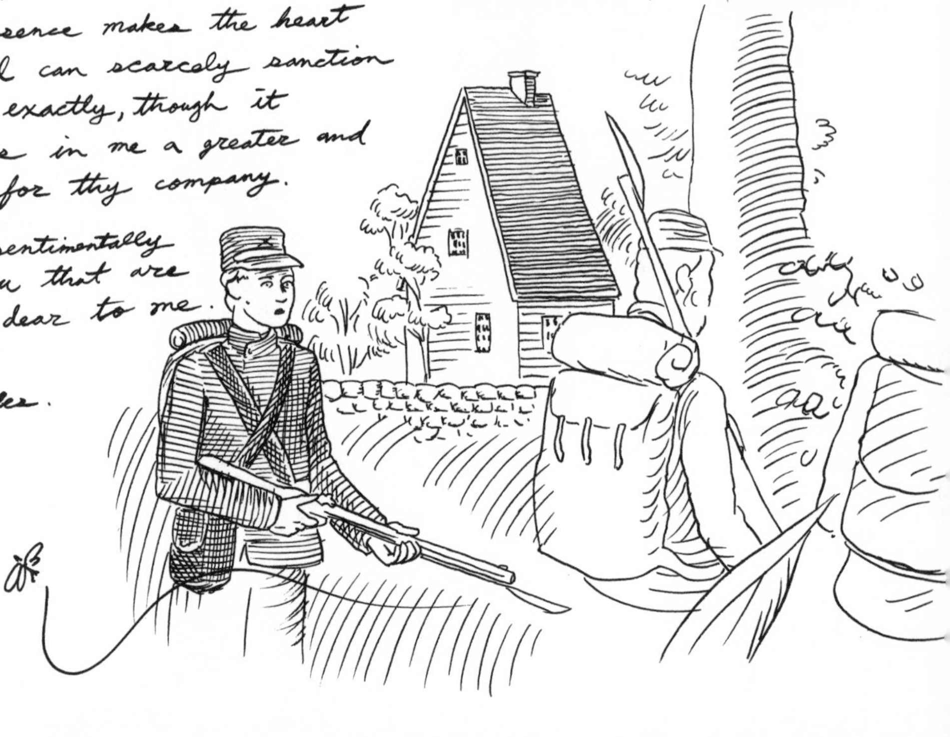

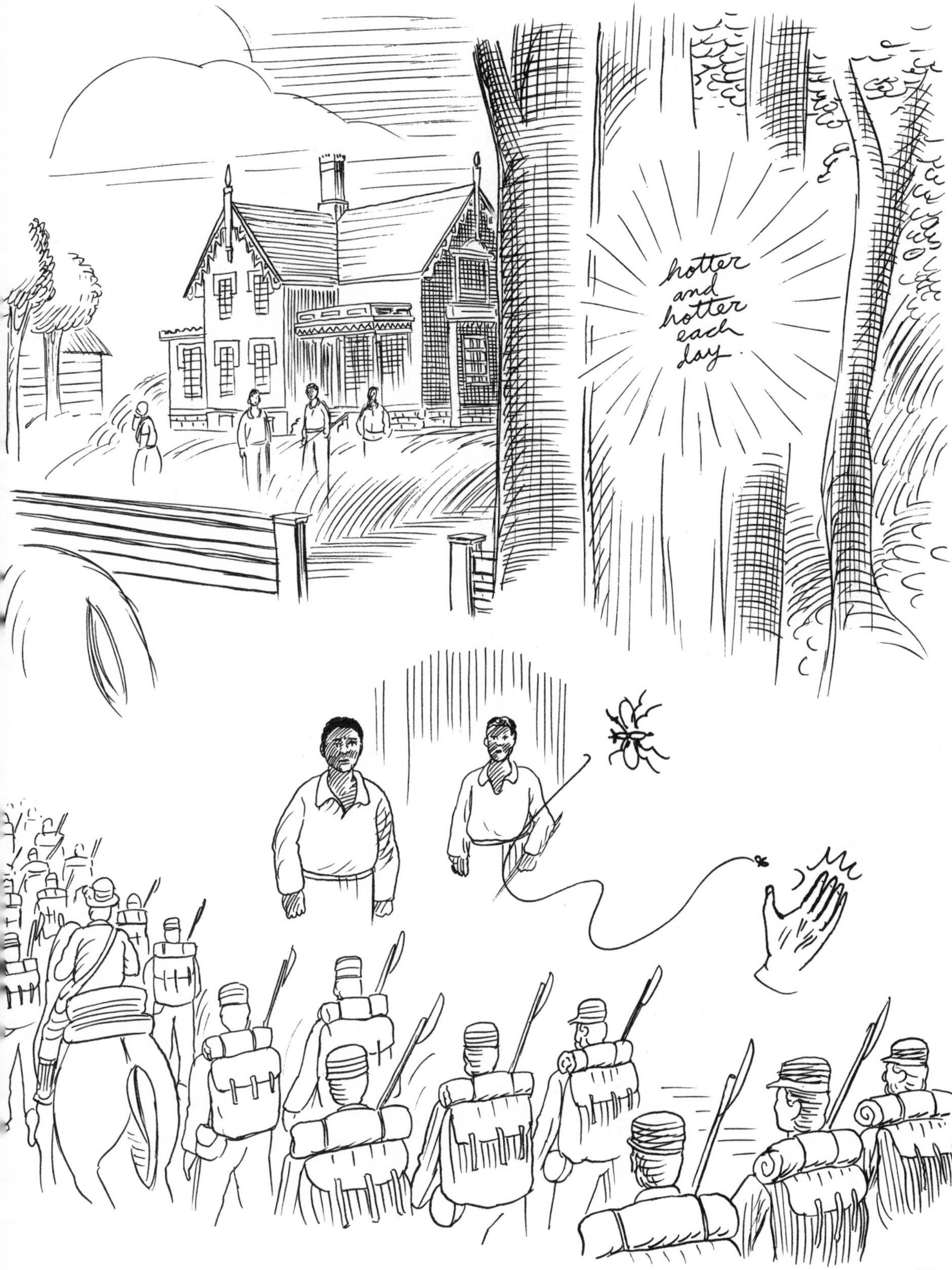
hotter and hotter each day.

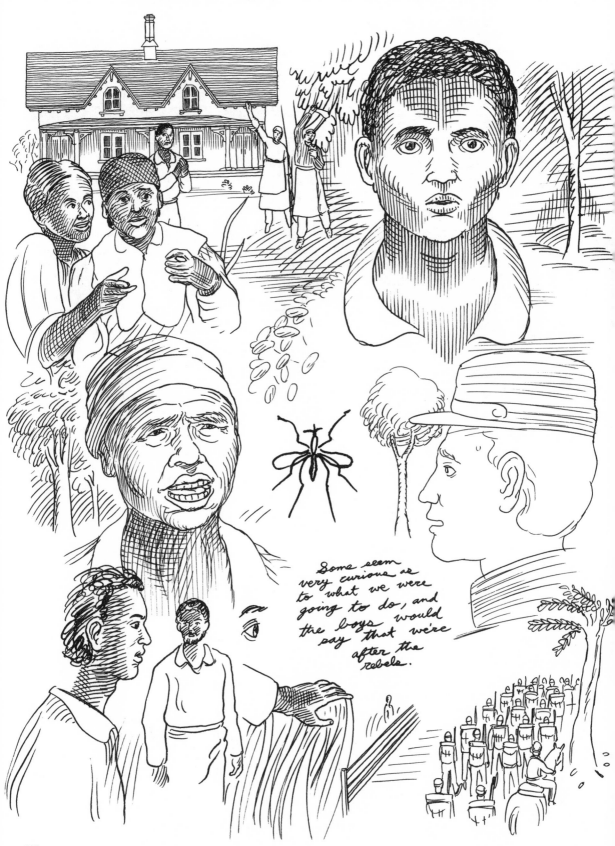

Some seem
very curious as
to what we were
going to do, and
the boys would
say that we're
after the
rebels.

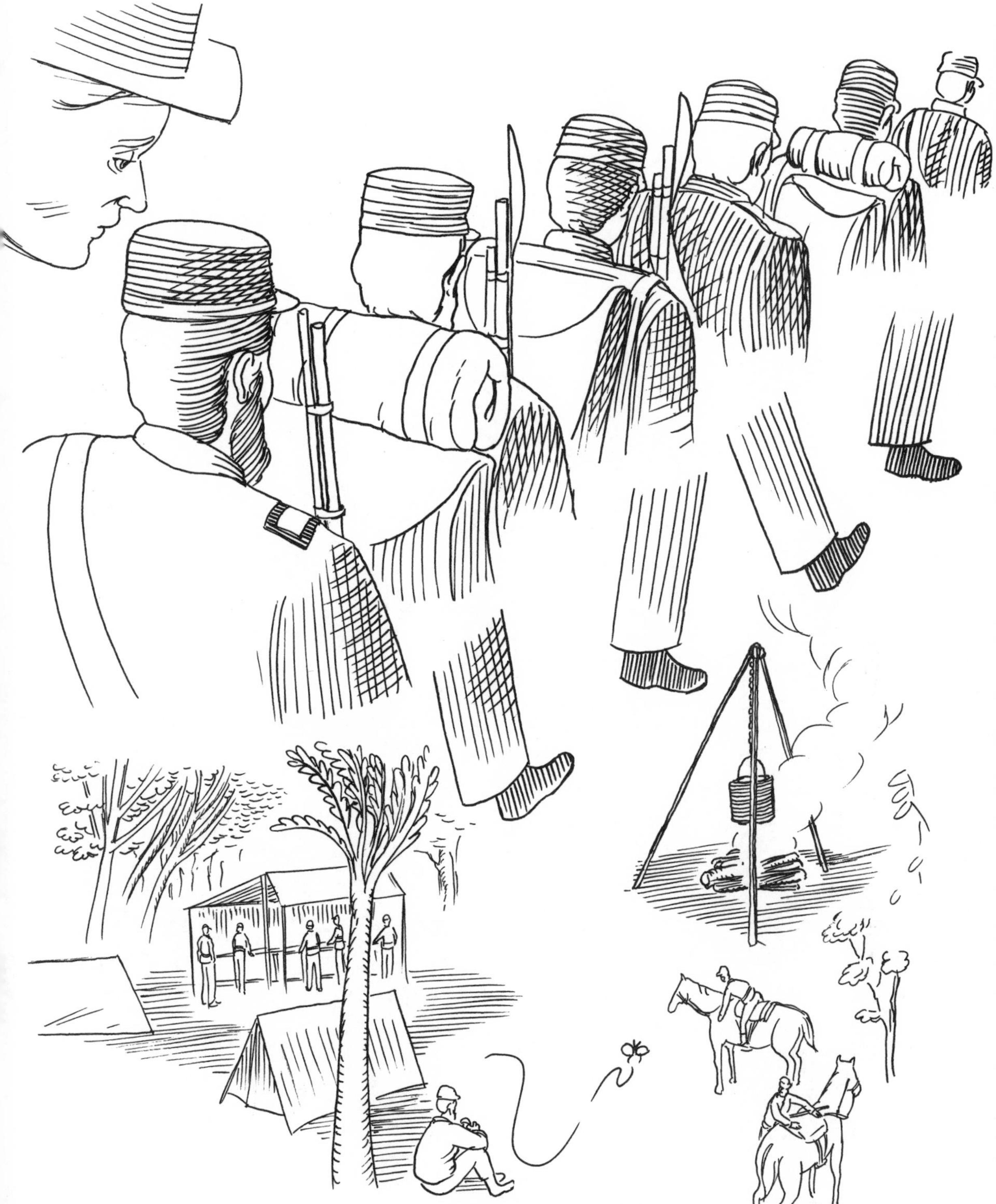

Edward and I are tasked as "bummers", to raid Secession homes for rations.

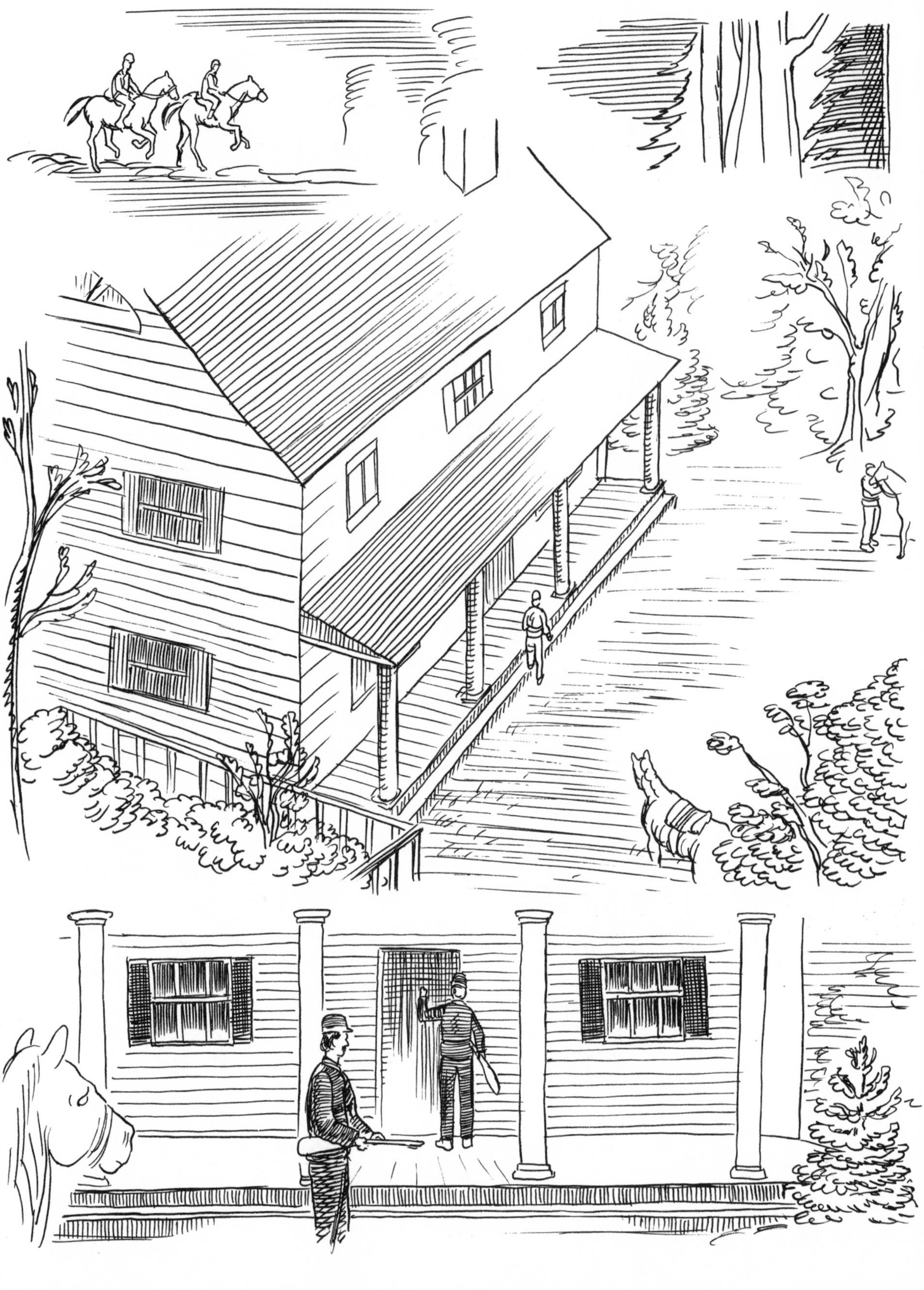

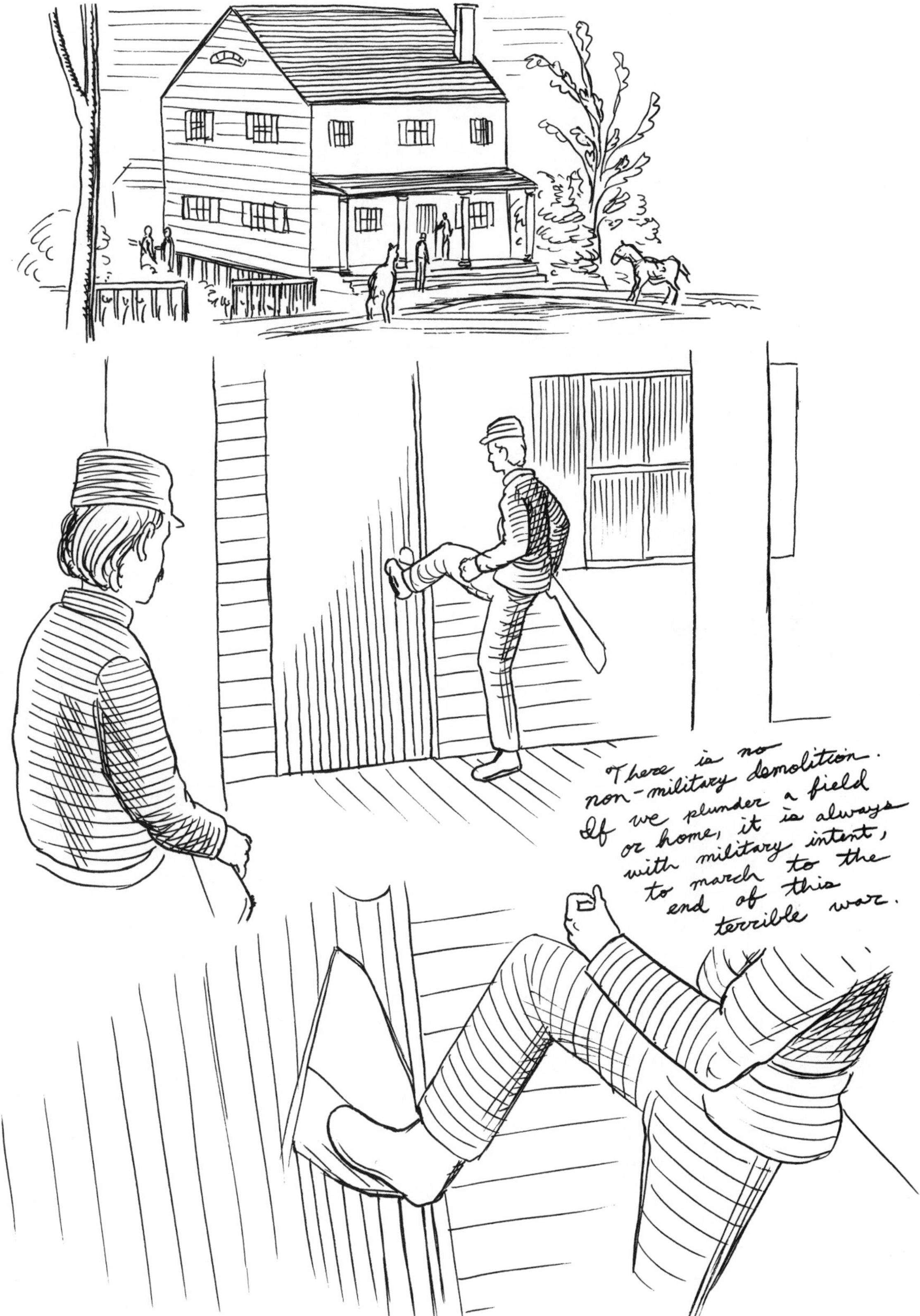
There is no non-military demolition. If we plunder a field or home, it is always with military intent, to march to the end of this terrible war.

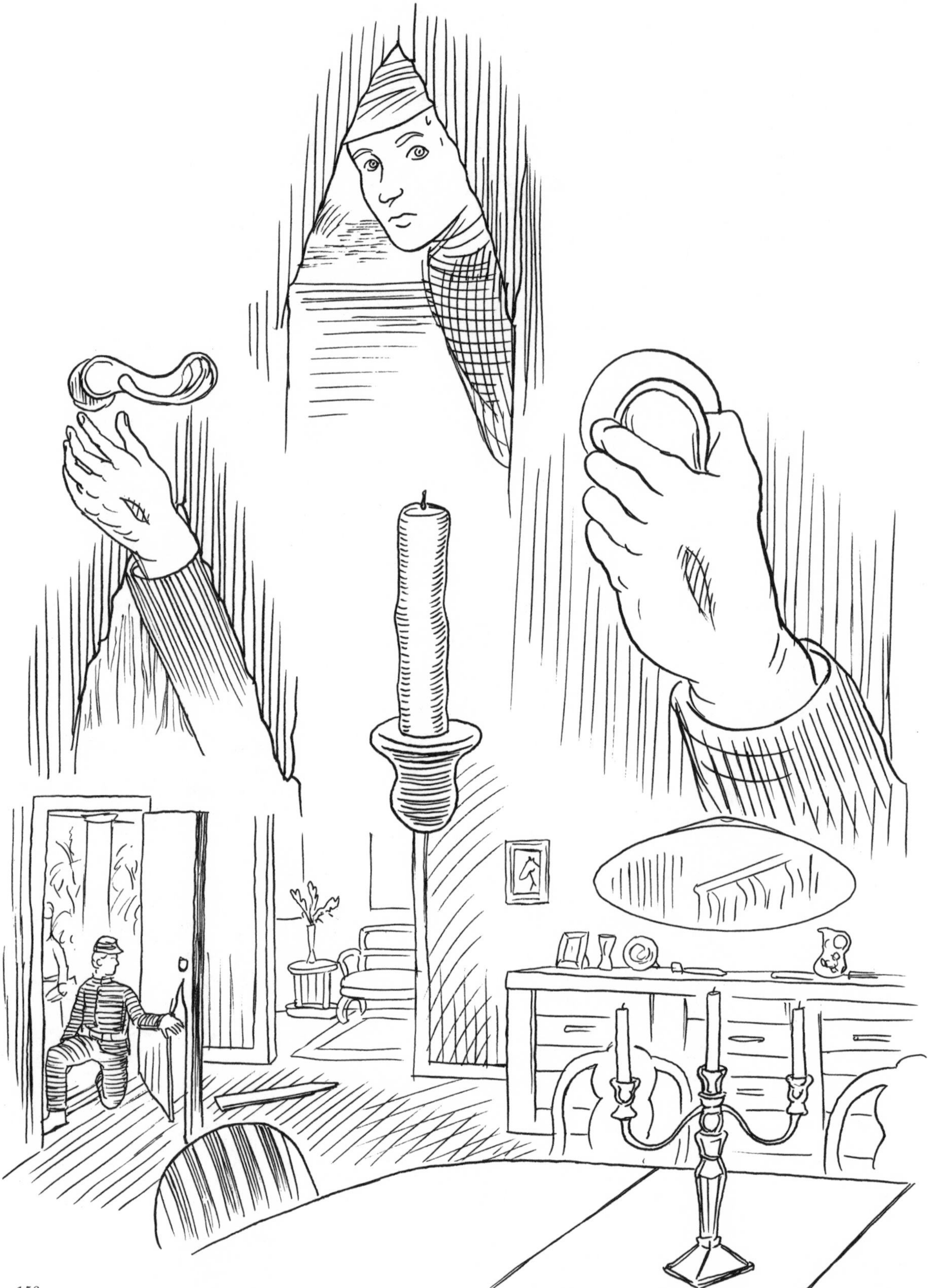

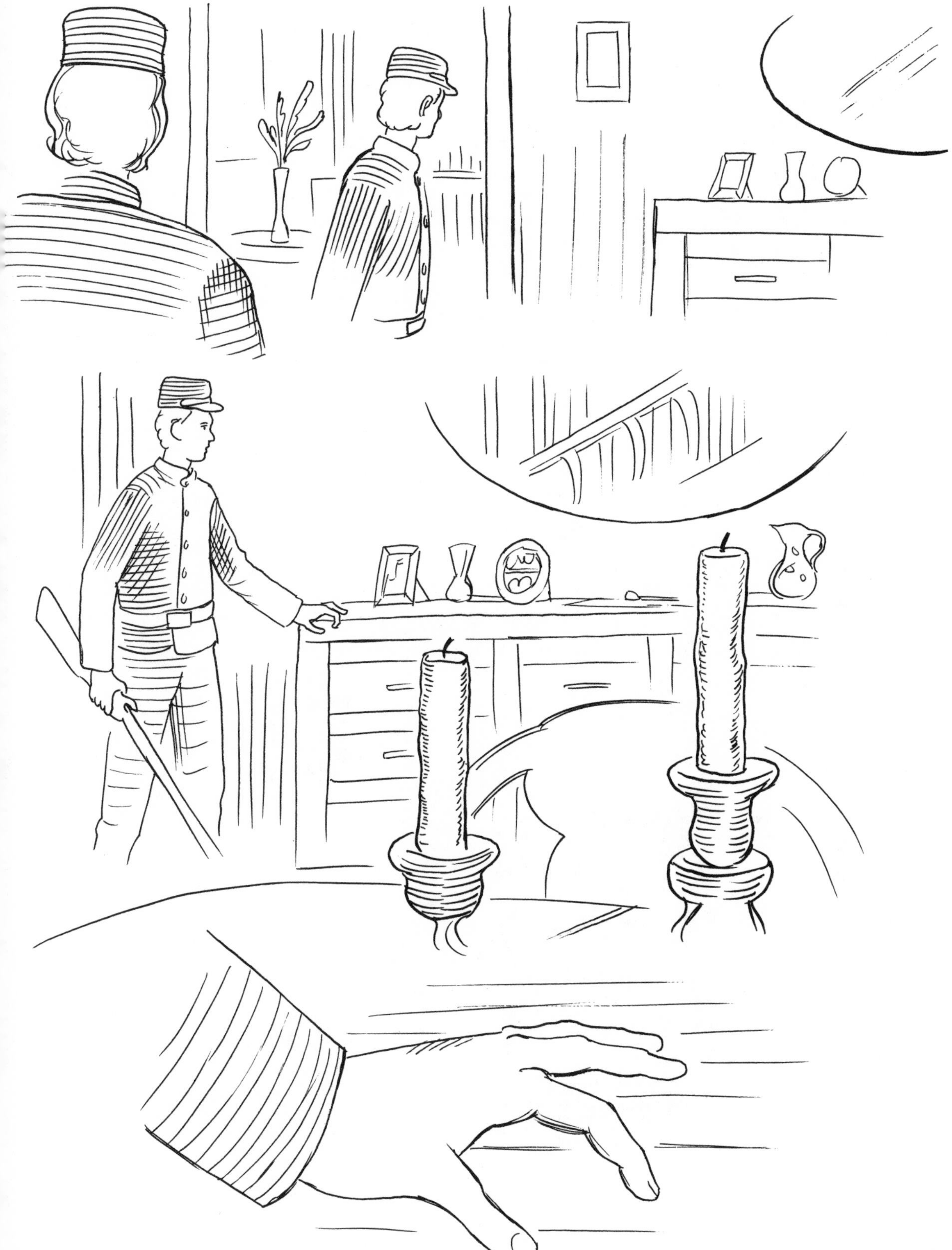

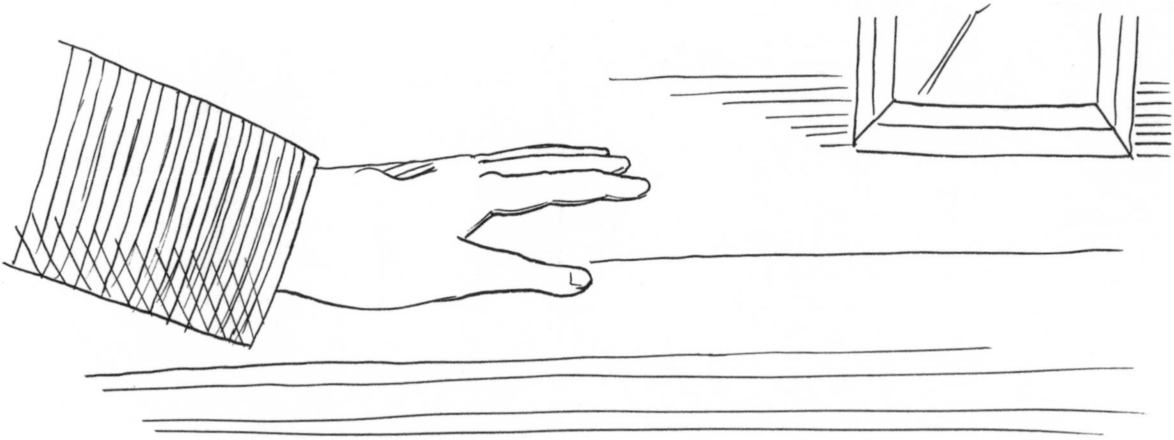

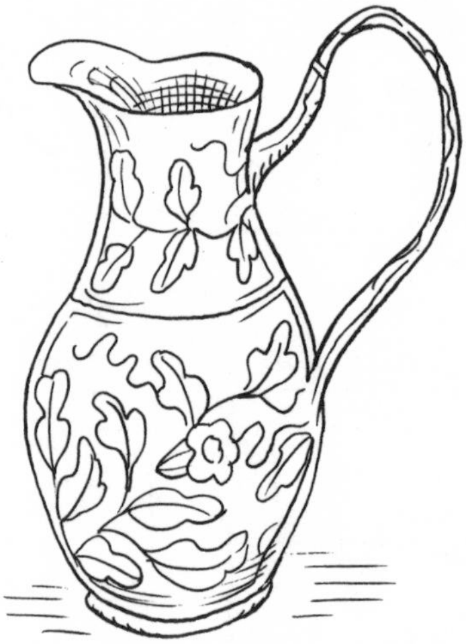

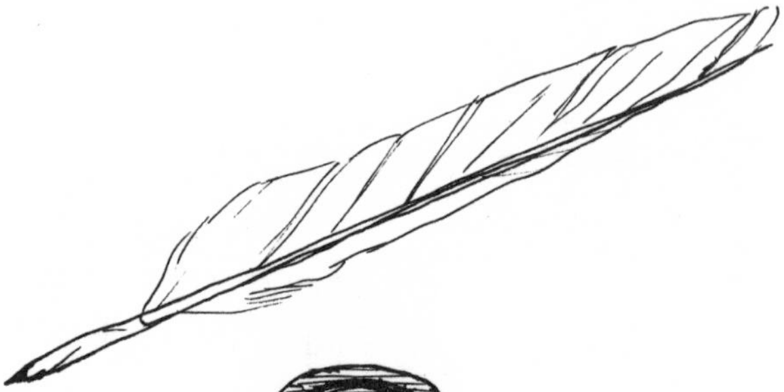

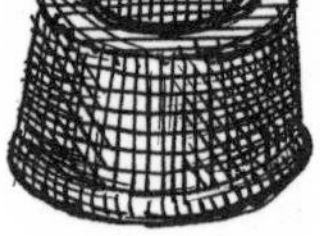

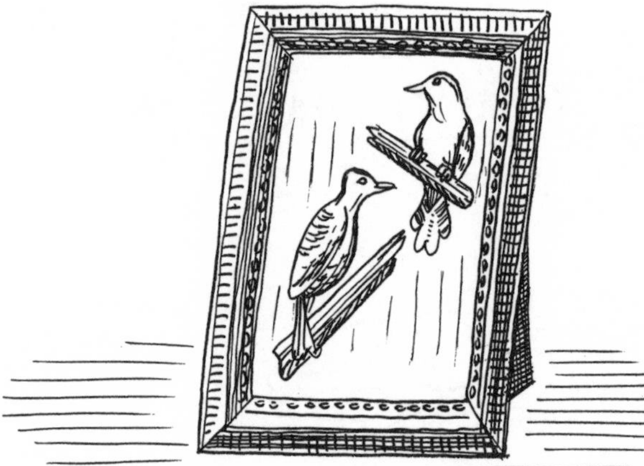

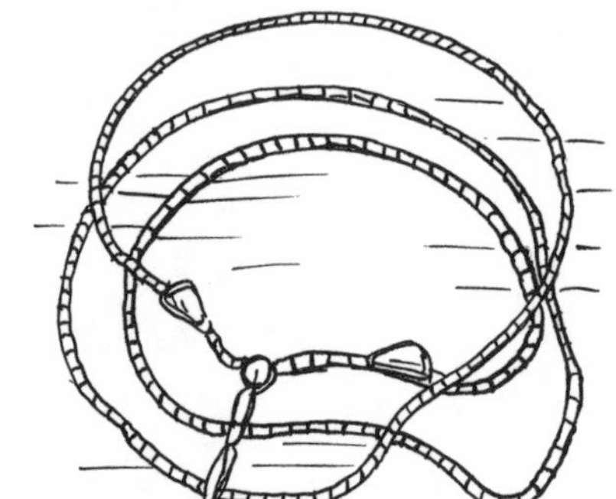

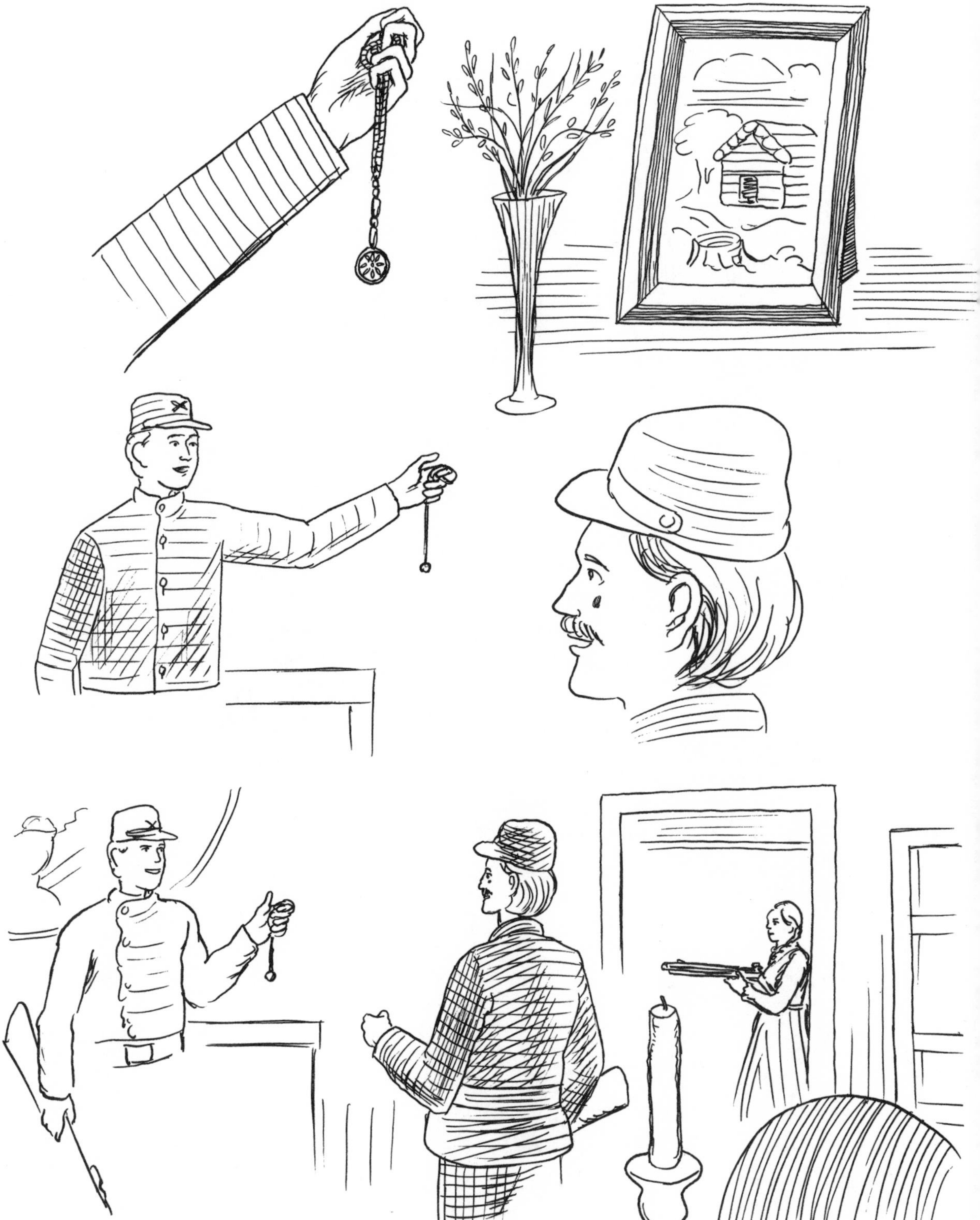

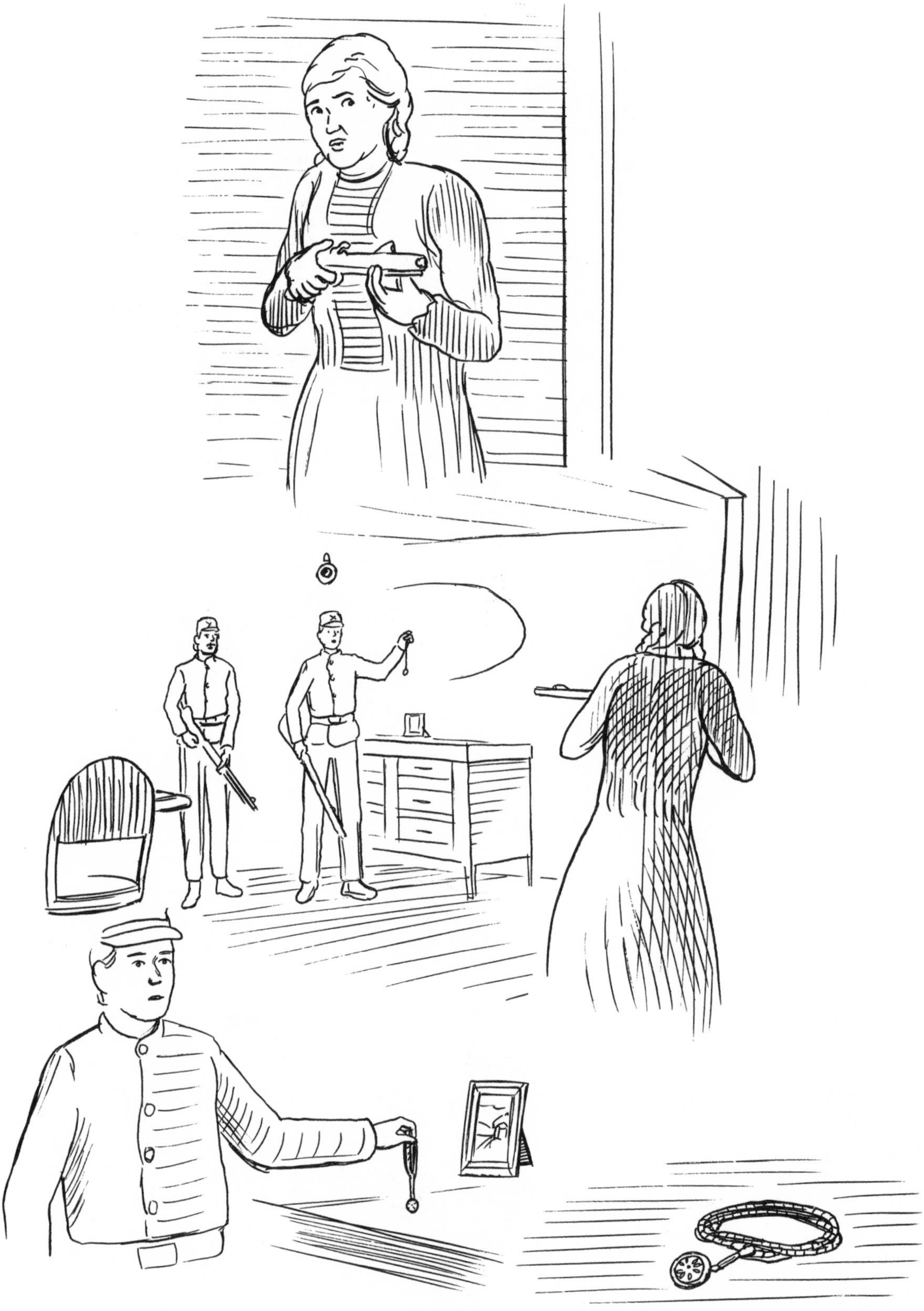

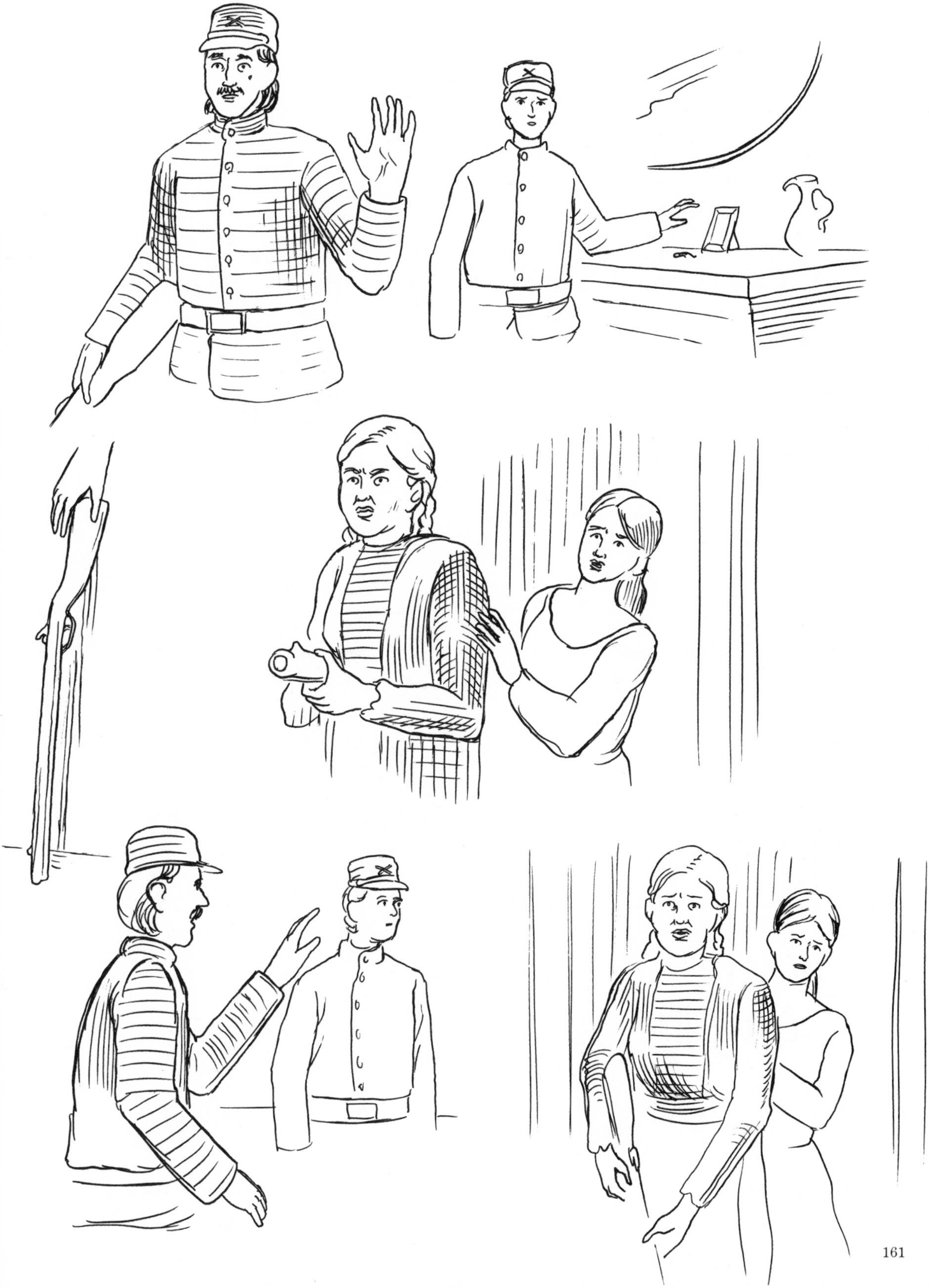

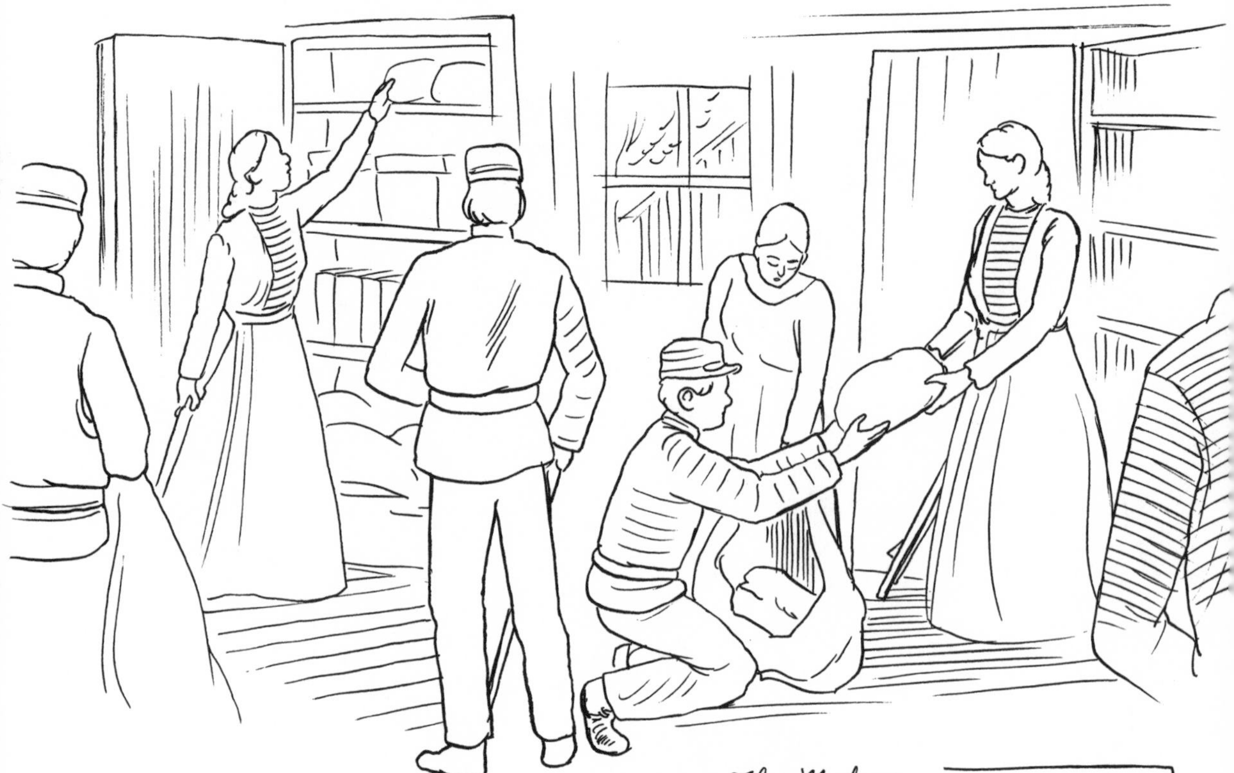

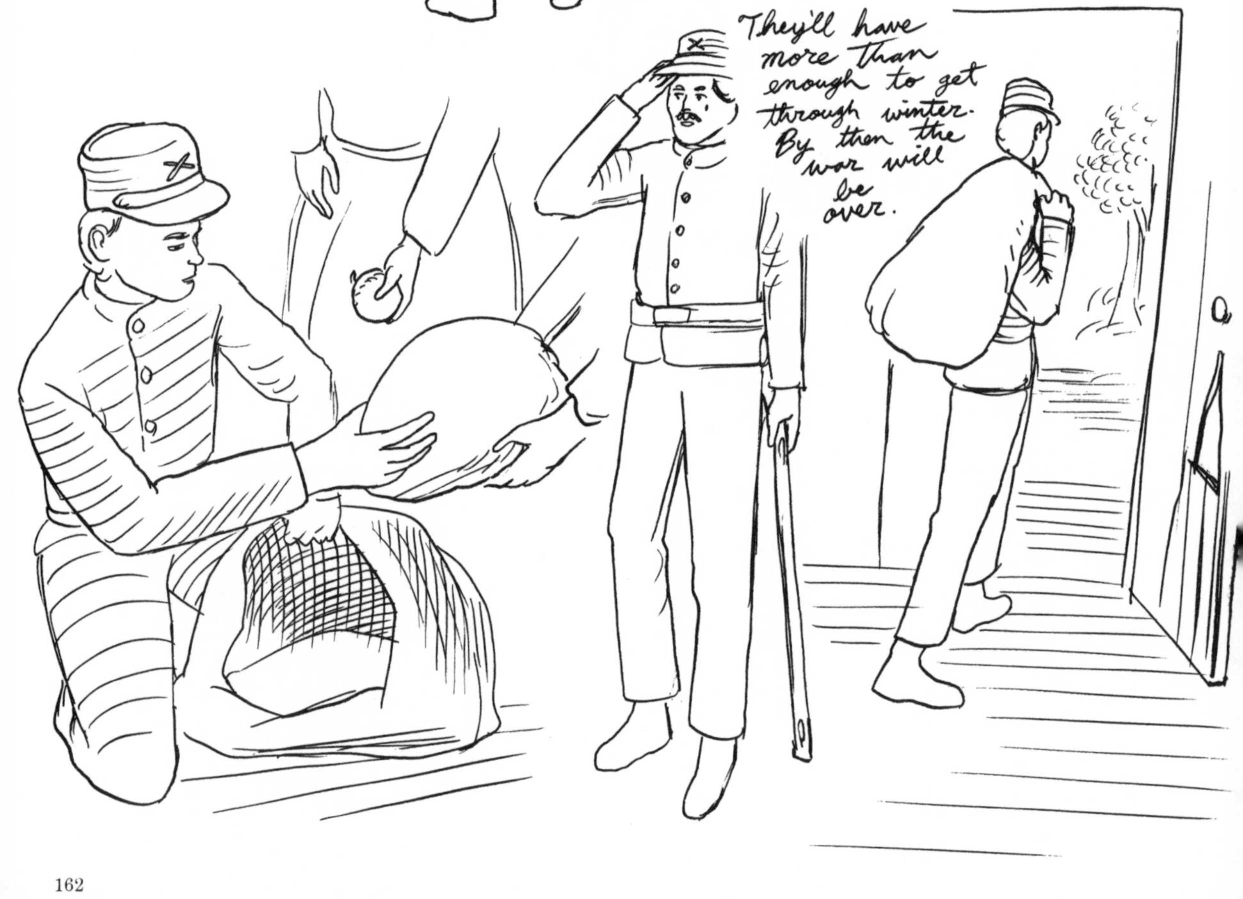
They'll have more than enough to get through winter. By then the war will be over.

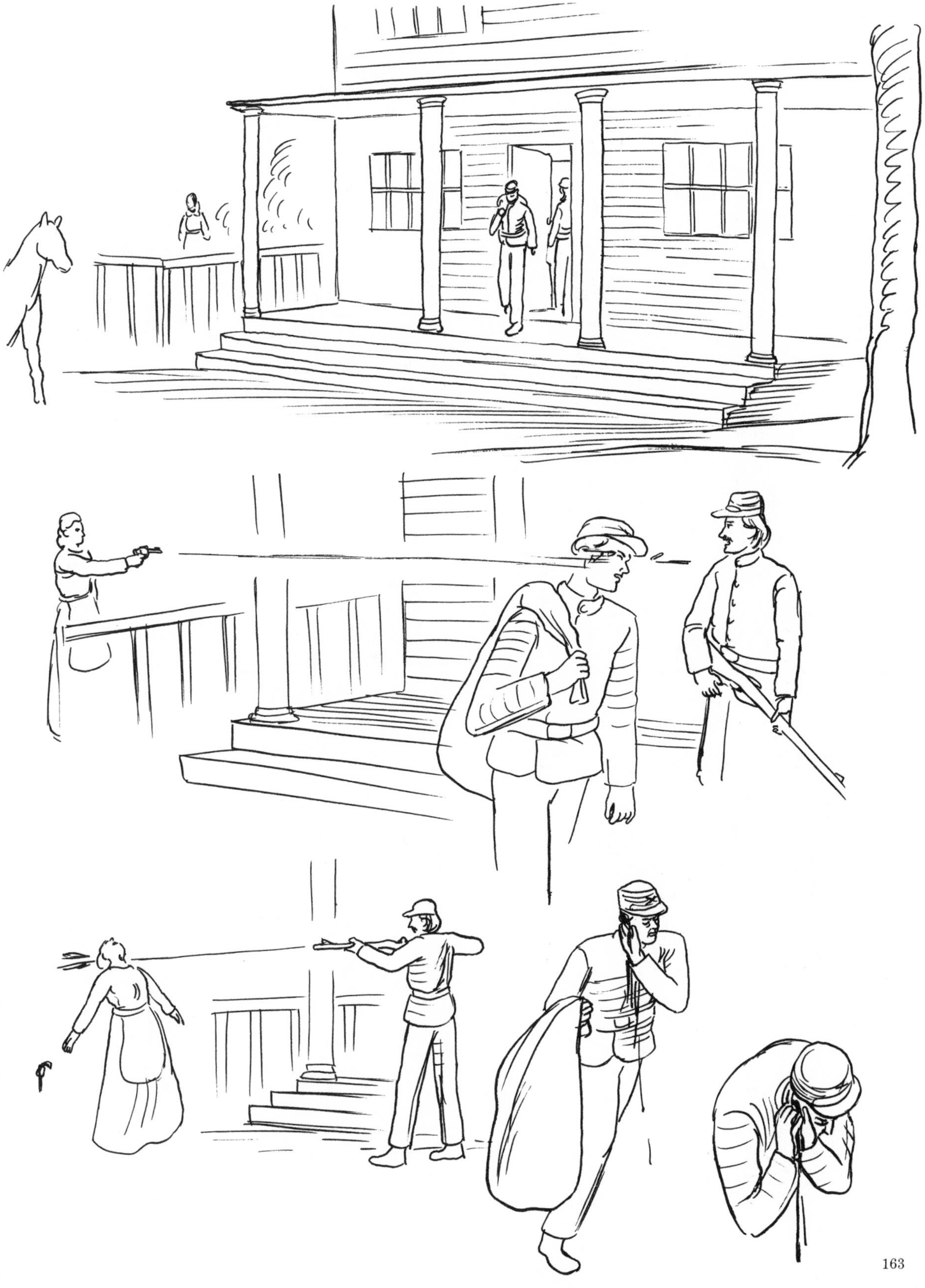

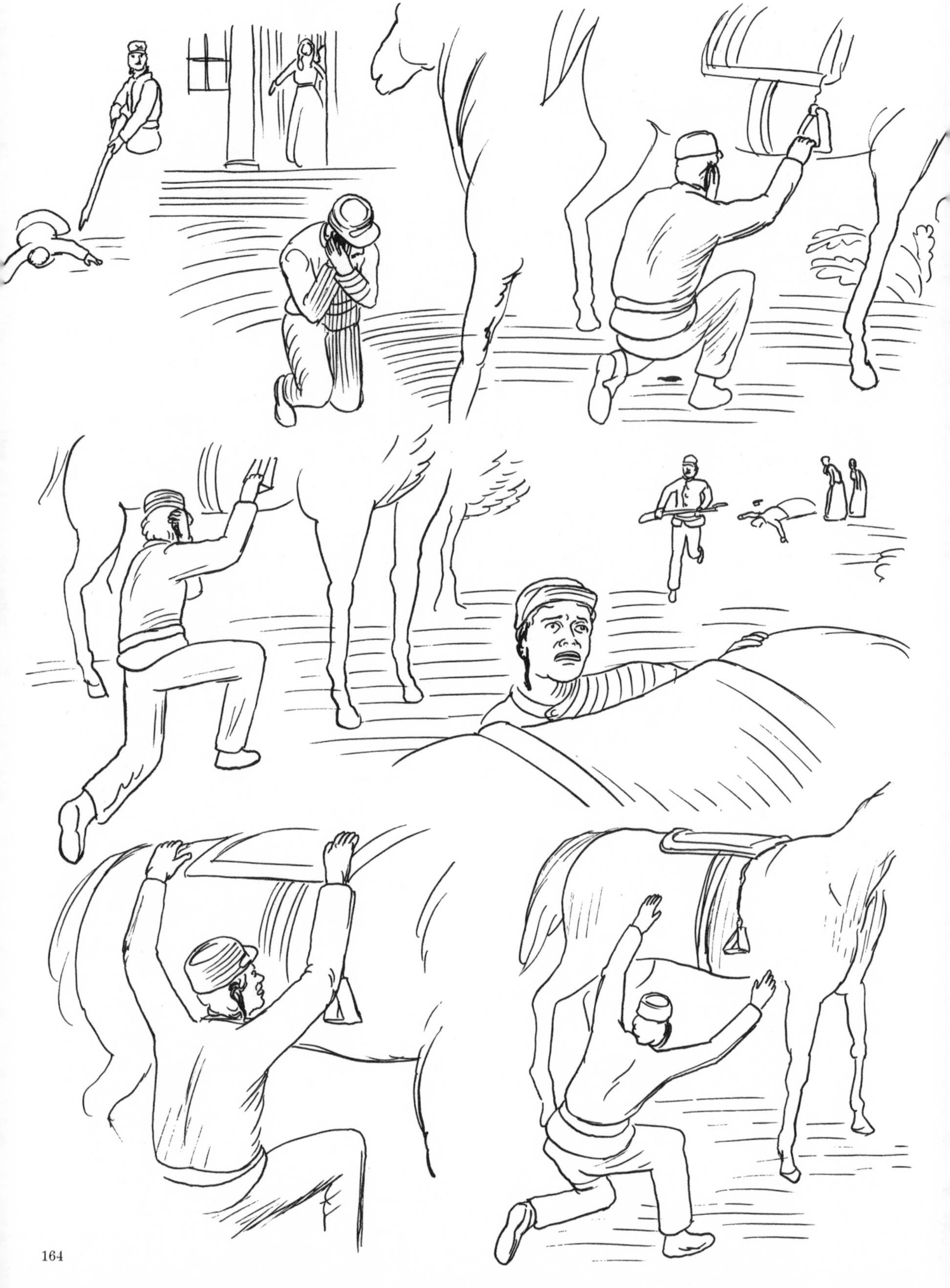

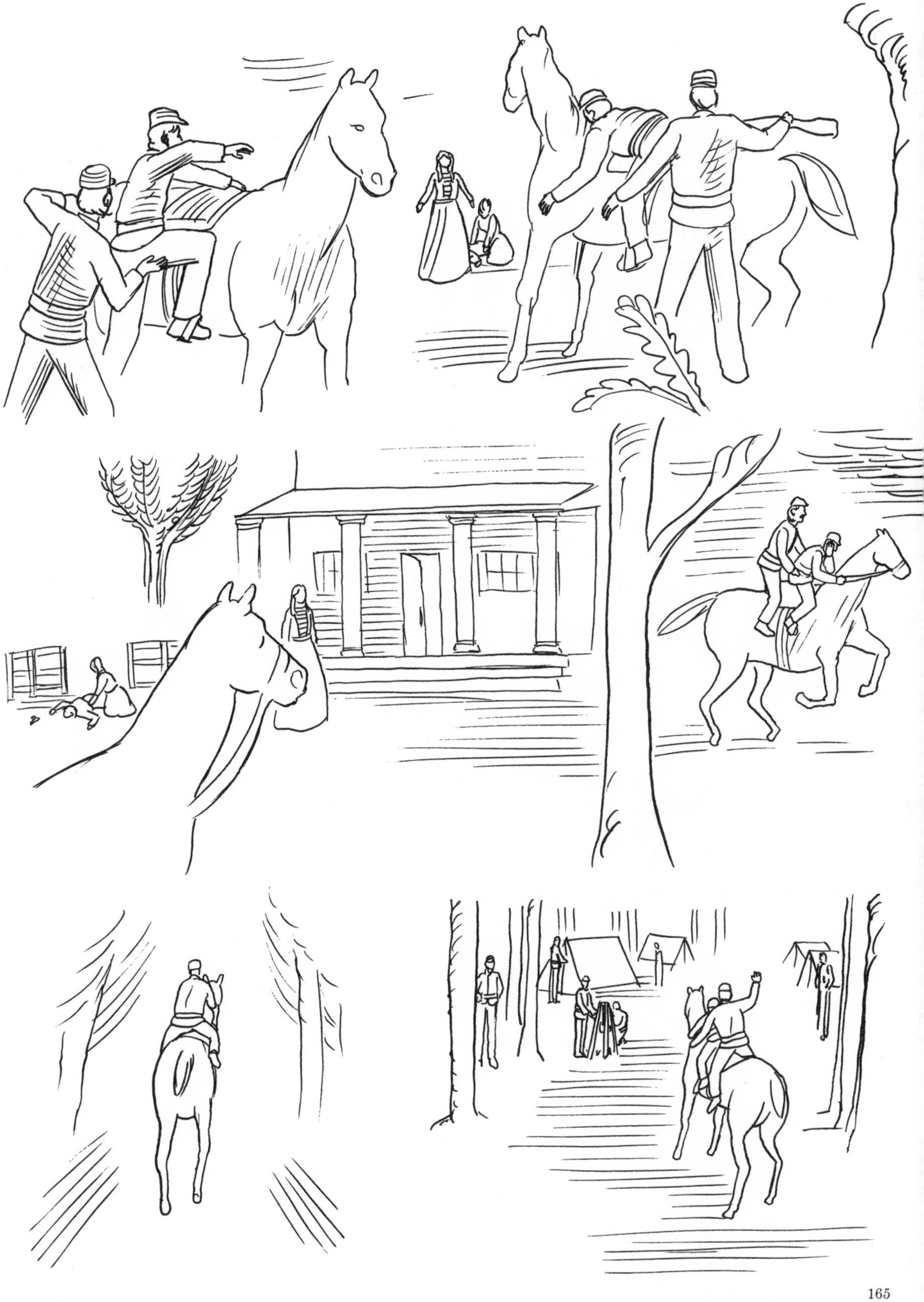

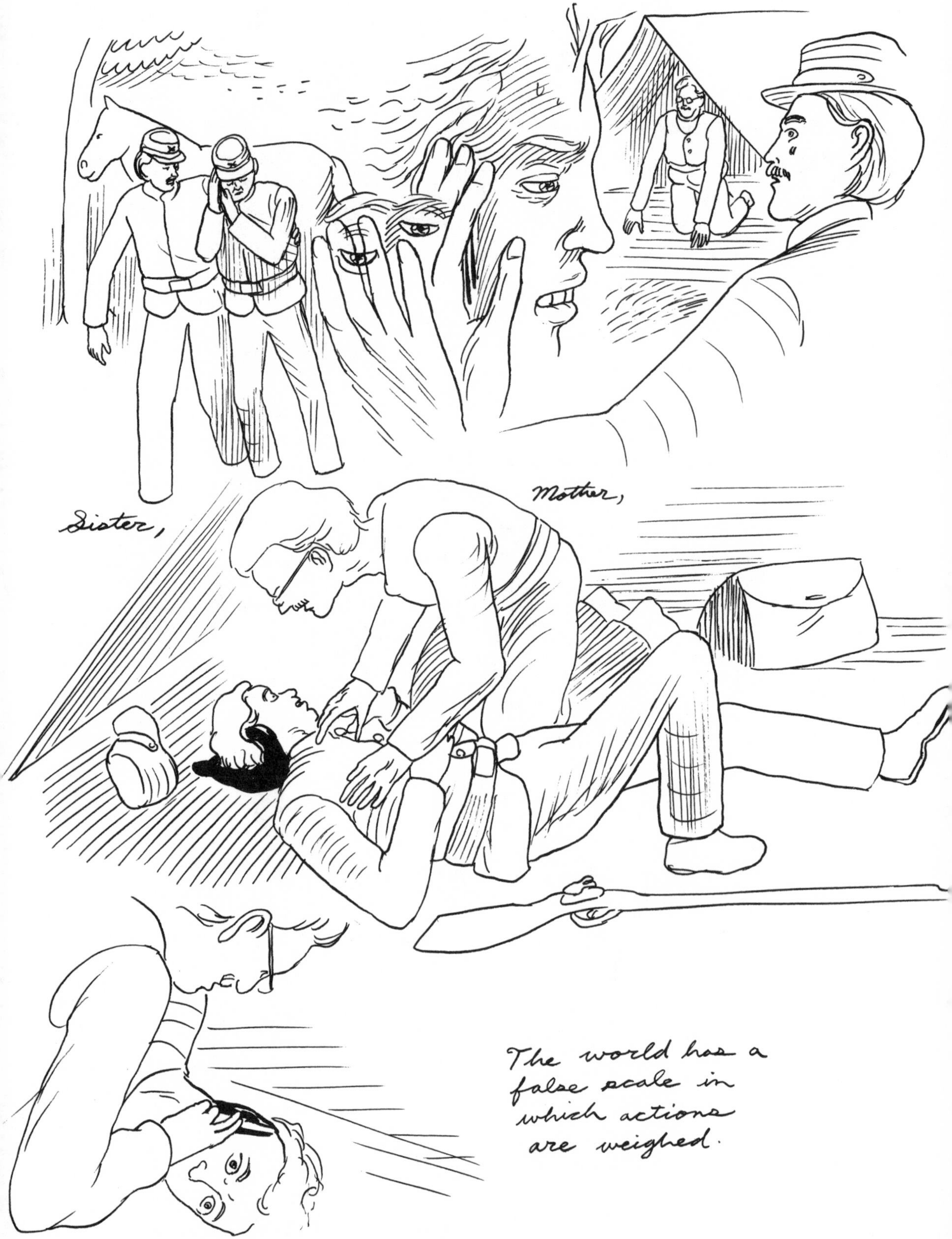

Sister,
Mother,
The world has a false scale in which actions are weighed.

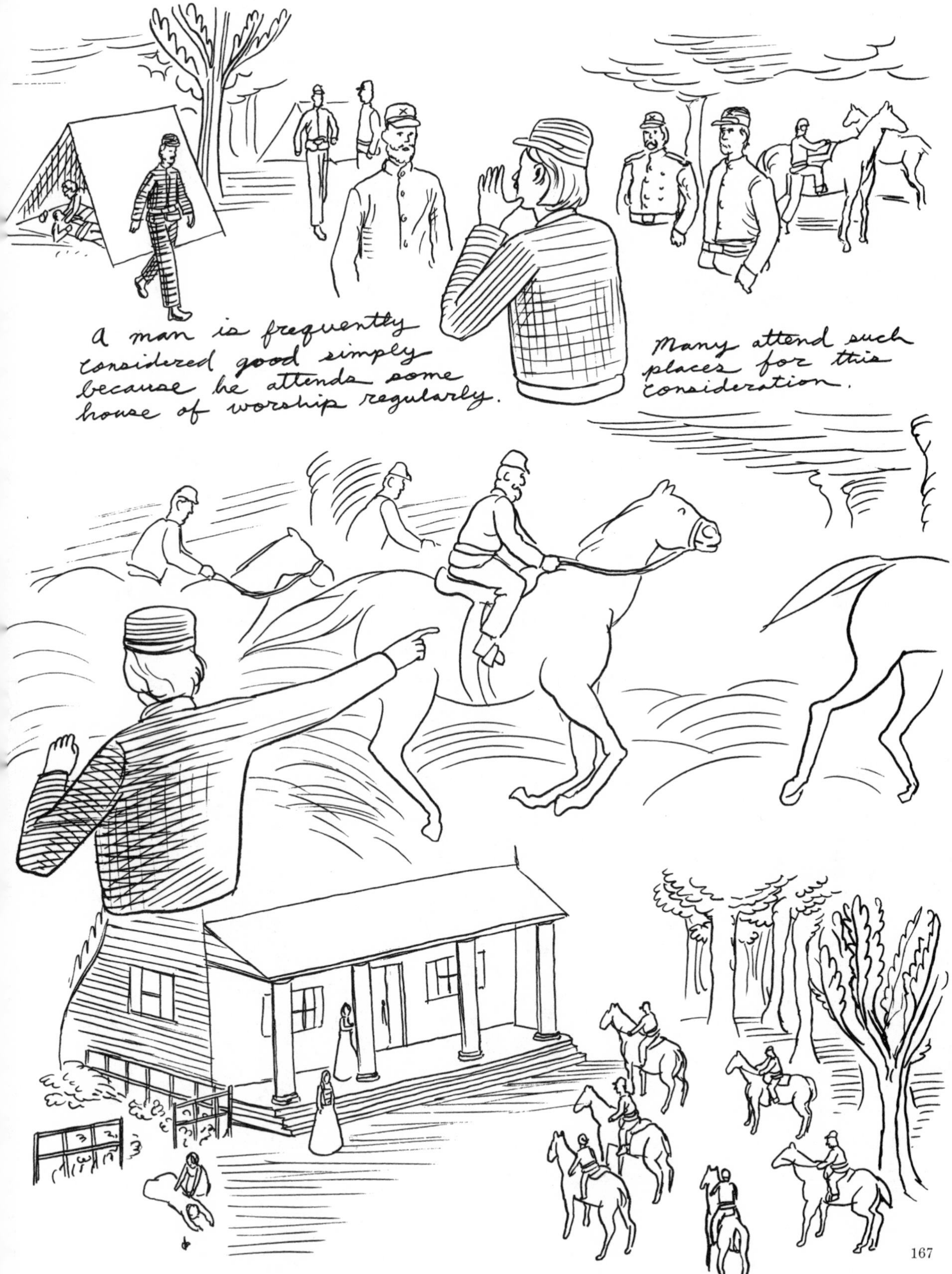
A man is frequently considered good simply because he attends some house of worship regularly.
Many attend such places for this consideration.

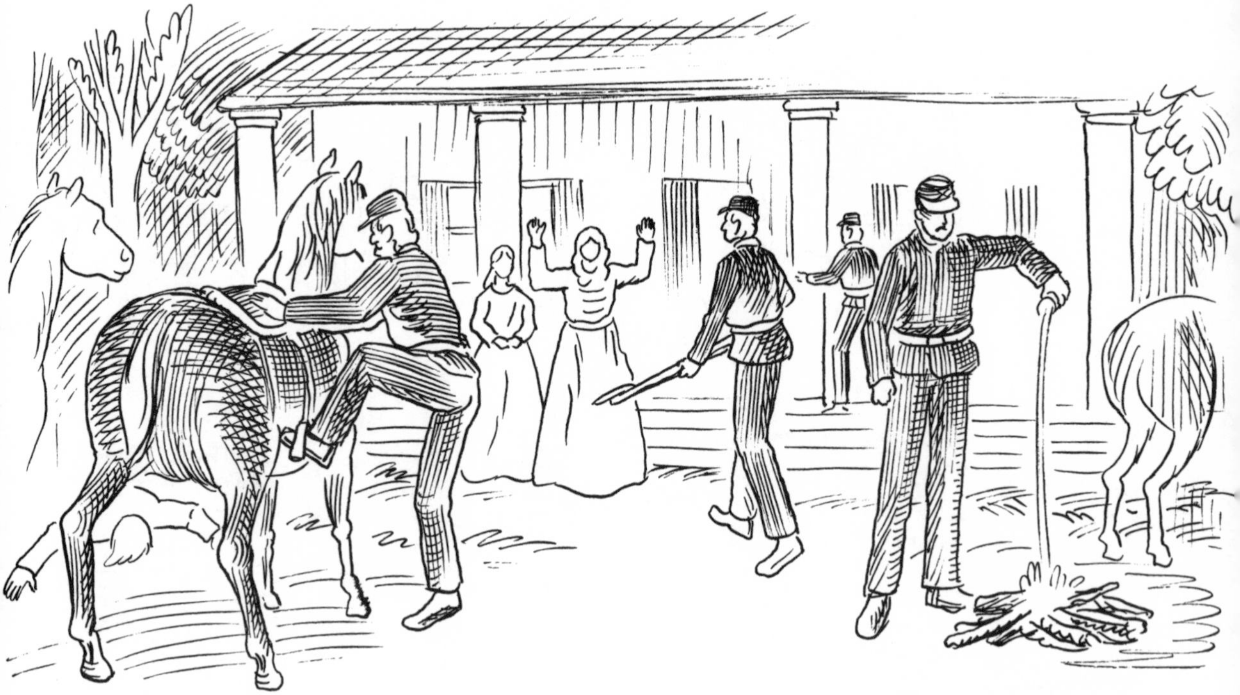

I would rather do one good act than go to church a lifetime without doing it, and would rather take the chance of the one act than all the professions in the world. Goodness is an active principle. It is simply acting up to thy own highest idea of right. Goodness is the fruit of the action.

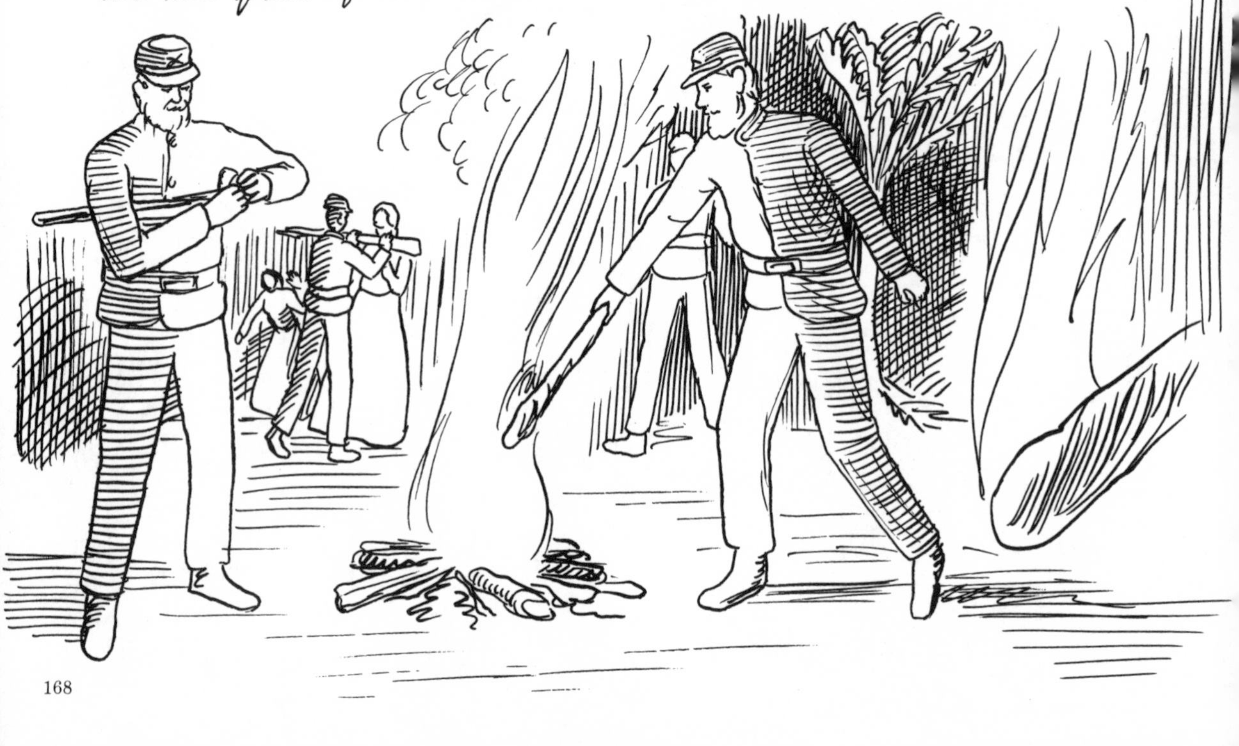

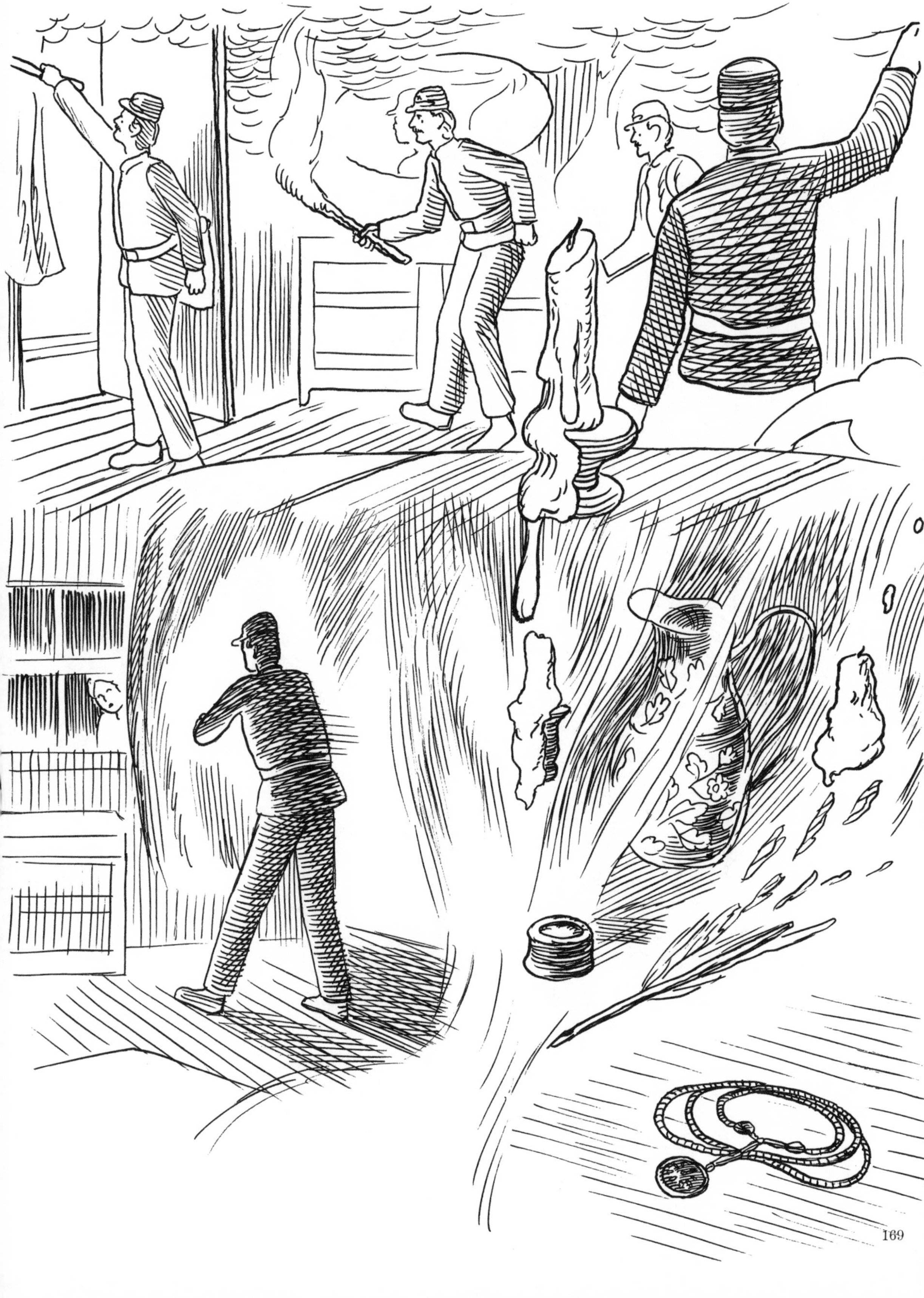

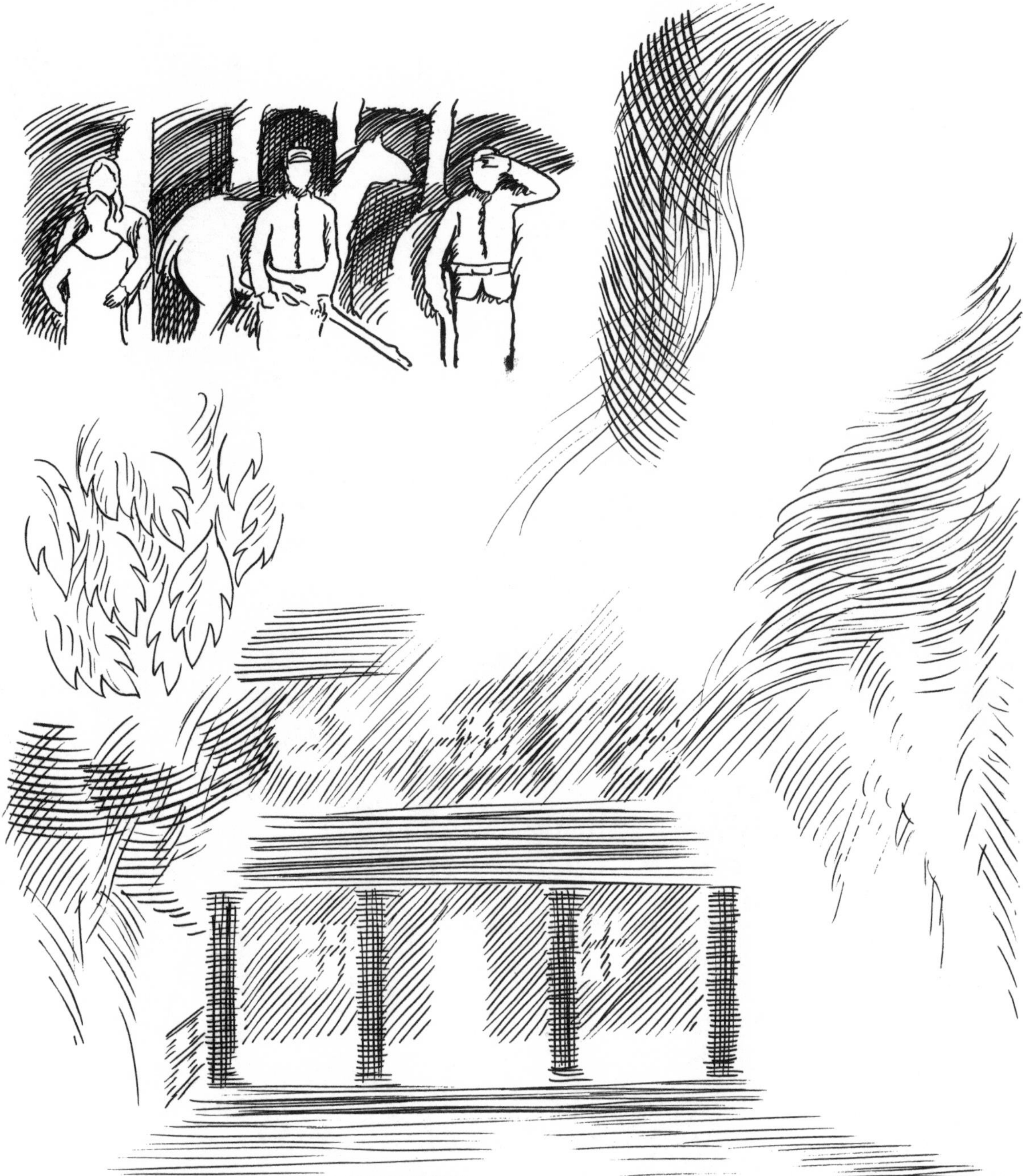

All we do to others is done in reality unto ourselves.
For every violation of his own inward light of truth
man must suffer, and he will soon cease to kindle
fires which burn only himself.

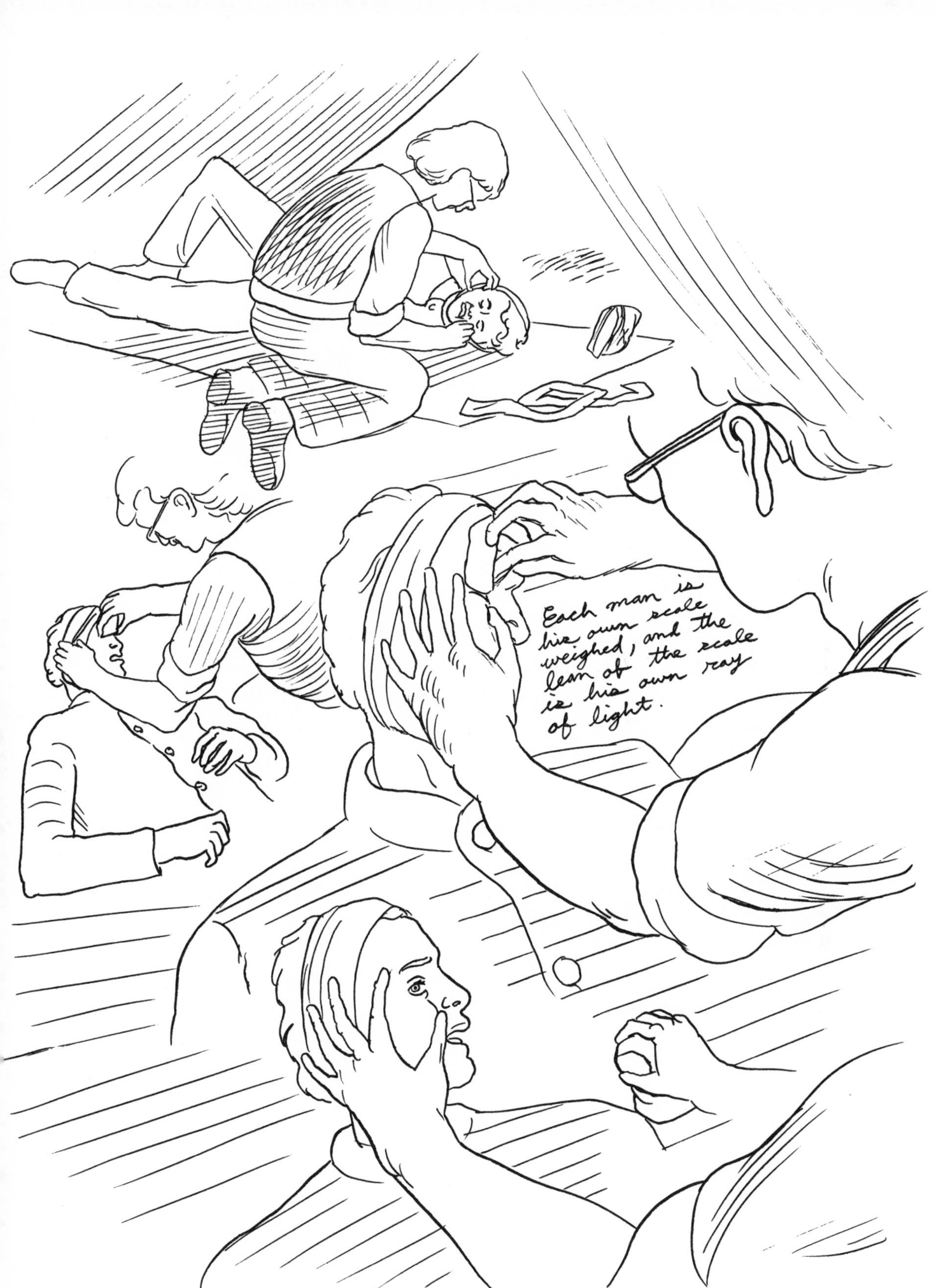
Each man is his own scale weighed, and the lean of the scale is his own ray of light.

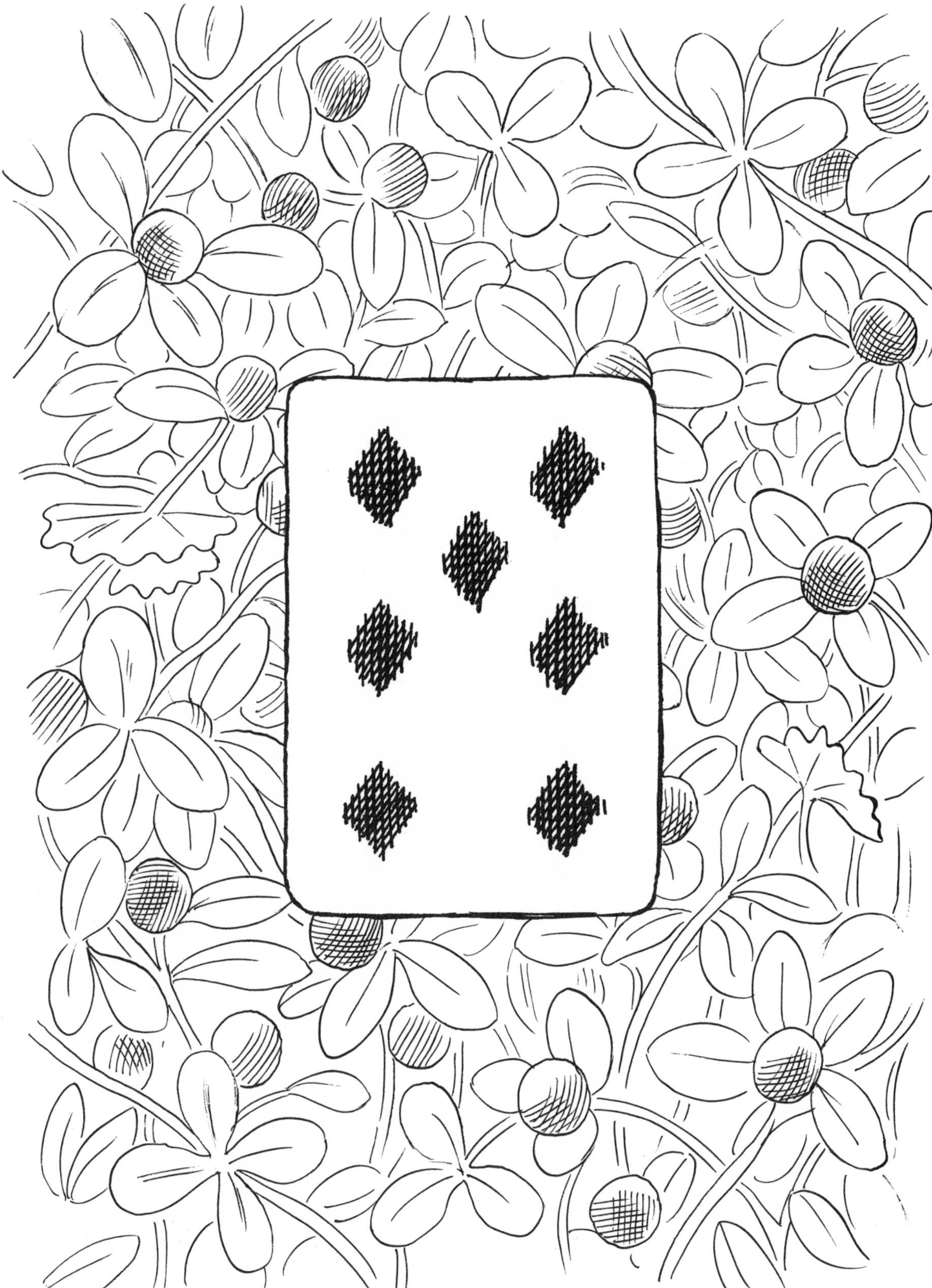

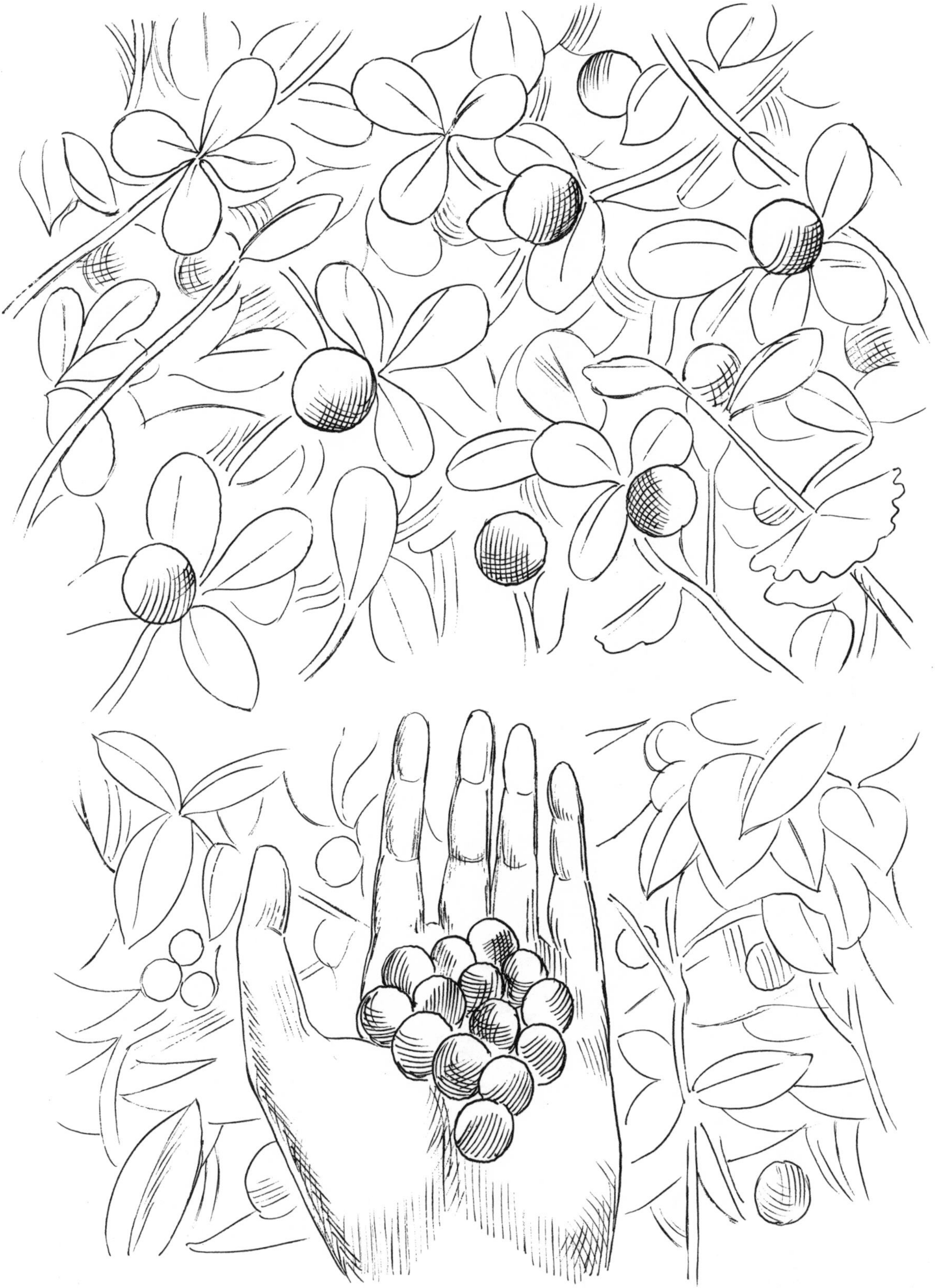

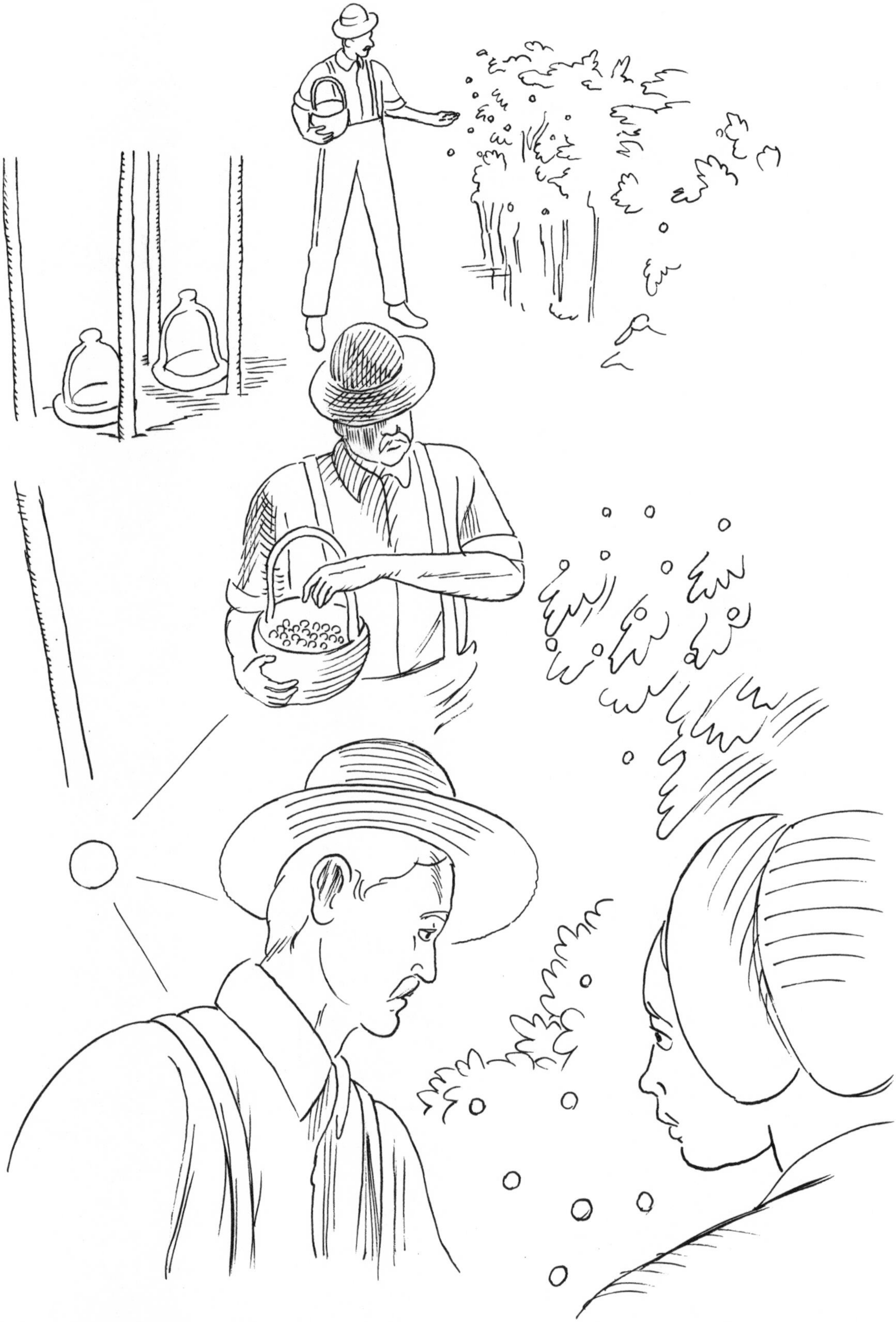

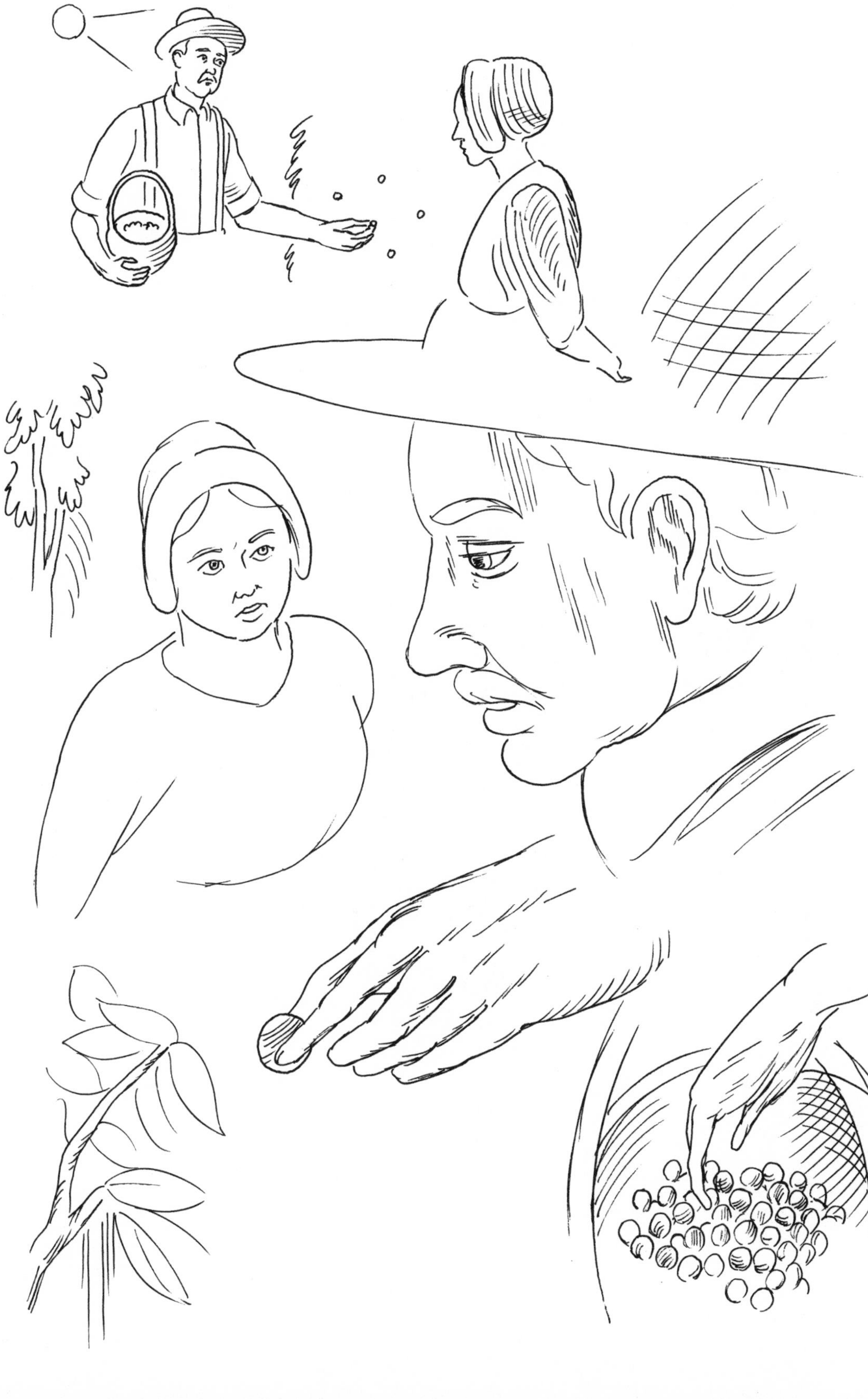

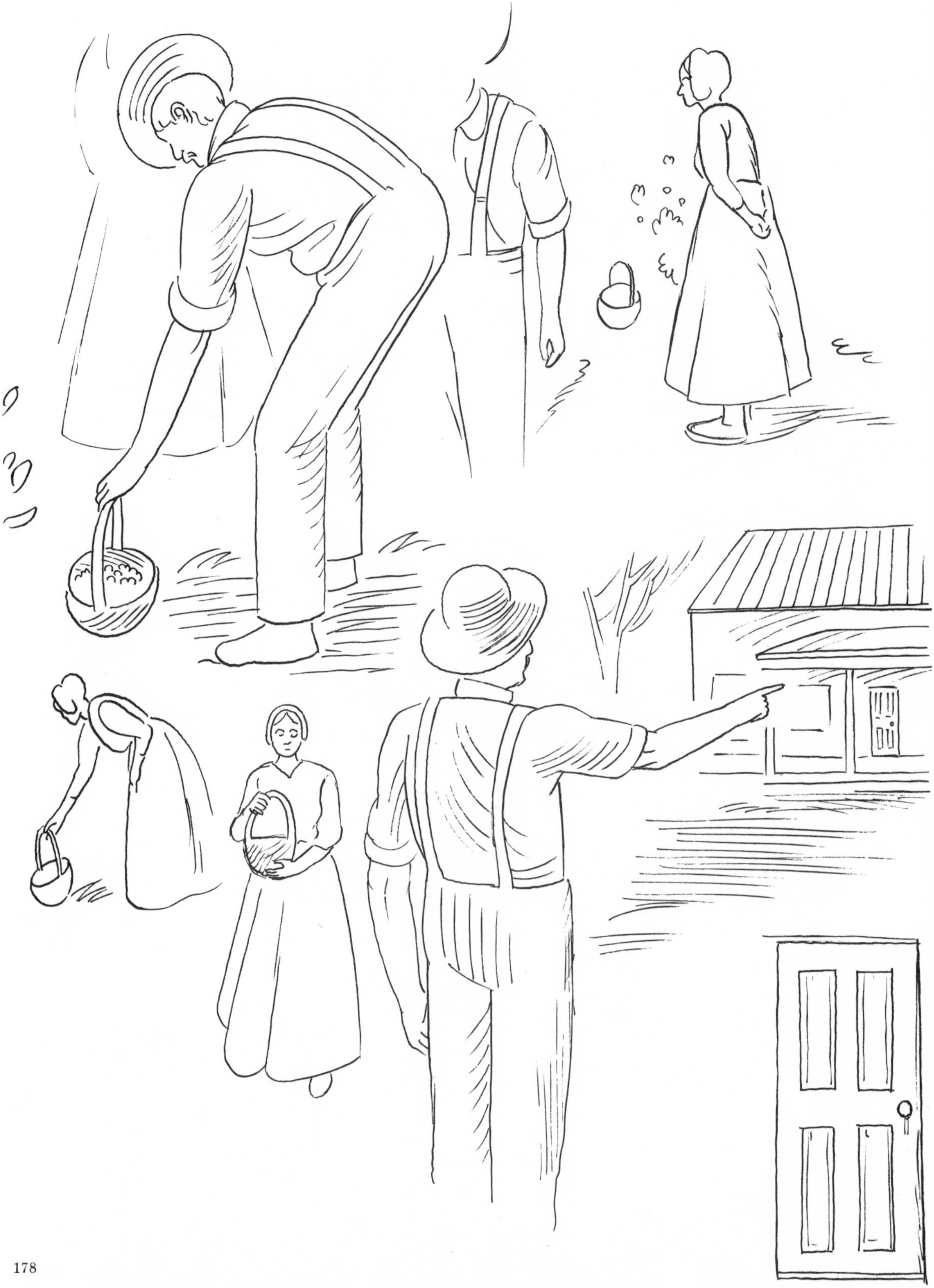

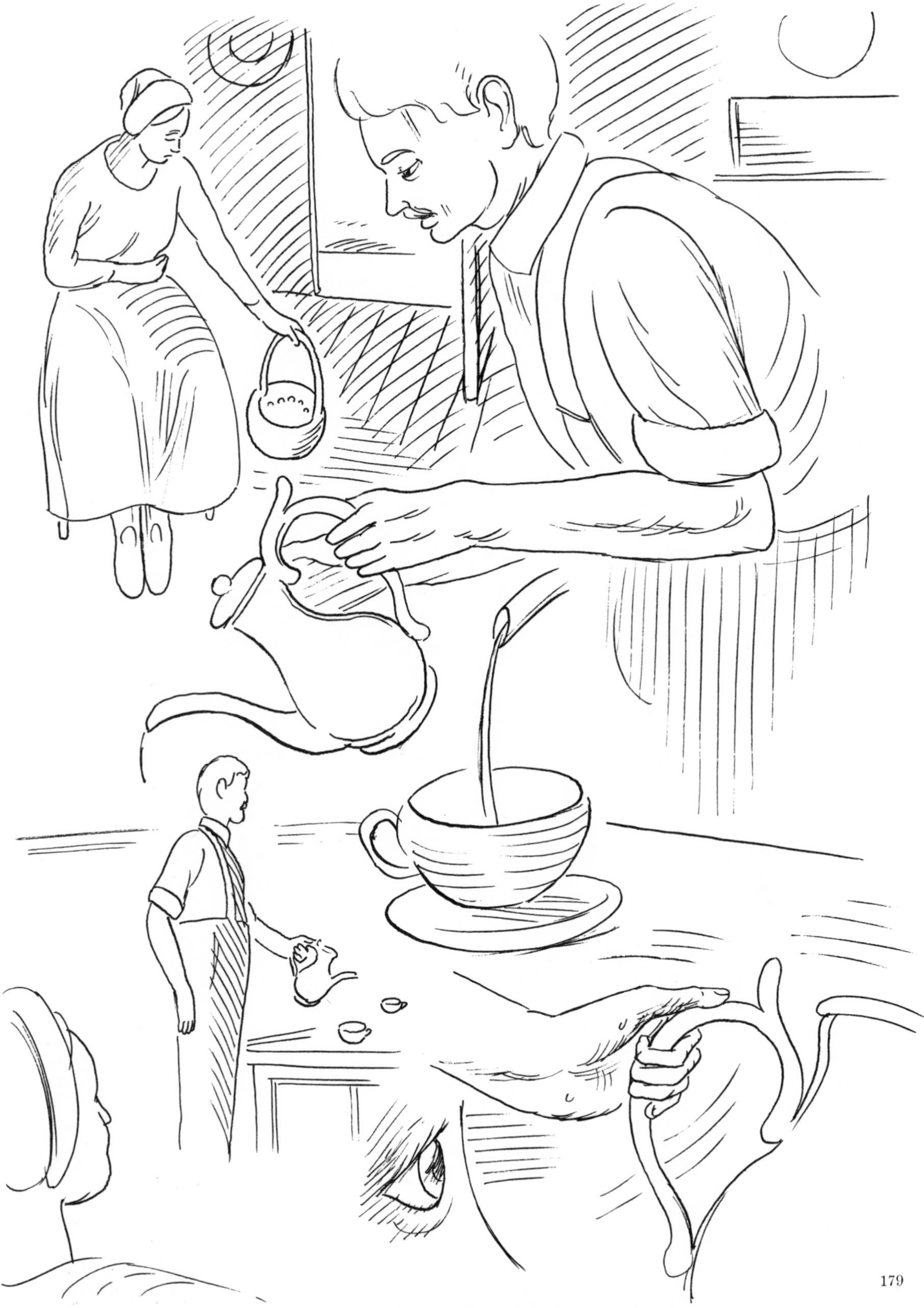

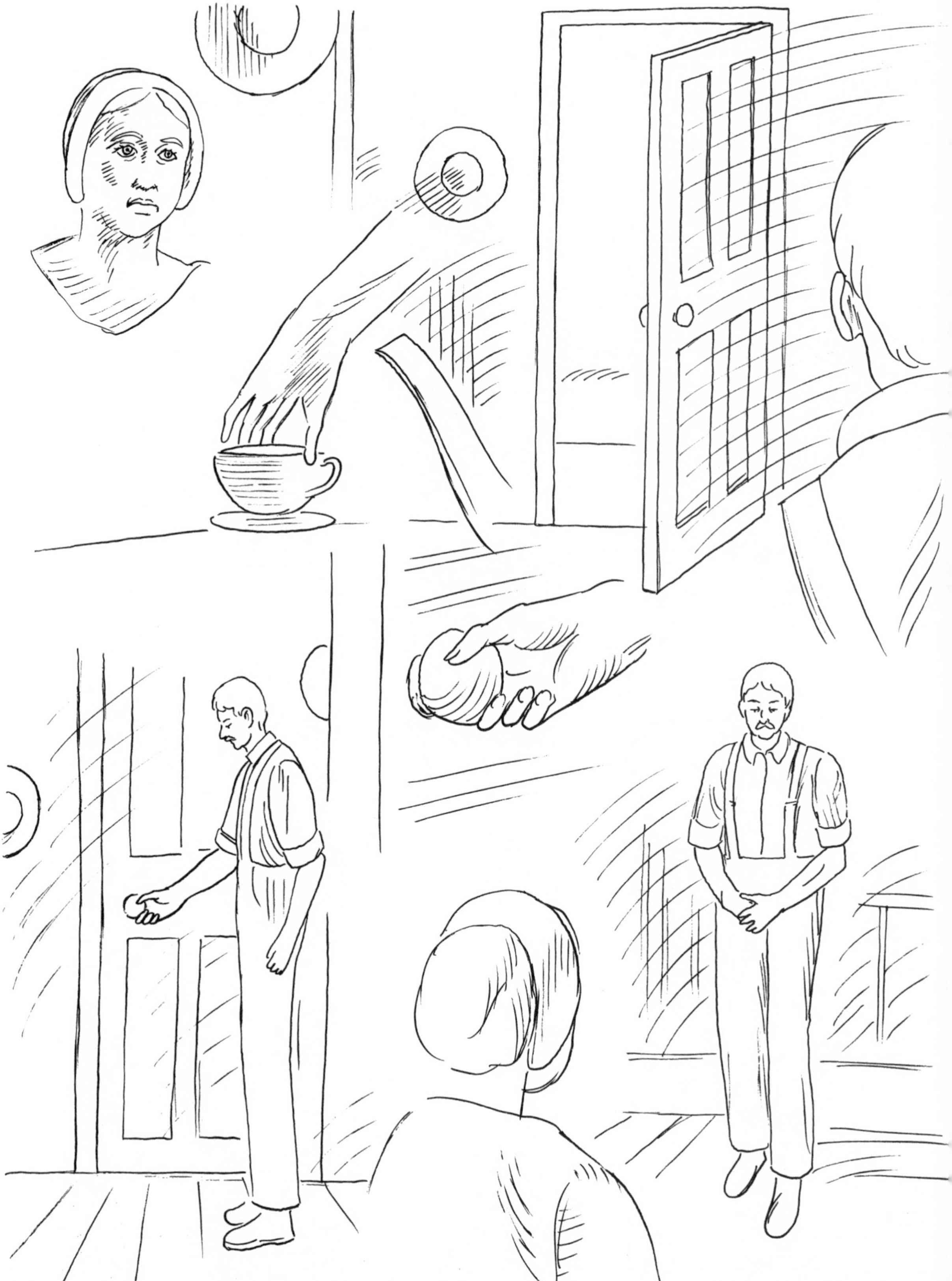

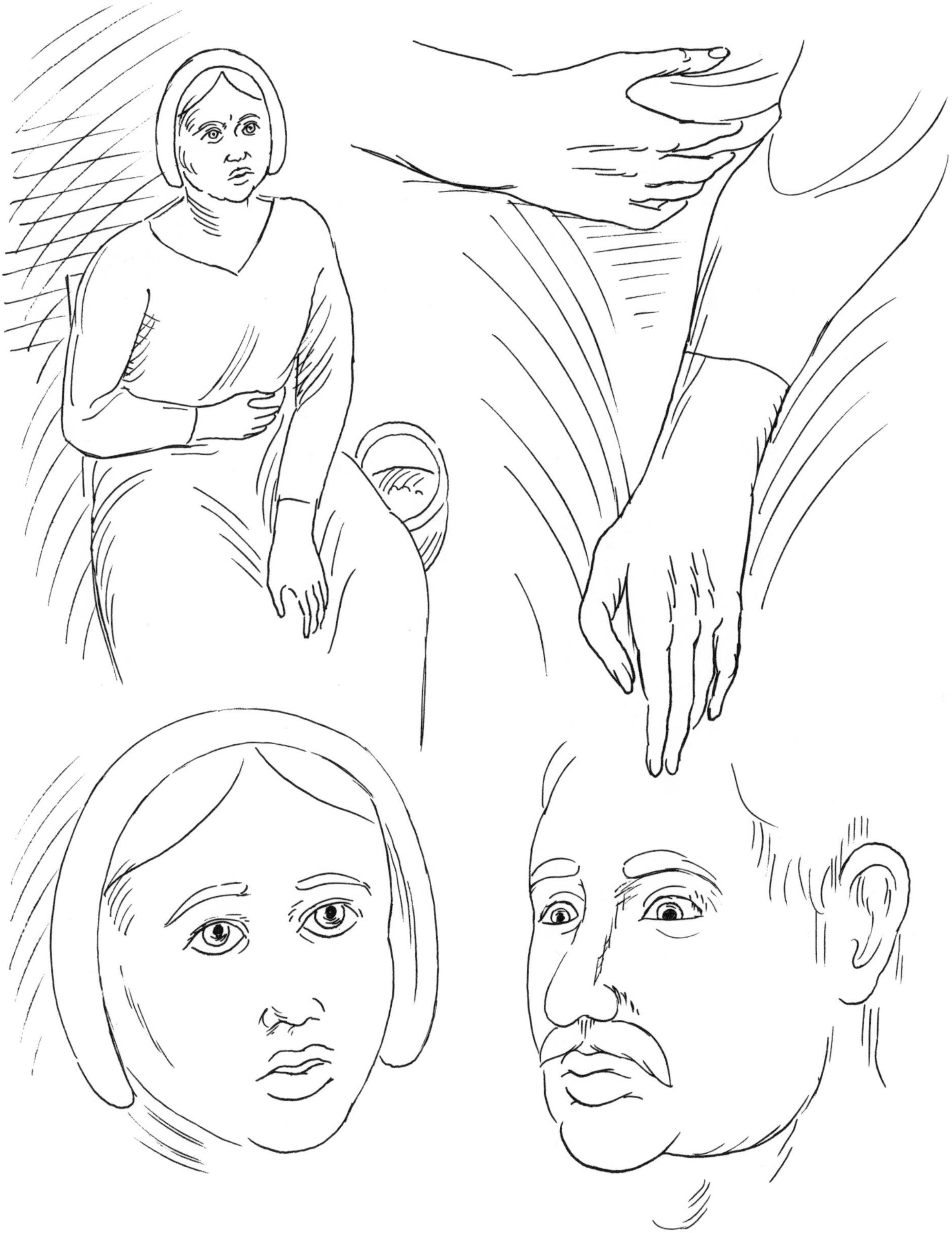

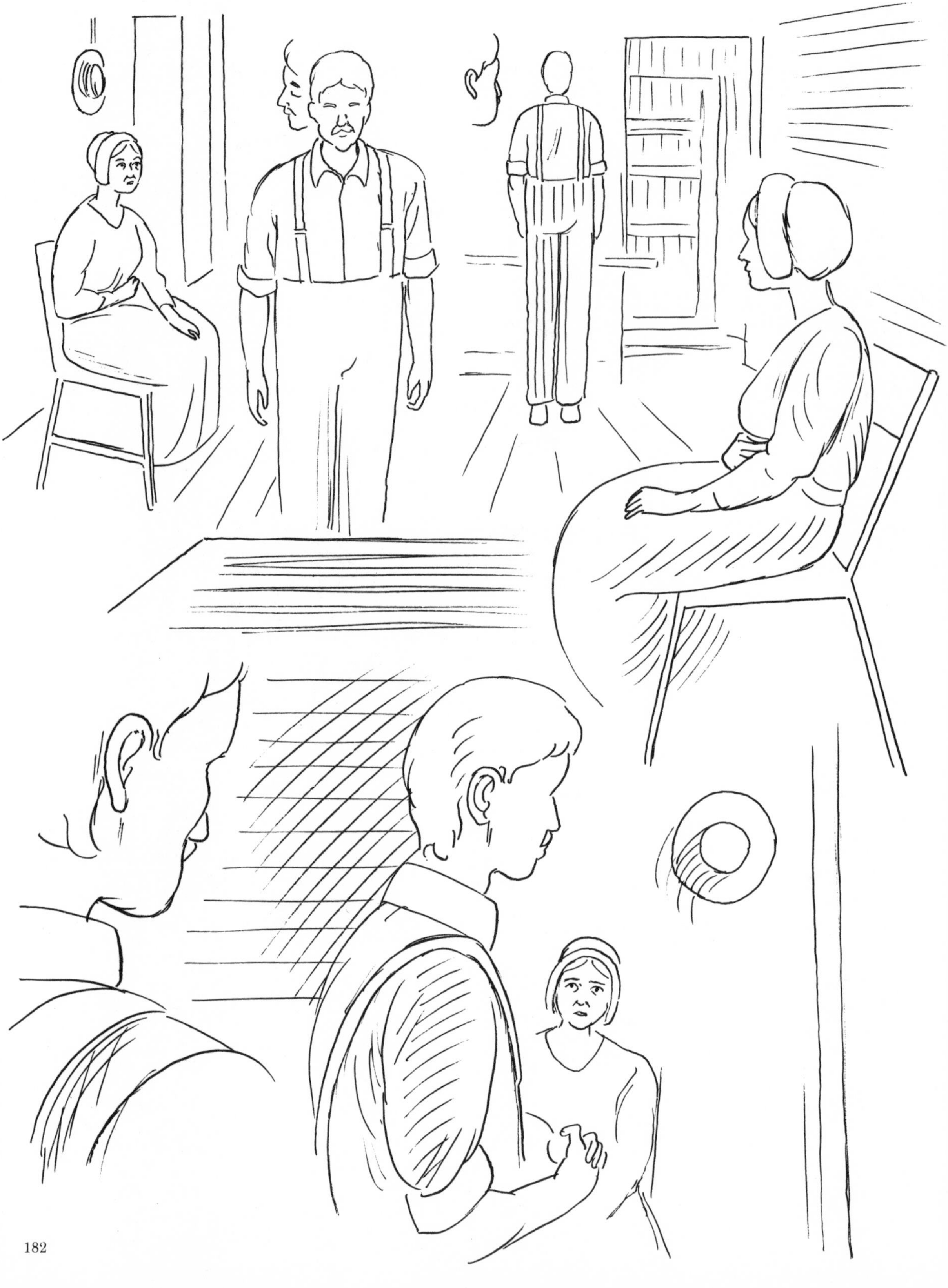

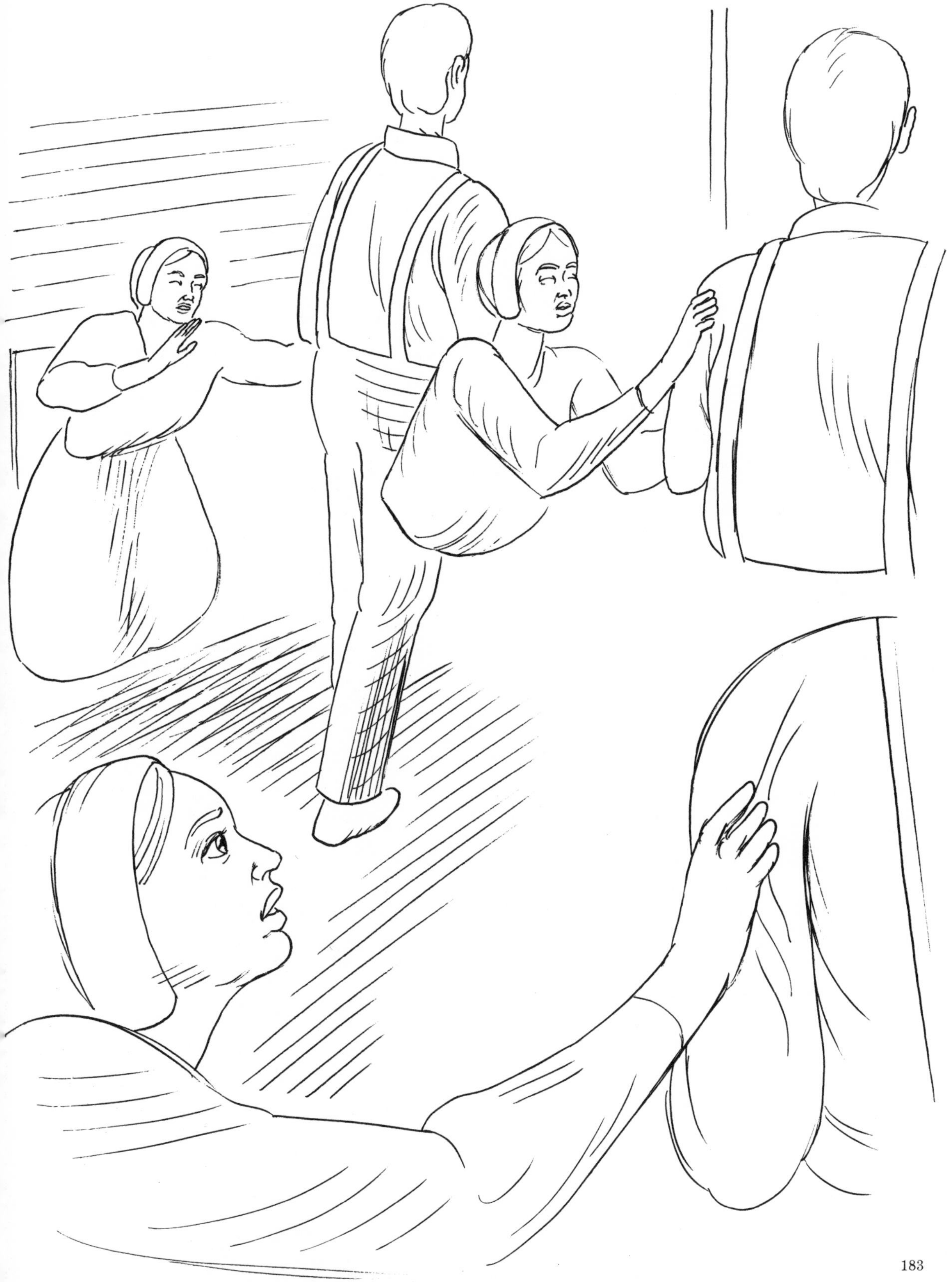

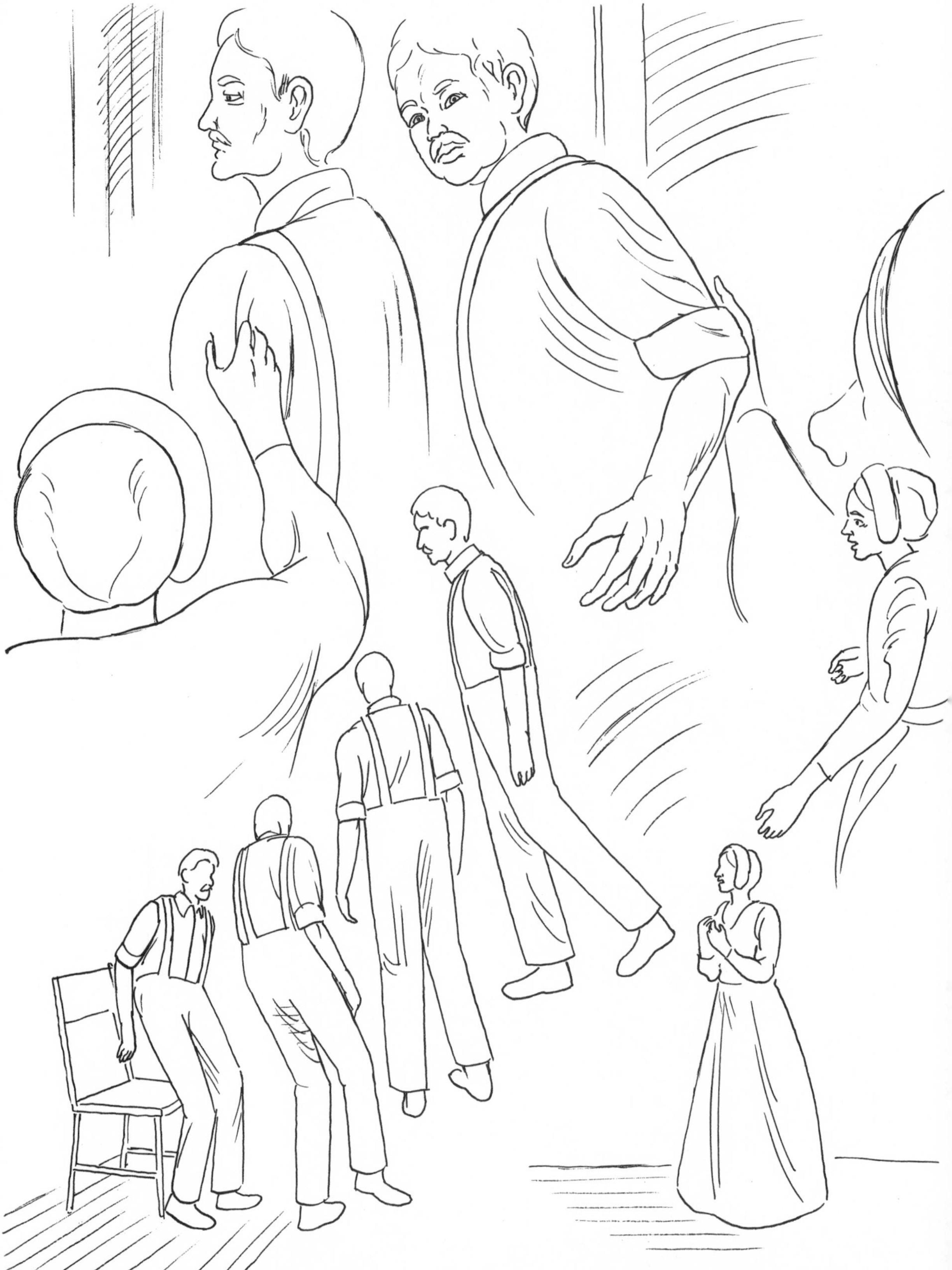

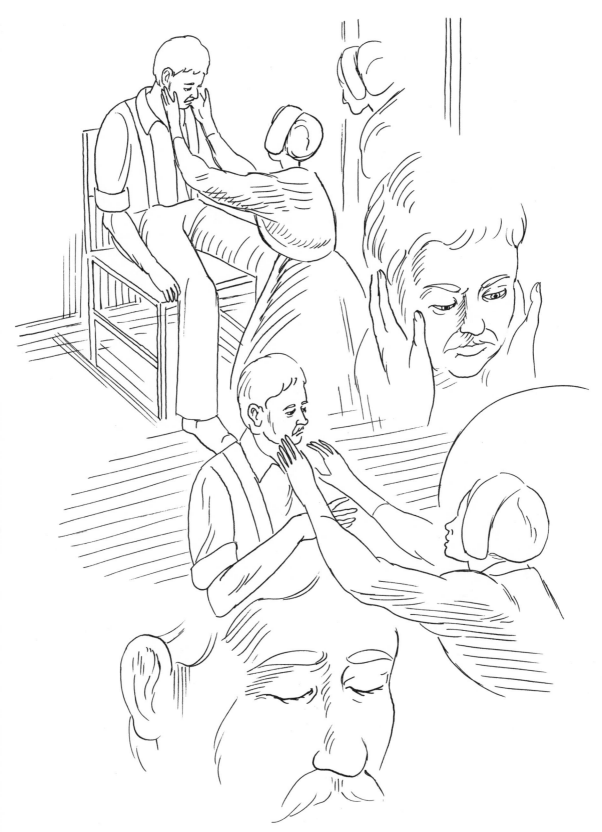

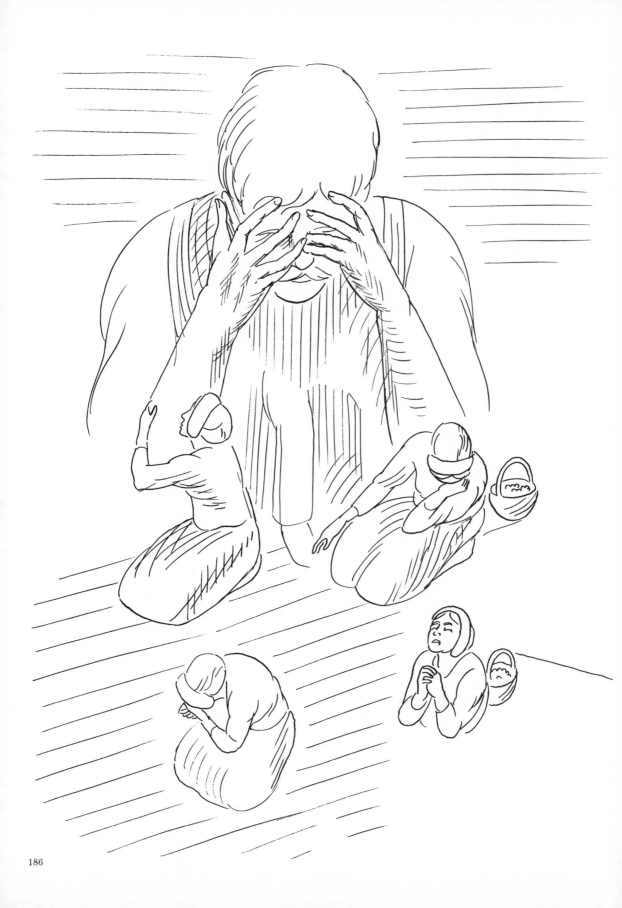

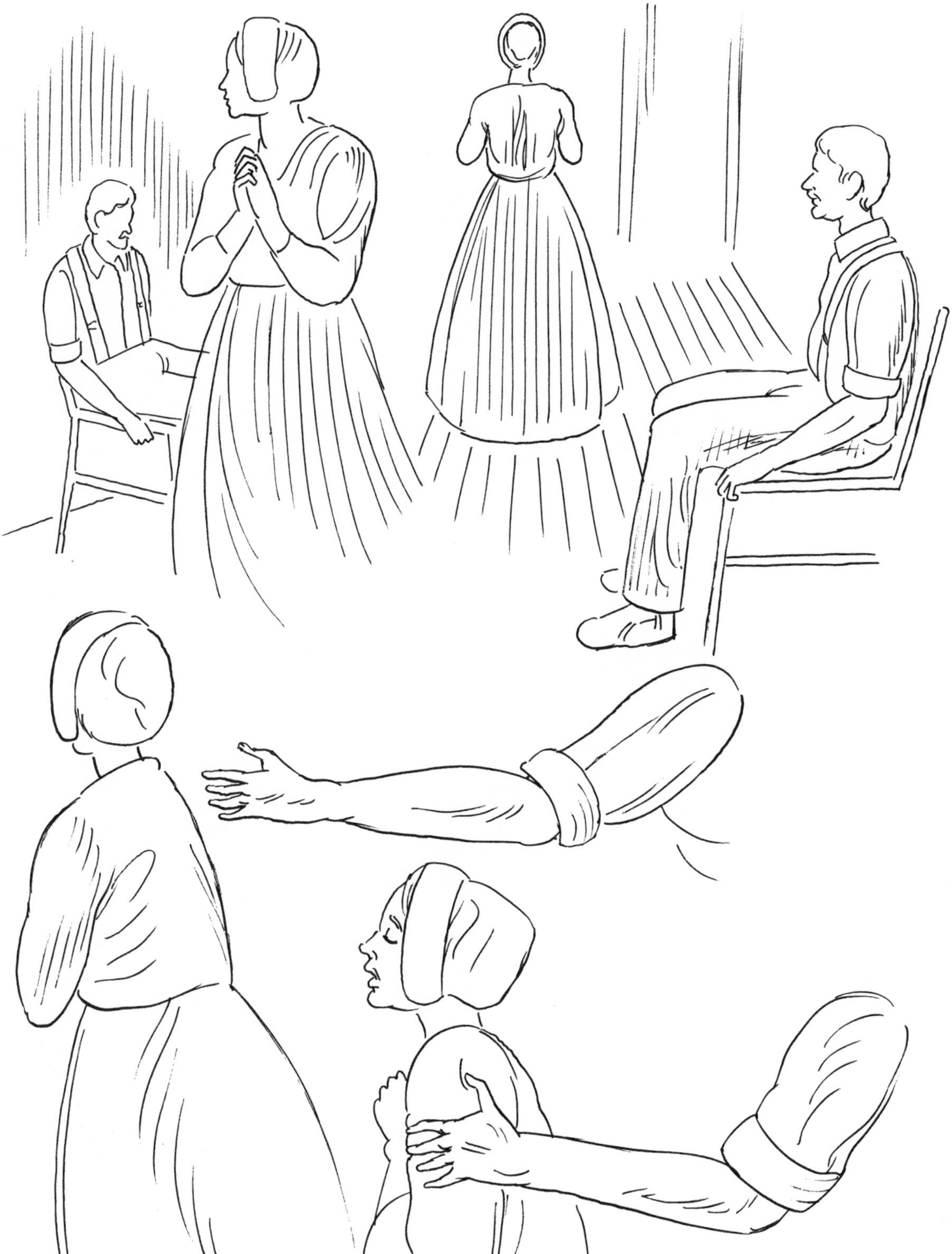

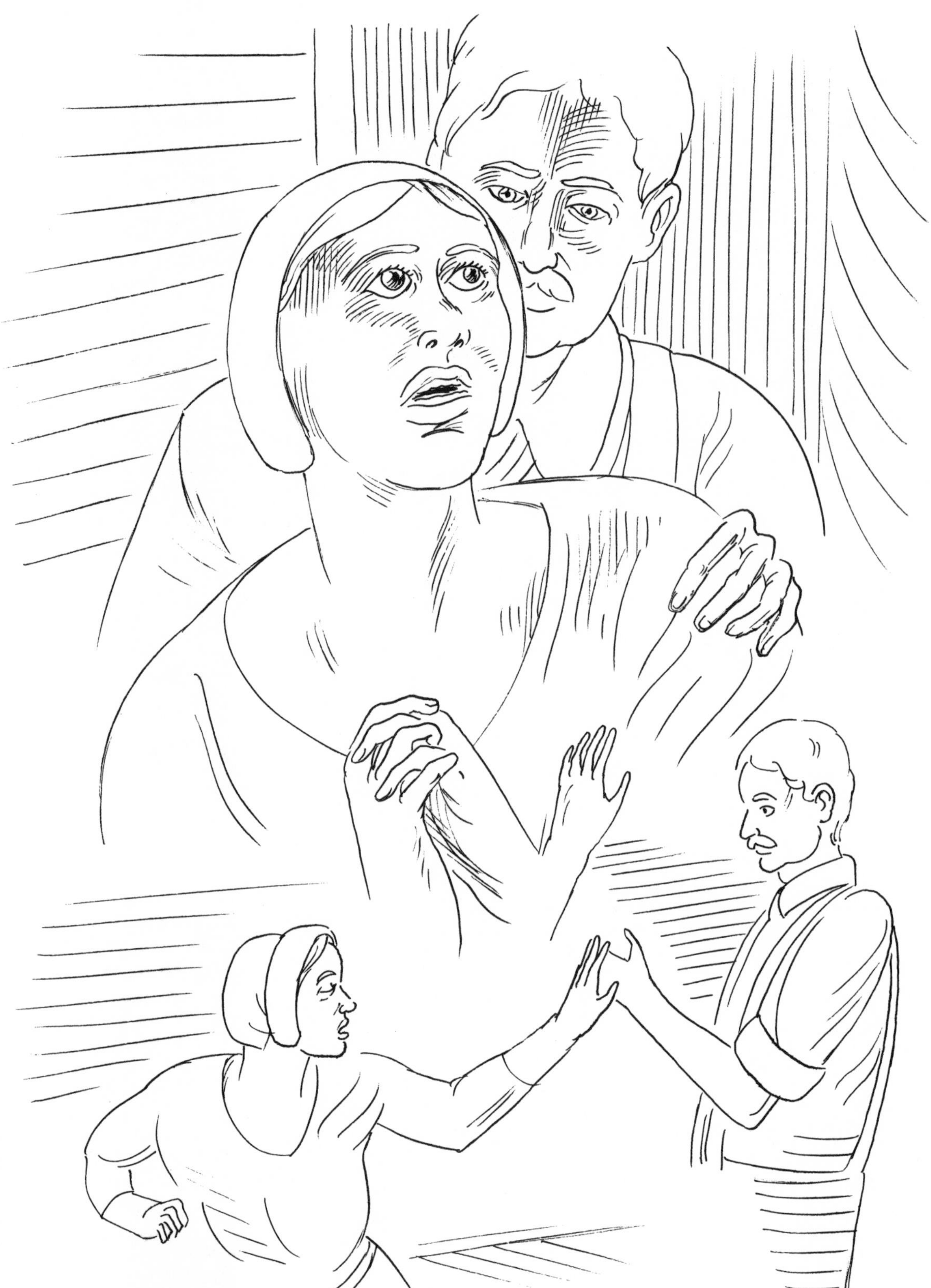

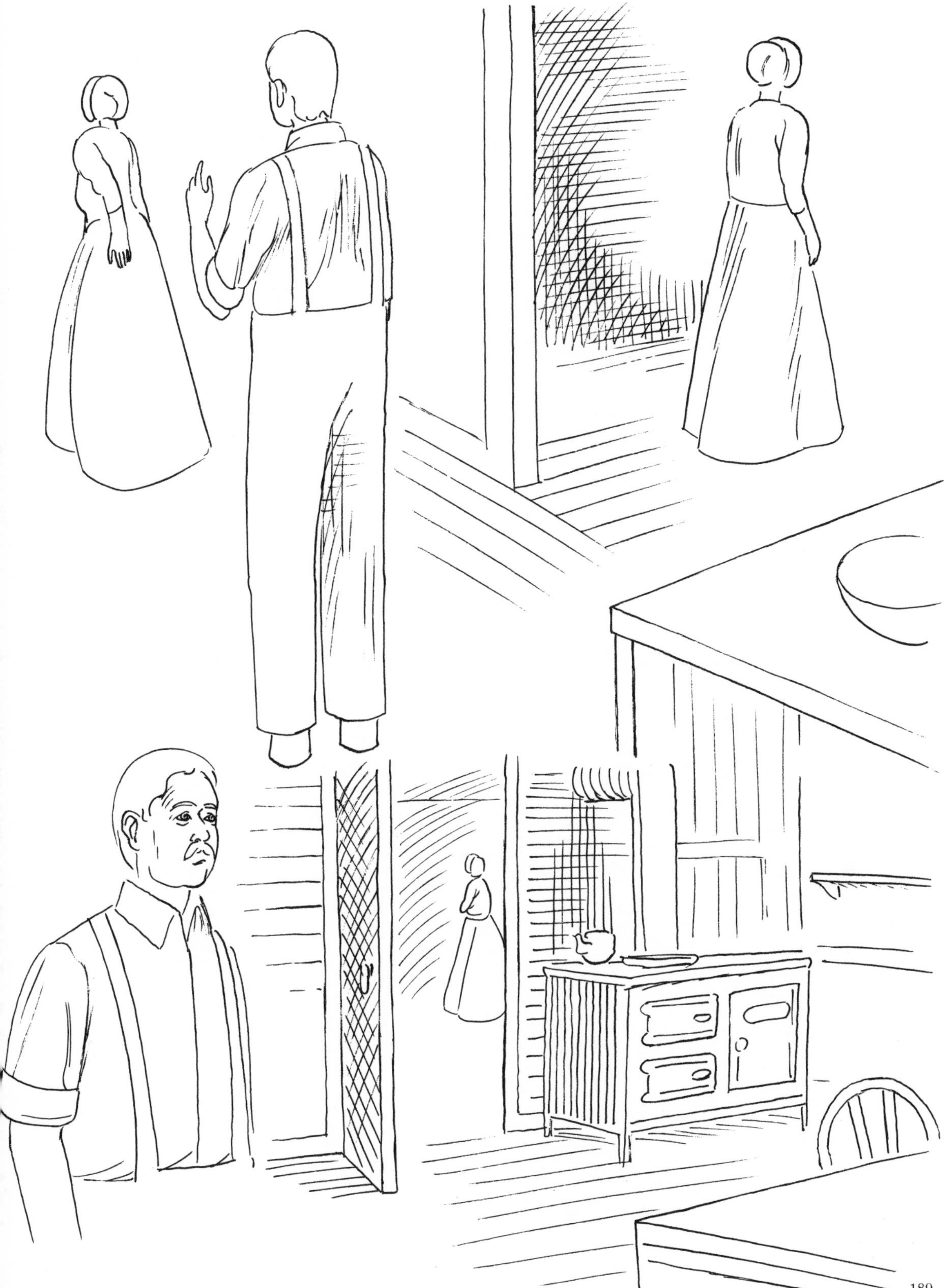

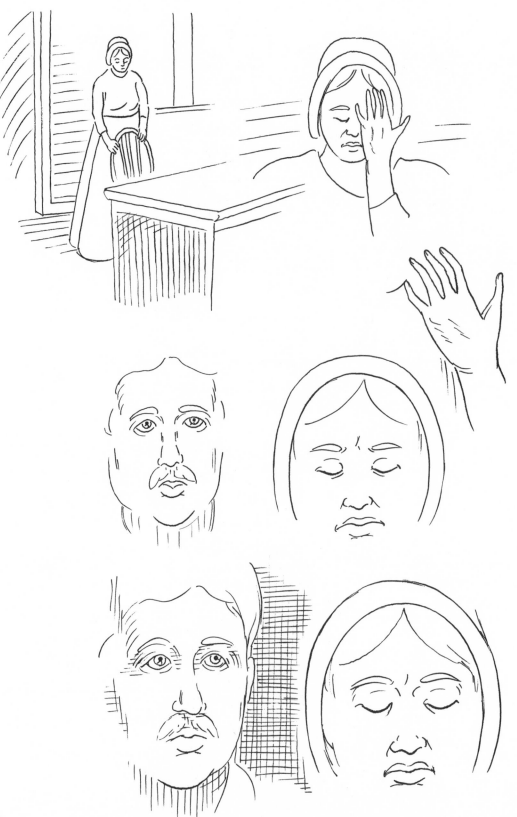

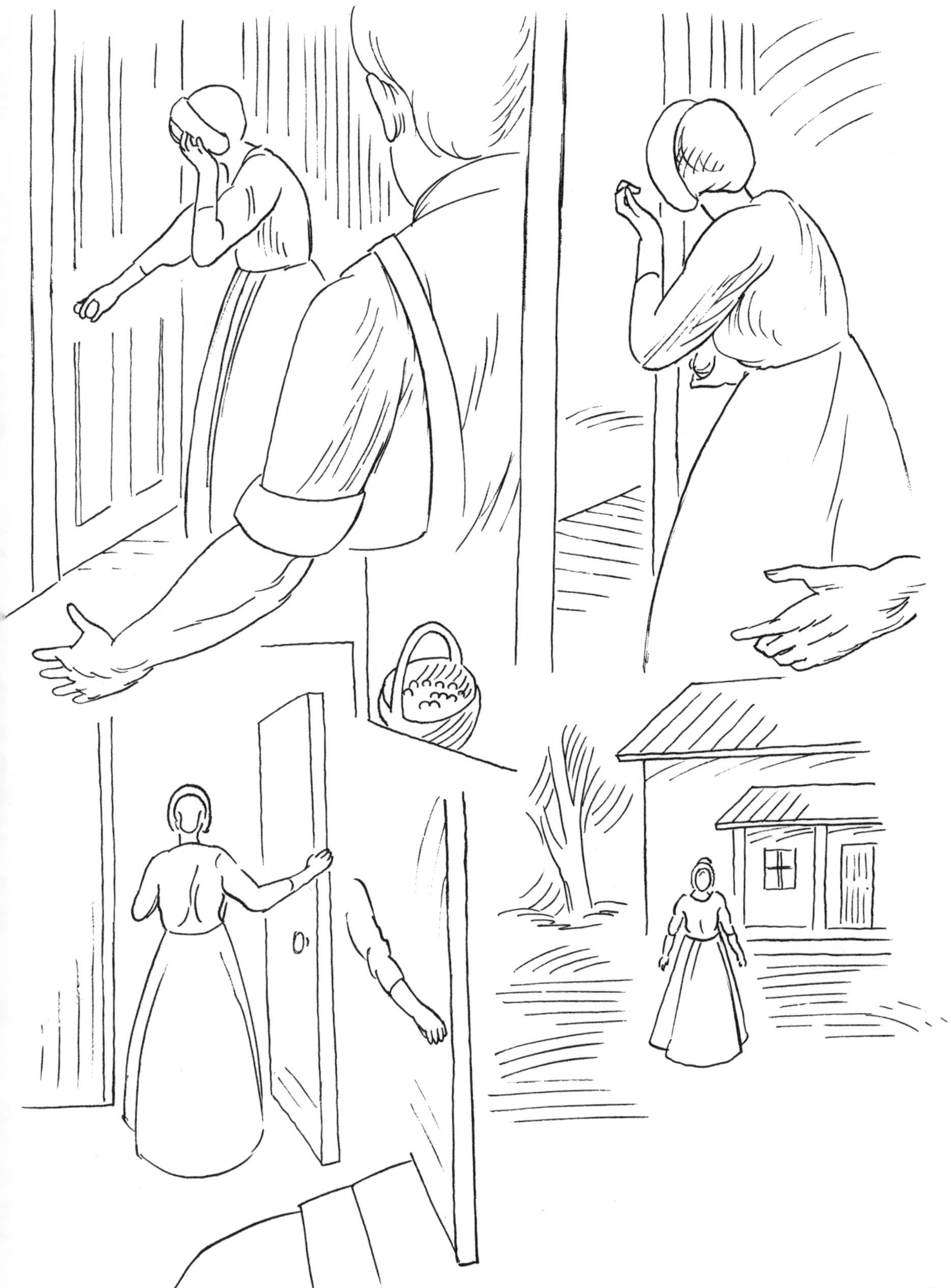

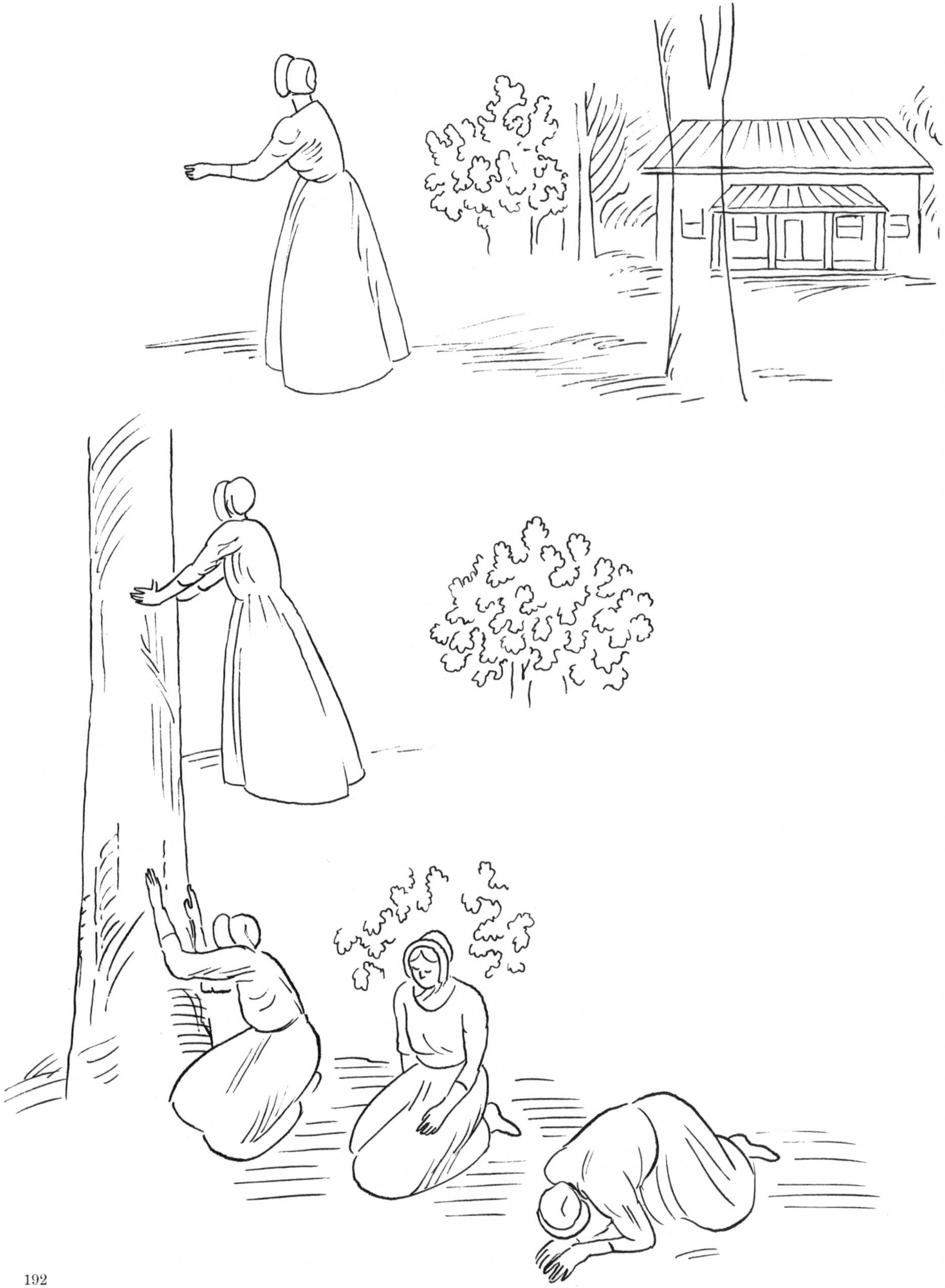

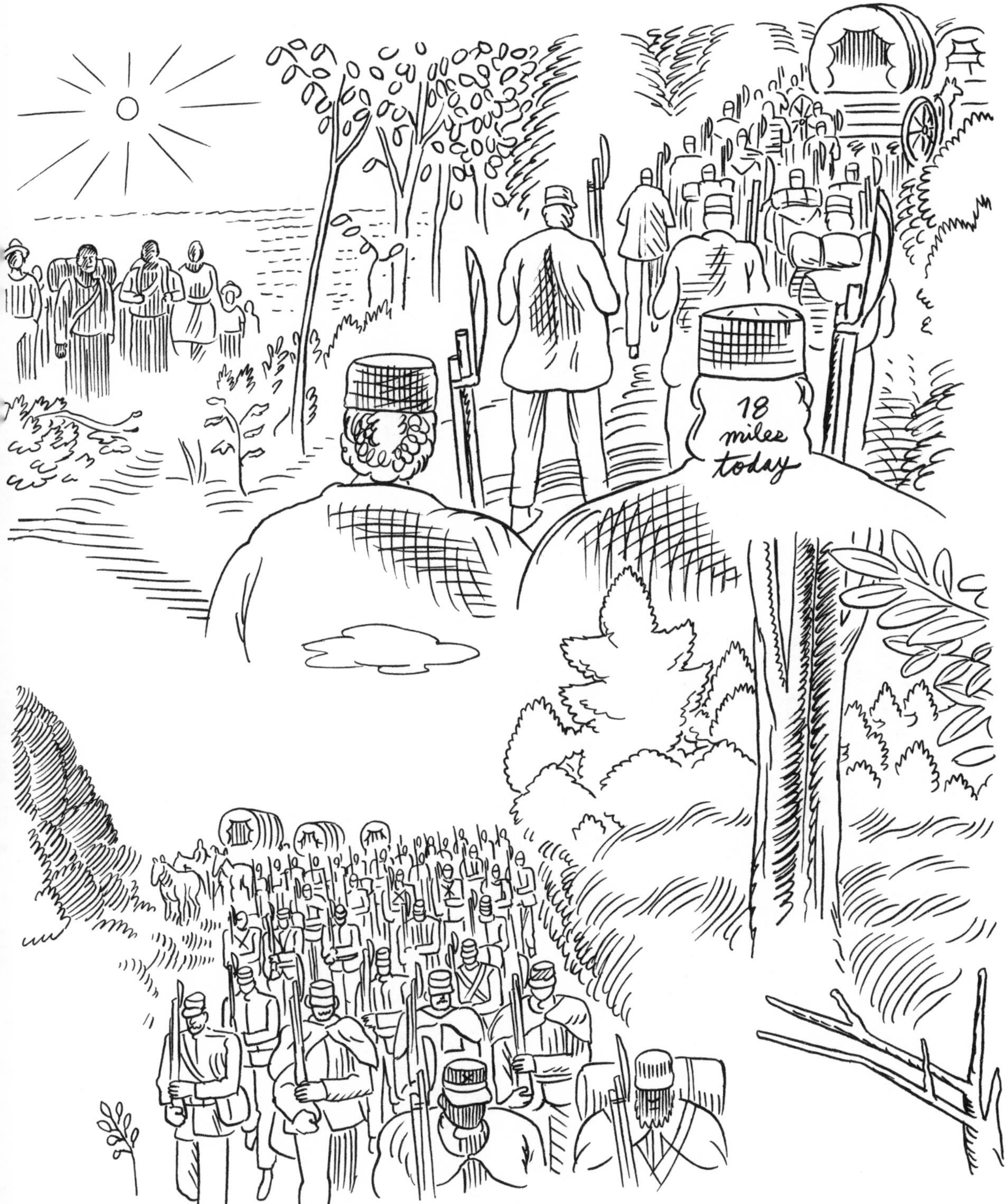
18 miles today

In the present we are most barbarous animals compared with our own high ideal of right and justice, of love and light. How will we look when man in the great future shall gaze back upon us?

Compare the bloody deeds of the present with our professions of love and mercy. The future loses sight of our professions and judges us as we are.

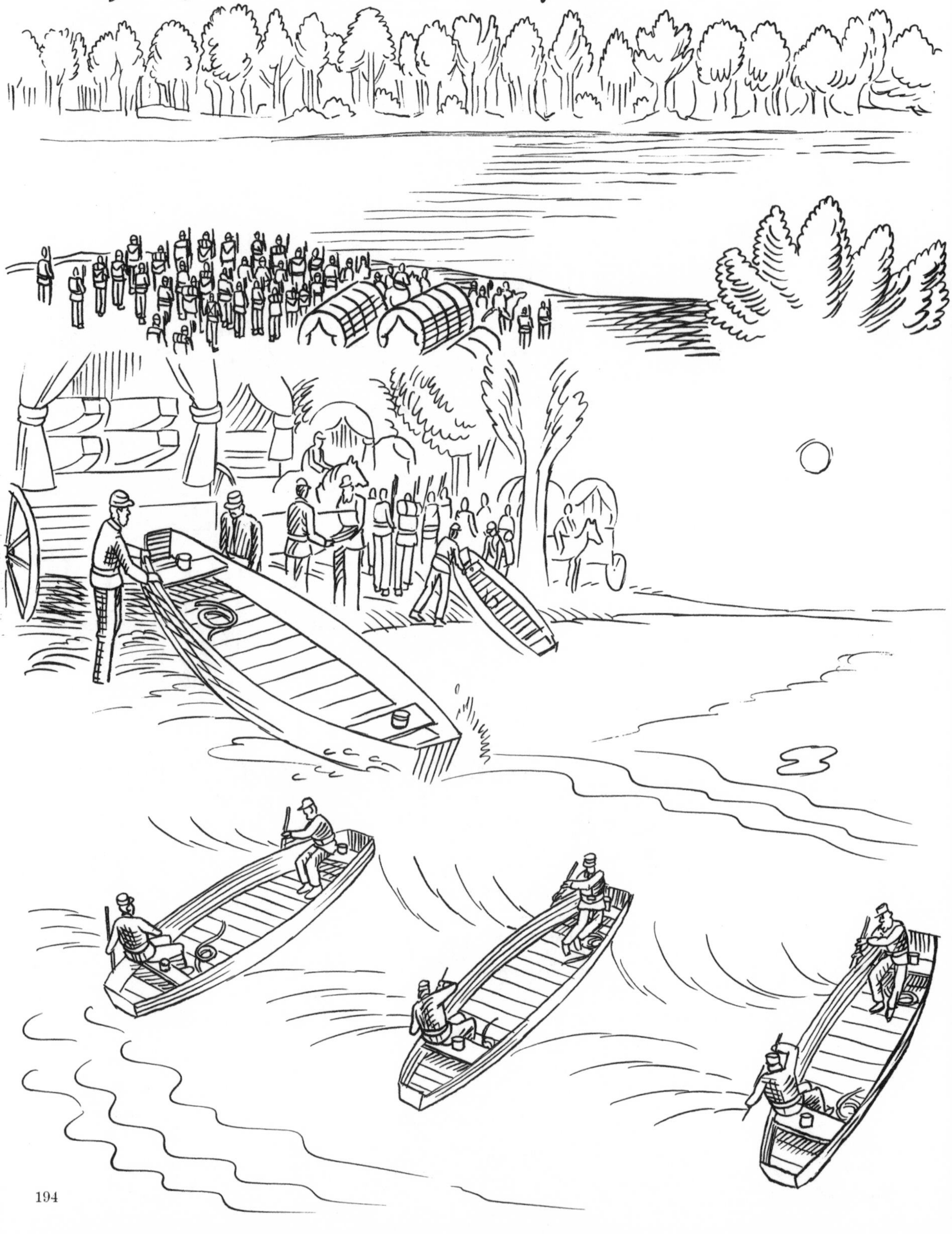

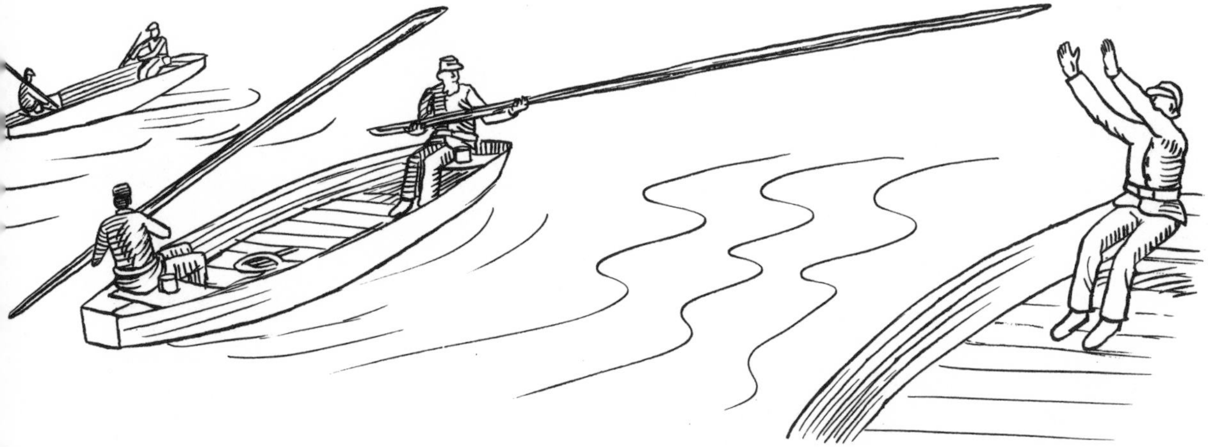

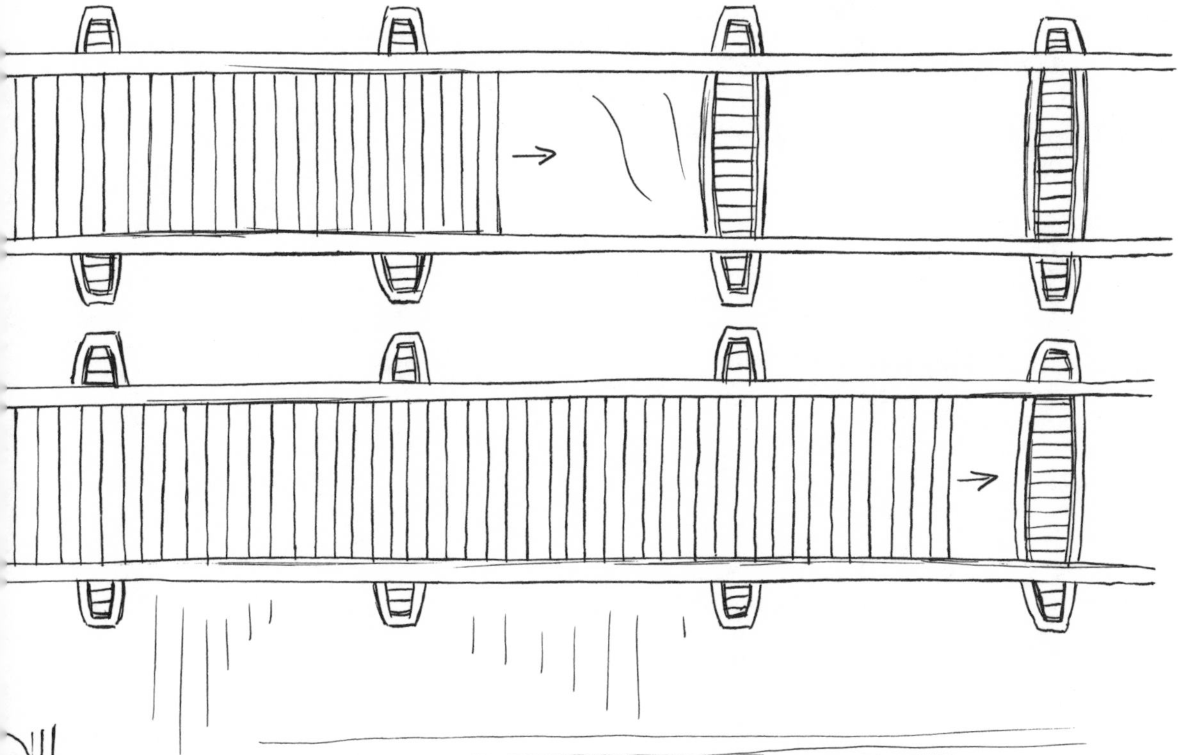

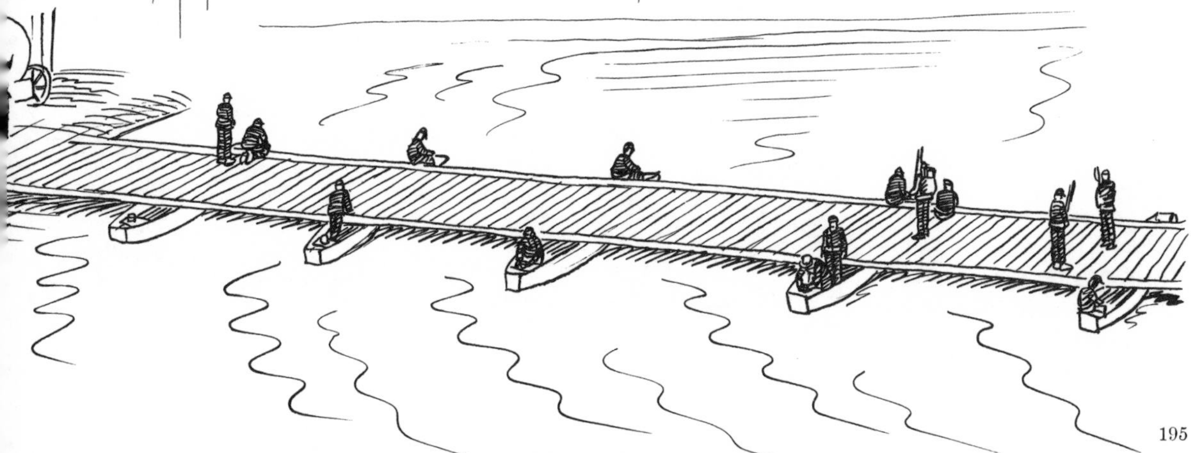

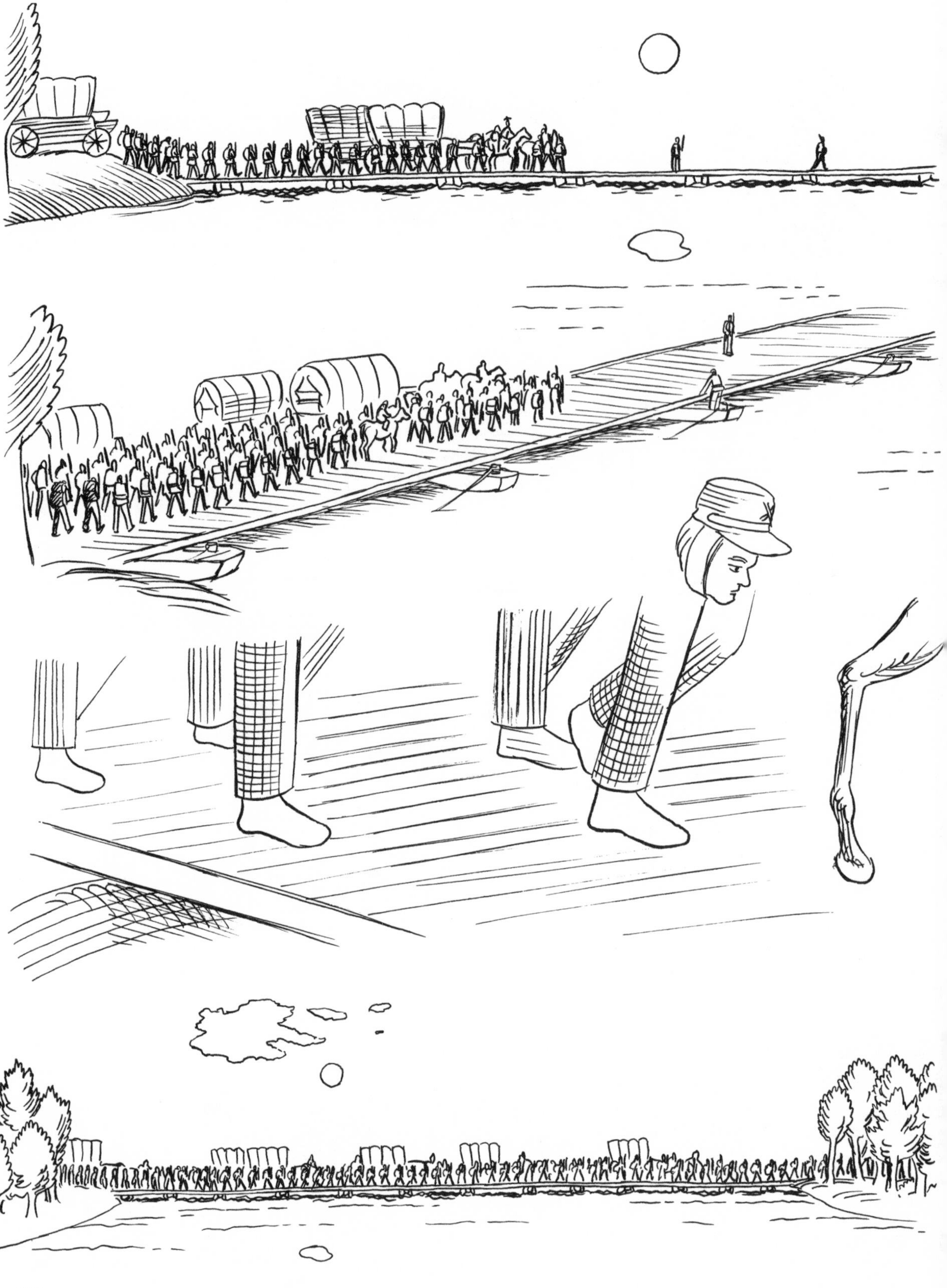

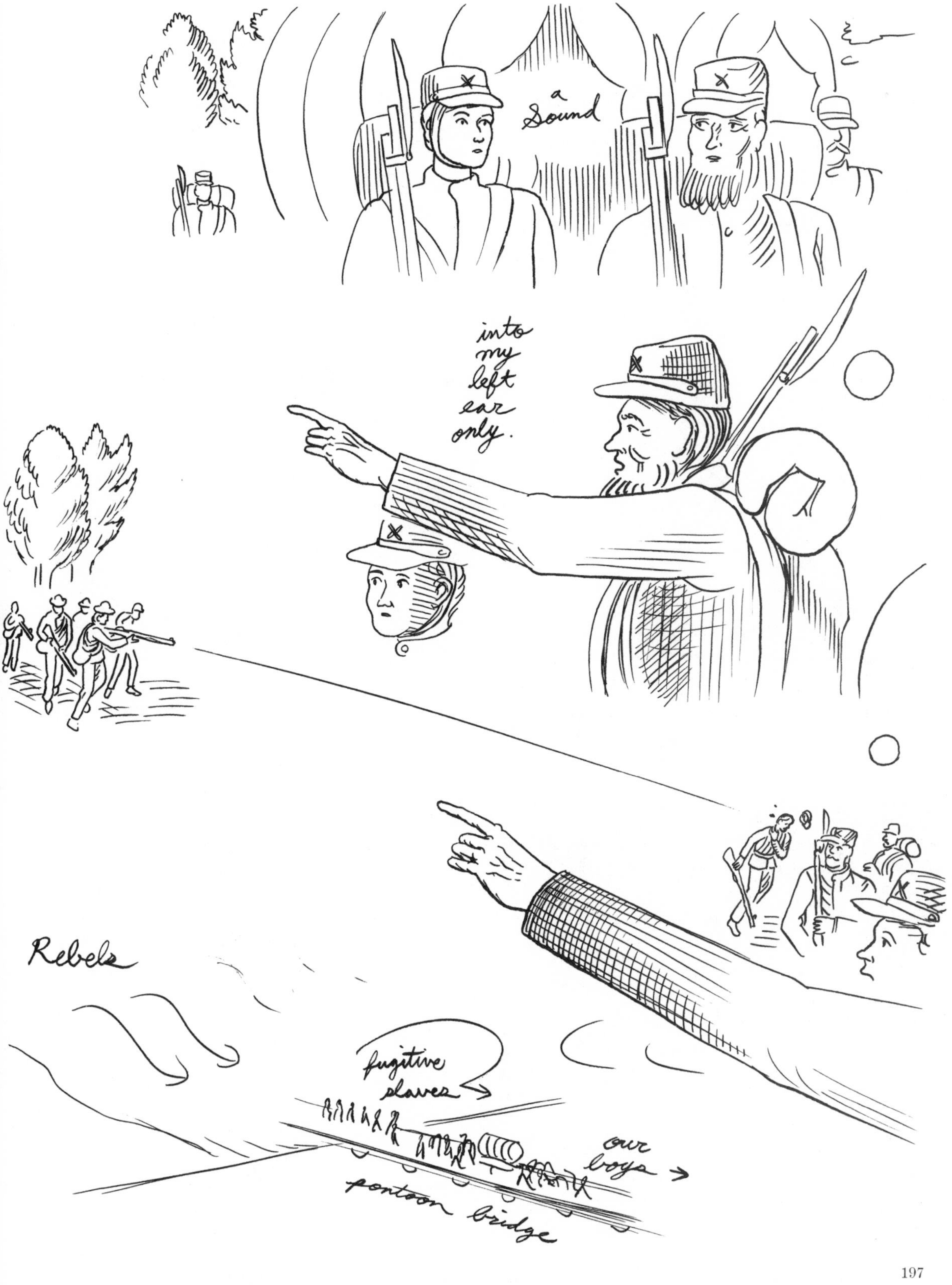
a Sound
into my left ear only.
Rebels
fugitive slaves
our boys
pontoon bridge

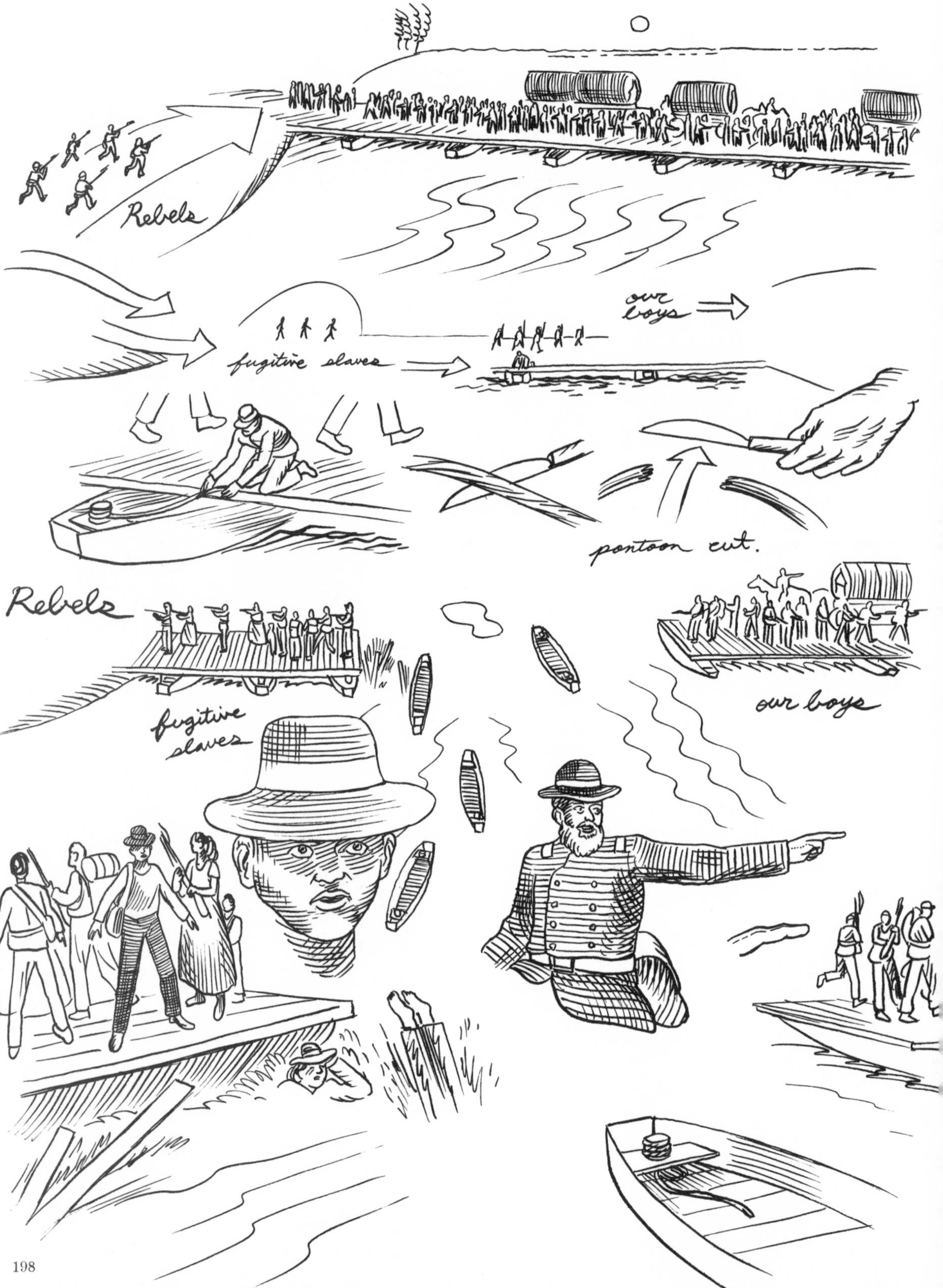

Rebels
fugitive slaves
our boys
pontoon cut.
Rebels
fugitive slaves
our boys

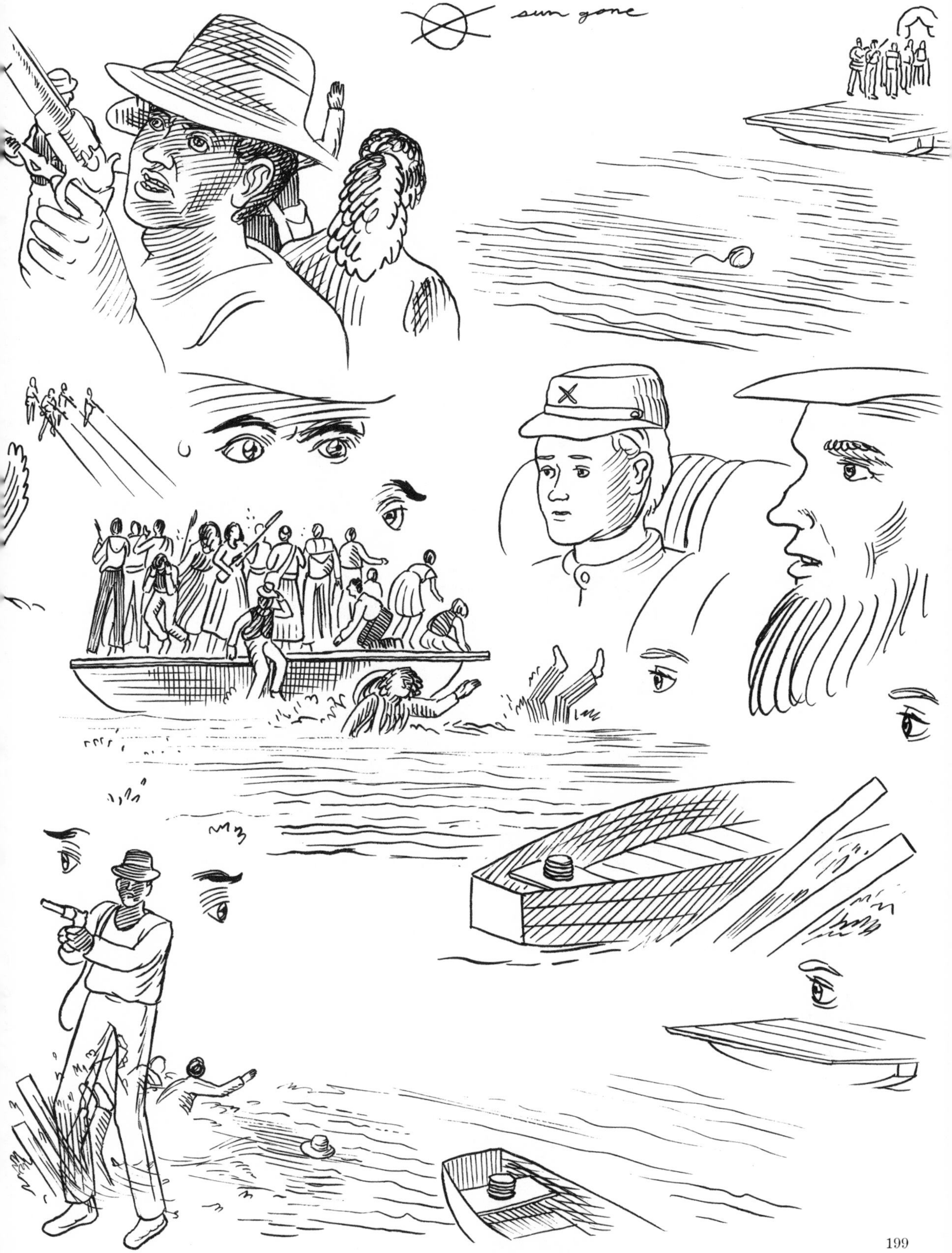
sun gone

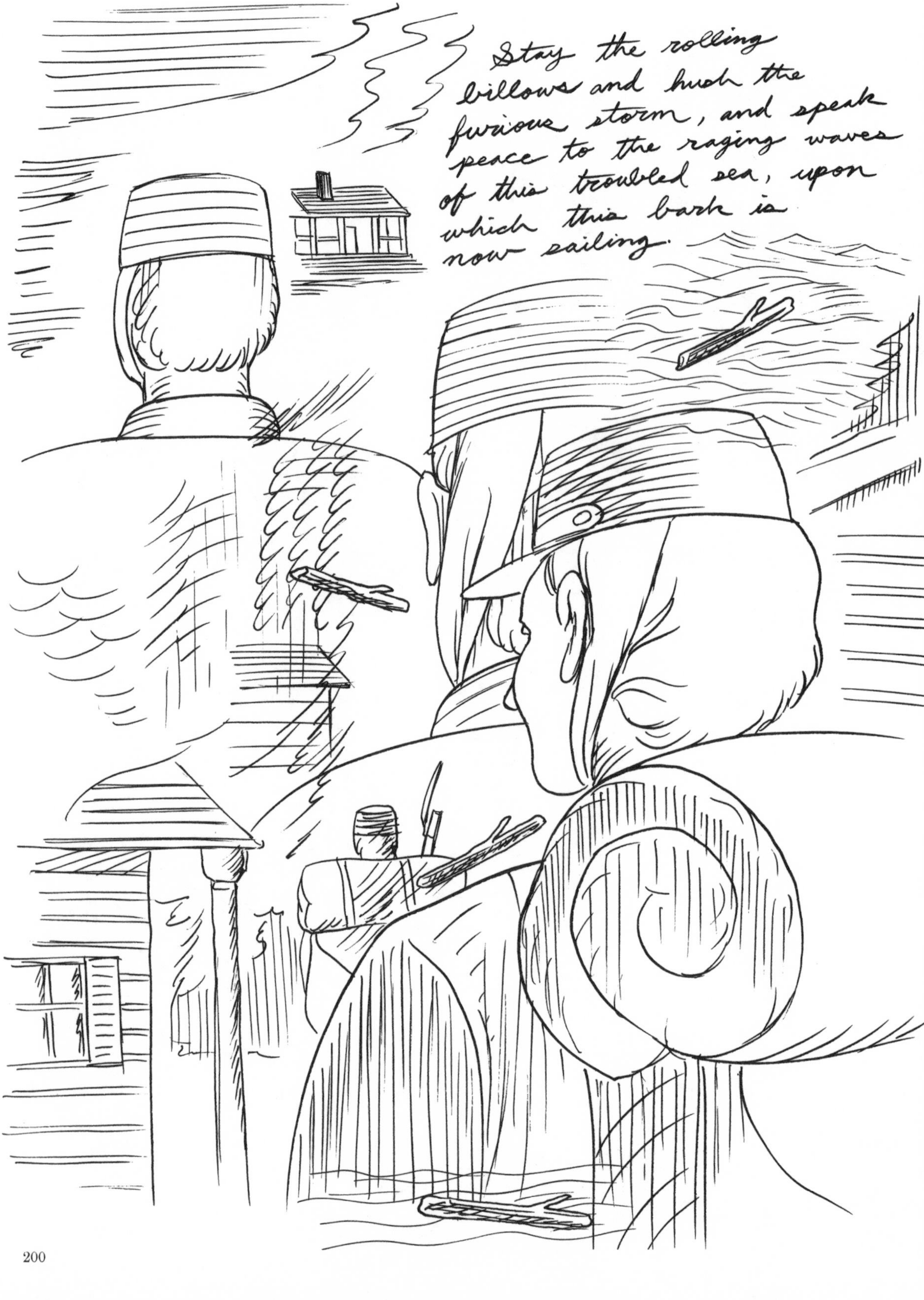
Stay the rolling billows and hush the furious storm, and speak peace to the raging waves of this troubled sea, upon which this bark is now sailing.

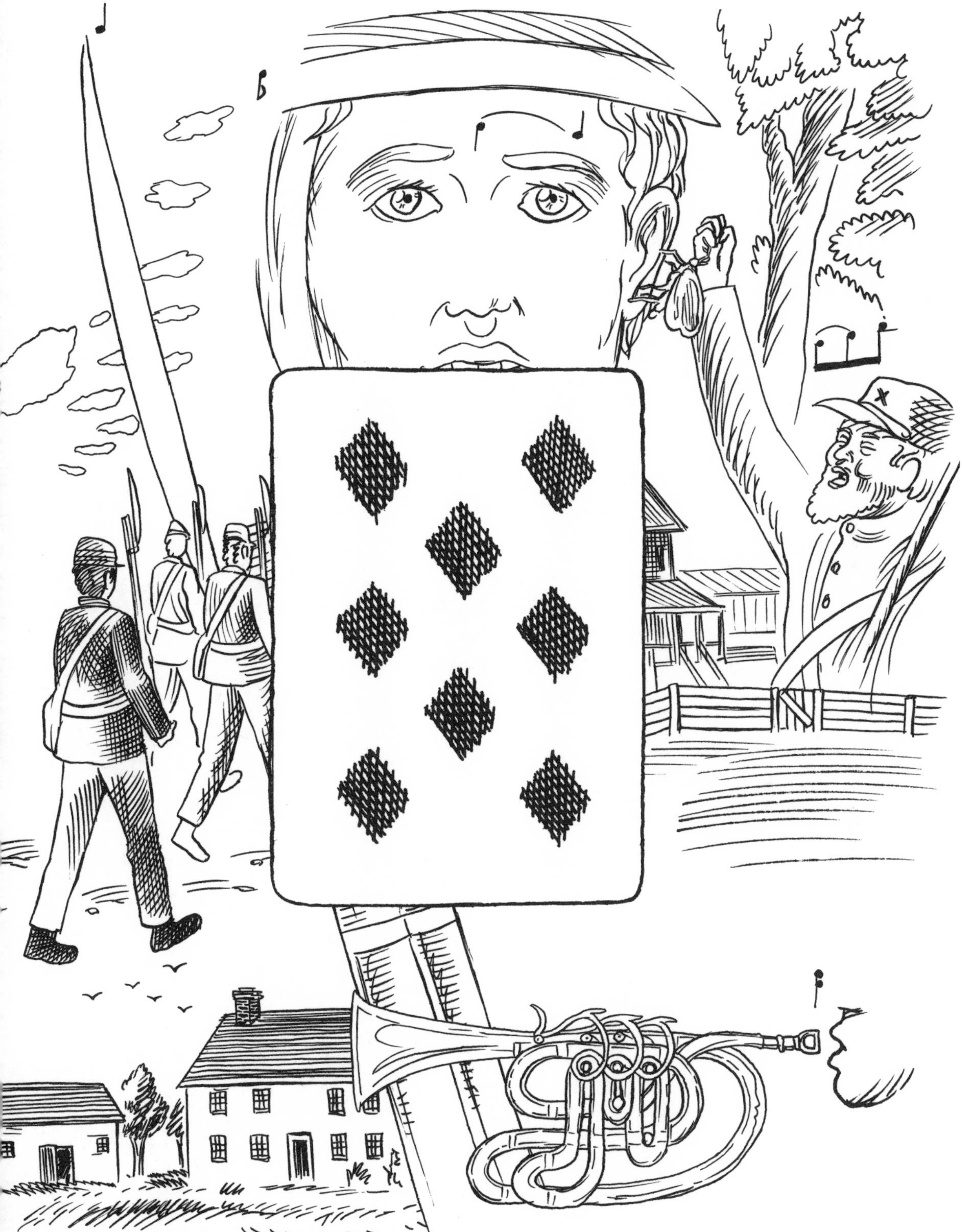

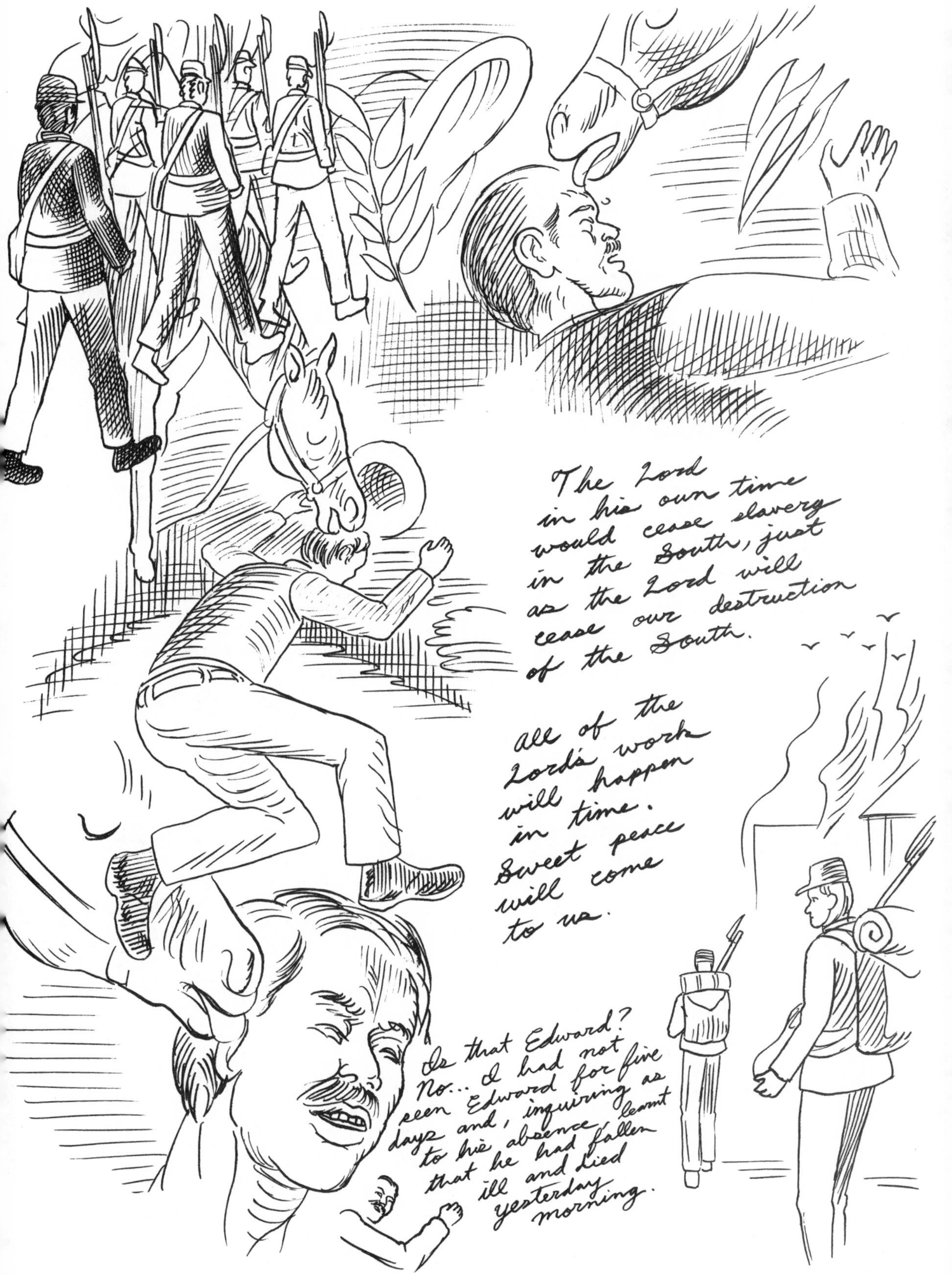
The Lord in his own time would cease slavery in the South, just as the Lord will cease our destruction of the South.
All of the Lord's work will happen in time. Sweet peace will come to us.
Is that Edward?
No... I had not seen Edward for five days and, inquiring as to his absence learnt that he had fallen ill and died yesterday morning.

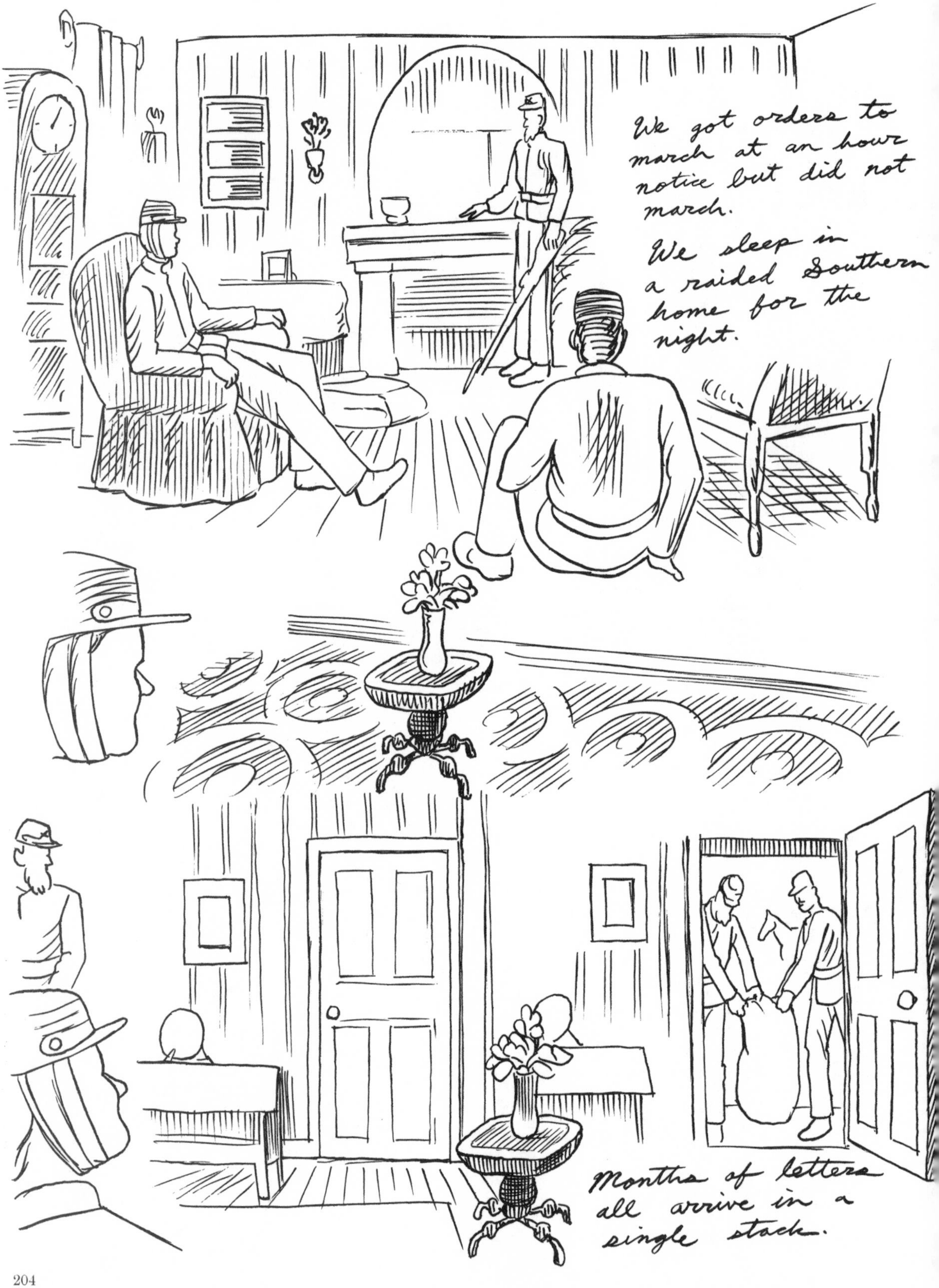
We got orders to march at an hour notice but did not march.
We sleep in a raided Southern home for the night.
Months of letters all arrive in a single stack.

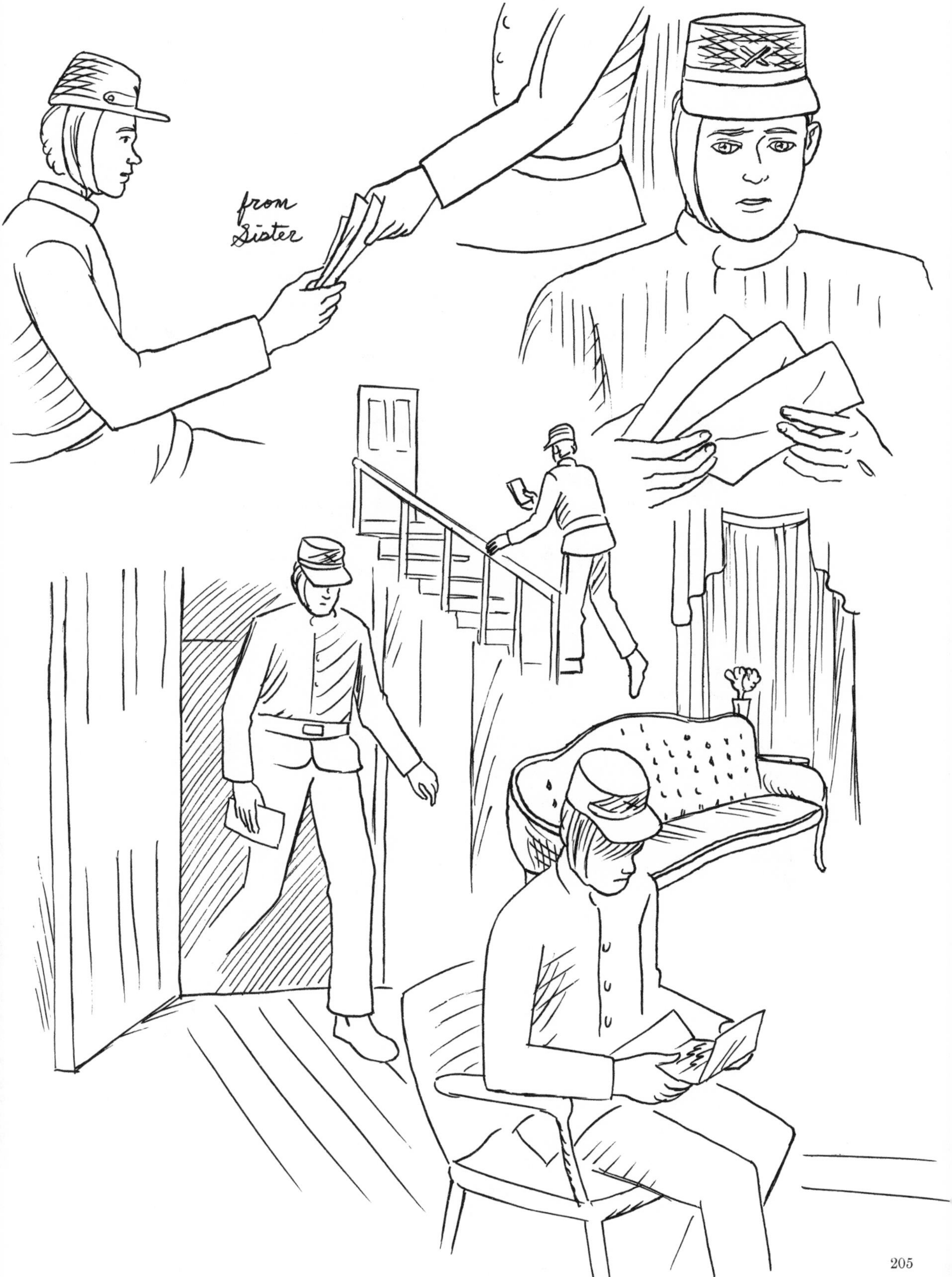
from Sister

May 2

Charles,

I am afraid this letter will be of a melancholy and upsetting character. Mother has fallen ill, from a disease of the heart. It began so slight at first, that I thought not to mention it.

I found her much worse on the third day, being almost unable to speak to me. I watched her most of the night and she spoke of thee in the most upsetting manner. Father and she wish and pray thee wast a peace-man and beside her. She grew worse. Ill health is certainly a deprivation of the powers of life.

Meeting was held this morning, and Mother was held in the light. Please, if thee receive this, hold her in the light, for her health is failing rapidly. She needs thee, and the protection of the Lord.

Love,
Fanny.

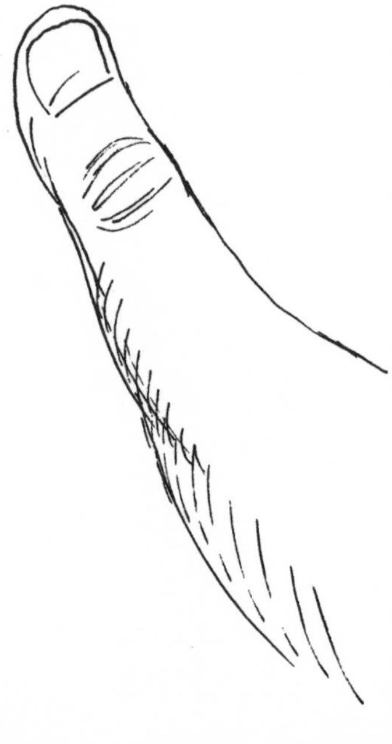

May 16

Charles,

I am sorry to say that Mother departed this life this morning about half past 11.

I am now occupied with arrangements expecting the funeral, which owing to Monthly Meeting to be held on the sixth day is to take place on fifth day.

The condition in this life is nothing compared with happiness in eternity. The violation of our discipline was a stain upon her conscience and jeopard her hopes of happiness in eternity.

Where art thou?

Our family has been twisted and now brutally torn apart.

I feel my heart so overburdened, I want someone to lean upon.

I wish thee wast here.

Fanny.

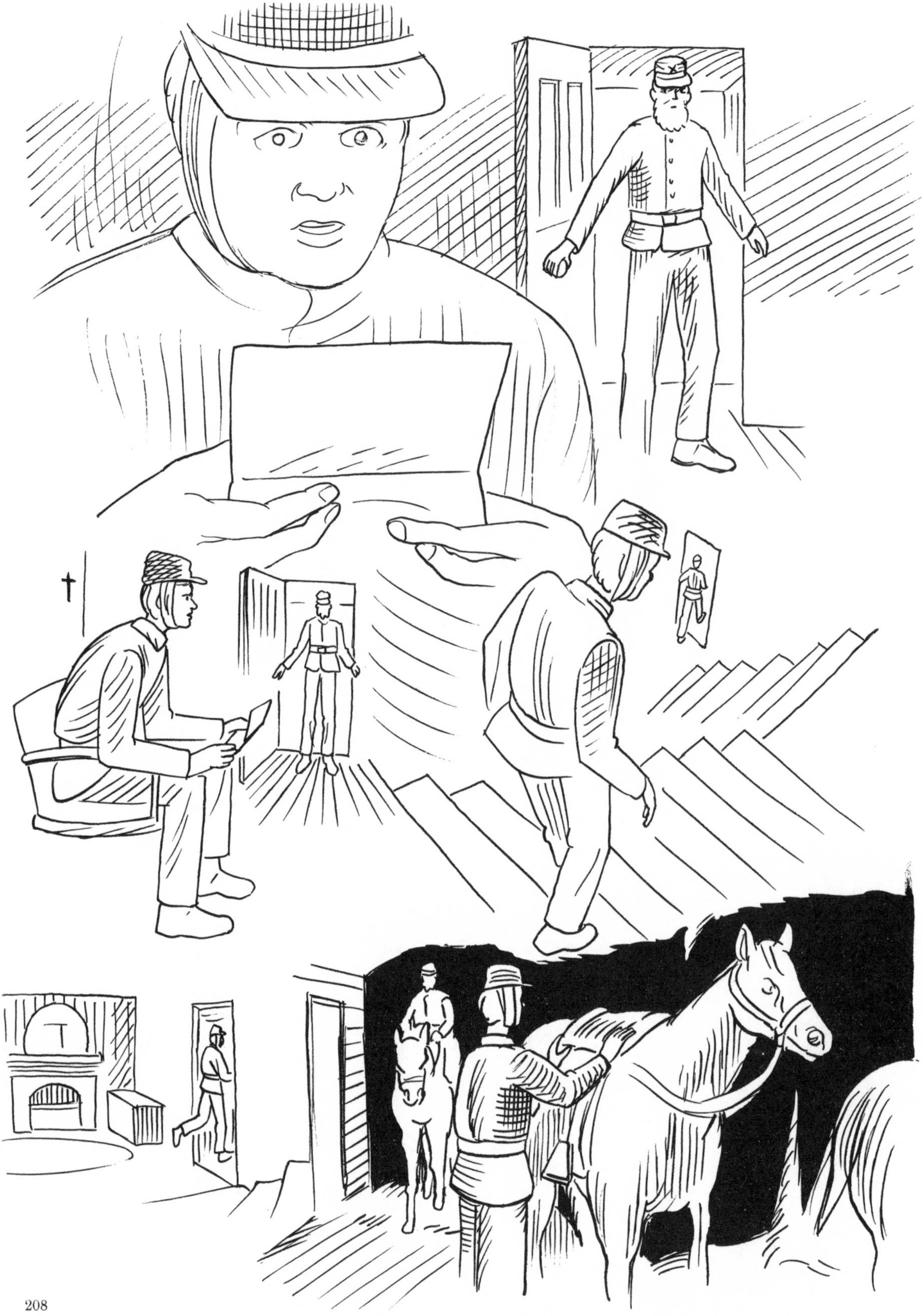

Mother...

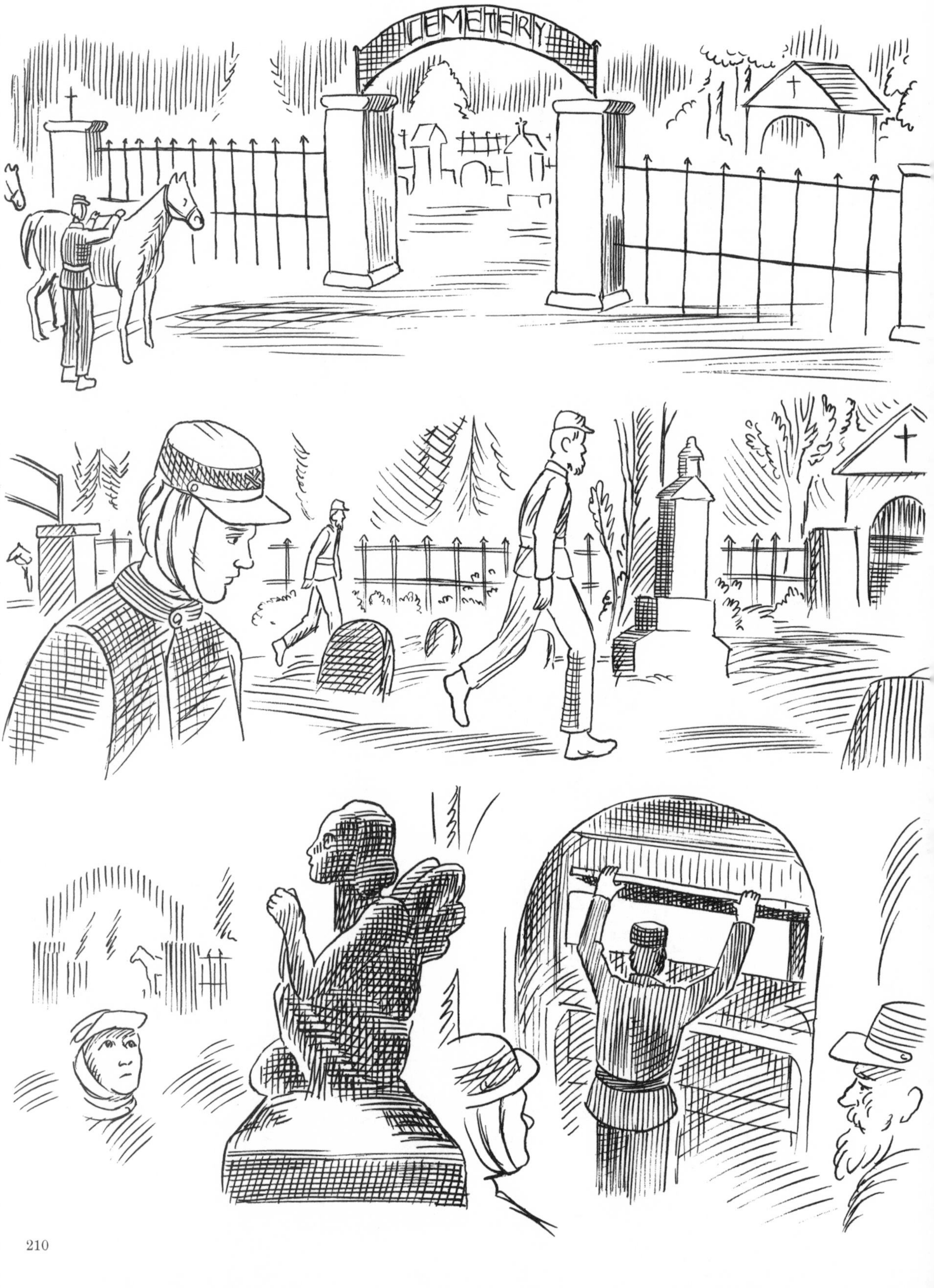
CEMETERY

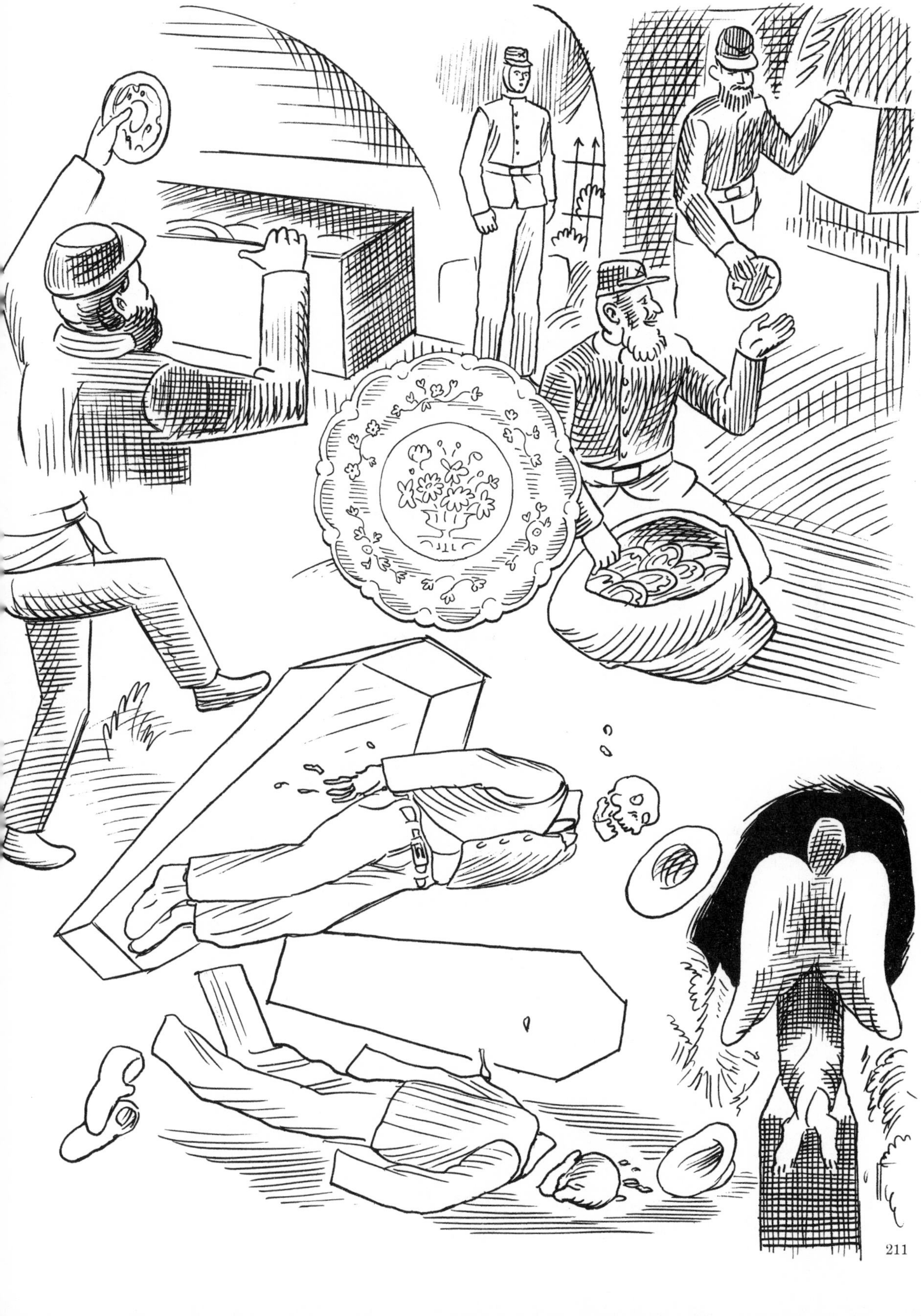

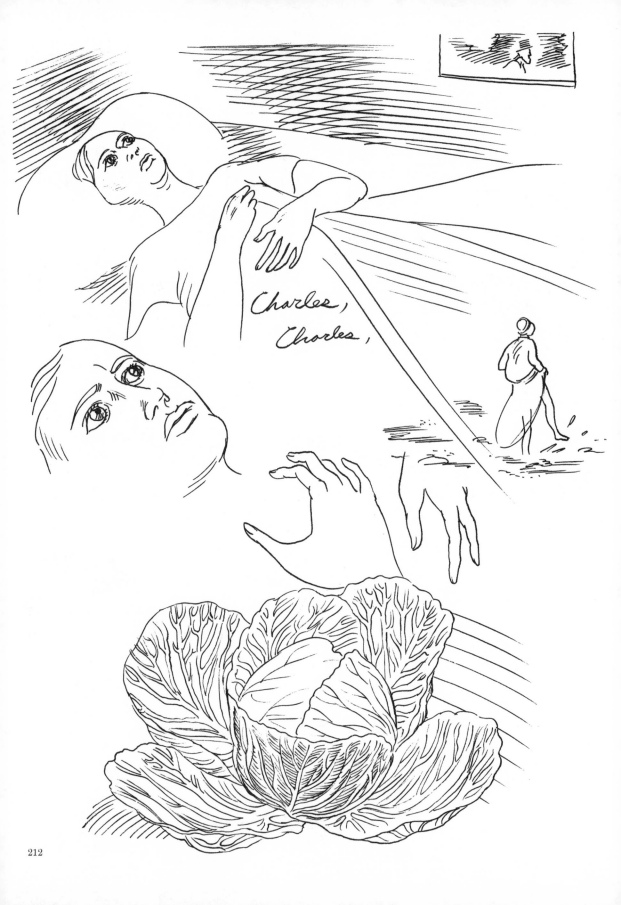

Charles,
Charles,

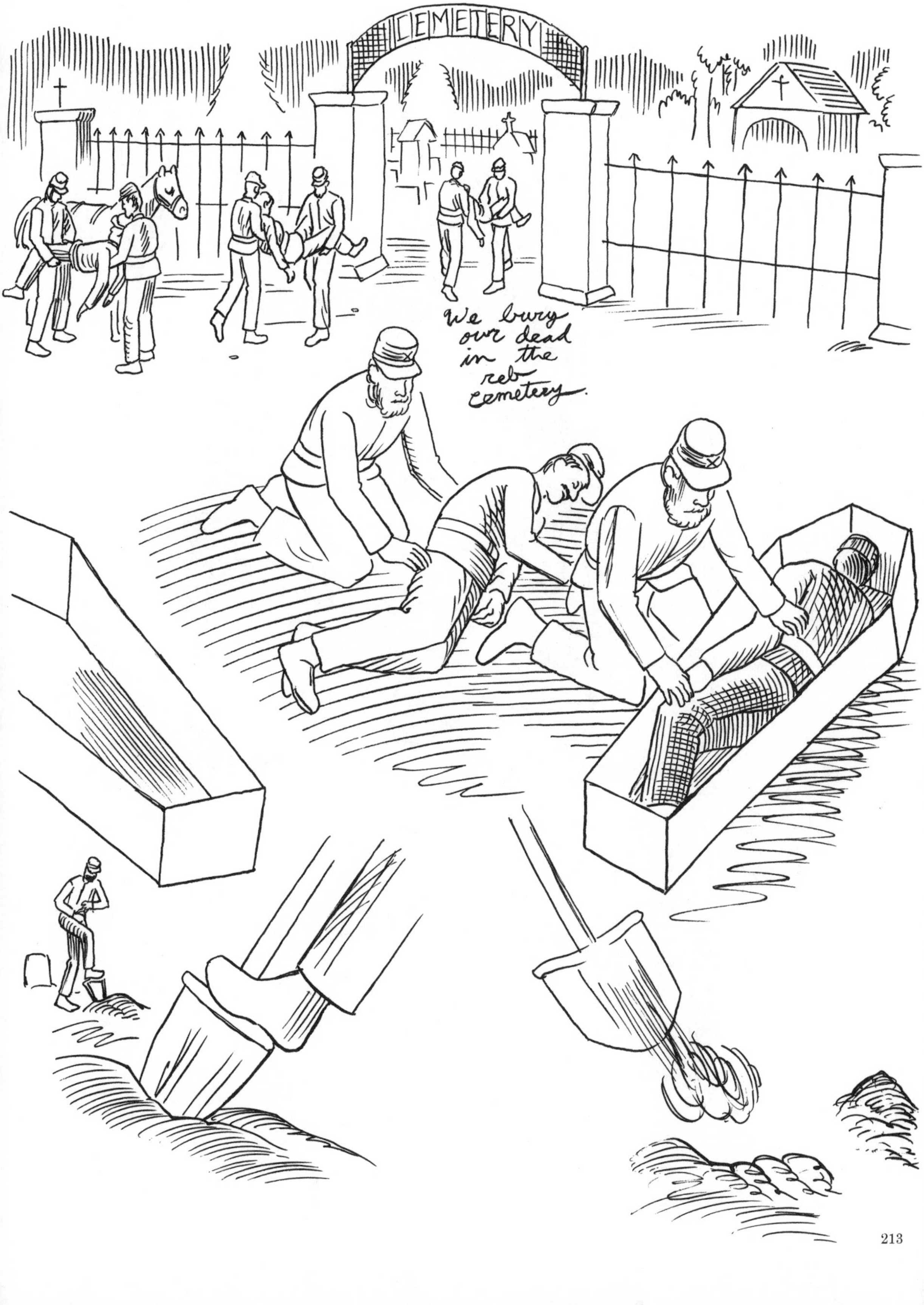
CEMETERY
We bury our dead in the reb cemetery.

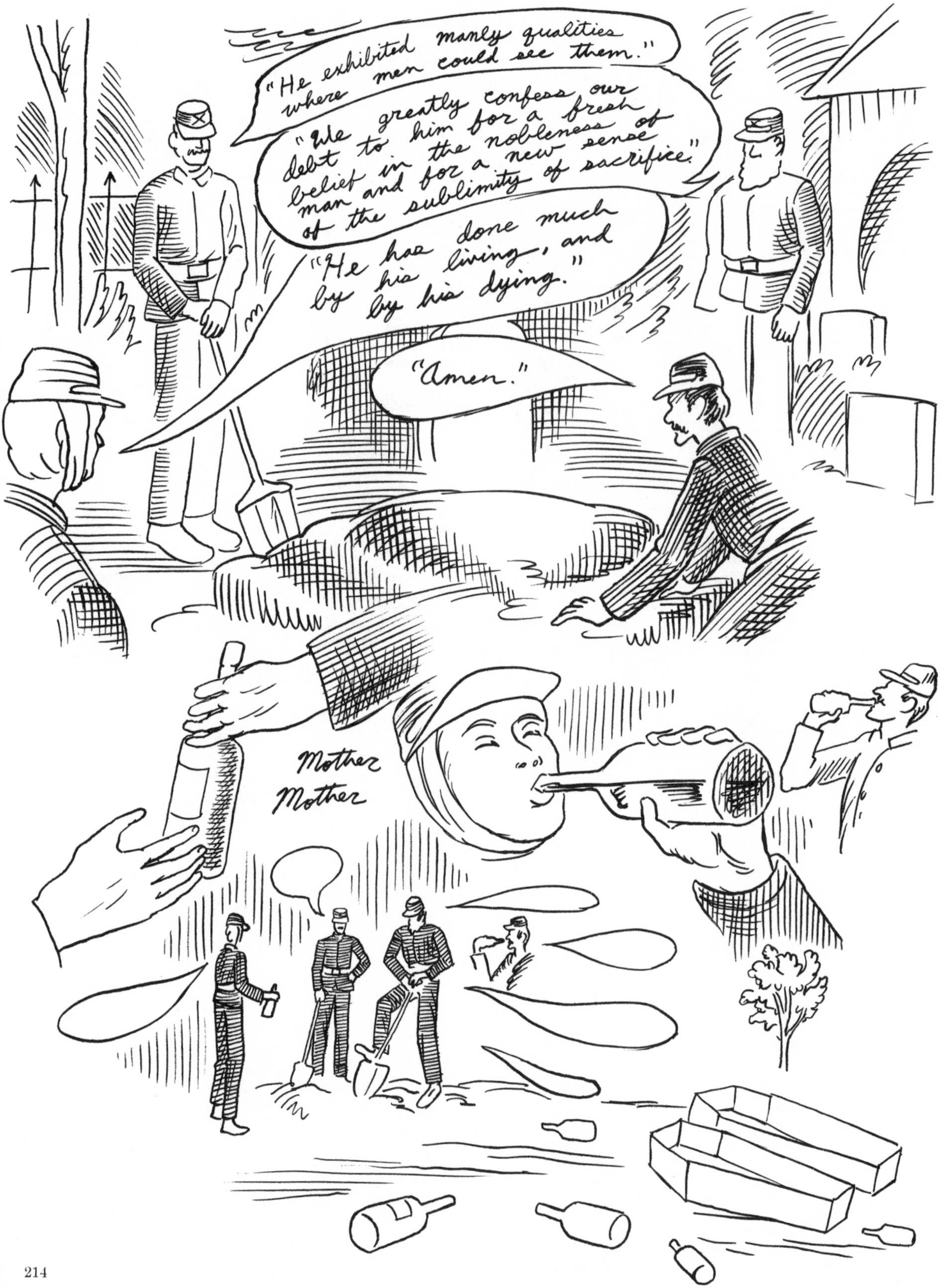
"He exhibited manly qualities where men could see them."
"We greatly confess our debt to him for a fresh belief in the nobleness of man and for a new sense of the sublimity of sacrifice."
"He has done much by his living, and by his dying."
"Amen."
Mother
Mother

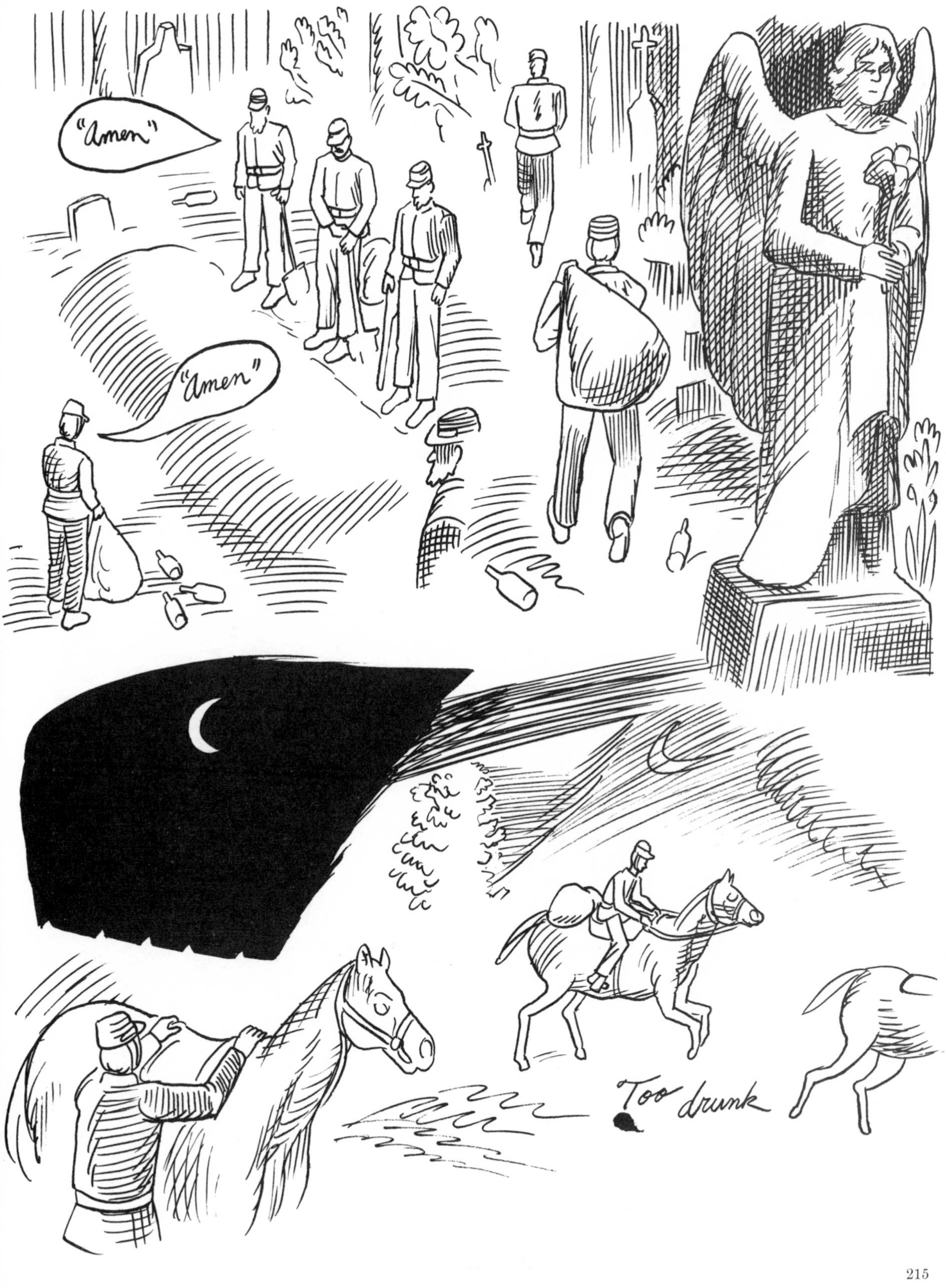
"amen"
"amen"
Too drunk

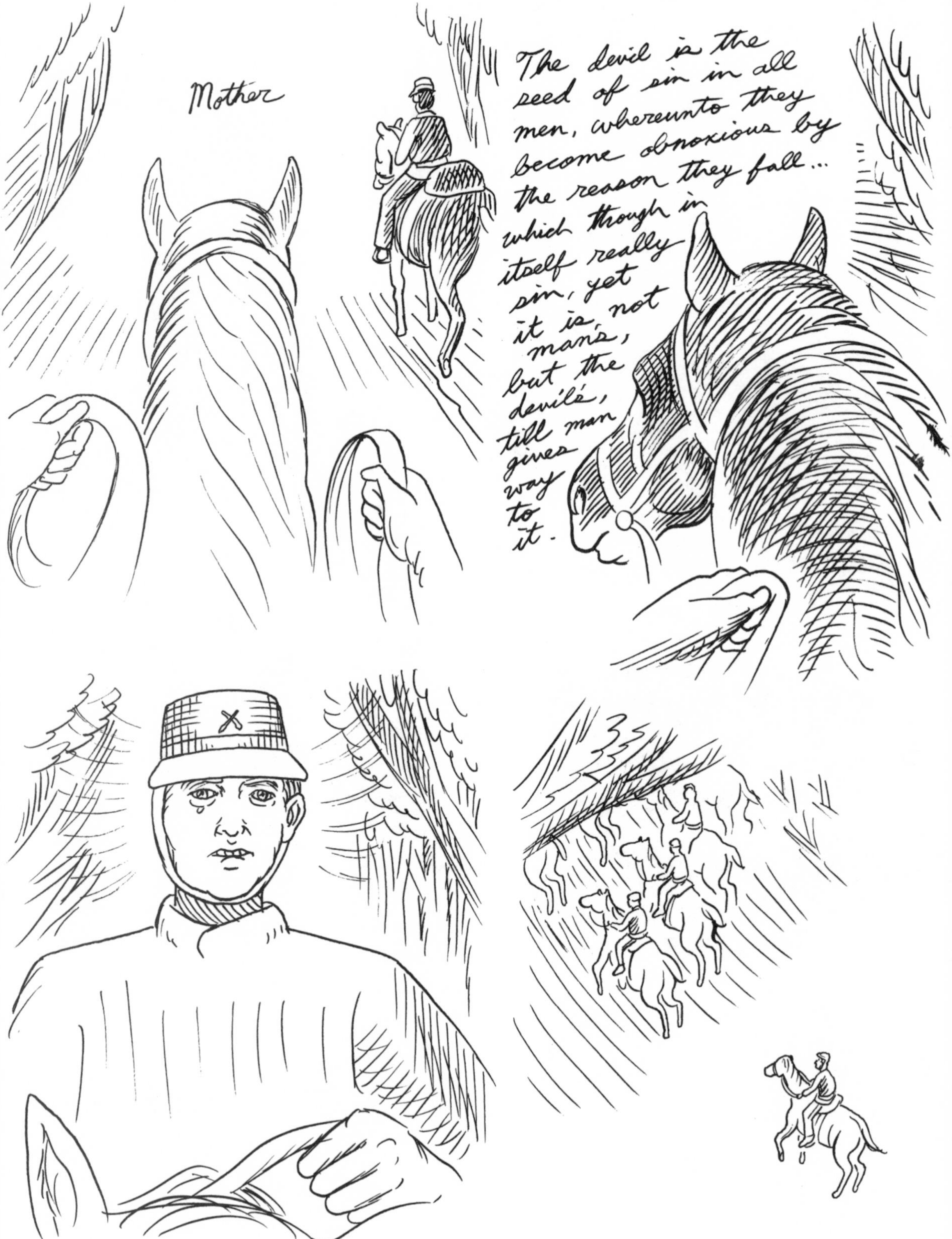

Mother
The devil is the seed of sin in all men, whereunto they become obnoxious by the reason they fall... which though in itself really sin, yet it is not man's, but the devil's, till man gives way to it.

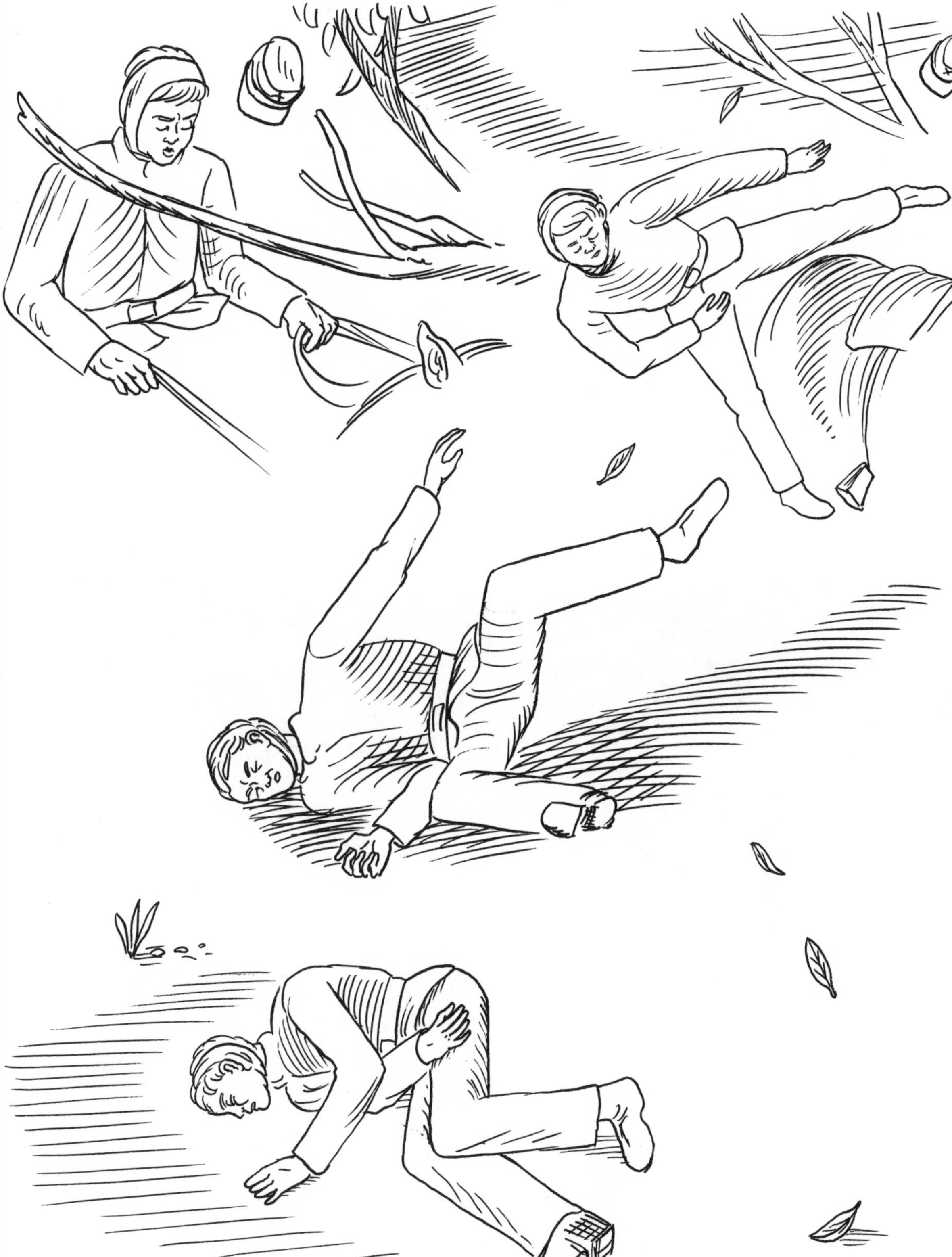

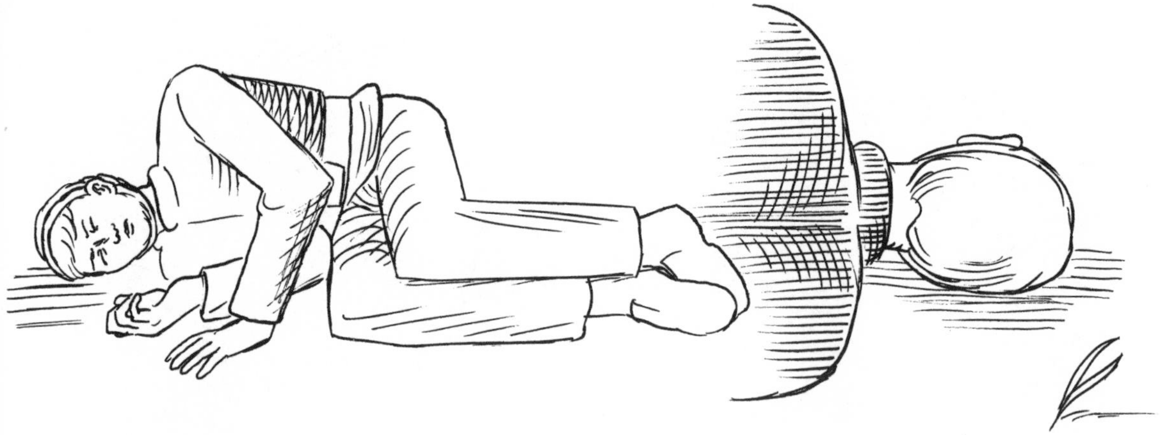

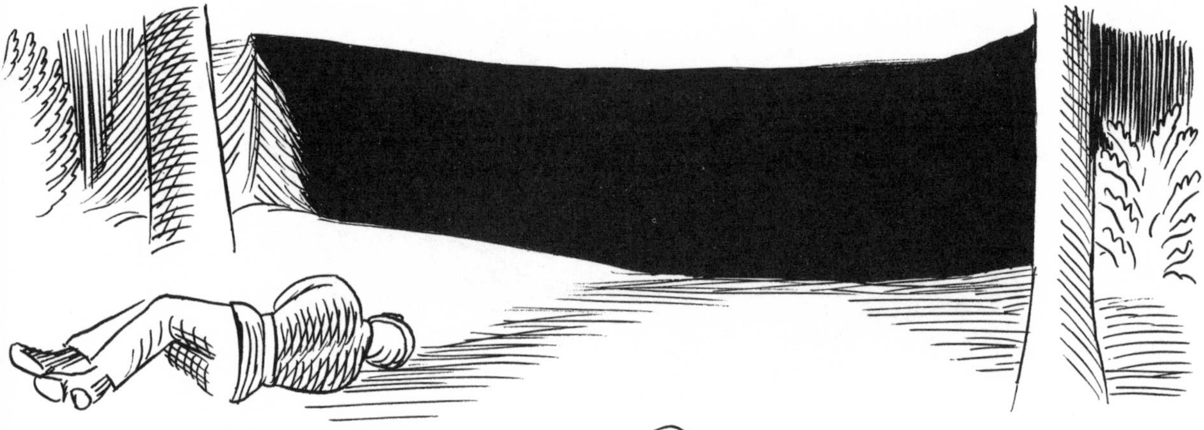

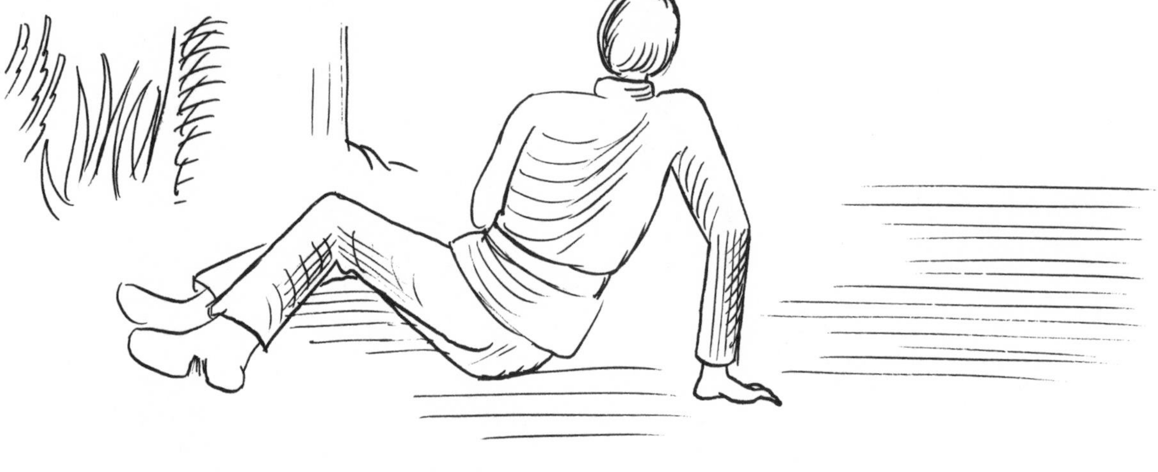

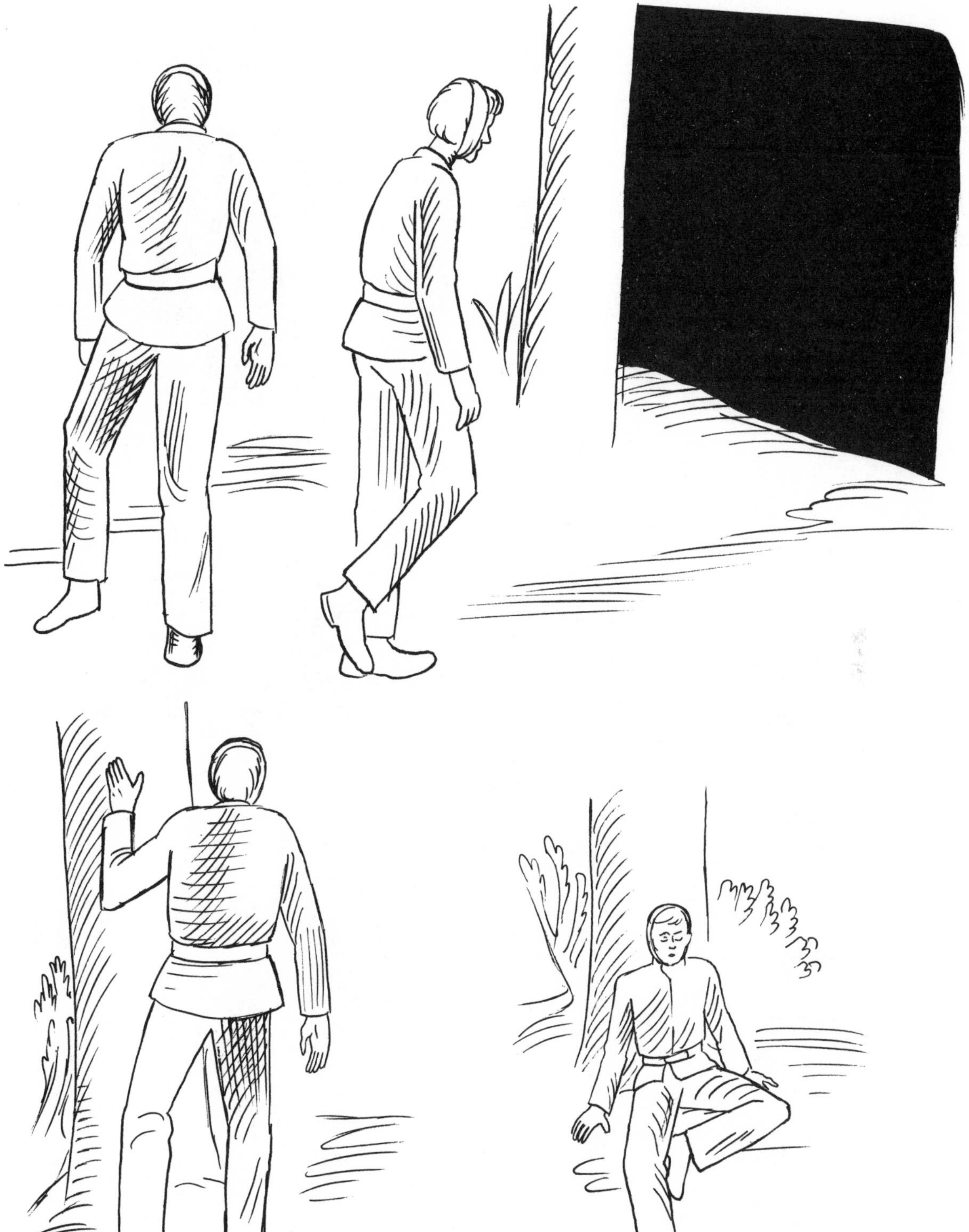

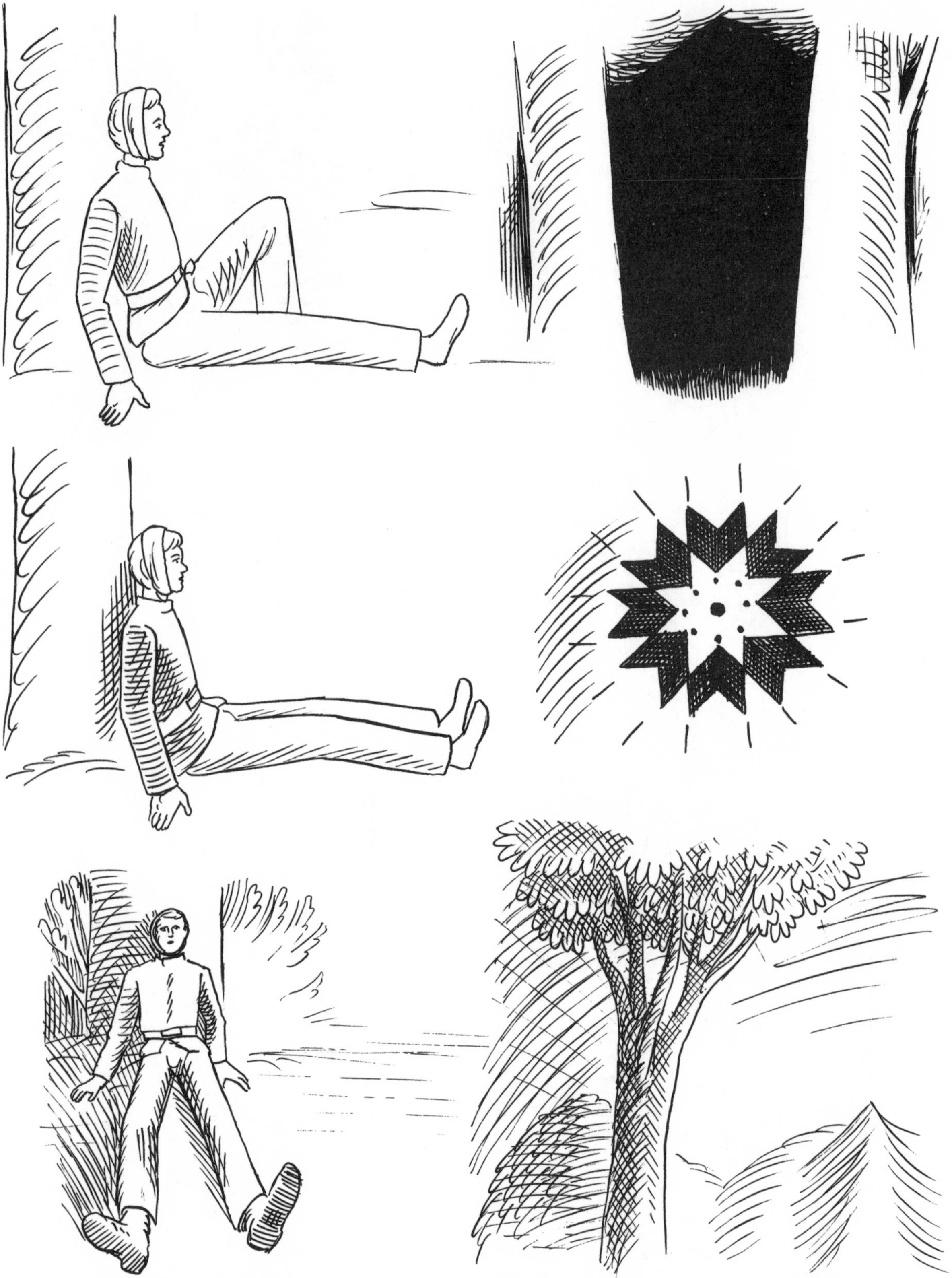

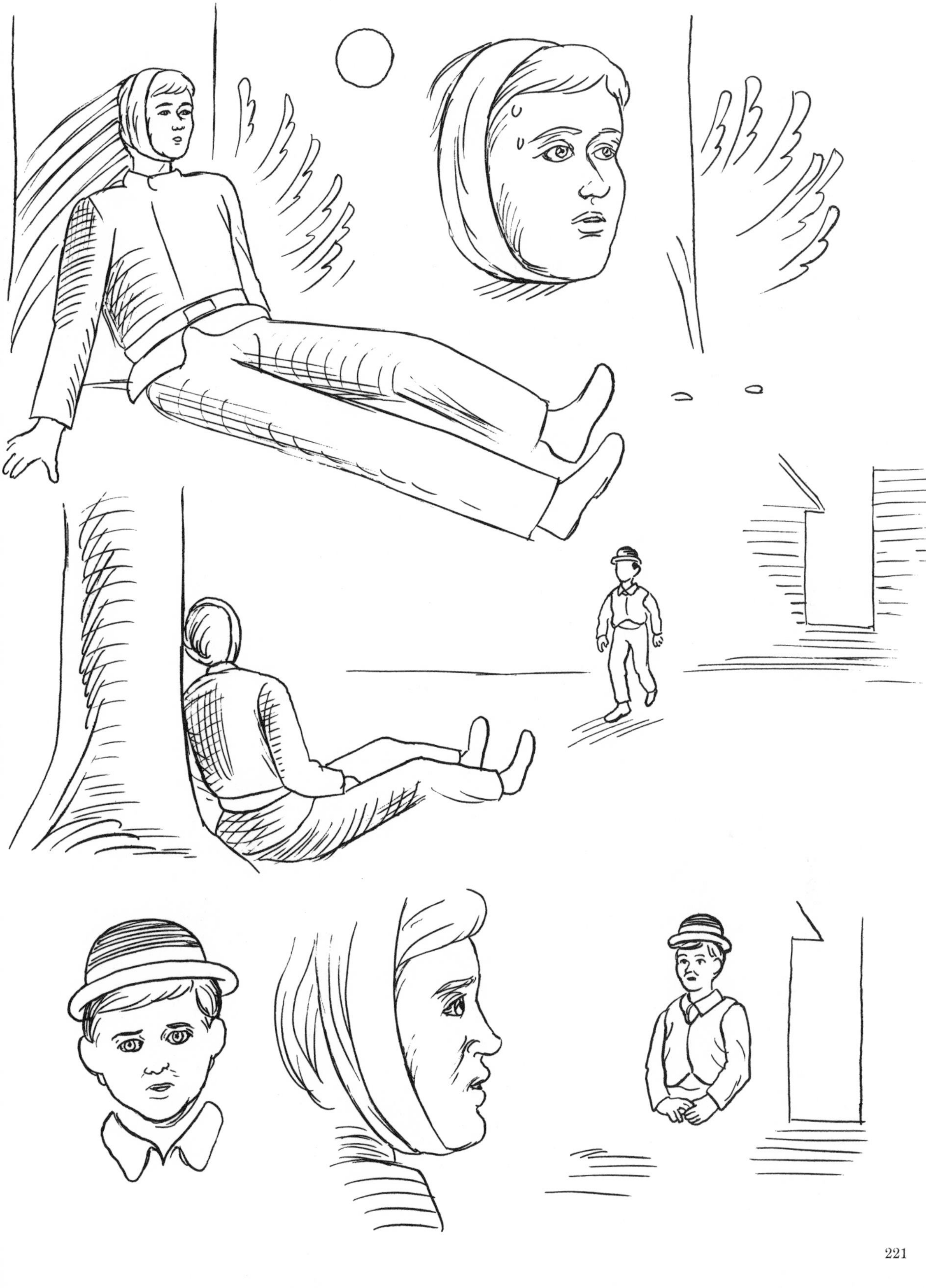

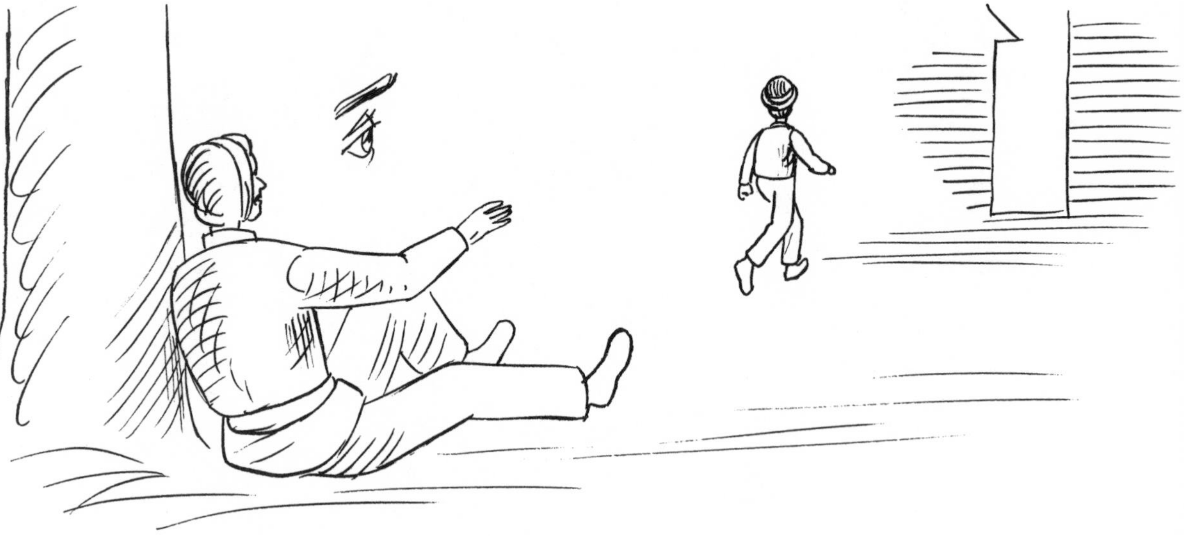

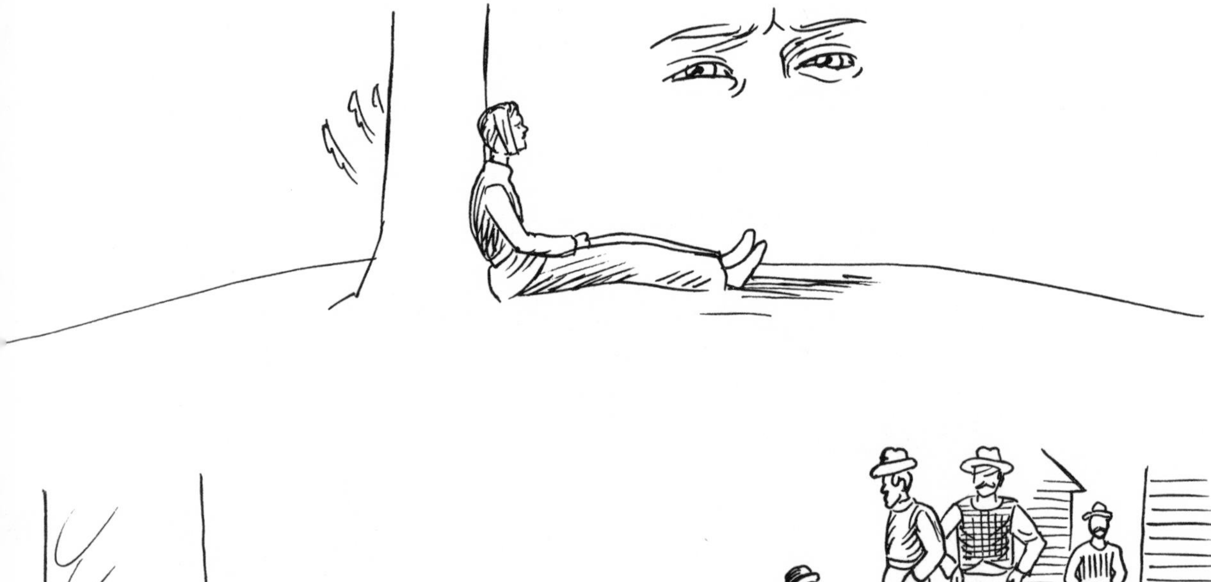

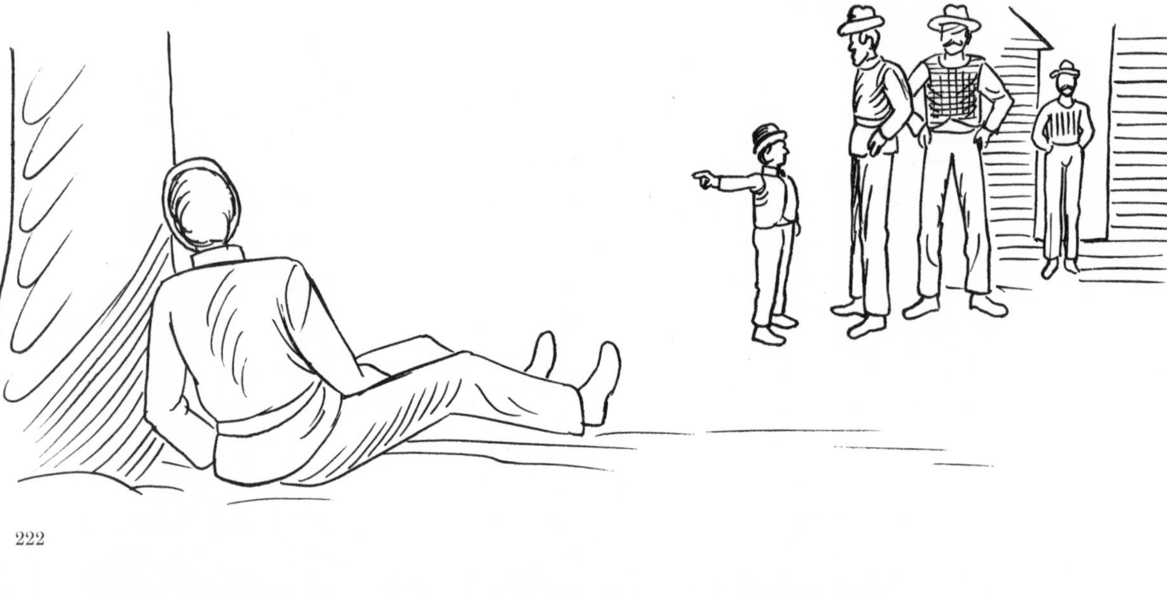

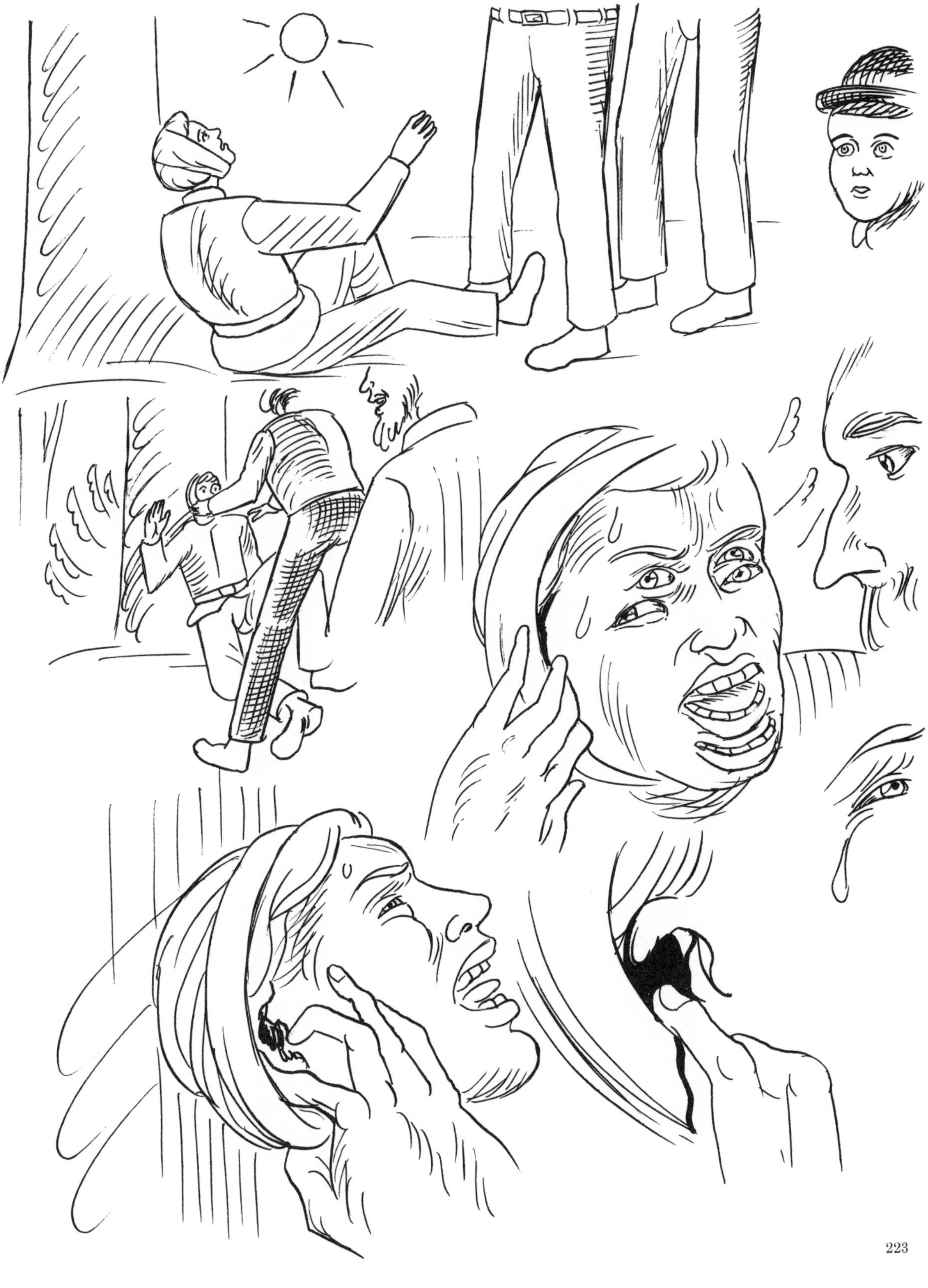

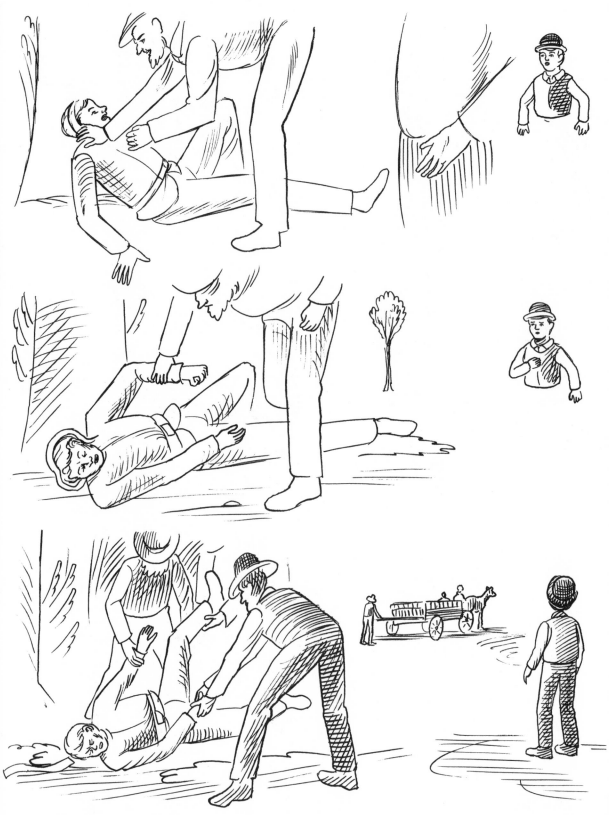

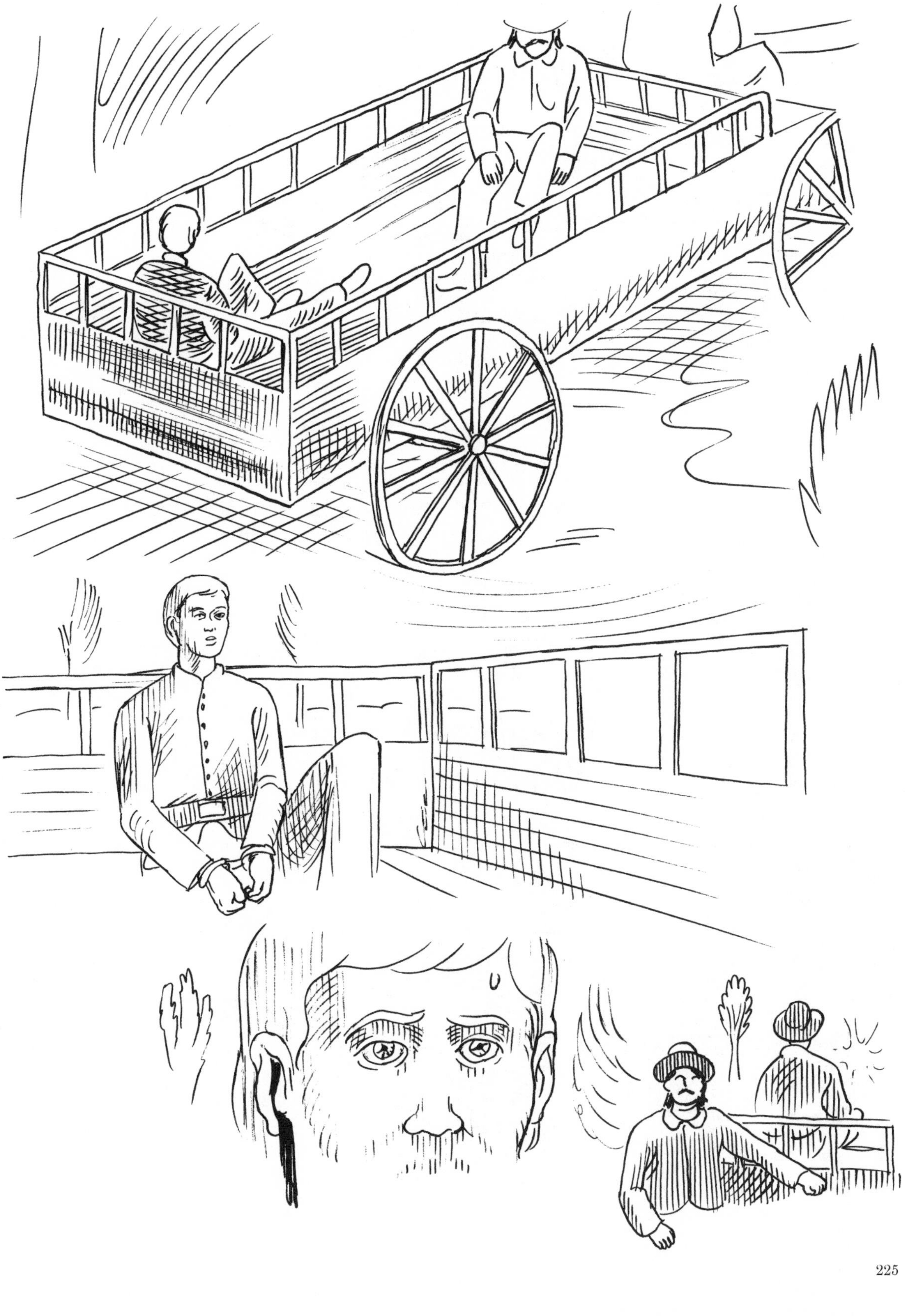

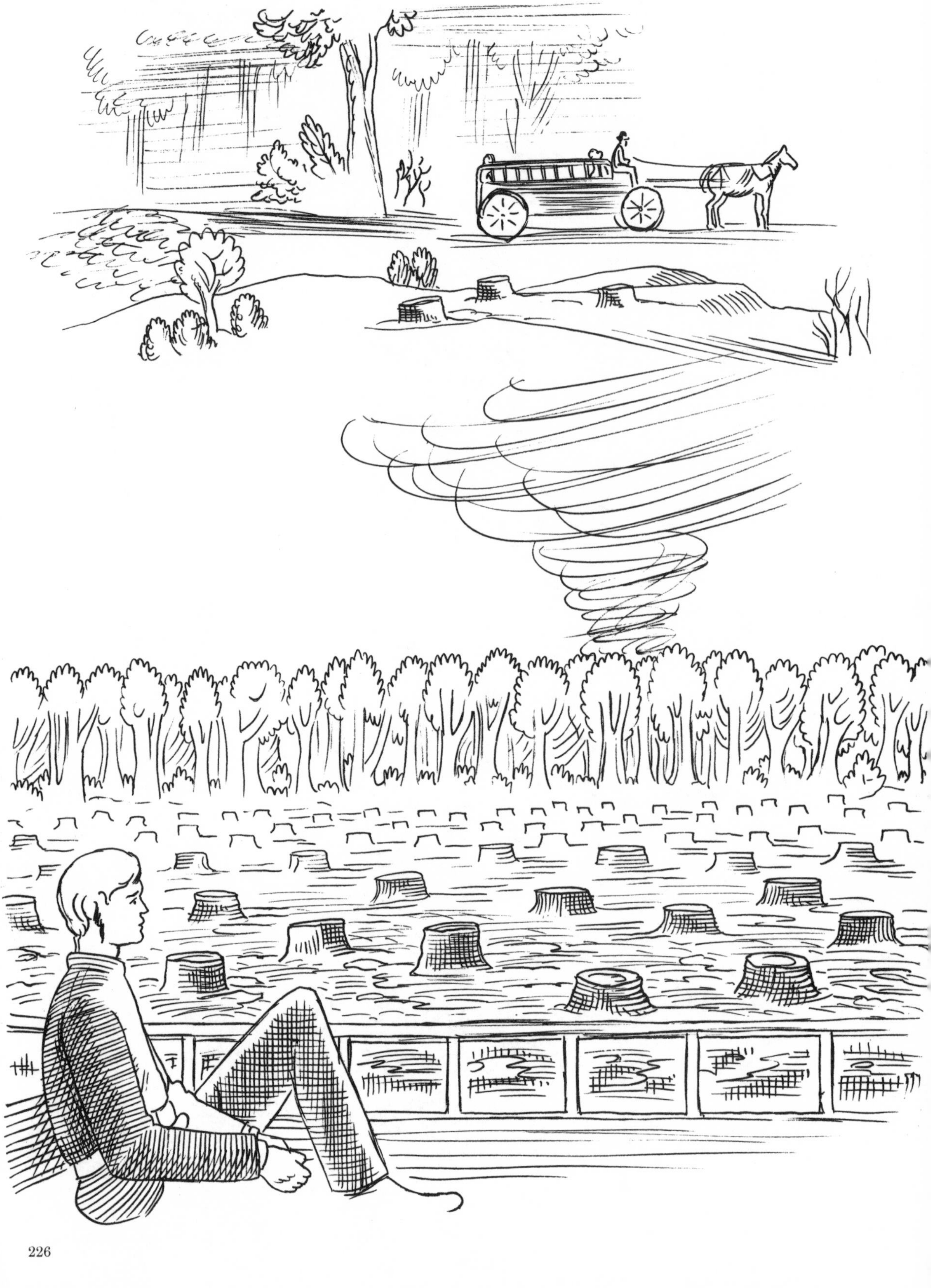

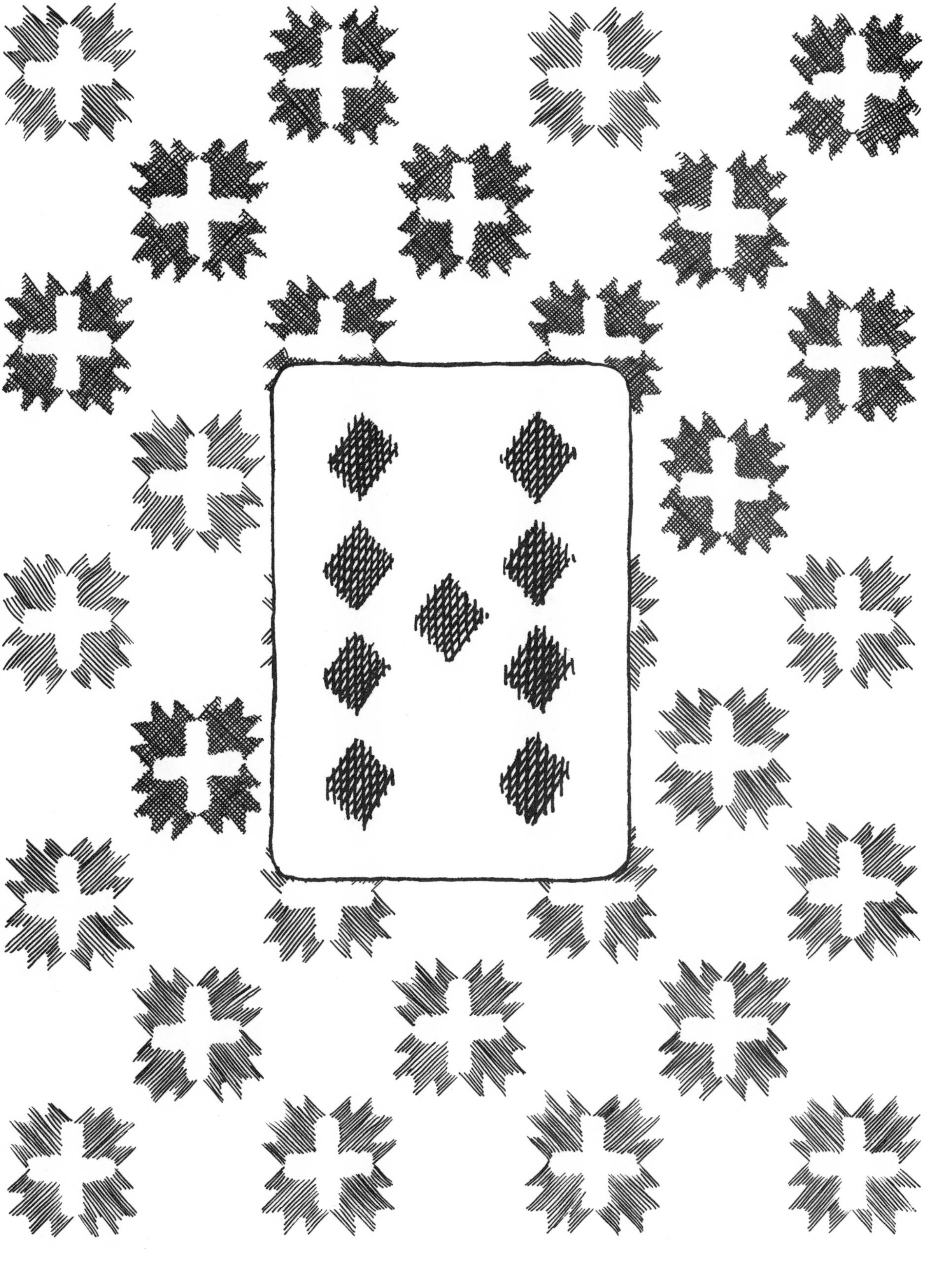

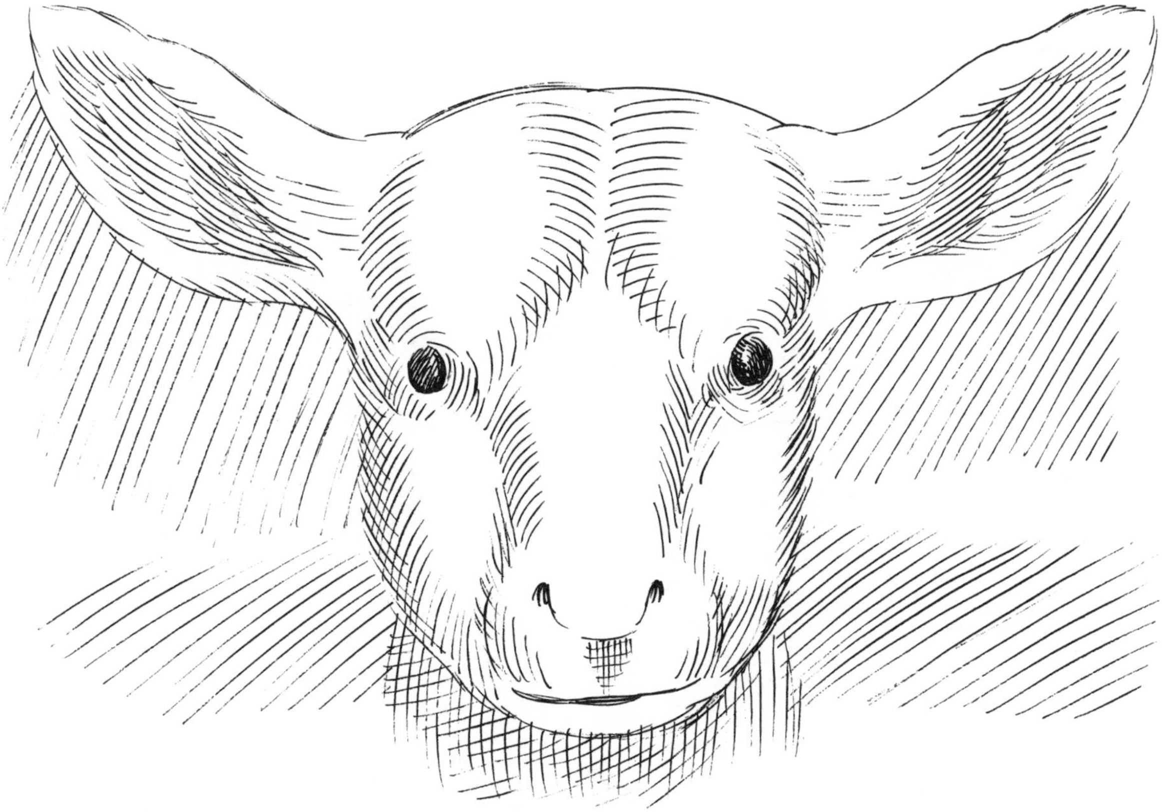

Our ancient testimony to the peaceable nature of Christ's kingdom has been made more dear to our hearts by contemplating the scenes of carnage and destruction that abound in our land. It was doubtless the intention of the Most High in sending his beloved Son into the world to bring mankind into harmony and fraternal love. This happy condition was shadowed forth in the figurative language of prophecy: "The wolf shall dwell with the lamb, the leopard shall lie down with the kid, and the calf and the young lion, and the fatling together, and a little child shall lead them."

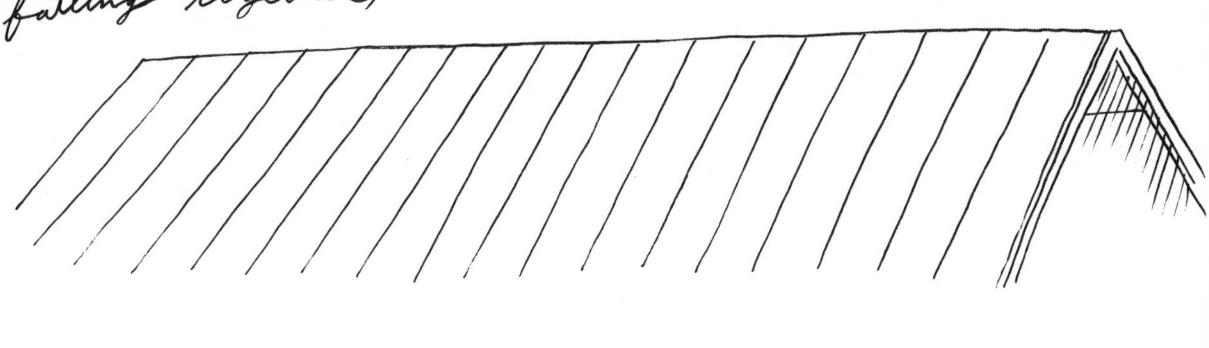

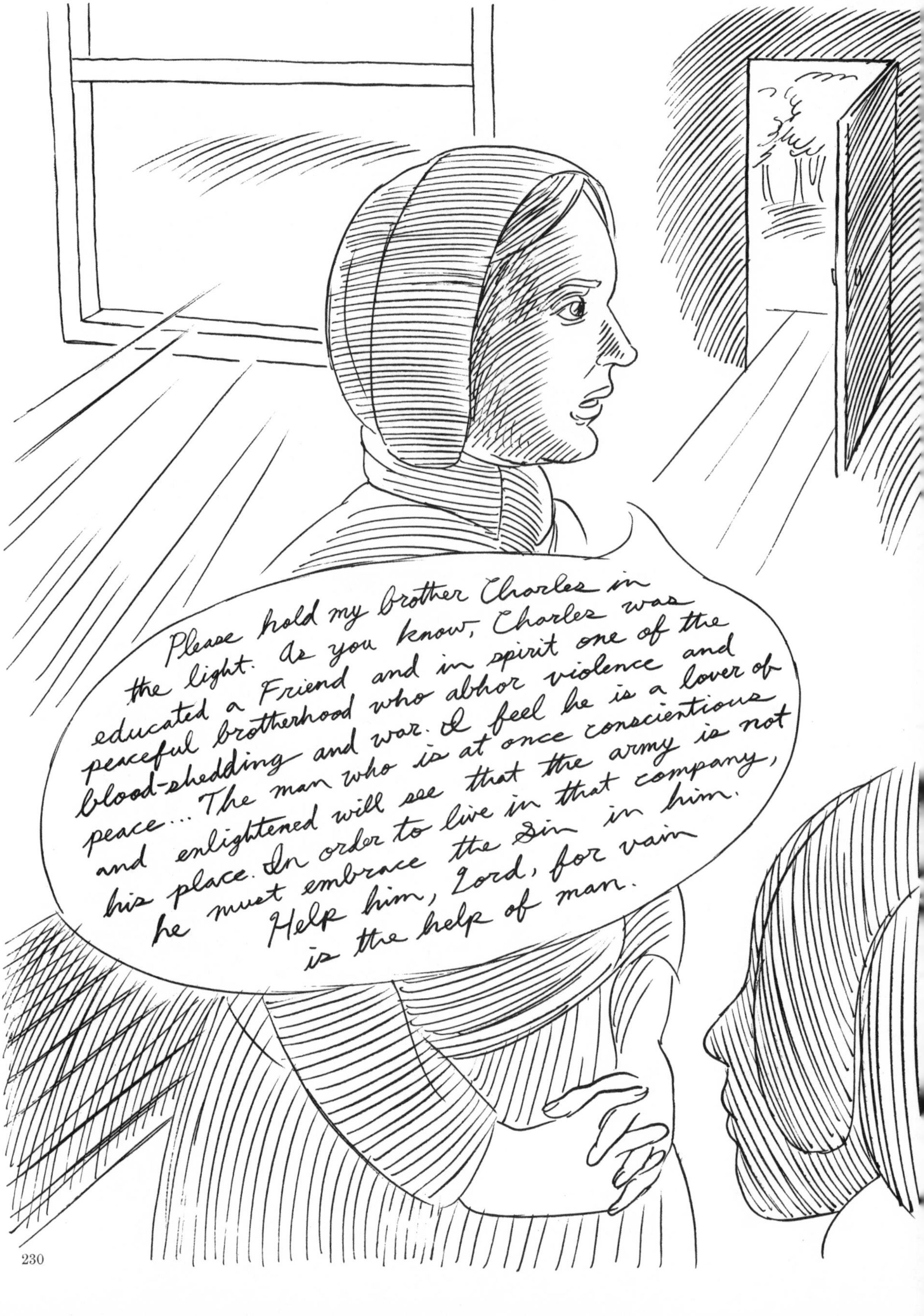
Please hold my brother Charles in the light. As you know, Charles was educated a Friend and in spirit one of the peaceful brotherhood who abhor violence and blood-shedding and war. I feel he is a lover of peace... The man who is at once conscientious and enlightened will see that the army is not his place. In order to live in that company, he must embrace the Sin in him. Help him, Lord, for vain is the help of man.

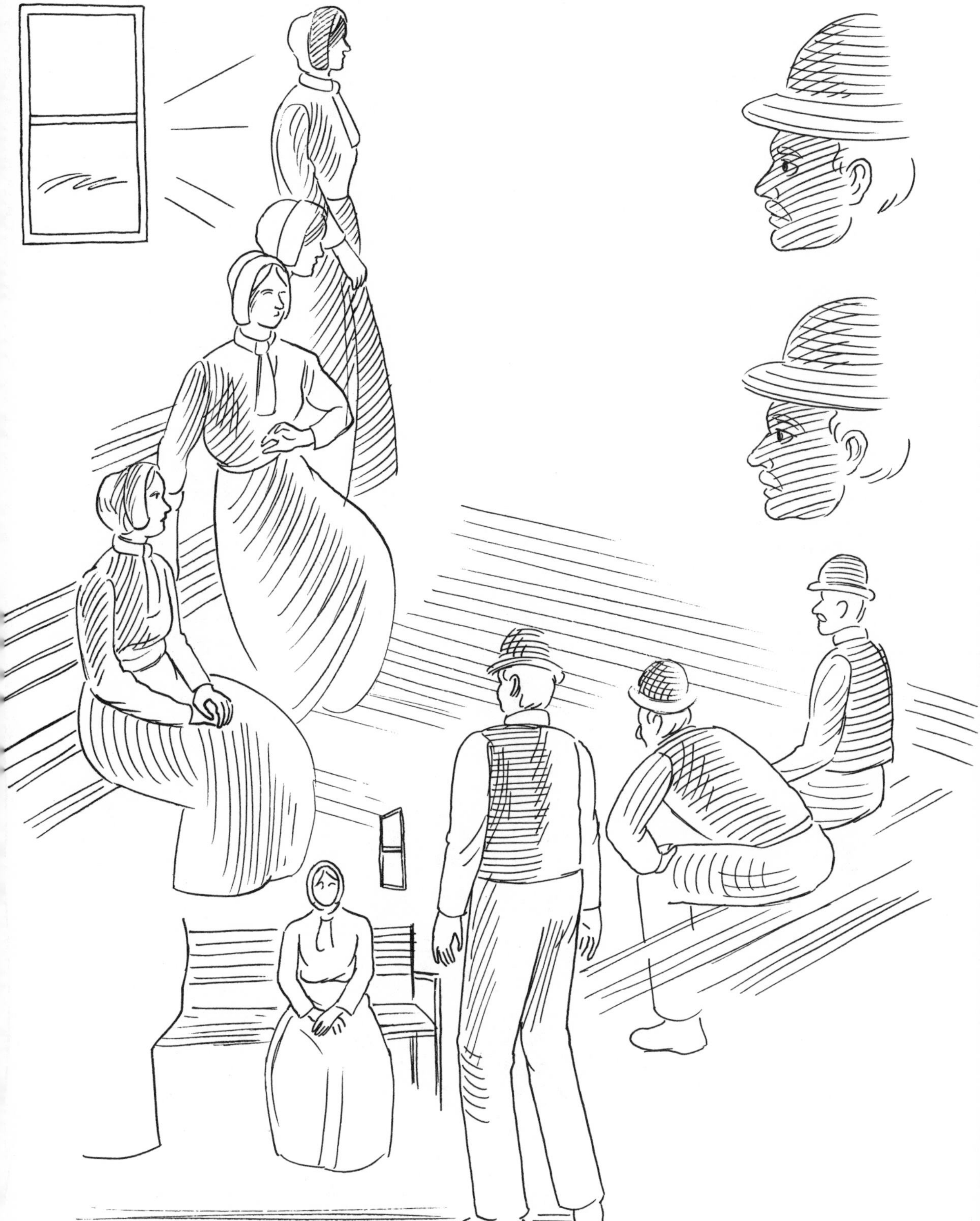

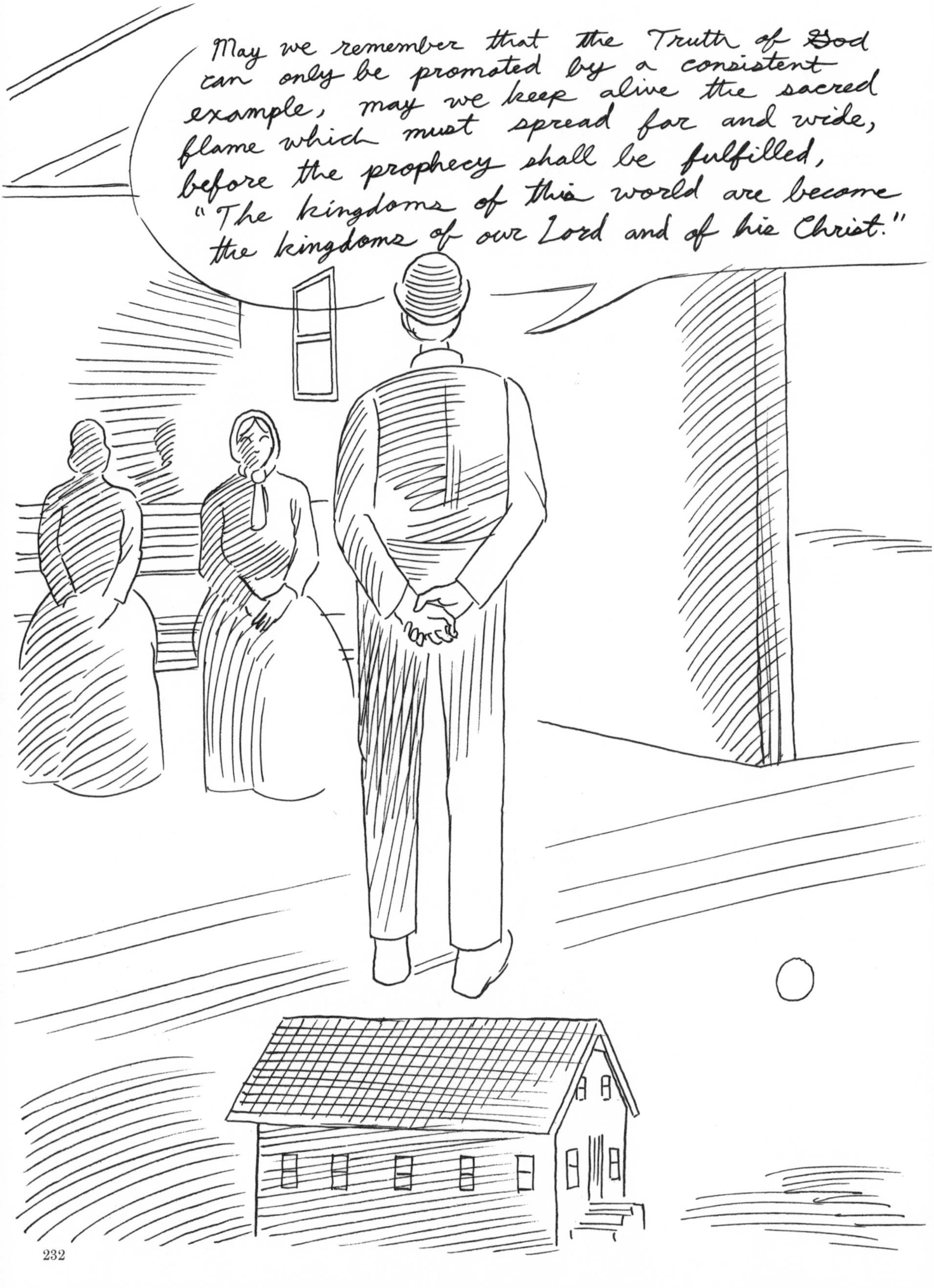
May we remember that the Truth of God can only be promoted by a consistent example, may we keep alive the sacred flame which must spread far and wide, before the prophecy shall be fulfilled, "The kingdoms of this world are become the kingdoms of our Lord and of his Christ."

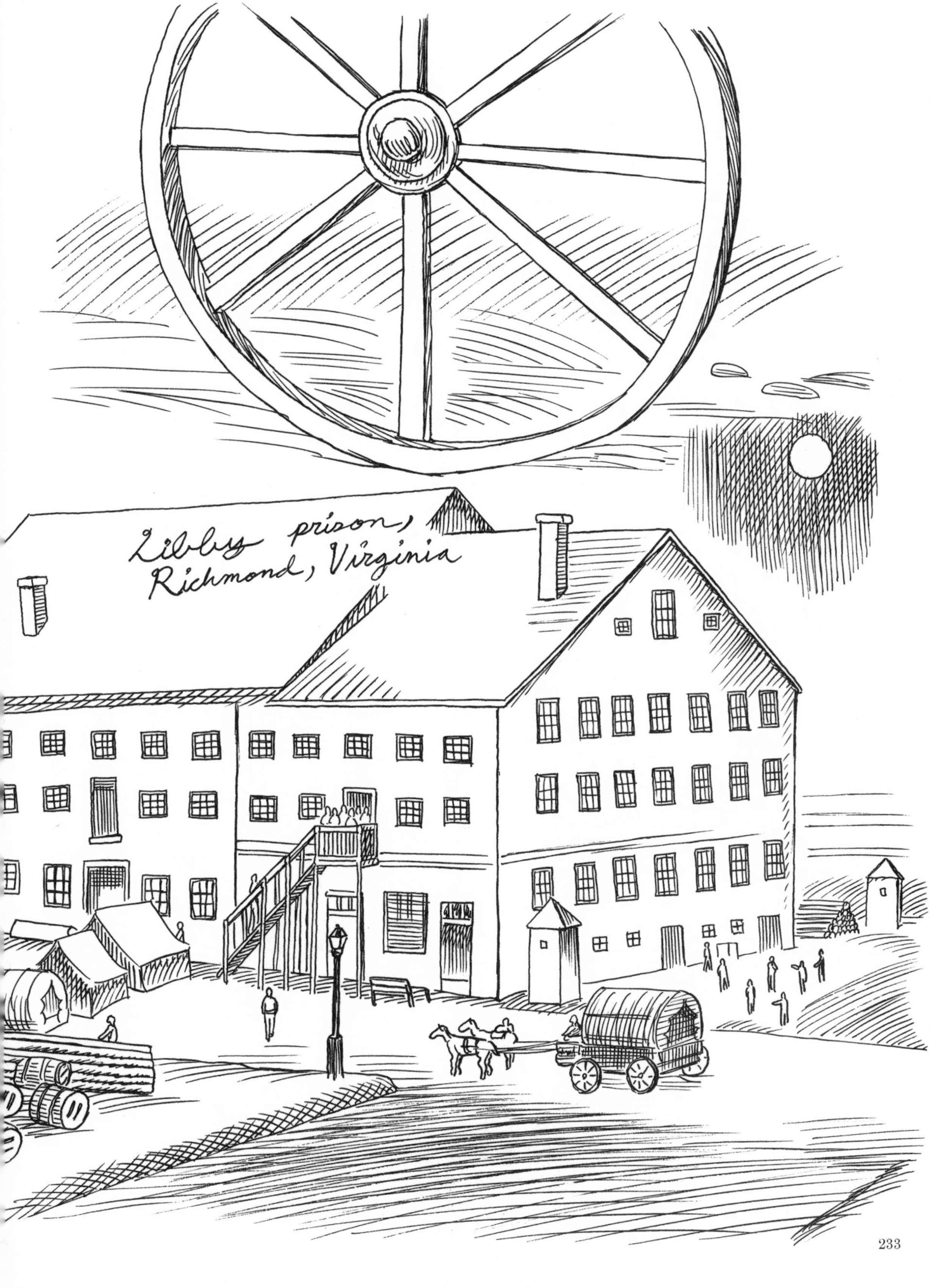
Libby prison,
Richmond, Virginia

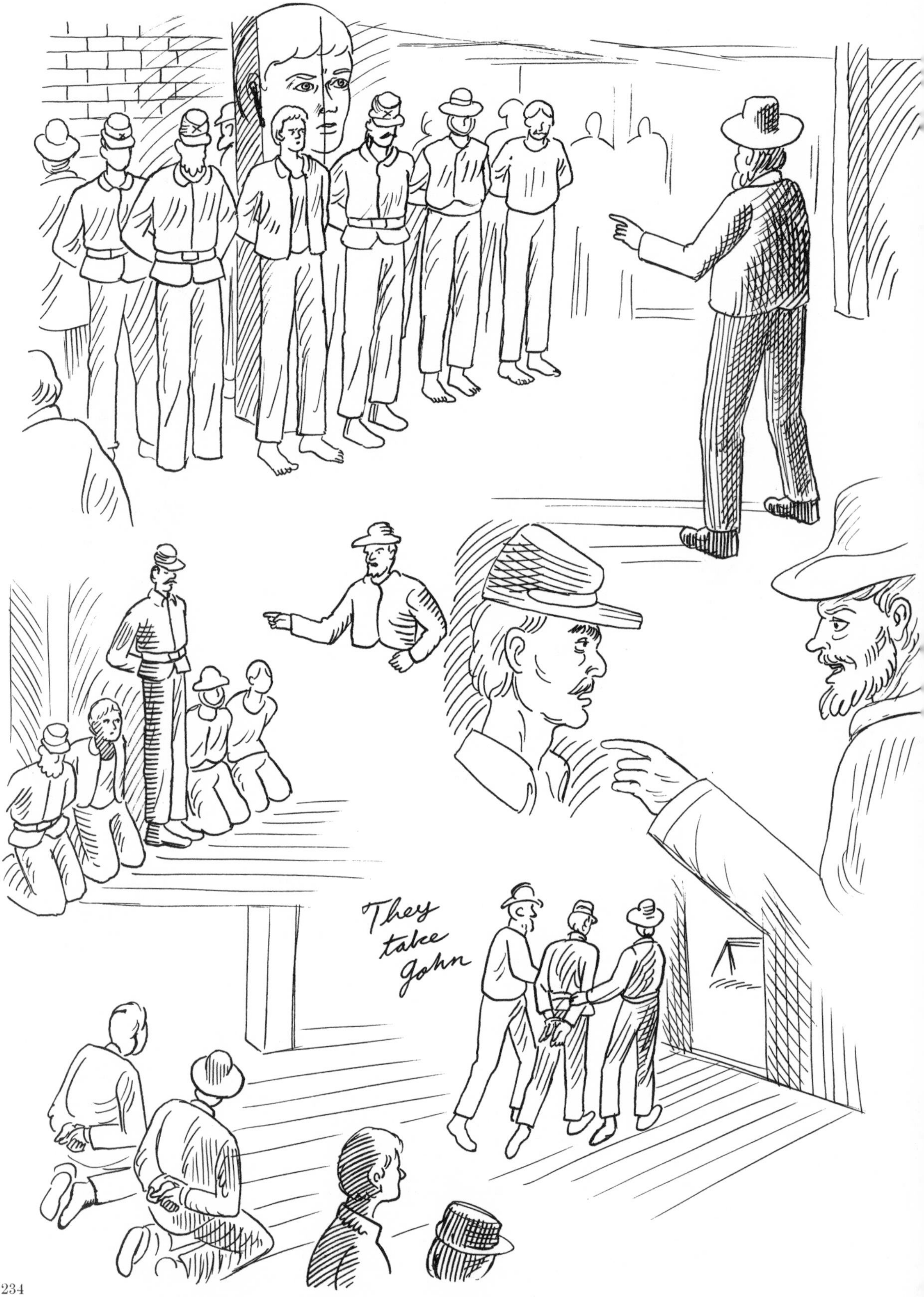
They take John

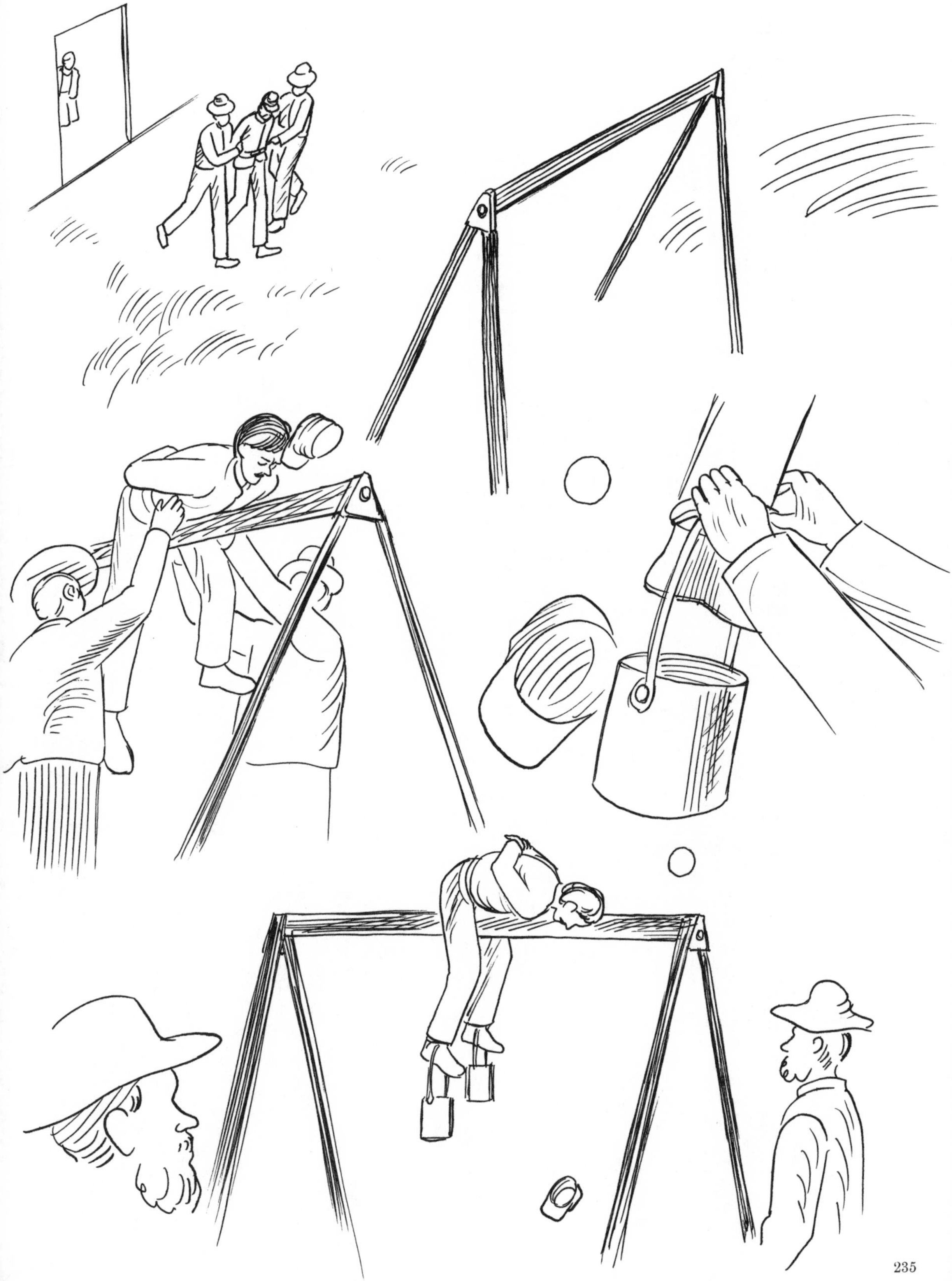

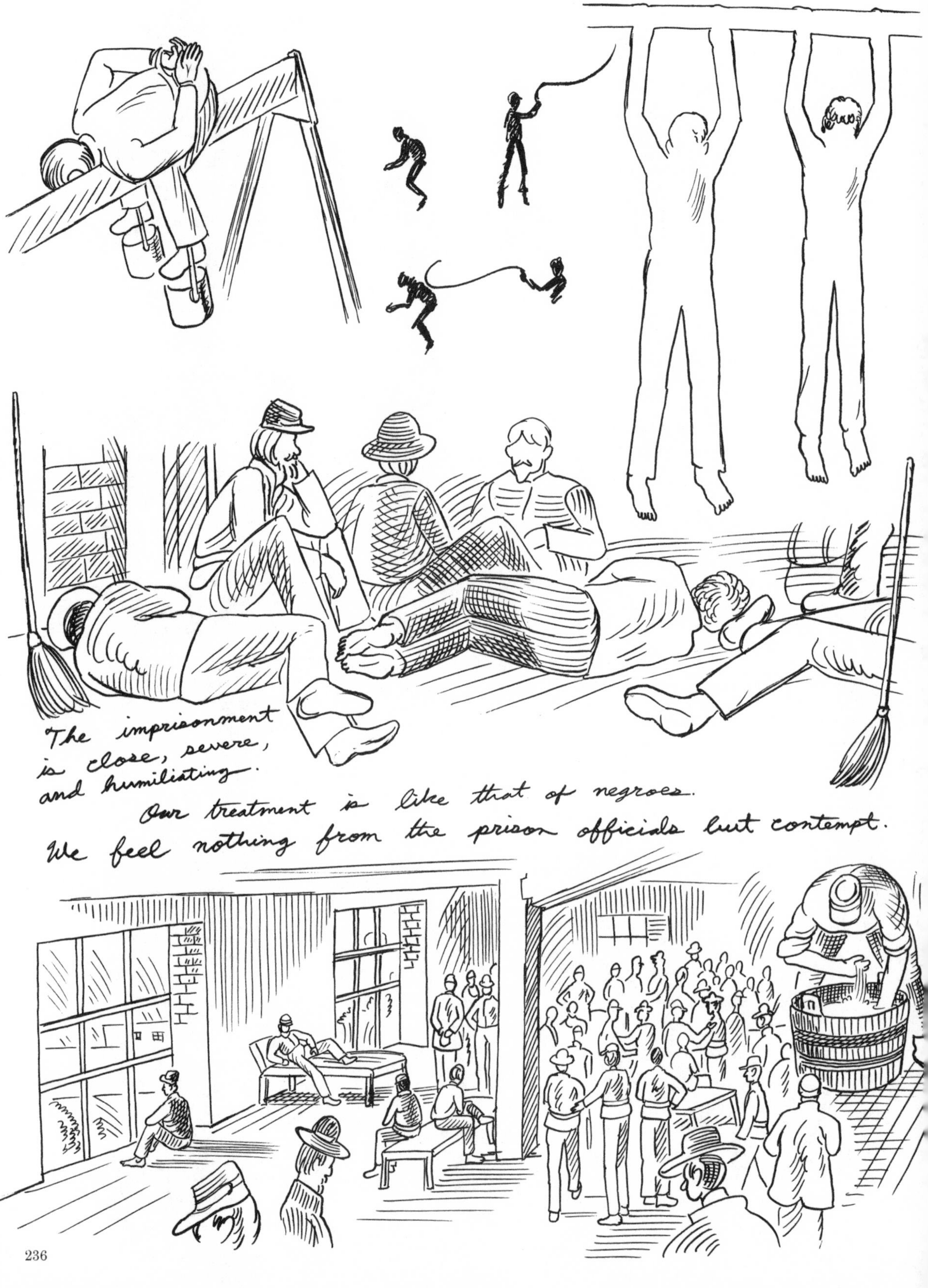
The imprisonment
is close, severe,
and humiliating.
Our treatment is like that of negroes.
We feel nothing from the prison officials but contempt.

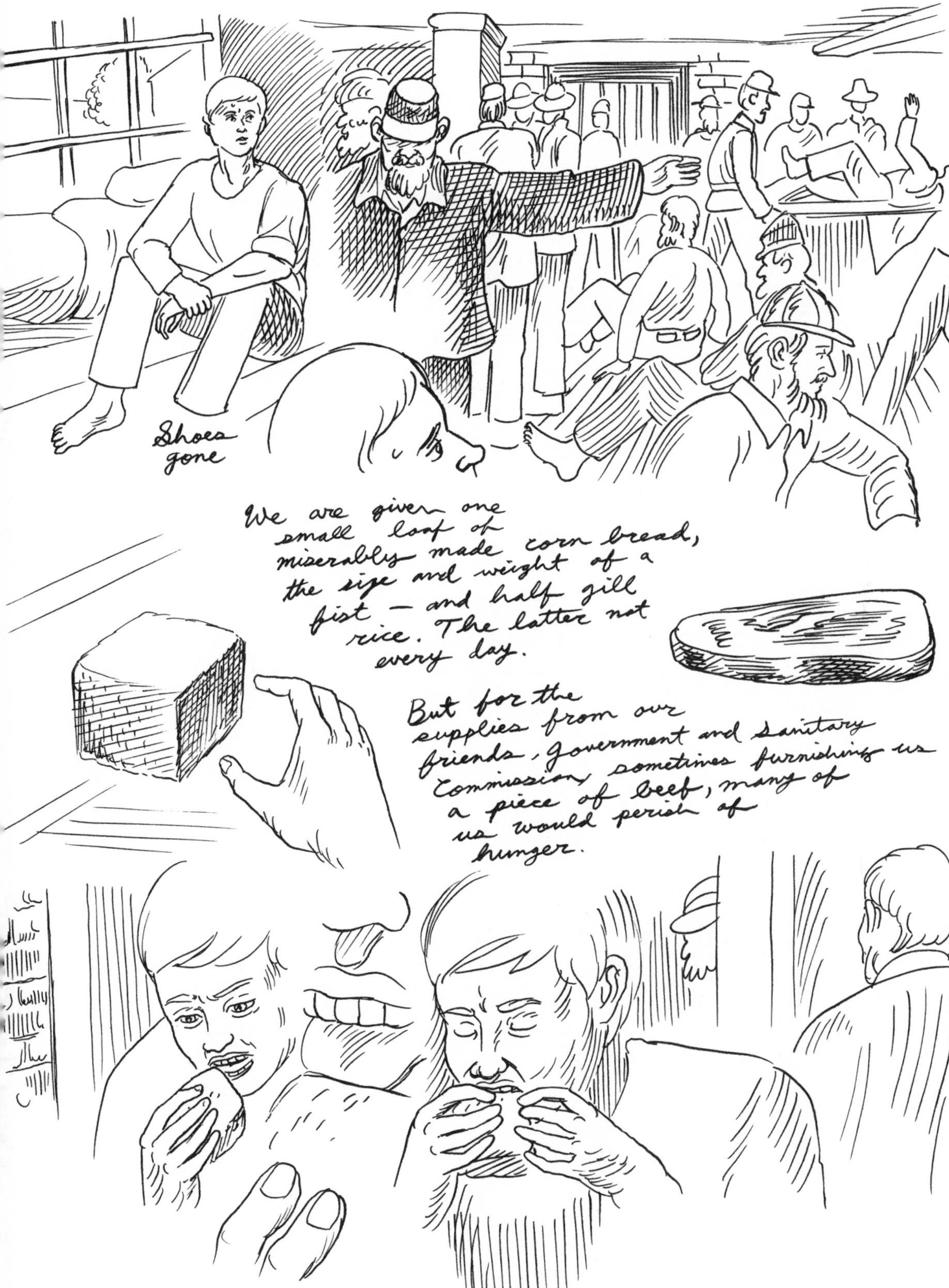
Shoes gone
We are given one small loaf of miserably made corn bread, the size and weight of a fist — and half gill rice. The latter not every day.
But for the supplies from our friends, Government and Sanitary Commission, sometimes furnishing us a piece of beef, many of us would perish of hunger.

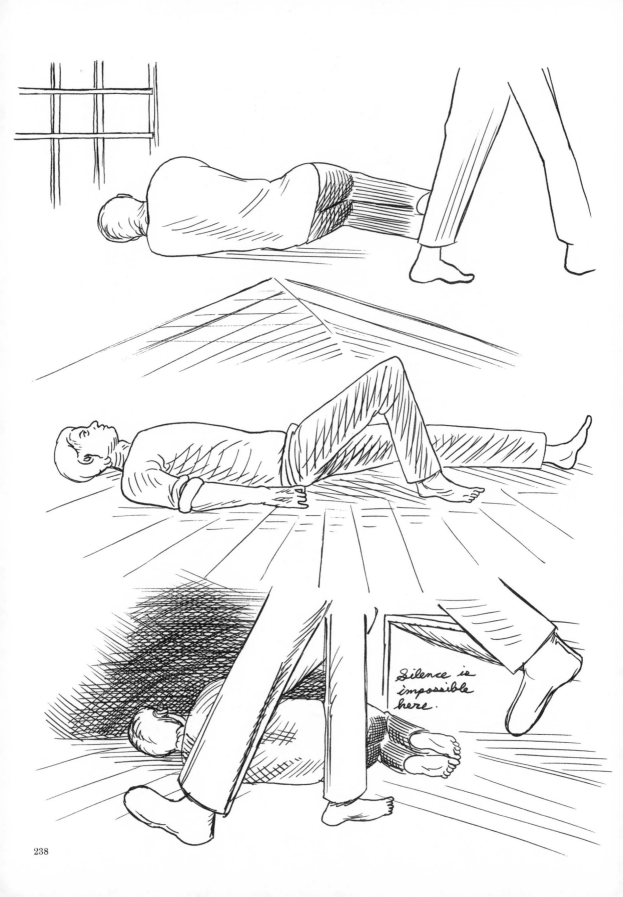

Silence is impossible here.

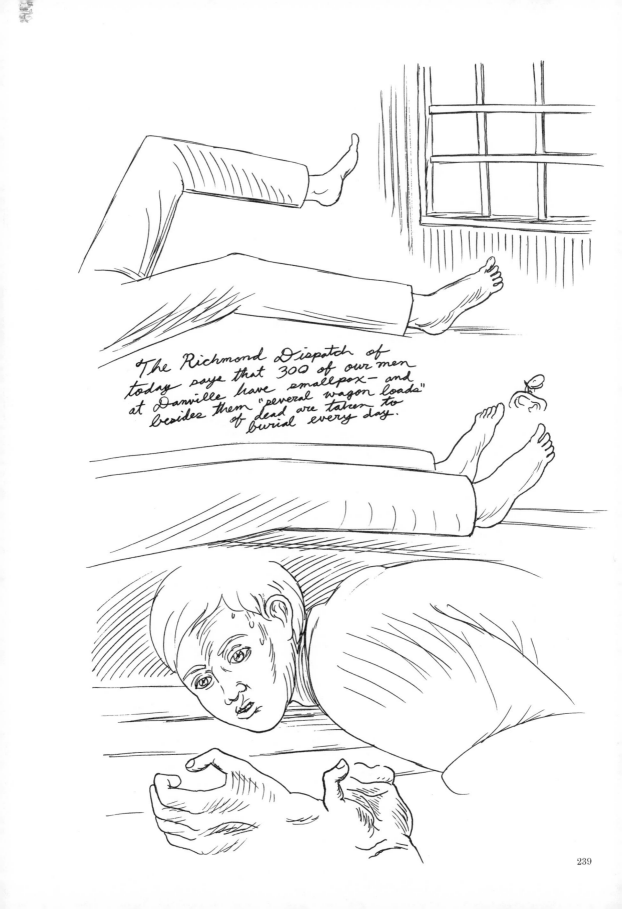

The Richmond Dispatch of today says that 300 of our men at Danville have smallpox — and besides them "several wagon loads" of dead are taken to burial every day.

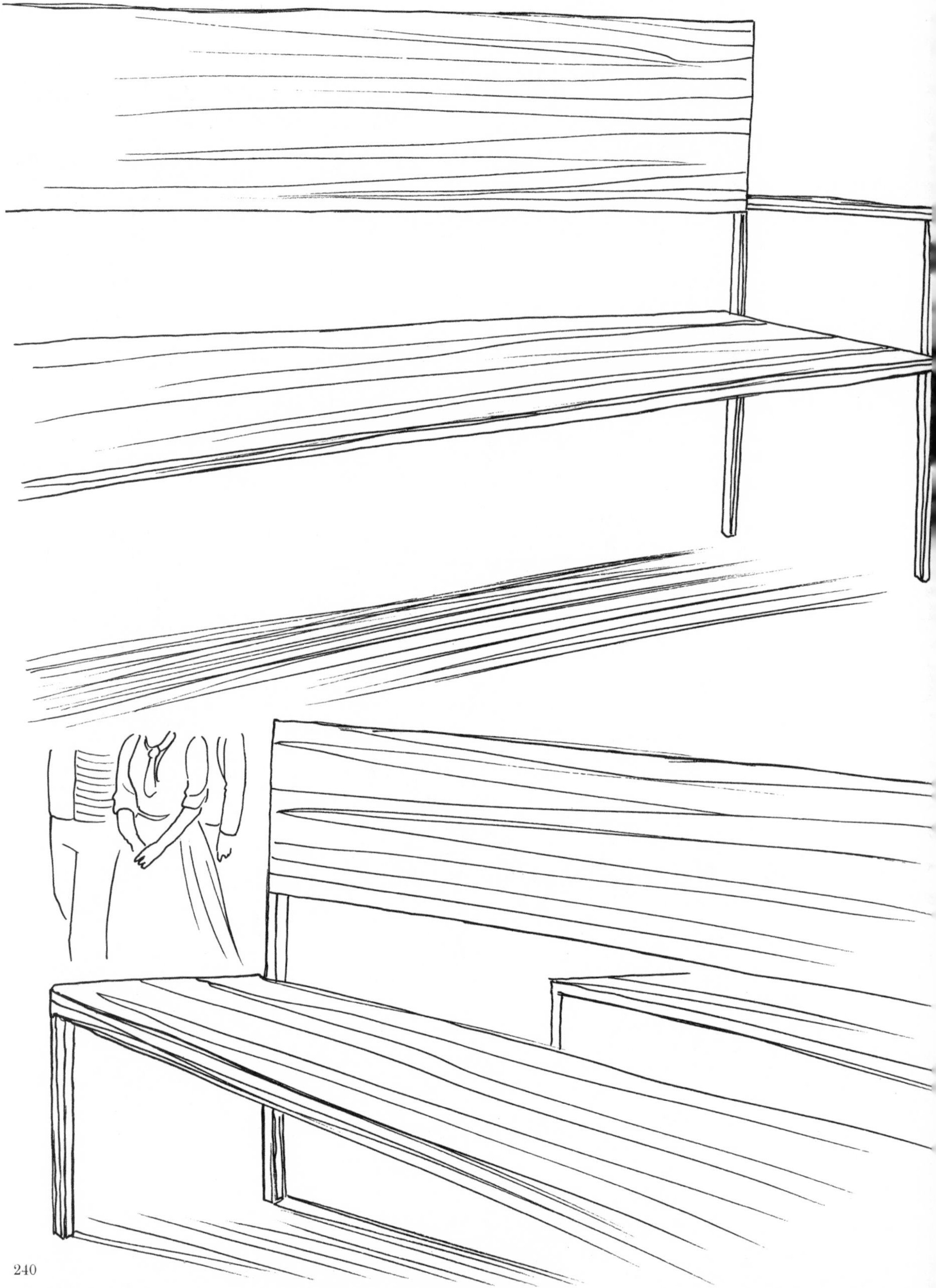

Of the Society of Friends was in a healthy condition, there would be some action taking place in meeting, in giving counsel and encouragement to strengthen the hands of Friends faithfully to maintain a Christian testimony against war and all warlike measures, including a present levying of a tax for the support of the war. The matter which my mother Elizabeth brought before the meeting, but the spirit prevails, and has ruled for years past, turned judgement away backward, and the honest-hearted, who had hoped for counsel from the Society, were discouraged through the position taken by the leaders of the meeting who endeavored to make it appear that our testimony did not require us to decline paying the tax now demanded.

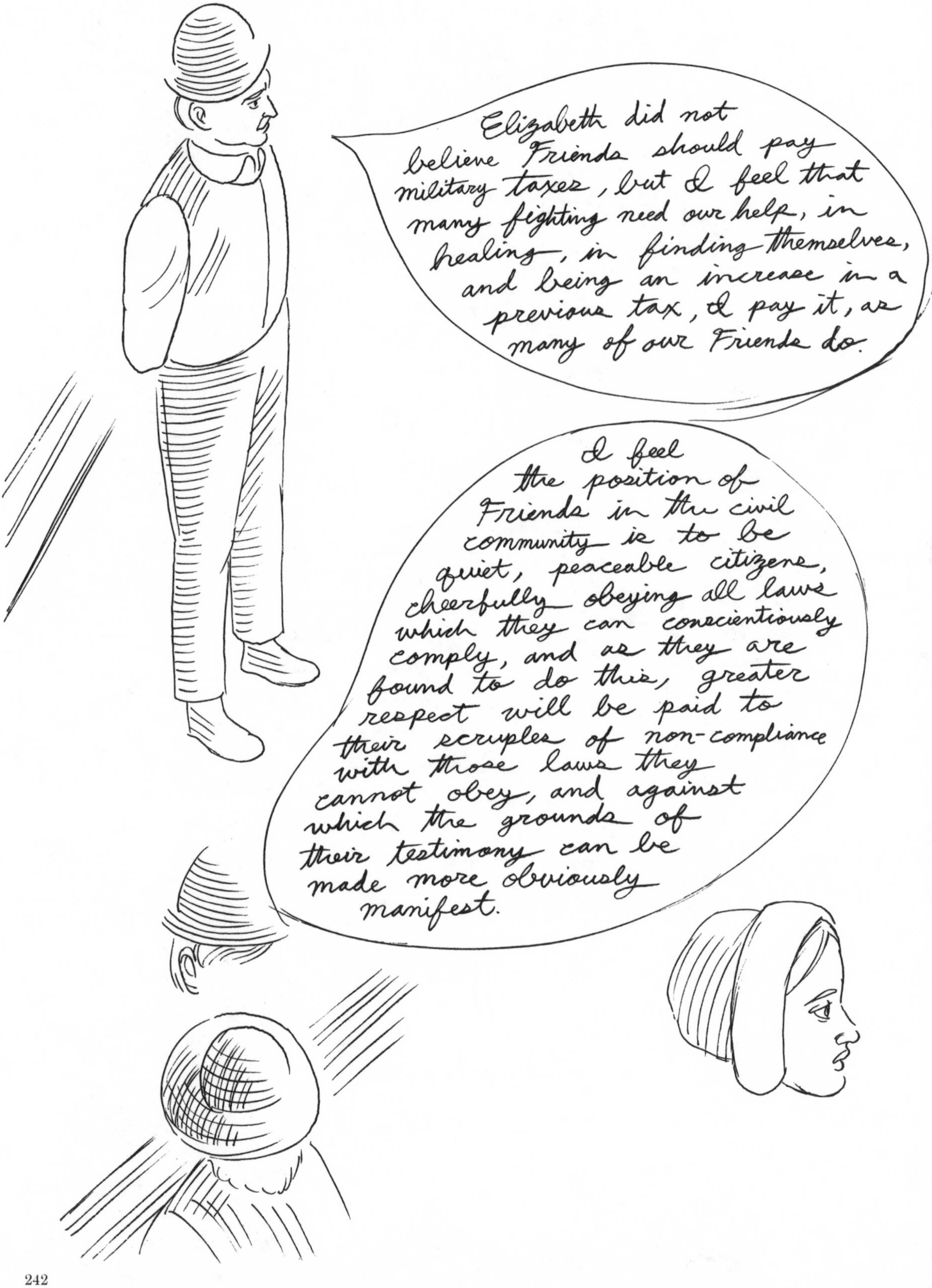
Elizabeth did not believe Friends should pay military taxes, but I feel that many fighting need our help, in healing, in finding themselves, and being an increase in a previous tax, I pay it, as many of our Friends do.
I feel the position of Friends in the civil community is to be quiet, peaceable citizens, cheerfully obeying all laws which they can conscientiously comply, and as they are found to do this, greater respect will be paid to their scruples of non-compliance with those laws they cannot obey, and against which the grounds of their testimony can be made more obviously manifest.

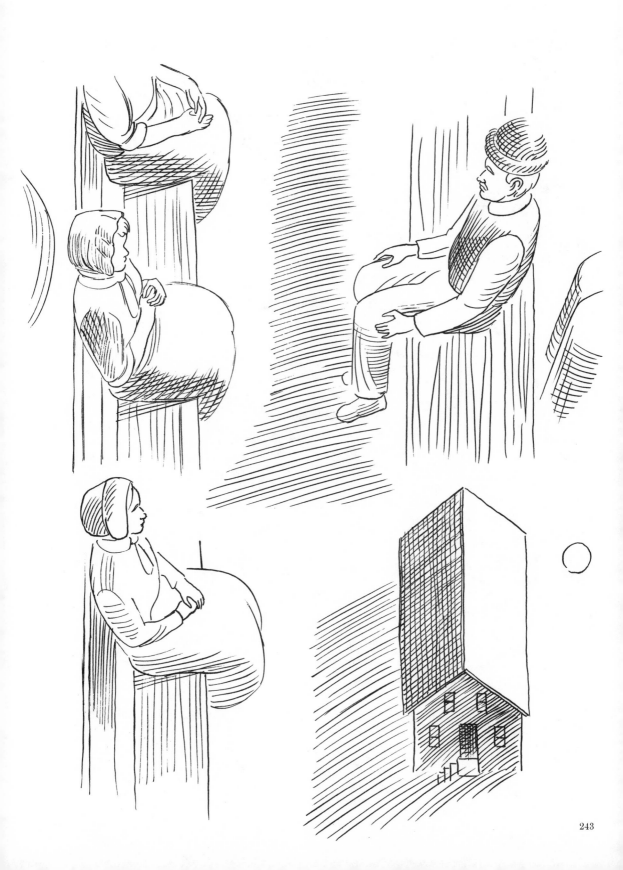

243

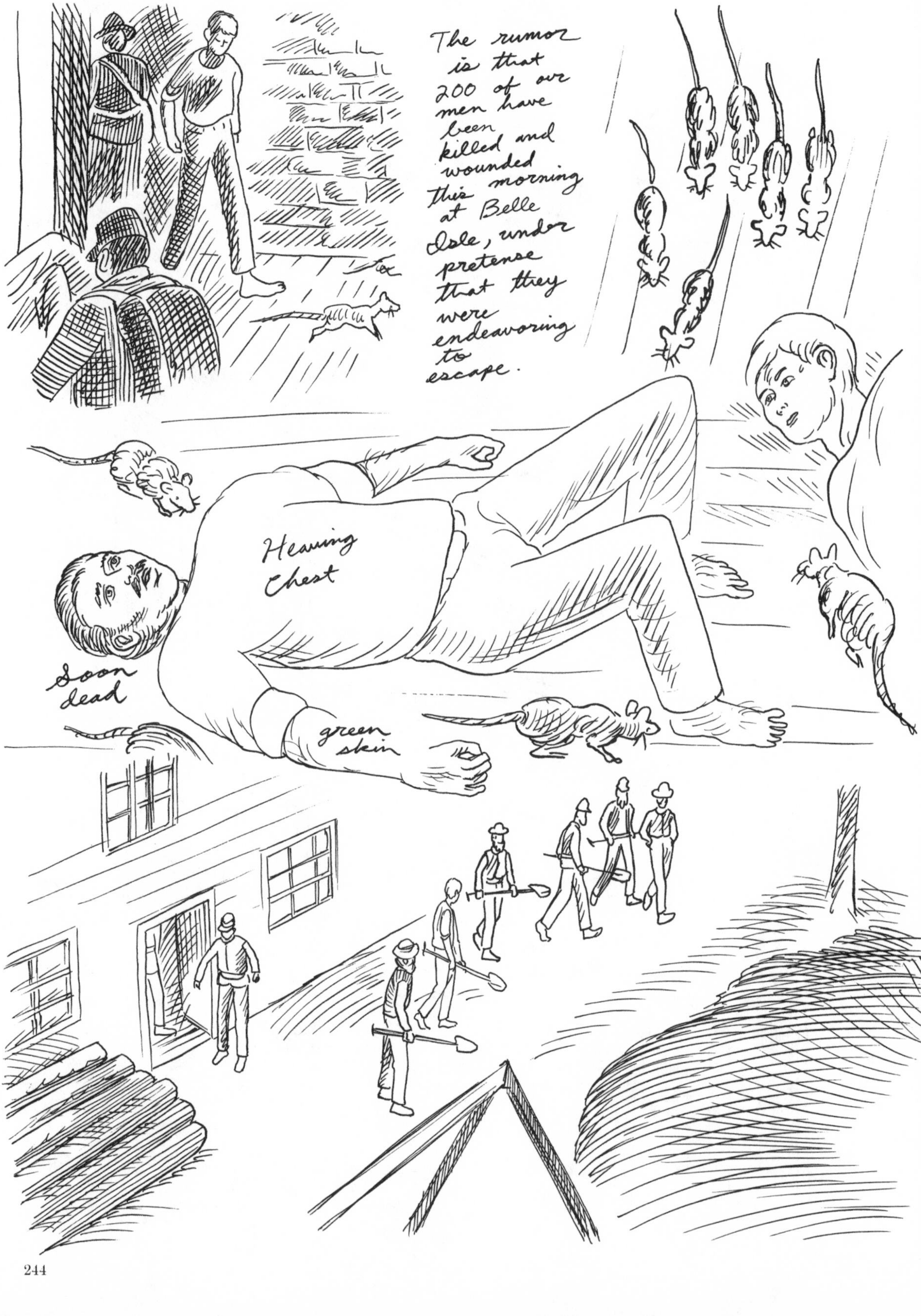
The rumor is that 200 of our men have been killed and wounded this morning at Belle Isle, under pretense that they were endeavoring to escape.
Heaving Chest
Soon dead
green skin

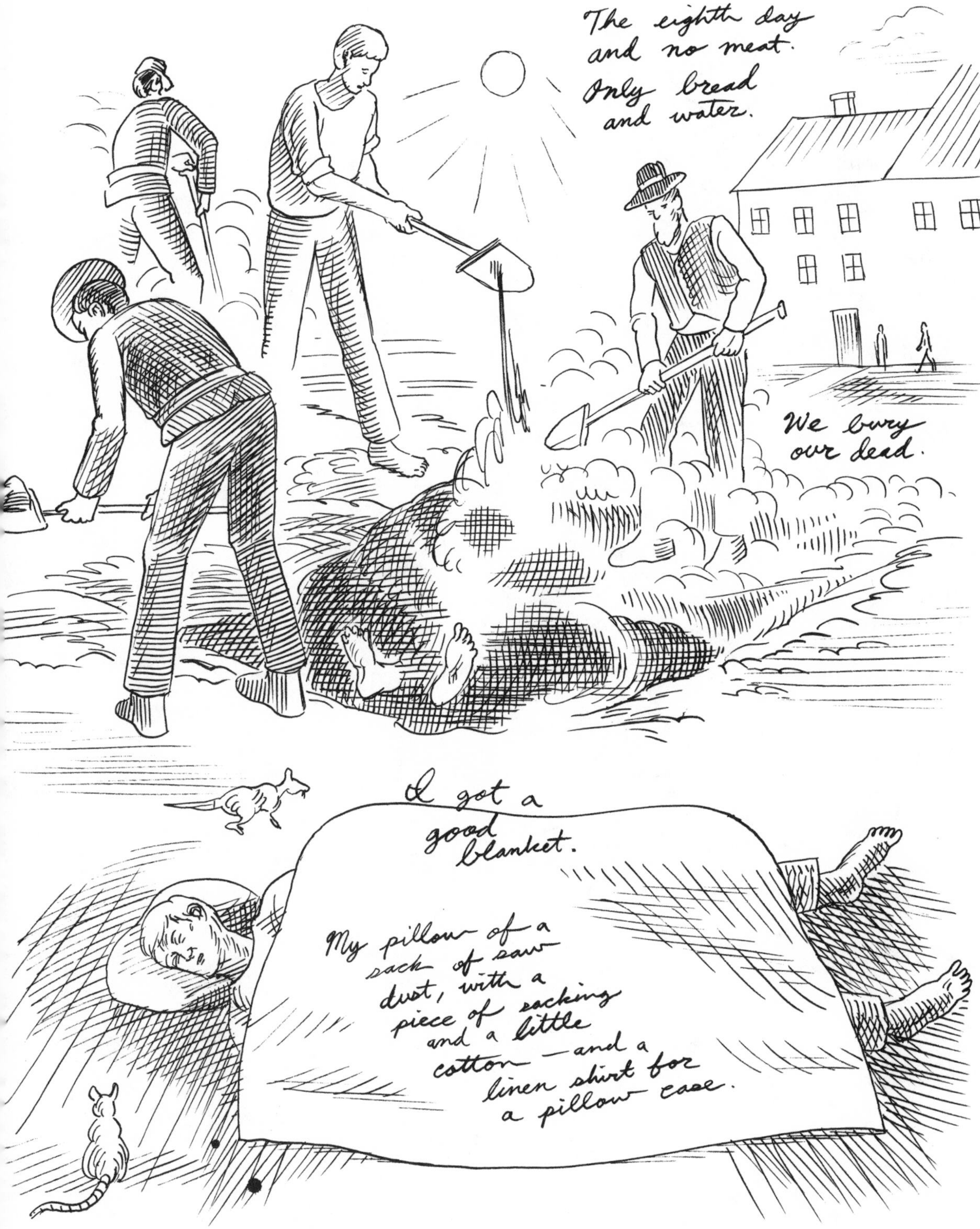

The eighth day and no meat. Only bread and water.
We bury our dead.
I got a good blanket.
My pillow of a sack of saw dust, with a piece of sacking and a little cotton—and a linen shirt for a pillow case.

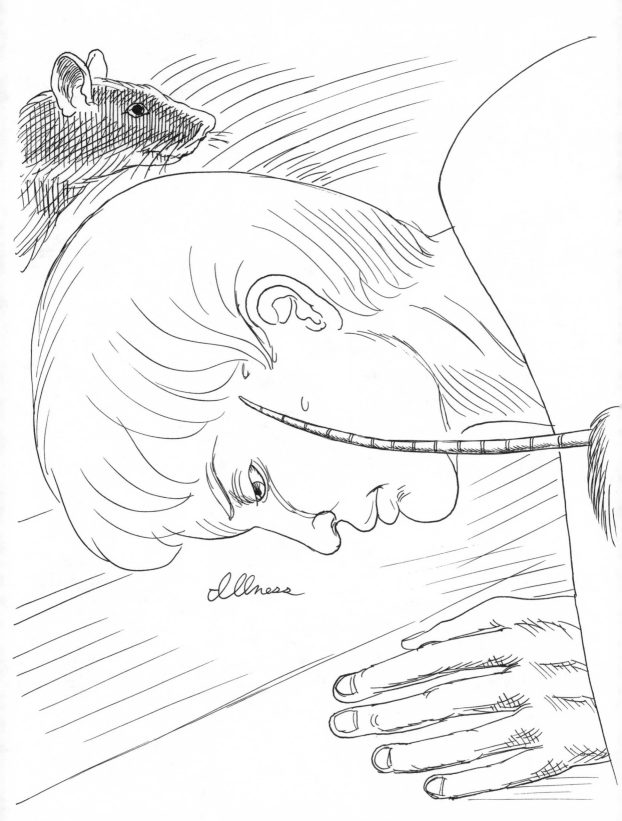

Illness

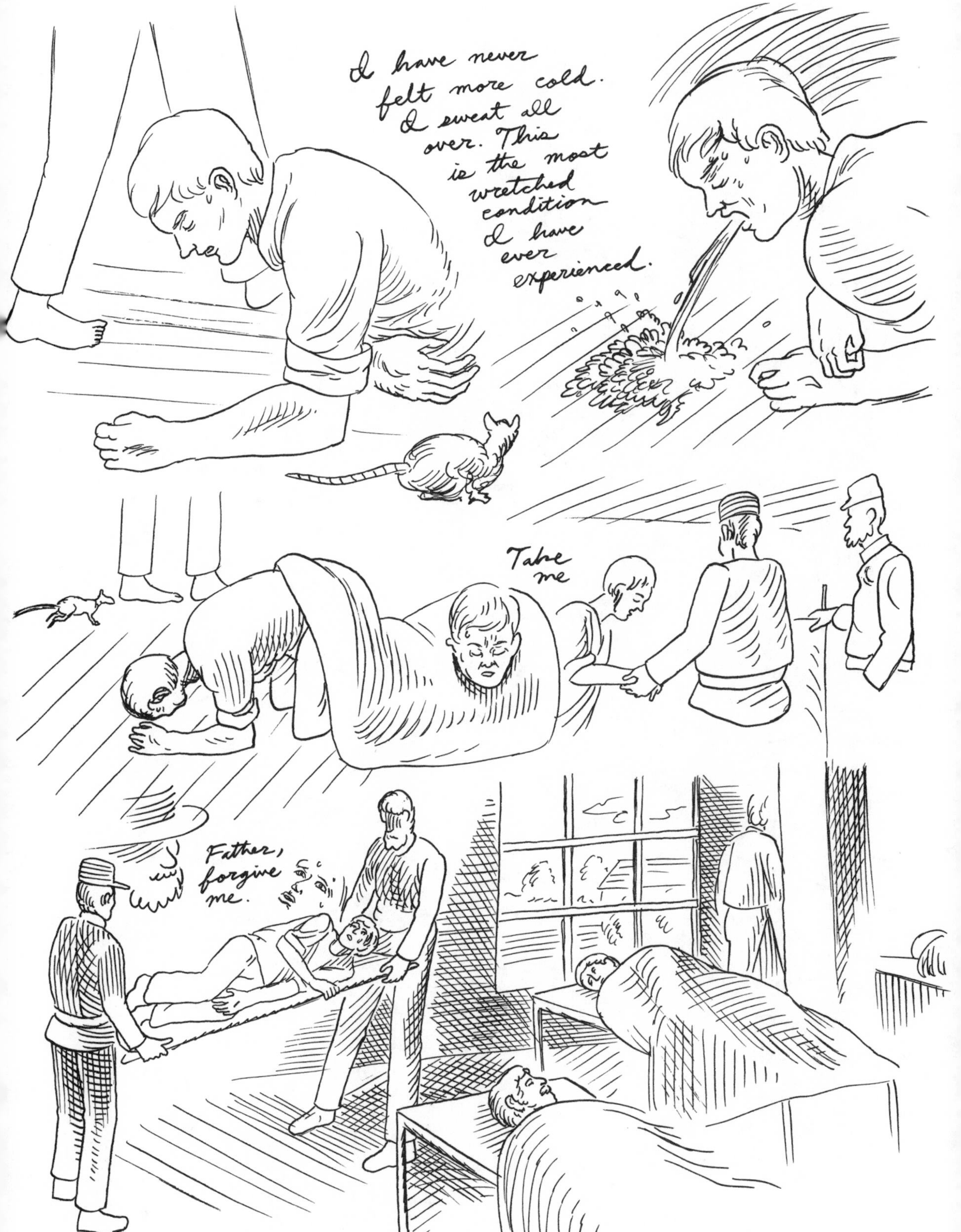
I have never felt more cold. I sweat all over. This is the most wretched condition I have ever experienced.
Take me
Father, forgive me.

I can sense
only parts of
my arm now.
Only a third of
my toes.
I have never
felt more
disconnected and
connected to my
body, this fragile
shell which
houses my
inner light.
Dear Lord, I
pray to
thee.

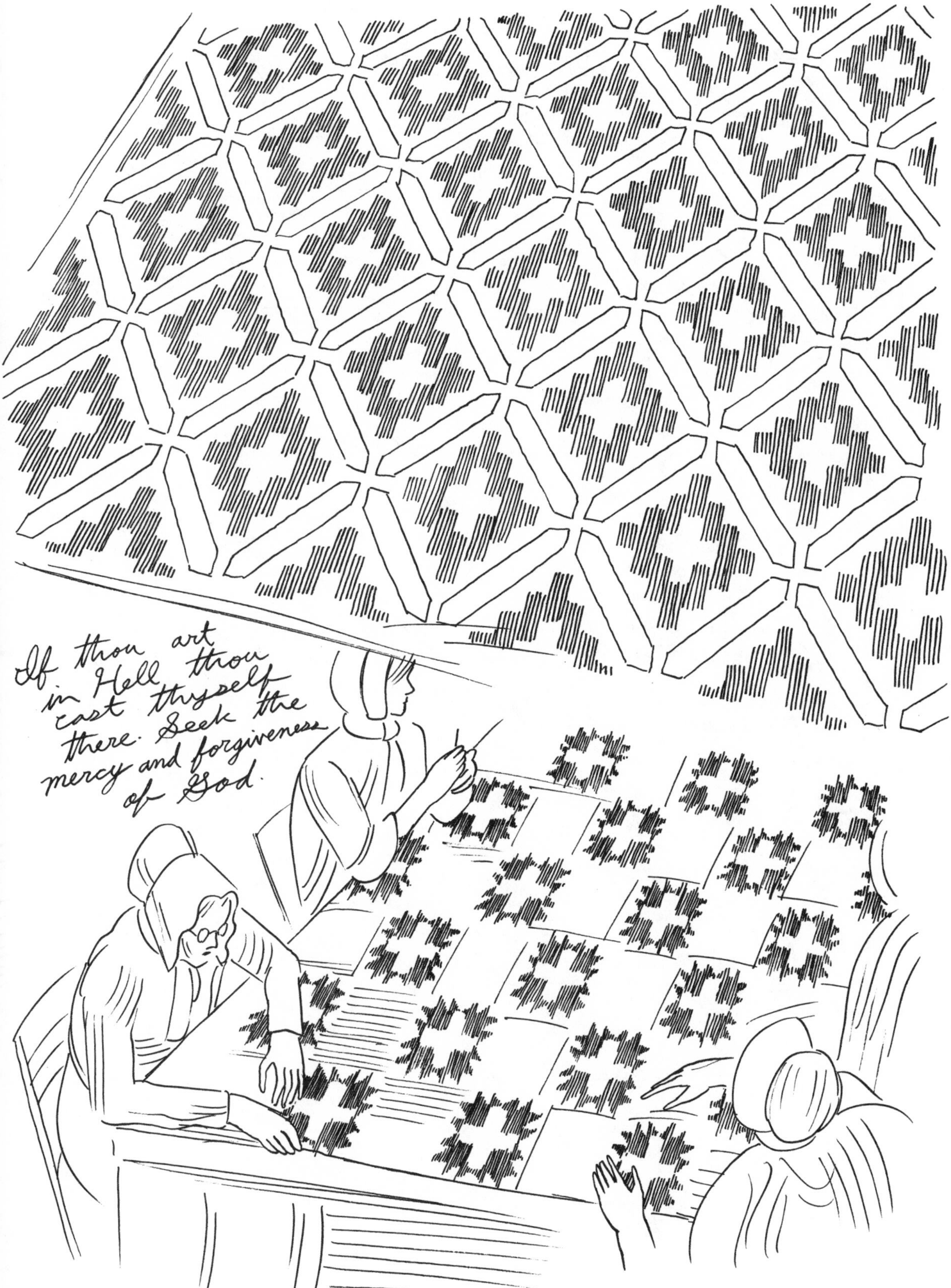
If thou art
in Hell thou
cast thyself
there. Seek the
mercy and forgiveness
of God.

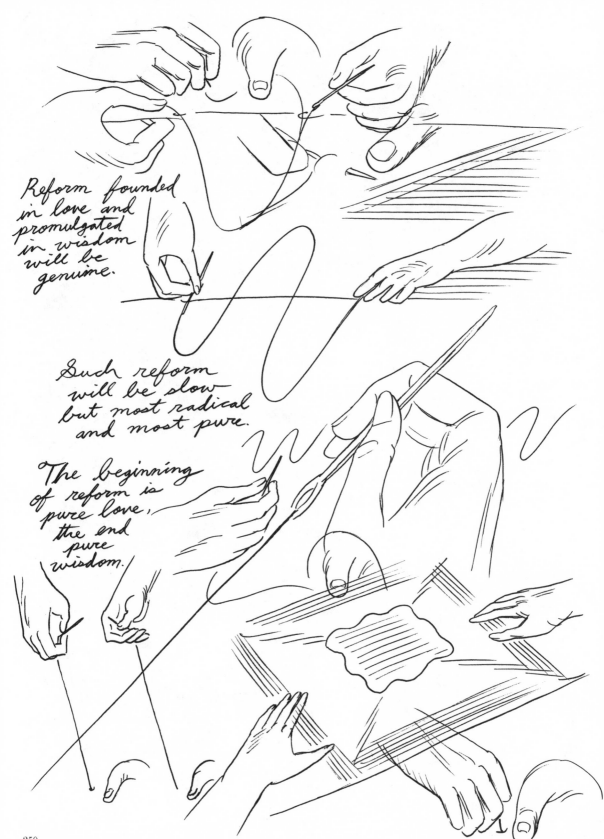

Reform founded
in love and
promulgated
in wisdom
will be
genuine.

Such reform
will be slow
but most radical
and most pure.

The beginning
of reform is
pure love,
the end
pure
wisdom.

If thou lovest mankind with a pure unselfish love, a love which desireth only his external good and thou dost feel God's light with thee opening the way, then walk thou in the light and every word thou shalt utter and every act of thy daily life will conspire to elevate man.

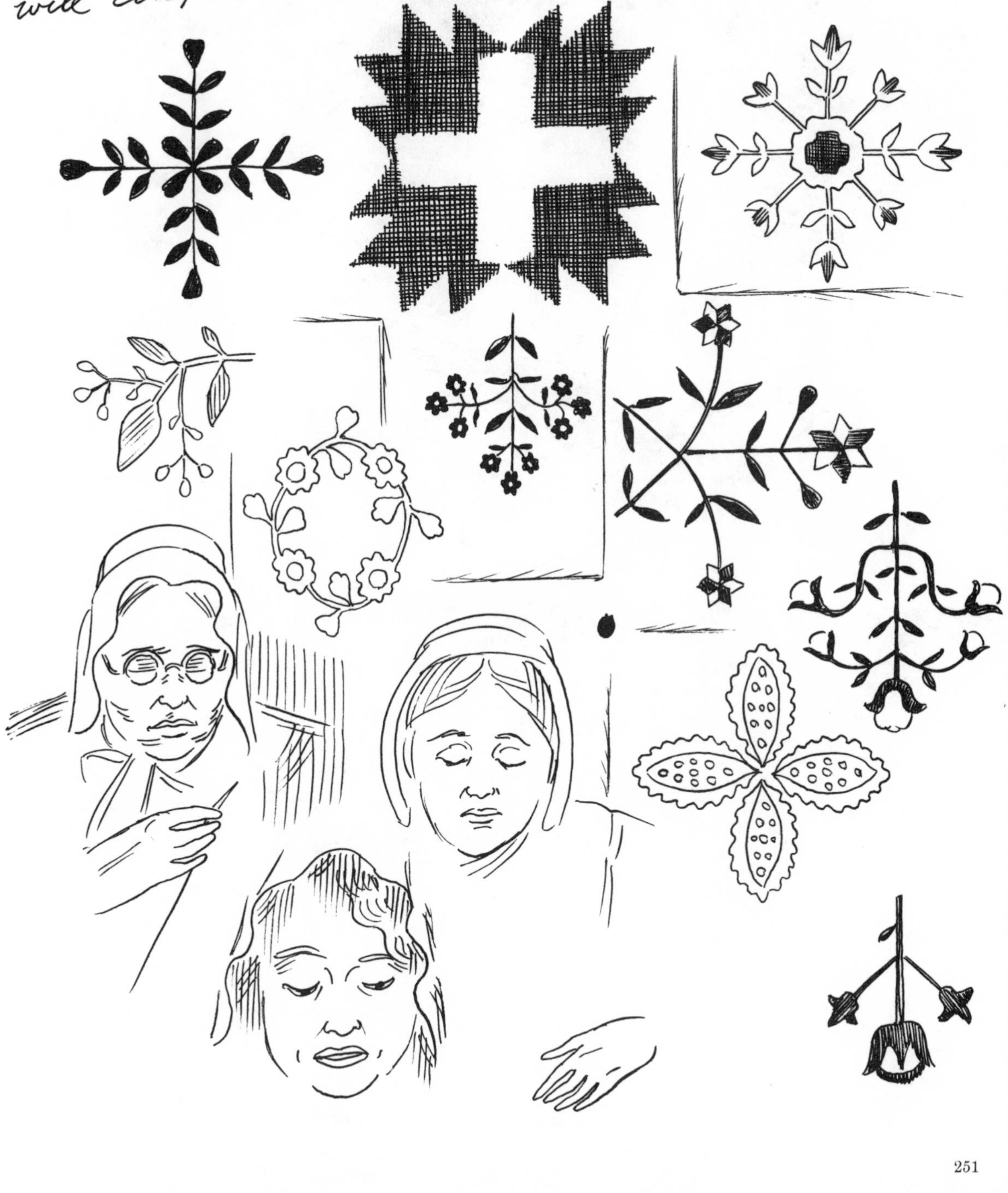

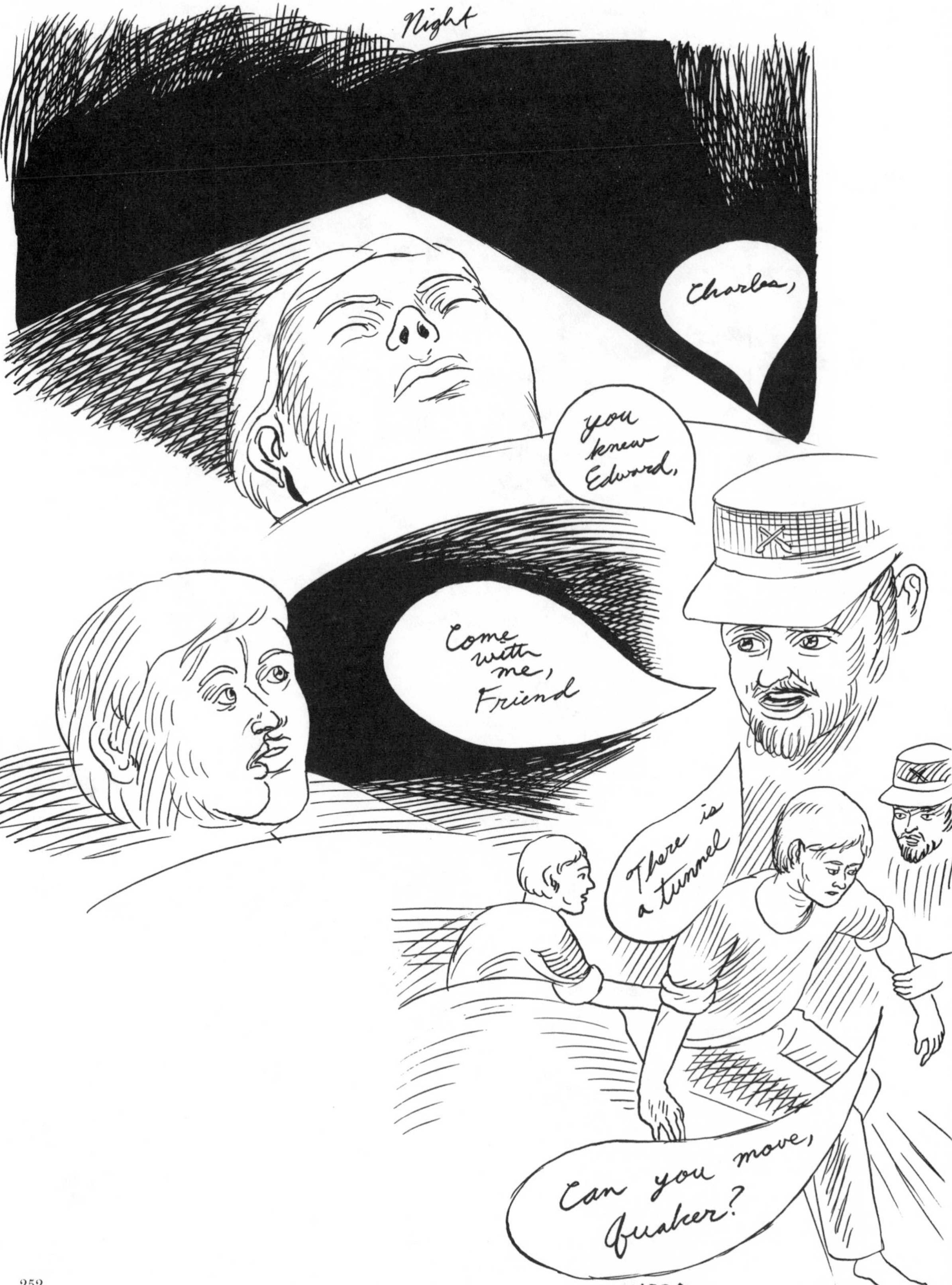
Night
Charles,
you knew Edward,
Come with me, Friend
There is a tunnel
Can you move, Quaker?
prayers answered.

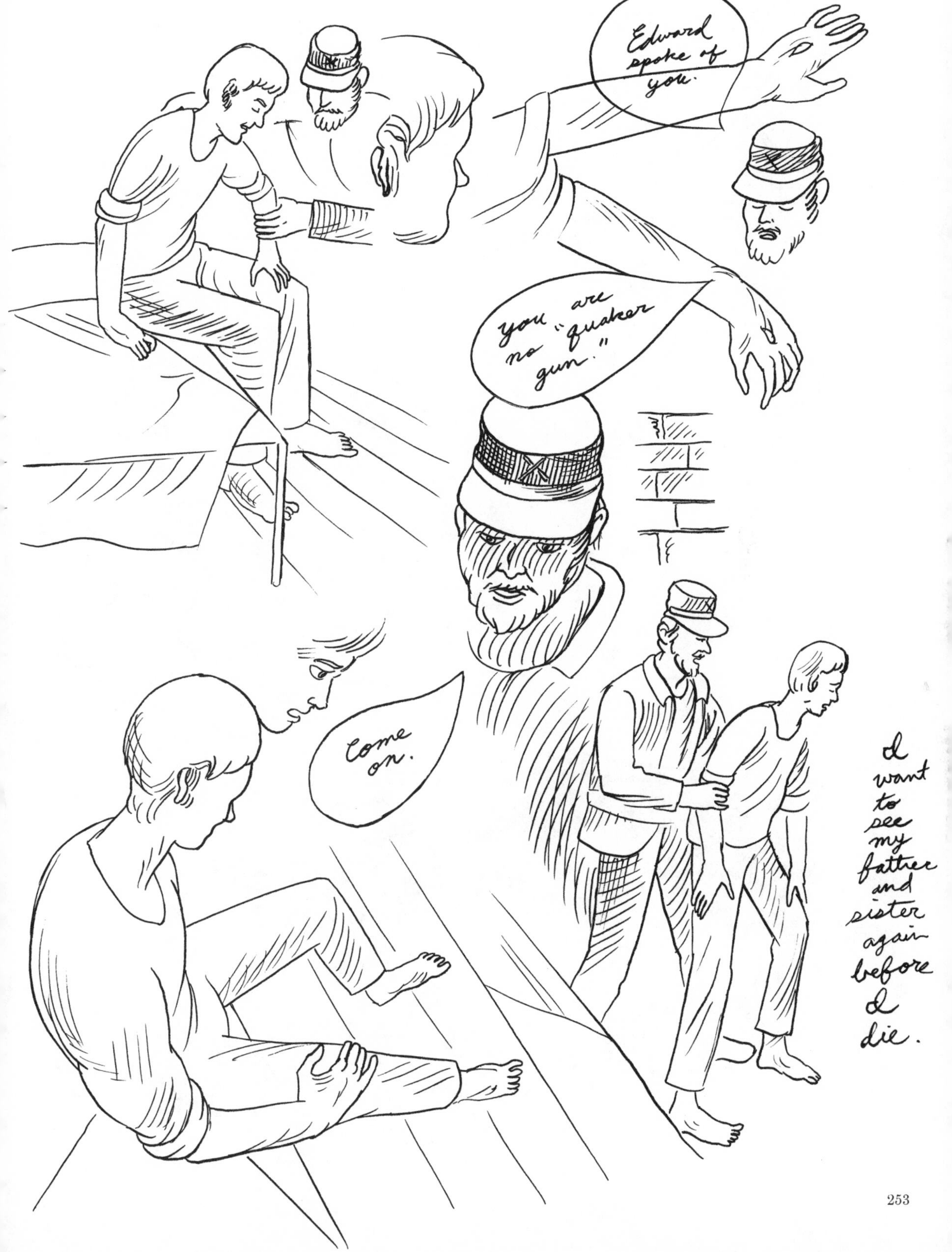
Edward spoke of you.
You are no "quaker gun."
Come on.
I want to see my father and sister again before I die.

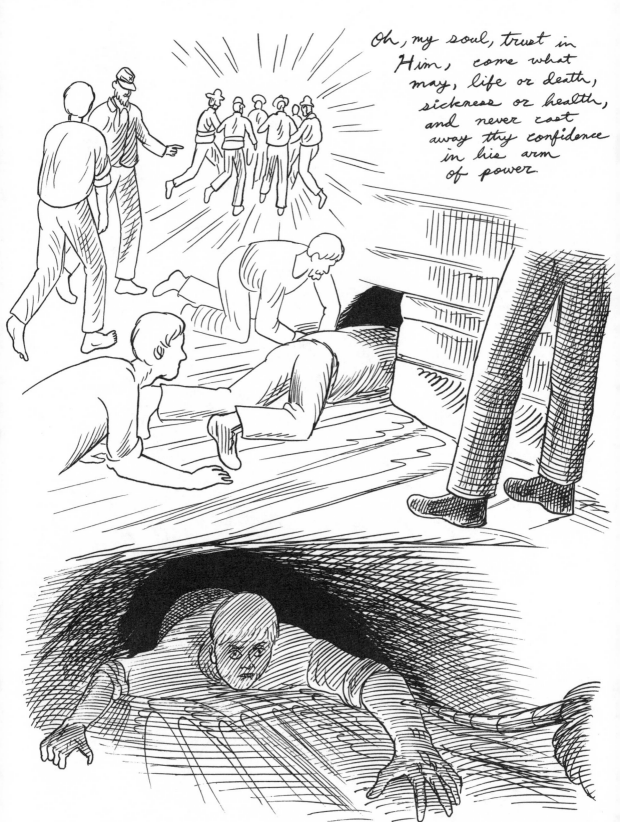

Oh, my soul, trust in Him, come what may, life or death, sickness or health, and never cast away thy confidence in his arm of power.

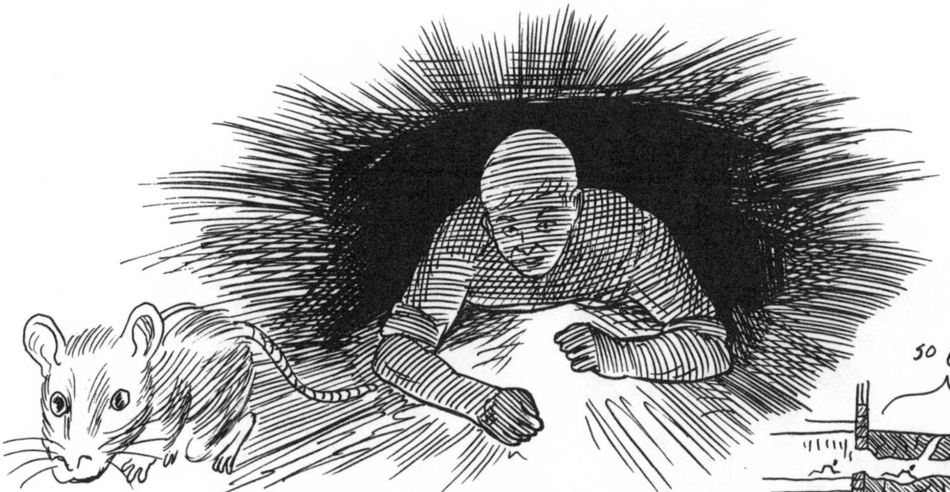

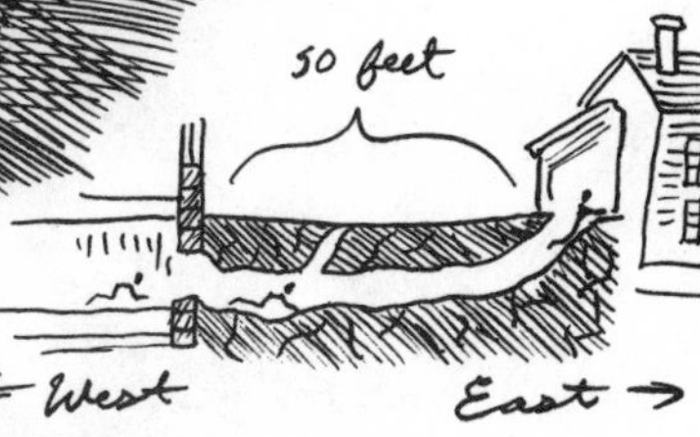

50 feet
← West
East →

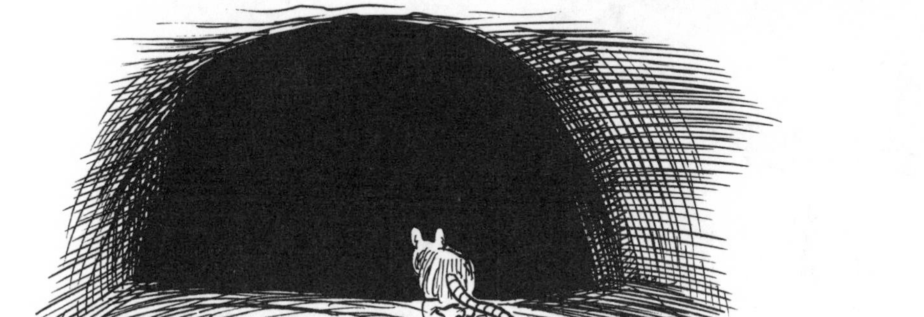

Heaven is not seen, it is felt and known. It is within thy spiritual understanding. It is not entered by force. Thou cannot batter down the doors of heaven and rush headlong in.

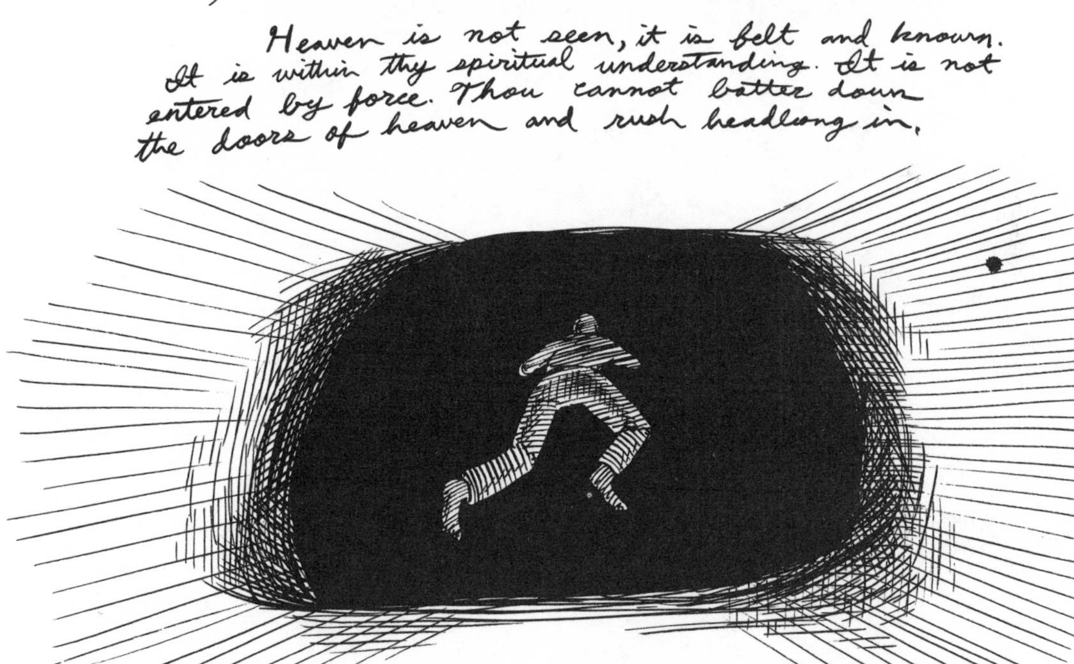

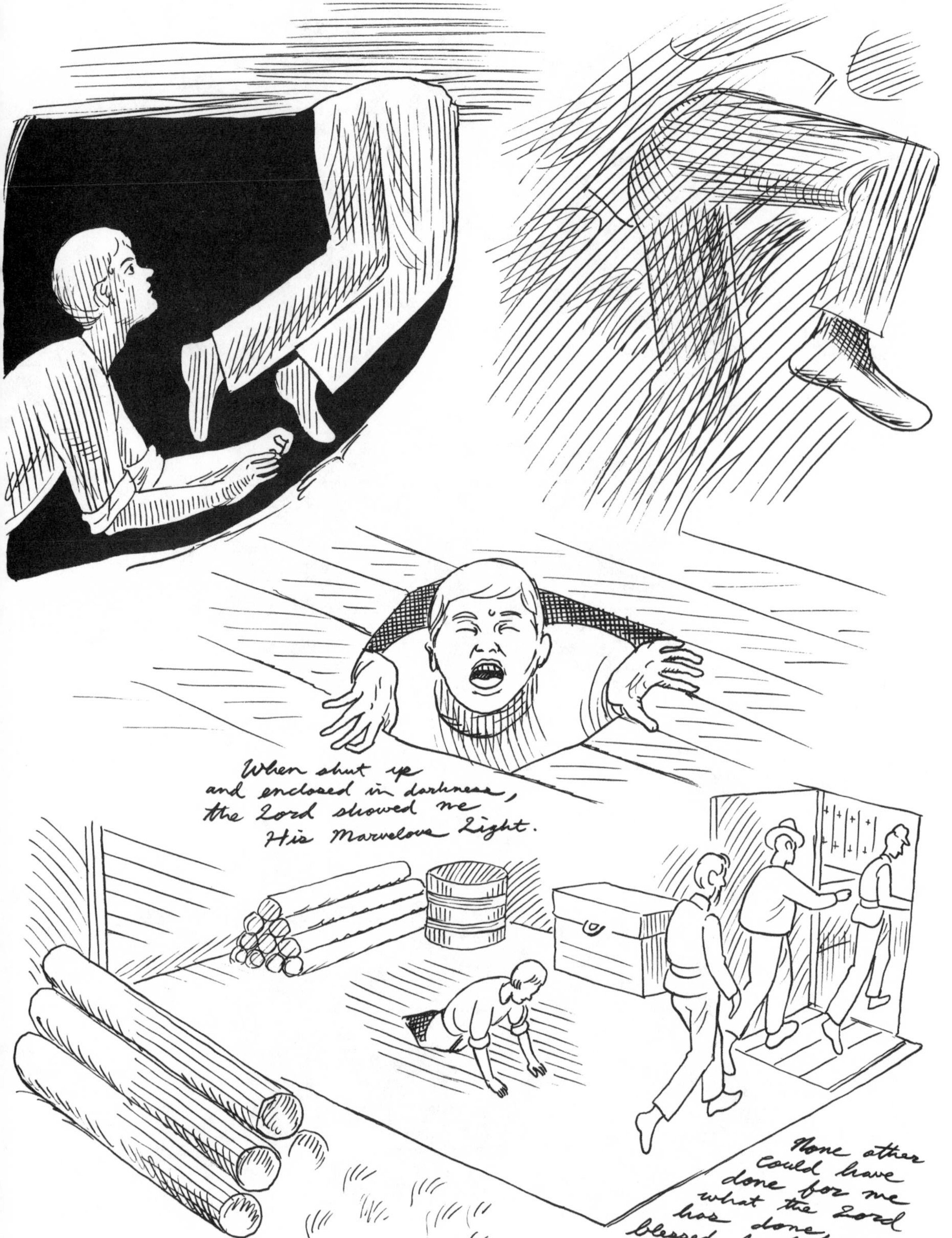
When shut up
and enclosed in darkness,
the Lord showed me
His Marvelous Light.
None other
could have
done for me
what the Lord
has done,
blessed be his name.

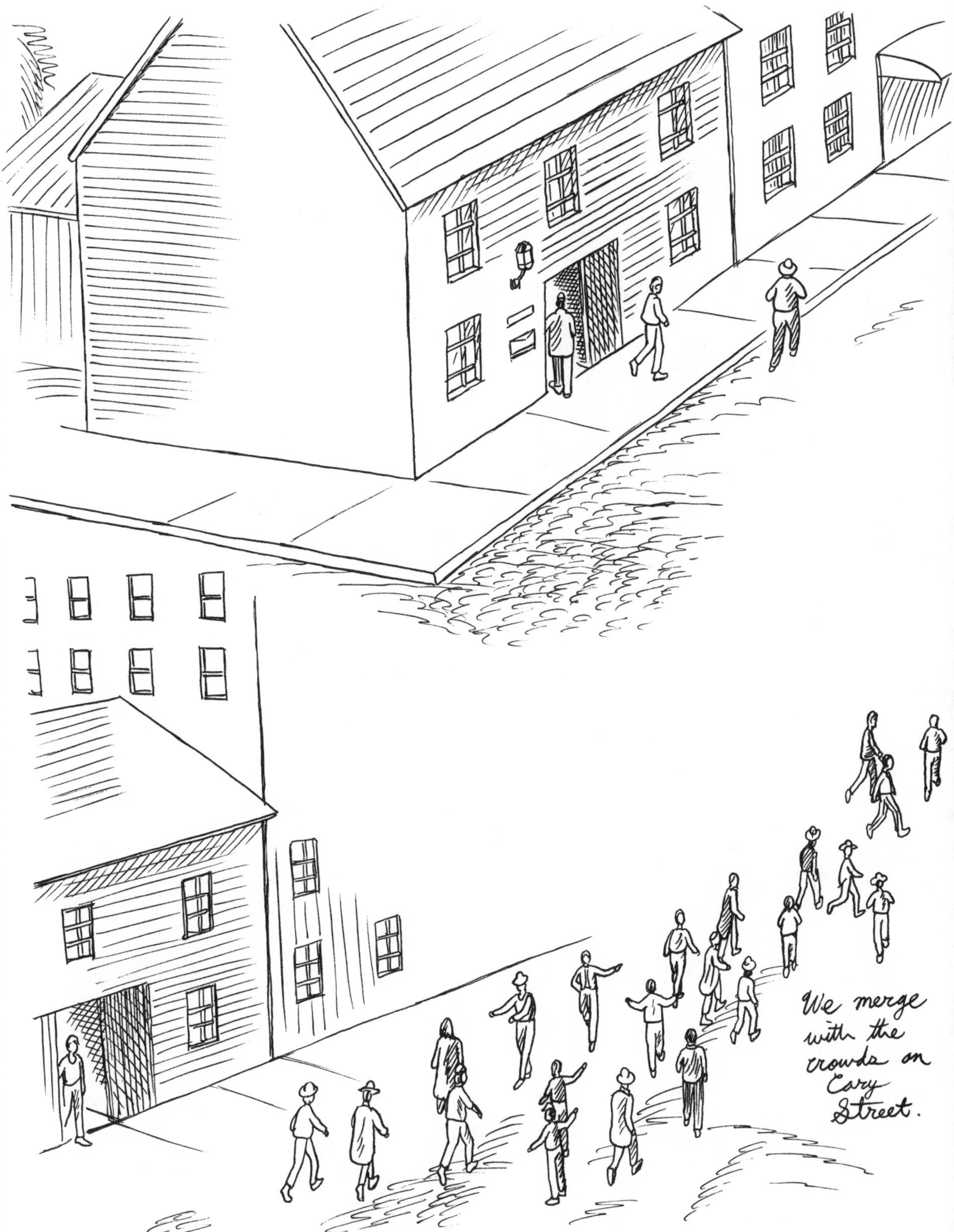
We merge with the crowds on Cary Street.

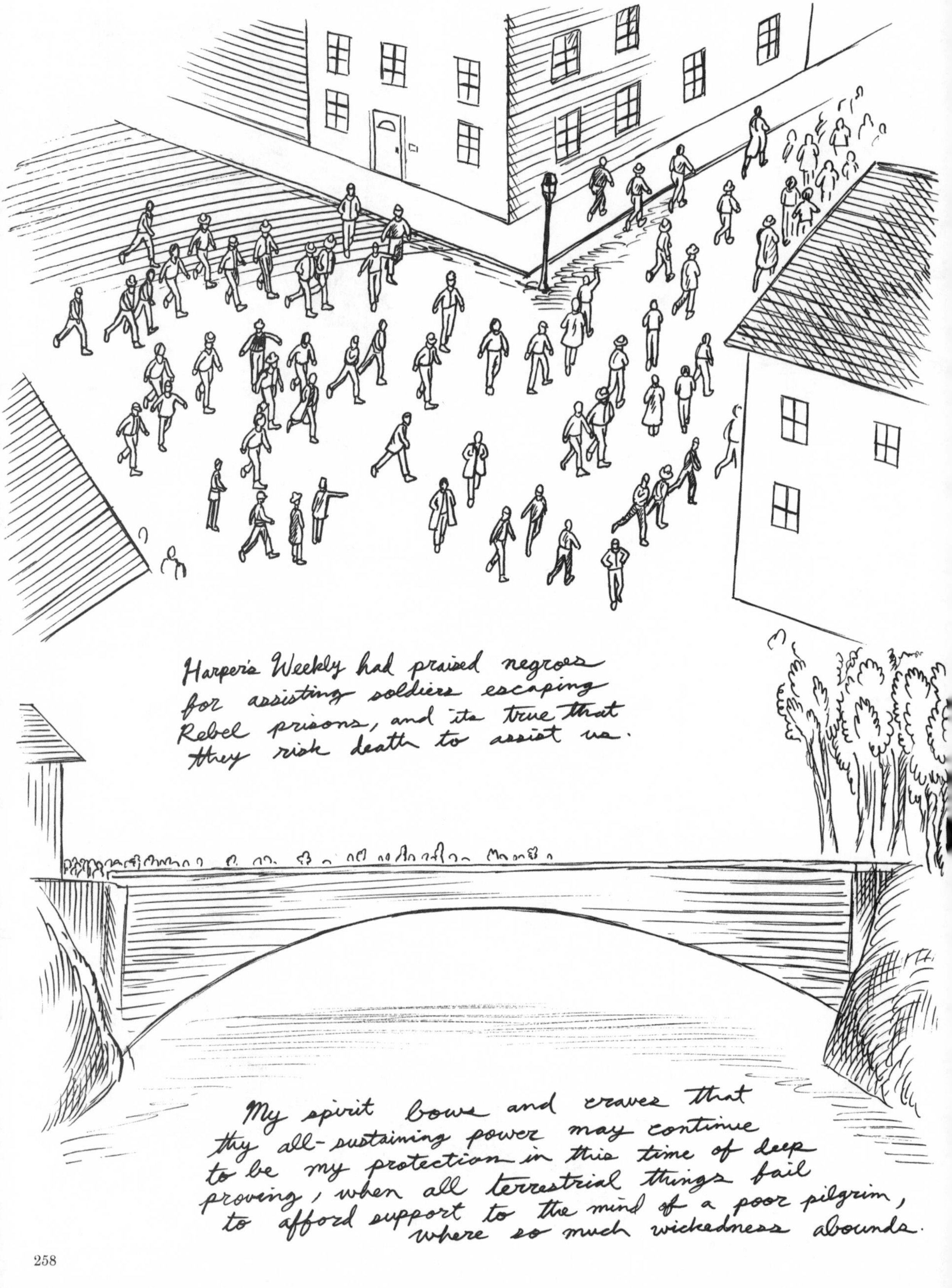
Harper's Weekly had praised negroes for assisting soldiers escaping Rebel prisons, and its true that they risk death to assist us.
My spirit bows and craves that thy all-sustaining power may continue to be my protection in this time of deep proving, when all terrestrial things fail to afford support to the mind of a poor pilgrim, where so much wickedness abounds.

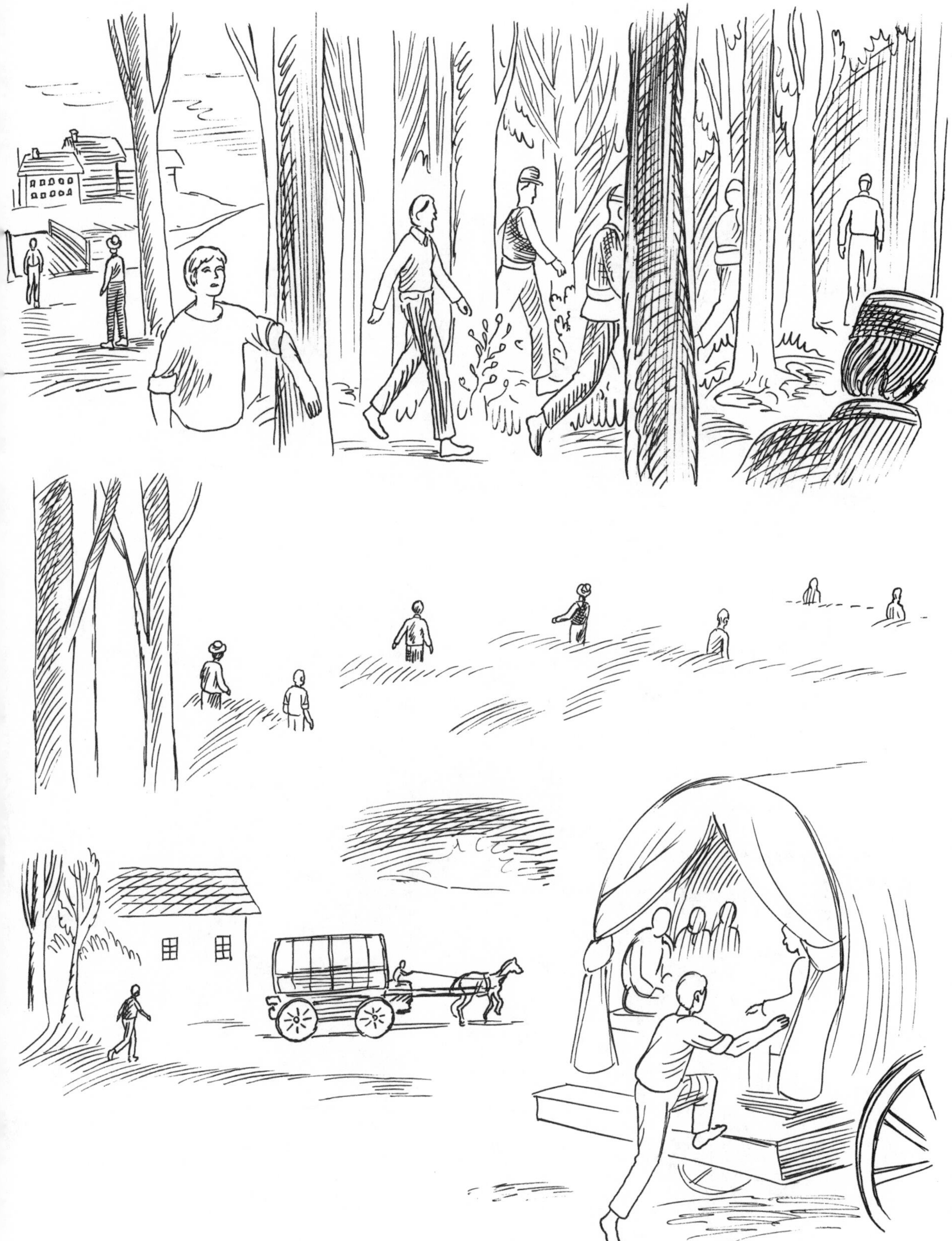

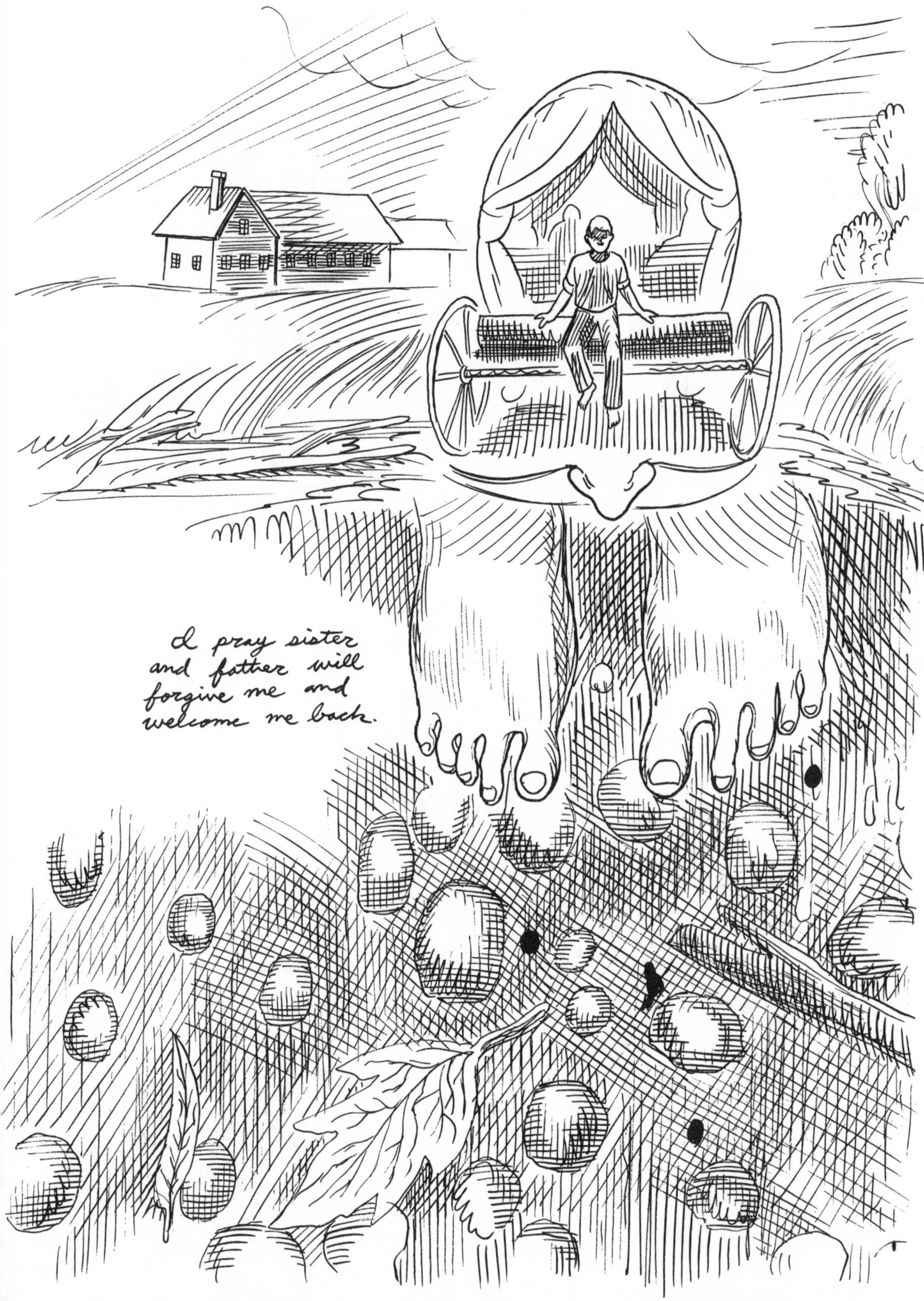
I pray sister and father will forgive me and welcome me back.

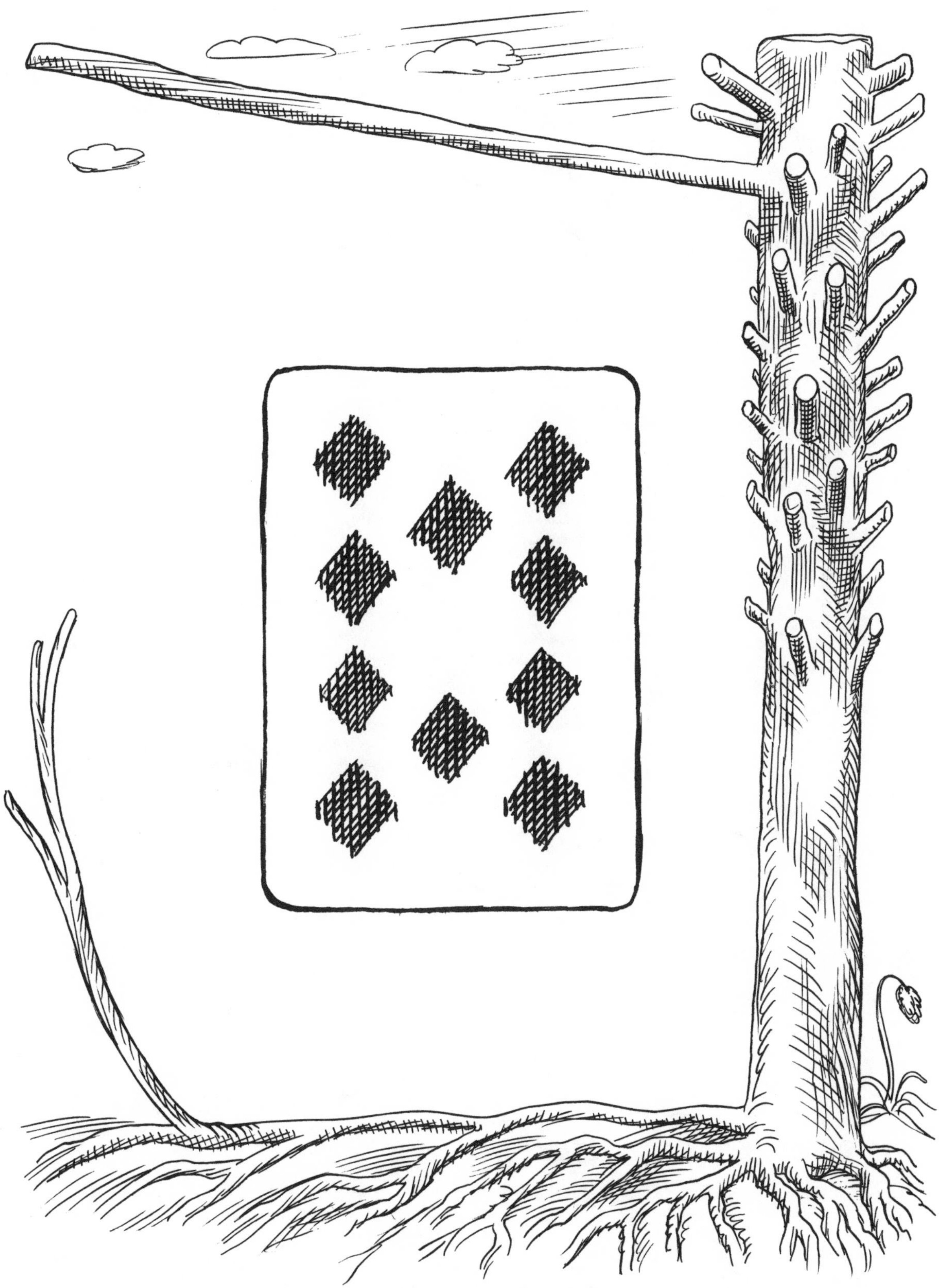

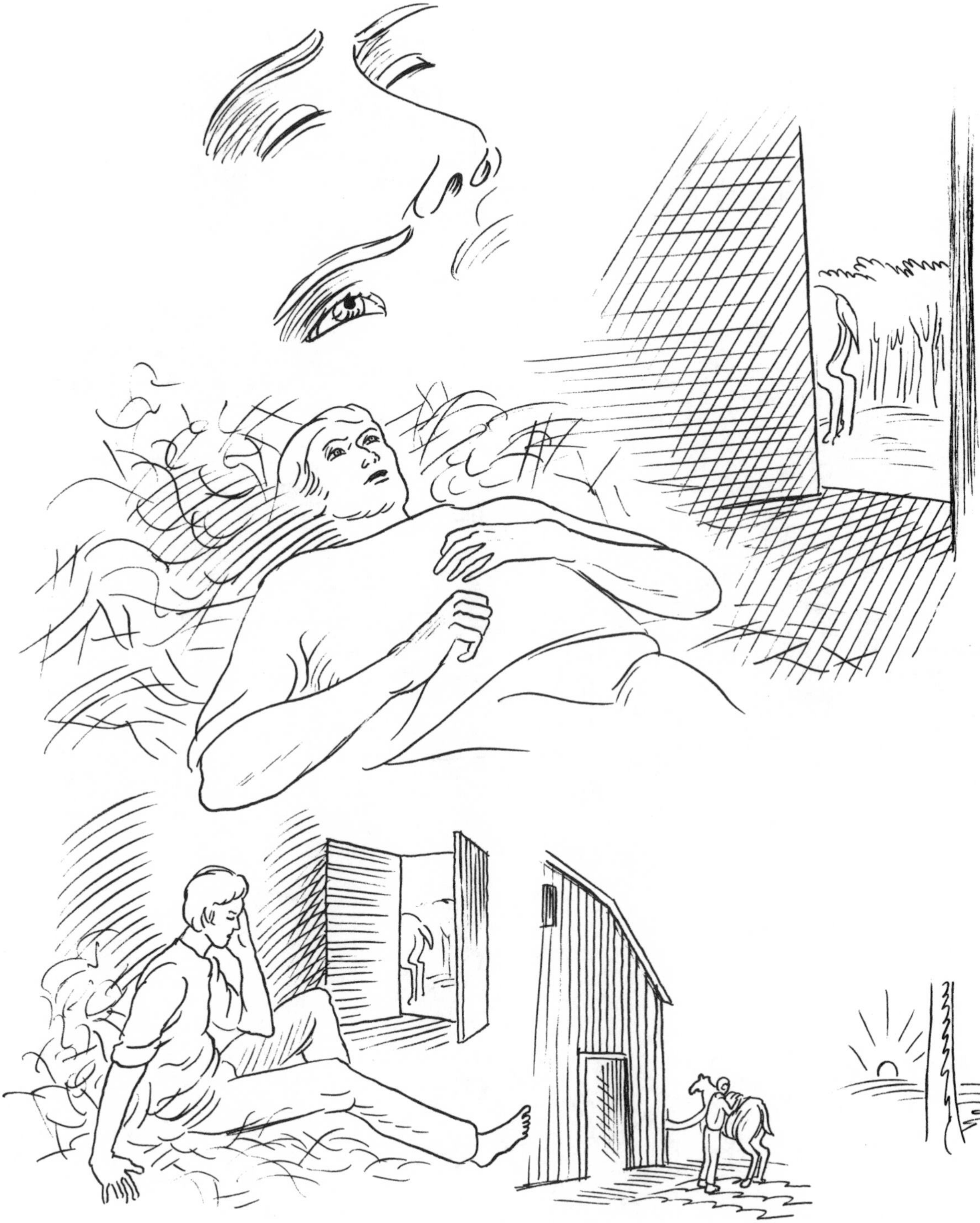

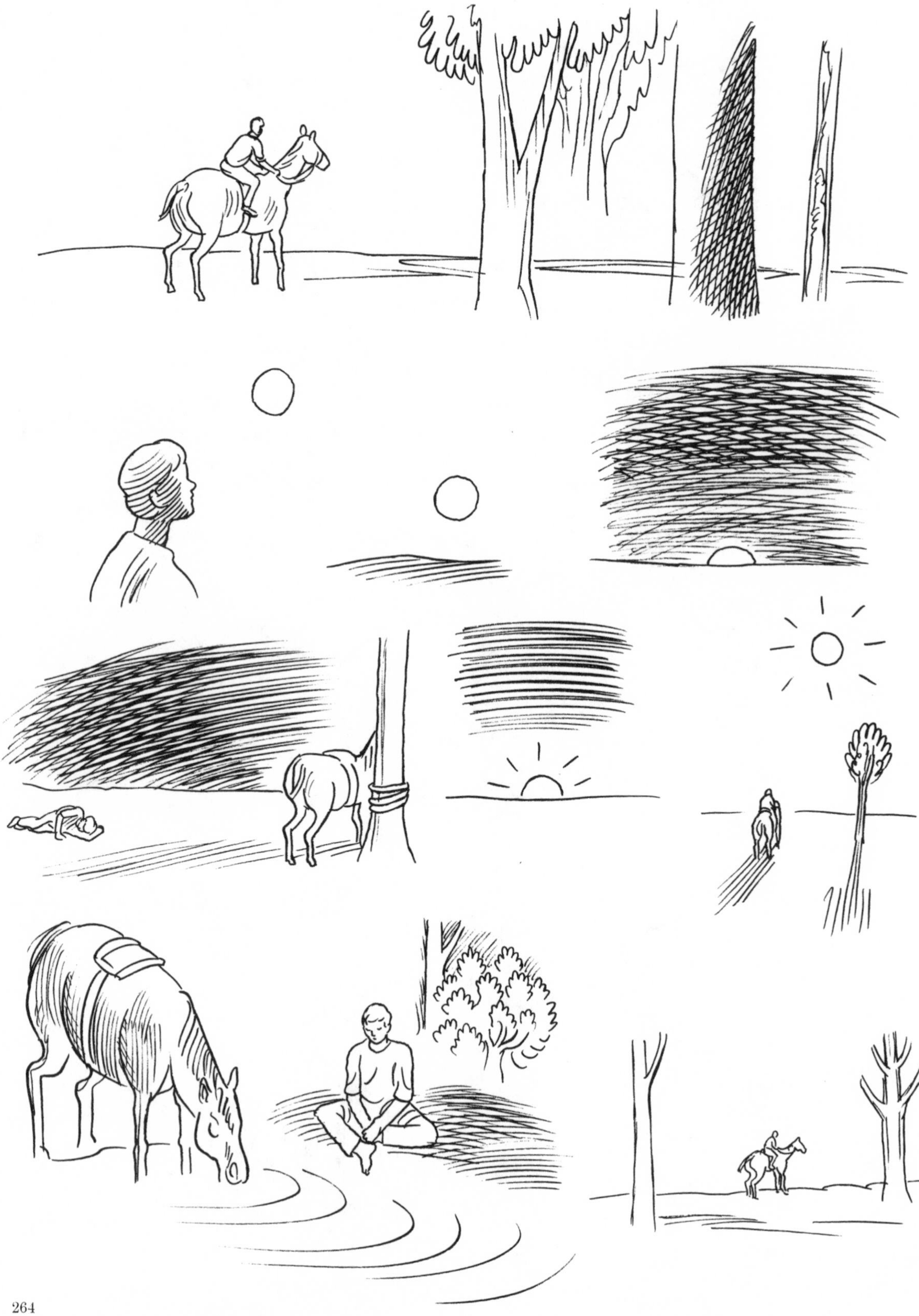

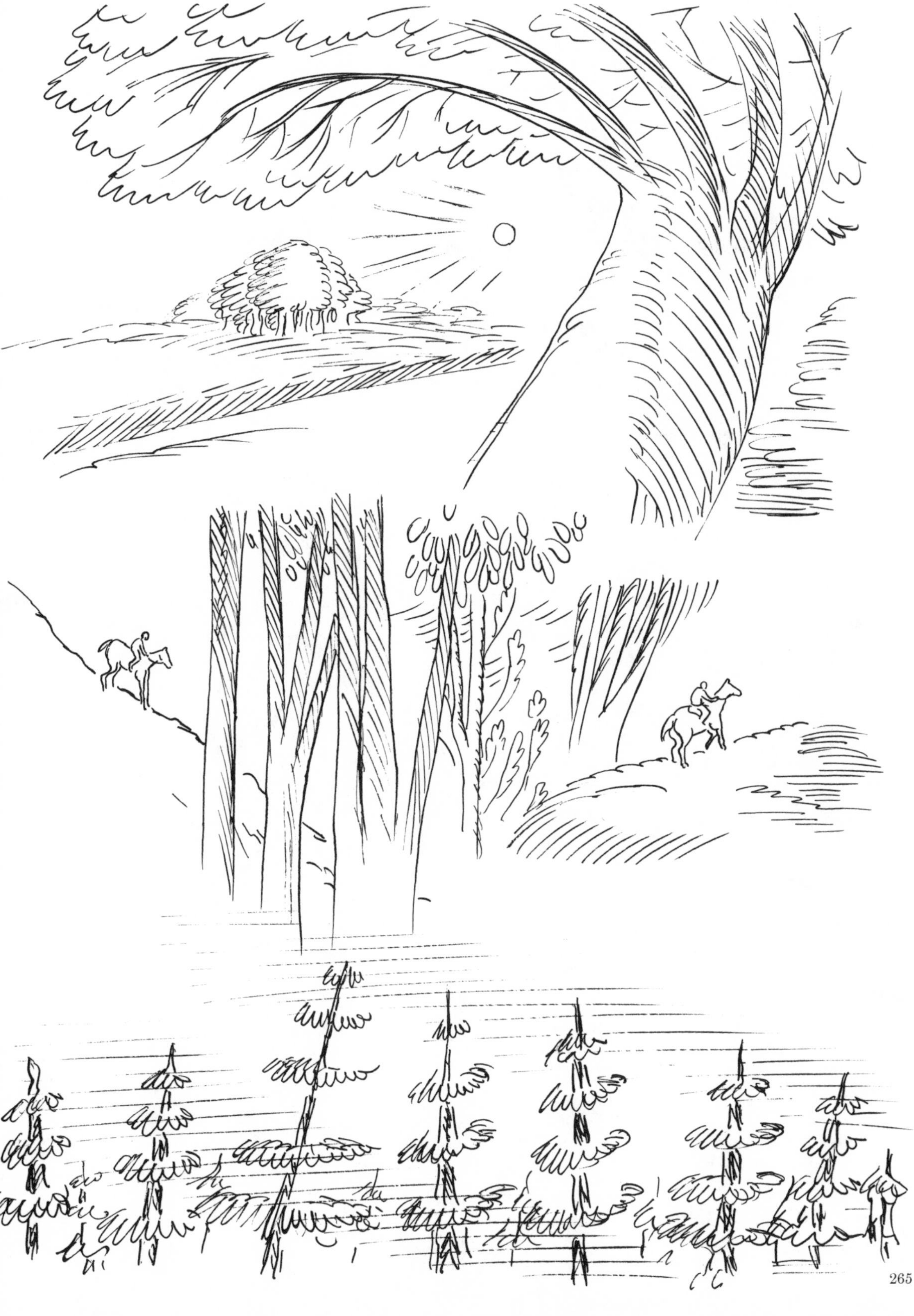

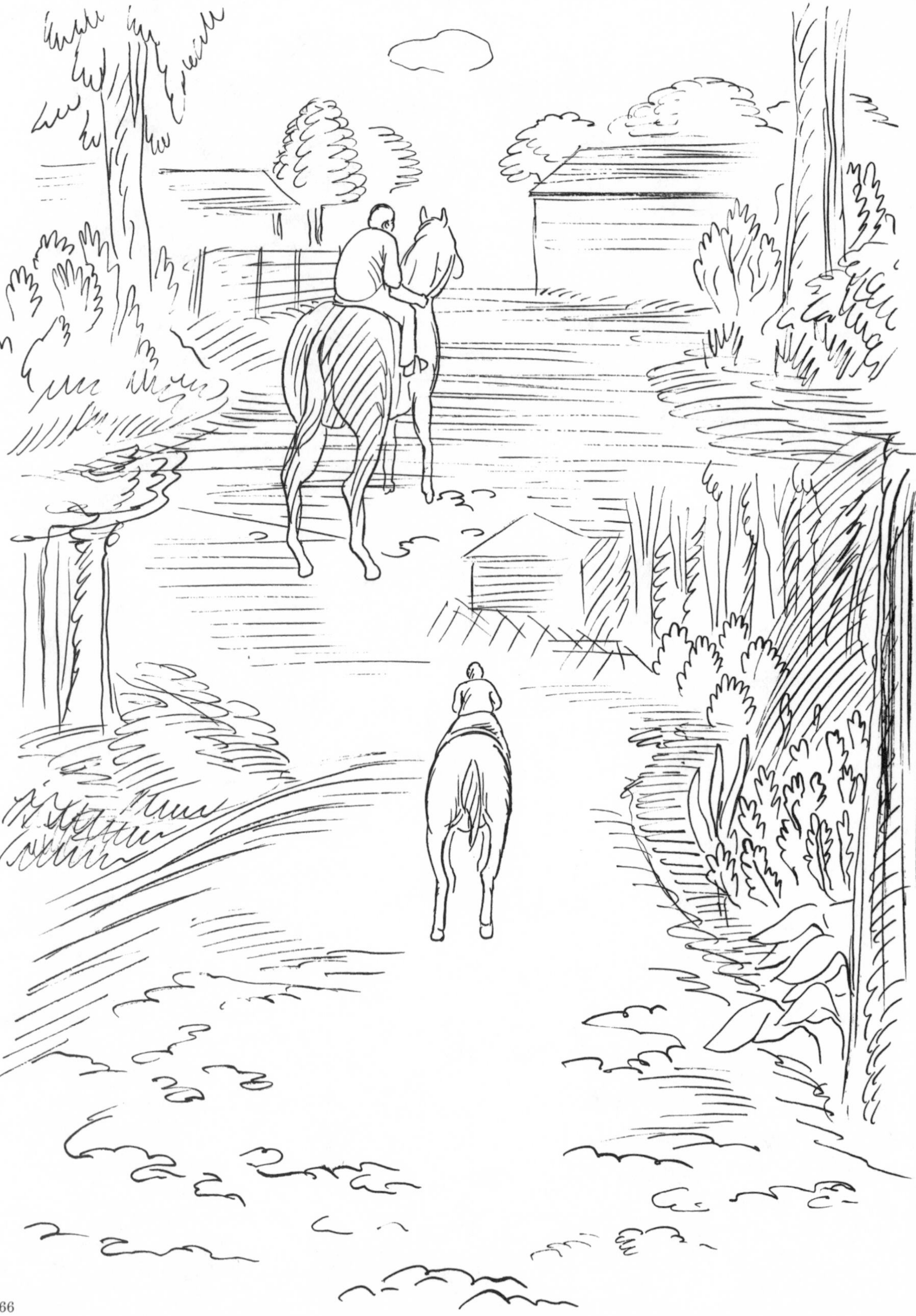

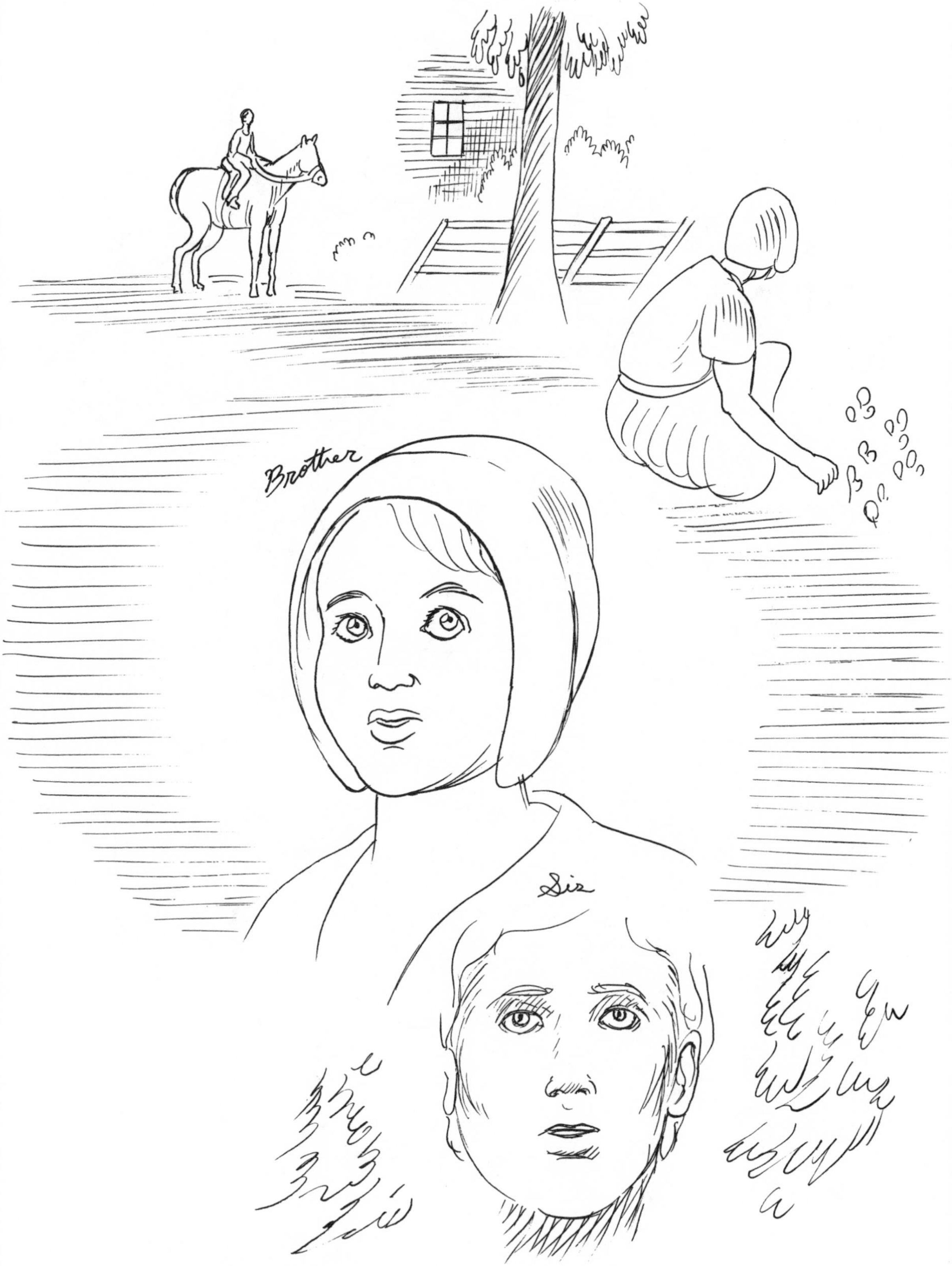
Brother
Sis

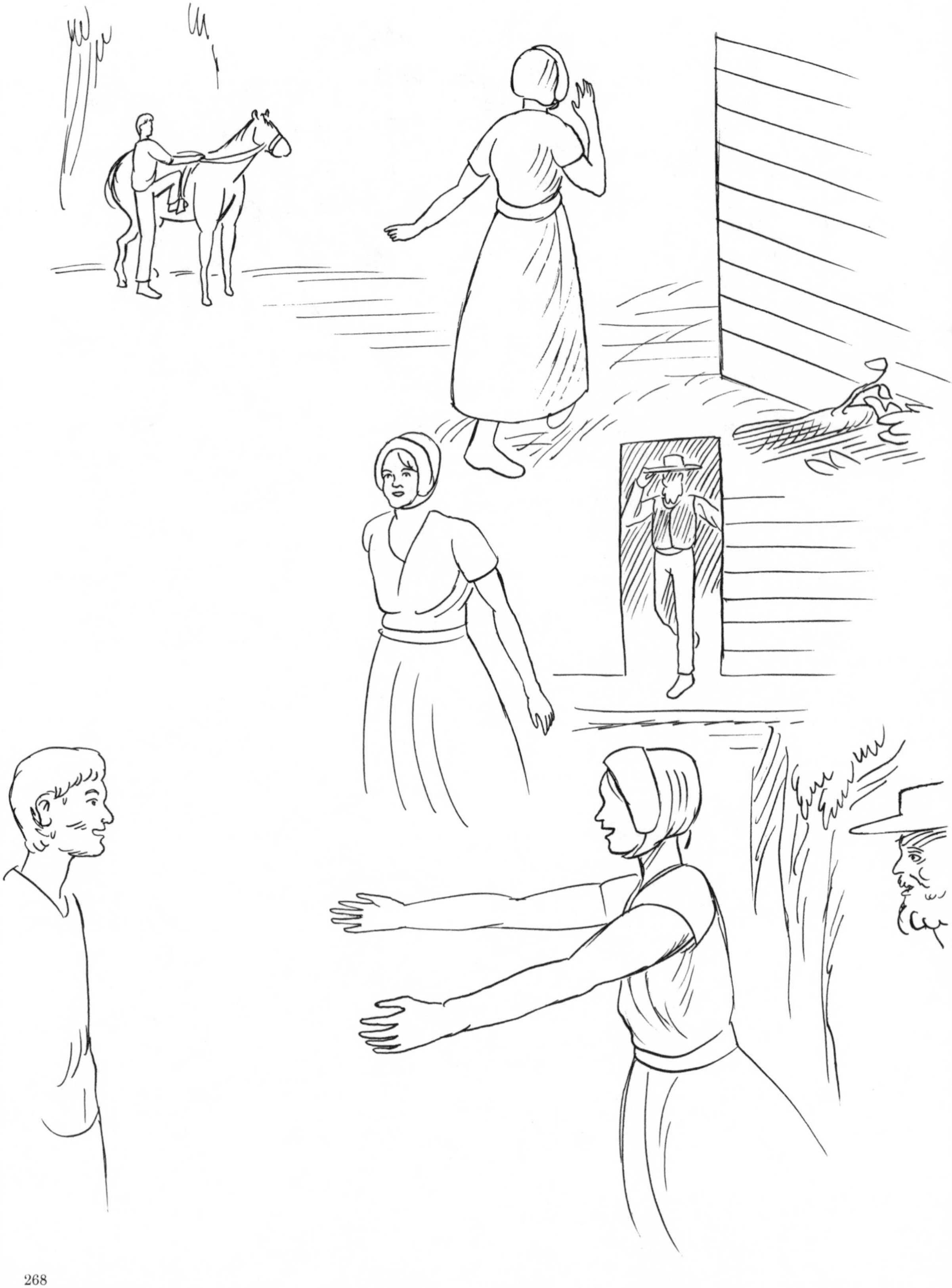

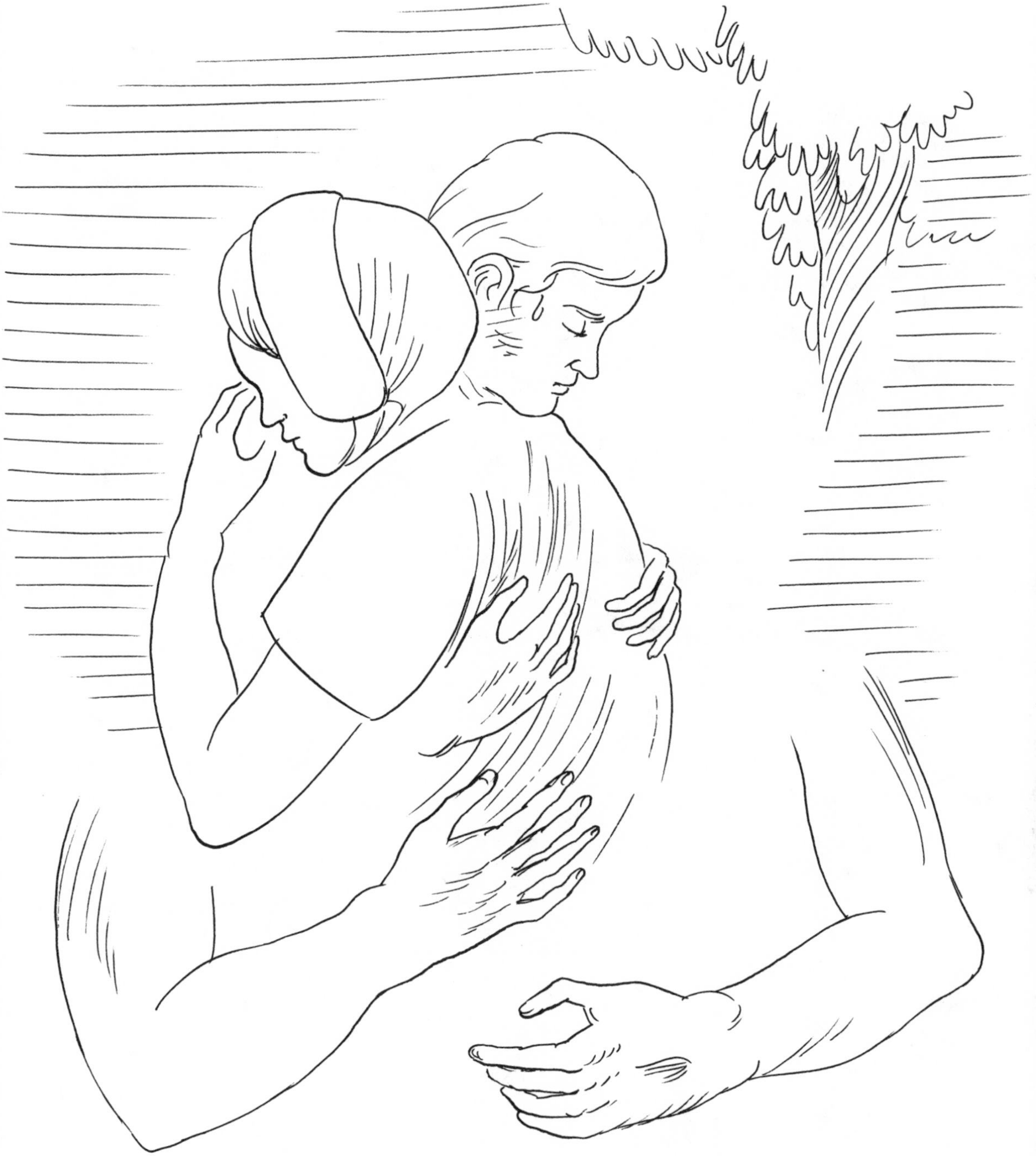

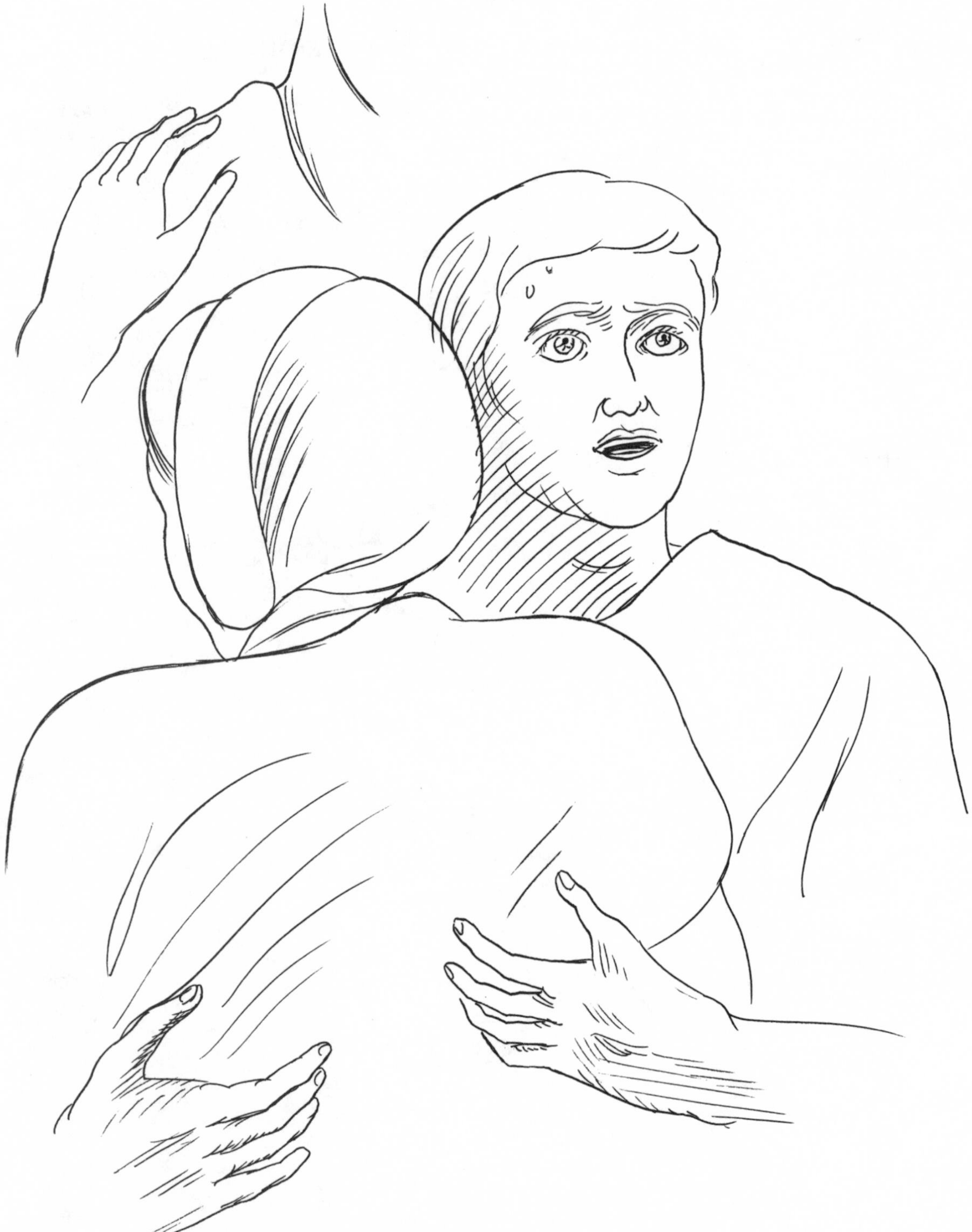

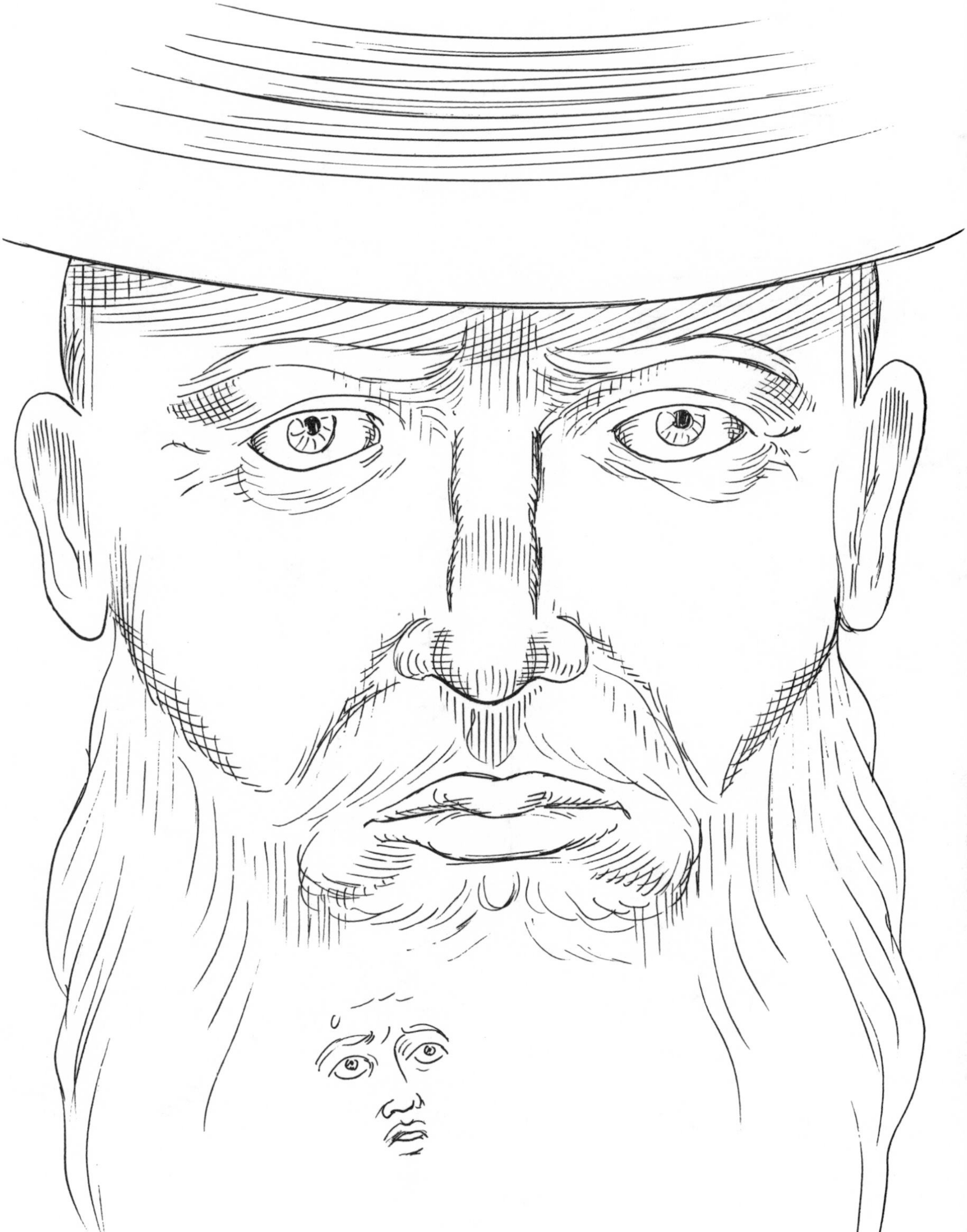

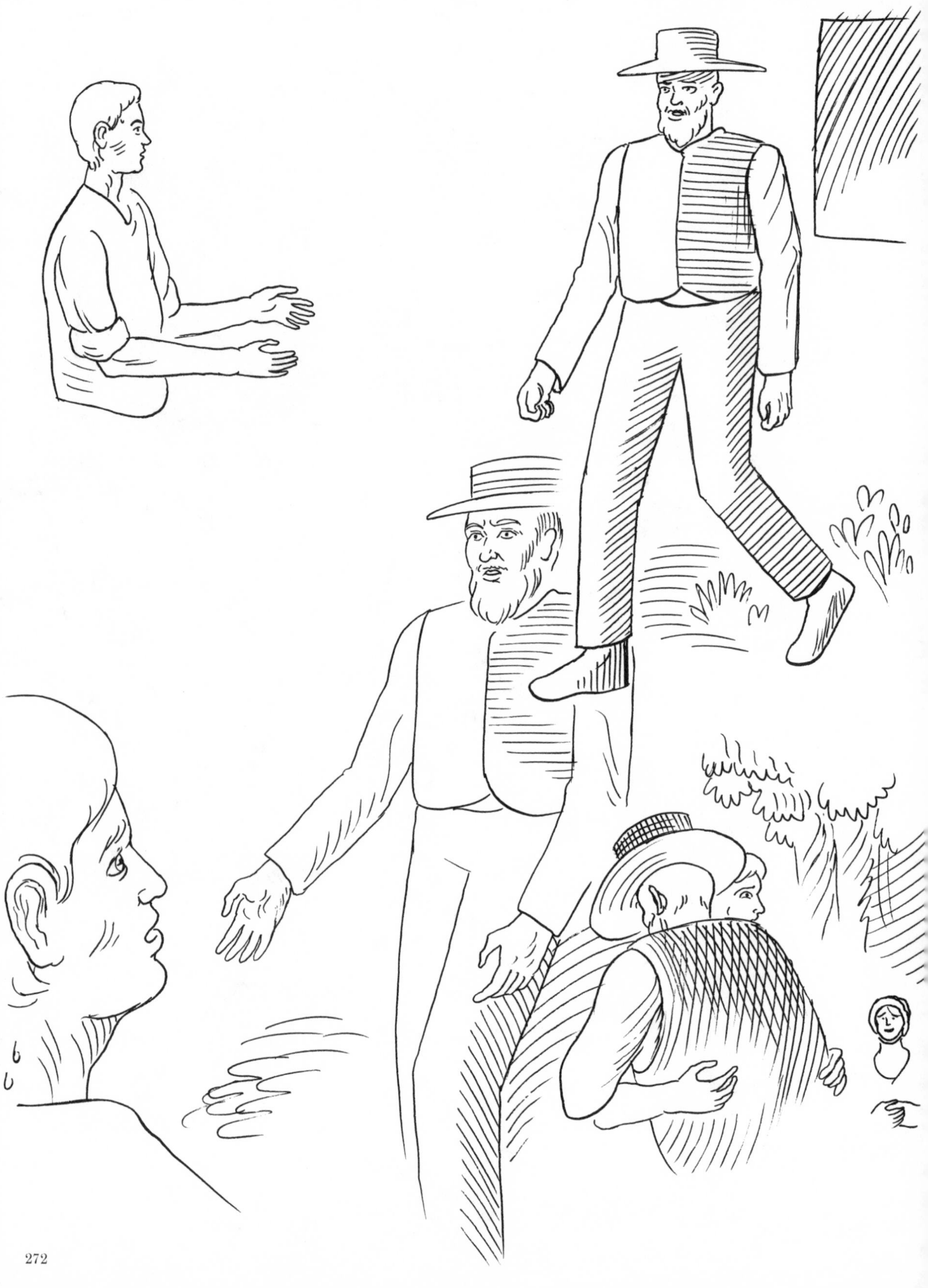

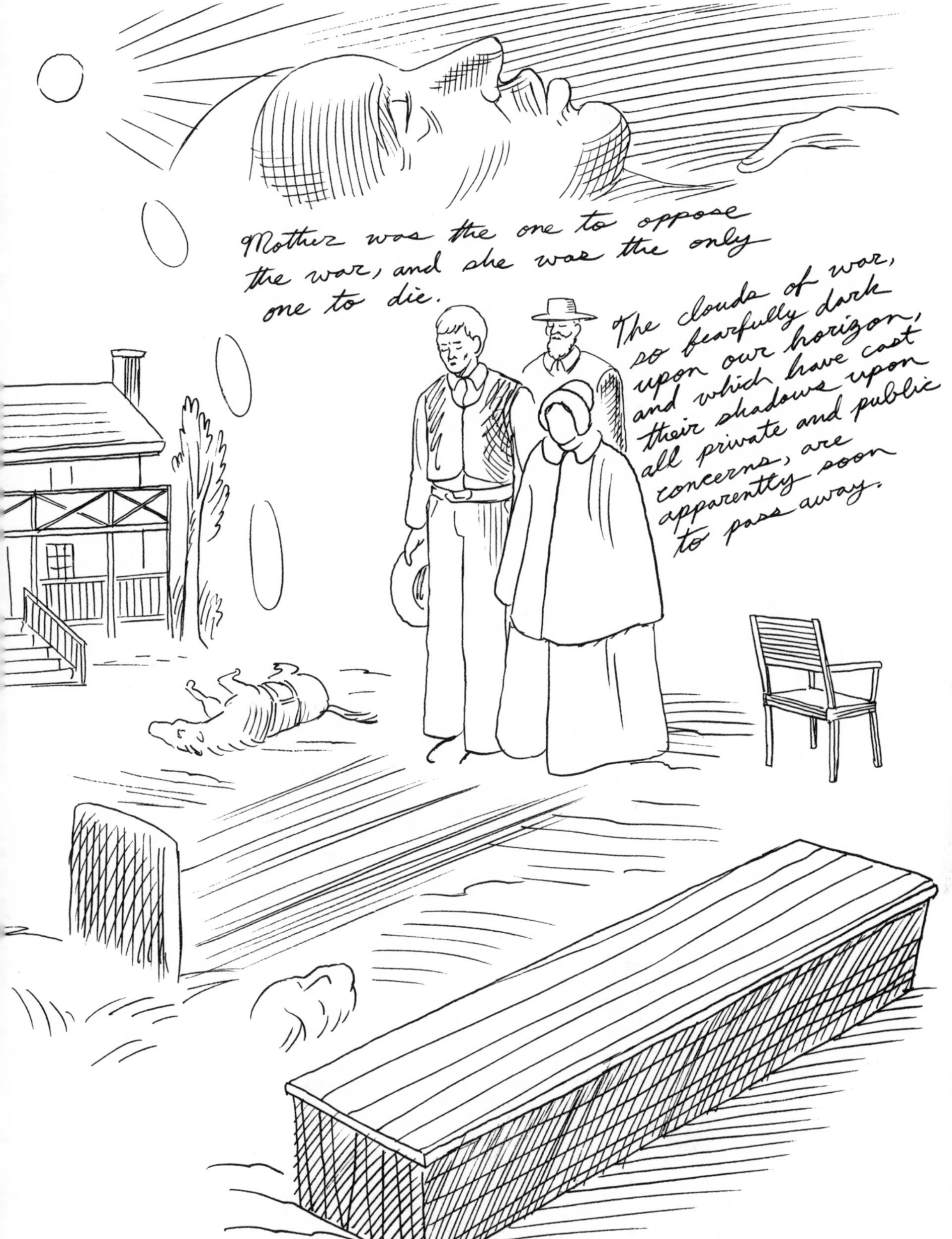
Mother was the one to oppose the war, and she was the only one to die.
The clouds of war, so fearfully dark upon our horizon, and which have cast their shadows upon all private and public concerns, are apparently soon to pass away.

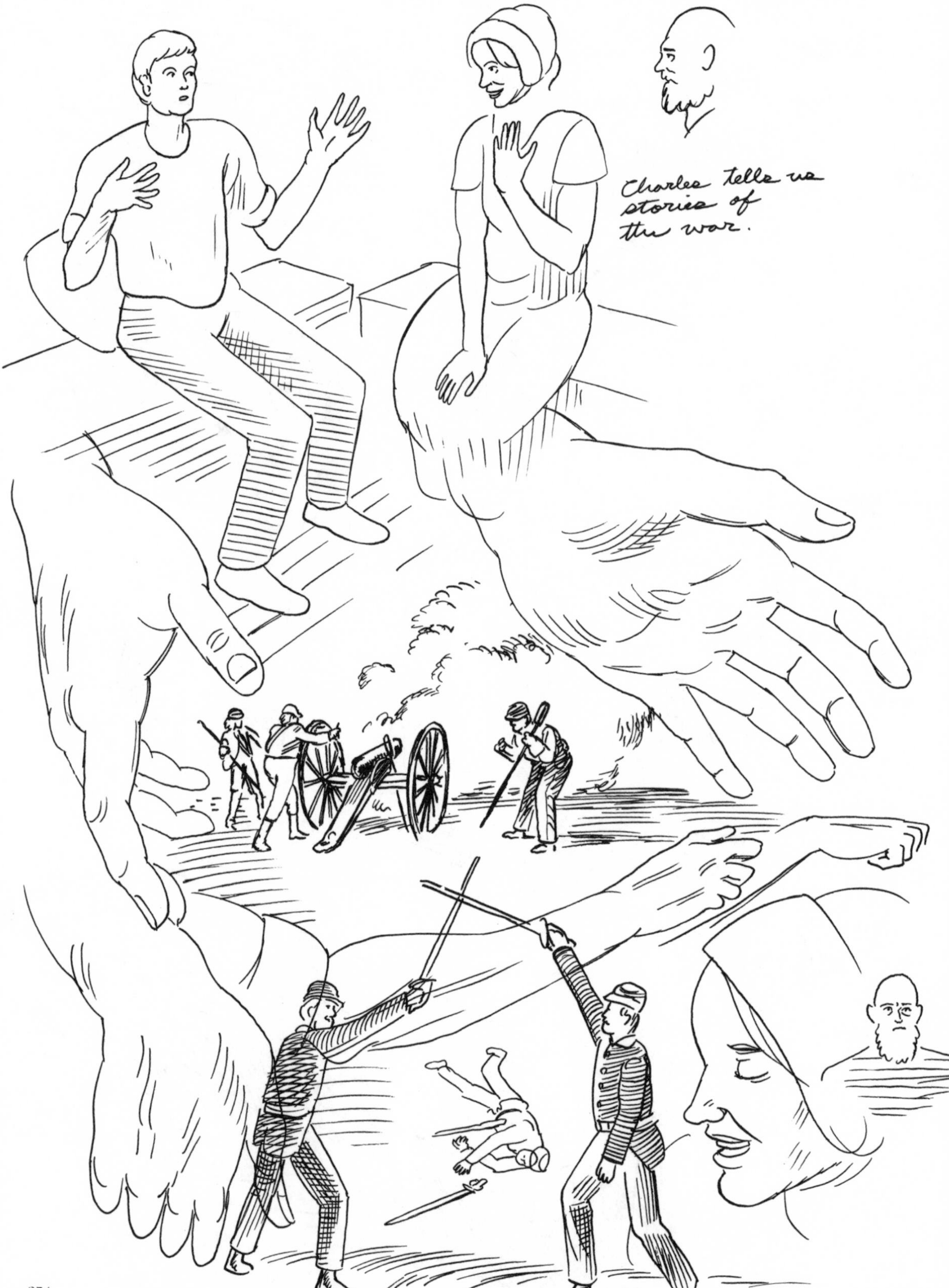
Charles tells us stories of the war.

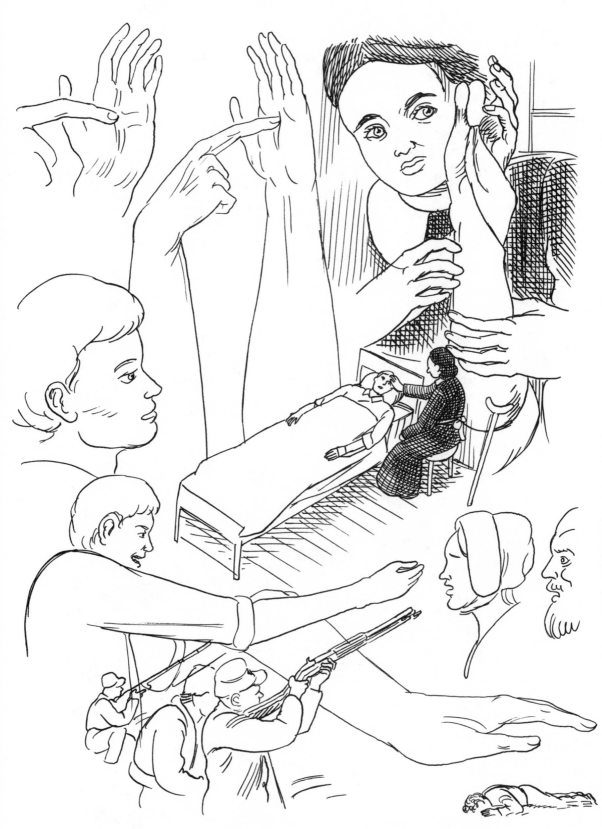

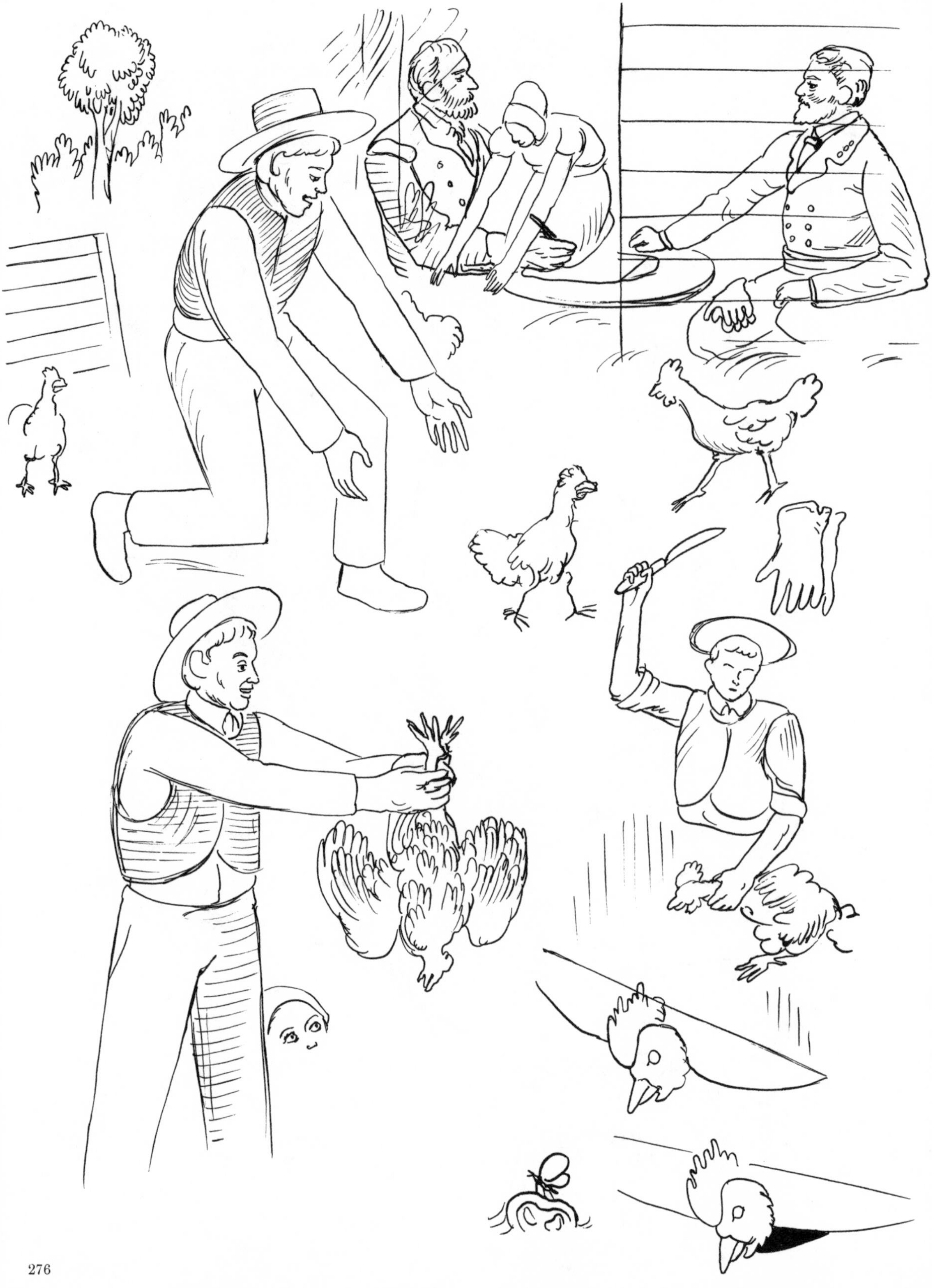

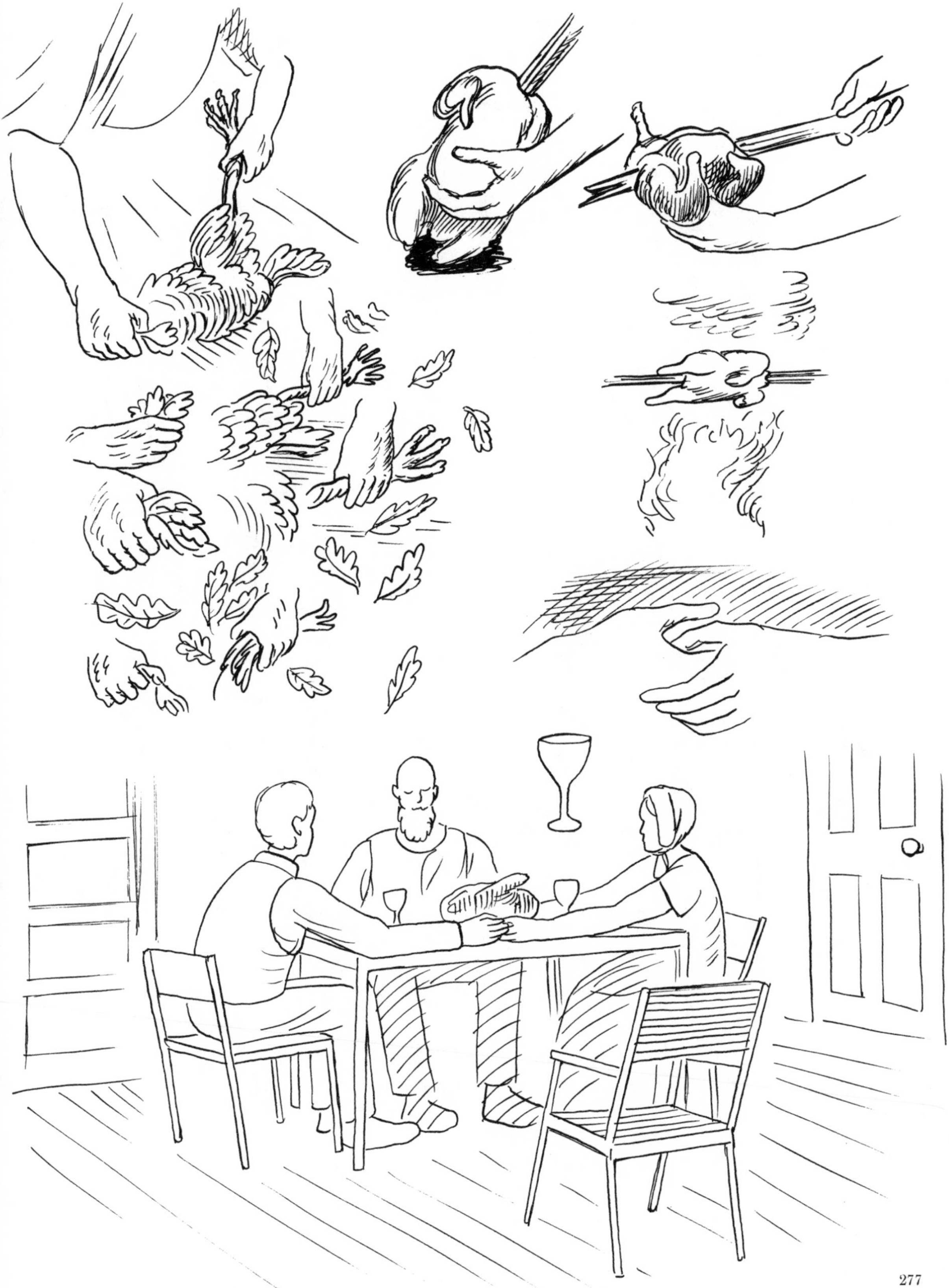

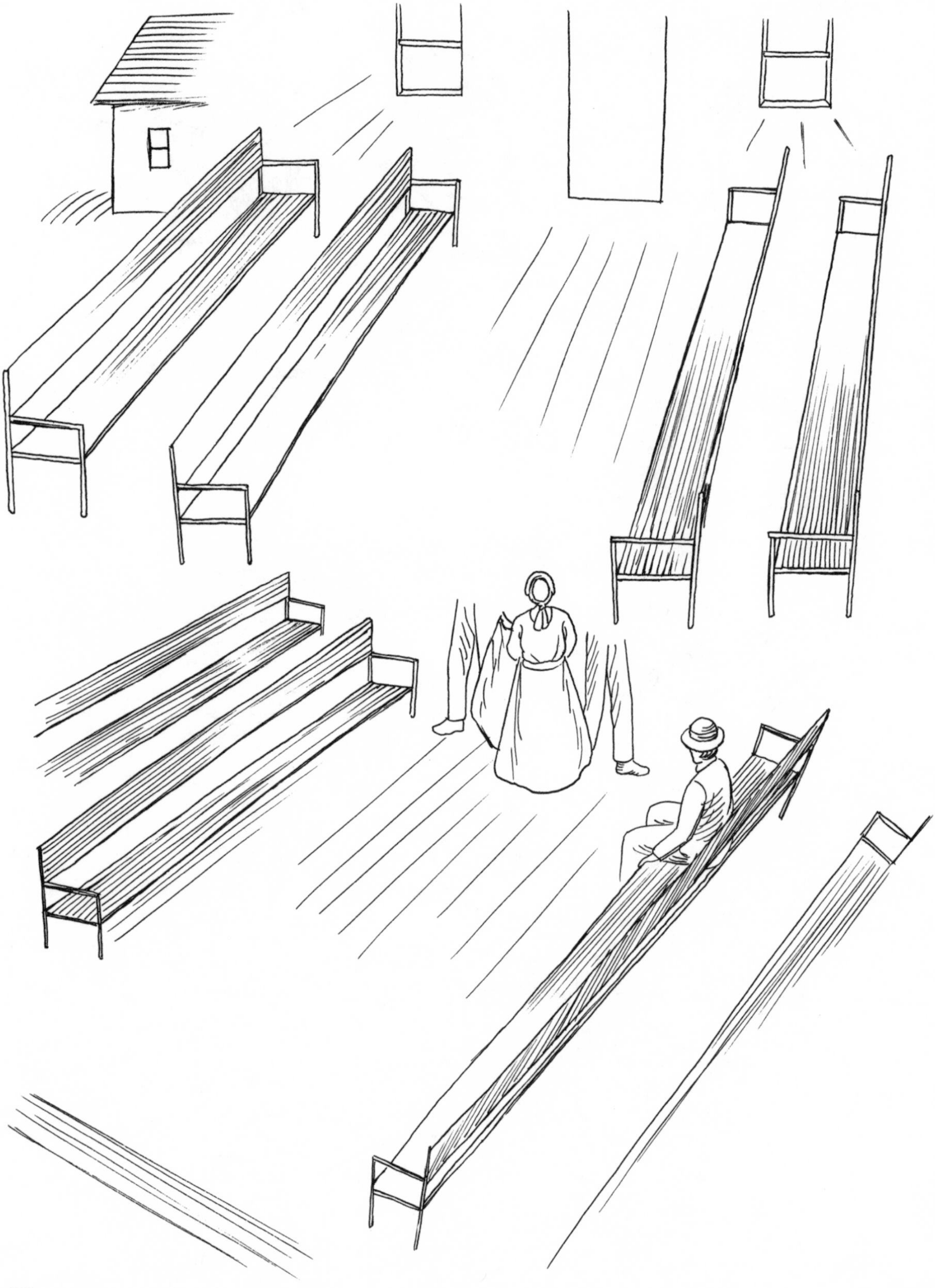

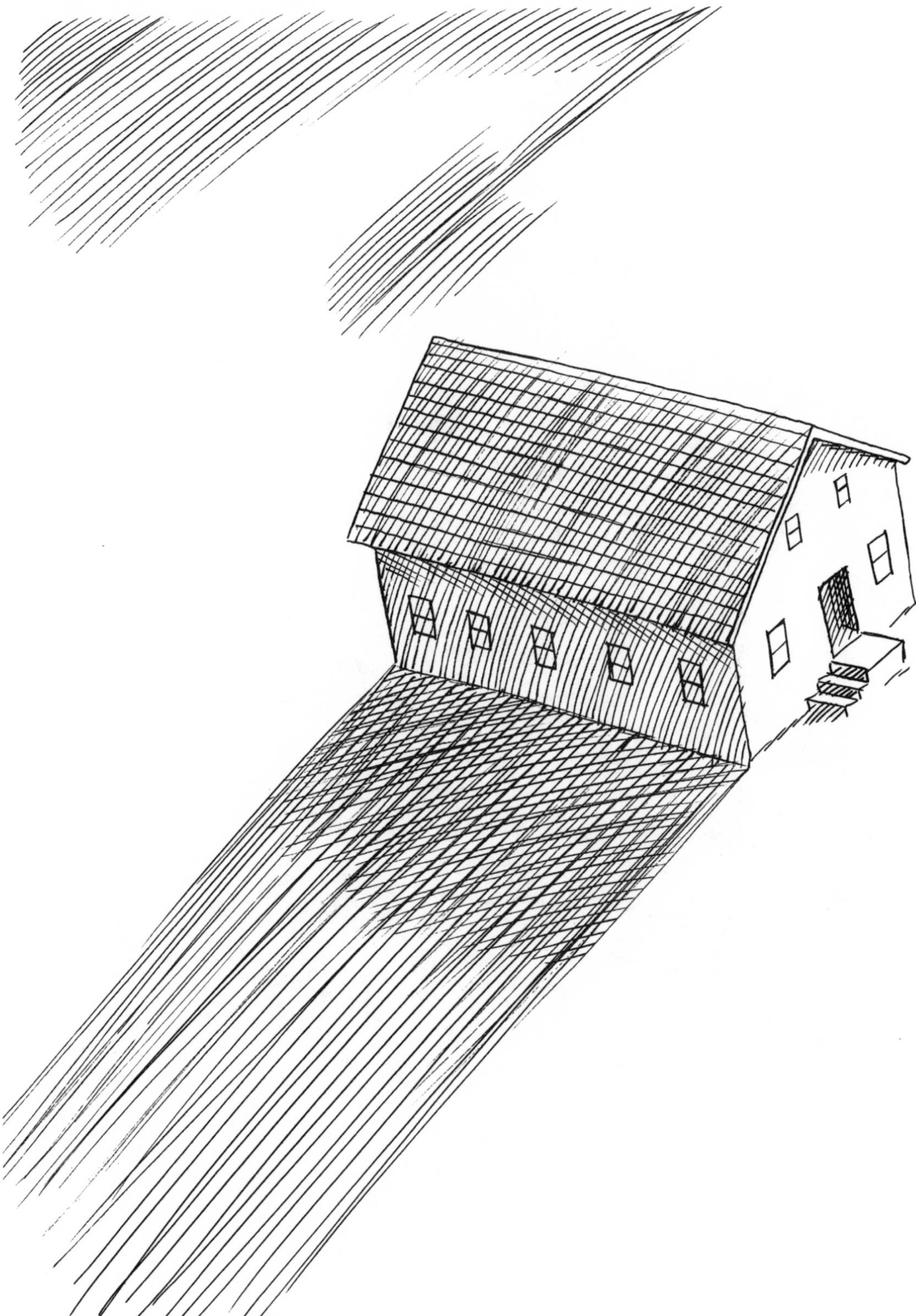

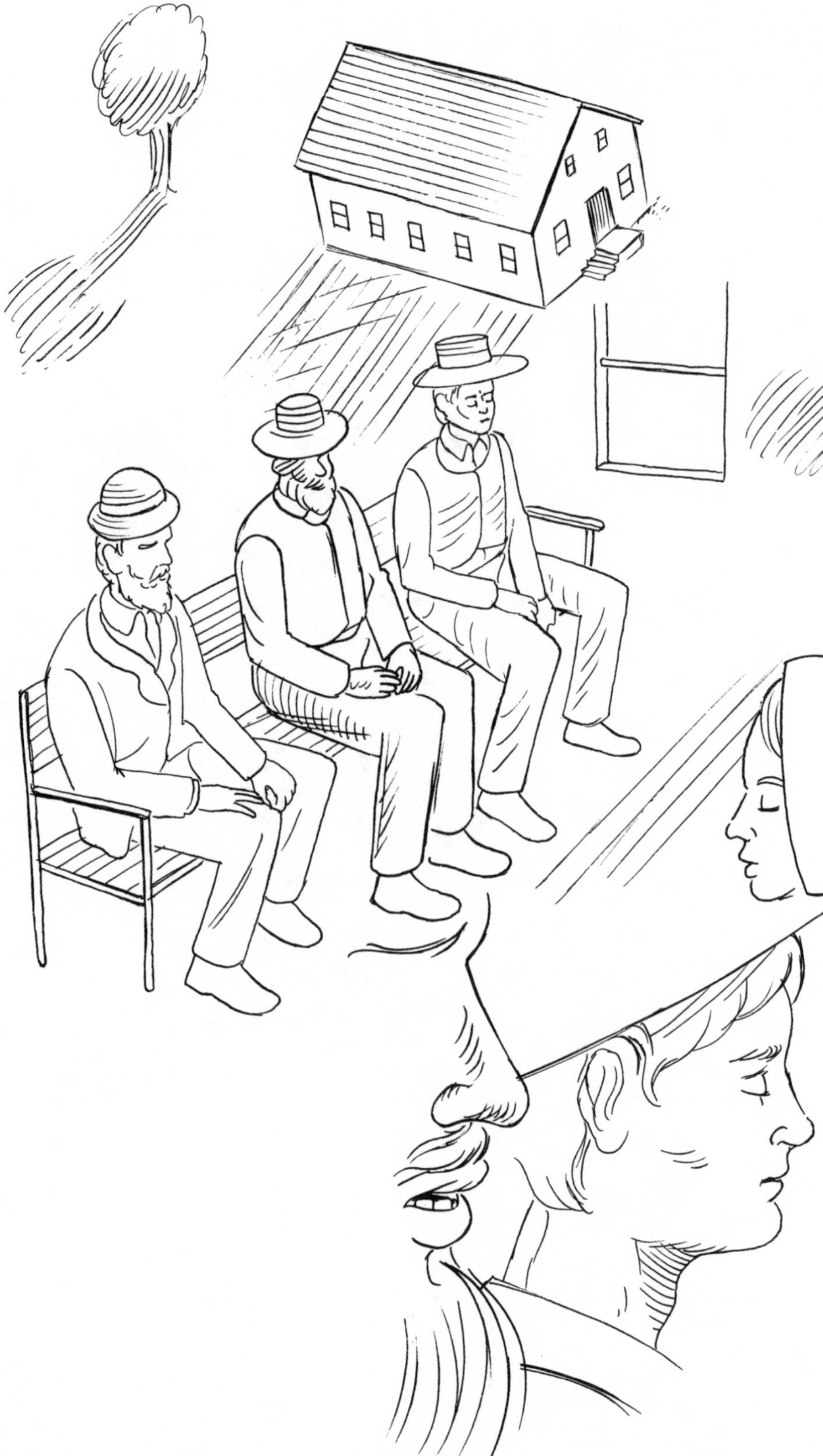

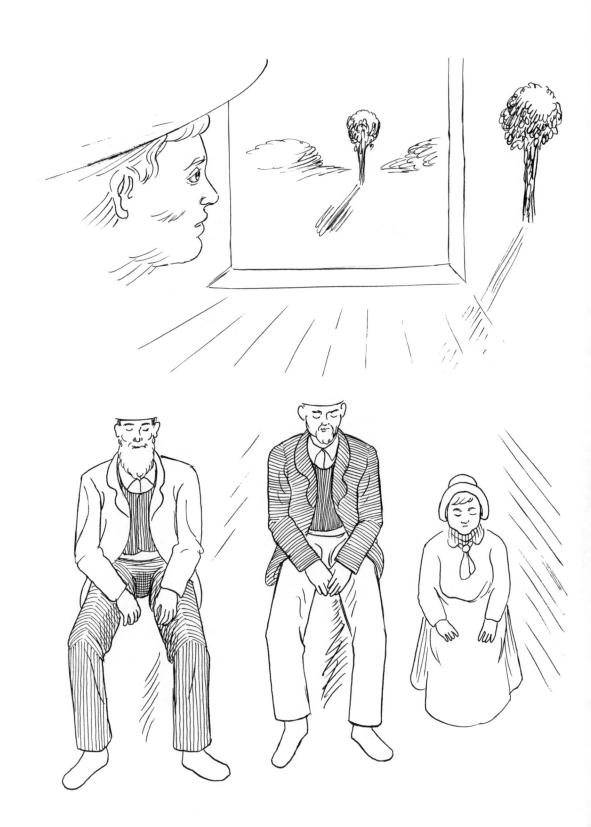

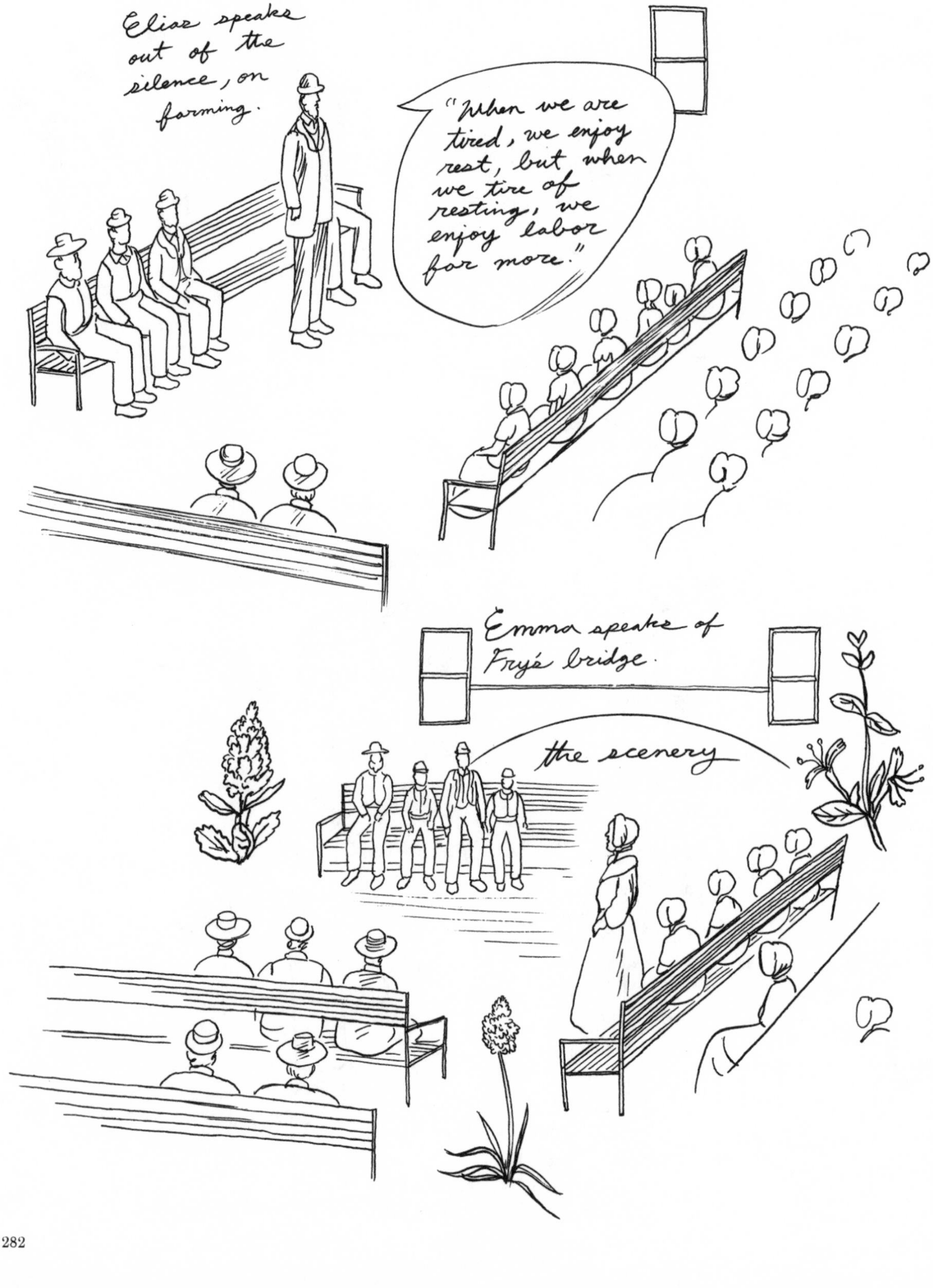

Elias speaks out of the silence, on farming.
"When we are tired, we enjoy rest, but when we tire of resting, we enjoy labor far more."
Emma speaks of Fry's bridge.
the scenery

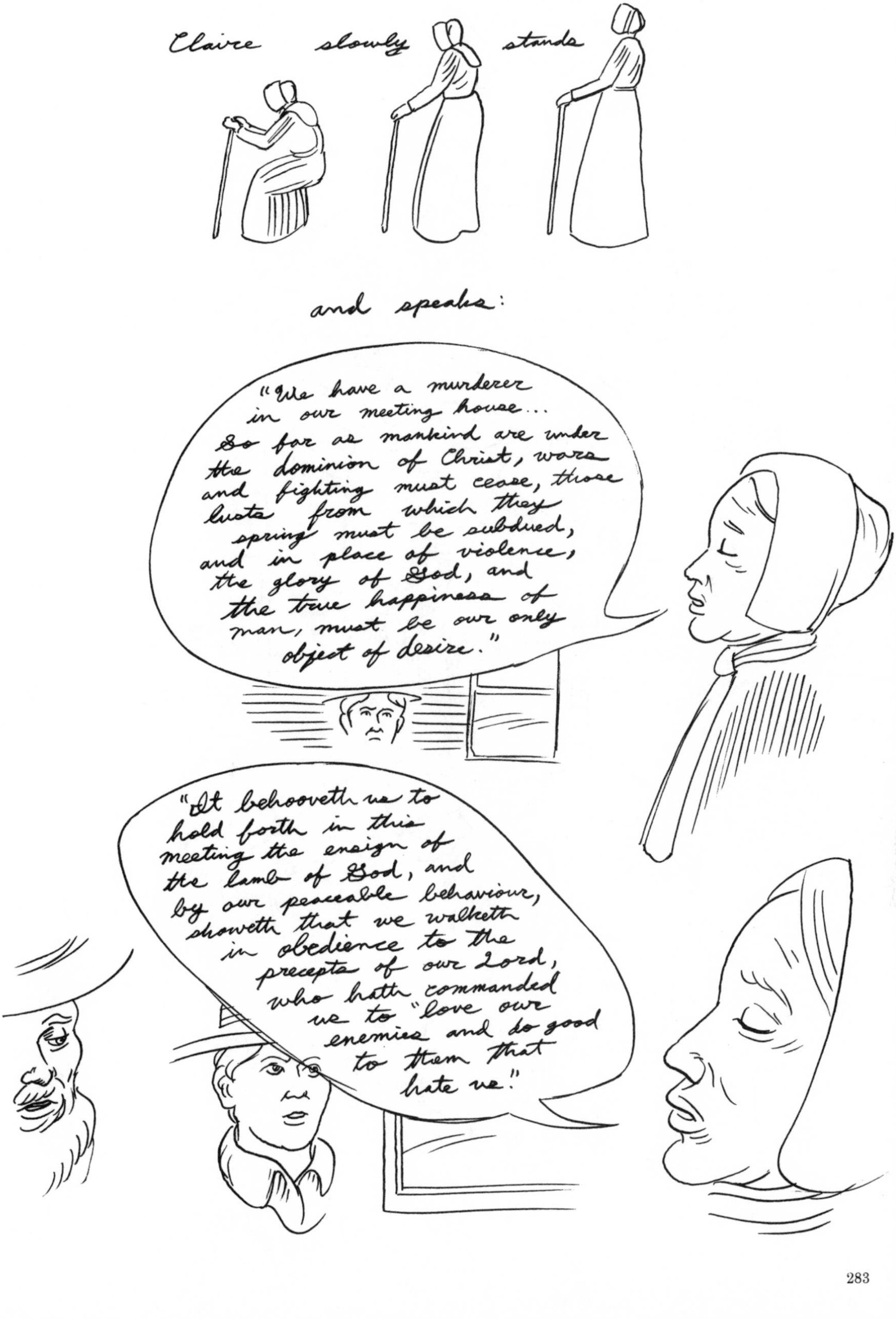
Claire slowly stands
and speaks:
"We have a murderer in our meeting house... So far as mankind are under the dominion of Christ, wars and fighting must cease, those lusts from which they spring must be subdued, and in place of violence, the glory of God, and the true happiness of man, must be our only object of desire."
"It behooveth us to hold forth in this meeting the ensign of the lamb of God, and by our peaceable behaviour, showeth that we walketh in obedience to the precepts of our Lord, who hath commanded us to "love our enemies and do good to them that hate us!"

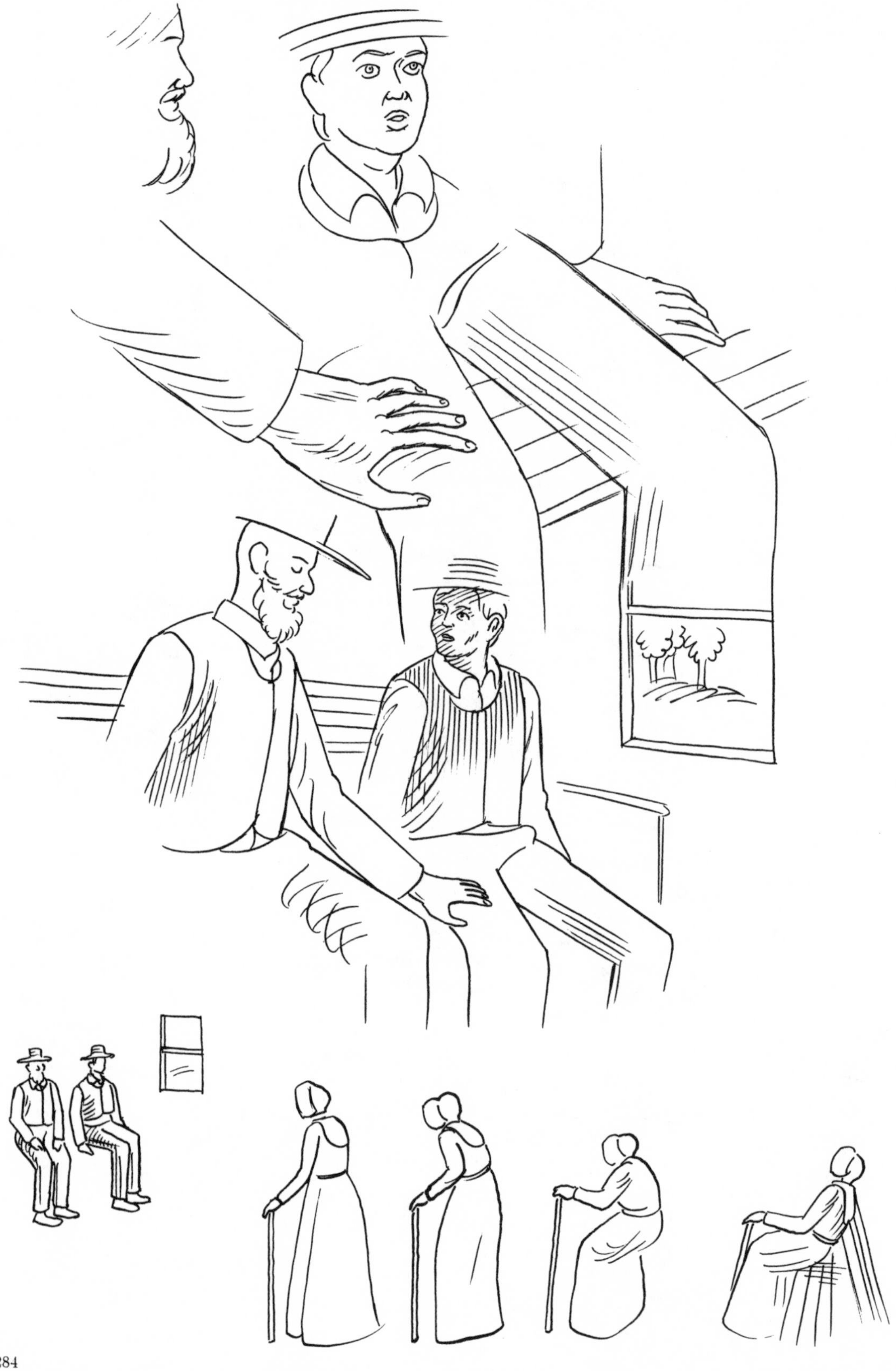

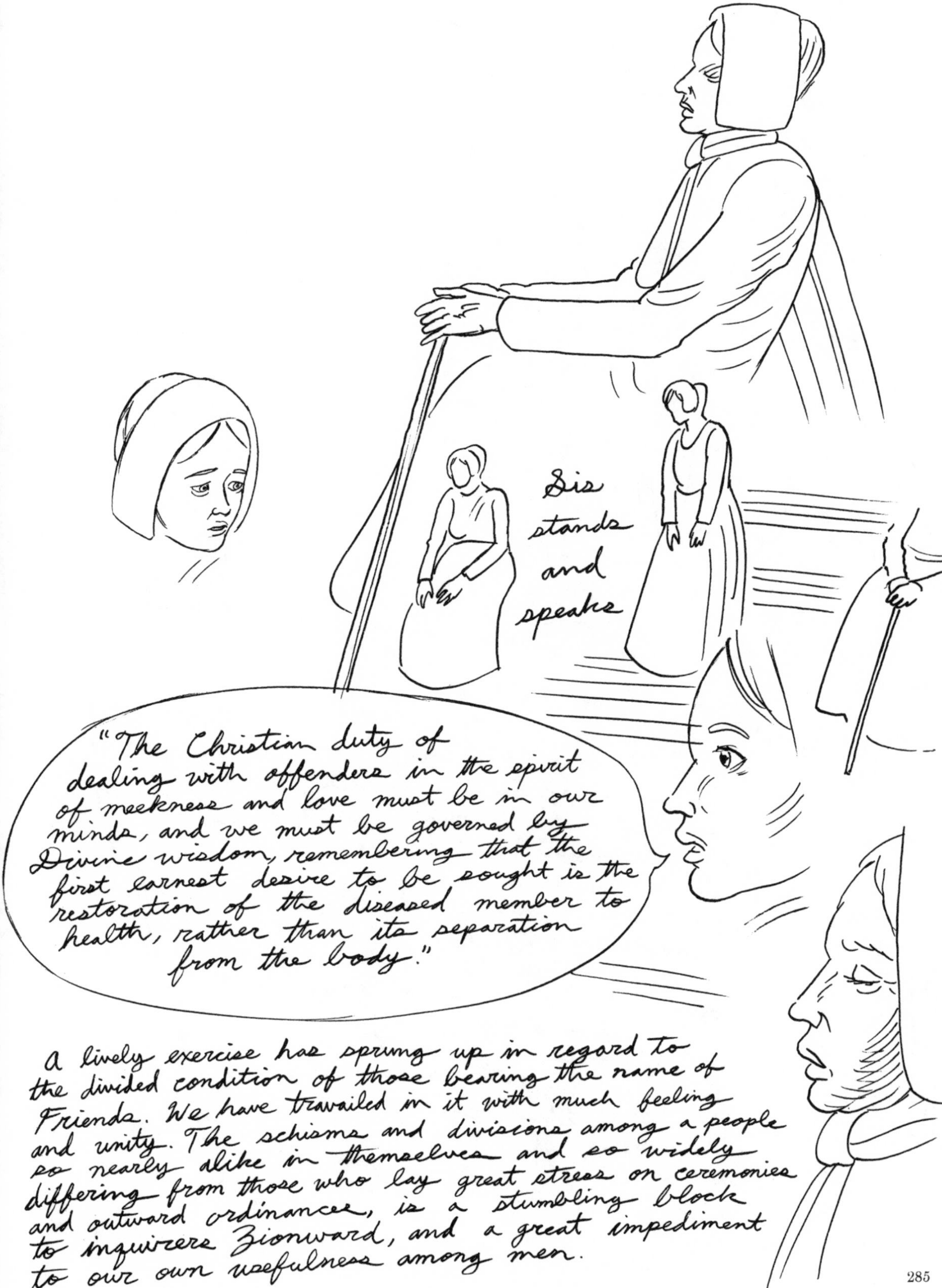
Sis stands and speaks
"The Christian duty of dealing with offenders in the spirit of meekness and love must be in our minds, and we must be governed by Divine wisdom, remembering that the first earnest desire to be sought is the restoration of the diseased member to health, rather than its separation from the body."
A lively exercise has sprung up in regard to the divided condition of those bearing the name of Friends. We have travailed in it with much feeling and unity. The schisms and divisions among a people so nearly alike in themselves and so widely differing from those who lay great stress on ceremonies and outward ordinances, is a stumbling block to inquirers Zionward, and a great impediment to our own usefulness among men.

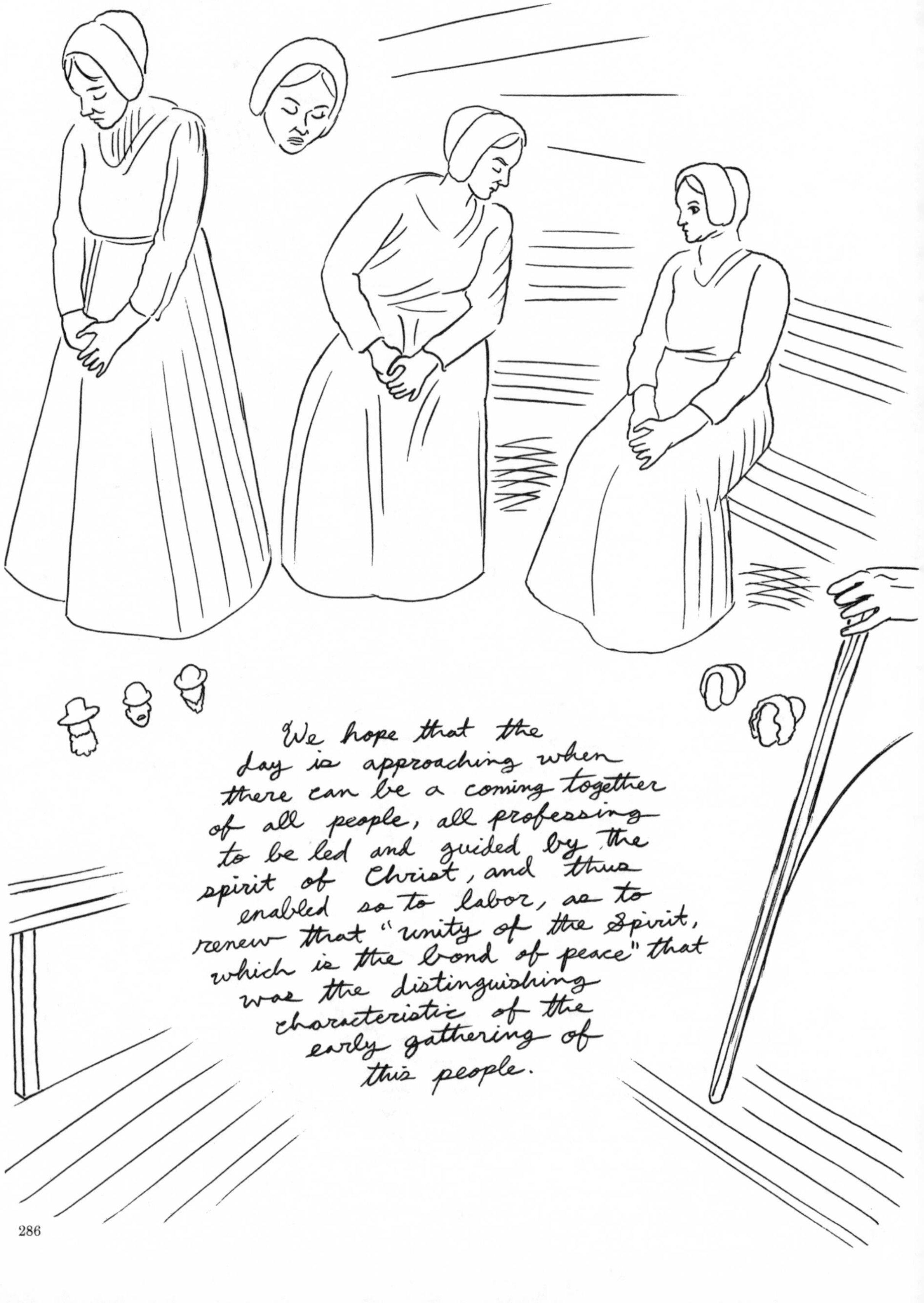
We hope that the
day is approaching when
there can be a coming together
of all people, all professing
to be led and guided by the
spirit of Christ, and thus
enabled so to labor, as to
renew that "unity of the Spirit,
which is the bond of peace" that
was the distinguishing
characteristic of the
early gathering of
this people.

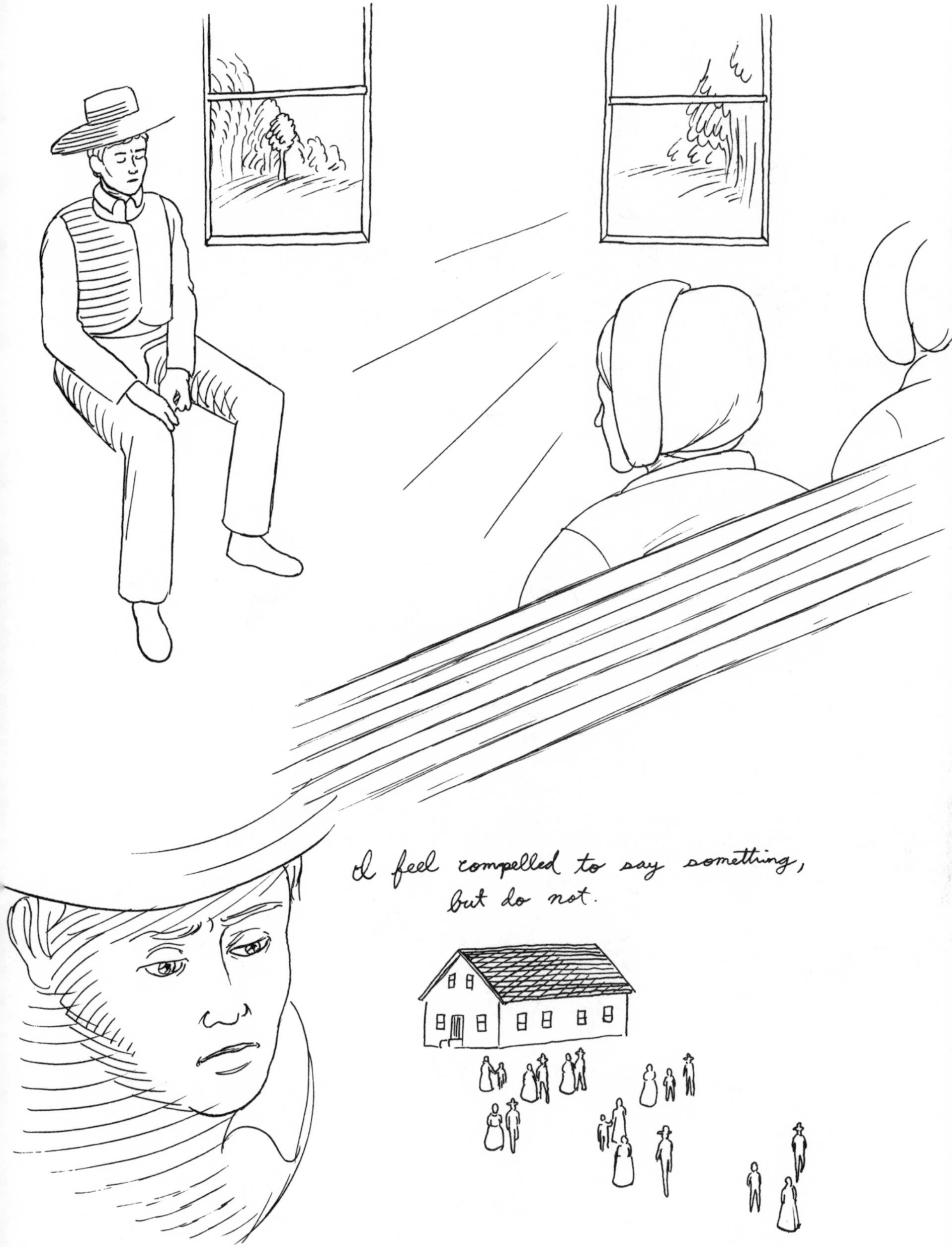
I feel compelled to say something,
but do not.

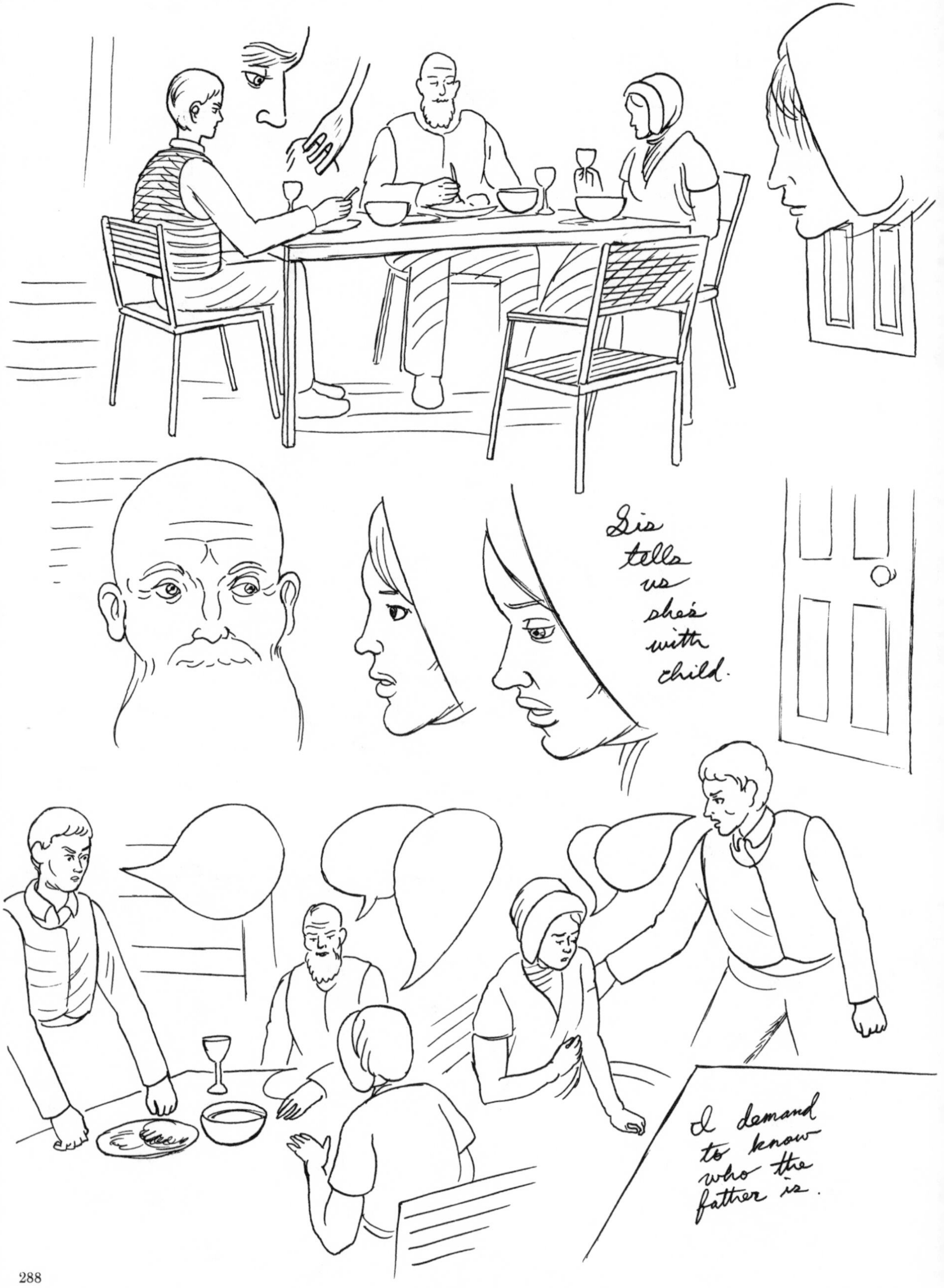
Sis tells us she's with child.
I demand to know who the father is.

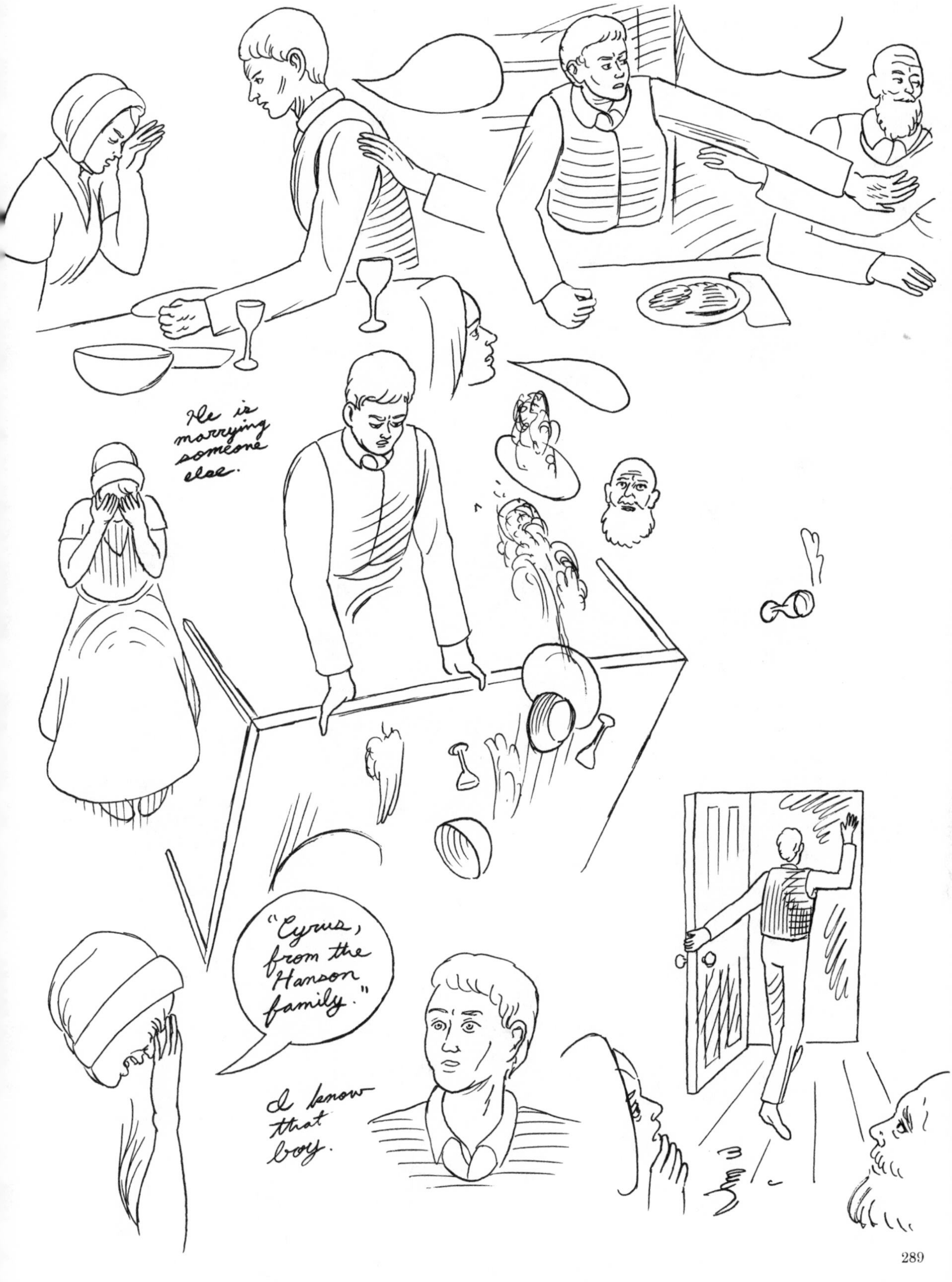
He is marrying someone else.
"Cyrus, from the Hanson family."
I know that boy.

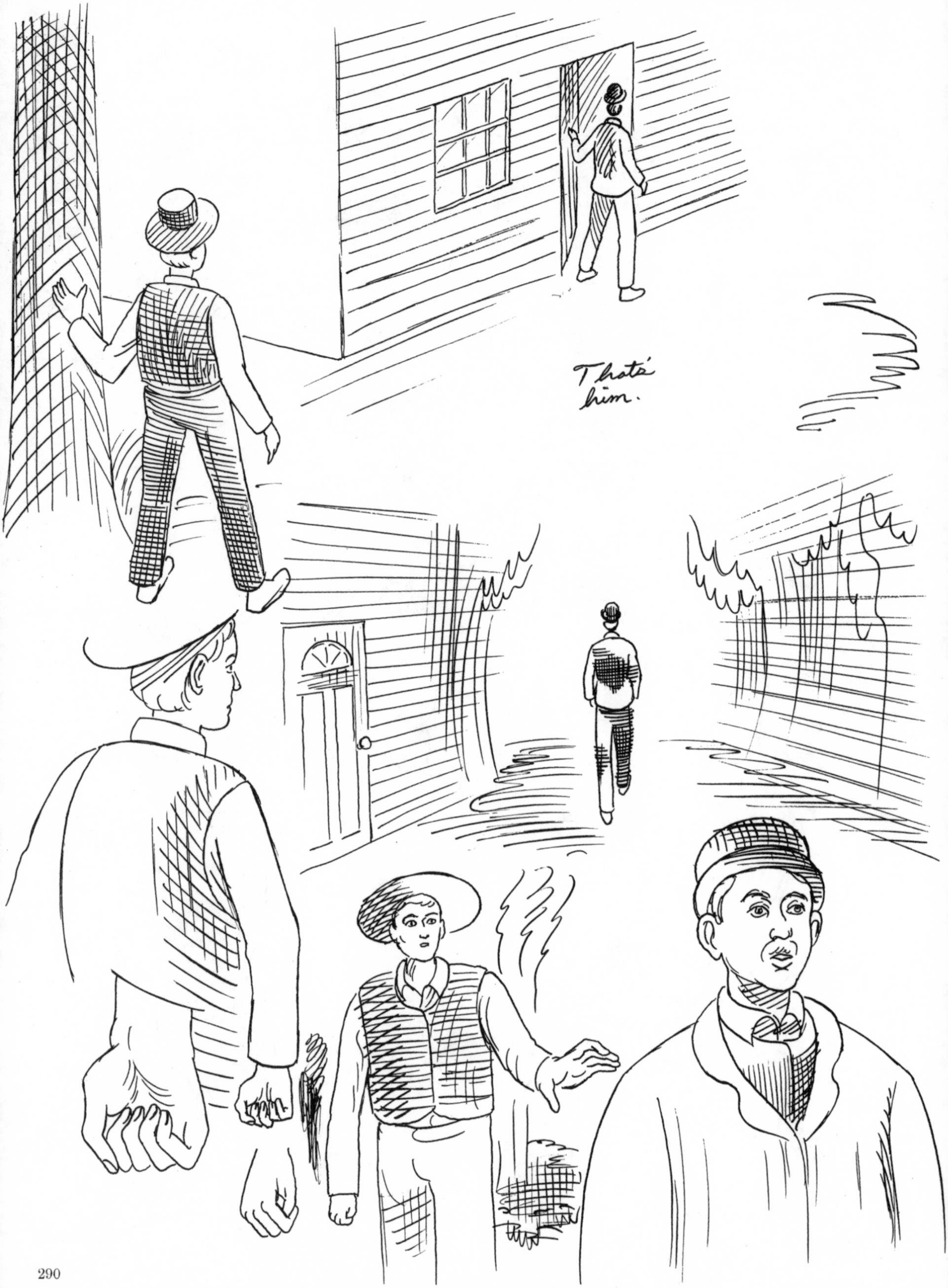
That's him.

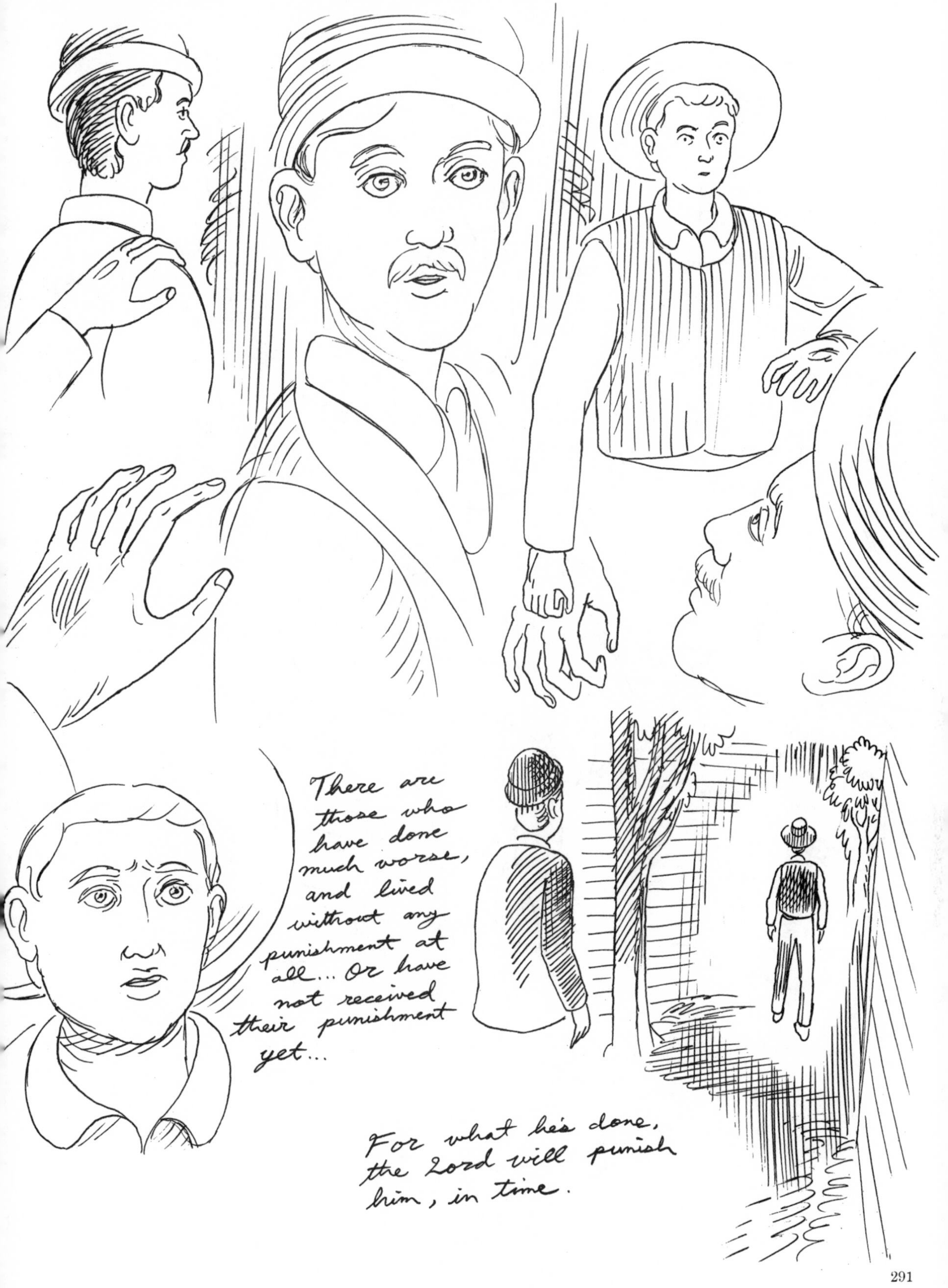
There are those who have done much worse, and lived without any punishment at all... Or have not received their punishment yet...
For what he's done, the Lord will punish him, in time.

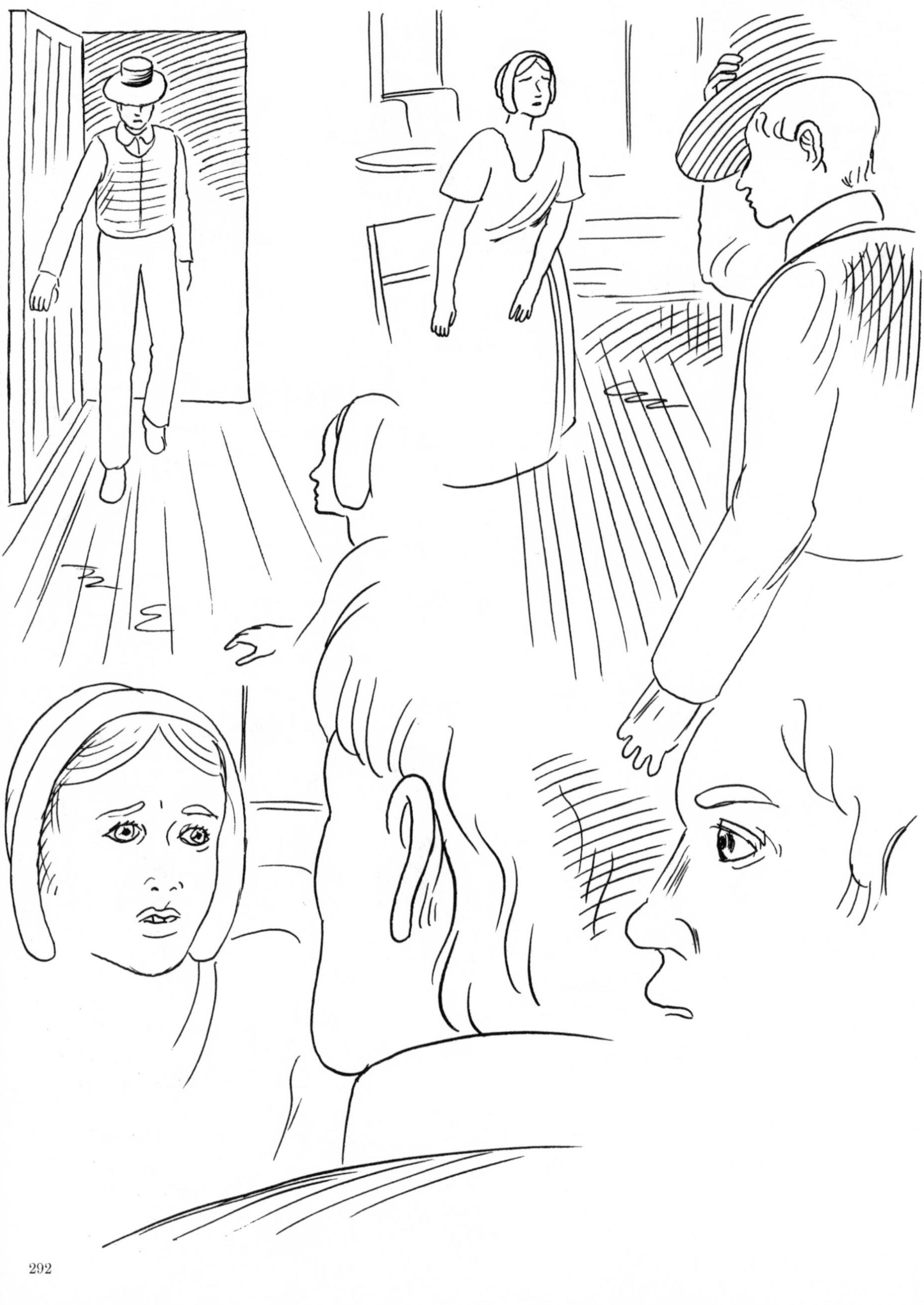

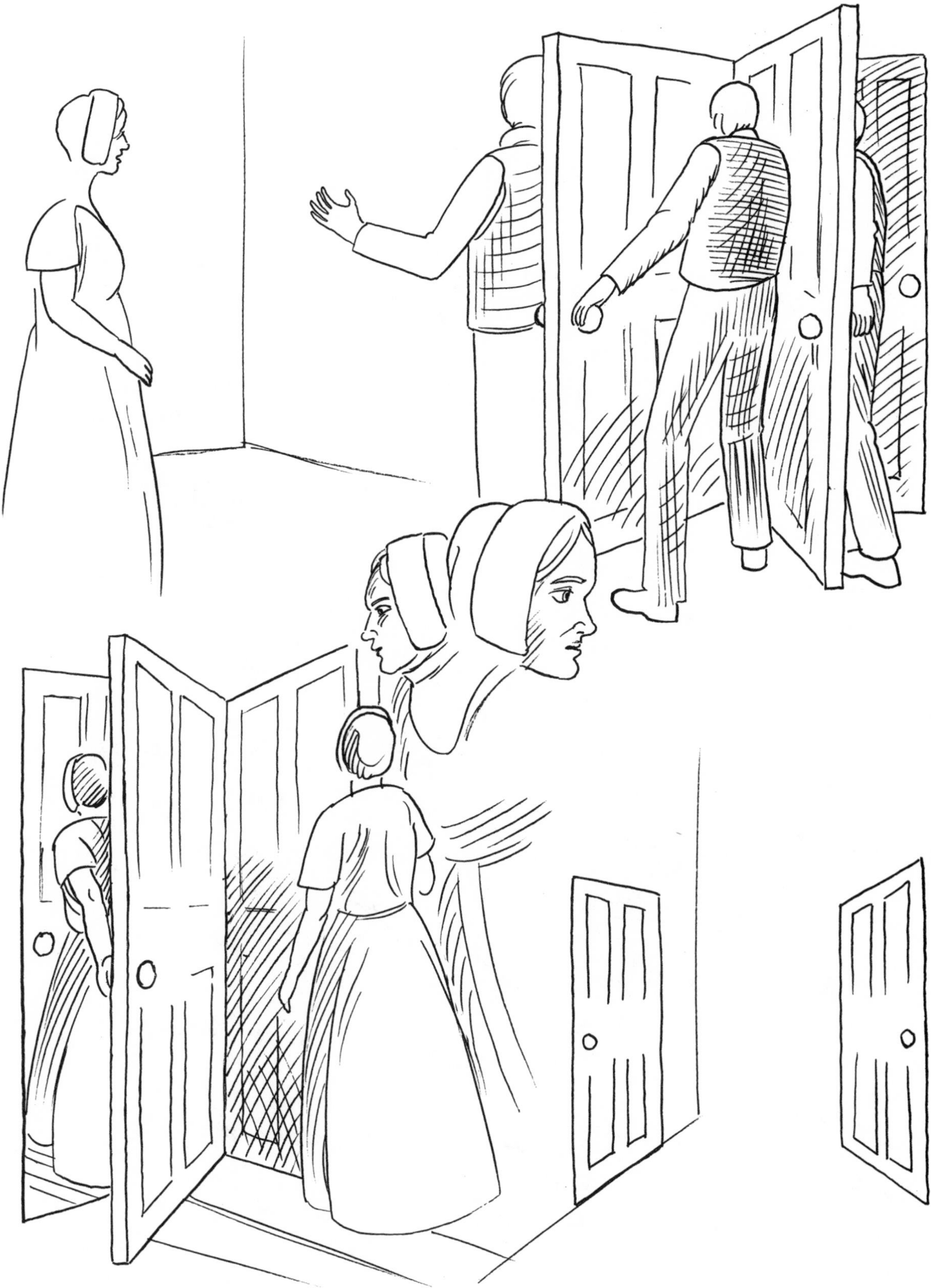

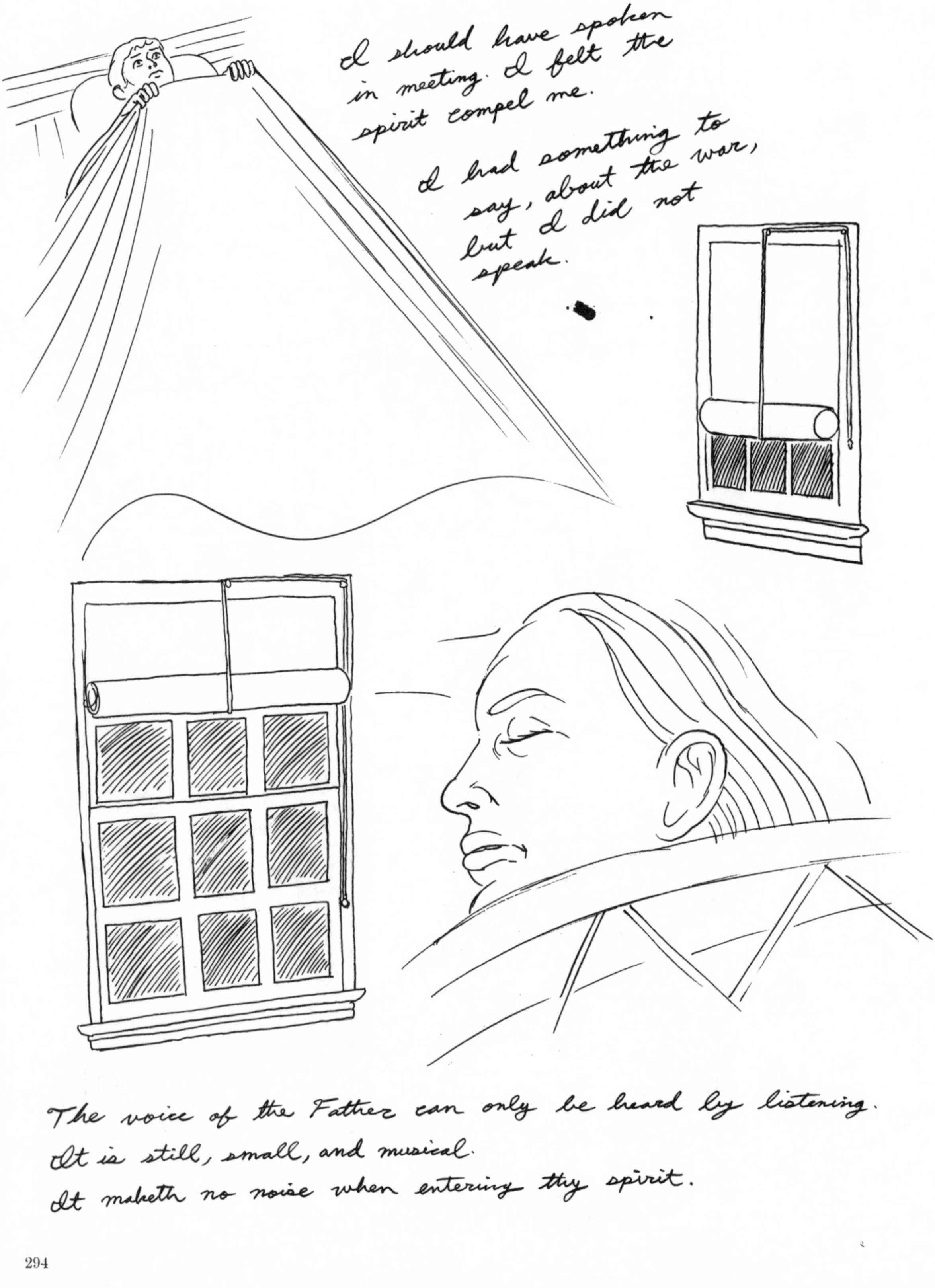
I should have spoken in meeting. I felt the spirit compel me.
I had something to say, about the war, but I did not speak.
The voice of the Father can only be heard by listening.
It is still, small, and musical.
It maketh no noise when entering thy spirit.

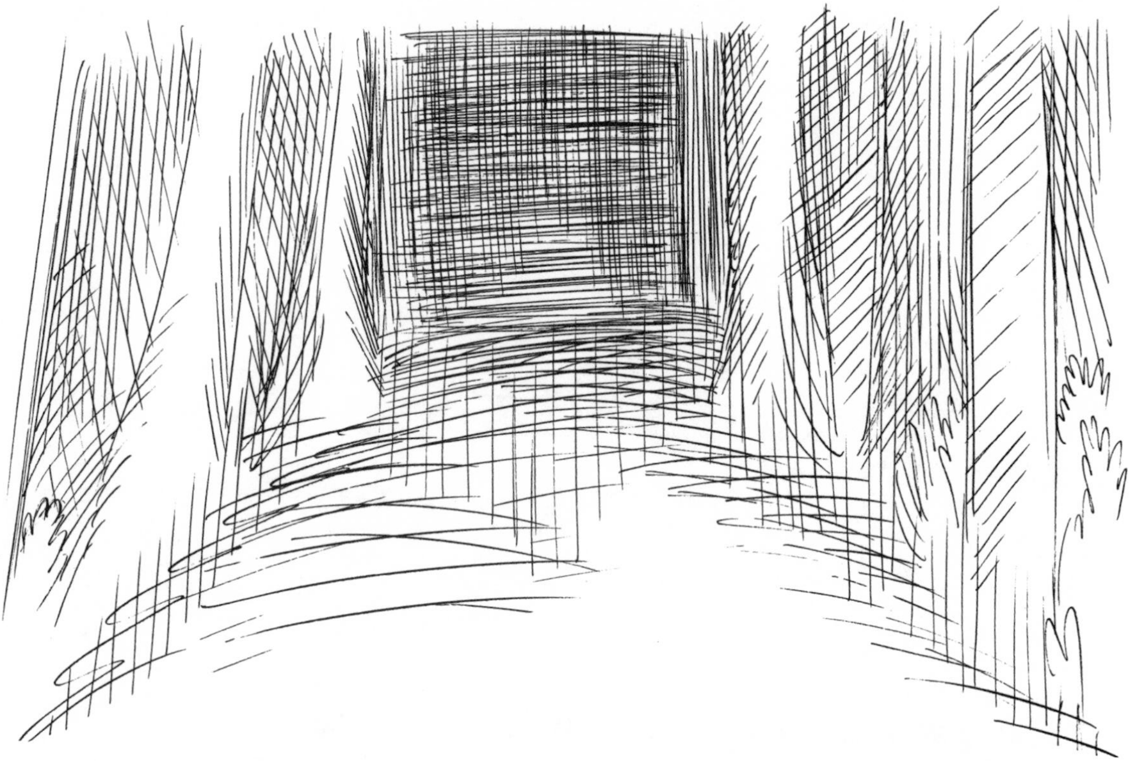

Therein is proof of thy nobility — no one can hear it, yet the tones convey eternal truth and vibrate in purest love.

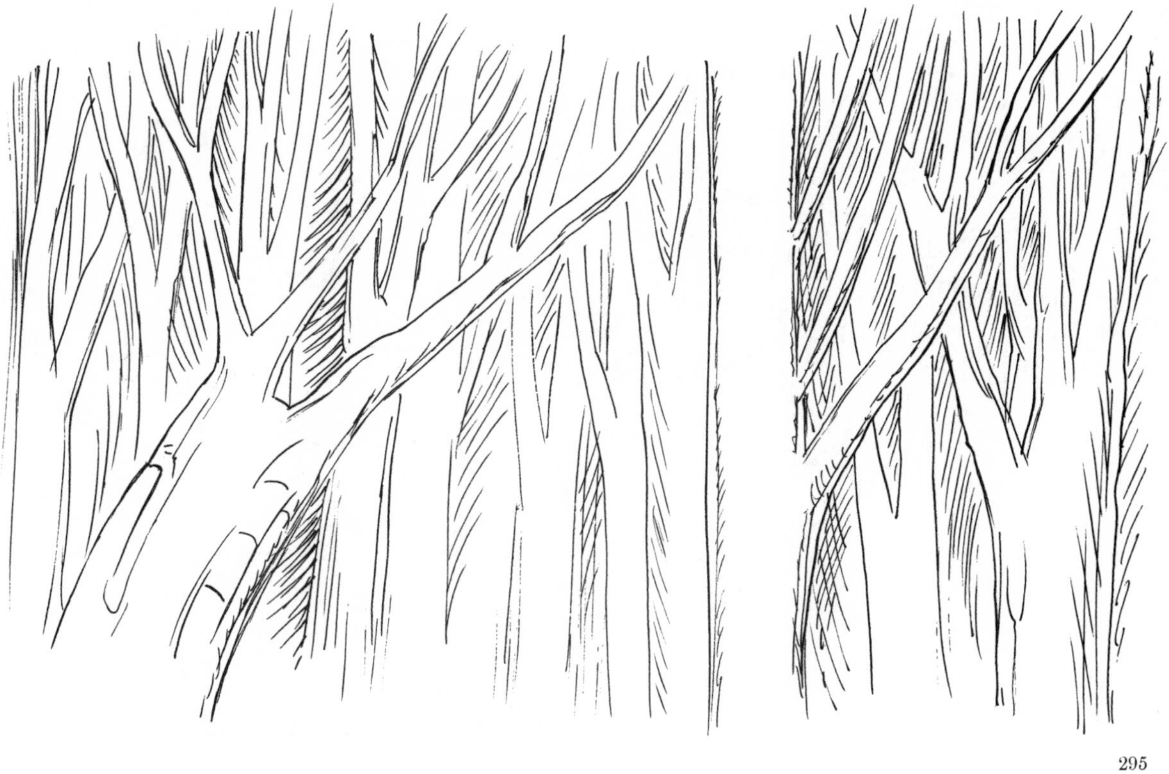

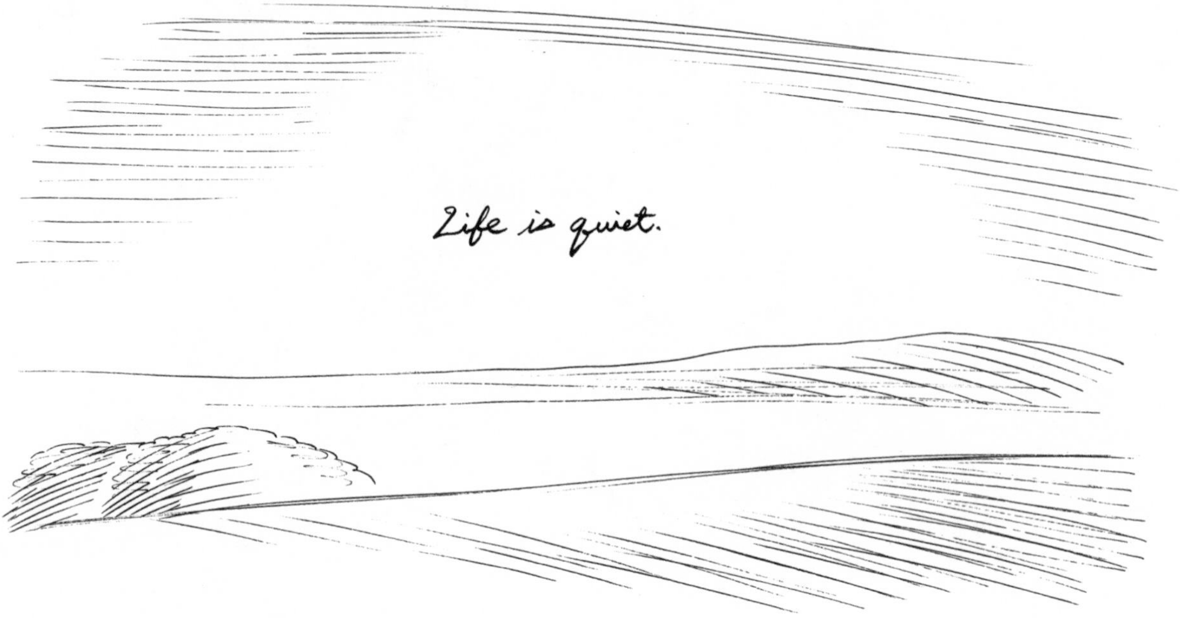
Life is quiet.

In all nature all things have their tone which will unite with every other tone when called upon, but the life of all, every bird, beast, fish and insect, is still.

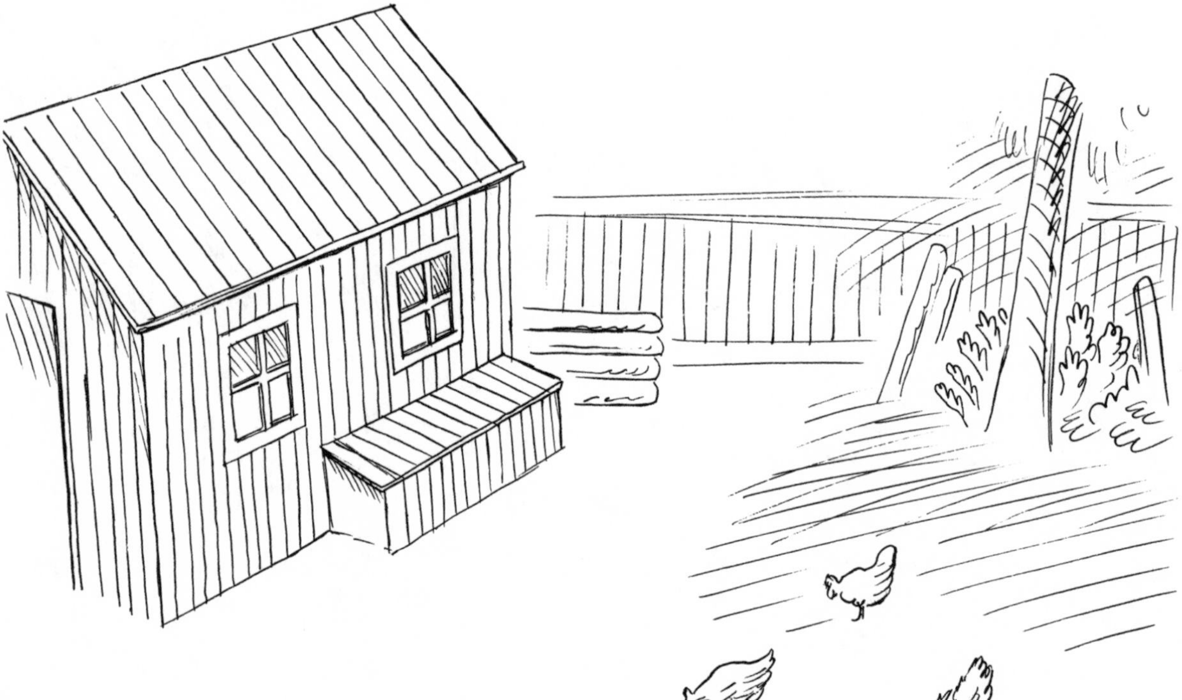

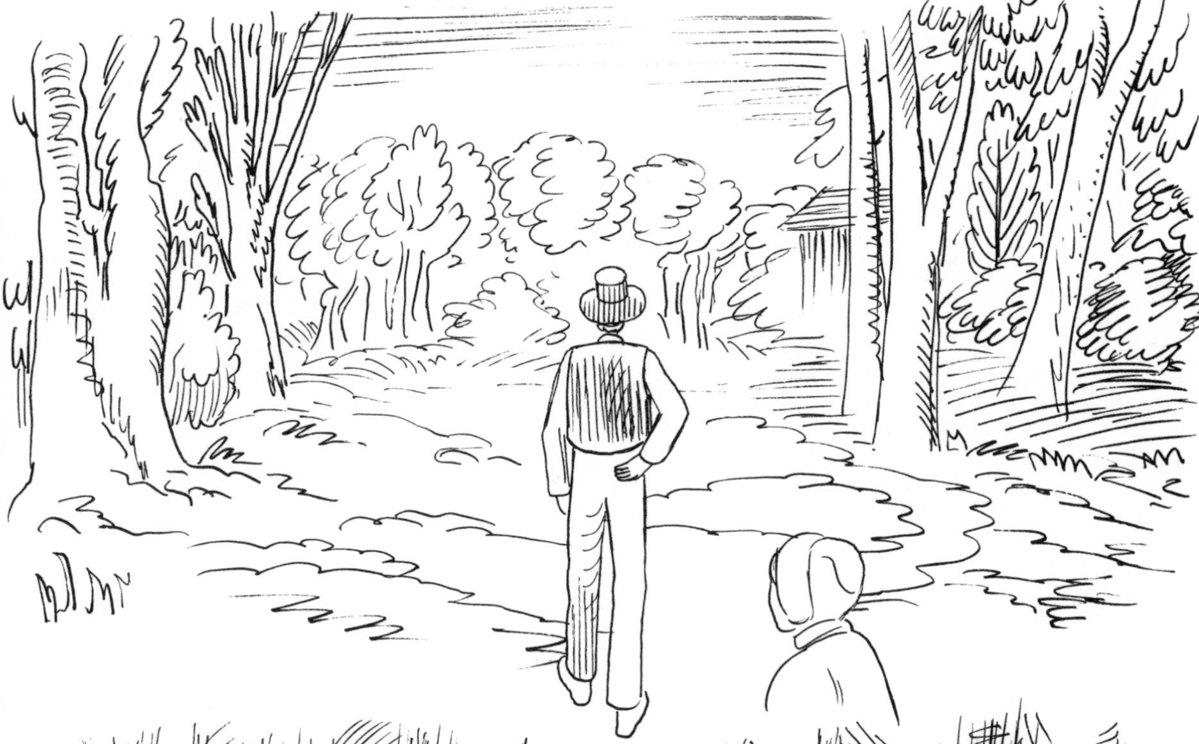

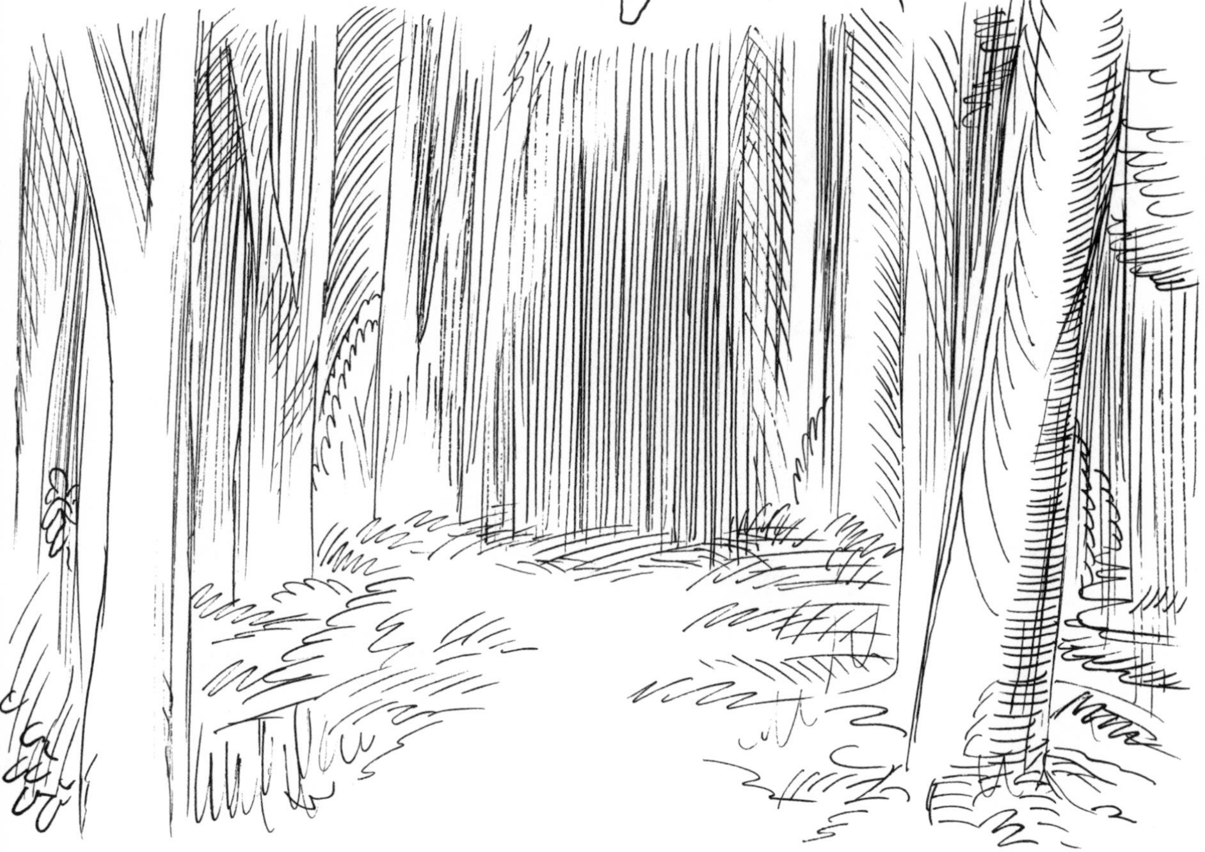

the end

Much of the text for this book comes from actual Quaker and soldier diaries and letters I found at the New York Public Library. I planned the book and completed the first hundred pages while an NYPL Cullman Center Fellow. A key source was *The Fighting Quakers* by Augustine Joseph Hickey Duganne, published by J. P. Robens in 1866, which is mostly composed of a correspondence between two Quaker brothers and their mother. On the following pages is a list of other texts that may be of interest and provide a more factual and literal understanding and rendering of the events than my approach.

This book owes a huge gratitude to...

Lucas Adams, Rick Alverson, Brian Baynes, Lance Edmands, Serge Ewenczyk, Hal Foster, Lauren Goldenberg, Sammy Harkham, Norman Hathaway, Ryan Holmberg, The Billy Ireland Cartoon Library and Museum, Alex Jacobs, Julia Jarcho, R. Kikuo Johnson, Evan Johnston, Joe Kessler, Chip Kidd, Shiamin Kwa, Lauren Lamborne, The MacDowell Residency, David Mazzucchelli, The Metropolitan Museum of Art, Dan Nadel, Gary Panter, Raj Parameswaran, Quaker & Special Collections at the Magill Library at Haverford College, Michael Robbins, Jane Samborski, Frank Santoro, Dan & Monica Shaw, Nick Shaw, Art Spiegelman, Jean Strouse, Matthew Thurber, Michael Vasquez, Chris Ware, and Gabe Winslow-Yost.

SELECTED READINGS

Abbatt, John Dilworth, ed. *A Victorian Quaker Courtship: Lancashire Love Letters of the 1850s*. York, England: William Sessions, 1989.

Barbour, Hugh, Christopher Densmore, Elizabeth H. Moger, Nancy C. Sorel, Alson D. Van Wagner, and Arthur Worrall, eds. *Quaker Crosscurrents: Three Hundred Years of Friends in the New York Yearly Meetings*. Syracuse, NY: Syracuse University Press, 1995.

Branson, Ann. *Journal of Ann Branson, a Minister of the Gospel in the Society of Friends*. Philadelphia: William H. Pile's Sons, Printers, 1892.

Brock, Peter. *Pacifism in the United States: From the Colonial Era to the First World War*. Princeton, NJ: Princeton University Press, 1968.

Chenoweth, Lynda Salter. *Philena's Friendship Quilt: A Quaker Farewell to Ohio*. Athens: Ohio University Press, 2009.

Crothers, A. Glenn. *Quakers Living in the Lion's Mouth: The Society of Friends in Northern Virginia, 1730-1865*. Gainesville: University Press of Florida, 2012.

Duganne, A. J. H. *The Fighting Quakers: A True Story of the War for Our Union*. New York: J. P. Robens, 1866.

Dugdale, George Henry. "Accession 27929." 4 leaves; photostats (negative and positive). Papers, 1864-1866. Library of Virginia, Richmond, VA.

Fager, Chuck. *A Quaker Declaration of War*. Fayetteville, NC: Kimo Press, 2003.

Fry, Elizabeth. *Elizabeth Fry: A Quaker Life*, edited by Gil Skidmore. Lanham, ND: AltaMira Press, 2005.

Gross, David M. "History of Quaker War Tax Resistance: The U.S. Civil War Period." *Sniggle.net* (blog), October 29, 2014.

Hesseltine, William B. *Civil War Prisons*. Kent, OH: Kent State University Press, 1972.

Hirst, Margaret E. *The Quakers in Peace and War: An account of their Peace Principles and Practice*. London: Swarthmore Press, 1923.

Janney, Paulena Stevens. *The Civil War Period Journals of Paulena Stevens Janney, 1859-1866*, edited and annotated by Christie Hill Russell. Baltimore: Gateway Press, 2007.

Katz, Harry L., and Vincent Virga. *Civil War Sketch Book: Drawings from the Battlefront.* New York: W. W. Norton & Company, 2012.

Linton, C., in the *Society of Friends* religious journal, no. 3 (1861-1866), in the Manuscripts and Archives division at the New York Public Library.

Nelson, Jacquelyn S. *Indiana Quakers Confront the Civil War*. Indianapolis: Indiana Historical Society, 1991.

Sheehan-Dean, Aaron, ed. *The Civil War: The Final Year Told By Those Who Lived It.* New York: Library of America, 2014.

Sinha, Manisha. *The Slave's Cause: A History of Abolition*. New Haven: Yale University Press, 2016.

Walter, William Harvey. *A Quaker Goes to War: The Diary of William Harvey Walter*, transcribed and edited by Carol-Lynn Sappé. Westminster, MD: Heritage Books, 2008.

West, Jessamyn. *The Friendly Persuasion*. San Diego: Harcourt Brace Jovanovich, 1991.

Wheelan, Joseph. *Libby Prison Breakout: The Daring Escape from the Notorious Civil War Prison*. New York: PublicAffairs, 2011.

Wilbur, Julia. 1863 diary. Quaker and Special Collections at the Haverford College Library, Haverford, PA.

Wiley, William. *The Civil War Diary of a Common Soldier: William Wiley of the 77th Illinois Infantry*, edited by Terrence J. Winschel. Baton Rouge: Louisiana State University Press, 2001.

Wright, Edward Needles. *Conscientious Objectors in the Civil War*. Philadelphia: University of Pennsylvania Press, 1931.

ALSO AVAILABLE FROM
NEW YORK REVIEW COMICS

YELLOW NEGROES AND OTHER
IMAGINARY CREATURES
Yvan Alagbé

PIERO
Edmond Baudoin

ALMOST COMPLETELY BAXTER
Glen Baxter

AGONY
Mark Beyer

MITCHUM
Blutch

PEPLUM
Blutch

THE GREEN HAND AND
OTHER STORIES
Nicole Claveloux

WHAT AM I DOING HERE?
Abner Dean

THE TENDERNESS OF STONES
Marion Fayolle

TROTS AND BONNIE
Shary Flenniken

LETTER TO SURVIVORS
Gébé

PRETENDING IS LYING
Dominique Goblet

ALAY-OOP
William Gropper

VOICES IN THE DARK
Ulli Lust

IT'S LIFE AS I SEE IT
Edited by Dan Nadel

FATHER AND SON
E. O. Plauen

SOFT CITY
Pushwagner

THE NEW WORLD
Chris Reynolds

PITTSBURGH
Frank Santoro

MACDOODLE ST.
Mark Alan Stamaty

SLUM WOLF
Tadao Tsuge

THE MAN WITHOUT TALENT
Yoshiharu Tsuge

RETURN TO ROMANCE
Ogden Whitney